Praise for *The Parisian*

"Dazzling . . . A deeply imagined historical novel with none of the usual cobwebs of the genre . . . *The Parisian* has an up-close immediacy and stylistic panache . . . that are all the more impressive coming from a London-born writer still in her 20s . . . Exquisite." —*New York Times Book Review*

"Assured and captivating . . . Ms. Hammad's acute evocation of place and personality ensures that we are never lost . . . This agile writer sets us firmly in place, fixing our attention on intersecting lives."

—*Wall Street Journal*

"Reminiscent of Michael Ondaatje's *The English Patient* and Sebastian Faulks's *Birdsong*, 27-year-old Isabella Hammad's epic debut novel surpasses both in its scope." —*New York*

"Stunning . . . a lush rendering of Palestinian life a century ago under the British mandate and a sumptuous epic about the enduring nature of love." —*Vogue*

"Hammad uses the features of historical novels to cut through the familiar dichotomies of West and Near East, placing her protagonist in a rich web of families, political intrigues, and cultural exchanges, and subtly reconfiguring the literary tropes of 'home' and 'abroad.'" —*New Yorker*

"Epic . . . Because the book takes place in the complicated time and spaces that it does, the narrative grapples with sociopolitical concerns as well as it does the intimate, human ones. It sweeps you along." —*Vanity Fair*

"Superb . . . Elegantly controlled . . . *The Parisian* makes history, and its actors, live once again." —*Boston Globe*

"[A] lush historical epic with echoes of Stendhal." —*O Magazine*

"It's hard to believe this sweeping, sophisticated historical novel is Isabella Hammad's debut—Hammad is truly a talent to watch." —*Refinery29*

"With historical sweep and sentences of startling beauty, [Hammad] has written the story of a displaced dreamer . . . Readers will be rewarded with a new voice worth listening to."   —*Christian Science Monitor*

"Isabella Hammad's *The Parisian* . . . seems to be a refutation of [Edward] Said's argument. Her book has a defiantly old-fashioned scope and pace, unhurriedly telling the story of one man's life against the backdrop of turbulent times . . . Hammad lets the action speak for itself. Considered as a work of Palestinian literature, *The Parisian* is also remarkable for not being about exile . . . [Hammad] evokes a Palestine that is grounded and self-sufficient: not a lost paradise or an isolated backwater, but a place with all the social jousting and familial intrigues that realist novels thrive on . . . real and urgent."   —*New York Review of Books*

"Provocative, testing and magnificently risky, this is an author writing for her life."   —*Telegraph*

"Lavish, leisurely and immersive . . . *The Parisian* comes across as both old-fashioned and modern-minded . . . Ms. Hammad's command of the broad picture and the filigree detail alike makes this paradoxical tone succeed. One of Midhat's French friends disdains the small stuff since he 'was an architect, not a carpenter.' Ms Hammad knows, and triumphantly shows, that a novelist of vision must be both."   —*Economist*

"Remarkably accomplished . . . Hammad is a natural storyteller. She sustains tension and suspends revelation skillfully, and interweaves character and theme, the global and the local, with the assurance of a much more experienced author. The writing is deeply humane, its wide vision combined with poised restraint . . . *The Parisian* teems with riches—love, war, betrayal and madness—and marks the arrival of a bright new talent."   —*Guardian*

"One of the most ambitious first novels to have appeared in years . . . Written in soulful, searching prose, it's a jam-packed epic . . . Hammad is a natural social novelist with an ear for lively dialogue as well as an ability to illuminate psychological interiority . . . Hammad is a writer of startling talent—and *The Parisian* has the rhythm of life."   —*Observer*

"Hammad has an exquisite control on her subject: this is precise writing, measured, and careful . . . Much of the pleasure of the book is to be found in Hammad's often strikingly clear, original imagery . . . She also provides many canny shifts in focus, from a cinematic, establishing wide-shots of a location, deftly sketched, to zooming in on the tiniest, most intimate detail . . . It is Hammad's sustaining of both perspectives, the minutiae that make up an individual life and the macro political upheavals that change a country forever, that makes *The Parisian* so impressive." —*Independent*

"Isabella Hammad shows rare maturity, both in her marshalling of a huge cast of characters and in her ability to illuminate such a politically charged period of history without didacticism or literary showboating." —*Mail on Sunday*

"Sumptuous and sharply observed—an old-school novel to lose yourself in." —*Metro*

"In her exceptional debut, Hammad taps into the satisfying slow-burn style of classic literature with a storyline that captures both the heart and the mind. . . . Richly textured prose drives the novel's spellbinding themes of the ebb and flow of cultural connections and people who struggle with love, familial responsibilities, and personal identity. This is an immensely rewarding novel that readers will sink into and savor." —*Publishers Weekly* (starred review)

"An assured debut novel . . . closely observed and elegantly written." —*Kirkus Reviews* (starred review)

"*The Parisian* is a sublime reading experience: delicate, restrained, surpassingly intelligent, uncommonly poised and truly beautiful. It is realism in the tradition of Flaubert and Stendhal—everything that happens feels not so much imagined as ordained. That this remarkable historical epic should be the debut of a writer in her mid-twenties seems impossible, yet it's true. Isabella Hammad is an enormous talent and her book is a wonder." —*Zadie Smith*

"*The Parisian* is a gripping historical novel, a poignant romance, and a revelatory family epoch. Above all, it is a generous gift. There is a kind of joy that can hold not only pleasure, but struggle, and even sadness. This novel tells that kind of joyful story, and evokes that kind of joy in the reader."
—Jonathan Safran Foer

"A lushly imagined, beautifully written, expansive powerhouse of a debut. Isabella Hammad is a great new voice." —Nathan Englander

"An exquisite, intricate and wise novel. I was utterly gripped from the first page until the last. This sweeping, historical epic marks the arrival of a wonderfully gifted author. Isabella Hammad is a marvel and *The Parisian* is an unforgettable read." —Irenosen Okojie

"*The Parisian* is extraordinary—wise, ambitious, and lavishly rewarding. With luminous prose and rare compassion, Isabella Hammad offers her readers an absorbing story of war and identity, of love and independence, of hope and history. It's an astonishing novel, heralding the arrival of a major talent." —Bret Anthony Johnston

"With masterful lyricism and unflinching insight, *The Parisian* captures the personal passion and political violence of a nascent nation's struggle for independence. Hammad has written a profound and intoxicating epic, brimming with unexpected, vivid imagery and unforgettable characters. Hers is a fresh voice of the first order." —Bradford Morrow

"A model of what the short story can do . . . [A] most ingenious and open-hearted work." —David Gates on Isabella Hammad's "Mr. Can'aan," winner of the 2018 Plimpton Prize

THE
PARISIAN

THE
PARISIAN

or
AL-BARISI

A Novel

ISABELLA
HAMMAD

Grove Press
New York

Published simultaneously in Canada
Printed in the United States of America

This book was set in 12-point Arno Pro by Alpha Design & Composition of Pittsfield, NH.

First Grove Atlantic hardcover edition: April 2019
First Grove Atlantic paperback edition: January 2020

Library of Congress Cataloging-in-Publication data is available for this title.

ISBN 978-0-8021-4880-3
eISBN 978-0-8021-4710-3

Grove Press
an imprint of Grove Atlantic
154 West 14th Street
New York, NY 10011

Distributed by Publishers Group West

groveatlantic.com

20 21 22 23   10 9 8 7 6 5 4 3 2 1

for Teta Ghada

لِكُلّ التَفاصِيل

Characters

The Kamal family
Haj Taher Kamal, textile merchant
Aziza Kamal, Haj Taher's first wife, deceased
Midhat Kamal, son of Haj Taher and Aziza
Um Taher (Mahdiya) Kamal, mother of Haj Taher, Midhat's "Teta"
Layla, Haj Taher's second wife
Musbah Kamal, eldest son of Haj Taher and Layla
Nadim, Inshirah, Dunya, Nashat, other children of Haj Taher and Layla
Abu Jamil Kamal, cousin of Haj Taher, carpet merchant
Um Jamil Kamal, wife of Abu Jamil
Jamil Kamal, son of Abu Jamil and Um Jamil, cousin of Midhat
Wasfi Kamal, cousin of Midhat
Tahsin Kamal, cousin of Midhat

The Molineu family
Frédéric Molineu, sociologist and anthropologist at the
    University of Montpellier
Ariane Molineu, née Passant, wife of Frédéric, deceased
Jeannette Molineu, daughter of Frédéric and Ariane
Marian Molineu, niece of Frédéric, sister of Xavier
Xavier Molineu, nephew of Frédéric, brother of Marian, law student
Paul Richer, Marian's fiancé

Other characters in France
Sylvain Leclair, friend of the Molineus, vigneron
Laurent Toupin, medical student
Samuel Cogolati, medical student
Patrice Nolin, retired medical professor
Carole and *Marie-Thérèse*, daughters of Patrice Nolin
Georgine, the Molineus' maid
Luc Dimon, vigneron
Madame Crotteau, socialite
Faruq al-Azmeh, professor of Arabic language in Paris, originally
    from Damascus
Bassem Jarbawi, Raja Abd al-Rahman, Yusef Mansour, Omar, and others,
    Faruq's friends in Paris
Qadri Muhammad and *Riyad Assali*, school friends of Hani and advisors
    to the Emir Faisal

The Hammad family
Haj Hassan Hammad, cousin of Nimr, landowner, member of
    the Decentralisation Party
Nazeeha Hammad, wife of Haj Hassan
Yasser Hammad, eldest son of Nazeeha and Haj Hassan
Haj Nimr Hammad, cousin of Hassan, shari'a court judge and scholar,
    mayor of Nablus in 1918
Widad Hammad, wife of Haj Nimr
Fatima Hammad, eldest daughter of Widad and Haj Nimr
Nuzha Hammad, second daughter of Widad and Haj Nimr
Burhan Hammad, youngest son of Widad and Haj Nimr
Haj Tawfiq Hammad, uncle of Haj Hassan and Haj Nimr, politician

The Murad family
Hani Murad, graduate of law school in Paris
Basil Murad, distant cousin of Hani, brother of Munir
Munir Murad, distant cousin of Hani, brother of Basil
Fuad Murad, Hani's uncle in Jenin, member of the Decentralisation Party

Sahar Murad, daughter of Fuad
Um Sahar Murad, wife of Fuad

Other characters in Nablus
Hisham, Haj Taher's agent
Butrus, tailor at the Kamal store
Um Mahmoud, maid to the Kamal family
Adel Jawhari, young man, former schoolfriend of Midhat
Abu Omar Jawhari, uncle of Adel, mayor in 1919
Qais Karak, young man
Haj Abdallah Atwan, soap factory owner
Madame Atwan, matriarch of the Atwan family
Eli Kahen, Samaritan tailor
Abu Salama, Samaritan High Priest
Père Antoine, French Dominican priest and scholar
Sister Louise, Sister Sarah, Sister Marian, and others, members of the order
    of the Sisters of St. Joseph, known in Nablus as "the Ebal Girls"
Ayman Saba, impoverished Christian farmer
Hala Saba, daughter of Ayman

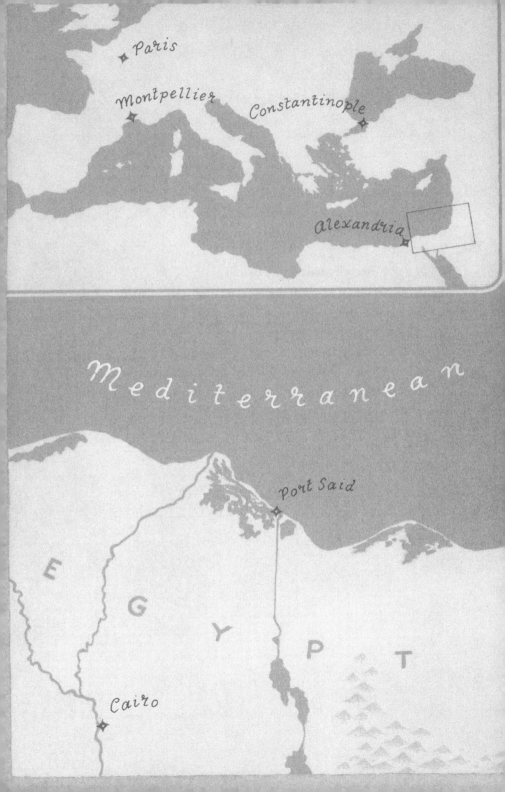

Beirut
Aley
LEBANON
Litani River
Damascus
Jabal al-Sheikh
SYRIA
Akka
Haifa
Safad
The Golan
Sea
Nazareth
Lake Tiberias
Anabta
Jenin
Irbid
Druze Mountains
Tulkarem
Mount Ebal
Nablus
Zawata
Tel Aviv
Mount Gezirim
Jaffa
Lydda
Jericho
Jerusalem
Dead Sea
Gaza
JORDAN
PALESTINE
UNDER THE BRITISH MANDATE
1923

PART ONE

1

There was one other Arab onboard the ship to Marseille. His name was Faruq al-Azmeh, and the day after leaving port in Alexandria he approached Midhat at breakfast, with a plate of toast in one hand and a string of amber prayer beads in the other. He sat, tugged at the cuffs of his shirt, and started to describe without any introduction how he was returning from Damascus to resume his teaching post in the language department of the Sorbonne. He had left Paris at the outbreak of war but after the Miracle of the Marne was determined to return. He had grey eyes and a slightly rectangular head.

"*Baris.*" He sighed. "It is where my life is."

To young Midhat Kamal, this statement was highly suggestive. In his mind a gallery of lamps directly illuminated a dance hall full of women. He looked closely at Faruq's clothes. He wore a pale blue three-piece suit, and an indigo tie with a silver tiepin in the shape of a bird. A cane of some dark unpainted wood leaned against the table.

"I am going to study medicine," said Midhat. "At the University of Montpellier."

"Bravo," said Faruq.

Midhat smiled as he reached for the coffeepot. Muscles he had not known were tense began to relax.

"This is your first visit to France," said Faruq.

Midhat said nothing, assenting.

Five days had passed since he said goodbye to his grandmother in Nablus and travelled by mule to Tulkarem, where he joined the Haifa line for Kantara East and changed trains for Cairo. After a few days at his father's house, he boarded the ship in Alexandria. He had become accustomed to the endless skin of the water, broken by white crests, flashing silver at noon. Lunch was at one, tea was at four, dinner was at seven thirty, and at first he sat alone watching the Europeans eat with their knives. He developed a habit of searching a crowded room for the red hair of the captain, a Frenchman named Gorin, and after dinner would watch him enter and exit the bridge where he supervised the helm.

Yesterday, he started feeling lonely. It happened suddenly. Sitting beside the stern, waiting for the captain, he became conscious of his back against the bench, a sensation that was bizarrely painful. He was aware of his legs extending from his pelvis. His nose, usually invisible, doubled and intruded on his vision. The outline of his body weighed on him as a hard, sore shape, and his heart beat very fast. He assumed the feeling would pass. But it did not, and that evening simple interactions with the quartermaster, dining attendants, other passengers, took on a strained and breathless quality. It must be obvious to them, he thought, how raw his skin felt. During the night he pressed the stem of his pocket watch compulsively in the dark, lifting the lid on its pale face. The ticking lulled him to sleep. Then he woke a second time and, continuing to check the hour as the night progressed, began to see in those twitching hands the spasms of something monstrous.

It was with a strong feeling of relief, therefore, and a sense that his sharp outline had softened slightly, that he smiled back at his new friend.

"What do you imagine it will be like?" said Faruq.

"Imagine what, France?"

"Before I came, the first time, I had many pictures of it in my mind. Some turned out to be quite accurate, in the end. Some were—" He pinched his lips and smiled in self-mockery. "For some reason I had an idea about wigs. You know, the false hair. I'm not sure where I got it from, possibly I had seen an old drawing."

Midhat made a sound like he was thinking, and looked through the window at the sea.

His high school in Constantinople was modelled on the French lycée. The textbooks were all French imports, as were half the teachers, and even most of the furniture. Midhat and his classmates had sat on ladder-back chairs with woven rush seats reading "la poésie épique en Grèce," memorizing the names of elements in a mixture of French and Latin, and only when the bell rang did they slip into Turkish and Arabic and Armenian in the corridor. Once formulated in French, certain concepts belonged in French, so that, for instance, Midhat knew the names of his internal organs as "le poumon" and "le coeur" and "le cerveau" and "l'encéphale," and understood philosophical abstractions by their French names, "l'altruisme," "la condition humaine." And yet, despite being steeped for five years in all things French, he struggled to conjure a picture of France that was separate from the furnishings of his classrooms, whose windows had displayed a hot Turkish sky, and admitted shouts of Arabic from the water. Even now, from the vantage of this ship, Provence remained hidden by fog and the earth's unseeable curves. He looked back at Faruq.

"I cannot imagine it."

He waited for Faruq's scorn. But Faruq only shrugged, and dropped his eyes to the table.

"Were you ever in Montpellier?" said Midhat.

"No, only Paris. Of course, the university is famous for medicine. Didn't Rabelais study there?"

"Ah, you know about Rabelais!"

Faruq chuckled. "Have some marmalade before I eat it all."

Faruq returned to his cabin after breakfast, and Midhat climbed the staircase to the deck and sat beside the stern. He stared at the sea and listened with partial comprehension to a group of European officials—Dutch, French, English—shouting from the next bench, first about the technology of the vessel and then about the German advance on Paris.

Boards quaked beneath Midhat's feet: a child was scampering along the deck. Beyond, a pair of young women compared cartes postales, and the wind harassed the tassels on their parasols. Those were the same girls who last night at dinner had displayed their lovely hair like hats, crimped and waved and decorated with jewels that sparkled under the chandeliers. At last, the door to the bridge opened and a red-haired man, Captain Gorin, stepped out and cracked his knuckles. A uniformed official leapt from the bench to address him, and as Gorin's lips moved—soundless to Midhat in the wind—the grooves in his face deepened. He cupped his hands over a cigarette, shook a match free of its flame, and held the lit end in his palm against the wind. The other man departed, and Gorin smoked over the rail for a while. His curls flung about; they seemed barely attached to his head. He flicked the butt overboard and retreated below deck.

Midhat decided to follow. He crossed before the shouting Europeans just as Gorin disappeared under the hatch, and swung after him down the metal stairs. The first door on the passage gave onto a saloon, which was full of people. In the corner a gramophone sang. He scanned for Gorin, and met the eyes of Faruq, who was sitting at a table with a pile of books.

"I'm glad you're here," said Faruq. He had changed his clothes and was now wearing a dark suit and a yellow tie with green hexagons. "I found these for you. They are the only ones I have with me. Some poems . . . poems again, this one is quite good actually . . . and *Les Trois Mousquetaires*. Essential reading for any young man on his first trip to France."

"I am very grateful."

"I will buy us something to drink, and then we shall practise French. Whisky?"

Midhat nodded. He sat, and to hide his nerves, reached for *The Three Musketeers*. The page fell open at the authorial preface.

> While doing research at the Royal Library for my History of Louis XIV,
> I accidentally fell upon the Memoirs of M. d'Artagnan, printed—as were
> most works of that period in which the authors

Two glasses half full of trembling liquid slid across the polished table.

"Santé. Now, I'm going to tell you some things. Are you ready?" Faruq leaned back against the bench, and pulled the prayer beads from his pocket as he reached for his drink. "First of all, women in France. Now, this is strange, but they are treated like queens. Always they will enter a room first. Remember that. Expect a few things that might make you uncomfortable. Try to have an open mind. Remain true to your origins, in French we'd say *rester fidèle à vos racines*, fhimet alay? You know I have many French friends. And Spanish. The Spanish are more like the Arabs—the French are something different. They are mostly Christians, so consider them like your Christian friends in Nablus. I presume you have met or at least seen French pilgrims in Palestine. Are there missionaries in Nablus?"

"Yes. But I also went to school in Konstantiniyye. I know many Christians."

Faruq was not listening. "Well you should know that missionaries are always different from the natives. The religion is less strong in France, first of all. So try not to be shocked by their kissing, and their alcohol, and so on."

Midhat laughed, and Faruq gave him a look of surprise. Desiring at once to prove that he would not be shocked, Midhat took a sip from the other glass. It was like drinking perfume; he tasted it in his nose. He had tried whisky once when he was sixteen from an illicit bottle in his school dormitory. He had only wet his tongue, however, whereas the owner and his accomplice finished the bottle between them, and when in the morning the schoolmaster smelled it on their breath they were whipped and banned from class for three days.

"There are many things you will like. The way of thinking, the way of life, it's very refined. In this I feel there is some affinity between Damascus and Paris."

"And Nablus," said Midhat.

"Yes, Nablus is very nice." Faruq sipped and exhaled. "Where will you live in Montpellier?"

"At the house of Docteur Molineu. An academic."

"An academic! Ah, yes. You will like that."

Midhat did not mind being told what it was that he would like. He took it as a sign of kinship. He wanted to agree with everything Faruq said.

He spent the remaining four days of the journey reading Faruq's books on the upper deck. Or, at least, holding the books open in his lap and looking out to sea, and occasionally pronouncing some sentence in French from one of the pages he had pressed down against the wind. His mind, newly relaxed, wheeled off into daydreams. He indulged three scenarios in particular. The first featured a thin-necked Parisian woman lost in Jerusalem, whom he directed in perfect French to Haram ash-Sharif. An onlooker, often a notable from Nablus, reported on the incident, rendering Midhat famous as a man of great kindness and linguistic skill. In the second fantasy, he sang a dal'ona—"ya tayrin taayir fis-sama' al-aali; sallim al-hilu al-aziz al-ghali"—inspiring awe to the point of weeping in those who passed under his window and heard him mourn the distance between himself and his imagined lover. In the third fantasy he saved another passenger from falling overboard by catching him around the middle with the grace of a dancer. The onlookers applauded.

These daydreams were fortifying. They increased his sense of fluidity with his surroundings and gave him confidence when entering rooms. He took a dose at regular intervals like a draught of medicine and emerged from the dream after a few minutes' elapse renewed and refreshed. Thus he managed, more or less, to soothe the hard outline of his body—which still at times oppressed him with its stinging clasp.

On the Marseille docks Faruq shook Midhat's hand and held his arm. "Good luck. And be brave. When the holidays come, you must visit me in Saint Germain."

The train to Montpellier departed an hour later. Night settled on the countryside, which looked rather like Palestine: similar rugged hills, dry greenery. Midhat slept against the loud, vibrating glass, and in the groggy morning waded through another two chapters of *The Three Musketeers* as the hills drew a wavy horizon line, and raindrops snagged and shuddered down the panes. He fell asleep again after lunch, and when the announcer called, "Montpellier!" it was a quarter to five: he stood and followed the other passengers onto the platform, fatigued and in need of a wash.

The fore of the Montpellier station resembled a temple. Midhat dragged his trunk between the columns and watched the figures and motorcars move over the quadrangle ahead. He had no idea what Docteur Molineu looked like. There had been no description in the letters from the university, and therefore every man walking nearby was a possibility. That thin person with long shirttails, was he looking at Midhat with interest? Or that elderly gentleman; with those spectacles he certainly looked like a scholar. At the moment when his true host would have turned towards him, however, each candidate continued walking. The man by the ticket booth was definitely staring, but rather too intently, and Midhat avoided his eye.

The crowd before the station thinned, and a lamplighter carried his ladder between the standards. A flock of nurses crossed into the foyer of a building opposite and shook their umbrellas. The lit end of a cigarette flashed double in a puddle, vanished, and someone passed Midhat close on the right. He had a large blond moustache. He was too young to be the Docteur, surely—and as he drew nearer Midhat saw the man's expression was not kindly, and that his eyes, encircled with blond lashes, were not on Midhat's face but on his tarbush. The man's own hat was lipped and shallow, and as he fixed Midhat he put a finger on its brim. Midhat recognised the French sign of respect, the gesture en route to the gesture of lifting the hat, which showed you weren't hiding anything underneath. But he couldn't help feeling that this blond man was pointing out the brimlessness of Midhat's own hat. He frowned, and the man disappeared down a side street.

"Monsieur Kamal?"

At the end of the concourse, a young woman raised her hand. Beneath her cap, short curls of brown hair hugged her ears. A diagonal crease across her lap switched from side to side as she approached.

He hesitated. "Bonjour. Je m'appelle Midhat Kamal."

The woman laughed, and wrinkles appeared beneath her eyes. "Et je m'appelle Jeannette Molineu."

Jeannette Molineu extended a pale hand with knuckly fingers. Midhat held them; they were rather cold. It was peculiar that the wife should come to collect him, but he thought of what Faruq had said about French women, and followed Jeannette to a green motorcar parked on the concourse.

"I hope you weren't waiting for long," she said, opening the door and squeaking onto the backseat. "How was the journey?"

"It was . . . for many days."

The chauffeur drove fast and the motor overwhelmed their voices. From the window, Midhat watched the city rise and fall and thin into alleyways, with shoals of umbrellas and overcoats swelling and contracting on the sidewalks. They turned down a narrow road on which the buildings were gridded with black balconies and roofed with terracotta. The car slowed.

"This city," said Midhat, "it is similar to Nablus. The two mountains, the stone buildings, the small streets. But it is bigger, and the stone is more yellow."

"Nablus is where you are from?"

"Yes. And you were born here."

"No," said Jeannette, in a low, smiling voice, "I grew up in Paris. My father and I moved here about four years ago, when he started working at the university. And I did my baccalauréat here."

"Your father is Docteur Molineu?"

"Of course."

"Ah. And your husband?"

"I'm not married. Pisson, will you take us through the centre? This is Rue de la Loge, the main commercial street. And at the end is Place de la Comédie. It's small, Montpellier, you won't take long to know it. It's a little dark now to see, I'm afraid."

Midhat looked over at Jeannette Molineu's face. Shadows falling between the streetlamps made her eyes appear black and large, blotting her pale skin and filling out her thin upper lip. The shadows rotated as they moved, and each time they entered the full glare of a lamp again the effect was reversed.

The road was broader now and the roadside grassy. Pisson turned a corner and decelerated to an open pair of gates, then crunched into a driveway checkered by windowlight falling from a large house. A maid curtsied by the door as Jeannette escorted Midhat into the hall. Electric lamps were mounted on the wall between framed pictures, and a large mirror hung beside a staircase that curved up to the right. One open door revealed cream-coloured walls and the shining black hip of a piano; from another, a jowled man had emerged, with grey hair and a close-fitting suit.

"Bienvenue, bienvenue, Monsieur Kamal. Frédéric Molineu. I am your host."

"Good evening, my name is Midhat Kamal. Enchanted to make your acquaintance."

"Come come, bonjour my dear, so—pleased, so—pleased."

Molineu shook Midhat's hand vigorously, clasping a second hand on top of the first. Midhat tried to copy the motion but now his fingers had been released, and his host was spreading his arms out at the hall.

"Please feel this is your home. We are honoured to have you as our guest and enthusiastic to show you how we live. Please, come have an aperitif."

The salon was blue, with quilted couches around a table crowned by a silver tray and four crystal glasses. Glass doors gave onto a terrace with an iron table and chairs, and a gloomy lawn.

"I notice your hesitation." Docteur Molineu snatched at the fabric on his knees as he sat. "This is not alcohol. This is called a *cordial*. Sans alcool totalement. S'il vous plaît, Monsieur, asseyez-vous."

Midhat took a seat on the couch and immediately felt exhausted.

Jeannette said, "When is Marian arriving?"

Now that father and daughter were beside each other, Midhat could see the likeness. There was a direct expression in the eyes. But where the Docteur's jaw was substantial, Jeannette's chin tapered, lightly cleft. She had removed her hat but her hair remained flat over the head, her curls released just at the ears. Her features were delicate and the tiny creases beneath her eyes only made her more beautiful. And she was slender, but there was a breadth to her shoulders—or perhaps it was the way she held them, slightly hunched. Midhat looked down, pressing his thumb into the stem of his cold glass.

"Later, dear. Marian is my niece. She is getting married next week, so you will see a French wedding! Marriage ceremonies are the key, really, to a culture. You see a wedding, you understand the society. How was the journey?"

"The journey was long. For that I am tired. This is extremely delicious."

"Your French is very good," said Jeannette.

"Thank you. I attended a French school in Constantinople."

"So, I'm interested in your first impressions," said the Docteur. "Did Jeannette take you on a tour of the town?"

"Papa, he's tired. We drove a little through the centre."

"It is a beautiful city," said Midhat.

"Well. I hope you are comfortable here. Montpellier is not large, and I suspect you will prefer walking to the Faculty while the good weather lasts. But Pisson will help you in the first few days. On Monday je crois qu'il y a une affaire d'inscription, and then, you know, tout va de l'avant."

There were several words in this speech that Midhat did not understand. He nodded.

"It's a lovely building," said Jeannette. "The Faculty. It used to be a monastery, you know."

"Ah, merci," said Midhat to the maid as she presented the decanter. "Bikfi, sorry, that's plenty. No, I did not know that."

Molineu leaned back, eyes to the ceiling. His face was lined and his hair was dappled with white, but his body looked limber. The waistband of his trousers was narrow, and the indent in the wide muscle of his thigh showed through the fabric. With his hands on his knees he sprang forwards again, and his heels clacked on the ground.

"We are so enthusiastic about your coming. I'm afraid we are going to ask you all sorts of questions. Professionally, I am a social anthropologist. The lining of my heart is sewn with questions."

Midhat did not understand this last phrase. But Molineu had put the tips of his fingers on his chest, and the words "question" and "heart" prompted Midhat's own heart to accelerate with the immediate fear that Molineu might be referring to medical practice.

"I have much to learn," he said. "I am very new."

"Absolutely, absolutely. There is always so much to learn. Of course we are not always so new."

"Do you live near Jerusalem?" said Jeannette.

One of Midhat's fantasies from the ship flared involuntarily in his mind, and he saw his invented Parisienne lost in Jerusalem's old city. Heat rose to the back of his neck and he said, in as rapid French as he could muster:

"We are north from Jerusalem. It will take five hours, six hours. It can be dangerous. You must travel through Ayn al-Haramiya, a passage between two mountains. After, perhaps, nine o'clock in the evening, there are thieves."

"Ayna—what is the name?" said Docteur Molineu.

"Ayn al-Haramiya, ya'ni, it means the place where the water comes. I don't know the word."

"Sea?"

"No, in the ground."

"River? Lake?"

"No, in the ground, it comes from under—"

"Well? Spring?"

"Spring, spring. Ayn al-Haramiya means the Spring of the Thieves."

A bell rang, and a second later the maid Georgine entered the room.

"Mademoiselle Marian et Monsieur Paul Richer."

"The very couple," said Molineu. "Midhat, please meet my niece. This is Marian."

The young woman at the door wore a green dress and shiny green shoes. Behind her came a head of red curls, and Midhat instantly recognised the captain of the steamship, Gorin.

"Bonsoir, Capitaine," he said.

Jeannette turned sharply, as the red-haired man replied: "Bonsoir." He returned Midhat's nod and reached out his hand: "My name is Paul Richer. With pleasure."

"Hello," said Marian.

"Marian is our young bride-to-be," said Docteur Molineu.

Midhat stared at the weathered face of the man he knew as Captain Gorin while everyone sat down. He felt feverish. The maid brought fresh glasses for the cordial, and the fatigue came in rushes; he batted it away by moving a leg, an arm, a foot, anything to keep him present, here on this couch, in this blue salon.

"Dear Marian, I cannot believe it is so soon," said Jeannette.

"This is our young guest du Proche-Orient," said the Docteur, "Monsieur Kamal, who has come to study medicine at the university. He has just arrived, in fact. We expect he is feeling a little désorienté at the moment."

"Papa."

"Vraiment!" said the man who was or was not Captain Gorin. "Where are you from?"

"Nablus, a town north of Jerusalem, south of Damascus."

"Magnificent."

"He is going to be a doctor," said Jeannette.

Midhat twisted his torso. The position kept him more alert. It also allowed him to look again at the man's face.

And as he looked now, a conviction solidified that this was not, after all, Captain Gorin. Those ginger whiskers were not familiar, nor the sunburnt cheeks. This was a stranger, his name was Paul Richer, and given the smile on his lips he was clearly aware that Midhat was studying him. The realisation jarred as strongly as the instant of his first mistake, and Midhat was overcome by a sour-tasting unease.

"Monsieur Midhat," said Jeannette. "You must be very tired. Would you prefer to go to bed? Georgine, perhaps Monsieur Midhat would like to see where his bedroom is? He looks—he must be very tired from his journey."

And so, shortly before seven o'clock in the evening, on the twentieth of October 1914, Midhat Kamal was shown into a corner room in the upstairs of the Molineu house in Montpellier. The window showed the dim garden, a large tree at the far end. The walls of the room were striped yellow, and opposite the bed, beside the fireplace, a wooden chair faced a table with a vase of lilies dropping orange dust on its shiny veneer. His trunk stood upright beside an armoire. He untied his shoes and lay down.

Flat on his back, he thought again of the stranger downstairs named Paul Richer, and tried to picture his captain. Red curls, grooves in his cheeks. The rest was harder to fill in. He felt the rocking motions of the sea, and the images of the day plotted themselves on the insides of his eyelids: the French coast that morning, emerging from the blue distance; the passengers abandoning breakfast to crowd at the windows; the port of Marseille, the bustle for gangplanks onto shore, the motorcars, the whistling; Jeannette stepping towards him with her hand out; the town from the car window, darkening; the cordial, the salon, the bedroom, the ceiling. He realised his eyes were closed, and opened them.

The colours had gone. He was on his side, and the floor by the window was quilted with moonlight. In the dark the bedroom was large and soft. Sleep was half off and half on. He pulled himself up; a chill seared. Jacket off, braces down, unbutton the shirt. And then a whisper, a patter—nothing human, the sound of two objects shifting past each other. He stared at the door, and watched it puff open with an intruding breeze. The latch had not clicked shut.

On his feet, he pulled the handle and the door turned silently on its hinge. There lay the upstairs hall. Grey and empty. No draught, although the air was a little cooler. The lip of the carpet that ran up the stairs lay supine at the top, slightly furled. Above it the banister turned, descending. And in the far corner at the other end of the gallery, where the gloom deepened, a lamp stood beside a closed door.

He retreated. He pressed the door until he heard the latch, and slid under the cold sheets. His eyes shut on the dark ceiling and soon the bed-clothes were as warm as his skin, and he could imagine he was back in Nablus. A memory rose up, of a time he had walked in his sleep, when he was fourteen or so. He had woken at the warble of the call to prayer to find himself in bed beside his grandmother, his Teta, with one of her arms around his waist. Confused, ashamed, he tried to pull himself upright, stuck a foot out onto the cold tile—until Teta stretched forward and touched his hair. You were talking, she said. Habibi don't worry, habibi, go back to sleep.

2

In the twilight years of the Empire, keeping time had become a problem. The official year still began in March, when the tax farmers plagued the fellahin. But the Christians used the Gregorian calendar, led by January with the leap years and a few variations according to their liturgies; and while the Jews adjusted their terms to accommodate the cycles of the earth, the Muslims followed the lunar Hijri and gradually fell out of step with the seasons as they turned.

While Midhat was a child everyone in Nablus, even the non-Muslims, followed the moon and, in spite of Sultan Abdülhamid's new Frankish clock tower, kept religiously to Arab time. According to the Muslims, the Almighty had so designed the universe that every day as the sun disappeared the timepieces of humanity should be set to the twelfth hour, in obedience to the clock of the world. And so as darkness fell and the muezzins called for the maghrib prayer, wealthy Nabulsis all over town pulled watches from their pockets, extracted the crowns with their fingernails, and fiddled to make the hands clap on twelve, before, if so inclined, rushing off to the mosque.

As a very young child Midhat would sleep beside his Teta, Um Taher, in the winter. When he was five they moved beyond the old city walls, from a house with a shared courtyard and rounded chambers to a modern building with private rooms and squared edges at the foot of Mount Gerizim. He watched the seasons from his new bedroom window with the snowy gussets of Jabal al-Sheikh on the horizon.

The day Haj Taher, Midhat's father, announced his second engagement, Teta declared she had seen the carriage on the mountain a month before. Teta's prophecies protected no one, for she never knew what they meant at the time, and suffered only from the haunting of retrospect. Among other things, she had foreseen her own husband's death.

"I had a vision of a coffin on a blue carpet. I saw the corner of the wood on the blue carpet. I was at my mother's house, and I saw it again when they brought the coffin from Jaffa and put it at my feet. My eye, this eye, looked quickly down and I saw the corner of the coffin and, underneath it, the carpet."

Haj Taher's first marriage, to Midhat's mother, was Teta's doing. The girl came from a good Jenin family, and Taher had loved her.

"Your mother had green eyes. Her face was almost flat under them, like this," and she pressed her fingers over her cheeks, "wallah, like a little boy."

If she had prophesied this girl's death by tuberculosis, Teta kept it to herself. Midhat was two years old. His father was in Egypt. The house was filled with women crying, and as they washed the body on the dining table the housekeeper brought semolina pastries out to the hall, which Midhat crumbled in his fists before licking the sweet grit off his palms. The moment his father appeared in the doorway Teta yowled and gripped the edge of the table as though she might fall over.

Haj Taher did not stop long in Nablus. His clothing business in Cairo was growing fast and required more of his attention, and though he had hired extra staff for the shop on Muski Street and more young men to bring silks from the Golan, he never forgot his own father's lesson about the importance in business of maintaining personal relations, and since "Al-Kamal" was entering the Cairene lexicon to signify clothing of particularly high quality, Haj Taher Kamal himself could not run the store as an absentee. Nor could he rely on anonymous couriers to collect the silks from the merchants. He must both appear regularly on the selling floor and travel north for the stock, using the new envoys only to keep pace with the turnover. This ceaseless engagement was exhausting but profitable: it ensured the loyalty of the consumers and the honesty of the traders. Besides, the journeys added variation to his life; he could visit Nablus on the way, stop in on his agent Hisham at the local store, spend an evening with his mother and young son, before returning to check the accounts on Muski. When he returned to Cairo after his wife's funeral, he would have liked to set out on a trip again, but business had no time for grief. The holiday was approaching, sales had escalated, and he needed to stay in Cairo to supervise the shop.

Haj Taher spent his mornings at a sandalwood desk in the back room marking up the books. During the afternoons he mingled with the customers. This was a regime worked out over years, with a rhythm so precise that on more days than not the moment his assistant knocked on his door for lunch he was just inking a final digit in the accounting book, and this temporal economy pleased him, this sense of moving from one activity to another without a moment wasted.

Shortly after his wife's death, however, his regime was disrupted. Catching wind of his bereavement, a medley of Cairene businessmen began to disturb him in the mornings, and the hours devoted to accounting spilled unhappily into the afternoons. Every other day another man appeared, entered with caution, and puffed out his chest before the desk to describe the virtues of his daughter. Haj Taher thanked each one for the offer and declined. But after several weeks the interruptions began to work on him, and some of his polite dismissals became resentful acceptances of their invitations to call. After a longer while the flattery began to work on him too, and his acceptances became ceremonious. For it was beginning to seem plain that of course he deserved to marry again, and to marry well. And with his nose for business, Haj Taher was aware of the inconstancies of fashion and favour, and that for the time being he was a rich merchant, famous among the ladies, and he would do well to make use of it.

Without any female relatives in Egypt, he had no one to inspect the contenders. He might have called on his mother, but he considered her continued grief for his first wife and decided against it. Instead, he employed a friend named Rabab, a light-blooded dancer to whom he often made love after her performances in Zamalek. For a small fee Rabab agreed to investigate the girls on offer, and sift, discreetly, through the reputations of their families. A week passed, and on the Thursday evening Haj Taher caught Rabab wrapping herself in a gown behind the stage. Smiling with her lips together she produced a list written on the back of a menu. This one had a wealthy family, she said, but the mother was a pig. This was one of four girls, and the least appealing of the four. A shame; her two older sisters were very nice. This one was not wealthy, but the family was pleasant. Popular, well known. Pretty? So-so, very small teeth. This one was a Copt. Irritating. This one was certainly the most beautiful of all of them—

"What is her name?" said Taher.

"Layla. The family is so-so. Well off, not terribly."

"What is the mother like?"

"A nice person. Attractive, too."

He did not take long to decide. He wrote to Layla's father, and within days they had arranged the signing of the book and the wedding date. Only then did he invite his mother from Nablus for the ceremony, where she did not join in the ululations, nor did she dance.

Layla had thick hair and a thin neck, and in keeping with tradition she did not take to her stepson. She was especially hostile to touch, and whenever she could she would detach Midhat's fingers from her husband's thumb. Since she preferred to stay near her own family, Haj Taher's visits to Nablus became infrequent. More often now he sent an envoy to check on the stall there and conserved his travelling time for the Golan, leaving Midhat alone with Teta on Mount Gerizim for longer and longer periods.

Around this time, Midhat's memories started to congeal. His father became a big knee, a voice on the other side of a room. Teta was a cushion of breasts smelling of rose water and sweet violet. Layla was a bony wall. His mother, a soft nothing.

As Taher and Layla's visits to Nablus became rare, gossip about their fortunes bred in the schoolrooms. Midhat's cousin Jamil, who lived in the house below theirs, heard a rumour that Haj Taher had won his wealth by uncovering pharaonic artefacts in his garden in Cairo.

Teta burst out laughing. She was crouching in the doorway, fixing something. "Remember boys, the most unhappy people are the envious ones."

But when Taher did appear in Nablus, Teta glared at his new wife. Taher cracked pumpkin seeds between his teeth and Midhat stood looking at the large knee, which bounced as his father reached for the bowl. He liked the square hole made by his father's shelved leg, one ankle on the other thigh, and, preoccupied then by an urge for fitting things into holes, he longed to climb under his father's lap and stand up inside that human cubicle. Then the legs crossed, and the big dangling foot with its shiny leather vamp became a swing, perfect for sitting on. Beside him, Layla watched.

One memory of his father prevailed over the others. Later Midhat could not have said how old he was—six perhaps, or seven—but with that uncertainty the image earned the status of a myth or a recited dream and occupied undue space in his mind, for while there must have been similar mornings this was the one that endured.

In the memory, it is dawn on Mount Gerizim, and the bread tin lid claps shut on the sideboard. Two valises stand by the door. And there is Baba, wearing a tarbush and brown wool travelling coat, and he whispers good morning and leans down for a kiss. His breath is human and sweet, and two red swollen pores are visible under his moustache. From the doorway Midhat watches his father attach the bags on either side of his horse. Baba mounts, and before he moves, pauses on the back of the animal to look at his son. The watery exhalations of the morning hover over the distant olive trees in a bluish haze, and Haj Taher, Abu Midhat, descends into the mist.

It was spring when a letter arrived with news of Layla's pregnancy. Teta clapped her hands, and the ladies arrived to congratulate her. After that, months passed without a single letter or telegram. Summer opened up and heat poured from the sky. The bricks of the houses turned ash white. Groundling plants yellowed and died. Samoom winds made suffocating visitations under the cover of dust and dried up four of Nablus's freshwater springs. When the rains finally came, they came in torrents.

At first Midhat thought it was the storm that had woken him. Then he heard voices. Creeping to the door he saw the shape of his father in the hall, standing in the glow of a lamp, shaking water from his arms. Teta stepped into the light beside him, collecting layers of clothing in the jerking dark. When Midhat woke again it was morning, and his grandmother was sitting on his bed. She put a hand on his ankle through the cover, and said quietly: "Your father is here. He is upset by the death of the baby." His father's clothes, deformed by the damp, hung for days from the hooks on the kitchen wall.

When the second baby came, Taher and Layla returned to live in Nablus. A short while later, Midhat was sent off to school in Constantinople. His cousin Jamil had already completed his first year at the Mekteb-i Sultani, so the departure was not as fearsome as it might have been. In fact, all year Midhat had felt envious of Jamil, who at thirteen was already so like a man, and careless of his schoolbooks, which he brought home during the holiday. Midhat had seen the pile on his cousin's bedroom floor knocked sideways so the spines were visible, and strained to decipher the lettering of the titles. When he himself was sent off, the change felt less like going away than going towards.

The Mekteb-i Sultani—also known as the "Lycée Impérial"—was a large yellow boarding school beside the Bosphorus, with black-and-gold gates and formal gardens. His classmates hailed from all over the Empire: Armenians, Greeks, Jews from Macedonia, Maronite Christians from Mount Lebanon, even Bulgarians and Albanians until that territory was lost; and though the majority were Turks and most of the others were sons of officials and officers, it was nonetheless here that Midhat had his first taste of cosmopolitan life. After an intensive course in French, he perfected his Ottoman Turkish, and learned a little English and a little Persian; he studied astronomy and mathematics, was bored by calligraphy and geography, and excited by philosophy and science. School timetables were set to Frankish time, so that instead of riding the twelve hours between sunrise and sunset as they did in Nablus, the schoolboys counted from noon to noon.

It was also at the Lycée that Midhat first discovered his own separateness. He was bathing in the shower room one morning, his feet on the varnished wooden boards above the drain, rubbing the suds as the water sheeted his legs and thinking vaguely about the boys in line outside while he was alone in here. Then it came to him. He looked down at his body and realised that his hands were only his hands, and that his eyes were only his to look out from. It was peculiar, provoked only by the barrier the door made keeping the water in and the other boys out. And it was not exactly something he hadn't already known; only he now felt it more concretely. It had never occurred to him before to question why Midhat should be Midhat, and that no one else should be Midhat, or that Midhat should be no one else. And at the same time that it now mystified him, looking down at his legs, red with heat and lightly tufted with straight black hairs, he also could not imagine how things might be otherwise. This realisation was like a tiny jolt of electricity that both locked him inside his body and alienated him from it. The jolt was as curious as it was painful, and when later he tried calmly to recall the feeling, he could not. He even tried to recreate the experience by entering the showers and looking down at his hands, but the jolt would not come. Over the next four years the sensation did visit him again, but rarely. Once or twice he felt it in a classroom when his mind wandered from the lesson and he looked at the pen between his fingers. And sometimes in that half state between waking and sleeping, when he was lying in bed and Jamil was snoring in the cot beside him, and his mind blurred the events of the day—then it came: the electric feeling of aloneness, victorious and agonising, unearthly.

During the holidays Midhat and Jamil took the ferry back over the Bosphorus to the Asian side, and then the train from Haydarpasha to Damascus, before travelling south to Nablus. The baby, Musbah, grew older in lurches. One year Layla was round with pregnancy again, the next year there was a second child, the following year a third. One year Midhat returned and found that his father and Layla had moved back to Cairo, and again he and Teta were alone on Mount Gerizim.

Then the Ottomans joined the war effort, and time literally began to change. There was an argument over some warships—the British wanted them back, the Turks sold them to the Germans—and though the Ottomans continued to pretend they were neutral, they signed a secret treaty with Germany in August 1914 on the Gregorian calendar. Mobilization began, and, in a bid for discipline, all the clocks were set to Frankish time.

At school, the Turkish boys were excited. But many wealthy sons of the provinces scrambled to avoid the barracks; the men of Haj Taher's generation paid a fee to evade conscription in the Ottoman army, but the rules had changed. Some young men in Nablus made use of a conscription loophole and married impoverished women from the villages; others hid in their family homes; others escaped to Europe. Jamil found employment as a military clerk in Constantinople and managed that way to avoid the front line, while the income from the Kamal store in Cairo was by now so plentiful that Haj Taher made plans to send Midhat to France.

Even though the Turks would soon be at war with her, France remained, in the minds of everyone at the Mekteb-i Sultani, the pinnacle of Europe and exemplar of the modern age. The great travellers of North Africa and the Levant always chose to visit France, and even European "Frankish" timekeeping was by an accident of etymology tied to the French. What an opportunity, therefore, to go straight to the heart of modernity and be educated there. At nineteen, Midhat Kamal was becoming ambitious. And he was pleased by the confidence in him his father's decision displayed, and the love that wished to put him out of war's way.

He travelled to Cairo for the first time en route to Alexandria. On the journey he thought about his mother. These thoughts had little substance beyond a familiar nightgowned shadow—often summoned, always deficient in reality—and an indelible sense that, despite the two years they shared on earth together, his mother had died so that Midhat might live. A fatal logic of correlation: when she was, he was not, and when he was, she was not. He observed the commotion of the Cairene streets as through a thick pane of glass. The Europeans surprised him, clustered in separate cafés from the Egyptians and the Greeks; they wore pale colours and cast distinctive silhouettes against the imperial sun. His father's house also surprised him. A white villa with two storeys, surrounded by fruit trees that knocked their goods against the windows. It did not surprise him that Layla scowled when he arrived, and whispered in the hall outside the bedroom where he slept, and tried to exclude him from conversation at dinner.

The evening before his departure, his father caught him on the stairs.

"Habibi, come with me, aal-maktab."

The office shutters pleated along their joints to disclose the remaining day, and Midhat watched his father reach over the desk against those pale slats of light, and heard the wheeling of a drawer. He returned with a handful of purple silk; amid the fabric something gleamed. A gold disc. He rubbed the silk over its engravings.

"This is for you, Midhat."

The watch was heavy and cool. Midhat popped the clasp. From an ornate enamel dial three tiny black hands protruded. One trotted around the rim, pointing at the Arabic ciphers.

His father produced a penknife. "This is how you open the back."

He slotted the blade into the edge, and the back of the disc swung open on an invisible hinge. Inside, a series of corrugated wheels were fastened with screwed silver plates, all motionless except for two: one spinning in a fury, and pushing a smaller adjacent wheel, which turned at regular intervals. The smaller wheel was clicking. Click, click, click.

"Thank you. Father, thank you."

"God keep you, habibi. Keep it safe."

3

"Where is the mother of the bride?" the photographer called, emerging from the curtain.

A woman ran across the lawn, the wind pushing her dress between her legs. The assembled group made a space for her in the first row. One flash and a loud pop, and the photographer emerged again to replace the slide.

"Hello Monsieur Kamal," said a large man in an ivory waistcoat. "My name is Sylvain Leclair."

Sylvain Leclair's moustache twitched as he spoke. Midhat returned the greeting, and Sylvain gave him a long impassive look. He removed his hat, drawing his fluffy hair up into a peak on the back of his head.

"Are you a relation of the bride, or of the groom?" said Midhat.

Leclair's expression did not change. He turned to Docteur Molineu.

"Frédéric, come here. I want to talk to you."

The two men moved off, and Midhat wondered if he had said something wrong.

"Monsieur Kamal, are you enjoying yourself?"

Jeannette was beside him, wearing a blue dress and white lace gloves.

"I'll tell you who everyone is," she said. "Bonjour Patrice! That—that in the big hat is Madame Crotteau. Her husband died last year of meningitis.

She can be a little annoying, you have been warned. And that one I said hello to is Patrice Nolin. Actually he used to be a professor at the Faculty of Medicine, although he has retired, unfortunately. He wrote a book last year about the social life of animals. And right up until the war he was in the Congo. His daughters are Carole and Marie-Thérèse, those two. That's Marie-Thérèse in the orange dress. God, isn't it hideous."

Marie-Thérèse's dress was more red than it was orange, Midhat thought, and he appreciated the diffuse quality of the satin. But he nodded nonetheless; it was unusual to have Jeannette's attention like this. Since his arrival a week ago she often smiled at him, but only from afar, and she did not engage much in conversation. Her father on the other hand pestered him with questions whenever he could, most often at breakfast. Sometimes Jeannette joined in these discussions—just that morning, for example, she appeared to enjoy explaining the difference between *très*, *trop*, and *tellement*, the last two of which they discovered had no direct Arabic equivalents. But more often than not she slipped from the table before they were finished and disappeared into some remote quarter of the house, and Midhat did not see her again until he returned from the Faculty in the evening.

"That man talking with Carole is Carl Page, he works in a bank. His mother is a friend of Sarah Bernhardt's. His son has already been called to Ypres. And that one in the red cravat is Xavier, my cousin, Marian's brother. He is studying law. And Laurent, he is also at the Medical Faculty. I will introduce you."

Laurent was a tall blond man, stooping to talk with a squat fellow in a bowler. Jeannette did not, however, make any motion to initiate an introduction. She continued:

"With him is Luc Dimon. He owns the largest vineyard in the region."

"And these are all friends of the bride?"

"The ones I have named. I don't know the groom's party. They are mostly from Nice."

Docteur Molineu was now in conversation with Patrice Nolin near the entrance to the dinner tent. There was something girlish about Nolin's appearance. His eyes were far apart and his cheeks had a high colour. Molineu's face was puckering with animation. That was exactly how he looked at breakfast, jumping with excitement whenever they encountered any phrase that could not be translated.

The crowd began to move, and a footman raised an arm by the tent entrance. Midhat's name, spelt "Monsieur Methat Kemal," was written beside Jeannette's on the board. They collected slices of fowl in brown sauce from the table at the back, and as they took their seats Sylvain Leclair appeared across the table, alongside Luc Dimon.

"Le jeune Turc!" said Sylvain Leclair.

"Actually," said Jeannette, "Monsieur Midhat would call himself a Palestinian Arab."

Midhat glanced at her. Something thawed in his chest.

"So, Monsieur l'Arabe," said Sylvain, pulling out his chair, "what brings you to Montpellier?"

"Medicine," said Midhat. "I am studying medicine at the university."

"Escaping the barracks?" Without moving the rest of his face, Sylvain Leclair winked. "This is my friend Dimon—Luc, this is a young Arab man, staying with the Molineus. Monsieur Mid—quoi Mid—ha? He is here avoiding the war."

"Sylvain," said Jeannette.

"I'm just playing. Dimon owns a vineyard. The largest in the region. With the best wine."

"Ho ho, how do you do. Sylvain is very modest, he is an excellent vigneron. But you know, we all had trouble with the blight, it was an awful thing."

"Some of us had more trouble than others. Did you know about this, Monsieur Kamal? It attacked the plants. They were very, very small." Sylvain curled his forefinger inside his thumb. "Phylloxera vastatrix. Une petite friponne. The little grues destroyed my entire vineyard. The vine leaves all had little balls on them. This is a Clairette Languedoc, would you like to try, Monsieur Midhat?"

"No, thank you. Yes, a little. Thank you."

"How did you come to know the Molineus?" said Luc Dimon.

"My father contacted the university, and Docteur Molineu kindly offered himself as a host."

"The sacrifices," said Sylvain. "Tell us some things. We'd like to know all about your way of life."

Midhat could not tell if Sylvain was mocking him. "Excuse me?"

"Midhat, may I introduce you to Monsieur Laurent Toupin."

Jeannette moved back in her chair to reveal the tall blond man on her other side.

"How do you do."

"Enchanted to meet you," said Midhat. He turned his head, and a crisp breath of wind from a gap in the marquee alerted him to the sweat on his face.

"He speaks French well," said Laurent.

"He does," said Jeannette. "Excuse me, gentlemen."

Laurent took Jeannette's vacated seat. His sleeve was rolled before the elbow, and his forearm was covered in wiry blond hair.

"You know, I think I have seen you at the Faculty . . . you are very recognisable. I am in my fourth year, but you have just started? How have you found it, the classes? The first year is a little boring, I remember, you have all the preliminaries in the sciences. But have you started the clinics?"

"Not yet," said Midhat. He took a deep breath. He was conscious of Sylvain Leclair, swilling his wine across the table from them. "Next week, I believe."

"And you are enjoying it? I love medicine, I really do, I love the Faculty. It's the best discipline in the world. We are at the very tip, the edge, pushing into the unknown. You know, they say you can look out there into the unknown, or you can look in here. People are so afraid of it, and that's why. But—is it common to visit France to study medicine, for men in your region? I imagine the traditions must be different. I mean, it was only two centuries ago they were using Avicenna's book in the Faculty, but I imagine things have diverged since then."

This mention of Avicenna struck Midhat as artificial. He realised Laurent was trying to impress him, and warmed to him instantly.

"We have a university in Cairo," he said. "It is a good university. There is another in Beirut. But more and more men from Syria are studying in Europe, in England, France, Germany. And the same is happening in the other direction. Though not for university of course. We do have good universities . . . they are not the best. The best is Europe, everyone knows that. But they use the French way, too, in Syria and Egypt."

"Interesting. You know it's very interesting to meet you. Jeannette tells me you are a Muslim. There was an Oriental who graduated from the Faculty the year I began, though actually now I think of it I believe he was Christian. Anyway, they aren't common here but certainly he was a good doctor."

"Midhat, how are you, is everything fine, everything going well?"

"Yes, thank you Docteur."

"Stop calling me Docteur now Midhat, I am Frédéric. You have met Laurent, I see. Laurent it's good to see you. Your hair is too long, however."

"The army will cut it soon enough."

"Ah, pff. Patrice, Patrice, come and meet Midhat Kamal. Here."

"Enchanté."

"Patrice is my colleague now, we are in the same discipline. It used to be the human body for him, and now it is the social one."

"Frédéric. Un livre, seulement un livre."

"So you don't think you will return to the university at all?"

"As I've said, the problem for me is that when the war begins . . . immédiatement c'est fini, ou sinon immédiatement, assez vite. No more free thought, no more free . . . exchange."

"Ah . . . yes, I know what you mean."

"Marian!" said Jeannette, who had returned and was standing behind them, addressing the bride on the other side. "I have not seen you since the church. You look so beautiful. Where is Paul?"

"Oh, Jojo I am exhausted. Ouf—I have to go."

Laurent said: "When is he going to Flanders?"

"After they return from Nice, I think."

"Are you not going, Laurent?"

"I'm exempt for a while, because I volunteered. Not for long though."

"Oh come on, you have to join us! You should just volunteer again. Don't be a mouse."

"Xavier is going."

"When?"

"With the others. Two weeks."

"And all the ladies will be nursing you."

"Did you hear about the Alberts' German governess?"

"Governess? No, I only know the story about the bank . . ."

"Maman . . . Maman . . ."

Around them the guests were rising with a racket of chair legs. Four pyramids had appeared at the back of the pavilion. Midhat followed Jeannette between the tables. The pyramids, he saw, were constructed of tiny round cakes.

"Midhat, may I offer you one?"

"Bonjour, I am Madame Crotteau."

"Bonjour Madame, I am Midhat Kamal."

"I know. How do you find Montpellier? Is it not beautiful. Has Frédéric taken you to Palavas-les-Flots?"

"Why in hell would I take him to the sea?" said Frédéric. "Imagine, you travel to an entirely new country and they say—let us show you the water on which you came! No, Nicole. He needs to see the culture, the city, the landscape of the interior. Hear the music, read the trobairitz . . . that's the important . . . the smells, the terroir of Occitan . . ."

"Only a Parisian could be tellement fier du Languedoc."

Frédéric raised an eyebrow. "My mother was from Dordogne."

"You must come for a walk with me, Midhat," said Laurent, shaking icing sugar onto the floor. "I'll show you the gardens. Yes?"

"Yes, that would be wonderful."

"Fantastic. We'll meet at the Salle Dugès when the sun is out."

They decided on Thursday, if the weather was good. Thursday came and it was raining, so they decided on the Friday. The morning session that Friday was an introduction to practical dissection for the first years; Midhat would meet Laurent afterwards, at noon by the statue of Lapeyronie.

Each week the crowd in the Salle Dugès had diminished. Now only a handful of French students remained, exempt from combat for medical reasons, to which some confessed while others remained rigidly silent.

Nonetheless eager to prove their nerve, all made pointed use of frontline slang, referring to the Germans as "Boches" and quipping about the weakness of the Prussian gene. Many younger professors had also been conscripted, and several names on Midhat's timetable did not correspond to the person who appeared at the front of the classroom. His classmates were mainly Spaniards and Belgians and there were also two Swiss and one Englishman. Midhat was the only Arab and the only student not from Europe, and in the morning atmosphere of the Salle he felt shy. He observed, remote from conversations, how someone could introduce an anecdote as funny, might even begin by outlining the final joke: the listening company would anticipate the ending and laugh in unison. Once a humourous tone was established, anything could be amusing, and each person was ready to laugh even at the weakest joke in the spirit of including everyone.

Despite his shyness, his accent was improving, and he pronounced "le thorax" and "le capillaire" with the precision of a foreigner. On the Rue de la Loge he bought a new French hat, an overcoat, and a black umbrella, and he brought all three items with him to the Faculty on the Friday he was to meet Laurent, despite the fact that their walk was dependent on fine weather.

Professor Brogante stood at the head of the operating table.

"Medicine is not an exact science," he intoned, stretching over the implement tray and flipping a scalpel so its blade faced the same direction as the others.

The walls of the dissection hall carried Brogante's voice far over the raked seats, so that, to the students standing close around the corpse, on which a white sheet rose to points at the feet and knees, the professor's statements seemed to boom.

"The fact that its data are so complex, that it deals usually with probabilities rather than certainties, does not destroy the scientific character of medicine." Brogante's hands descended to the lower edge of the sheet. "It only adds a reason for greater scientific caution."

The students rustled for a view.

"Every point I, the physician, observe is a suggestion. I look for other indications to confirm my diagnosis, or I try a certain procedure, the outcome of which will decide whether I have read the situation correctly."

A head of black hair appeared at the top of the sheet, shining blue in the glow from the high windows. The waxy shaven face of a man emerged, followed by his torso. Brogante flattened the sheet over the legs, wrapped his fingers around a scalpel, and approached the grey neck.

"In order to expose the thoracic and abdominal cavities, we will make the first incision from the sternum . . ."

Professor Brogante's voice expanded so much it seemed to have no edges, and Midhat no longer heard the individual words. He saw the blade pierce the skin of the neck, and watched the top layer of epidermis split quickly, as though it had been tied tightly shut and was just released. The first long incision complete, Brogante cut a second lateral line. Then he turned the flaps of skin back, one by one, four dry slaps. Inside was an inhuman assemblage of organs. Overripe red and purple and sick yellow. Midhat looked at the bloodless strings of sinew lacing the stomach, and gave way. His vision thronged with black spots, which crowded together and closed the cadaver from sight.

The next thing he knew he was sitting alone, in the front row of the auditorium. He saw the backs of the other students ahead, and Brogante's voice continued, more distantly:

"The gallbladder lies to the extreme right of the epigastric zone. The caecum in the right iliac compartment and, can you see, that there is the ascending colon. Can anyone tell me what region that is in? Monsieur Havonteur?"

Midhat could not see the body for the students. One head turned: it was Samuel Cogolati, a Belgian. Cogolati twisted his neck to check no one was watching him, then bounded over and crouched beside Midhat's chair.

"Tout va bien?"

"Qu'est-ce qui se passe? I fainted, didn't I."

"Yes." Cogolati breathed a laugh. "Ça va, I caught you, you didn't hit the floor." He shook his head up and down very quickly. "I have to go back, but . . . Ça va?"

"Fine, fine, go back. I'll take a moment. Thank you, Samuel."

"De rien."

In spite of the bread roll Cogolati brought from the dining hall, Midhat's legs were still trembling when he met Laurent at noon beside the statue, and he was grateful for his umbrella to lean on.

"Philosophically speaking," said Laurent, as they moved off down the boulevard, "your reaction was totally natural. I recall my first practical dissection. Not a . . . not a pleasant experience."

"Thank you. But I still can't help feeling ashamed of myself."

"It will be less abhorrent, you'll find, observing the living organism. Unfortunately they must start you on the dead because it's better for pointing out the organs. I think there is something of the *object quality* of the dead that is alarming. But what one must realise, what we must accommodate, as students of medicine I mean, is that death is absolutely a part of life. And as we progress scientifically, as a race, we must overcome those social taboos that relegate death to a separate sphere. What I mean to say is, don't worry about it."

Midhat took a deep breath and tried not to sigh. "I am still—I feel—"

"Human nature . . ." said Laurent. He looked up at the sky, eyes half-shut against the sun. "The meaning of illness . . . We are never without death, in life. You could argue we exist in a constant state of dying, like a flame, unstable, decaying. And what is sickness, therefore? Sickness is a part of life. We talk of life as renewal, but really it is decay. The fight against decay, sometimes, but decay nonetheless."

While Laurent spoke, Midhat thought of the tour they had taken on the first day of term, during which he had followed the other new students into an enormous hall with a trompe l'oeil ceiling. The walls of the first gallery were lined with cabinets, and everyone had gasped as they turned to look.

Deformed foetuses pressing against the glass walls of jars. Human and animal skeletons hanging from nails; skulls branded with the names of diseases stacked at jaunty angles. In a glass-topped cabinet lay a mummified head, chemical black, the brain half-exposed. The cabinets extended: more brains, quartered and labelled, bodies strung up, black like the head. Burnt,

perhaps. The diagrams on the walls, the paintings, all of them depicted
gaudy excrescences, specimens of monstrosity, phases of venereal disease.
Charts compared abnormality with abnormality, infection, atrophies, pal-
sies, leprosies. A two-headed baby with twin tufts of hair creased four eyes
at him.

Laurent brought them to a stop. At the top of a tall, pale-green gate a
curlicued sign of beaten iron stated: UNIVERSITÉ DE MONTPELLIER, JARDIN
DES PLANTES, FONDÉ PAR HENRI IV EN 1593. The gate scraped open over
the gravel, and they faced a track up a shallow incline that split in two: to
the right alongside a hedgerow, to the left by a stone wall finished with an
urn. They took the hedgerow path. Beyond, white paths sliced green lawns
and a stone building arched upward, speared with cypress trees.

"This garden is one of the oldest in Europe," said Laurent. "It was created by the king for a famous scientist called Belleval. They added parts to
it in the last century, though I'm afraid I can't remember which is which."

The air carried a cool fecund smell. Smoke-white leaves from the
trees above lay in heaps where the turf met the pathway, the light shafting
between the boughs scattered shadows, and Midhat soon lost any sense of
direction. They passed a thicket of bamboo, and a pond of giant water lilies
basking in the sun, and geometrical flowerbeds lined with shrubs. They
shaded their eyes at the greenhouse windows and saw underwater plants
reaching large green hands from their berths.

"What was it you were saying," said Midhat. "About death, and life?"

"Oh, I don't know. I'm always pontificating. That's what my father says.
Too much talking, not enough doing, he says."

"It was interesting . . ."

"What is life? That is interesting. From whence did it begin?"

Midhat laughed. A blast of sunlight replaced Laurent's shadow on the
glass: he had abandoned the greenhouse and was facing the shrubbery.

"God, of course," said Midhat.

"Yes. But well the problem now, it seems to me, is there is starting to be
too much knowledge. It cannot be contained by a single brain. Before, we
could—more or less, I mean—hold it all in. But now, practically speaking,

we are all more or less brains floating in a sea of knowledge." Laurent touched a fern and the wand jogged under his finger. "That's not quite the image I wanted to conjure."

"Did God create the universe, or was he coexistent with it."

"Quite. You should talk to Jeannette, she studied philosophy."

"The syllogism of life is an impossible thing," said Midhat. "We cannot trace the endless stream of cause and effect."

"How have you found her, by the way?"

"Because if we try to go further back, to the father's father's father and so on, it is like trying to reach Him, up there, by building a tower. What did you say?"

"Jeannette. As a house companion, how is she."

Midhat paused. "We have not talked very much." He imitated Laurent and touched the end of a fern. "I like her."

"Yes. I'm sure it must seem odd to you, how we treat women here."

"In some respects. There is more freedom. What is this way?"

"Just another lawn. Have a look."

They returned to the path. Under the sun the embarrassment of the morning was washing off, and the umbrella helped the rhythm of Midhat's footfall. Insignificant thoughts bloomed in French in his mind, and in an access of sincerity he released a few and described the scene around them: the beauty of the human touch on the unseeing bark of the tree trunk, labelled by age and species, which continued to stretch according to its nature, sideways and upward, blistering knots and rough fuzz.

"This is so unlike anything I have seen before, even though I know many of these plants. Sometimes I feel tired from looking at new things, but sometimes it makes me feel . . . more awake! But look, that is an olive tree. That is everywhere in my country, but I see it now and it sets off a curious system of joy in my mind, to have found it here, in a place so strange to me."

"I am delighted you like the garden so much."

Although his new friend's tone was not unkind, Midhat felt deflated. Of course, it was difficult to communicate any profound sensation, let alone in another language.

"I'd like to travel around Europe," said Laurent. "Like you, I suppose. My grandfather kept a diary about his travels to Greece and Rome. When I go to war I might travel, if they send me further than Picardy."

"The world is dilating," said Midhat. "Or—perhaps not 'dilating' . . ."

"Developing?"

"No, I mean—the trains, for instance. The trains are all over the world . . . they sell oranges from Jaffa here in Montpellier. I saw them!"

Laurent laughed. "Ah Midhat Kamal, you are a special case."

Beside the path, four young women sat in the shade of an oak tree. Midhat watched one bite into a peach. He felt pricked by Laurent's laughter, and wished he had said nothing.

In his last year at the Mekteb-i Sultani, the divisions between the Turkish boys and the rest of them had appeared like a sudden chasm in the earth. He and Jamil returned from Nablus after Ramadan to find a variable network of alliances drawn up without their consent, and sometimes the Arabs and the Armenians were together and sometimes they were apart; similarly with the Jews and the Greeks; for the children had listened to their parents during the holiday, and following the newspapers and the example of the teachers they enforced the external currents within the school corridors with surprisingly little resistance. After lessons Midhat and his cousin sought each other out, fearing the game they were being forced to play whose rules were often unclear. You never knew when someone might turn on you, and if you never shot an unkind glance or whispered behind your hand you risked being accused of disloyalty and getting your arm twisted by a member of your own side.

Midhat had experienced pressures he was sure Laurent had not. He felt an urge to prove that his enthusiasm was not a sign of unworldliness.

"Do you know what you will specialise in?" said Laurent. "I'm doing psychiatry."

They halted by a ruin in the classical style, a roofless set of arches laced with red blossoms.

"Psychiatry?" said Midhat. "That's not the body."

"No. But I have developed an interest in it. And if you must know, it was because of a woman."

Midhat could not reclaim the energy of a few moments before. He remained silent. Just as Laurent started walking off from the ruin, he threw out:

"I had a mistress in Constantinople."

Laurent glanced back. Midhat continued, casually: "She spoke neither Arabic nor Turkish. I rented a chambre in the Etiler neighbourhood, for privacy."

He felt a hand on his arm.

"I am impressed," said Laurent. Again, he laughed. "I am also rather amazed!"

"Her name was Marie."

"Where was she from?"

"Sweden."

"Bra—vo."

He had drawn them in a loop: ahead was the green gate, the letters in reverse. Midhat also felt amazed, and even a little alarmed. Apparently, it was quite as easy to invent something as to put on a new hat and coat.

4

The water in the garden pond was shallow and did not completely cover Jeannette's knees, which rose above it like pink islands. The fountain had stopped working and the cherub's jug was empty. A white scar around the stone perimeter marked the water level from the previous summer. She heard the wind in the trees before it reached her; a second later, goose pimples rose on her submerged legs.

A head bobbed in an upper window. It was Georgine, in Midhat's bedroom. Jeannette had spent the morning in the room adjacent, her father's study, organising a box of photographs into two leather albums. The box contained images of her mother as a young woman. Some Jeannette had never seen before. She had not thought intently about her mother in a long time, and the photographs were hard to look at. And yet she had looked, and for hours, searching ravenously for signs of herself in her mother. She came to when Georgine called for lunch. Then she decided to sit in the garden pond and meditate.

As a child, Jeannette had resembled her father and everyone thought she would take after him. Like Frédéric she was energetic: she spoke quickly, she liked drama. But over the years she had changed, and now she loathed the beating of her mind, and deliberately sought out boredom in order to avert it. Her father liked to call her "the Sphinx."

When she thought about her childhood, she thought of her bedroom in Montparnasse. She thought of the pink and white wallpaper, embossed with gold curls that sprouted into tiny flowers, which she loved to pick in secret near the skirting board behind the chairs, digging her nail into the flowers and scratching out the cakey plaster underneath. A row of dolls dressed in coloured lace ran the length of the window seat, with heavy cold hands, white bisque faces, and real hair. Jeannette rarely touched them. Her favourite toy was a sticky tarot deck, which she spent whole afternoons arranging and rearranging on the floor, casting incantations. The girls from school were jealous of the miniature ivory elephants, the music boxes, the tin ship with the painted crew, and when they came round to play they wanted to wind them up and work their limbs, and at first Jeannette would sit patiently and allow them to do so. But sooner or later she demanded the other girl play with her instead, and together they would invent religions on the window seat, directing spells at the hats of passersby. Jeannette selected chants from a book of poetry, and her favourite was on page 92, from a poem called "Resignation":

> As a child, I dreamt of the Koh-i-Noor,
> Persian and Papal richness, sumptuous,
> Heliogabalus, Sardanapalus!

Héliogabale et Sardanapale! they called from the window, pointing their fingers at solitary men, watching how they reacted or did not react to the effect of the witchcraft, and the doom that lay ahead of them.

Papa was the patron of the toys. Jeannette had no brothers or sisters, and her mother Ariane was affectionate but withdrawn, and often kept to her bedroom. After lessons, or when she came home from school, Jeannette read the books her father gave her under the bed until her elbows were sore from the carpet bristles. When she thought about her childhood in later years, she thought of the view from the bedroom floor: the spaces beneath the chairs were shelters from equatorial typhoons, the woodwork below the window a carving from an ancient civilisation. On the bookcase she could remove the panel behind the encyclopaedia to access a round hole in the wall, which was a hiding place for scrolls and treasures. As she grew older she imagined different kinds of adventures and began reading novels, which she bought on her way home from class and concealed inside the dust jackets of history books.

One Friday afternoon, the year she turned sixteen, Jeannette returned from school to find their neighbour sitting with a policeman at the kitchen table. Her mother, they said, had shot herself with a pistol in the courtyard. Her father was not yet back from the university. The neighbour heard the shot and called the policeman, who had already called the undertaker. They looked at Jeannette with frightened eyes and offered biscuits and tea. She was surprised to find that she could not even open her mouth to form a yes or a no.

In the aftermath, all parental reserve evaporated and Frédéric told his daughter everything. Her mother had expressed the urge to end her life on at least two other occasions, but those episodes were so far apart that he had not considered them cause for serious alarm. "Forgive me," he said, pulling a handful of his hair near the crown. Every now and then he would say, "Oh," and cover his mouth, and she knew he was remembering something.

Jeannette seized at these details with appetite, at every memory that slipped out of her father's mouth between his silences, while he sat in the living room staring at the floor, mouth contorted with regret. Death had loosened the truth from him and he was miraculously unguarded: gone was the man who cantered off midconversation; in his place stood a mass of uncatalogued private facts. Thus exposed he gave Jeannette everything. In the days leading up to the funeral he described his courtship, his impressions of the woman who became her mother at each stage of knowing her, how she changed and did not change over the years.

Without meaning to, with these stories he opened a whole hemisphere of his daughter's imagination, so that once the coffin was finally laid in the earth and he began to close his wounds Jeannette was still picking at hers. A woman was taking shape in her mind. Not only was this woman her mother, she was also Mademoiselle Ariane Passant, and Madame Ariane Molineu, a figure made out of the darkness from before Jeannette was born. Before long, in the natural way, her father learned to live with sadness, and soon that sadness lost its sting, and what had been unsealed in shock began to clam up again, and he would not release any more of what he knew. He brushed Jeannette off when she asked him to, with an appalled look, as if forgetting how much he had already told her.

They moved to Montpellier after Jeannette finished school. Frédéric's sister lived in town with her children Marian and Xavier, and also nearby was the vineyard of Sylvain Leclair, an old friend of Ariane's. Frédéric took up a position as maître de conférences at the university, and Jeannette enrolled to study philosophy, becoming one of only nineteen women in her year.

Father and daughter settled in quickly. They entered the society around the university and formed acquaintances that became friendships. It did not matter here if you were indigenous or from elsewhere since within those lecture halls and libraries all accents converged on a standard, and the commerce of knowledge dissolved regional difference. Sylvain brought the Molineus into the orbit of the vignerons, who also accepted them, albeit with reservations. The society of the vignerons had clotted over the last fifty years under pressure of various external disasters, including the droughts and the Algerian wine surplus. In distinction to the northern Gauls, they clung to the archaic identity of Occitania—although that was a name so diluted by now that half the restaurants along the seafront had it daubed in enamel on their front boards. But between the vines Sylvain was such a beloved and strange personality that he secured invitations for his friends "les Molineux" without any trouble, in spite of their voices and clothes, which recalled Paris through and through.

At the end of each weekday, father and daughter reunited in the blue salon to discuss philosophy. They drank from new china and debated Bergson's notion of freedom experienced through time, which Frédéric liked for its emphasis on the action of the mind. Jeannette preferred Boutroux's point that formulae can never explain anything because they cannot explain themselves, which she sometimes mistakenly distilled into the view that there is no point in commenting on any phenomenon since we are all part of the same fabric, which meant you could at most grasp the corner of something but never see the whole. These discussions, in which Frédéric encouraged the expansion of his daughter's sympathies to consider alternative points of view, often touched on themes of significance but they were never applied to their own lives. Although father and daughter avoided candour, these evenings brought them into a new kind of intimacy from which each drew strength.

Since Jeannette earned her diploma, even this had dissipated. Her friends from the university were all married, and though she had no desire to leave her father their discussions had stopped, and without an emotional repertoire to buttress the intellectual bond they grew apart. Now Jeannette relied on her own powers of stillness for succour. Her philosophical education had sharpened the apparatus of her mind, which she had repurposed into ramparts. She let the hours of the day fall by remotely, and her thoughts slid from object to object without engagement.

Lately she had encountered a few difficulties. The arrival of Midhat was one cause. She had kept a distance from their visitor, but even at a distance his presence made it harder to submerge herself in her own mind. The war was another cause, and although that too was distant it was all anyone wanted to talk about. At least, she considered, they were fortunate to have left Paris—though, of course, the boys would be leaving soon, Xavier, Paul, Laurent. These small changes wrought vast work, and the corners of Jeannette's mind had begun once again to glimmer with activity. And then that morning, the photographs of her mother. Her face and figure before the photographer's painted screen. The freckle under her eyebrow, the lace around her collar, the stray hairs curving out, marked in immortal grey lines on the gelatin silver.

"Bonjour, Mademoiselle."

Jeannette started. Midhat Kamal was standing on the terrace at the back of the house. He held an umbrella between his graceful hands, and his thin black eyebrows were raised in greeting. As she lifted her arm to wave, he bowed, but remained on the terrace amid the iron furniture. He could have been a European from this distance; the coppery tone of his face, and his dark brow and eyes—these were the only signs that he was what her father would call "Semitic." If she hadn't known she might have guessed he was Italian.

"How are you?" she called.

"Quite tired, but I am well. I have walked from the Faculty, it was beautiful. I am afraid I have interrupted you bathing."

"Not at all, I was going to come in. It is getting cold."

She stood, and as the chill air whipped her wet legs and flapped the bathing suit on her stomach she saw the whites of Midhat's eyes.

"Let me get my towel, I am sorry. One moment. Perhaps then, would you like to take a coffee? One moment, Monsieur Midhat."

She tried not to run. She crossed the lawn, lowering her eyes as she wrapped the top edge of the towel over the fabric on her breasts; wet feet on stone, on floorboard, on carpeted stair. In her bedroom she peeled out of the swimming costume, rubbed the damp off her body, and dressed quickly in a cotton house gown. At a dignified pace, she descended the stairs. Georgine was already bringing in the coffee, and curtsied as Jeannette passed.

"Alors," Jeannette exhaled, meeting Midhat's sidelong glance. He was sitting very upright on the sofa. She chose a wicker chair and drew her sleeve out of the way to pour the coffee into two cups. "Tell me, Monsieur Midhat. I haven't asked about your family at all. Your parents, are they . . . do you have siblings?"

"My father is a merchant. From Nablus. A merchant of textiles and clothing. He is quite successful."

"How lovely. And your mother?"

"My mother was from near Nablus, a town called Jenin, but she died, Allah yirhamha, when I was very small."

"Oh dear, I'm so sorry. But you are like me then, Monsieur Midhat. We are both without our mothers."

"My mother died from *sill*, in Arabic, *la tuberculose*, in French."

"That's very sad, I am extremely sorry."

"How did your mother die?"

"I was also young." She looked through the doors at the terrace, where her wet footprints slashed the paving stones. "She was ill, also. A problem with her heart, I don't know precisely. Perhaps when you are a great doctor you will be able to explain it to me!" Her mouth smiled, her eyes were closed.

"Yes I do hope I will be a doctor," said Midhat. "Sometimes, in Nablus, men do not always profess as they studied."

"Profess?"

"Profess . . . comme une profession."

She faced the garden again. The silence lengthened.

"What is Nablus like?"

"Nablus is a little village. It's a town, I mean a city. It's not large but we call it a city. What I mean is, even when you leave Nablus, you take it with you. Do you know what I mean?"

"I think so."

"I don't mean I don't love Nablus. I do. Only, everyone knows about everyone else's life. It can be a little . . ." He made a clawing gesture at his throat until she smiled, albeit weakly. "I'm sure that is why my father likes it in Cairo."

"Egypt?"

He nodded.

"And for you, you chose medicine . . ."

"That was his choice, my father's. He founded, I mean he is one of the founders of, a new hospital in Nablus. He considers it very respectable, you know. But I am also very content from it. I love science, I always loved science. So it is my choice too. I am excited by . . ." He looked down, thinking of the words. "The work is so exact, so particular. But," he sighed, "one has to be too detached, you know."

To his surprise, Jeannette erupted with laughter. He looked up to see her face glowing, her whole body rippling with amusement. When after several moments she was still laughing, he tentatively joined in, watching her carefully to know when to stop. An abrupt little cough was the signal, and as she sighed back into silence and he dropped his smile, it occurred to him that she could not possibly have known he was thinking of the dissection, or of the legless man he saw that morning in the clinic, neither of which seemed to him very funny. He looked at her still-smiling eyes and tried to imagine what she thought about him.

"I have been walking with Laurent regularly," he said.

She squinted and drew her cup to her lips.

"We walk to the botanical gardens, sometimes we walk into town. He shows me the city. I enjoy him."

Jeannette chuckled again but without sound, pinching her lips together, examining her fingers as they turned the cup in her saucer. Midhat's hand involuntarily twisted palm-up, questioning, but she didn't notice. He was not offended by her laughter, the way he was by Laurent's. It was mystifying but did not seem spiteful. In fact her continued hilarity was drawing a smile again to his own lips. His eyes kept falling to where her dress exposed the upper part of her chest. The skin was pale but freckled, and shiny—perhaps with sweat. Or with water from her bathe.

"Why did you sit in the pond?"

Her smile vanished. "Why?" she said. "Oh. I was feeling a bit hot."

He considered her, and hung fire. Since arriving in Montpellier a month ago, he had developed a habit of pausing whenever he felt uncertain. Ever mindful of his ignorance of convention, he strongly wished to avoid making a fool of himself. And it might well be customary to sit in a pond when hot, and how would he know? On the other hand, Jeannette did look discomfited by the question. Then again, that might be because of something else; for example, her own preconception about his discomfort with outdoor bathing. About which, if the truth be told, she would not have been wholly incorrect.

"How is Laurent?" she said.

"He is well. He will study psychiatry. He is a very kind man."

"He is."

"I find him—he makes me laugh. He has what in Arabic we call 'light blood.'"

"Rather than heavy blood."

"Exactly."

"That seems right, Laurent has light blood. But I wouldn't call him frivolous. He is quite a serious person really."

There was a pause. Midhat said: "I love it here. I hope I shall stay."

"You should stay. We love having you. You are very . . . I don't know." She met his eye. "Graceful."

A strong red blush started at her chest and covered her face. It was Midhat's turn to look at the garden. He wanted to give her privacy, but he was also waiting for the grin to subside from his own cheeks. Outside, the clouds turned the grass grey, and the tree at the far end was animated with wind. When he looked back, Jeannette was still red, staring at her lap. Neither of them said anything. Something in Midhat's chest began leaping wildly about as a fly zoomed into the silence and browsed the coffee things. Together they watched the fly inspecting the corner of a sugar cube, and then sitting on the silver rim, rubbing its hands together. He made a decision to look at her again. He found, to his amazement, that he was unable. Staring at the sugar cube he marvelled at his shyness. It occurred to him that so far his imperfect French had made most conversations obtuse—but what if, since by the same token one could not afford ambiguity, everything also became more direct?

"Bonjour les petits." Docteur Molineu knocked on the back of the open door. "How are we today. Is anyone hungry?"

"We're drinking coffee."

"Let's have an aperitif sur le patio. Georgine, will you bring the crémant, and a cordial for Monsieur Midhat."

The wind was still blowing. Midhat helped Jeannette carry blankets from the hall, observing where her short hair revealed her neck, and when they returned outside Docteur Molineu was sitting on an iron chair with his legs crossed.

"I wonder." He addressed his daughter: "I was thinking today about consistency of character. Is that something you believe in, consistency?" He stroked the lip of his champagne glass.

"I'm not really sure what that means," said Jeannette.

There was a weary note in her voice, which made Midhat crane round to see her face, but her face no longer gave away anything. She wrapped her gown close and hunched her shoulders against the wind.

"What do you think, Monsieur Midhat," she said. "Are you consistent?"

"I think he is consistent," said Docteur Molineu. "Yes, I would go so far as to say that is even an unfair question to ask him."

"Excuse me?" said Midhat.

"I didn't mean to offend. You know, Midhat was telling me yesterday about some of the superstitions where he comes from. Particularly with regard to the Samaritan community, yes? Who live in his town."

"How interesting," said Jeannette. "I only ever heard of the Good Samaritan."

"Yes, I mean, and that whole episode allegedly happened on the mountain where he lives. It's thrilling. He was saying—would you tell Jeannette what you told me?"

Midhat, unsure whom he should be addressing, switched his eyes between father and daughter. It disturbed him that he could not read Jeannette's expression, and he wondered if she was bored. "I mean, it is only superstition, as you say. People pay them to do certain magic, and so on. You know, the evil eye, jealousy—but I don't really—"

"Absolutely fascinating. This was a tribe—tribe? A sect who split off from Judaism. Or was contemporary with. There was a great travel diary by a woman who went to stay with them, I should see if I can get my hands on it."

"It is only folklore," said Midhat.

A smile tweaked the corners of Jeannette's mouth. "How interesting. Papa."

"What? He wants to."

"It is not always appropriate."

Docteur Molineu relented. In the ceasefire, the image of Jeannette's thighs recurred in Midhat's mind. He looked out at the grey lawn.

"Excuse me, sir," said Georgine, opening the door. "There is a letter for Monsieur Midhat."

"Mm." Molineu clanked his glass on the table and stamped his foot on the flagstone. "It is getting chilly, too, and I am rather hungry."

"I can heat the soup," said Georgine. She waved familiarly at Midhat. "Come, please."

She led him to the hall table. The letter was from his father, and dated three weeks prior.

My dear son Midhat,

God willing you are safe. Travel has been difficult because the British are defending the Canal against the Turks. However, I heard from my brother that there are no problems yet in Nablus. A German commander is staying at the Hammad house. The foreign post offices have closed in Jerusalem so do not expect any letters from Palestine. In Egypt the postal service is still fine. Trade is also fine, alhamdulillah. Layla and the children are fine, alhamdulillah. Work hard in your studies.

Regards,
Your father

Outside, Jeannette was folding the pink blanket.

"Georgine will do that."

"Papa."

"What? Don't look at me like that."

They shut the glass doors on the wind, and as they passed through the salon Jeannette saw her reflection in the mirror. A cloud of wind-loose hair was suspended around her head. She drew three pins from the back and slid them over the top, gathering and twisting some locks to keep them in place, and pressing her temples. Then she followed her father into the dining room, where he was addressing Georgine.

"Is he coming?" he said.

"Oh, yes, Monsieur."

"Patience," said Jeannette, drawing out her chair.

Nevertheless, Jeannette required only the lightest suggestion from her father to rise again and fetch Midhat for dinner. Yesterday she would have insisted on giving him privacy. But now she felt so unmanageably agitated—not only by her father but by the entire day, whose many strands lingered, threatening different undefended parts of her, so that a panic was already welling up—and it seemed to her in that particular moment that the only remedy for this unruly beating of her mind would be to walk into the hall and apologise to Midhat on her father's behalf, and so settle at least that quarter of her agitation.

She saw their guest through the banister. He stood half-framed by the door to the salon, where the piano was stretching out, coffin-like, and the sun in the window lit a few threads dangling from his forehead, which was bent low with reading the letter in his right hand. His whole attitude was frozen. Then he shifted his weight to his other foot, and put his left hand limply on his hip. He pulled a face, a part-frown, as if straining against a bright light: the squint of trying to discern something. Although she was certain she had not made a sound, he suddenly jolted to face her. She sprang to life as naturally as she could, as though she was just entering from the dining room. But the motion of her arms was theatrical and from his expression she knew it was obvious she had been watching him. His fingers quickly folded the letter.

"I wanted to tell you," she said, sliding her hand down the banister. She saw his eyes drop to her mouth.

"Yes?"

"I'm sorry," her voice caught as her own eyes fell, to his sun-dark neck, and she shut them. "I wanted to say . . ." Everything rose; she inhaled, grasping after what she meant to say. Her thoughts slithered from her grip. "I didn't tell you the truth."

The silence that followed gave her just enough time to register what she had embarked upon; it was not enough time to think twice.

"When?" said Midhat.

"When I told you," she began, "about my mother. The truth is, I do know how she died. She, she shot herself. With a gun."

Midhat's reaction to this was minimal. His eyes widened, fractionally, which she might not have even seen were it not for the way the light was falling. Nevertheless, Jeannette immediately repented. She wondered how on earth she had so quickly given in to that glimmer of a desire to expose herself to him, which had arisen like a sudden shard among the many other thoughts and concerns that were whirling around, disorienting her and setting her off-balance. In ordinary circumstances, she would have seen such an impulse and neatly stepped aside. But today nothing was ordinary. Here she was, burdening their houseguest with this uncomfortable piece of her personal biography.

To her alarm, Midhat started walking towards her. He still hadn't said anything. His forehead was wrinkled with confusion and interest, as if she resembled someone he knew, and he was trying to work out who it was. She felt a hand reaching into her stomach and squeezing.

"Dinner is ready," she threw out.

He stopped, seeming to understand what she really meant, and nodded, corrected.

"All right."

"I'm sorry," she added, in a forced casual voice. "I shouldn't have told you that."

"Don't be sorry."

She gave him a breathy smile and directed her steps towards the dining room. There was a pause of a few seconds before she heard him follow.

Midhat was unsettled by this exchange. Jeannette's intention in telling him this was by no means obvious. What he did not admit to himself now, although it would strike him with force later, was that her confession seemed to glitter at him, like a fresh wound, or a point of entry. For now he reflected only that her divulgence did not really correspond with the restrained manner of its delivery, and that this was rather bewildering. He had been approaching her to examine her face, and after she departed, he hung in the hallway wondering how else to read her. That catch in her voice occurred to him as a symptom of distress—the only apparent symptom, in fact—although to be distressed at having lied to him did not seem plausible. She was more likely distressed from remembering her mother's suicide. He looked at the space she had vacated, between the banister and the shadow-braided wall, and felt a lunge of pity.

At the dinner table, he tried not to look at her. He was afraid of what his face might give away. Frédéric slipped his napkin from its silver ring, and as Midhat set the envelope beside his placemat and picked up his spoon, his mind, shutting out Frédéric's monologue about his colleague at the department, drew some shaky maps of interpretation. Had Jeannette told him about her mother to excuse herself, her aloof manner, perhaps? Or something else she had done that he had not noticed? Or was she really ashamed that when he had been honest with her, she was not honest with him? Or was she explaining something else, referring to another part of their conversation he had failed to understand, some nuance in French— and as he mindlessly applied the butter to his bread roll he found himself picturing what Jeannette might have seen as she entered the hall. This set off an unexpected burst of pleasure, imagining himself from the outside, standing in this house.

"Was the letter from your family? Are they well?"

He lifted his head, and saw Frédéric dabbing his lips.

"Yes, well. Thank you."

Midhat glanced at his envelope. The label was visible: "Opened by Examiner 257." He reached out and, pretending to scan the address, flipped it over.

Frédéric was the first to stand. He put his hands on his hips and regarded the door, as if the task ahead, of taking a digestif in the salon, was going to require the orchestration of a regiment. "Will you join me, Jojo?"

"Not tonight. I'm tired."

"Goodnight, then."

"Goodnight."

Midhat also declined. He mounted the stairs, thinking of the letter. Work hard in your studies. He couldn't prevent that sudden, double vision: the external view of all this, of what his father might think of it.

5

Carl Page heard it first from Madame Crotteau, who said she had heard it from the Nolins, but when the Nolins were asked they knew nothing about it. On the Friday before the party, Georgine went in to collect an order of tartelettes and she heard it from the baker. Sylvain Leclair, it was said, had been hit by a motorcar on the Avenue de Toulouse. He was alive, but both his legs were broken.

On Saturday it began to snow, very lightly, and after dropping Midhat in town to buy an evening suit, Pisson drove Jeannette to Sylvain's vineyard with a bouquet of pink lilies beside her on the backseat. Later, Midhat walked home carrying his new suit in a box. Afternoon was turning into night and the lampposts sprinkled yellow snow in perfectly triangular beams.

It was December, Midhat's third month in Montpellier. His walks with Laurent had become a fixture, and the best consolation for his loneliness. Besides his breakfast interrogations by Docteur Molineu and the occasional exchange with Jeannette, they were also his principal opportunity to practise French beyond the scientific vocabulary required at the Faculty. The guests at tonight's party would provide another opportunity; he needed to be agile, alert. He tramped up the drive to see Pisson shutting the car door, and heard Jeannette's voice as he stepped into the hall.

She was in the cream-walled salon with her father, reporting loudly that it was a lie. Sylvain had no trouble walking, and though it was true he had fallen to the ground, the car had barely grazed him.

Docteur Molineu laughed. "Midhat, you're welcome to come in. It's not quite a lie, is it dear, only some of the details were exaggerated."

"I am extremely embarrassed."

"Oh, la. One ought to telegraph in advance I suppose. I did say you should take Midhat. It's not really appropriate for a young lady, I'm sure everyone must think I'm horribly irresponsible." He picked up a wooden table and set it down behind the piano. "Humans and rumours. Would you help me with the chaise longue, Midhat? I think we'll put it in the hall."

"Don't you see how embarrassing this is? I brought him flowers and there was nothing wrong with him, and he was so . . ." She expelled a syllable of air. "I'm really in agony."

"I don't see why you are making such a fuss. Did you explain yourself? Sylvain is not stupid, I'm sure he knows you only meant to be kind. It's an easy mistake. The guests will be here from seven o'clock, and I'm going to work before then. I'm a little afraid we may have invited too many. Not usually a cause for—since one counts on half to stay at home. But these days it seems people are in need of a party . . ."

Midhat put his hands under the chaise.

"Thank you, Midhat," said Molineu.

"Not at all," said Midhat. "It is my pleasure."

Jeannette flicked her eyes to him, but her expression did not change.

In the mirrored doors of his armoire, Midhat's white collar threw light up at his face. He licked his fingers and touched his hair. Georgine's voice came through the floorboards.

"Les Mademoiselles Carole et Marie-Thérèse, et Docteur Patrice Nolin."

He pushed up his tie, plucked at his sleeves and shirttails, and started down the stairs.

"It's the Arabian man," said Patrice Nolin, shaking the droplets off his hat by the door. His cheeks were especially red with the shock of heat on cold skin.

"Good evening, cher docteur," said Midhat.

The girls took turns greeting Midhat, and coils bounced behind their ears: both had attached artificial hairpieces to their chignons.

"Good evening, ladies."

Docteur Molineu led the Nolins into the salon. There was no sign of Jeannette.

"How is the Faculty?" said Patrice Nolin, passing Midhat a champagne glass.

"My classes are interesting. But it is only the preliminary sciences in the first year. We also have had the introduction to dissection, and we are beginning to attend the clinics in the mornings, where we observe the doctors and the patients and make notes, and we discuss afterwards. And sometimes—" He stopped. He had just remembered that Nolin used to be a professor at the Faculty, and surely knew all this. "But yes, what I mean is, I am enjoying it. This snow has also been remarkable."

Molineu presented an open case of cigarettes. "Patrice, I have been wanting to ask your opinion. How do you think it will turn, now that we've won at Flanders? The picture I draw from *Le Matin* and the wireless is very indefinite."

Nolin cleared his throat. "I think we can expect to see a few strategic manoeuvres. I'm no military expert, but of course they'll obviously be look-ing for ways to weaken the enemy. At the same time, we've got to keep our eyes on the other corners of the globe, on the balance of forces. And Russia is next, so, my guess is we'll see a push to draw the Germans over from the Eastern Front, to ease up that side of things. But this is just speculation." He waved his hand and the smoke from his cigarette squirmed above him. "It's up to the generals. We just have to wait—and—see."

More guests arrived. Madame Crotteau kissed Midhat's cheek with a husky giggle, and her cold fur, wettened into prongs, rubbed against his neck. As he turned to greet Marian, Midhat caught sight of Jeannette through the open door, standing at the mirror by the bottom of the stairs, dressed in green and black. She touched her collar and looked herself in the eyes. Then her gaze slid over and met Midhat's. He held it until she looked away.

"I love tennis," said a woman with a lilac shawl. "I play it on the lower lawns with Ma'moiselle Briquot. Won't you join us when the spring comes?"

"But we're getting away from the central point," came Docteur Molineu's voice from across the room. "What was the central point?"

A young lady in a high-necked dress and an elderly gentleman cried greetings as they entered.

"When we exchanged our remarks, that it was a very moving funeral procession, and burial . . ."

"It was tremendously entertaining. It's a shame you weren't there . . ."

"But do you see anything hopeful?"

"It seemed that the family had been the ones comforting all of us, saying you have to go on, and so on."

"Sometimes I do worry about Georgine." Docteur Molineu was at Midhat's side. His eyes were red. "I wonder if we ought to hire a second girl, to be her friend, you know." He finished his drink and breathed.

"Laurent," said Midhat, reaching for his friend's shoulder. "I didn't see you enter."

"Cher Midhat," said Laurent, turning around. "It's good to see you. Goodness you look well. What a lovely suit. Do you know Carl Page?"

"Yes, I think we met."

"I know you of course," said Carl Page. "You are the famous Oriental guest. Well then what's your take on this, as an Oriental? We're talking about Flanders."

"Oh," said Midhat. He cleared his throat. "If you're asking about the Turks, then . . . I think there are still losses from the Russian war that are . . . hanging over everything. But in terms of Europe—I mean, I think we'll see some strategic manoeuvres from the French generals in the near future." His voice deepened. "The balance of power, and so forth. And the Eastern Front, of course, with Russia. There might be a strike sooner rather than later, keeping eyes on all corners. And so forth."

"I see."

"Carl did you hear," said Madame Crotteau, leaning across the back of the sofa, "about Mistinguett's lover?"

Laurent grasped Midhat's neck and laughed. "You very nearly sounded as if you knew what you were talking about. Oh I haven't eaten a thing, those look quite edible." He reached for Georgine's tray of fish rolls. "I have the most hilarious story to tell you. About your professor, what's his name, Brogante."

"Oh yes," said Midhat.

"So he was cycling to the Faculty in the rain, I heard this from a surgeon, and by the time he arrived, this Brogante, he had a rash on his legs. The trousers were woollen, I suppose. And he's apparently quite a large fellow, is that right? He borrowed a spare pair from someone else, but they were too small for him and he couldn't do them up. But now the funny part is that he had to teach a class, so he wore them anyway and taught the entire lesson while standing behind a chair with his buttons undone. Isn't that just the funniest thing."

"Very funny," said Midhat.

"Have you heard about Sylvain?" came a woman's voice. A thin blonde, addressing a group of people Midhat didn't recognise. "He was hit by a car and is very badly injured."

"Isn't true," said Docteur Molineu, behind them. "Jeannette went to see him."

The group made sounds and inclined their heads, as if to say: ah, indeed?

"He's coming tonight, I think."

A low chord sounded from the piano.

"Saint-Saëns!"

"They caught him within a week . . . poor fellow wasn't *built* to fight."

Carole Nolin was conferring with a silver-haired man in tails who had one knee on the piano stool. The man played the chord a second time, and Carole sang a probing note. Then they began in earnest, nodding together, and her voice swooped upward, and the room fell quiet.

"Prin-temps—qui—comm*en*-ce! Portant l'espér*an*-ce, aux coeurs amour*eux* . . ."

"I saw it in Hamburg thirty years ago. With Talazac, before the French revival."

Midhat's glass was empty. His head thrilled with Carole's singing. At the next crescendo the room seemed to lose interest, and the murmur surged again into a loose babble. One final clanging note, applause, and it changed to a spirited tune about Paris. A dozen guests joined in, tilting their glasses with gestures that resembled dancing. Someone opened a casement at the far end and blew a cool shot of air over their faces.

Midhat looked around for Jeannette, with a pleasant nervousness in his stomach. His glass was full again, and the room listed as he turned his head. Sylvain Leclair was in the corner by a tapestry, hair parted to the side, curled and oiled, catching the light from a side lamp.

Paris c'est une blonde
Qui plaît à tout le monde
Le nez retroussé l'air moqueur
Les yeux toujours rieurs!

"Shut the window!"

It had jammed in the frame and a gentleman in a wine-stained waist-coat was attempting to wrest the handle from a Russian doctor named Andryashev whom Midhat recognised from the Faculty. He looked very drunk. Wine-stripes triumphed over Andryashev, and the Russian smiled and threw up his hands as though letting an opponent win at cards, before falling on the lady behind and dissolving in a wind of apologies.

Laurent was eating another fish roll. "Everything is old gossip. People are still talking about Henriette Caillaux, you hear her name all over the place. Half their sons—oh, this song's by the woman who insured her legs for a million francs. What's her name, she wears those funny hats."

The tune had accelerated into an aggressive chromatic counterpoint, and two girls hopped near the piano, grabbing each other's elbows. Midhat turned—where was Jeannette? There was Sylvain Leclair again, his silver hairline a crescent moon. And there she was, beside him, Jeannette, listening to Sylvain.

"I think I still love her," said Laurent.

Midhat started. Laurent was looking in the same direction.

"They don't go away easily, those things."

"You love Jeannette?"

"You didn't know."

"No." A cold liquid poured down Midhat's spine. "I did not know that."

To his right, a woman with pink cheeks spun round and smiled at him.

"Nothing comes of nothing," said Laurent.

Midhat peered at him. "What do you mean?"

"Hm?" Laurent ran a hand through his hair. "Only that it's meaning-less in the scheme of things." In a sober tone, he added: "One can still love from afar, of course."

Midhat tried to dwell on this remark. It kept escaping him.

"Sylvain does rather seem to be annoying her, doesn't he? She looks angry."

"Does she?" said Midhat. He studied Jeannette's lamplit face. To him, her features appeared limp and without expression.

"Yes. That is what Jeannette looks like when she is angry. You'd do well to learn it fast, if you want to get along with her."

Midhat directed his eyes down at his glass, seized by an undertow of resentment. He had thought Laurent was his friend. But then, how many months had they known each other? Three, three and a half. He made a prompt resolution to turn cold towards him.

"Everyone asks me that," he said. "How am I getting along. As though it were the most difficult thing. You know, the hills here are the same as our hills. They seem to think I live in a desert."

He swung his head back and slipped the remainder of his drink down his gullet.

"That's not really what I meant," said Laurent. "But, yes, that is silly. Try not to take it to heart. Unless a man has travelled, how is he to know?" He cleared his throat. "Actually Midhat, I have some news. I need to tell you."

Midhat stared again at Jeannette. Her face cracked into a clear scowl. Her lips moved, she was saying something to Sylvain. Then she turned, and forced her way out of the room.

He must follow her. Bodies gave way under his hands like palm fronds. He reached the hall, and the doorway grazed his shoulder. Checked the exit points: front door, no; back door, no. Dining room, no. Stairs, no. He moved over to the coat stand by the front door and looked down at the handle of his new umbrella. An elegant pleat was carved into the bend.

"Do you know," came Laurent's voice behind him. "You look like you've drunk rather a lot."

"So have you."

"No, I haven't. I just feel quite relaxed."

"I didn't know you loved Jeannette."

"Yes. We were close at one point. You know how these things are. But I was being serious, I have something to tell you."

"You love Jeannette."

"No, not that. It's that I'm going to war. In three weeks, after Christmas."

The umbrella fell from Midhat's hand and sighed as it lay upon the others. Laurent faced the open salon door, hands in pockets, arms very straight, as if he were cold. Midhat reached for his elbow.

"Of course it's wretched," said Laurent. "But we knew it was going to happen. I'll be working as a doctor, actually, or something medical, which is . . . I mean, it means I won't be on the front line. I worry about Xavier. You know"—he turned—"I feel guilty. They need doctors, but I can't help feeling . . . but nothing is perfect, is it? It will be sad to say goodbye to you, dear Midhat." He gripped Midhat's shoulder, and shook it a little. "It has been wonderful. Oh, please don't be like that. I'm supposed to be pleased."

"My friend," said Midhat, stricken.

"Yes."

"Wait. Wait. I have a gift. Please wait, just here."

Laurent closed his eyes on a half smile and nodded. Midhat climbed the stairs, keeping his eyes on Laurent's blond head, watching as he shifted the pile of coats on the chaise longue and made a space to sit down. Around Laurent's head Midhat drew a careful, stumbling circle, holding the banister. He grabbed the gold watch from his bedside and cradled it back down in two hands.

"Laurent. Please."

"Oh no, Midhat. That's too much."

"You must. Please take it. I am ashamed of myself." He sat on the coats. "Open it. It's Turkish, but it does tell the time. Laurent. Oh, Laurent."

Laurent ran a finger around the clock face. "It's very beautiful."

Midhat leaned back and looked at the ceiling, streaked yellow by the lamps. He closed his eyes, but the spinning dark was intolerable, and he opened them again.

"You know, there was a drunk in Nablus. They called him al-Musamam, the poisoned one. He lived on the outskirts. He was always wandering around in the daytime, begging, and collecting vegetable crates. And he stacked these crates where he lived on the outskirts. And one day I was with my friend, and we walked past al-Musamam. And my friend was bold, he was my cousin actually, and he asked al-Musamam why he collected the crates and stacked them. And the poisoned one replied: I am building a tower to reach the moon. But, said my cousin, if you reach the moon, you will go blind. It is better up there, where it is, and we can all see the town by its light."

He heard the sounds of the party again, as though they had been switched back on.

"I am so grateful for your friendship," said Laurent. "God willing I will return before long. I thank you, many times over. I am very moved." He held his hair back as he looked down at the watch. "I think I should leave now. I don't think I can bear the party anymore."

Nor could Midhat bear it. He kissed Laurent on both cheeks. Laurent smiled and put on his coat, saluting as he stepped into the sharp night.

Midhat shut the front door and returned upstairs. He was drunk, he needed to go to bed. He hauled himself up by the balustrade. At the gallery, a noise caused him to halt, and he held on, straining through his murky ears to discover the direction it came from. He had no idea what he was going to say to Jeannette, but he knew that they must speak. A scraping sound, and the high murmur of a woman's voice came from further down the hall. He passed the doors of the Molineu bedrooms, and saw, beyond the bathroom in the corner, two bodies standing against the wall: a man and a woman. His heart jumped into his mouth. The corridor did not admit much light from the window but the pair were clearly embracing—the man's head moved and Midhat caught his oiled hair. Sylvain Leclair. He stepped left to see the woman, and the floorboard cracked. Both faces turned. It was the maid, Georgine. Her red mouth fell open.

"Oh. Pardon me," he said.

He hurried back. The door of his bedroom slammed much harder than he meant it to, and the bed rose to meet him. He pulled at his tie, closing his eyes, and saw Sylvain talking to Jeannette, accompanied by a violent surge of feeling, as he had felt in the salon against Laurent but directed now, in a drunken, zigzagging fashion, at Sylvain; he listened, dazed, to the laughter and chatter dampened by the floorboards. He thought of Jeannette smiling at him, and his body softened. He undressed chaotically, lay on top of the covers, and was quickly asleep.

When with a powerful thirst he awoke, the room was silent. The sky between the open curtains was completely black. He reached for his watch. The table smacked his hand three times before he remembered what he had done.

6

When Ariane Passant was a child, she complained to her mother that she felt nauseated when she looked at certain men.

"Maman," she said, "why does Uncle Charles make me feel sick?"

"That's not a nice thing to say, Ariane."

"I feel sick in my nose."

"Do you mean you don't like Uncle Charles?"

"No." She considered. "I like Uncle Charles."

Ariane first met Frédéric Molineu at a ball in the Seventh Arrondissement, and they danced a polka. Frédéric's cravat was patterned with small black plumes like the clubs on playing cards, and as Ariane concentrated on her steps she watched that the size of the plumes did not change, to regulate the distance between their bodies.

Frédéric Molineu called on the Passant family soon afterwards. Monsieur and Madame greeted him with surprise and offered him a seat beside the fire. The cook had just sent up a fresh plate of salmon sandwiches. Ariane locked her fingers and stared at the flame. She was very pale and beautiful, and her eyes were a transparent blue. Monsieur Passant asked Frédéric about his profession, and Frédéric explained that he was a doctoral student at the École Normale. He made sure to allude to his father's landholdings near Normandy, which he was due to inherit. He could feel the silence coming on and tried to forestall it: he complimented the furnishings of the room, this lovely mantelpiece, was it original to the house? He remarked that salmon was probably his favourite type of sandwich. Monsieur and Madame Passant's responses were economical: polite, not encouraging, relapsing each time into silence. Frédéric could not understand their reservation. It was obvious that he was an excellent match for Ariane, who was already nearly twenty. Unless, of course, he was misreading something. He stole glances at their daughter, which she never returned. A large freckle underscored Ariane's left eyebrow, and she had a delicate, tapering chin.

Frédéric persisted. Once a week, sometimes twice, he knocked on the door and was invited in for coffee or a glass of wine. Monsieur Passant began to imply, with meticulous indirection, that Ariane had other suitors; but over the months that followed Frédéric never met a single one or heard any of their names. The conversation did not flow with time, and each visit was as stilted as the first, so that Frédéric found he must restrain himself from commenting on the appearance of the room to avoid sounding mechanical. He watched Ariane for short bursts, resigned to the fact that she would never look back at him. She spoke only if asked a direct question, and then in a quiet, soapy voice would answer as briefly as grammatically possible.

Sometime in the third month Frédéric became aware that the Passants were serving him a salmon sandwich every time he visited. A sign, at last, which he might interpret. He waited a few more weeks to make absolutely certain; and yes, each week a salmon sandwich, flavoured with dill and salted butter. He summoned the courage, and one evening asked for a conversation alone with Monsieur Passant.

Passant led him into the dining room. A brass coat of arms hung on the far wall and the table was dressed for dinner. Frédéric barely needed to introduce his proposal with the various flourishes he had practised before Passant was giving his consent with his hands clasped. He led Frédéric back to join mother and daughter by the old fireplace, and Ariane fixed him with her transparent eyes. There was no need to tell her. She bowed her head.

The engagement lasted for two months, until the end of the semester. Ariane and Frédéric were married in the spring of 1891.

After the age of thirteen, Ariane would tell him later, her nasal nausea had almost disappeared. But on occasion she would still catch sight of certain men and feel the same revulsion. It was usually a man's face, turned sideways, that set it off, becoming more vivid than other faces in the room. She would look again hungrily at the face, but the sensation always drained quickly, the imbalance neutralised. During her engagement to Frédéric, however, Ariane found herself once more as she had been as a girl. At night she thought of the muscles in Frédéric's hands, his quick manner, his eyes, his full, masculine eyebrows. It was as though the change from courtship to engagement had utterly changed his face. Soon he was invading her dreams. She recalled them in the mornings and felt the old flutter in the chest, and the strange sickness in the nose, like being in a tanner's shop and inhaling leather fumes.

This proved a problem only on their wedding night. Dusk was falling when they arrived at their new apartment; they climbed the stairs, hung their coats behind the door, and Frédéric led the way down the corridor to the bedroom. Before he had even turned on the lamp, Ariane moved past the bed and stood in the far corner. One section of her face was blue with moonlight, the rest in darkness. Neither of them spoke. Then, Frédéric took a step forward.

"Don't be scared, Ariane."

Ariane said nothing.

"I will sleep out there, if you prefer."

Her blue lips made the shape of "no," but no sound came out.

Minutes passed. Frédéric took the plunge, looked at the ground and began to undress. To make it less of a performance he tried to stand side-on, but when on a reflex he reached for the wardrobe to hang up his suit he accidentally exposed himself, and hesitated midgesture, extending his arm and retracting it again. A laugh caught in his chest. By the time he was under the covers he felt he had run a long distance. Ariane remained in the corner. He turned over and she began to weep. Gently, slowly, he heard the flicking sound of buttons, followed by the soft rasp of cotton, and then he saw the white cloud of her petticoat as she slipped into the bed. He felt her wet face on his shoulder. The weight of her head, her warm small body curled up like a creature's. He caressed her hair until the jagged breath became calm, and then deep, and then fitful and heavy with sleep.

It did become easier. The following morning Ariane smiled at him as they packed their things for the journey south. On the road between Lyon and Grenoble, she said: "I think this man needs a haircut."

She was pointing at a calèche in front of them. Long sheaves of hay stuck out from the rear of the vehicle. Frédéric laughed, and Ariane gazed at him, then joined in laughing, drawing breath and laughing again.

Ariane even laughed when they first made love, in the rented guest room near the water. Her body was soft but her limbs were strong, and her legs gripped him from behind. At the moment of entry she gazed up at him with her transparent eyes, and Frédéric let out a strangled moan. For a week they slept late and made love on waking, then bathed and walked along the shore to drink coffee by the pier where the sea smacked against the wall.

After they returned to Paris, Frédéric took on the teaching of two more undergraduate anthropology courses, while he worked to make his dissertation worthy of publishing. His manuscript was particularly ambitious in trying to combine two lines of contemporary thought under a single thesis: one being the recent theories of cranial development and criminality, and the other the program of physical anthropology that was emerging at the time from scholarship in the African colonies. On their return from the south, however, Frédéric discovered to his dismay that during the very week of his honeymoon an old doctoral colleague named Émile had published his own manuscript, a work on the anthropology of crime based on firsthand knowledge from the Central Prison Infirmary. The news was a blow to Frédéric's confidence. Émile's work was fairly pedestrian but it was undeniably thorough, and its flaws paled before the simple fact that he had published before Frédéric had—and at that Émile was three years younger than him. The whole thing cast a shadow over Frédéric's manuscript, which had been proficient at the time of defence but now seemed unwieldy and even in places a little thin. If his first publication did not meet with the esteem of his peers, if it failed to win him prestige, Frédéric feared humiliation and an irreversibly minor status in the development of the discipline.

Ariane was his relief. She was like a crocus, her blades just starting to part. Her cheeks shone with new colour as she set about decorating the apartment. All by herself she bargained over a salon set from Saglio on Rue de Vaugirard, and marshalled the neighbours to hoist a bowlegged commode up the stairs. The misery of his days at the university was soothed when Ariane met him at the door and showed him the walls almost finished in a sprigged paper, or a new lacquer on the skirting board. Over dinner she offered him simple but sound wisdom; she said better to take longer than to rush and regret, and Frédéric was delighted at least as much by her confidence in providing solace as by the actual solace provided, and said yes, you are right, thank you my darling. After a year, he had still not published. But after thirteen months, Ariane was showing the first signs of pregnancy.

The baby was born earlier than expected. Her limbs were meagre and she cried through the night. They hired a Swiss nurse named Ingrid to help, and when Jeannette turned four, Ingrid left and was replaced by a nursery governess named Eva. When Jeannette turned eight, Eva left and was replaced by Lorena. It was during the epoch of Lorena that Ariane's health began to suffer most noticeably. She spent more and more time in bed with various ailments, cheerfully resigned to the slow progress of recovery. No sooner would she be physically well again than she would plummet into a state of despair and confine herself once more to the bedroom. This behaviour was inexplicable to Frédéric. Ariane expressed extreme feelings of guilt over minor mishaps, often as trivial as misspeaking, or picking up the wrong glass in company. When he returned from the university in the evening, she would report the anguish of her day, how she entered a room wanting to do one thing and did another, and it was not right, it was not right, and Frédéric, bewildered, tried to soothe her as she had once managed to soothe him. The pattern of his days had reversed. His fears of ignominy had been unfounded, and he had secured a good position in the department following his publication. It was when he came home that the terror began.

How much did the neighbours know? Too much. The walls of those Montparnasse apartments were thin, and sometimes Ariane even went onto the balcony to wail. Though she said her pain was compounded by the dread of what other people knew and thought about her, even that did not stop her. Fearing their censure Frédéric did not confide in the Passants, nor did he want to send Ariane to a psychiatric hospital. For nine years she had been healthy! If it was an endemic neurological condition, he was anthropologically certain that she would have exhibited symptoms before now. Instead he took her to see a psychiatrist associated with the university, and employed a doctor to visit the house.

The child Jeannette suffered. All things circled around her mother, whom she could not reach. Ariane was the void in the whirlpool. The family moved to the edge of the Fourteenth Arrondissement and the new, thick-walled house was filled again with nightly wailing, and whispers and fingers on lips, as Lorena the governess pulled Jeannette from her mother's door, dangling toys. Sometimes, during a particularly bad flare, the governess would simply join Jeannette by the door and cover the child's ears as she peered through the crack.

When her mother lapsed, Jeannette became frantic and tormented the governess with crying, and her resentment persisted throughout her school years. But when her mother died, and her father confessed the details of this foregoing account, Jeannette's anger was overlaid with other emotions. Some of what she felt was guilt. Some of it was the same curiosity that made her governess put an ear to the door. For the next four years she examined and rearranged the fragments of the narrative, like her tarot deck spread over the carpet, until the moment had arrived when the hold of the past became unbearable, and for a while she could not think about it anymore.

In the spring of 1915 the fighting started again at Ypres. The Germans were using poison gas. Sudden clouds, yellow-green, whistled free from canisters along the front between Steenstraat and Langemarck. They rallied and advanced as a single luminous mist, just as the French troops were called to the firing line. Among the dead were the Molineus' chauffeur Pisson, and Marian's husband Paul Richer. Marian wore her wedding dress to the memorial service. The photograph from the newspaper announcement was framed by a garland, and where "Paul Richer" had curled beneath his chest now a line of roses nestled. The Tricolore was propped beside it, and when the breeze paused the flag furled, its colours tipped vertical, so that it resembled, to Midhat's mind, a cloak with a stained hem.

A few days afterwards, Marian announced that she was joining the volunteer nurses. She was posted at Divonne-les-Bains on the Swiss border, and in her letters to Jeannette she described the disfigured men whose wounds she was cleaning. One was paralytic, and another had lost the use of both hands. One had no thumbs, one had a leg as fat as an elephant's, one had lost the lower half of his jaw and smoked cigarettes through his nose. And the violets were blooming in the fields, she said, more fragrant than at home, and yellow primroses lined the forest floor.

Given that Paul was the first relative of the Molineus killed in action, Midhat expected Jeannette to withdraw further from him in her grief. Ever since the party in December, his feelings towards her had become tangled with his feelings about Laurent. Even though, to examine it logically, Laurent's confession that he still loved Jeannette implied that Jeannette had not responded in the first instance, he remained helplessly jealous all the same, not only because someone had usurped him by desiring Jeannette first, but also because Laurent was French, and more advanced than Midhat in his studies, and had gone off to war, and was from every angle more suitable to be Jeannette's husband than a Palestinian from Nablus who was a citizen of the enemy.

But, in fact, after the news of Paul's death Jeannette turned towards Midhat. She sought him out after meals, asking him questions about his studies; she knocked on his door while he was reading, apologised for the interruption, but would he like a biscuit and a cup of tea? Midhat's classes at the Faculty were in the afternoons, and the clinics in the morning were optional for first-year students. So the mornings became time to spend with Jeannette. They parted at the breakfast table, and when the door banged with Docteur Molineu's departure, they reunited in the hall, as though casually, without acknowledging the subterfuge.

The first time came about by accident. Midhat was in his bedroom trying to learn the bones of the body. Ilium, sacrum, patella. Tarsus, metatarsus. He copied the lines in his notebook, and the words became paler and paler. He shook the pen. Tibia, fibula, calcaneus.

The door of Docteur Molineu's study was ajar. He pushed it open, and found himself in a surprisingly grand room. Three of the walls were lined with books up to the ceiling, and the fourth gave a view of the neighbouring farm and the blue hills through a bay window flanked by maroon curtains that sprawled from a tasselled pelmet. The woodwork was painted dark turquoise. In the corner stood an armchair, and in the centre a large desk with a leather work surface, spread over with piles of paper and a few volumes. Two inkwells sat on the far edge, both half-full of black. One was rimmed with green, the other with red. He hesitated.

"Monsieur Midhat?"

He spun round. Jeannette was standing in the shadow of the door.

"I have run out of ink," he said.

He noticed that her neck was red, and a couple of hairs from the front of her head had trailed down from their pins. Oddly, at his words the redness spread over her entire face. It was an opening, he saw: they were dislocated from their usual positions—across a table, seated—and neither had the usual composure. He took a step to the side.

"Would you like to go for a walk?"

"Oh." Her dark pupils cooled, and in a moment she replied, with renewed self-possession: "Thank you. That would be lovely."

They met in the hallway wearing their coats, left the house without speaking, and walked up to the Boulevard du Jeu de Paume. Day was brightening, the streets were full of people, and there were enough distractions for them to ignore their mutual silence. The Beaux Arts steeples, the Palais de Justice decked with flags, submarine windows bulging out from slate roofs, shining with daylight. Midhat led the way to the Botanic Garden. Ilium, sacrum, patella, sang in his head. They reached the green gates.

"I used to come here with Laurent," he said, touching the railing.

But he found he knew the park no better now than on that first visit, and he slowed his pace. He chose the hedgerow path, and after that did not force any particular direction. Spring had brought out new colours in the beds, and violets spread rampant along the paths.

"Tell me more about yourself," said Jeannette.

"What would you like to know?" He was happy they were side by side and he did not have to look at her; otherwise he might have found it hard to speak.

"I don't know. What about your school."

"Well, it has one long building, like this. And on one side there is a big gate, and on the other side is the Bosphorus."

Sensing that this wasn't quite what she wanted, he changed direction and described how with two friends from the dormitory he used to sneak out at night by climbing a wall behind the oak tree. Once, they were caught on their way home from the city, and gave the warden false names.

"Samir became Izz ad-Din Izz ad-Din, Ilhan said Simeon Simeon, and I said my name was Ahmad Ibn Ahmad. It was very funny. The warden laughed and rode us home, and we weren't even punished. I mean, we never went anywhere really, we only walked around the streets for a while. Sometimes we bought ice cream. Ha! We didn't know what to do with the freedom. It was just for the sake of being free."

Next Jeannette asked about the different religions, and Midhat listed the various groups in the Empire, running a mental finger over the boys in his Mekteb dormitory. Again, this clearly wasn't what she wanted. So he elaborated some details of his own experience, and described how there weren't many Christians in Nablus, but his neighbour Hala was one of them, and he used to play with her when they were very young. They made a house in the woodshed and his Teta would bring them tea.

"It sounds like a very free childhood."

"It was, I think so. We lived at the bottom of a mountain. My father wasn't at home often, because he worked in Cairo, works in Cairo, and I had a nurse when I was small but mostly I grew up with my grandmother."

More and more fluently, he asked Jeannette about her own life. He wondered if she would tell him more about her mother, but she did not, and he did not ask. Slowly she unravelled some other facts about her childhood in Montparnasse, and narrated some amusing stories to match the ones he had shared. Then, as they reached the greenhouse, she burst out that she had felt uneasy during her studies at the university. There among all those men—she laughed, the little creases beneath her eyes clarifying in the sunlight.

They met again the following morning at eleven o'clock. This time they walked around the neighbourhood, and peered up the driveways at the other houses, their shutters and paintwork cracked and faded by the hot breezes that came off the Mediterranean. Conversation moved beyond simple facts and memories into the realm of speculation: perhaps I feel this, perhaps I feel that. Midhat reeled from the blaze of Jeannette's interest and tried to temper his enthusiasm about what she shared with him. But his joy was precarious, and attended by strong gusts of anxiety. At times he felt their privacy threatened by the hypothetical judgements of other people, and became distracted by the view he imagined from the windows they passed, a man and a woman seen from above, unchaperoned. This notion sent his thoughts on a worn path: first back to his school friends, and his cousin Jamil, with the query accompanied by a slightly gleeful pride as to whether any of them were encountering women the way he was. Directly this thought would sink under the thought of Laurent, and his shadowy history with Jeannette, and Midhat's comparative ignorance of European convention, in which for a man and woman to walk side by side and discuss their childhoods might quite easily signify nothing at all. He began expending considerable effort trying to stop his mind from enlarging upon the looks she gave him, and the remarks she made, and the silences she allowed. Everything about it was new to him. Presumably, it was not new to her. He wondered if she used to go walking with Laurent, and this thought alone was often sobering enough to check the elaboration of his fantasies. And yet, though he knew it would in all likelihood appease his conscience, he could not summon the courage to ask her about Laurent, nor even to mention his name.

One morning, while he was studying in his bedroom waiting until it was time to meet Jeannette in the hall, he heard crying downstairs. He hesitated, then resolved to remain where he was and pretend he had not heard anything. The wailing became more intense. An upstairs door creaked, and Jeannette's voice said:

"What on earth is going on?"

Midhat opened his door to see Georgine, face aflame, bursting out of the salon. She grasped the balusters at the bottom of the stairs like the bars of a jail cell.

"Please," she said, rattling the bars.

Docteur Molineu came after her, and raising his hands, which were full of letters, directed a dark look up at Midhat and Jeannette in the gallery.

"I'm sorry but we just cannot afford it," he said. "I'm really sorry, Georgine."

"What's happened?" said Jeannette.

Glancing at Midhat, Molineu said, with apparent reluctance: "They are reducing funding at the university. I've looked at the numbers and we can't keep the staff anymore. We are only three, we don't need—"

"No," said Georgine. Her mouth stretched wide, and fresh tears ran down her cheeks.

"Any day now they will start rationing."

"I can ask my father," said Midhat.

"No no no no." Molineu flapped his hand.

"Where is your family?" said Jeannette.

"She's from Normandy," said Molineu. "Georgine, listen to me."

"Shall I go?" Midhat mouthed at Jeannette.

She shook her head, and held out her hand, low down, to indicate that he should stay. This hand, being hidden, seemed to Midhat to refer to their secret walks, and it pulled taut a bond between them.

"Are you worried about your family?" said Molineu.

Georgine took a shuddering breath and nodded. "Please, professor, master, please—"

"Let's talk about this calmly. For God's sake, Georgine," he added, as she erupted again and covered her face, "you must calm down."

Gradually, she did. Then, to their collective amazement, she proceeded to convince Molineu—still addressing him by a variety of hyperbolic titles, which may have helped her case—to keep her employed at a low rate of pay until further notice.

Midhat and Jeannette did not go walking that day. Jeannette helped Georgine to close off the cream salon, the guest bedrooms, and Pisson's apartments, where they threw white sheets over the furniture. They ate dinner together in weary silence, Georgine serving them with swollen cheeks and glossy eyes.

The dead stacked up. Every morning they read the tableaux d'honneur: John Bertrand from Port-Marianne on April 28th, Maurice Carrignon on the 30th, Jean Rival the dentist's son at St. Julien in early May, Basile Vallon at Ypres a few days later. Convents, seminaries, colleges, high schools— every large building in Montpellier was crammed with beds and wounded soldiers. Jeannette volunteered to read to convalescents. She began walking into town with Midhat after lunch carrying books and magazines, and from the main roads they heard the singing of the peasant women bearing stretchers. Sometimes they caught sight of their swinging brigades: four women to a pallet, their skirts knotted to keep their legs free.

A matter of months, they had said last year, and the posters in town were peeling; some of the older ones had ripped through. A soldier kissed a child, a buxom woman triumphed in a kitchen. A tattered Tricolore waved as an elderly man passed packages to a trench. There were few gatherings or parties now in Montpellier, and at those few, news from the Front was all.

In the Molineu house, death had its old way of unbuttoning the truth and loosening tongues. Under the general sadness Jeannette found she could no longer bore herself into unfeeling. Her thoughts returned to her mother, and she let them. And she began to confide in Midhat.

They were sitting on the terrace one morning in May, holding books they had no intention of reading. Wildflowers interrupted the lawn ahead, and where the lip of the terrace met the grass, the spears had cracked the grouting to poke up between the flagstones.

"No, it had nothing to do with the supernatural," she said. A brief spring cold had left a croak in her voice. "It was all her. I think she made herself ill on purpose. I think it gave her something to focus on. Because the moment she was well again she would do something extreme, like make herself vomit by eating too much, or starve herself and leave the house on a rainy night with no shoes on. They called her a hysteric afterwards, but that never seemed right to me."

"Hysteria," said Midhat, resting his jaw on the heel of his palm. "Yes."

"My mother was all I wanted, and I couldn't touch her."

"I had the same. I felt the same about my father."

"Not about your mother?"

"Well, I was two when she died. Sometimes I think I have a memory of her. But it's blurred, and I'm not certain. I remember her sitting on the floor, doing something with her hands. I don't know."

"All my memories of my mother are of her lying pale in bed. She was happiest when she was ill, I'm sure of it. I used to visit her bedside when she had the flu, and so on. Isn't that strange? And when she wasn't ill she was a terror, a ghost, and those were the times I hated her. The house was in disarray, she used to whip up the . . . the servants, they were all over the place, my father . . . But illness—that was when she thrived. I mean it's difficult now even to try to imagine these things. I don't have anything to hold, it's just little bits my father told me. And some things I remember. But even then, how can we know if it's real or not, or if we made it up ourselves, as you say."

"Will you explain it to me though," said Midhat, shifting along so he could face her. "Because I still don't understand exactly. Psychiatry is not until the third year."

Jeannette chuckled, then sighed and looked serious. "They called it a nervous illness," she said. "Which meant it was neurological, in the brain. Which part did you not understand?"

"The part about her being happiest when she was ill."

"Ah, well—nor do I. It's just that, as far as I can remember, her time was divided between being sick, physically, and healthy. Only when she was sick was I allowed to see her. Do you see? I mean, this woman stayed more or less the whole time in her bedroom. Then there was a certain period when

Sylvain used to come, and she seemed to get better again. She wasn't in bed. He was there for dinner quite often, Maman would be there, and he would bring me little gifts. I remember these glass grapes, like this, they were purple, and the stem was carved from wood. Anyway, Sylvain came for a few years. And then I don't remember what happened exactly. But it was unexpected, certainly, her suicide. I was sixteen, I think I told you."

"Yes. I am so sorry, Jeannette. Really. It is a tragedy."

"Well. There was a time when I thought about it a lot, trying to work it out. Then I realised there wasn't much point in becoming preoccupied with these things. I had this idea that when she was ill it was as though she was filling up a doorway with stones, so that she couldn't leave the house, then spending days pulling out stone after stone, until she could see the street outside. But then the moment she would have been able to walk out freely, she would just pick up new stones. I do think . . . I think it's true she distracted herself . . . I think being alive was hard for her. I don't know, I don't know anything, this is only from what my father told me, and some things Laurent was reading about a few years ago."

"Laurent."

"Yes."

There was a pause. Midhat ventured, "I miss him."

"So do I." She sniffed. It may have been from her cold. "I had a letter from him last week."

"Oh," said Midhat, unable to restrain his surprise. "Is he well?"

"He is fine, he is well. He is coming back, in fact, soon. Would you like to see the letter?"

"If it's private—"

"Not at all. I'm surprised he has time to write letters, to be honest. One moment, I will run up for it."

He walked by the pond to wait. He was compelled by a sudden, powerful wish that Laurent should die. But even the salutary prospect of Laurent's disappearance was swamped by the likelihood that Jeannette's love for him would only swell with his heroic memory. The water in the pond had risen over the winter, and lines of reflected light wriggled on the inside of the wall.

The lower part was covered in a greenish fur. He turned around and Jeannette was on the terrace again, holding an envelope. She came towards him. "Take it."

28 April 1915

Dear Jeannette,

I was sent to the Dardanelles in the end, not to Ypres. I'm working on the Pioche cruiser under a hero named Bastien who has already been offered five stripes. Most of the boys here are from Lyon and Toulon. Two days ago more French landed with the English on the European coast, while our regiment set about taking Koum Kaleh, and they say a quarter of our men are down. It has been difficult to make a hospital on a boat in which thousands of men have been crowded for weeks, let alone in the middle of battle. Nearly all the cabins for the wounded were still occupied by soldiers at the height of it, so I spent the afternoon dragging saddles and mailbags into one of the kitchens and replacing them with sterilised sacks and bandages and drugs.

From twilight until dawn the convoys of wounded followed one after another and we spent those hours working constantly. I was in the children's playroom of the ship where we have some big tables—I'm meant to be a junior but all the ranking gets forgotten once you're in it. The first casualty was a Senegalese—he lay unconscious on a raft. One bullet had gone through his ear, another two through the abdomen. He died at noon without waking up. Then a master corporal came back with his chest shattered by shrapnel, and for a moment I saw his naked heart, still beating. This is the fastest I have learned anything, Jeannette, honestly it makes a mockery of old Dean Rivaut's "observation and inference" at the Faculty.

The sight of the Dardanelles these last two days and nights has been unimaginable. You can see a mass of dead on the Koum Kaleh shore. On the European side Krithia is burning. Before Yeni Sher there are ships everywhere—battleships, cruisers, torpedoes, dredgers—a whole fleet surrounds the peninsula—and on the Pioche men are sleeping in every corner. This morning the smoke from the cannon is mixing with the dawn mist and the whole thing seethes and smoulders.

All yesterday the Gallipoli Peninsula seemed to be on fire—the castle of Sedd-el-Bahr was burning. The Australians joined us and fired on the Asiatic coast directly on Koum Kaleh, and sent up cascades of fumes and dust and flames. When the soldiers were waiting in the dining-saloon, someone got hold of a gramophone and played it as though it was the end of the world while the Charlemagne shelled Besika Bay. Since then our warships have been firing unceasingly. We're an auxiliary but even so we saw a shell fall just in front of us today, and a second sent up a jet of water in the same place, and then a swarm of other shells came soaring above our heads. Since then we've been hit a number of times, and with our very thin plating a single shell does a great deal of harm, so there's always more work to keep the place in order.

By 12 o'clock Yeni Sher was destroyed. The Pioche directed her guns on Intepe and we all got up on deck to watch. Firing continued all through the night and the ship trembled. In the morning the corpses were heaped before us along the front for a stretch of about three hundred metres.

Enough. It feels good to have written after so much seeing, though I hope it is not upsetting to read. I hope Midhat is well, and enjoying his classes at the Faculty. It is very peculiar to think about that now. I still keep time by his watch, though it is necessary to hide the Turkish numerals from the other soldiers. When this battle is over I will be released on furlough, which they say could be next week, or next month. Either way, I look forward to seeing both of you.

With love and affection,
Laurent

"He's coming back."

"The battle ended on Friday. We haven't heard from Xavier . . ." She turned over the envelope.

"Did you love Laurent?" he said, forcefully.

"Excuse me?"

"Laurent said he loved you."

Jeannette stared at him. "When did he tell you that?"

Blood hooted in Midhat's ear. He looked down at his shoes. "It was at the party."

"Midhat." She expelled a throaty syllable of breath. "I—I'm not sure what I should say." She held out a hand for the letter. Her face had fallen. She looked distraught.

"Jeannette, please, I'm sorry."

She left him on the lawn. Her skirts folded and unfolded as she climbed the steps.

Over dinner, she did not meet Midhat's eye. The following day after breakfast he waited on the terrace, but she did not come. He left for the Faculty without his umbrella and, as luck would have it, within a few minutes it began to rain. Umbrellas sprouted around him, and his shoes smacked through the puddles, his socks spreading the cold around his ankles. Before long, the entire avenue was ablaze with watery pavements, and when he arrived at the Salle Dugès a scent of damp wool was rising from his coat.

7

Docteur Frédéric Molineu's office at the university was smaller and far less grand than his study at home. Still, he worked at the university most days: if he wanted a promotion after his next thesis he needed to accentuate his presence there, which meant being physically present as much as possible. He arrived in the morning at eight o'clock, lectured until noon, then retired to the office to continue his own research and answer questions from any students who came by. So few were left now; one lectured to a mere handful in the auditorium, most of them women and foreigners who regarded Molineu and his pointer with the glazed eyes of victory statues, delirious with so much sorrow.

The office was a corner room on the second floor, accessed by two sets of swinging double doors before the final one with the frosted window. Inside, west-facing windows gave him afternoon sun and a view of the courtyard, and two watercolours above his desk depicted the Hérault River. The offices on the other side of the hall had views of an actual river, a small tributary of the Lez. Frédéric's desk knocked up against the window, and he kept his liquor in a low cabinet on which he stacked books that wouldn't fit on the shelves. Any visitor or student would sit in the chair, while Frédéric sat on the desk. He often caught himself thinking about the other, spacious offices in the department, emptied now by war—though of course one would never ask.

The door opened a crack. "Good evening Frédéric."

"Patrice. Come in, take a seat."

Frédéric sat on the desk and rested his foot on an open drawer.

"What time is dinner, I told the girls . . ." Patrice hung his hat on the back of the door.

"I think we said eight?"

"Good."

"What can I offer you, I have whisky, absinthe—"

"Absinthe?"

"Oh, it's empty, pardon."

"I'll take a cognac—if that's cognac. How is the work going?"

"I have been working on a few ideas. I am making some progress. One has to test the kinks, you know."

"Tell me."

Frédéric swilled the liquid in his glass. He did feel threatened by Patrice's new interest in anthropology. The truth was that he also still relied on Patrice to be his fresh pair of ears: he was the only person with whom Frédéric felt he could sound out his thoughts without being judged. That was in part because Patrice remained outside the department, which made any competition between the two of them personal rather than professional. While Patrice was certainly intelligent enough to have made a career in the discipline, even at this late stage, he had not; he was only, as he called it, "dabbling in his dotage." "Inspired by your good self!" he even said last year when he published that book on animal behaviour, and Frédéric had reacted with a panic, and hurtled into his own work with new fervour. Clearly professional advancement was not enough to motivate Frédéric Molineu; for that he required a rival with a face.

"First of all," said Frédéric, pushing the drawer open slightly further with his heel, "language."

"Go on."

"Language and the progress of civilisations."

"Well. That sounds quite—"

"German, yes. I wouldn't publish until after the war. I mean I haven't started writing yet. I haven't finished *reading*."

Patrice rested an elbow on the back of the chair, sending his shoulder into a hunch. "So it's a philological treatise?"

"I'm not sure, to be honest. I have two strands. One is, yes, philological, linking philology and development. A word can deviate from a grammatical rule, so why not a human being? And what would that mean, exactly? I'm thinking about this specifically with relation to the Muslims."

"Islamic civilisation."

"The Muslim as a deviation from the onward progression. That's the sort of thing you might say." Frédéric released a clumsy gust of laughter.

Patrice frowned. "Certainly, determinism is something I'm intrigued by."

"No, of course. But what I meant was, and this is more interesting to me than the onward march to the universal what-have-you, that they chose the wrong messiah, Muhammad not Christ and so on—which to be frank has always been slightly apocalyptic for my taste. . . . Then the question becomes, for me at least, the extent to which one might actually recuperate a deviation. Do you see what I'm saying?"

"You mean, one would teach them to conform?"

"More or less. The value of liberty, for example. What isn't present in their religious texts."

A car sounded on the road outside. Patrice fixed on Frédéric, and said: "You're thinking of your Oriental."

"Midhat?" said Frédéric. "Well, in fact, I suppose yes I did feel somewhat inspired by—I mean, clearly, this is evidence that one can teach the Arab."

"Just because he is a student." Patrice shook his head. "Rich Turks are constantly sending their sons abroad. And you're talking about civilisation as a whole. There are always exceptions. It's a bit of a leap."

"But look, what about language. Humboldt says—"

"Don't quote a German, there are people in the hall. And I never want to be a defeatist but I would also point out that you don't read Arabic."

"Yes. I was thinking about that." He tapped his forefinger on his glass. "But really I am . . . Patrice, not everyone has a person living in his—who has such remarkable . . . But yes, it's only thoughts at the moment. As you say, if I'm calling on the Boches with all their—their *Weltansicht*, of course I must wait. And I want to be more empirical. As you say. You are right. As always."

Frédéric sipped and watched his friend. Patrice looked up at the window, pursing his lips in little contractions.

"I suppose it could be interesting. It's ambitious, Frédéric, especially if you don't have the language. Perhaps—you know I don't want to discourage you—keep playing with the ideas. But if you're using German scholarship as your framework, it's tricky, you know? It might be worth waiting."

Patrice was right, Frédéric was ambitious. But he was ambitious in a particular way. After his first publication at L'École Normale Supérieure more than twenty years earlier, Frédéric had derived the most lasting pleasure not from the actual promotion the book had secured—which was a victory quickly assimilated, as victories usually are—but from the reaction of his colleague Émile. Émile was gracious: he congratulated Frédéric, complimented the scope of the work, described it as "admirable" for the way it breached disciplinary boundaries, even if those boundaries were internal to anthropology. But beneath his grace Frédéric heard accents of jealousy. He spied hostility in the notes Émile presented for discussion, and in the haughty way Émile greeted him in the dining hall thereafter. At that, Frédéric had felt nothing but glee.

After four years as maître de conférences at Montpellier, however, he had yet to produce the thesis required for promotion to professeur, and all the while was becoming embarrassingly senior for his lecturing position. But he had been galvanised by Patrice's publication last year, and now that the war had magnified his youth—since he happened to be at the younger end of those too old to fight, saved by a margin of eleven months—Frédéric was spurred to replicate his previous success while the corridors of the department were still quiet. He would continue as he had begun, by breaching boundaries. The majority of scholars these days specialised ad infinitum, carving out a piece of terrain so minute that each became an expert on a single detail, a speck of dust, trusting with the capacious vagueness of religious faith that his small corner would in the end contribute to some entirety. What a dreary, unglamorous life. Frédéric was an architect, not a carpenter. And this time he would stretch even further than anthropology. Philology was the new terrain—the life of words, which led one back to the life of humans with fresh paradigms.

That was a technique with German origins. But what could he do, while the men were on the battlefields? Study in secret. Only bring to the university notes written in French, lest a colleague catch sight of an umlaut and cry traitor.

Unlike most, however, Patrice Nolin was highly critical of the war and took no care to conceal it. Which also made him the only man Frédéric knew who wouldn't flinch if he happened to cite a scholar who came from the other side of the Rhine.

They finished their drinks, put on their hats, and walked back through town for dinner. Night fell slowly on the empty street.

"And what was the second?" said Nolin.

"Second what?"

"Strand. You said there were two."

"Oh, Hegel. He has a passage on Herodotus. He says the ancient Greeks drew most of their art and philosophy from the Orient, from Babylon and so on. Egypt. Pallas Athena coming from the moon goddesses. Which might lead you back to the same point about the Orient deviating from the line of progress, but it summoned something else for me too, about origins, primitive form. It sparked a thought, anyway. I must blow, and see if it catches fire."

In the driveway, the car windows were collecting dust.

"Bonsoir Georgine."

"Bonsoir Monsieur." She curtsied as they entered. "Ma'amoiselle Jeannette et Monsieur Midhat sont sur la terrasse."

Frédéric led Patrice into the blue salon and saw them through the glass, his daughter and the Arab. The firelight shot long shadows down the lawn. Jeannette was smoking a cigarette, and as she turned to look back at them a rush of wind pushed her hair over to one side, exposing a tender white spot of scalp. She held the cigarette away and opened the door.

"Is it time for dinner?"

"Almost. The girls aren't here. Nor Sylvain."

She stepped back to let Monsieur Midhat pass into the room.

Midhat bowed. The black robe he was wearing signified, Frédéric knew, that he had visited the clinics that morning. It was strange, even amusing, that he had not changed out of it for dinner. Perhaps the boy was proud of his education and wanted to parade it. But as he sat down and responded flatly to Nolin's questions about his day, Midhat's overall solemnity became conspicuous. He must have seen something terrible at the hospital. Or perhaps he was simply worried about his upcoming examinations. Certainly he would need to do well if he was to pass into the second year. At least that was something Frédéric could look forward to: it was going to be very interesting to see how Monsieur Midhat performed.

Frédéric was almost correct. Both the prospect of the first year assessment and the scenes of the war-wounded and dying at the hospital were causing Midhat anxiety, and he was feeling increasingly uncertain about his capacity to become a doctor. But Frédéric had failed to identify the overriding factor, the one that eclipsed the others; for despite his knowledge of the human brain and of society, in which like any anthropologist he knew the structural significance of marriage, Frédéric never dwelled much on the part played by love in the life of man, outside his own experience of it. Love was something else entirely, little studied in anthropology precisely because it was capricious and often eluded diagnosis: it might appear to its victims like an illness, or be experienced as a state of grace. Often it manifested itself simply as anxiety. Thus Frédéric could not at sight diagnose the major cause of Midhat's suffering, since it never occurred to him that the young Arab might be in love.

A week had passed since Midhat's exchange with Jeannette on the lawn, during which she had continued to avoid him at every turn. In the daytime the house seemed empty, except when Georgine clattered along a passageway with her bucket of sudsy water. Apparently Jeannette spent all day in her bedroom, for Midhat only saw her at mealtimes, and then briefly: always she arrived after him and left before and looked down at her plate throughout, so that the impression of the whole was a rustle of skirts and an impassive face onto which Midhat could paint nothing. Apparently she even managed to cross the hallways when he wasn't there. Sometimes he thought he heard footsteps and would quickly open a door, but it was eternally too late, or it was Georgine, who started, alarmed, the bucket in her hand rocking drips onto the floor. In moments of deep anguish he felt he might reach her only if he broke all bonds of propriety, and all the laws of host and guest, and stood at the top of the stairs and cried out her name.

His jealousy that day over Laurent was unwarranted to be sure, perhaps even insensitive, but it was only because he loved her. He could not comprehend what had so gravely caused offence. Was it the fact that, as with Laurent, Jeannette simply did not return Midhat's love, and so his jealousy had embarrassed her? Or, was his frankness inappropriate in and of itself, the kind of blunder that destroyed delicate webs of peace and decorum? That much was surely true, even he knew that; but he also felt certain that indelicacies were where real life resided, and that people usually forgave a blunder if it turned out well in the end. Or was it that Jeannette loved Laurent after all, and Midhat's question had touched a nerve? And with that letter in his hand—he knew enough of romance to understand what absence might have done to her feelings. And in addition Laurent was in danger. And in addition Laurent was returning. So, there was nothing to be done: if she did not love him, she did not love him. If she loved Laurent, she loved Laurent.

As a child, Midhat had loved a girl in Nablus: the Christian girl, Hala, whom he had mentioned to Jeannette. She came from an impoverished farming family on the edge of town not far from the Kamal house, and when Midhat was young, Teta encouraged him to go over there with bags of flour and eggs on Fridays. Often he would wrap a secret handful of sugar in a roll of muslin and carry that down too, hidden in his pocket.

Hala had red hair. Some said her ancestors were Crusaders who settled there centuries ago; but since neither her parents nor any of her siblings were red-haired, the family denied this. Hala's hair was dark at the root and pale orange at the ends where the sun seemed to have washed off the colour, and her skin was pale and freckled. Midhat loved Hala as children love; he loved her beauty, and her smell, which in his mind was faint and white, and linked forever to sitting beside her in the woodshed in summer, looking through the doorway at the scuffed earth and tufts of green. When he turned eleven he was no longer allowed to spend time with her and, just like the Muslim girls, Hala donned a veil and stayed indoors. Then Midhat left Nablus for Constantinople, and he never saw her again.

His love for Hala was unnameable except in the terms already available to him, and so he used to whisper that he would marry her, and little Hala would bite her lip and smile. Even at the ages of seven and eight they knew about shame, and that fiancés should not spend so much time alone together, and that the differences in wealth and faith would cause problems between their families. And so "marriage" was a secret word, al-zawaj, he breathed in Hala's ear, and from their small hands the steam of mint tea went on rising.

In Constantinople, his understanding of love changed. The curriculum at the Mekteb-i Sultani exposed him to the poetry of the pre-Islamic Jahiliyyah and Abbasid verses which he committed to memory, and the chronicles of the grammarians, the works of Imru' al-Qays and the love lyrics and ghazals. Some texts they read in class, some they passed between their bunks on pages torn from books, or transcribed by the Iraqi boy Rafiq, who did the best calligraphy. Midhat's child-love for Hala was blotted out by these older stories, which, saturated with time and retelling, described the kinds of madness wrought by a beautiful woman: a universal, faceless figure that devastated the viscera of men and inhabited their minds, a lawless revenant composed of verses, hypnotising the inner ear. There were no real girls at school, but on their nocturnal adventures Midhat and his friends would joke about meeting young women on the streets, although the most they ever saw was a skirt in a doorway. As they passed the waters of the Bosphorus clicking in the darkness, the boys shared stories in arch tones that implied expertise in the ways of their bodies and those of the other sex, always pretending there was more to tell, and they were withholding only for the sake of decency.

Hala endured as Midhat's model of a female. She was the only girl he could picture who did not have the face of Teta, Layla, or a hazy something of his mother, which looked a bit like his aunt. Hala could not age: she was always ten years old. Her hair was always long and triangular over her shoulders, her knees were always muddy. Those poetical abstractions learned by candlelight could not be animated with Hala's face and body, for she was unchangeable and unsexual. The ancient poems took force in Midhat's mind as the engines of a vaguer longing, which lacked a face, ached for flesh but thrived on deprivation. The madness of the poet could never be brought off by a woman herself, she in possession of a living body: it was only ever her imprint in his soul, that ideal echo itself the true Beloved, compound of his mind and her being. Midhat knew this much of love before he left for France, and Teta had secured that knowledge: during the school holidays in Nablus he always asked for stories before bed, and Um Taher lay happily beside him unwrapping slivers of her history, her almost loves and secret encounters, her long breasts spilling down her sides. Teta took refuge in the past, repeating the same turns of phrase as she recited her prophecies about the man she fell in love with as a girl, a poor relation who left jasmine flowers on her balcony in the months before she was married off and became the wife of the wealthy merchant they knew as Abu Taher. Stories of longing were the only stories. To desire was as good as to possess.

But here in the Molineus' house things seemed to be different, and Midhat was not equipped. He had not read the right books. Even French words felt thicker lately in his mouth, and like a heavy screen they separated him from what he wanted to say. Each day he was more the fool, the foreigner unable to control his own meanings, lost in the wild multiple of language. And Jeannette was no echo, no Beloved in any sense that he could map. It seemed to him that he desired her herself, not her imprint; he wanted to hear her voice again, to see her eyes again—but if she responded so badly to jealousy, how was he to express that desire? He did not enjoy longing for her, as Teta had seemed to enjoy longing. Even to remain in the house made him ache, because she was also in the house, in another room, choosing not to speak to him. At the same time, he resisted going out because then he might miss an opportunity to encounter her. So he waited, exhausted by a perpetual state of readiness, his stomach clenched as he grasped after eye contact at dinner, hoping to meet her by accident in the hall, distracted, ashamed, heavy with an explosive and unwieldy desire which only increased in strength the longer she ignored him.

Meanwhile, his old shocks of separateness were coming thick and fast. More than separation now, it was that purer loneliness he had felt on the ship to Marseille. During classes, walking to the Faculty, in bed at night, the outline of his body oppressed him as a hard shape. He felt no curiosity about the sensation, which was pure unalloyed pain. His awareness of his limbs was an agony, he wanted to get out of them, to be elsewhere; but he was locked inside his body, and relief from its pressure came only with sleep. And yet even sleep did not sustain him, for he rose already tired, and when he arrived home in the evenings he was too exhausted to change his clothes, and he wore the robe he had worn all day to the dinner table.

That morning Docteur Molineu had announced that Sylvain Leclair and the Nolins were coming to dine, and on returning from the Faculty Midhat chanced a rare sighting from his bedroom window: a flash of yellow silk blown into view by the wind. Afterwards he would wonder if that was deliberate, somehow, whether she knew he was watching for a signal and had made him wait before giving him one.

She did not turn around when he opened the glass door. He left a space between them on the terrace, and looked out at the darkening lawn. It was difficult to speak. At last, he managed: "I'm sorry."

A silence followed.

"Well, that's something."

She said this with such an air of moral authority that he turned his entire body to glare at her in disbelief. Unperturbed, or perhaps unseeing, she offered him a cigarette without meeting his eye. He declined. She did not even register this gesture: she had seen her father through the glass door, and was opening it.

Dinner was a roasted fowl divided between eight—Docteur Molineu, Jeannette, Midhat, Patrice Nolin, Marie-Thérèse, Carole, Sylvain Leclair, and Georgine, who ate in the kitchen—swamped on the plate by beans seasoned with tarragon. Flour-thick gravy sat in jugs between the candelabras, and the steam through the kitchen door misted the spring-cool glass.

The faces lit up and went dark as they leaned in and out of the candle-light, which shot theatrical shadows up from Sylvain's eyebrows over his spherical forehead. Docteur Molineu stumbled out a prayer, and the clinks and sounds of eating commenced, and murmurs of polite conversation.

"What truly is the difference," Nolin broke out, "between a man making arms in a war factory under military control, and the man who dons a uniform and holds a gun?" He wiped his lips. "We are imagining these boundaries. Is it just the women and children who count as 'civilians'? What am I, or you, Frédéric? Are we also incapable of our own defence?"

Docteur Molineu made a stretching gesture of consideration and Midhat perceived that Molineu admired Nolin and wished to impress him. In an instant, his understanding of his host was changed, and he saw him as a man who yearned. He thought of Molineu's wife, and wondered whether he continued to suffer the way his daughter did.

Marie-Thérèse flickered a wine-stained tongue, and tittered. "Carole and I are volunteering at the Auguste Comte School. The mathematics exercises encourage the children to buy war loans."

"My daughters have also both become marraines de guerre. Do you know what that means?" Nolin's eyes narrowed pre-emptively, and he pursed his lips as if tasting the words before he released them.

Midhat shook his head.

"It means they are writing letters to soldiers. But they don't know who they are writing to, they just pretend. It's meant to give the soldiers comfort, a letter from their 'godmother.'"

The three Frenchmen laughed.

"I think it is a very nice thought," said Jeannette.

Nodding, Midhat tried and failed to catch her eye. Sylvain rumbled another laugh, and Jeannette turned so sharply that her hair shook around her head. A memory sprang to the surface: Jeannette distressed, talking to Sylvain, on the other side of a room. With it rose the echo of a powerful dislike, and an obscure imperative to protect her.

"But our view of war is practically picturesque," Nolin said, ostensibly to Docteur Molineu, but loud enough for the entire table. "We continue with our cavalry charges, dashing, Napoléon, you know? These exotic escapades.

I was there when Carl lost Sébastien, so I'm not being flippant. I only mean the glamour will fade."

"Mm."

"We were young, Frédéric, during the Prussian war. But my brother fought and I remember even as a child I knew it was a sore thing, a low thing, and this being the largest we have ever seen—it is not an escapade, at any rate."

A sigh came from across the table. It was Jeannette.

Sylvain said: "We all know it is not an escapade, Patrice."

How odd this was, thought Midhat. These three men too old to fight, dining with three young women left in a world of women and fathers and crippled absentees, and himself a rarity, not only as an Arab but as a young man. No one spoke for a few moments. Midhat made a decision that he would speak. His stomach flipped. He cleared his throat.

"I have been thinking, cher Docteur."

All faces turned towards him.

"About what you once said to me regarding consistency."

Molineu looked surprised, but also delighted. He put his elbows on the table and interlaced his fingers.

"And I have been thinking," said Midhat, "that there is always a cause of *in*consistency, since nothing is without cause. I have been studying Newton." He laughed, anticipating smiles of condescension from the older men. But Nolin and Molineu merely continued to look expectant. "Docteur Molineu and I were discussing what it means to be consistent. Whether it is in our nature or—but I have come to understand it all as a puzzle of two," he wobbled his upturned palms like scales, "that covers more than a few questions about human beings. It stayed in my mind, this conversation we had, and I have concluded that it has to do with causes. There is a lovely phrase by one of our philosophers in Islam, Ibn Rushd, who believed in a beginning and an end . . ." At once, his point about Ibn Rushd didn't seem relevant. "I mean, if something appears to be without cause it is usually an aberration . . . with regard to the body, at the least. And even if there doesn't appear to be a cause there is *always* a cause, only that cause might be obscured, and being obscured, we may deduce from its obscurity that almost certainly something is seriously wrong with the body internally, the apparently causeless aberration . . . say a rash, or great fatigue, or a strange pain . . . being therefore a symptom of something invisible. And similarly I think that if we look at the mind and character of man, aberrations in behaviour will always have a cause. That is if we could map mind onto body—but if we could, and if we looked at motives and experience and we *still* cannot find the cause of the inconsistency, it would tend to mean that there is something quite seriously wrong, something that is causing aberrant behaviour. Madness, for example."

These were thoughts he had begun to play with on the days he walked alone to and from the Faculty, and they were not ready to be shared with others. Though he had not decided whether as a whole they held water, he liked to return to the various themes, and derived from them a private confidence in his own mind, as he had once derived confidence in his body through daydreaming. But as his words about the invisible left his mouth he suddenly saw their flaws, how they didn't address other invisible causes. Crucial among the invisible being, of course, God.

"That sounds interesting," said Nolin. "Invisible causes as a sign of pathology. But it could be sophistical. Let me think."

Midhat was flattered by Nolin's tone, though he knew he had spoken with the accidental definiteness of a person using a second language. He looked at Jeannette, hoping to be admired. Instead he saw a pair of outraged eyes.

"Wait a minute," said Nolin. "Are you saying that madness *is* a discrete invisible cause? Or that it has one? I mean, are you calling madness an aberration, or is it the cause of aberrant symptoms? For one thing, it's often not particularly invisible, and for another, it is most often extremely difficult to ascertain causes. Unless you are of the modern camp. Other than neurological, you know."

"I think I meant to say that madness was a cause. But I suppose it's not so invisible, no . . ."

"Yes, it's a little vague. In the end," Patrice Nolin addressed the table, "one must ask of a speculative paradigm first and foremost whether or not it is *of use* when we are going about our daily business of trying to understand phenomena. I admire your originality Monsieur Midhat but your thinking is caught in a kind of tautology . . . or system of infinite regress."

"Thank you, Patrice, for that lesson," said Frédéric, with a jolly smile.

The damage was done. Midhat wished he had not spoken.

"I think," said Sylvain, after a pause, "the Muhammadan speaks very good French, however."

"Sylvain," said Jeannette, harshly.

"Jeannette," said her father.

"Are we all going to say each other's names?" said Carole.

"Carole," ventured Marie-Thérèse, but nobody smiled, and she blushed a painful shade of red that leaked onto her forehead and nose.

"In addition to which," said Nolin, "I can't believe your world is so perfectly *consistent* with itself, Monsieur Midhat, pardon me. There are several things I can name right now as serious aberrations in this world, behavioural or otherwise, and we know exactly what the causes are."

"I am sorry," said Midhat, enunciating with some force.

"That's enough Nolin," said Sylvain.

Midhat looked at his unlikely defender, and remembered in a flash that it was at the party—that was where Sylvain had upset Jeannette, and he, Midhat, had followed her into the hall.

"Pardon me," said Nolin in a haughty voice, though it was followed swiftly by an earnest "Ah," as Georgine took his plate. "Thank you."

Georgine squeaked the trolley around the table.

"Why don't you sit with us for dessert?" said Molineu.

Georgine hesitated a fraction too long. Already Molineu was suggesting that Jeannette might shuffle down towards Patrice, and slip a chair in there, three on each side is perfect, first perhaps bring in the soufflé and dessert spoons, if you might Georgine. Midhat caught a raised eyebrow from Jeannette to Carole. Not out of unkindness towards Georgine, he understood, nor out of disrespect for her father; it was just a necessary concession that something was out of the ordinary, to avert gossip that the Molineus always dined with their servants. Molineu's face was quickly showing signs of embarrassment as his whimsy took effect. Georgine seated herself between Jeannette and Sylvain and whispered, "Good evening."

Midhat looked at Sylvain and Georgine right-angled on the corner of the table. Her head was bowed, and he was swigging from his glass. The embrace Midhat had stumbled on at the party presented itself vaporously to his mind. He watched them in amazement, side by side, ignoring each other. For the first time it occurred to him to question whether Georgine had been willing. He felt a wave of confused disgust.

"Yes, that's better. Isn't it." Docteur Molineu pushed his spoon into the soufflé.

Midhat returned his attention to Jeannette, who was staring at her bowl. He was always watching her distress from afar, across a room, a garden; he blinked as the image recurred of water falling off her thighs. The anger he felt on the terrace was already cooling, deposed by her apparently worthier annoyance at his mention of madness. That hardly seemed much of an indiscretion, especially given that the speech in its entirety had drawn enough embarrassing attention to himself that no one would be thinking of her mother. All the same, he had forfeited his high ground. Was it a game of one-upmanship, of who could be more annoyed with whom? At least, if it was, then she could not be indifferent to him. At this thought he was surprised to feel a hot little glow of hope.

"I think we ought to change the subject," said Nolin.

"Which subject?" said Marie-Thérèse.

"Somebody pass Georgine a spoon," said Molineu.

"Thank you."

"And how are your studies, Monsieur Midhat?" said Carole.

"My studies are fine, thank you Mademoiselle. I am now beginning the preparations for my final examinations before the summer break. And then in the winter term I will be starting to perform my own dissections on cadavers. In the summer term it will be histology, physiology, and biological physics."

"How nice. It sounds challenging."

"We received . . . or rather, Jeannette . . ." He glanced across and saw with relief that her expression had softened. "A letter came from Laurent." She nodded her permission. "It seems he has been putting his learning into practice already."

"Good luck to him," said Sylvain.

"He'll be on leave soon," said Molineu.

Nolin said, "What is the news from the Front?"

"Oh, please let's not talk anymore about the war," said Jeannette.

"Yes," said Sylvain. "Let's—let's talk about cinema, or literature or something. Has anyone seen *The Heroes of Yser*?"

"What the hell are you talking about?" said Nolin. "You think talking about cinema is not talking about the war? What do you think the subject is of *The Heroes of Yser*?"

"Oh, shut up," said Sylvain.

"High culture has become totally sterile."

"Patrice."

"We are actually talking about the *cinema*. There is nothing left to discuss. Which leads us to the more interesting point that leisure is the grounds for innovation, and that in a state of war . . ."

"I think we are surfeited with this line now, Patrice," said Molineu.

Nolin closed his mouth and quivered a frown. What a bore he was, thought Midhat. He noticed the wine was gone from the bottles and their glasses, and wondered if they had all slipped into extreme versions of themselves.

"Have we finished?" said Molineu.

Jeannette had barely touched her dessert; Sylvain's bowl was empty; the Nolin sisters had made admirable dents. Midhat did not particularly like the soufflé, it tasted too much of egg, but it was sweet and he liked sweet things, and accordingly had eaten half of it. Georgine's bowl was wiped clean, and at her employer's question she jumped to her feet and scraped herself free of the chair. Setting off with the squeaking trolley again around the table, she disappeared into the kitchen with the plates.

"Coffee, anyone?" said Molineu.

"I think we have surfeited," said Patrice Nolin, with a quick smile.

He bowed his head at his daughters, who stood and cooed: the food was delicious, such a treat, really, in these dark days. Sylvain patted his chest, he couldn't fit in a drop more. They gathered their coats in the hall, and shook hands and kissed goodbye.

In the silence after their departure, Molineu said something about coffee and returned to the dining room. Jeannette hesitated in the hall, and Midhat felt the breath of something resuming. She walked to the door of the cream salon, and turned the key. When he saw she had left the door ajar, he followed.

She was sitting on the piano stool, which was covered in a sheet of canvas, like everything else in the room. The covered piano extended vast and glacier-like before her. There was a strong smell of varnish. He hung in the doorway.

"I understand," he said.

She looked up at him wearily. He wondered if she would disavow their previous exchange and pretend she didn't follow.

"Did you drink wine tonight?"

"No," he replied, with a sharply falling intonation, as if that were a ludicrous suggestion. Then he stepped forward and lowered his voice. "I wanted to say again that I am sorry. Please accept my apology. I understand you are angry. And that I should not have talked with Laurent about you. And that I should not have presumed . . ."

She faced him. She was painfully beautiful in the yellow dress. Her skin was like soft paper, those blue veins. He could tell by her eyes that she was experiencing some kind of emotion, but he hesitated to name it, so often was he getting things wrong.

"I am not jealous of Laurent. But you know I—I did mean what I said." He swallowed. "And I'm sorry if you do not—if you do not feel the same, I will not . . . But, I miss you, Jeannette. Really." He reached out for the nearest covered piece of furniture, wanting to sit and meet her level; but whatever he had gripped wobbled and he let it go. "I miss talking to you. It meant so much to me, walking with you, and without it, I can't say what it is, but I lack . . . Really, I—I loved . . . And I want to help you to find out what happened to your mother. I will do anything I can."

Jeannette's eyebrows rose, though she did not actually look surprised. "My mother. That is kind of you, but there is nothing to be done. As I think I told you I don't think it's healthy for me . . ."

"But as long as you know that—that I am listening."

Here, at last, she smiled. He had said the right thing.

"There is a line in *The Three Musketeers* . . ."

"Oh no, don't quote *The Three Musketeers!*" She laughed, leaning back. "You know, you shouldn't feel you have to rely on what other people have said all the time." Her eyes rested on him for a moment, then she twisted and tucked her feet under the piano. "I'll tell you. When I was studying at the university, I was always surrounded by these young men being knowledge-able." She laughed again, a chain of exhalations. "And it was intimidating. I felt I was less than they were. They were men after all—and who was I?" Her fingers traced where the lid of the piano was hidden beneath its dress. She lifted the lid. The fabric caught on the back of it, like the skin of an eyelid. "I used to come home from the library and go through all my work with Papa. Then I found myself parroting him in my seminars, and I would say exactly what he had told me the night before. And then, after a while, I realised I didn't need to. It was just language these men were playing with. I would listen very carefully to the arguments they made, the way they discussed things outside class. Leaning on this philosopher and that, adding clause after clause, and I realised it was just language, not life. They knew nothing about life, and this was everything to them, and it was small. And thinking that suddenly liberated me, and I was no longer afraid to speak up. And my speaking became better." With her forefinger, she marked the cracks between the keys under the canvas, making indentations that disappeared as she moved from one to the next. "I could have disparaged them in my mind and made it easier for myself that way. I could have called them petty young men or something. But I didn't, because what would have been the point?" She had outlined five keys, now six, her hand moving across the front of her body. "I'm trying to tell you that you shouldn't think you have to be intimidated by things on the surface, like conversation."

"I'm not intimidated."

"Well, I'm just saying. You are not beneath them in any way. You may be much younger, but you have for one thing far more goodness than Patrice Nolin."

She pressed a key. The sound was manifold and deep, glassy and warm at the same time. She gazed up at him as if she had voiced a dare. The challenge was so direct he should have felt embarrassed. He didn't: he felt amazed. He felt an exhilarating exposure, the stinging relief of salt air.

"I think I am in love with you," he said. His mouth was dry. "I also think you are quite unreasonable."

She remained looking up at him, until they heard the grate of a floorboard.

"Ah, pardon me," said Georgine, closing the door again.

The interruption solidified the moment. Jeannette whispered that she should go to bed, and moved past. Midhat waited alone for a few more minutes amid the covered furniture, hearing the rain mutter on the window.

In the kitchen, Georgine was drying a stack of wet plates.

"I hope you enjoyed the dessert tonight," said Midhat, opening a cabinet.

"I did Monsieur, thank you. I hope you did too."

"Georgine, if it's not impolite of me to ask . . ."

"Yes, Monsieur?"

He selected a glass and hesitated.

"I was wondering. Could you tell me, why is Docteur Molineu a friend of Monsieur Sylvain Leclair? It is only—because they are not neighbours, I was wondering . . ."

"Monsieur Leclair was a good friend of Madame Molineu," said Georgine. "Who died."

She looked so serene, wiping her hands on the towel at her waist. He thought of Sylvain Leclair, and his heavy, impassive insults. Nolin was a pedant, but Leclair was nasty. Midhat turned the faucet on to fill the glass, and as the water rushed, his imagination began to whirr.

8

He did not sleep easily that night. He consulted an alarm clock he had borrowed from the Docteur so frequently that he barely saw the hands change
their angles, but instead felt he was moving with them, pushing into the
night in one continuous movement. Fatigue won out around four thirty,
and he woke after a few more hours to find the room flushed with sunlight.
Seconds later, the clock burst out singing.

Jeannette entered for breakfast after he did and delivered a general
good morning. The tablecloth shone in the light between them and the
steam twisted from the coffeepot. Docteur Molineu began to read aloud
from the broadsheet.

"Fifteen hours. Bad weather continues, no event on the Front during
the night . . . to the east of the Yser, two attempted attacks by the enemy
stopped by our gunfire. And the Dardanelles . . ." He crackled over two
pages. "Brigadier General Cox pushes an attack . . . serious loss of the
enemy . . . good. Considerable progress . . . German general killed . . . Aus-
tralian submarine lost in the Straits."

Folding the paper Molineu noticed a blob of jam on the tablecloth and
reached for his butter knife. The blob slid easily onto the blade but as he

tipped the knife upwards it stretched and crept over the other side, falling off in three red drips.

"Jojo, pass me your napkin."

Jeannette was replacing her letters in their envelopes, and still she had not looked at Midhat. He watched her brazenly: it was not possible that she would treat this the same as other mornings. He would not miss the moment she turned her eyes to his.

"Thank you," said Molineu, enclosing the mess under the napkin. "Did Marian write?"

"Yes, she wrote."

"She is well?"

"Yes, she is well."

And still she would not turn to him. She was sealed; she made not a single unnecessary movement. Her arm reached for the coffee cup, her head remained immobile as she moved her eyes.

Her hair had grown, he realised. When he first arrived, there had been little to pin up, and the rough curls had bloomed out of the back of her head, cutting away to her thin neck. It could not have been any shorter yesterday but it was only now he noticed, perhaps because she had arranged it in a new style: with a parting on one side and a series of large coils wound and fastened on either side of her head. The sunlight throbbed over her hairline. Breakfast over, they stood to part. Jeannette was nearest the door and left the room before him as usual.

Since the blunder over Laurent, when Jeannette started avoiding him, Midhat had used the mornings to study for his examinations. Most days he remained in his bedroom until lunchtime, combing through his books subject by subject, recording any concept he had trouble with, and compiling a list of queries that he carried despondently to the afternoon class. Today the prospect of this routine was a particular strain. He dragged himself upstairs. The physics textbook already lay open on his desk. Was it possible, had he misread the look she gave him from the piano stool? As the rods of the chair hit his back he felt a thrash of anger that she should be so cruel, so intent on making him suffer.

The first section of the chapter "Motion, Velocity, Acceleration" was titled: "The Motion of a Train." He read it through, then realised he had not absorbed anything. Had it been shock, that look she gave him, and he had taken it for love? It would not be the first time he had failed to understand her. Had she not smiled? Then again, a smile could mean several different things. He began to read aloud.

"The Motion of a Train. Let us suppose that a locomotive stands with steam up . . . steam up . . . ready to make the run to the next station . . . the next station . . . When it starts, we notice that at first it moves slowly . . ."

A soft knock at the bedroom door. "Good morning, Midhat," came Jeannette's voice.

"Ah," he said, up and turning the handle, "come in, come in," his legs seemed to have no bones; he saw Jeannette's face and her hair pinned, her hands holding a book, and his anger fell away, overcome by that Arab impulse to encourage strangers over thresholds. Jeannette looked taken aback. Yet, what else could she have expected, knocking on his door? She stepped inside and stood next to the prayer mat.

"I wanted to show you something."

"Please, please."

He pulled out the chair for her, then sat on the bed and locked his hands as though they were in public. To calm himself, he breathed out slowly through narrowed lips.

"I found this the other day when I was going through old photographs," she said.

She pulled two pieces of pale green paper from the book but did not hand them to him. He was delighted to realise she was trembling.

"It is a doctor's report."

"About your mother?"

She looked him in the eyes. "They didn't diagnose her with hysteria, it says here. But with 'hystero-neurasthenia.' Do you know what that is?"

"I can find out."

"Do you think I'm ridiculous?"

"Of course not. Of course I don't think you're ridiculous. I think"—he bent forward, speaking gently—"we have faith that life means something, and the attempt to resolve it, to seek it out, this is what keeps us going. And that's the same for things in the past, if they are important to us."

"Well, that is very rational. Here, this is the list. Nausea, migraine, headaches. Intercostal neuralgia, cramp, tinglings, prickings . . . rheumatism, pains in the forehead, the gums, the back of the neck, the throat . . . occasionally in arms, chest, loins, stomach, knees, feet, ankles . . . upon examination genital parts all tender." Jeannette made a little shocked motion of her eyebrows—she had been reading without processing, he saw, and perhaps had not intended to read that part aloud.

"This is a long list," he said. He had learned from his grandmother to skip over shameful things. At the same time he was playing a doctor, with a doctor's dispassionate attitude to matters of the body. He could not help admiring himself.

"And this," Jeannette continued, "this one is a list of symptoms she seems to have written herself, in her own handwriting. I'll read it to you— she says: 'The walls of my father's house were totally transformed. I was woken up by the sensation of weight on my leg, my bed being beside the window, the man had stepped onto it. I screamed and quickly he climbed back out again. It took a while to settle as my sleeping mind woke fully, and when it did, I saw the walls had vanished. Or rather, they had become simply walls, plaster and wood and brick, just a structure with no inside or outside. Inside and outside were an illusion.' That's that one, and here, another, she says: 'There is little keeping me alive. When I am well I cannot be from too high a height or I will make myself fall on purpose.' Let me know if there's any word you don't understand, by the way."

"What does that mean, do you think? I understood it, I mean, but generally, what is she saying."

"What she *means* . . . I don't know if it's something we can necessarily . . ." She left off.

Midhat loved that *we*. "It sounds," he said, "as though she was in pain all the time, most of the time. Physical pain. Even when she was healthy. Don't you think?"

She turned over the page and read from the bottom. "Listen: 'I feel sometimes as though my head were being stirred with a stick, and at other times as though my head were being alternately opened and closed. Nausea, almost daily. Sometimes it feels like motion sickness, as if I were going somewhere. Often it is in the nose again, and I have the old dreams.'"

"She is mad."

Jeannette gave him an irked expression.

"I'm sorry, I didn't mean that. It seems, I think, that being alive is to stay inside the body." He could hear, returning into his voice, that note of glib certainty. He tried a more tentative intonation. "This is one way to look at it. And if the body is a place of pain, then that makes it difficult to stay there. So, I suppose, your mother wanted to leave."

Jeannette nodded. She reached across the gap to touch his arm, and inhaled as though to speak. Then she pulled back, and rubbed her hands.

"I will let you alone, of course. You are studying."

"You don't need to," said Midhat. "I want to help, I told you so."

"I know you did," she said, rising. "I don't know why I'm fixed on this, I shouldn't be. You must think I'm . . . I don't know. I'll see you later then, I suppose."

On one of his visits to the university hospital, Midhat had taken part in the observation of a patient suffering from a stomach ailment. The patient was a teenage boy whose abdomen was distended and painful, resulting in some vomiting and loss of appetite.

The boy's ears were pointed and pale. The four students stood against the wall by the door while Docteur Brion spoke to him. Seated on the bed, shoes off, dressed in a hospital gown, he looked past the doctor at them lined up with their notepads, wearing black robes; his eyes were wide, chin loose, thin legs bent open from the hip and trousers hanging, while Docteur Brion spoke to him in a bright voice. Brion examined the boy's tongue and the four students hovered behind. The tongue looked angry and raw. His bloated stomach was sensitive to pressure. Brion instructed the boy to push his head forward for the soft-rubber stomach tube, and to open his mouth while he, Brion, directed the tube down the throat. He asked the boy to swallow.

"This attempt at swallowing will first cause the pharyngeal muscles to grasp the tube . . . and then as they relax it may be pushed downwards until the stomach is reached—in the average individual a distance of about sixteen inches from the line of the teeth."

The boy's eyes widened further. He gagged, and his bent knees convulsed.

"Good, well done. Now, the attempts at retching will usually cause the contents of the stomach to come up through the tube. And . . . here they come."

A trickle as the liquid came up through the tube and poured out the other end into a glass receptacle. It was thin and yellowish, with mealy grey lumps and a few strands of bile.

"If the contents do not come up at once," said Brion, pulling the tube up out of the boy's gullet while the boy rasped, "the patient should be told to strain as if making an effort to pass stool. Or, alternatively"—he reached for a rubber bulb the same red as the tube—"one may aspirate the stomach contents by attaching this to the extremity of the tube, compressing it and gradually, very important that it be gradual, allowing it to expand."

He slowly compressed and expanded the rubber bulb. The boy's mouth hung open. A globe of spittle dangled from his lower lip.

What they discovered when they strained and examined the liquid was a low level of hydrochloric acid and a great deal of mucus. Brion's diagnosis was chronic gastritis. Such a diagnosis always required further tests for lactic acid and the Boas-Oppler bacillus, which were symptoms of cancer. Accordingly, Brion reached for a bottle of Gram's solution from a shelf, and using a pipette added some of the filtered contents to a small container of the solution. The solution turned bright blue: the Boas-Oppler bacillus was present.

The boy stared over at Midhat and his colleagues while all this was going on, until the solution turned its shocking colour. Docteur Brion trembled uncharacteristically—perhaps he had not expected the test to come up positive, perhaps he would otherwise have chosen to conduct the test in private—and for a moment seemed not to know to whom he should pronounce the diagnosis. They could all see the evidence, however, and although the boy might not know precisely the rule that the Boas-Oppler bacillus stains blue with Gram's solution, it seemed somehow so obviously a sign of alarm, the solution now the rich hue of a low sky gathering at the meridian.

"Carcinoma of the stomach," said Brion. "You'll have to see the surgeon this afternoon."

For the first time, the boy spoke. "But I have to get back to work." His voice was unexpectedly high-pitched.

The boy stayed in Midhat's mind for days afterwards, and on his next visit to the hospital he sought out Docteur Brion to ask after the status of the carcinoma. Distracted then by a new flood of soldiers arriving wounded from the front, Brion looked confused and said he could not remember, waving Midhat out of the way as he pushed the swing doors of the next ward.

It was the look of fear on the boy's face that weighed most heavily on him. That was the fear of discovery. The boy had glimpsed the malevolence within his own stomach, a thing living there inside him.

After Jeannette left, Midhat ran through his physics notes in a fever, and without time for lunch set off at a sprint for the afternoon class. There were only five other students in the classroom and they all sat in the first row of desks. Midhat raised his hand to ask the professor if they could go over Coulomb's law of charged bodies, and was relieved to see that he was not the only one writing down the formula. In the corridor afterwards, he caught sight of his biology professor, and running up behind him asked if they could briefly go over the chromosome theory of inheritance. "But there is not much to go over," said the professor. "You understand the theory, do you? Simply, that chromosomes carry genetic material. That's all there'll be in the exam. What is it you don't understand?" Midhat hesitated, and then expressed his gratitude, yes, at last he understood. He turned around and crossed the courtyard to the library. It was almost half past two. *I feel sometimes as though my head were being stirred with a stick*, he thought, as he heaved against the massive door.

Samuel Cogolati was the only other person in the library. He sat at a table on the far side and did not look up from his book. From this distance, Cogolati's hairless, waxy complexion resembled a child's. Midhat approached the medical dictionaries and pulled down the latest edition of Larousse. He sat in a chair and turned to "N."

Page 746 showed an illustration of a wheeled machine captioned "Nettoyage par le vide." On the opposite page was the definition he wanted:

Neurasthenia: – (Syn: Nervous exhaustion, nervousness, neuropathy, cerebro-cardiac neuropathy, hyperaesthesia general, general neuralgia.)

SYMPTOMS. Neurasthenia may be manifested in two very different ways. Sometimes the neurasthenic has a healthy appearance, a fresh complexion, and a confident air. And on the contrary he is sometimes a depressed individual; emaciated, pale, holding his head down, answering with difficulty even the simplest of questions. These two varieties of patients generally complain of the same ills: headaches occupying the top of the head, limited at the neck or various parts of the skull, increased by sounds, smells, and intellectual fatigue, and decreasing after meals.

This fitted with the stick-stirring, in any case.

Insomnia is frequent and painful. The patient feels the need to sleep after dinner but soon wakes up, failing to fall asleep again until morning; and so *he rises already tired*, since during the interval he has been persecuted—

A page of photographs intervened illustrating "Nettoyage par le vide." A man stood in a street beside a vast black machine labelled: VACUUM CLEANER; the same man then knelt indoors, pressing the end of a tube into the floor; then two women in aprons raked the ground with various metal prongs.

—by a kind of jittering of thought and many distressing sensations, so that even when he seemed to rest he was assailed by nightmares.

Dizziness sometimes occurs: an empty feeling in the brain, flies before
the eyes, staggering without falling.

A finger down the other symptoms: Digestive disorders . . . Respiratory
and circulatory disorders . . . Disorders of the genito-urinary tract, one
of the causes of the disease . . . Ringing, observed in the ear . . . Extreme
sensitivity to hot or cold, causing pain . . .

The constant study of his health to which the neurasthenic applies himself
causes him to perceive a thousand sensations, unnoticed by everyone else,
which he interprets and exaggerates.

The treatments included a diet without crustaceans, with the addition of
raw egg yolks and broth.

"Bonjour, Monsieur Midhat."

Cogolati stood above him, holding a book with a finger between the
pages.

"Ah, Samuel. How are you?"

"What are you reading, the dictionary?"

"I am, yes. I am researching neurasthenia."

"Interesting. May I sit? What have you found."

Midhat's stomach rumbled. He coughed.

"Oh, not much," he said. "The only unifying trait seems to be strange
physical sensations. Apart from that, it seems you diagnose a patient as
a neurasthenic if you can judge them to be a hypochondriac. Isn't that
strange? They are ill if they are not ill. There is no specific ailment, nothing
physical or neurological, just this subjective, doctorly reading of the patient
herself. Or himself."

"Yes. That is vague. Perhaps this is what Rivaut means when he says
we are part of a developing science!" Cogolati tipped his head back with
silent laughter.

Midhat was already elsewhere. His mind was seeking out its well-
worn channels and now streaming back by the gravity of habit to that
shamed idea of his: the idea of invisible causes, that there might be other,

hidden sources of Ariane Molineu's pain. He thought of Jeannette's resistance to the idea of madness. He thought of the babies in the jars, labelled and locked.

"We should look in the Psychiatry section." Cogolati set down his own book and marked his place with a slip of paper.

Midhat was glad of the company. Together he and Cogolati examined the titles on spines, consulted contents pages, and set books in piles, mapping recurring terms. Midhat found no mention of "hystero-neurasthenia" anywhere but he seized on "hysteria" and other terms that appeared alongside it.

"What is the nature of the research?" asked Cogolati.

"I was just reading about neurasthenia in a . . . novel."

"Aha! The best kind of research, led by the imagination. I admire that."

Briquet's "Treatise on Hysteria" contained 430 case studies. Almost all concerned young women, frequently lower class. A few mentions of aberrant sexual activity.

"Ho ho, listen," said Cogolati. He elbowed aside a discarded volume on the table to rest open the one he was reading. "This writer says: 'It certainly happens that neuroses above the belt are far more clearly understood than those below.' How amusing. How awfully unhelpful."

The rumble in Midhat's stomach was sharpening into hunger. The clock said three; breakfast had been more than seven hours ago. In a recent issue of *L'Encéphale* he found an article entitled "Les Cénestopathies," and he read through the six case histories at manic speed. The article argued that the cause of lesionless pain was disordered bodily sensation. *Incorrect inhabitation of the body,* Midhat wrote in his notebook, a little shakily.

The sun faded through the windows. Cogolati yawned.

"This has been instructive, but I am not quite sure what we have learned. That definitions are often in conflict? Or that the mind and the body should remain different spheres. You know, I have a friend you should talk to, majoring in psychiatry. At the moment he is working with traumatised soldiers. Would that be helpful?"

"Wait, listen. This is in," Midhat shut the cover to see the jacket, "*La Conscience Morbide*, Blondel. 'Morbid consciousness is a kind of cenesthetic instability,' he says . . . 'a rebel to logic' . . . 'a refractory in our conceptual regime, and different in kind from normal consciousness.'"

"Yes, it's . . . I mean, I don't know. I'll have to go, Kamal. But this has been fun—we should—anyway I'll see you in Botany tomorrow. Good luck. I look forward to hearing your conclusions."

"Thank you," said Midhat. "It has been wonderful having you here."

"I am so glad the library is your home," said Cogolati with a wink. "Until soon."

The library door gonged shut, and echoed up the stacks. Midhat's hunger was fading, as during a fast. He returned to the thread he had just dropped.

Perhaps Madame Molineu had not been normal. Perhaps she was "morbid." But really, what did that prove in the end? It seemed worse to him than blaming an evil spirit. At least people would try to expel a spirit, and the victim was not isolated, they did not disbelieve her, nor diagnose her because they thought she did not have the symptoms she claimed. How could one tell if a symptom was not there, if it was not the kind of symptom that could be seen?

La France Intellectuelle, with her granite monuments engraved with birth dates and death dates and graduation dates, was a place of such unerring certainty that Midhat felt he was often gazing up her plinths in awe. Even in wartime the French argued from their lecterns, formulated between four walls; while in Nablus—in Nablus they reached for the supernatural when they were helpless, whether with prayers to God or the charms of a sheikh to protect them from the evil eye. Nabulsis spent their lives close to their graves, at nature's mercy, and sought antidotes to the world's pain in the vapours of ritual. Here in Europe the trains always ran on time, the streets were paved perpendicular, one did not feel the earth—and yet it seemed now to Midhat that these structures were also illusory. They gave only the appearance of rightness. For at times and in certain lights you could see it was a baseless fabric, which could be lifted. And one could reach a hand beneath, and beyond it feel the thin air.

His hunger had disappeared. Four hours in the library and he had no new information for Jeannette, except that the doctors had failed to help her mother, but that much had already been clear. Here he was, exploring the same diagnoses the doctor had given. It was these that must be discarded in the first place. He returned the books to the reshelving trolley and stepped out into the courtyard. The streets were quiet but for the distant singing of the stretcher-bearers, and his feet clacked in the cool.

He turned a corner and the moon revealed itself suddenly, huge and white behind a flowered branch, an interloper before the sun had even gone. He stopped, and tried to consider outright what might have happened to Ariane Molineu in her lifetime. What interferences might have been made. What damning course of action. What—or who—in her life might have proved a *cause*.

9

Sylvain Leclair lived on his vineyard on the left bank of the Hérault, and spent his days between the trellises or in his vaults monitoring the barrels. At the same time, he was a figure about town, a feature at most major gatherings and many minor ones, in a way that had little to do with his profession. Possibly, it had more to do with his connection to Paris: his maiden aunts lived in the Fifteenth Arrondissement and he visited them several times a month, and was apparently popular at salons in the neighbourhood. But Sylvain never masqueraded as a cosmopolite, nor falsified his southern vowel sounds, or the nasal accent that rounded off most end-stopped words with that inconclusive syllable "uh." On the contrary, Sylvain Leclair was unashamedly parochial, and always disgruntled, aggressive, self-righteous, and somehow this was his ticket to all classes and parties, in which he was famed and praised for his bad temper.

Jeannette's relationship with Sylvain was based, like her father's, on his friendship with her mother. All she knew was that Sylvain had first befriended Jeannette's maternal grandmother in Paris, and then had befriended her child. Sylvain filled a certain space for the girl with no siblings, and when Ariane turned sixteen he became her ally at the balls, and her comfort when she felt ill at ease, which was often. She hung on his arm and, naturally, rumours soon developed that they were engaged.

When Ariane turned eighteen and there was still no sign of a proposal, her father addressed Sylvain: he must either make clear his intent or put an end to his attentions. Sylvain was surprised, he said he was sorry, he had no intention of proposing marriage. After that, except for the odd sighting across rooms, Ariane and Sylvain did not meet again for several years.

By a series of improbable coincidences, in the winter of 1901 Frédéric Molineu found himself sitting beside Monsieur Leclair at a dinner party in Fontainebleau, to which he had been invited at the last minute by a professor at L'École Normale. Their conversation took its turns and it emerged that Monsieur Leclair had known Frédéric's wife Ariane as a young girl. Naturally, it occurred to Frédéric that there might have been some romantic attachment; but it seemed so physically unlikely—this large provincial man, his delicate young wife—that the notion was instantly usurped by the possibility that such a friend from her past, capable of reciting such happy memories, might provide some comfort to Ariane, who by now experienced every human interaction as though it were a violent scratch.

Sylvain accepted the invitation to dine, and to Frédéric's astonishment the effect was nearly immediate. Reunited with her old friend—who was twenty years older than her and had by now gained so much weight he could be taken for her grandfather—Ariane began to resemble her old self. Sylvain's visits became a monthly event, and she continued to relax; she slept and ate well; she was once again that cheerful woman Frédéric had known in the early days of marriage.

It did not last long. The patterns in Ariane's mind could not, it seemed, be reversed, and little time passed before she fell again into darkness. No one ever knew the precise nature of Ariane's bond with Sylvain Leclair. The only important thing was that even he was not capable of saving her.

When Frédéric and Jeannette first moved south to Montpellier four years earlier, the vignerons' unrest over the falling price of wine was a recent memory for the townspeople. During Sylvain's visits to the Molineus he had not, they thought, made particular efforts to conceal his political activity, but nor was it something he discussed much, and if he did mention it they tended to imagine he was exaggerating for effect. As they settled into Montpellier, however, it became apparent that nothing was exaggerated, and that Sylvain was famous throughout the town for thundering to the front of the crowd at Place de la Comédie, where the syndicalists and royalists and Occitan separatists had all gathered to protest the fraudulent powder then swamping the market, which could be turned into wine with the addition of well water. And when Marcelin Albert screamed from the podium, Sylvain Leclair had roared back his slogans, and roused from the crowd the energy of a bonfire.

Such open fever had not recurred since in Montpellier, but Sylvain was always alert to other kinds of contagion. Ostensibly, the war had settled the region with the double balms of employment and bereavement. But something else was boiling underneath. The unconscripted who feared censure were quick to denounce others, and public squares were rife with scraps of hearsay, transmitted from mouth to ear, mouth to ear, until in some warped fashion they were returned to the doorstep of the accused as a talisman of wrongdoing.

It is hard to say just how the word first spread about Patrice Nolin. In all likelihood it was some indiscretion of his own, a passing remark, probably, that caught in the windpipes of a nervous patriot who proceeded to spread it around, until in the space of a single evening Nolin's name was carried across town, and in the morning the whole of Montpellier was against him. And, naturally, Sylvain Leclair caught word of this on his morning ramble, and swiftly brought the facts as he could discern them to the house of the Molineus. Midhat had just left for the Faculty. Frédéric Molineu was about to follow when he saw Sylvain Leclair's portly frame in the driveway, swinging his cane.

"Good day Sylvain."

"Good morning. Have you heard?"

"Heard what?"

"Nolin is gone. He came home from dinner, there were letters on his doorstep. He was scared, he left."

"Come in, what are you talking about. What letters?"

"Thank you," said Sylvain, brushing his feet on the rug. "There were three or four of them. Some were anonymous. At least one," he grunted, "was written by Luc Dimon." He shot a glance down the hall.

"Luc?" said Frédéric. "What does he have against Patrice?"

"Oh, you know. Traitor, this, that. German, selfish, all the rest."

"My God. Should I, do you think, visit him? Or, should we avoid . . ."

"There isn't time," said Sylvain. He glanced again in the direction of the kitchen. "He and the girls were ready to leave an hour ago."

"You've seen them then."

"I passed by. I told him what I had heard."

"What did you hear?"

"This, that. We'll have to be very careful now. Shall we sit? I could do with a coffee."

"I—oh dear. We could do, I suppose," said Frédéric. "Well, what is the time? My watch has stopped."

"Eight thirty."

"In fact, you know, I must go. I lecture at ten. I'm sorry, Sylvain, another time."

"What are you sorry for, my friend. Everyone is always walking over your hospitality. I suppose I am no less guilty. I'll follow you out."

"Well, you know, thank you for telling me."

That was a lie: Frédéric was not lecturing at ten that day. He walked calmly beside Sylvain down the driveway to the road, but once they separated and he rounded the corner he began to march so fast that by the time he reached the department his collar was damp with sweat. He leapt up the steps two at a time, pushed through the first double doors, charged through the second, reached the last door with the frosted window, and unlocked it as fast as his shaking hands could turn a key.

Everything was the same as last night. His desk drawer was still open, the pair of glasses from which he and Patrice had drunk stood together on the cabinet, bottomed with yellow cognac circles. He dropped his briefcase and began to assemble his papers. He opened drawers and pulled out pages, stacked them on the desk and flicked through. It was no use, he would have to take all of them. Even if they were in French—here, there, references to

German philosophers, scattered all over the place. He snapped open two leather folders and slipped the papers inside as neatly as he could without bending the corners, collected his three most recent notebooks and an English translation of the Quran, and scanned the room one last time before running out again.

Jeannette, meanwhile, had left the house for the convent. As usual she had taken her copy of *Les Mystères de Marseille*, but en route she also stopped at a newspaper stand to purchase a selection of dailies. There was one convalescent on the second floor of the convent named Albert who came from Béziers and did not have any legs, and who always asked Jeannette why she never read any stories that were true. The wound on Albert's face was slow to heal, and some days it split open and wept pus, and he was constantly complaining about the position of his bed beside the window, which was so bright in the mornings he couldn't sleep in. The doctors said he was too delicate to move, and anyway, most people would be fighting for that bed. Look at the view you have sir, they said, of the garden wall. Albert's tone on the subject of true stories unnerved Jeannette because she could never work out if he was joking or sincere, though it was similar to the tone he used to complain about the bed. By now he had said it so many times that she decided to take him at his word, if only so that he would stop repeating it.

Between the pages of the novel she also brought the two slips of paper she had shown to Midhat that morning. The doctor's diagnosis of her mother, and her mother's own handwritten description of her symptoms. There was no time to look at them again, but she did not want to part with them. She squeezed the book for fear they might fall out.

The low voices of doctors echoed on the stairway. Jeannette reached the second floor, shy as ever for her lack of a white nursing habit. The corner by the window where she usually sat was bright with daylight, and extra chairs had been brought from other parts of the ward. The men cheered as she approached. The bed nearest the window was bare, taut with a fresh sheet.

"Where is Albert?"

"He's gone."

"Third floor, they finally moved him."

"He's still alive, don't worry! Look at her," said the one named Jerome, pointing at her from his pillow, "she thought he was dead."

A new convalescent sitting on one of the chairs in his pyjamas pinched his face and ducked his head with mirth.

"Fine," said Jeannette drily, as she sat beside him. "Do we want *Les Mystères* today? I also have the newspaper."

"I don't know what you're doing with that, Mademoiselle," said Jerome. "No newspapers, thank you very much. Give us the story."

"Fine, fine. Are you all ready? Bien. Chapter five, où Blanche fait six lieues à pied, et voit passer une procession . . . Blanche et Philippe quittèrent la maison du jardinier Ayasse au crépuscule, vers sept heures et demie."

She did not pay much attention to the words as she read them but she was a good reader all the same, and she turned the corners of each phrase with expert modulations in her voice, cued by certain words and elements of punctuation, as though she were playing a piece of music. The men were rapt, and even the nurses who came to change the bandages spoke in whispers and wound the cotton very slowly. On occasion Jeannette would glance up from the page to see faces propped around her like children, their lips falling apart.

She left early in the afternoon. "Les braves" needed to eat—and also to sleep, the nurses said. The moon was already rising. She could not help it: before she even reached the house she opened *Les Mystères* and pulled out her mother's note and, pausing at the corner before the drive, unfolded the paper in the dwindling light.

Sometimes I feel I am getting larger and larger, and then at other times that I am shrinking. I am going both fast and slow. The cavity in my mouth is enormous, and I feel a great pressure.

Sometimes I can smell death. Some people, I look at them, I don't know if I smell it or see it or feel it. I feel it in my whole body. It is not totally bad. Some days have a particularly strong smell. I find myself wanting to keep them or I want to keep the feeling but I can't and it washes over. It is like being turned upside down. When I feel it I think this is the real life, the not imitated and not performed. My marriage is a fact like a house I live in, these four walls. Frédéric is a house. That feeling is a reaction to something foreign. But then is that actually true? Because even a known thing can become unknown

"Jeannette."

Midhat was running up the road. His eyes were wet and bright; his hair flopped loose from its oil. He whipped one large strand back from his face.

"Jeannette. I saw you walking, I ran. I have been at the library. I have not found anything new. But," he caught his breath, "I have a theory."

He was shining with excitement. She felt the urge to touch his hand, and although she did not, something of that impulse must have expressed itself because his face gave off an encouraged smile.

"Shall we . . ."

"Tell me at the house, not here."

They turned the corner and walked up the drive, and Docteur Molineu opened the door on them. His expression was grave.

"I have some very sad news, mes petits."

Midhat noticed a letter in the Docteur's hand, and with a falling sensation guessed what it was.

"No," he said.

"Our friend Laurent is dead."

The letter was from Laurent's mother. He had been killed in a bar at Ypres on his journey home. A drunken officer had mistaken him for someone else and stabbed him in the arm and the chest. Laurent had died quickly from severe loss of blood.

The door still open, the three stared at the floor in silence. Molineu touched his daughter's neck. Then he reached to pull the door shut and suggested in a restrained voice that they rest before dinner.

Jeannette's face was completely white. Midhat invited her into his bedroom, and she accepted without embarrassment, and sat in Midhat's chair while he sat on the bed. Both faced the window, through which the last of the day erased itself from the garden. The cherub with its dry jug was stripped of detail as all the features of the landscape were unified in shadow, and the lamps of the interior turned the window into a mirror that reflected back their faces. There was his, the whites of his eyes gleaming, his body hunched on the edge of the bed. There was Jeannette's. Her lids hung low.

"We were children," she started to mumble. Tears fell out of her eyes. "When we were children we used to pretend that we were orphans."

He could not reply. Very soon, he would feel unbearable pain. It was only a question of waiting.

"We all wanted to be Cosette. Or La Petite Princesse."

The fact was, Laurent remained Midhat's superior in every way. Laurent, whom he had started to resent, and even—yes, even to hate. And he had even—for a moment, only—wished Laurent would die. He squeezed his fists together and shut his eyes. But perhaps it was not the real Laurent he hated. Perhaps it was only the idea of him. The idea of a person who so exceeded him in virtue, as well as in intellect, and in manner and culture, and even in appearance. Laurent Toupin, his stoop, his blond mop and easy gestures. At the edge of these thoughts was the unmanageable fact that the man no longer existed. He could not face that just yet. He must think about Laurent alive.

Jeannette was still talking, something more about orphans. What did she mean by it? Did she mean that Laurent had been like a parent? He could not face that yet either. He dared himself to picture a bloody corpse, a ruptured arm and chest. It was a horrible image, but it did not move him. Possibly it was difficult to believe in something he had constructed himself. Nothing yet could overpower the picture still beating in his mind: Laurent ahead on the garden path, trouser twisting around the knee, eyes half shut against the sunlight as he murmured some absurdity about human nature.

Jeannette had stopped talking. Midhat spoke aloud, without control.

"He was my friend!"

Even the bitter sound of those words; he hated it.

The gold watch occurred to him in the middle of the night. He woke to the sound of the windowpane rattling in its frame, and as he brought his cold arms under the warm covers his brain flicked awake. The watch. Lost, undoubtedly. He saw it in his mind's eye, ticking away in the mud. The fragile casing blown off like the wings of a beetle, the heartbeat exposed.

Then he remembered that Laurent was killed not on a battlefield but in a bar. He turned over in bed.

In the morning, he was not sitting for long at his desk before he heard a knock on his bedroom door. Jeannette stood in the hall, face as white as it was yesterday. She reached for his hand and gripped it with her dry fingers. They did not say anything. He leaned forward and, gently, touched her lips with his. When he pulled away, her forehead crumpled and her mouth twisted open.

The memorial service was held on Friday. The congregants gathered in an old dome-vaulted church with marble arches, dressed in suits and ties and austere gowns, the furlough soldiers in their blue belted uniforms. Midhat sat with the Molineus in the second pew below a large unlit chandelier. Ahead, plaster mouldings of saints and supplicants leaned out above the altar. Midhat did not listen to the service. He had caught sight of Laurent's father as they entered: he knew it was him because of his height and posture, although his hair was brown. But now the man was on the other side of the aisle, and there were too many heads in the way. Sobbing at the end of the same pew was a young blond woman who might have been Laurent's sister, or his cousin, perhaps. Midhat wondered if they had found the watch on Laurent's body, and if so what they had thought of it. Perhaps that Laurent had stolen it from a dead Turk; that he was a hero, and this was his booty. Heads bowed for the prayer. Beside him, Jeannette started to shake. He wanted to put his hand on her arm, but he restrained himself, lest he appear to be denying her the right.

After the service, Midhat and the Molineus separated from the rest of the mourners to walk back home through the town. The end of the boulevard spread into a manicured square and above them a veering crowd of pigeons alighted on the bronze arms and head of Louis XIV. Out of nowhere, Docteur Molineu announced that they deserved a trip to the beach.

"No question about it," he said, voice rising as he steered them down the promenade. "Not one of us has left Montpellier all winter. Midhat has not even seen anything but the inside of his university! Ergo, a change of scene," and he leaned out to look at their faces with an attitude of rebuke, "will be essential. Nothing good comes of being dreary. I don't care what other people say about it." He paused. "We mustn't care. War or no war. It is not healthy to deny ourselves all the time. In fact, Laurent would probably quite like it if we went to the beach. I believe it is just the sort of thing he would prescribe. Was he not always talking about how much he wanted to travel abroad?"

Jeannette sighed, and, unexpectedly, began to laugh. The skin on her cheeks looked tight with dried tears.

"Do you like to swim, Midhat?" said Molineu.

"I have been in the sea."

"You have been *on* the sea, certainly, but have you entered it voluntarily. Have you felt the cold salt crossing over your bare back. Because that is a completely different sensation."

According to Molineu's decree, the following morning Midhat, Jeannette, and Georgine met him in the hallway dressed in their linens; and equipped with parasols and a bag of pears, they set out for the train to Palavas-les-Flots, where they requisitioned an entire cabin and shut the door. Frédéric insisted that Midhat take the window to observe the view, and they sat as the engine began to moan. This time it was Midhat who could not look at Jeannette, who was opposite him. He spent the journey scrutinizing the contents of the window, the landscape he had not seen since his arrival as it materialised abruptly from behind him and receded slowly into the distance behind the body of the train, the olive groves rattling past and tapping at his memory, that sight of olive groves in France as well as in Palestine, as around them the ligaments of the train clattered and banged.

The news that morning notwithstanding—half a mile advanced at the price of sixteen thousand dead—the shore at Palavas was dense with bathers beneath an obscenely colourful sky. A concrete jetty elbowed far out from the coast and the water thrashed against its walls. Among the thistles bordering the beach, Georgine discovered an unmanned booth stacked with deck chairs, dark green, salt-stained; Midhat volunteered to climb over the counter and extract one for each of them. He and Frédéric carried them to a spot between a tent and a coloured hut. Midhat removed his shoes: between his toes the dune was ice-cool. He unfolded a chair, and pointed it out to sea.

Docteur Molineu was the only one who swam in the end. He tried his best to cajole Georgine but she refused, going redder and redder in the face until finally Jeannette admonished her father for being so insistent, and he let it go, and tore off into the water on his own.

The waves were still breathing in their ears when, speechless and sand-heavy, they took the train back to town. Through the windows the sky glowered purple, and on their way from the station they were forced to take shelter in the awning of a closed café as the clouds suddenly emptied their weight with great force on the city. They waited and watched the rain shiver down the awning. Jeannette paced from end to end. Out on the road the water was falling in dollops that splashed upwards, so copious they looked like bowls of silver. After a while she sighed and upturned a chair, arranging over the damp seat the canopy of a half-closed parasol. She perched, looking uncomfortable.

Molineu, who was peering out with his arms behind his back, said: "I think we should run. We can use the parasols as umbrellas." He turned to look at them. "What do you think? Otherwise we really will be here for hours."

"Run?" said Georgine. "But Docteur, my shoes . . ."

"Oh come on Georgine, it'll be fun," said Molineu. "You can have an old pair of Jeannette's. All right, everyone ready? Get on your feet Jojo. Don't be morose."

They could not help laughing as their linens turned transparent, and at the parasols, which did not function as umbrellas at all but were completely useless against the downpour. Midhat tried not to look at Jeannette's dress which, going grey, was sticking to her waist, revealing the socket of her navel. He increased his pace to catch up with Docteur Molineu and left the women shrieking behind. They reached the house out of breath and dispersed to change.

When Midhat came back downstairs, the door to the cream salon was open; he could see Jeannette inside, standing with her back to him. Courage flashed. He stepped in and, after bolting the door, turned and jumped to find her already right behind him. She laughed, then he laughed, and he took her body in his hands, and to the soft wet of her parted lips his heart reacted violently.

Grief excused intimacy, but was also real and demanded it. Even their spasms of guilt, felt on occasion over the next few days, could only be assuaged with further closeness. It was a miracle they kept it a secret. Their colour was always rising in company, they could not help smiling at each other across full rooms, and clasping fingers just out of sight, under the skirt of a tablecloth or behind backs as they filed through a doorway. And yet the most Docteur Molineu seemed to notice were the shadows and red fever spots that appeared beneath Midhat's eyes.

"Nothing is worth losing sleep over," he said, saluting Midhat and wishing him good luck before class. "Remember they are only exams. It will turn out fine in the end. And if the worst comes to the worst and you do need to repeat the year," he opened his arms, "we will still be here. Provided we are not bombed, of course. All right, off you go."

All day long Midhat's insomniac brain vaulted between euphoria and fear, and Docteur Molineu's sympathetic speeches only doubled the terror of confronting him. He would postpone the proposal to Jeannette, at least until the end of the academic year, and yet the prospect remained an agony even at that distance. The rules of guest and host were so ingrained, he knew the shame of trespass in his bones. From this again he sought refuge in Jeannette's lips and whispers, and her head resting softly on his shoulder.

It was also during this period that he discovered a side of the Molineu house that was entirely new to him. For the first time he understood just how limited his experience of the building had been, confined, as a guest, to his bedroom and the ground floor, and that single glimpse he once stole of Docteur Molineu's study. The house was far larger than he had imagined and most rooms were, like the cream salon, closed off with sheets thrown over the furniture, turning them into secret white ranges, labyrinths of approximating silhouettes that evoked a past with imprecision, more pungent, somehow, for how they forced the imagination to carve and colour and populate. Midhat's soared off, conjuring ghosts of inhabited rooms, always projecting this imagined past onto an imagined future. In the corners, dust collected in spirals. When Georgine creaked along the corridors the pair of lovers hid beneath the dusty sheets, biting their fingers and stifling their breath under the tinkle of Georgine's quarter bar of soap dipping into the bucket.

Only with hands and lips did he and Jeannette touch, and their restraint became an exquisite torment. Fingers on palms, fingers on faces. They deliberately avoided their bedrooms: at most one would teeter on the threshold while the other retrieved something, but even that felt dangerously close. Sometimes in a frenzy Midhat did pull her to him, and bruised her lips so that the skin around her mouth turned pink, and seeing the mark he had made he would pull her to him again, and she responded easily. But mostly they delighted in the agony of resisted desire, which being resisted was sustained, and in this mutual abnegation they colluded like thieves.

Further along the upstairs corridor, beyond Georgine's door and a dim bathroom full of brass, a narrow set of stairs led to an entire third floor. Midhat was amazed. The windows up there were so small they did not from the outside even suggest a space tall enough to stand up in. Yet two unused rooms of full height held a miscellany of objects, and a third was a slope-roofed attic of boxes and abandoned furniture, much of it rickety and broken, and a little alcove with a velvet chair where Jeannette spent her time searching, "among my mother's things," she said, pointing at a glass-fronted cabinet through whose windows, smoky with dust, loomed shelves of trinkets, porcelain ornaments, printed books, a candlestick with a bare stub of old wax, and something made of lace bundled in the corner.

It was a morning love. They were forced to leave the house before noon, he to go to the Faculty, she to the convent or to stand in line for the bread ration. And so it was a love with morning's freshness, and they never saw the shadows of evening seep through those unclean windows. Midhat often woke before dawn, and in that hour before the sun rose caught Jeannette in the corridor, and they whispered in the dark unselfconscious with sleep. Then the day began in earnest, and with a thumping heart Midhat staggered until evening on a precipice of exhaustion.

Aside from confronting Docteur Molineu, the other terror, of course, was his own father. That reckoning too must be postponed, at least until after he had spoken to Molineu, perhaps even until the end of the war. He fantasised about spurning his inheritance and striking out on his own. Each of these thoughts rippled with fear. At least Teta would love Jeannette, he could be certain of that. In the afternoons over his textbooks he pushed a finger into his soft cheek and felt his teeth between his eye socket and jaw. All of it must be postponed, all of it: June was upon them now, the holiday was in sight, and regardless of whatever Docteur Molineu said about staying on longer the examinations required serious work if he were to pass into the second year.

A physics practice paper he completed in the library one afternoon was returned the next day with a 45 scrawled on the first page. The pass grade was 70. He entered the lecture theatre in a trance, and sitting at the back heard the lesson only intermittently, as though the lecturer's voice were carried to him on a fitful wind. When he emerged an hour later he felt someone tap him on the arm. It was Samuel Cogolati.

"Hello, Midhat." He smiled, grimly. "I just want to say how sorry I am. I am very, very sorry. Unexpected but, I mean, these things . . ."

Midhat looked down at the 45 on his physics paper. "How on earth did you know?"

"Pardon?"

"I only received it this morning," said Midhat. "Oh," he caught himself, "you are talking about Laurent. Oh yes! It is really terrible. We are in despair. Thank you, Samuel. I, I really appreciate it."

"But there's another thing, wait. Would you consider, I was wondering, would you like to study together?"

"Study together?"

"I enjoyed our time in the library when we were researching psychiatry. And I was impressed by your interest, your curiosity in these different areas of medical science. I think that you and I, we could make revision for the examinations rather pleasurable."

Cogolati's large nostrils spread open with his smile. Midhat hesitated. Then, he held out his hand, and as he shook Cogolati's the thought warmed up in his brain that this man had been sent to save him, and Cogolati began to chortle at this eagerness, now shaking his entire arm, saying I'm so pleased, I'm so pleased.

The following day at eleven o'clock, armed with several sets of example papers, textbooks, and element tables they had drawn up themselves, the pair met in a recess behind the cathedral.

"Let's start with botany, shall we?" said Cogolati.

That corner, in the shade of the cypress trees, became the place where they sat every day from eleven until two as June turned into July, and the summer heat struck the ashy stone of the anatomical theatre, bleaching their eyes so that when they turned away they discovered green and purple oblongs floating across the pages of their books. From the first it was apparent that, after a year of diligent study, any further revision of the material was for Cogolati merely a pleasant supplement. This caused Midhat even more anxiety, which he tried to disguise under his enthusiasm, asking questions and tutting at the responses as if to say, oh of course, yes I knew that. If Cogolati ever felt irritated by this he hid it well, for he only giggled and tipped his head back as Midhat asked, for the third time: "And catalysis? Remind me what that was again? Oh yes, oh yes, of course."

They sat the examinations in the first week of July. Two hundred seats were arranged in the hall with metre-wide gaps between, and a dead space at the back where the examiners marched and congregated. Zoology and botany came first. Midhat thought both the written and the oral tests went well: there were questions on photosynthesis and the agents of seed dispersal, which he and Cogolati had studied thoroughly, and a section on vertebrates and invertebrates; in the zoology oral Midhat confidently identified the gill raker, the spiracle, proboscis, cilium, and tentacle, and outlined the history of a frog before a panel of two professors; in botany he sketched the life of an alga, a fungus, and a liverwort; he listed the characteristics of a gymnosperm, a monocotyledon, a dicotyledon; he defined respiration and triumphantly discussed the life of the deciduous.

Physics was also relatively straightforward. The key to it, Cogolati had explained, was to memorise the formulae and then recognise from the question which of them was needed. After that it was a simple matter of substituting numbers. "This is the problem with rudimentary science assessment," said Cogolati. But if he wanted Midhat's collusion in his disdain, he was met only with the astonished face of a man who felt he had just been saved. "Thank you," said Midhat. "Thank you."

The real trouble came with chemistry. It was not that Midhat didn't know the material; he had spent the three days' interval between the physics written test and the chemistry one beside Cogolati in the library, completing practice papers and discussing their answers, and on the day of the examination he entered the hall feeling prepared. The problem was rather that, looking down at his paper in the cool plaster-walled chamber, with the sound of two hundred pens scratching, and the hollow clop of the examiners' strides between the desks, he was distracted. He read and reread each question without haste; he worked on one answer and then another, abandoning calculations mid-tally.

Today, on the day of the chemistry written test and the final day of the academic term, Sylvain Leclair was due to dine at the Molineus'. Since Laurent's death, Midhat's romance with Jeannette had been flowering of its own accord, and his theories about Ariane Molineu and the cause of her suicide had moved to the periphery. But though he had not consciously dwelled on them, something had continued to develop down below, and now unsettling ideas of abuse were floating up, along with strange remembered images: Sylvain sneering across a table, Jeannette leaving a room in distress.

He looked up from the exam paper and saw a young woman ahead of him in the adjacent column of desks. She was agitated: rattling her pen on the desk, twitching the heel of one foot over the other ankle. The young man at the next desk swivelled around.

"Shh!"

She started, and the pen made a final dying movement between her fingers.

"One hour remains," said the examiner. His chalk squeaked on the board: "ENCORE UNE HEURE."

It was then that Midhat finally jumped into action and looked down at the paper, on which only one question had been completed. He had made a start with number 5: he turned to it again.

5. (a) Calculate the weight of sulphur in 50 g. of $Cr_2(SO_4)_3$. Find the result to three significant figures. (Atomic weights Cr 52, S 32, O 16.)

When the hour was up he had answered half of the questions, and at the call, "Put your pens down now!" he rose from his chair dizzy with concentration. They were released alphabetically. Midhat found Cogolati outside, standing on the steps in exaggerated contrapposto.

"How was it for you?" he asked, as they fell in line.

"Fine, I think."

Across the courtyard, the cypresses shushed and waved.

"Would you like to take a coffee?"

"Thank you," said Midhat, "but you know, I'm quite exhausted. I think I should go home."

This was their goodbye then, because Cogolati was leaving for Geneva in the morning. Midhat thanked him, and Cogolati grinned awkwardly. They embraced and parted at the gate.

Summer was in full flare. All around him trees expressed tiny pink flowers, clouding the streets with blossom. Everything was calm. He walked back to the house in slow motion, set free from the regime of academic time, the blocking of days into hours and half hours. He reached the house and climbed the stairs: the door to Docteur Molineu's study was ajar. In the slit he saw, on the floor by the bay window, the back of Jeannette's head. He knocked.

"Come in."

Beside her on the floor were a stack of albums and a small pile of photographs. The first photograph showed a woman wearing a lace collar and a flower in her hair.

"How did it go? Come, kiss me."

"It was fine. I am tired, my brain is tired. Keep reading, don't let me disturb you."

The last time Midhat had entered Docteur Molineu's study was in that furtive search for inkwells. It was not a room they chose on their secret mornings; it was implicitly out of bounds. And yet standing now in the centre, the woman he loved reading before him, he experienced a new sense of entitlement. The desk was covered in a mess of papers and a few stacked books with bookmarks flopping out like tongues. Resisting the impulse to sit in the chair, he indulged a momentary vision of the future, in a room just like this one. He closed the image, and moved to join Jeannette on the floor.

It appeared in his mind before he realised he had read it. His own name. He reversed his steps.

Near the edge of the desk was an open notebook. The page was titled in large letters: "Notes Préliminaires—Midhat Kamal." Underneath the title were a variety of illegible markings in green ink, sometimes at angles up the margins. Midhat picked up the notebook. At the bottom of the page he made out two inscriptions: "Naplouse—deux montagnes, Ebal et Gerizim," said one, and the other, "Les Samaritains—la magie? L'Araméen & l'Arabe & l'Hébreu." He turned the page. "Proverbes" was the next title. Three were listed: all of them proverbs Midhat had heard as a child in Nablus and had translated for Docteur Molineu in a conversation last winter by the fire, here transliterated. "Newspaper talk" said one; "Kalam jarayed—something that is hard to believe." Another: "Kalamo waqif—his speech is standing—i.e. aggressive"; "the words of the night are coated in butter—will melt in the sun—promises not kept." At the bottom of the page was written: "La langue peut affecter le cerveau? La traduction pure est impossible."

"What is this?" said Midhat.

"What is what?"

"Your father . . ."

"My father what?"

"He has been writing about me."

Jeannette got to her feet. "What do you mean, writing about you?"

He turned back to the desk. Among the volumes there were two translated copies of the Quran. He passed the notebook with his name in it to Jeannette and picked up the first Quran, an old French edition bound in brown leather with a ridged gilt spine, entitled: "L'Alcoran de Mahomet Tom 1." The second was a more recent translation in English.

"He has been studying me."

She turned a page, and Midhat looked over her shoulder. One passage was large and legible.

The Effect of a New Language Learned by a Primitive Brain.

It is as if learning the word makes room in the mind for its meaning—its usage, nuance, connotation, and distinction—so that even if the word were forgotten, an indent in the surface of the mind would remain, an imprint, or cavity. Thus a wordless man may be capable of complex thought, except that he must once have learned to speak.

Jeannette did not move to turn the next page. They were silent.

"Did you know about this?" he said, after a moment.

"Of course not."

"Do you . . . think . . . do you think I am . . ." His voice strained. "I must speak to him."

He held the chair back for balance.

"Yes. I suppose you should." She placed the book carefully on the desk. "Would you like me to come with you?"

"No. You and I—this is not the time for it. I need to sit down."

Jeannette followed him to his bedroom. He sat on the bed as she watched from the doorway. Her eyes were red with suppressed tears.

"You can sit."

He could not look at her. As her figure moved past he stared through the open door down the hall, where a light thrown from a window out of sight dispersed on the floorboards. He stared at the shapes framed by the door until they were estranged from his eye, and the banister became a woman's arm, and the shadow in the far corner by the bathroom door a black shoe, with a long lace, which was in fact a shadowed gap where one of the floorboards had warped upwards.

He felt a cramp in his stomach. He was a guest, but the host had trespassed. And he too had trespassed, and transgressed, with the host's daughter. Whose then was the crime? The spectre of his ignorance rose again before him. He thought he knew their public codes now, more or less—but the private ones? He had thought himself in the bosom of the family, capable—almost—of sitting in a chair in the study. He had thought his difference no difference. But if he was the father's subject, how could he be the daughter's husband? One did not study one's sons-in-law.

Darkness was engulfing the view through the door, and the shadows widened and the light patches contracted, and the shoe in the corner disappeared in the pooling shade.

"Midhat?" Jeannette's eyes were wide. "Midhat I just heard the door. They're here."

He heard himself respond.

"I should change," she said. "They will have a drink first."

She entered the field of the doorframe, moving in and out of light, and then she was gone.

He moved slowly. He put away his books and notes on their shelf in the cupboard, and pulled off his examination robe. He dressed himself in a dark grey suit, with a silver tiepin and a butterfly brooch on his lapel. He looked at his reflection in the mirrored door of the armoire. He tried to see what Frédéric saw. Something moved. It was the reflection of a branch from the garden tree, wagging in the breeze like a shaken arm.

In the hall the floorboard creaked; he opened the door and saw Jeannette at the top of the stairs. She wore a dark yellow gown with black lace over the shoulders.

"Come down," she said.

"I will wait, and come after."

Sylvain Leclair and Docteur Molineu were already at the table when he entered. Sylvain was beside Jeannette, and a place was set for Midhat beside the Docteur opposite her.

"Good evening Monsieur Midhat," said Sylvain.

"Good evening, Monsieur Leclair. Docteur. Mademoiselle."

Leclair had lost some weight since he last came for dinner in the spring, though he was still large, and his face sagged slightly. His pointed eyebrows were grey; for some reason Midhat had remembered them black.

"Well. You will have to forgive us for the simplicity of the meal," said Docteur Molineu to Sylvain. "I'm afraid we were unable to find any fowl or meat. But we do have butter, so hourra for that."

Georgine brought bowls of pumpkin soup, and Molineu poured the wine.

"You have finished your examinations, I understand?" said Sylvain.

"Yes, I have finished."

"And they went well?"

"I hope so. We shall see."

They sipped from their spoons. Jeannette ripped a bread roll and began to butter it.

"And when will you be returning to your country?"

The spoons were silenced. Even Jeannette turned her head.

"When will I be returning?" Midhat heard a tremor in his voice. "Soon, possibly."

"And will you practise medicine in your hometown?"

"Will I what? Oh . . . I don't know . . ."

Molineu reached for the butter dish.

"I was sorry to hear about your friend," said Sylvain.

There was no reason why this above all should have been the statement to provoke him. It may simply have been that Midhat was already primed to react. But in a quick moment, his anger gushed and rendered him wordless, filling the front of his head like a wall of water. When he finally managed to speak, his entire body was shaking, and he could only whisper.

"Who are you?"

"Monsieur Kamal," said Jeannette, "are you all right?"

"Am I all right? Am I all right? That man, that man . . . Mademoiselle, I am afraid to tell you, but that man . . . he is a worm and a, a thief."

"A thief?" said Frédéric.

Sylvain laughed. "I am afraid I have set him off," he said in a high, ludicrous voice. "Your guest is feeling guilty, perhaps, that his compatriots are at war with us and have killed our friend."

"You are disgusting. You have no respect for women, or for anything that is sacred."

"Midhat," said Jeannette.

She had blanched. Midhat felt a blast of panic—her love for him so precious, so fragile, so long earned—and what control he had gained over his own voice was lost in an instant.

"No—This man, he is a cancer, he has slipped into the heart of your family. But I know him for what he really is."

Sylvain met his eye. "You know nothing."

"Calm down, Midhat," said Molineu. "You are—I think you should calm down."

"You!" said Midhat.

He looked at Jeannette again: her eyes were shiny with tears. It was the wrong time; he breathed, he steadied himself.

"What on earth is wrong?" said Molineu.

"Wrong! What is wrong, I . . . I . . ." The orange bowl blurred in his vision. "I have found . . . I had planned to talk to you . . . about this . . ."

Jeannette warned him with a tremor of her head. No, said her lips.

"Later, I had planned to talk about it later."

"Talk about what?"

"Nothing—nothing."

"It is not nothing," said Sylvain. "You have made two strange and aggressive accusations, Monsieur, and at the least you should explain yourself."

"Your wife!"

"No," said Jeannette. "No, Midhat."

"My wife?" said Sylvain.

"No. *His* wife."

"Midhat!" said Jeannette, shocked.

Something in Midhat broke. He tried to hold on. "He is a bad man," he said. It surged up: "I saw—I saw, on your desk . . ."

"My desk?" said Molineu.

"I did not mean to enter, I did not mean, I was curious—forgive me!"

"There is no need," said Jeannette, "to talk about this now. We are all excited. Let us collect ourselves."

"No, Jojo, let him speak," said Molineu, in a tone for addressing a child. "You went into my study?"

"Forgive me, I saw, on your desk . . ."

Alarm crossed Molineu's face. "Midhat—"

"Do you think I have no insides?" He dropped a slack fist on the table. His spoon tipped, and lukewarm orange soup splattered over his hand and the tablecloth. He gaped down at the mess. Jeannette reached across with her napkin to wipe his hand.

"I can . . . I am only . . ." said Molineu.

"You have been studying me."

"No, that is not it at all . . ."

"Do you think I am not, you think I am *uncivilised*?"

"I should have asked your permission, of course, I see that very clearly now—"

"Do you think I am uncivilised?"

"No! Heavens, no, I was, on the contrary, Midhat, I have been inspired by your presence, by your elegance, and your—humanity . . ."

"My humanity?"

"Yes! Yes, your humanity—please, let me explain. On the contrary, I have been aware of the stereotypes that abound in our, in European culture. I believe there is some progress to be made, in the study of civilisations—"

"Docteur Molineu," said Midhat.

"No, let me speak. On the contrary, I am attempting in my research—a humble attempt, Midhat! A preliminary monograph, only! I have been, was attempting, on the contrary, attempting to humanise you!"

In came the tinkling of Georgine's tray. Sylvain, nearest the kitchen door, shook his head at her, and she stopped and tinkled away again.

"To humanise me?" said Midhat, after a breath. "I am—really, I am amazed. Monsieur, I am a person. I am—no—" He stood. His napkin fell to the floor. "Excuse me," he murmured. "I must go. Good night. Good night."

They were talking as he left but he could not hear them. He grasped the banister and mounted, very slowly. The gallery rotated into view. At the top he heard footsteps, and Jeannette caught him before his bedroom door.

"Oh, Midhat," she whispered. "I wish you hadn't."

"I'm sorry."

He lowered his head, and her hands caught him on either cheek.

"I wish you hadn't. Sylvain is . . ."

"I know about Sylvain," said Midhat.

"What did you mean by that? Sylvain is a friend."

He took a deep breath and stood upright. "I have reason to believe that he is at least one of the causes of the problem with your mother."

Jeannette looked at him blankly.

"When I was searching for the possible reasons for her illness, for her great unhappiness, it seems that in most cases of nervous illness, there is an event that is the first cause of the degeneration. And I have reason to believe that Sylvain Leclair may have abused . . ."

Her face was not reacting. Doubt set in. He could not go back; he would remain firm, in this at least.

She dropped her gaze. "Oh, Midhat. You are wrong about him."

"I am not wrong. He is a bad man. He does not have a clean heart."

She shook her head. "No. Sylvain was a friend to my mother."

"Listen to me." He held her by the arms. "You are in danger from that man."

"What?" Her eyes were sharp. "What is it you think you are doing?"

"Listen, Jeannette. I'm trying to—"

"No, Midhat. I said, you are wrong."

With a slow, certain gesture, she turned her face to the side. And then, she shut her eyes.

Midhat waited, close to amazement. As if he had just watched a glass bowl fall and smash, and was not yet able to believe its shattered fragments were irrevocable, he clasped her arms, watching, waiting for her to turn back to him. She did not say a word. If there were any tension in her expression he could think it was an impulse of the moment, of passion, that would pass. But there was no clenched jaw, no tight lips, no tears. Only a quiet sadness, in those eyes that opened slightly and looked at the ground. She would not defend him against her father. It was broken. He had broken it.

The corridor began to change shape. The shadows flexed, as though a light were swinging to and fro on the ceiling and contorting them. He shook her once more, in desperation. The edges of the gallery were already blurring in his vision. Even this thing, this one thing, Jeannette, even she was far from him. He loosened his grip on her arms and stepped back. She did nothing to protest. It was obvious to him that he could no longer stay in this house.

PART TWO

1

As is often the case when a city is ancient, and the names of her tenants are centuries unchanged, the gossip carried on the winds between the two mountains of Nablus had settled over the years into legends. Tales of marriage abounded, and tales of rivalry, and of curses and charms cast by the Samaritans. And the cockerel sentenced to death for crowing on the mayor's land, and the Moroccan hakawati who stole only gold jewellery, and the Bedouin prince who slept on his horse and shot his bullets at the sky.

One such story concerned a French Crusader queen of Jerusalem named Melisende, who inherited from her Armenian mother a pair of dark eyes and a love for riding in the sun. Her mother had borne no male heir, and on his deathbed the king her father divided the kingdom between Melisende and her son Baldwin. When Baldwin came of age he wanted the kingdom for himself, and for this purpose amassed an army to besiege his mother and force her into exile. Banished from the Holy City, Melisende spent the rest of her life in a palace at the centre of Nablus. Every day the prison guards let her go riding, and she would take her horse past Mount Gerizim, out to where the valley spilled into the fallow plain.

Eight centuries on, in the year 1915 by the Gregorian calendar and 1333 by the Hijri, the foundations of Melisende's Crusader palace were still to be found near the mosque in the Yasmineh Quarter, and the land where she would go riding was now part of the village of Zawata. On that same piece of land lived a man named Haj Hassan Hammad, who in the heat of one August afternoon had just lain down in the shade of an olive tree when his wife came running down the lawn. A Turkish messenger had arrived, summoning him to a tribunal with Jamal Basha in Aley, a city twelve miles uphill from Beirut.

In the spring of that year, the Turks had begun to deport the Armenians. First they rounded up the intellectuals in Constantinople—Krikor Zohrab, Daniel Varoujan the poet, Rupen Zartarian, Ardashes Harutiunian, Atom Yarjanian "Siamanto," Yervant Srmakeshkhanlian the novelist—more than two thousand in total taken to imperial holding centres, many tortured, most killed. Then the Turks forced every remaining Armenian civilian to march into the desert without supplies. The Empire was dying and in its last throes killing with paranoiac ferocity all dissidents. Now even race could be a mark of treachery. The women were raped before they were throttled, and the Euphrates was strewn with corpses. Under the pressure of the Great War, the Empire that so recently had been reforming towards democracy now attacked without mercy whoever was not, and did not want to be, a Turk.

The messenger told Haj Hassan that his friend and colleague Fuad Murad had also been summoned to the trial, and had already left Nablus for Aley. Hassan assured the messenger that he would set out at once, and sent him on his way. Hassan shut the door and found his wife Nazeeha, who had been listening, in tears. It occurred to Hassan that his uncle Haj Tawfiq Hammad, who represented Nablus in the Ottoman parliament, might intercede for him with the authorities. He composed a message to Tawfiq and sent it with his servant to the telegraph station in Nablus. He would wait one more night on his farm for Tawfiq's reply, and catch up the hours lost the following day.

That evening, after their meal of lentils and lamb, every member of the family disappeared to sleep or pray, except for Hassan, who took the opportunity to sit in his garden. Nazeeha wanted to join him, but he sent her away. He looked down from the ledge at the swimming pool glittering with starlight, and listened to the irrigation system watering the pomelo trees below.

In his study he packed a small bag for the journey—two fresh shirts and a pair of his best French trousers; the Quran; a bar of soap—and as he was buckling the straps the maid entered with a visitor. It was his friend, the merchant Haj Taher Kamal.

"Jamal Basha has become an anxious and bloodthirsty man," said Haj Taher at once. "You must not go, it will be certain death. Al-Lamarkaziya, Al-Ahd—every group that wants independence is a threat. It will not be a fair trial."

"We never asked for independence," said Hassan. "We are the Decentralisation Party. We ask only for reform."

But Haj Taher was convinced of his danger, and urged Hassan not to go to Aley. Hassan did not entirely disagree with him, but he had made up his mind, and of course he was counting on Tawfiq. Haj Taher meant well, but he was not a politician.

A telegram from Tawfiq arrived before midnight: yes, he would intercede. Hassan could be sure of a pardon.

He woke at sunrise, kissed his sleeping wife, mounted his horse, and rode north through the hills. By the time the sun had started to heat the air he reached Jenin, where he stopped at his cousin's house to exchange his horse for a carriage and driver. He napped in the carriage seat as his man drove them on. Through the wooden wall he listened to the uneven contours of the road, and woke to the quiet roar of wheels on rocks as the temperature dropped by Lake Tiberias. He ate one of the pieces of bread he had brought and offered the other to the driver. As they approached the Litani River he began once again to feel hungry, but all they had left was a bag of seed for the horses, so he requested a stop at the travellers' inn that was coming into view on the hilltop ahead.

While the driver fed the horses, Hassan approached the building. The exterior had recently been refurbished and plaster clung to the leaves of the carob tree outside in a sticky crust. The innkeeper appeared in the doorway, a short, black-eyed man in a dirty apron. No food, he said. Haj Hassan scowled, and the man remembered they might have a couple of eggs left over after all—if effendi could wait just a moment. Handing Hassan a newspaper to read, he limped out of sight.

Hassan sat on a stone in the now midmorning sun and opened the paper. There were the usual deaths and births, news of the British rebuffed at Gallipoli, and a long review of a book about a Syrian immigrant in America. He skimmed the review. Turning the page he read the title: "Eleven Nationalists Crucified in Beirut."

In the middle of the list was the name of his friend, Fuad Murad. Murad was already dead! And his own name was listed, with a *photograph*—Hassan Hammad was a wanted man. The photograph was two years old and showed him clean-shaven. He touched his beard and rose to leave. He found his driver relieving himself against a tree, and at the sight of him felt another spasm of panic. The driver had made a poor choice of tree and was struggling to avoid the splatters as his piss cascaded down the knots, and while he was occupied Hassan made a quick decision. He mounted the driver's seat and whipped the horses into action, ignoring the yelps of confusion behind him.

He crossed the Litani River by a crumbling bridge, only letting the horses stop to drink on the other side. From there he drove east, away from Beirut but otherwise in no particular direction. Whenever he saw a village he took a circuitous route—he could not risk being noticed as the only stranger in the souq that day.

After an hour and a half of eastward meandering he came upon a Turkish soldier alone by the side of the road, his ankles white with dust. The soldier stood and hailed Hassan. Gold buttons shone down his front, and a bayonet glinted by his side. His large moustache was waxed in the Ottoman style and a box of oranges lay on the ground by his chair. Hassan stopped the horses and dismounted, and the soldier demanded in accented Arabic to see some identifying papers. His eyes narrowed, taking in Haj Hassan's attire.

"Is this your carriage?"

"Yes," said Haj Hassan. He continued, in fluent Turkish: "I'm looking for a place to eat, do you know of anywhere nearby?"

Apparently delighted by Hassan's flawless Turkish, the soldier clapped his arm and offered him an orange. Haj Hassan accepted and began to peel it; the zest spat at his dust-covered hands. The soldier added the rind to a small pile in the box, and as they each ate a segment Haj Hassan decided it was necessary to damp any suspicions he had already aroused. He told the soldier that he had in fact set out with a driver, intending to visit his family in Beirut. But when he asked to stop at a caravanserai, the driver had robbed him and escaped. Taking pity, a kind old shopkeeper lent him this carriage, on oath that he would return it.

"I have no papers, nothing," he added, watching the soldier's face for a reaction.

"My lodgings are nearby," replied the soldier. "And I have a telegraph machine, if you would like to send a message to your family."

Hassan hesitated. The man might appear trustworthy, but he was still a Turk. And if he had guessed Hassan was on the run he might be hoping for a reward. Hassan considered his options. He could run fast. He would leave one of the horses unharnessed in case he needed to flee.

The soldier led him to a small hut downhill from the road, above which the zigzag of telegraph wires swung gently in the wind. As the soldier entered, Hassan unbuckled the tugs from one of his horses and fastened the saddle strap with a length of rope to the carriage frame, presented a handful of seed to the big lips, and rubbed the warm muzzle. Inside, the soldier was already boiling water on the stove. In the corner stood a table covered in electrical equipment: an upright box resembling a radio, its sides crowded with differently sized knobs and copper tubes; another box beyond covered in more knobs, with coils and armatures bracketed to every perpendicular plane and gleaming.

"Do you know how to use it?"

Hassan said nothing. The soldier laughed.

"Don't worry. Write down what you want to say and I will send it for you. Please."

Hassan accepted a piece of paper and wrote an elliptical message in Turkish. It was not for his wife, however: it was addressed to his friend Haj Taher Kamal.

The soldier sat and began to tap it out on the transmission key. The water boiled and the coffee frothed; Hassan turned off the flame.

"Now we just have to wait for a reply. There are clean cups over there."

The hut had only one chair, the one by the machine, and the soldier insisted that Hassan take it while he leaned against the wall. Between long spells of silence Hassan asked the soldier trivial questions about his post, cautious of their divergent roles in this game of empire, of any question that might shine the torch on the barrier between them. An hour passed, and the possibility dawned on Hassan that the soldier had counted on Hassan's not knowing Morse code, and had in that tapping pattern actually communicated his own message to his superiors, who might appear at any moment to arrest him. Perhaps there was still time to escape. He thought of the horse. On the other hand, if the soldier did turn out to be honest and had indeed sent the message to Haj Taher, Hassan would miss the reply. He eyed the route he would take past the soldier to the front door and sat erect, fingers flexed for the rope.

The machine started to emit a very loud clicking. Hassan jumped up in alarm and the soldier replaced him at the table, where a wheel was turning, unreeling a thin strip of paper under a gnashing gold foot into his receiving hand. When it stopped, the soldier tore off the strip, examined the marks upon it, and scrawled a note on a card.

"I have a cousin in Damascus near the citadel stop go to him stop his name is Abu al-Kheir al-Muwaqqaʻ stop," he said aloud.

He handed Hassan the transcript.

"Thank you," said Haj Hassan. "Peace upon you."

Hassan, lover of symmetry, fed the second horse a handful of seed before he reattached the first to the carriage. He resumed his pose of humble driver, and with a whip crack turned in the direction of Damascus.

At nightfall he reached Jupiter Gate on the southwest side of the old city. From his seat he hailed a street seller late in packing up his wares, and asked where he could find the house of Abu al-Kheir al-Muwaqqaʻ. The seller gave him a complex series of directions, and following them to the letter Hassan arrived at a doorway striped in pink and grey stone.

A silver-haired, thin-lipped man opened the door. He shook Haj Hassan's hand and directed him to the stables to park the carriage.

"Welcome, please," he said. "A friend of Haj Taher is a friend of mine."

He led Hassan to a bedroom with a mashrabiya window where the maid was unrolling a mattress. Hassan slept deeply and woke at dawn to pray, then slept until the second call. In the hallway he found a note: the family had left early to visit a grieving relative but would return before nightfall. The maid served him eggs with sumac, and as he finished eating there was a knock at the door.

Twelve Turkish soldiers entered the house. Haj Hassan immediately introduced himself as Abu al-Kheir al-Muwaqqa', praying silently that his beard was an adequate disguise. He had not welcomed any runaway Nabulsi, no, but he was happy to let them look through the house, and please to take a glass of lemonade. There was not enough space for all twelve to sit in the salon, so the senior personnel sat while the younger men stood around, drinking from tall glasses. Haj Hassan leaned on the windowsill and tried to adopt both the courteous manner of a host and the comfortable air of a proprietor, restraining his gaze from the many ornaments as if he had seen them thousands of times before. The men emptied their glasses. They thanked Abu al-Kheir for his time.

Haj Hassan remained a wanted man, and it became clear that he would need to remain in hiding for longer than a week. He discussed this with Abu al-Kheir and they decided he would marry the eldest daughter of the family, a plump girl named Rasha with wide-set eyes. Hassan gave one of his pocket watches as the dower—fortunately he had brought two—and promised his host in writing that he would repay any debts incurred during his time in hiding.

Months passed and Hassan's face continued to appear weekly in the newspapers, annotated with the details of his treason and the reward for reporting his whereabouts to the authorities. Abu al-Kheir decided on an alias for him, and under the new name "Qassem Khatib" Haj Hassan grew his beard long and thick, and lived quite happily with his new wife in the house of his father-in-law. But as the months accumulated he began to miss his first wife and children, and the pool on his farm in Zawata, and the florid company of the men in the Nablus courtyards. And as there was no safe way to transport money from Zawata, he began to feel uneasy about his dependence on his host, with the list of promised repayments growing longer. Before the year was out, he had decided to make a return visit.

One Sunday night in the spring of 1916, after news of a Turkish victory in Kut al-Amara, Hassan donned the cotton abaya and kufiya of a farmer and rode his horse south from Damascus. He reached the outskirts of Irbid as dawn broke like an egg yolk over the Druze Mountain; in its pale light a Bedouin woman was entering a tent in the valley, and catching sight of him she gestured that he should join her. He tied his horse to a tree and entered the tent to find the women battering pestles in coffee grinders between their feet and singing a mournful song to the rhythm. The white-haired elder of the family came to greet him, and they sat together in silence through the coffee ritual. When the coffee was brewed and they had emptied their cups, Hassan asked if he might take shelter for the night. The elder prevaricated. Hassan offered what little gold he had with him in exchange for one of his daughters in marriage; the deal was struck, and Haj Hassan had his first secure home on the way to Nablus, in a valley between Irbid and the Druze Mountain.

The second home was established by another marriage, this time to a farmer's daughter in a village south of Safad. The third, by marrying the daughter of his cousin's friend in Jenin.

By the time Haj Hassan returned to his first wife in Zawata, therefore, he had already acquired four more. He stayed at home for a month, tending to his farm and arguing with the fellahin over the return from the crops. When the month had passed he travelled back to visit his other wives, to sleep, dine, and give them money, en route to Damascus and the house of Abu al-Kheir.

Over the next year and a half Haj Hassan made two more covert journeys between Damascus and Nablus, visiting each wife and collecting the money from the farm. In Nablus, rumours continued as to his whereabouts, and whether he was alive or dead. Then in the winter of 1917, while Hassan was en route to Zawata, the Ottomans lost Jerusalem to the British. Hassan had only reached Jenin when his cousins brought him news that the Turks had retreated to Nablus and were establishing their new stronghold for northern Palestine inside the walls of her old city. Hassan turned back up the road by which he had come, went straight to Damascus, and did not renew his attempt to return. A year passed before the British finally ousted the Turks and seized Nablus. But only when Jamal Basha had fled to Europe did Hassan deem it safe to make a public return to his home in Zawata, where he was immediately recognised as a hero.

The year was 1918, and his cousin Nimr was the new mayor of Nablus.

*   *

At the Ottomans' overthrow, the streets of Jerusalem had flooded with revellers, and the citizens danced and whistled and cut down the telegraph wires to take home as trophies. But in Nablus the reaction was quite different. There the crowds gathered outside the municipal hospital, that symbol of Nablus's modernity, not to support but to protest the British capture of Jerusalem, and the Nabulsis had chanted their way to the temporary Turkish encampment to display their fervent displeasure. Although the city was a centre of Arab nationalism, her citizens still feared the defeat of the Empire. The known was better than the unknown, they said uneasily; the Ottomans had been bad, but who wasn't in a time of war? And besides, in those Turkish garrisons their sons were half the soldiers. And in addition Balfour had made his declaration: Nablus guessed what the British had planned for them, and they were afraid.

Somewhat out of character, Haj Nimr decided to host a party in celebration of his cousin's return, to which he invited the city's leading men. Haj Nimr was a religious man, and had been a shari'a court judge before he became mayor. The only parties he ever hosted were gatherings of the learned on the second floor of his house, where the men sat in a circle to drink tea and discuss scripture. While it was not unheard of for an alem to be a sociable man, Haj Nimr was not known for attending parties either; at the announcement of this gathering, therefore, his daughters became very excited, even though they would not be allowed to attend. His wife, Widad, arranged for extra help, including her sister-in-law's two maids and manservant. Yellow irises from the garden were arranged in diamonds on the tabletops. Huge plates were laid out of stuffed things—courgettes and vine leaves and aubergines—heaped on piles of baked tomatoes slipping from their skins. The best maker of kunafe in the old city was hired, and he set up his equipment in the kitchen to ensure the cheese was perfectly hot at serving time.

Nimr invited Haj Hassan to take coffee with his family before the party started. This was an event his daughters and his wife were allowed to attend. Hassan wore his best cravat and his shiniest pair of Damascene shoes and rode his horse from Zawata into Nablus at midday.

Set back from the road, the triple-arched windows of Haj Nimr Hammad's house were visible over the high stone wall. Passing through the gate, Hassan climbed the steps alongside a chain of trellises wound with vines. He reached the triple-arched doorway, and ascending the pyramid of steps before the entrance, turned the handle and entered the vast hall with its enormous vaulted canopy, full of light.

Haj Nimr's three children were waiting on a couch on the far side. Haj Nimr himself had already seen his cousin since his return, but he greeted him again now with four exuberant kisses as if for the first time. Nimr was tall and slender, and the thick black brows curving down the sides of his eyes were shot with grey; his eyelids hung low. Hassan was much shorter, and his cousin had to bend slightly to reach his cheek. His beard was already white, and shaved close to mark the end of exile. The tip of his nose reached down over his moustache; and though his eyebrows were high and thin, still Hassan resembled his cousin in the eyes, which like Nimr's slanted at the outer edges, giving him a mournful appearance. Hassan bowed to the children and approached. The two eldest were girls, Fatima and Nuzha, and they leapt up to greet him; the youngest child, Burhan, sat silently.

For all his local fame and achievement Hassan was both modest and somewhat severe. His gaze did not deviate, and his presence could be unnerving for anyone who could not match his self-possession. But whenever someone quite reasonably described Hassan as aloof, another would snatch the chance to claim more intimate acquaintance and feign surprise, since on the contrary Haj Hassan was, in his own experience, a remarkably warm man, honest, and loyal.

When Nimr kissed him Hassan gave a rare laugh, and now that he was seated the family waited in silence. Nimr had heard versions of Hassan's tale, among them several naming Russia as his site of exile, but, trusting none, he was as eager as his children to hear the truth from the man himself. Unlike his children, he concealed his enthusiasm under a sage smile and deliberate shakes of his venerated head.

After asking courteously about their schooling, Hassan gratified the children with a more interesting question:

"Almost three years and you are all just the same as I remember you—only taller and wiser and more beautiful! Do you know where I have been?"

"England!"

"Were you in Egypt?"

"Oh no—no, I was in Damascus."

He told the story drily, using the best turns of phrase he had practised on the house of Abu al-Kheir and his own family, which now rolled off the tongue without forethought. He described the warning from Haj Taher Kamal, his journey from Nablus to Aley, and the newspaper at the inn. The boy slapped his thighs at the encounter with the affable soldier on the roadside, and slapped them harder at the lemonade offered to the soldiers who searched Abu al-Kheir's house.

The keenest listener was Fatima, the eldest daughter. She absorbed the story without laughing, as she absorbed all the stories her brother shared of the men who were returning to Nablus with war wounds and foreign certificates. Among the returnees, she knew, was Haj Hassan's son Yasser.

Fatima's mother firmly believed that Yasser was a perfect match for her. She mentioned him frequently at home, though less for Fatima's benefit than for her father's; although Haj Nimr adored and respected his cousin, he remained evasive on the question of his cousin's son. Yasser was a reasonable choice, was a member of the family, had attained a high office in the Ottoman army, and was heir to most of Haj Hassan's lands in the Jordan Valley. But Nimr prized Fatima as both his eldest girl and the more beautiful, and consequently was hoping for someone even wealthier. When they talked about Yasser he regarded Fatima from across the table, and she would blush and avert her gaze. But, confined by the demands of his new political office, Haj Nimr had neither the time nor the opportunity to seek out other suitors, and his wife continued to push for her choice. Yasser was a good man, she repeated. Fatima rather thought that at thirty-two he sounded too old for her, but since the thought of marrying anyone was terrifying, at least if he was a relative she would have more access to her family.

Haj Hassan Hammad's land in Zawata lay in the shadow of Mount Ebal. A third of the way up the mountainside, a large perpendicular rock protruded.

Near the centre of the rock was a cave, and in its western corner was another smaller adjoining cave, its entrance blocked by stone. The story went that a female Islamic saint called Sitt Salamiyeh had died in Damascus, and when she was placed in her coffin her body rose through the air and vanished, appearing in this cave through the western corner, which had miraculously opened to receive her. The rock was now a pilgrimage site where oil was burned in her honour. The floor of the cave was scattered with earthen bottles, the walls studded with lamps.

That evening, while her father entertained his guests, Fatima escaped through the kitchen garden and climbed the mountain path. When she reached the cave she removed her veil and struck a match to light one of the lamps. Shadows shook and sprang across the chamber wall. She lit two more, knelt by the tomb, and prayed to Sitt Salamiyeh that whoever she married would have a habit of kindness withindoors.

Fatima was sixteen. She had stopped attending school two years ago, and was now apprenticed in the art of running a household. In the mornings she packed away the bedding, rolled up each mattress and tied it with string, folded the sheets and slotted them into the cupboard. Even though they had a maid who did most of the laundry, her mother was emphatic that Fatima master everything. She herself came from a poorer family and knew the importance of self-reliance in case of hard times. And so, after packing away the nightclothes, Fatima began the ironing, heating the coals first in a brazier and inserting them with tongs into the flatiron. Afterwards she set the iron on a trivet to cool, and helped the maid fold the sheets and garments into piles. Then she joined her mother in the kitchen where she would usually eat a piece of bread before helping with the preparations for lunch.

Until that year and ever since Fatima could remember, the upper part of the house had been occupied by Turkish soldiers, who used it for accommodation and sometimes as a meeting house, and with that curious mixture of fearful deference and the pride of the chosen Haj Nimr had made no show of resistance. Turkish cuisine infused the Hammad kitchen, and Fatima learned to cook white bean pilaf, stewed spring lamb, and stuffed chicken at the side of the Turkish cook. With the onset of war the Turks were replaced by Germans, who helped stock the kitchen as prices soared in the markets. And now, three years later, Fatima's family at last recovered the use of their upper rooms, and her father's rise to prominence in the town was matched by her mother's delight at being in charge of the house again.

Once lunch was on the boil or in the oven, Fatima returned upstairs to her clothes iron, which she brushed with hot beeswax to ward off rust. She spent the time that remained reading magazines and stitching, and just after four o'clock her sister and brother came home from school and the family gathered for lunch.

Fatima had lately developed an awareness of the length of life. Now that she was entering a new phase she saw both that it was long, and that it was a portion with an end. She considered the two mountains that formed the shoulders of Nablus and gave the city its finitude; however much the city might attempt to mount the crags and spread its suburbs, the earth was its body and it was bound to the valley. If Nablus grew at all it would have to spill out between the crevices where the valley ended in the plain, and even then it would only reach so far.

But the war had wrought changes, and in its wake Nablus was for the moment troubled with uncertainty. Trade was restored, the rationing was over. But tales of Salah ad-Din and Crusader battles were surfacing in the common memory as newspapers read aloud in coffee shops reported the redrawn maps, and their beautiful city, which had always been the southern sister of Damascus, officially became a province north of Jerusalem. That dignity the ruling families had so coveted under the Turks, developed over centuries, and campaigned tirelessly to protect, was at once under a far greater threat.

Travel was again possible between cities; Jerusalem was electrified, and under the new lamps and to the tunes emanating from the shiny phonographs, modern nightlife arrived in the Holy City. Young men rode down from Nablus to rent apartments within the old city walls, counting the hours on their watches as they passed into the night, smoking by the roadsides and dancing in bars.

Fatima dreamed of the Nebi Rubin festival. She had been ten years old when they went with their cousins from Lydda and spent two weeks in a big tent by the sea in Jaffa. Markets, cafés, and restaurants were set up for the festival; in the daytime there were horse and camel races and at night theatre troupes performed, and singers from Egypt and Lebanon, and in roped-off circles magicians played tricks, poets recited, and dervishes whirled. She doubted she would be allowed to attend Nebi Rubin again until she was married.

As Fatima finished her prayer a wind blew into the cave and curled the dust at her feet. Through the cave's mouth she saw night settling over the town, and hurried to extinguish the three lamps she had lit, then pulled her veil back over her face. The oil and matches in one hand, the other grasping the rocky entrance to the cave, she stepped out onto the mountainside. At once she pulled her muslin tighter and bent to keep steady against the wind. The movement of something black in the trees jolted her attention. But it was only the branches as they wagged and crossed each other, blocking sections of the violet sky.

Everything was close in the dark. She gripped the tiny bottle and listened, heard only the nightjars, the crickets, the broken call of the wind. She padded down the slope, clicking the bottle against the rocks for balance, her heart pounding. By the time she reached the town, her fear of the wild darkness had turned into a fear of the scolding she would receive for being out so late alone.

Closing the door, head bowed, she walked straight towards the bedroom she shared with her sister. But her mother was listening for her, and came rushing up from the kitchen.

"Where have you been?" she screamed. "Shame! Shame on you!"

"I was praying, Mama, I'm sorry."

"Why are you praying at this hour? Imagine who could have seen you! Shame on you Fatima!"

Fatima raised her arms to protect herself.

"Get to your room before your father whips you!"

For good measure, her mother reached out to pull down Fatima's arms, and then her veil, and slapped her hard across the face.

2

After the night of his disgrace, Midhat left the Molineu house without saying goodbye. Before the sun could rise the next day he had softly closed the
front door and dragged his trunk to the centre of town, where he bought a
ticket to Paris and sent a telegram ahead to his friend from the ship, Faruq
al-Azmeh. He arrived at the Gare de Lyon several hours later, his lungs
raw with loss.

As he took his first look at Paris—the cluttered pavements, the zinc
roofs, the faceless rush—that same changing sensation of the night before,
when he realised he would have to leave the Molineus', stirred again within
him. The people seemed less to walk down the street than to hurtle; he
heard the cry of a seagull and the earth muttered beneath his feet as though
somewhere below water was churning.

With all the clothes he had bought over the last year there was no space
in the trunk for his overcoat and tarbush, so he was wearing them now
and he was sweating. Surrounded by black bowlers and blue uniforms, he
noticed Tricolores angled from the military bureau and realised he could
not have marked his difference more obviously. There were some frowns
of confusion and clear distaste. But no: he would not take the tarbush off.

"Taxi?"

Above the bridge the gulls applauded. The taxi window showed a river and wide tree-lined banks. He wished he could recall the name of the neighbourhood where Jeannette had spent her childhood, and her mother had taken her life. As they crossed onto the farther bank a light rain began to pester the roof of the taxi; they drove alongside the river past a fenced park, and easels lined up on the quay, and the buildings rose on either side as they turned inward to where the city thickened. At last they halted on the Rue du Four, and Midhat opened the car door and paid the driver.

"Monsieur Kamal!"

At a metal table under an awning, a pair of spectacles dangling from his neck, sat Faruq al-Azmeh. The globe of Faruq's forehead seemed to have grown with his receding hair. They shook hands.

"I was so pleased to receive your telegram. My good friend, how are you? Turn around, this is our front door."

"I have missed you," said Midhat, as they climbed the stairs. "On the ship, do you remember, you told me all those things about the French. I wish somehow you might have stayed near me, there was so much more I needed to ask you."

"Mais bien sûr," said Faruq. "There will be time!"

The apartment was on the third floor of the building, with a balcony onto the street, and a window at the back onto a shared courtyard. The main room was furnished sparely but richly—dark green wainscoted walls, full bookshelves, windows ceiling-high and hung with damask curtains. Faruq helped him carry the trunk into a bedroom, rubbed his hands, instructed him to sit, and reached for a bottle of whisky and two glasses.

Thus began Midhat's life in Paris. His days of medical study were behind him. He enrolled in the history course at the Sorbonne, and by the end of the summer was attending lectures in wood-panelled halls smelling of chalk dust alongside other foreigners, young women, and elderly men. He spent his days in cafés with books on ancient Greece and seventeenth-century Spain, and Faruq supplied him with additional reading, stories of forbidden love, mystical texts, narratives of peripatetic foreigners living in Paris. Among them were Goethe's *Sorrows* and the story of a Lebanese priest's daughter trapped by her marriage and in love with someone else. These books were preoccupied with the senses, Faruq pointed out. Their authors pleaded openness to the world.

"We are all scarecrows turned philosophers," he said, "with crows living under our hats."

Sometimes after dinner Midhat would go out with Faruq to bars and cabarets. As the city moved from her mood of wartime grief to one of revelry, Parisian nightlife began to thrive on the electric atmosphere of the home front. Ration-dimmed streetlights greyed the boulevards but cinemas and theatres still packed out nightly and even stayed open during zeppelin attacks. Under the sustained pressure of war, the people of Paris behaved as though they had approached the end of the world. Faruq liked to joke that an atmosphere of "désastre" led to "déshabillement"—but Midhat said no, this was something greater, far more significant and penetrating. It was a charge shared between strangers, it was a pure thrill of Being. It lived in the body like a drug, this being alive in the jaws of the full, flying night.

His first sexual experience was with another student at the Sorbonne, named Claire. Claire was petite and blond and, Midhat was shocked later to learn, almost thirty years old. She expressed disdain for men who were not at war, and when he tried to defend himself she reached out and placed two fingers on his lips.

"Je ne veux pas entendre vos raisons."

He caught sight of her first at a lecture on the origins of religion. She was on the opposite side of the lecture hall, and as she watched the professor Midhat watched her. When the students flooded out into the courtyard, he felt a tap on his shoulder and turned to find her standing there with a hand on her hip.

"Je veux voir la wreckage, du raid la nuit dernière."

They found a five-storey building on the Rue de Ménilmontant where the wall had been ripped off, the cross section exposed, the remaining support wall now a coastal profile, half a bathroom rudely displayed, a kitchen, stocked shelves. He stared up in silence at the chair suspended on the top floor. He was thinking of a note Jeannette once read aloud to him, written in her mother's hand, about a house that stopped being a house once a thief had entered.

Claire took his hand in hers. "My God." Her dress was cut low, the skin on her chest pale and patterned with freckles that gathered below her clavicle. She placed herself closer to him. What a strange person, he thought; stripped of fear. She released his hand and moved past him to the garden wall. She pulled up her skirt, put her foot in the crevice, hauled herself over, and disappeared.

Midhat looked around. Only a few people were walking on the street. He heard a voice say, "Maman, regarde," but nothing more. He approached the wall and jumped up, and a thin vertical plate of concrete crumbled under his weight. In his haste he scraped a knee, sharp dust grooved his hands; he landed on dry grass and debris and saw Claire moving towards a shed with a collapsed roof. The corrugated door lying on the ground clanged with her footstep. She giggled, and slipped her body through the remaining gap of an entrance. Midhat followed her into the darkness.

Inside smelled of sawdust, and the dented roof left barely a space to stand. It was a woodshed: some logs remained in their stacks, most had scattered over the floor. A bucket glinted with fissures of daylight; Claire laughed, kicked it over. For no reason, and they heard the swish of the water as it tipped. It disturbed Midhat, this display of havoc. His shoe released a squelch as he raised it. Momentarily he feared her—but as this fear struck her little grip pulled at his jacket, and he fell forwards and reached for the wall. Her breath was loud in his ear. She kissed him. He tried to mimic her courage and, tensing the muscles in his hand and arm, slid his fingers under the collar of her dress, revealing her pale shoulder. Even in the gloom her eyes were bright. She stole a hand down below to where he was already hot and stiff and unbuttoned his trousers, and for a cruel second Midhat was reminded of his nurse, the only other person in his life who had ever undressed him thus. Claire was laughing softly, pulling her skirt up, her drawers down; he reached out and gripped her instinctively under the legs, braced her against the wall. She kissed him again, and with her hand helped him to enter her.

An eruption of sensation. He drew an enormous breath. His fingers clawed into the backs of her thighs. She was squirming, whispering in pain. Let me go. He checked his gasping, he held himself; she pulled back and forth, he copied her and tried to thrust. The pleasure surged and for a long, staggering moment he was totally unselfed. Then he was out again. Feet sounded on the street outside and faded. Claire released a puff of exasperated laughter and Midhat turned to catch his breath, his left foot completely wet with the bucket water.

Though at first the experience was painful to recall, before long it was a triumph in Midhat's mind. It was easy to rewrite a story in a city of strangers, and reporting it to Faruq over cognac Midhat changed the location—to Claire's apartment—and laughed, as a man who has done something for himself laughs, fortified by action. And then, having conned himself with this picture of manly achievement, and having teased out some details of Faruq's own affairs under the guise of sharing knowledge, he found the next time infinitely easier.

This girl was from Lyon, also a student at the university; he saw her across a lawn in the Bois de Boulogne, and reversing his direction met her as if by accident where the paths intersected. He complimented her on the ribbon in her hair; accepted the dinner invitation; helped when her corset-clasp snagged on her underdress, and touched the small hole it had torn with its little harp of exposed fibres. Then there was a society girl with bony shoulders who wore flannel suits and shoes with canvas spats. Sometimes she wore a monocle at parties. Another woman sold charity badges on the Rue de Rivoli; her curls were the colour of marmalade. He met her in June, and in the sunny mornings found orange hairs spiralled on the pillow beside him. He befriended a whore at the Café Napolitain who was slight and flat chested, and addressed Midhat as "Mon Exotique." After a month of evenings in rented rooms and breakfasts by the Seine this girl left the city for Provence with her mother, and Midhat regretted the loss of her scornful voice and her firm thighs. He began to visit the whorehouses in Pigalle, in part searching for another such woman, in part simply for the physical release.

Two whores he visited, but soon there was only one, for the first became syphilitic and was transferred to the local infirmary. The other was a woman named Pauline, whose skin was very soft and who sprayed herself with rosewater to mask the sewer-stench that reached the windows in summer. Pauline had a comic pout. When the Americans joined the war effort and filled Paris on furlough, she mimicked their voices with a wah wah drawl and swagger of her head, and lighting a cigarette watched Midhat produce the franc notes to pay the madam.

But after a while he began to feel the dullness of paid pleasure, and, of course, with all the soldiers on rotation one needed to be careful of venereal diseases. Still, on occasion, when induced by cheap wine, he could happily leave a bar in a group of men to carouse in the foyer of Le Chabanais, and accept without much forethought whichever boudoir he was shown into.

Through all this, Jeannette lived on in his mind. The more experience he gained, the less he could commit to any of these women he met in the Folies Bergère, or the Concert Mayol, or in the salons of cocktail parties. Sometimes in the dark he felt Jeannette's lips, and sometimes smelled her over some woman's head. Emerging from the fantasy to find a stranger in his arms, he would hear a high ringing sound and make love half in disgust before returning to Saint Germain heavy with renewed shame and longing. That sound moved into and out of his awareness for whole weeks at a time, and yet he carried his longing with him always like a crest of seriousness, and it gave him a gravity both real and performed, which the women of Paris sensed on him like a cologne and were captivated by.

One day, in the summer of 1916, he crossed the Rue de l'Odéon on his way to the university and caught sight of the back of a woman's head through the window of a bookshop. With a leap in his chest he recognised Jeannette's hair. She had cut it short again, it was blooming out the back of her head. What was she doing in Paris? She could not know he was here, he had left no forwarding address. There she was, Jeannette, in a matching shirt and skirt, pale grey.

But as she turned to face the window through which Midhat was staring she moved under the sheen of the reflected sun, and he could not tell if she had seen him. His body trembled as it took him through the tinkling shop-door. She was facing away, picking up a book to examine the spine.

"Jeannette."

At his voice, she turned. It was not Jeannette. Her brow furrowed, she blushed. Her eyes were small and lower down than they were supposed to be, and she was too short, and although she was perfectly fine looking the sight of her was to Midhat monstrous. She was at the counter, and now she was approaching him, whispering, "Excuse me"; he fumbled aside to let her exit, and the door chimed shut. Her face haunted him for several moments. A panic loomed: he could not remember what Jeannette looked like. He tried to conjure her face, but all he could see was this new anonymous woman with her low eyes and her grey skirt. He walked out in a concentrated daze, ransacking his memory. Then—at last—there it was: the little chin, tapering, the eyes, the look in the eyes, the smiling, the kiss, the ending. She was still there, intact.

It seemed the universe would not let Midhat's conscience lie. Only a few months later he spotted Monsieur Samuel Cogolati, his Belgian friend from the Faculty of Medicine at Montpellier, in the audience of the Théâtre des Bouffes-Parisiens during the performance of a comic opera about a magical pear. When their gazes collided, Cogolati jerked his head back in surprise. During the interval Midhat found him by the bar.

"Monsieur Kamal! I did not expect to see you again. I thought you had returned to Palestine."

Although only a year had passed, Cogolati looked older and his waxy face had at last grown some down. Midhat himself had grown an inch and been forced to buy new suits on the Rue Royale. He was also starting to comb his hair with a side parting, and carried a steel-topped cane.

"No, no, I am in Paris . . . I decided . . ." He stopped. "I decided that I needed a change of scene. And, you know how it is, new experiences, and so on."

"What do you mean?"

"New scenery, new people . . . I never wanted to outstay my welcome. And to see Paris! How can one visit France and not see Paris?"

"Indeed. I am here for the weekend on my way to Geneva. But we miss you at the Faculty, I was not expecting you to leave. I heard you did well in your examinations."

"Oh, well, all thanks to you. How—have you heard from my host family at all?"

"The Molineus haven't written?"

"Of course, only, it was a while ago . . ."

"The last I heard, Jeannette went off to be a nurse, but I'm sure you know more than I do."

"Well." An usher in red lapels was calling for the second act. "We should meet when you next come through Paris."

Midhat reached for a napkin with a shaking hand and drew a fountain pen from his pocket. *Rue du Four*, he wrote. He did not recognise his handwriting.

"Who was that?" said Faruq, as the curtain went up and the cast reassembled onstage to general applause and a few whistles.

"A Belgian."

Midhat struggled to focus on the remainder. All that time he had been studying at the Faculty of Medicine, and in the end it was she who worked in a hospital! Insipid images of Jeannette as a nurse tending wounded soldiers, stolen from newspaper illustrations; imprecise jealous pangs. And there was something uncomfortable about seeing Cogolati, an anxiety that he might not have presented himself as he wanted translated back to the Molineus. If only, in his vain haste to impress upon an old colleague his new urbanity and poise, he had borne in mind what Jeannette might have thought of such a Midhat, had she caught wind of it. Midhat the Levantine, with his mouchoir and new suit, now thoroughly estranged: the figure of the Parisian Oriental as he appeared on certain cigarette packets in corner stores. Cogolati surely only saw him as a colleague and an equal—and yet, that innocent, hardworking man would be forever linked in Midhat's mind with the moment he was awakened to his own otherness, when on the day he completed his examinations and said goodbye to his classmate he returned to the house to discover the other way in which he had been examined—by his host, and without his knowledge. Harrowed by the glimpse of a strange outside view of himself. And in just a year he had undergone such an alteration, from that stranger who had once desired to become European both inside and out, closer already in appearance to the pale Italian or Greek—when he was not blithely offering his genealogy to anyone who asked—than to the inhabitants of those apostasized subaltern continents who had so defected from civilisation as they occurred in picture books and nursery rhymes and the imaginations of French children. He had fallen so easily into the compromise available in Paris, this type, by an embrace of otherness that at first he had admired in Faruq but which now appeared in his mind a skewed, performed version of what it was really like to be in a place but not of it, not to know it truly. Docteur Molineu lurked at the edges with his notebook and his analysis, his charts of cranial development, observing him at the dinner table.

The husband had been duped! The pear was not magical, after all. Applause; the curtain, the bow.

That same summer, while preparing for a seminar on the history of modern philosophy, Midhat returned one evening from the café where he had been reading Spinoza to find the apartment fuller than usual with Faruq's friends and clouded with smoke. Faruq raised a hand in welcome; he had rotated the desk chair away from the desk, and standing, now offered it to Midhat.

The men around the room were animated with discussion. Most Midhat recognised; all were Syrian Arabs. The coffee table and floor were spread over with periodicals and papers, cups of cigarette stubs and saucers of spilt coffee.

"You cannot extrapolate and extrapolate, saying *we* for *I*," said someone from the sofa. He turned his head and Midhat saw it was Bassem Jarbawi, with his long chin. The Jarbawis were among the founders of the Lebanese Alliance in Paris, a diaspora body that lobbied for French political support for the Lebanese nationalist cause.

A man with close-set eyes leaned his elbows on his knees and looked about to speak, when Raja Abd al-Rahman, an accountant and aspiring poet, broke in.

"Yes, I speak for myself. I am not Christian, Muslim, Turkish, French, Chinese, or any of these things. I am just one among humankind."

"Raja," said the man with close-set eyes in an exasperated voice. "That's . . . You're misunderstanding—"

"I misunderstand nothing."

"No, we have to fight as a jama'a, or people like you will suffer."

"Omar," said Faruq.

"What?" said the exasperated man. "His own actions will make him suffer. If he wants to be on his own, let him."

"Khaleek shway," said Faruq.

"What 'khaleek shway'? They have just killed our best men. This is not about being one of humanity. We are from the East, every one of us in this room, and we have suffered enough. Lazim, kuluna, rise up."

"Using the same tools as our oppressors?" said a warm, level voice.

Midhat did not recognise this speaker. He was tall and thin, with hooded eyes, reclining on the sofa with one leg crossed over the other.

"Really, if you were given the chance, you would colonize Europe?" he continued.

"Yes!" said Omar. "Of course! All this, you don't want all this?" He gestured at the room around him as if the room itself, its green walls and mahogany chair legs and velvet cliffs, was the city of Paris in all her glory. "Come on Hani, be realistic, ya'ni. Think. Use your . . . you know."

"I am thinking. Are you thinking?" said the thin man named Hani. "I don't think this is enlightened talk, habibi."

"Hani is right," said Faruq. "You know we have to be modern in our thinking."

"Modern?" said Omar. "Ya zalameh, they may look like they are modern when you're in . . . in Saint Germain, when you're on a nice train, when you're in a cinema, but believe me, believe me, they are as brutal as the Turk in their empires, in their wars, in their cannon. You are not listening to me. Isma'nee. What does Arab tribalism look like? It looks like each town is his own country, and his country is better than the next town a hundred feet over. A united East is not Arab tribalism. By the definition." He pinched his thumb and forefinger together and shook them, as if he held a piece of paper with the definition on it.

"Wallah, I don't know," said Bassem Jarbawi. "You know? They have killed us. They are killing us. Like the Armenians."

"Who have they killed?" said Midhat.

"You didn't read the paper today?" said Yusef Mansour, a Maronite Christian from Aley with an ivory moustache. "Midhat, you have to start reading the paper."

"Another round of executions, nationalists," said Hani. "Twenty-one Syrians hanged in Beirut and Damascus."

"People from Palestine, habibi," said Faruq.

"They will lose the war and then we'll win," said Jarbawi.

"Who, who from Palestine?"

"A Shihabi, a Nashashibi," said Faruq, reaching behind him for a newspaper. "Ali Nashashibi, you know him? Salim al-Jaza'iri . . . wallah. They have cut out our eyes."

He passed the paper to Midhat and pointed at the relevant paragraph.

"An jad," said Omar, turning to Bassem Jarbawi. "You really think there'll be independence that easily?"

"Ana . . . assez confident." Bassem swivelled his hand.

"Abd al-Hamid al-Zahrawi," said Faruq. "He chaired the Congress here three years ago. Important people, Midhat. We're lucky to be where we are now, really."

"Exactly," said Raja Abd al-Rahman. "They'll kill us if we go back, just like the Armenians, just like Zahrawi. Or enslave us, turn us into Turks."

"So how did they catch them?" asked Midhat, handing the page back to Faruq.

"Papers at the French Consulate in Beirut. Habibi would you pass me that ashtray."

"We've been colluding with France, amo," said Bassem Jarbawi.

"I'm not returning until the war is over," said a portly man from a cushion by the fireplace.

"That's because you're a chicken," said Omar.

"They're shutting down the newspapers!" said Bassem. "You really want to go back there and become a Turk? Omar, look at the," he grabbed a journal lying beside him on the sofa, "at this, look, death, death, death. No alliances, nothing."

"I think," said Hani, still reclining, "that actually, the missions of the Christian countries, ya'ni, this will be our greatest obstacle. Because at the moment, they want to undermine the Turks, yes. But then later . . . I mean, they are empires. We know what empires do. They are hungry. The muthaqafeen in this country, at least, they see Zionism as a project to make, you know, make the Arab world this European thing."

"I don't know that Zionism is really the issue," said Omar, frowning.

"How can you say that?" said Hani, with an energy that pulled him upright. Midhat noted the yellow scarf that slid out from under his lapel.

"Our issue is independence," said Omar.

"What? The two are completely intertwined."

"I have to say," Raja Abd al-Rahman raised his hand. "You're forgetting that the Europeans don't want the Jews here. You heard the story about this Dreyfus? Yahud, Muslimeen, we're all the same to them, they don't trust us. Just put us over there. So it's not a matter of colonialism. It's more a matter of disposal."

Yusef Mansour heaved to his feet. "Glass of cognac anyone?"

"Please!" said Raja."

"Careful. Anyone else?"

"So what was I saying," said Raja, "yes, so, the Jews in Europe."

"Is that glass dirty? Forgive me, I'm going blind."

"Shush, let him finish."

"Sorry."

"Whereas we, on the other hand, we have always had Jews. Always, there have been Jews in Syria. They'll just be Syrian Jews."

"Raja, habibi, listen to me," said Hani. "They already have their own stamps." ("Stamps?" said Yusef to Bassem. "Ya Allah. We don't even have our own stamps.") "Exactly. So this really is the issue."

"Still, at the moment, France is the bigger threat," said Omar.

"You are all talking about independence as though Britain and France had won the war," said Bassem. "The Turk is still fighting, there might be a truce or something. We don't know what's going to happen."

"But if you look at the news," said Midhat, weighing in for the first time. "And now that the Americans are in, the Germans are really . . . I think it's only a matter of time."

"Midhat, come sit here. You look uncomfortable."

"I'm fine. The chair is just a bit broken."

"Faruq your place is falling apart," said Yusef.

"That's because I have fifteen Arabs sitting on my furniture every night."

"What are you talking about, we are as thin as reeds."

"Speaking of which, is there any food?" said Raja. "I brought carrots."

"It used to be chocolate we'd bring to a party," said Bassem. "Now it's carrots and potatoes. And bread."

"Did you bring bread?" said Faruq.

"No, sorry, I was just saying . . ."

"Well we don't have bread. But we do have some biscuits," Faruq slid off the desk, "they're in the cupboard, there should be enough. And there's a stock boiling."

"I actually bought some bread on the way home," said Midhat.

"Habibi that's marvellous."

"Midhat the Messiah," said Yusef. "Oh, it's warm, ya Allah."

"But what I was saying is," said Raja Abd al-Rahman, carrying his carrots into the kitchen, "the Jews are good agriculturalists. You know? They might be a boost to the local economy."

"That's because you're in Damascus, Raja," said Hani. "You're not Palestinian."

"We are all *Syrians*," said Yusef. "None of this 'Palestinian, mish Palestinian.' We are united, we will be one nation."

"Enough," said Omar. "I'm starving, I can't think anymore."

"See?" said Yusef to Faruq. "How could we break your chairs. Look at Omar's stomach. He doesn't even have one."

As Midhat grew in confidence he became more vocal during these evening conversations. Remembering what Jeannette had once said to him, about how she began to speak up at the university without fear of making errors, he felt his ability to argue develop like a muscle, which he exerted in his essays on the Revolutionary Wars and Jeanne d'Arc as much as over coffee and cigarettes, and which, though not totally detached from any notion of truth, seemed discrete from it, as if words could wind around and through the truth without manifesting it link by link. Besides, the fluidity of these debates and the changing political facts meant that none need be held to any assertion he had made, and each was free to swap between positions as served the present conversation. Then came victory in the Hejaz, and finally, the Ottoman Empire fell. Emir Faisal came to Paris for the Peace Conference, and what had been speculation, mere banter in high rooms off a boulevard, now these questions of nation or not were on the very threshold, and the blissful years of exile and indeterminacy were coming to an end.

It was three years since Midhat left Montpellier for Paris. Over that time, his life had become multiple. At one moment he was the student of history, meeting acquaintances after class in barrooms and cafés; at another he was the companion of women, with a gentle manner and easy laugh; then he was the mysterious lover; then the debater; and then he was the Arab. The divisions, though sometimes porous, were abiding, for with all the talk of origins and truth in his university essays and among his Syrian friends, Midhat was learning to dissemble and pass between spheres and to accommodate, morally, that dissemblance through an understanding of his own impermanence in each. But as despondence broke out among his friends, Midhat found it was the arguing Arab, that least interesting of roles, which he performed more and more. He loved this country, he loved her lines of rationalism, the sciences that put a veil on the unknowable, the lines of verse about the Orient, which Faruq read aloud on Sunday afternoons, even as they pinned him and his ancestors into effigies of themselves. Standing on Faruq's balcony, looking down at the black cars in the street like a procession of hearses, he felt that some great frame had cracked. He turned back to the apartment and the scene trembled through the quartered glass, the room appeared dislocated, the faces of his friends unfamiliar. Faruq was dressed in a velvet waistcoat, there was a stain on his shirttail that had been washed and preserved, like a pale brown birthmark.

Once the war ended, the meetings in Faruq's apartment became less frequent, and when the friends did assemble the tone of conversation was sober and apprehensive. Yusef Mansour was fixated on news of the famine in Beirut. Omar became inarticulate in his anger against the Triple Entente. Midhat drew closest to the other Nabulsi in the group, Hani Murad. Hani was the only one directly involved in politics, and his insights did not provide any of them with much hope.

When it came to Bonaparte and Bismarck, Hani Murad sympathised with the Germans. It was clear to him that to unify a country was the supreme goal of mankind. And after all, the people in Alsace did speak German.

Though enthusiastic about his own analyses, Hani had learned not to air all of them in public. The one occasion when he broached the question of Bonaparte and Bismarck, with a French colleague at *Le Matin* where he was working as a translator, the man looked up at him through the steam issuing from the kettle as though Hani had just blasphemed, and only later as they stepped into the street at dusk did the man address the issue gently, explaining as if to a child that language is not the source of nationhood, that there are other things that mark a person's origin and nature. Hani could not have disagreed more, but realised he should hold his tongue.

In December 1918, Hani was sitting at the typewriter in his room at a pension in the Latin Quarter, a fire flapping in the grate, the wallpaper peeling with damp. For the last year, while moving back and forth between journalism jobs and the boarding school where he took children to visit castles and gave spontaneous, imaginative lectures on French history, Hani had been spending his evenings with a pen in hand. He was translating a book from Turkish into French, and in the process had turned his desk into a morass of handwritten papers. A few weeks ago, a series of urgent letters had arrived at the pension from one Monsieur Payot, who agreed to publish the book on the condition that Hani present a typewritten manuscript as quickly as humanly possible. France, said Monsieur Payot, was peaking in her curiosity about the Ottomans, and now was the time to strike and see the gold wink beneath the rock.

The title was "The Historical Fate of Turkey." The original author was a Turk named Ahmet Rasim, who had written the four volumes almost a decade prior. The Empire's defeat now coloured the whole thing differently, of course, and over the month since the armistice Hani found himself taking particular authorial liberties, inserting proleptic glosses in some places and on other occasions simply marvelling that certain passages already held their own shadows within their stances.

He paused over one of his own remarks, contrasting Bismarck's designs to unify Germany with the brutality of the Young Turks and their "Turkification" policy. Was this another vanity of the amateur historiographer? Doubt was a sign: if one doubted, one must not do. He ripped the page from the typewriter with one hand, wound the next one up the platen with the other, snapped across the lever, and was about to begin typing out the first paragraph again when there was a knock at the door.

"Monsieur Hani Bey Murad!"

Grinning at him from the hall, holding their hats, stood two old school friends, Qadri Muhammad and Riyad Assali, grown into balding men, and sporting twin woollen suits and coloured scarves.

"Mon Dieu! Ha! What the hell are you two doing here? Ya salam I'm shocked! Kiss me, kiss me, you frightened me . . ."

Qadri and Riyad embraced him, laughing. Qadri smiled under his thick moustache, and Riyad, the taller, bowed his polished head.

"Sweet Hani, we are back to see you."

"Come in, please, itfadalu, itfadalu."

"No, Hani, we can't come in," said Qadri.

"We have important news, ya'ni," said Riyad. "Emir Faisal is here in Paris, for the Peace Conference. He is staying at the Continental Hotel, a guest of the French government."

"Hani, we want you to come with us to see him. Tonight." Qadri widened his eyes. "His Highness needs another man to lead the Arab delegation, and there isn't much time. We think you'd be perfect, Hani. What do you think."

"I don't know what to say. Can't you come in for a moment and we'll talk? I haven't seen you in years—I have tea and bread."

"Well, ya'ni, we're at a disadvantage." Riyad sighed. "They only told us last week that Faisal was welcome at the Conference. So it was last minute, ya'ni. We have us two, Nuri Said who fought in the Revolt, and the British man, Lawrence. Everyone else is here and we are not prepared. The point is we have to work fast."

"Hani, just come, now. We'll talk on the way."

Before he knew what was happening, Hani was knocking the logs apart and placing the guard in front of the grate, grabbing his hat, locking the door, and swinging an overcoat over his shoulders.

At the sight of the car outside Hani's heart swelled. The black paintwork shone silver with the streetlight. The three stood looking at the vehicle from the sidewalk, piping out garlands of cold breath, before Riyad clapped Hani on the shoulder and opened the back door. Frost lined each crevice of the windows. The chauffeur was wearing two coats.

"The emir is the son of the Sharif Hussein, of the Hejaz," said Qadri, turning to Hani from the front seat. "His father led the Arab Revolt against Turkey. He is a very, very brave man."

"So is his son, ya'ni," said Riyad, "and he is looking forward to meeting you."

Paris flashed by. Her banners of victory dangled in shreds from the lampposts. Hani's nerves were fired. All these years of scavenging for work in Paris, temporary posts for which it was necessary to hide his qualifications, directing his energy instead into nightly translation work, which was such a slow way to help one's country, and so oblique, such a weak salve for the guilt of exile while his uncles were being hanged by Jamal Basha. Now everything had fallen into place. His law degree was not for nothing. It did not matter that he had not heard of the Emir Faisal until this moment; what mattered was that he had been summoned.

The Continental Hotel was a palace of lights, red plush chairs and carpets, liveried servants pushing silver trolleys. A clean-shaven man with dark curly hair, greased in a side parting, met them in the lobby. He was wearing a khaki military suit.

"This is Nuri Said," said Qadri.

"Enchanté," said Nuri, ducking his chin to smile at Hani. He led them down a corridor.

The suite was as tall as a chapel, with vast street windows that shone with the electric chandelier and their reflections. Rising from a gilt chair before the fireplace to greet them, and dressed in azure sacerdotal robes, was His Highness, the Emir Faisal.

Faisal was Bedouin-slight. His eyes were liquid dark, his long face curtained by a heavy white kufiya of embroidered silk; his heavy nose tended handsomely off-centre and the jewels of a dagger handle flashed between the pleats of his abaya as he leaned across for Hani's hand. His palm was very soft. Behind the emir, Qadri and Riyad took their places beside Nuri, and Hani noticed they had already removed their scarves, and covered their own heads with white kufiyas and gold i'qals.

Faisal gestured for Hani to sit; Riyad, Qadri, and Nuri remained standing. Hani mumbled respectful salutations, and there was a moment of silence. Then Faisal spoke.

"What is the public opinion of the Arabs in France?"

His voice issued from his mouth like a murmur of the earth.

"Your Highness. I believe . . . It is my impression that the citizens of France read only the French newspapers, which mislead them about the Syrians. About the Arabs in general. So even the university students here believe the Arabs are a race of men that live in the manner of the Middle Ages. Before the Middle Ages, even, ya'ni."

Faisal said nothing. His hands were folded in his lap. Hani tried again.

"I believe that France dreams today of annexing Syria, and even of ruling her fate, as she has already done in Algeria, and Morocco, and Tunisia . . ."

Faisal raised one hand a few inches above the other.

"Do you think," he said, "that we can change France's position, if we wage a war of independence."

It did not sound like a question. Hani hesitated.

"I fear, Your Highness, they will not easily . . . relinquish their policy of colonization. This has been the central tenet of their overseas behaviour for decades."

Now, Hani must not let himself be carried away with his analyses. He had often reflected that French foreign policy was determined by the fact that France was poor in manpower where her neighbour Germany was strong. And the reason for this was that the typical French family did not produce many children. And the reason for *this* was that the French treated their women with impractical latitude. French women were far too free. French women were always at the theatre, rather than spending their evenings in the home preparing to reproduce. This behaviour of French women was a systemic problem, and the result of it was that the French nation wished to adopt more children, since the women produced none, and this they hoped to achieve by annexing land. Thus, war broke out with Germany.

Hani's lips parted, ready for speech. The emir waited. But once again Hani recognised in his own hesitation the signs of that arbitrating deity, doubt. If one doubted, one must not do. Such theories should perhaps not have their first airing in a meeting with Emir Faisal of the Hejaz, son of Sharif Hussein of Mecca.

The emir's eyelids were tight and swollen with fatigue. Yet even in this state he could judge the figure before him as a man of restraint and honour. He liked Hani's aristocratic profile, his thin limbs; he liked the pauses in his sentences, which spoke of prudence and control; and therefore the answer was yes, they would employ this man, Hani Murad, to lead the Paris office for the affairs of the Arab Delegation. Faisal nodded with closed eyes to Riyad.

Besides, they had run out of time, so they had no choice.

In September 1919, Hani Murad was sitting at the same desk, at the same typewriter. His view was no longer of the peeling wallpaper of his old pension apartment, however, but of pedestrians on Rue Spontini ambling by in summer pinafores. Near his elbow was a plate of sandwiches, and beneath his hand was a letter from Faisal in Damascus.

With a pencil Hani had underlined the statement: "Ask me the political situation in Syria, and I will tell you that the stones of Syria are asking for the country's independence." The question was how to convey that sentiment in robust, diplomatic French, in the letter he was currently typing for Clemenceau in Faisal's name.

The progress of the Peace Conference had been difficult. From the first the French were more interested in entertaining Faisal than negotiating with him. A twenty-minute meeting with the president, not a word of politics, all smiles and politesse and sitting down and standing up and holding hands and admiring his robe, what was it called? A lunch with the foreign minister, plates of sliced pineapple brought especially from the Caribbean, wouldn't His Highness like to try? Three handshakes and a violin quartet, not a word afterward; a tea party in a park of the chancellery on a blue sky day, the exposed bodies of dancers wiggling their legs to the chords of a piano, arranged in your honour, Your Highness. In Faisal's honour! Not one of them cared for the Arabs, not one.

Eventually Hani had persuaded Faisal to visit a French tailor, and since the emir removed his abaya and donned a trouser suit things had begun to improve. But Hani's task was still extremely taxing, charged as he was with balancing the personality of His Royal Highness with the iniquities of the French. After eight months, his hair had turned grey at the root.

There was a knock at the door. The voice sounded before Hani could turn in his seat.

"Habibi, keefak."

Midhat Kamal strode into the room. He wore a pinstriped suit, hair oiled in a side parting, whiskers on his upper lip trimmed. A red sweet william dangled from his pocket, squashed between the folds of a green mouchoir.

"Midhat bey. Habibi, come sit."

"You are working?"

"I am, but I needed a break. Take a sandwich. Sit, Midhat."

"All right. No, I can't sit. I have to talk. Hani, I know you're busy but I have to talk to you. I'm sorry to interrupt."

"It's fine. What's wrong?"

Midhat Kamal was never not in a state of agitation. As long as Hani had known him Midhat was always either laughing down a boulevard with a woman on his arm, or silent with a woman on his mind, obsessed by the next and the next, discarding the last with sweat on his brow as though looking for something he had still not found; rifling through the women of Paris, driven by a magma of sadness that could flare without warning in a salon over cups of tea.

"I am leaving. My exams are finished, the boats are going again, I've run out of money. I have to face up, finally, to what my father expects of me. I have to go back to Nablus. I have to do my duty."

"That sounds very well, Midhat. That is what we all must do, eventually."

"Oh but Hani I . . . I can't. I can't just leave."

"Habibi, sit down."

"I don't know what to do."

"Is this Jeannette?"

"Yes, Jeannette."

Hani laughed. "After all these women and you are still obsessed. Really, you are so much like a character from a poem."

Whenever Midhat laughed his eyebrows reached upwards, as though laughter and surprise were allies; he also had a strange habit, Hani had noticed, of switching his facial expressions between laughter and distress, silliness and sadness, which sometimes made it difficult to grasp his mood. The eyebrows went up.

"Should I write to her? What do you think I should do? I know, so much time has passed. She's only a woman. But she has remained with me. I forget about it for periods. It slips my mind for whole weeks, it becomes the background, and I don't notice it. And then, I start to hear it again."

Apparently exhausted by this speech, Midhat finally sat in the chair Hani had offered. He played with his tie, running it between two fingers. He laughed, switched, frowned.

"Ha, I know, you don't need to say it, yes, it wasn't my fault, I tried to do the right thing, the Molineus were not honourable. I should be proud of how I acted. I didn't mean to become so . . . I just want to know if you think I should write to her." He leaned forward and looked into Hani's face. "You are a man who makes good decisions, Hani. And it's not because I think she'll reply. Though if she did then at least it might clarify . . . but no, it is because I want to write. I am capable, now, of writing what I could not say before. Do you see? I have many things to say, which I have not said."

Before answering, Hani waited to make sure Midhat had finished.

The character of Jeannette Molineu had become famous among the Syrians in Saint Germain. Hani first heard about her from his Damascene friend Faruq al-Azmeh, in whose apartment Midhat was lodging. This young Nabulsi, said Faruq, he is tormented. I find I must be his philosopher as well as his friend, he clings to my every word as though one of them might save him.

"Midhat, I think you should write the letter," said Hani, in a reasonable voice, picking up one of his sandwiches. "Even if you don't send it."

"I have to send it."

"Well then. But mostly it will be beneficial to get out the words. I have always found that about writing." He took a bite of the sandwich.

"I have already written it."

"Oh, I see."

"Can I read it to you? And you can tell me if I should send it?"

"Please, itfadal."

3 September 1919

Dear Jeannette,

I write to you from Paris, though I am soon to leave it. After these four years I am returning to Palestine. I am sorry that I did not write to you before. I wish I had. Regrets pile on regrets. You see I had hoped I would forget you. In my mind you were bound up for so long with pain that to think of you was always to feel again the sting of everything else. I hoped that somehow my memories of life before I came to France might be the ones to stick, and that you would slide off them, and I would remain the same beneath. But I fear that on the contrary my experience with you has in fact become one of those primeval shapes of the mind, to an imprint that burdens everything that comes afterwards. The sting has weakened with time, a little. My memories of you have not.

I have many things to apologise for. I am sorry I did not tell you where I was going. I am sorry that I left suddenly. Three years ago I met M. Samuel Cogolati from the Medical Faculty and he told me that you had become a nurse. I imagine you have returned to Montpellier now. It is funny that I should have studied medicine, but you should have been the one to practise it. I hope that you have not seen too many terrible things. I feel shame at the thought that you probably have.

Jeannette, you have stayed in my mind for four years. You are always, always here in this mind. Not only because pain has lasted: you have lasted. I hear your voice every day. I see you beside me on the terrace. I see your hair—all those different shapes on different days! I recall your smell. And your yellow dress. I remember your breath when you kissed me. I remember your anger when you turned from me.

I hope you understand how painful it was to discover your father's writings. I had hoped to marry you, but I was shy and could not say so. For this, again, I am sorry. I do stand by what I said, however. I became myself here, in this country, and for that reason I cannot represent anything. I belong here as much as I belong in Palestine.

I wish you to know that I always meant well. It was all out of love for you.

I wish you a good life. I shall never forget you.

Yours,
Midhat

"Well," said Hani. "You're not a bad writer, Midhat. I'm impressed. Here's an envelope. There are stamps in the drawer."

3

In October 1919, the unrest in Egypt was still simmering. Britain had denied her request for independence at the Peace Conference, and when the leaders of the resistance were exiled to Malta the women of Cairo marched in protest. But the general strike had at last been called off and trade was returning to healthy levels between Egypt and the Levant. As a result, Midhat's father, Haj Taher Kamal, had set òut from Cairo for Damascus to purchase more silks, and on the way he decided to stop in Nablus.

The autumn heat oiled the faces that passed under the midday sun. Haj Taher went by the khan, saluted his agent Hisham through the hanging yards of canvas outside the Kamal store, accepted a coffee heavy with sugar and cardamom, and chatted with some old customers passing through. They praised God for the end of the war; they grumbled over the liberties of the British soldiers; they acknowledged the provisions of seed grain and livestock, and the happy revival of normal commerce.

Haj Taher Kamal was a merchant because his father had been a merchant, and his father before him. Merchants were the glue that bound Nablus to the surrounding villages: for the village people they functioned as credit lines, patrons, employers, even friends; for the city dwellers they were both harbingers of novelty and pillars of tradition, and when the festivals came around the Nabulsis danced through the markets sprinkling the ground with coloured ribbons and pistachio shells. As far back as living memory could reach the foundation stones of Nabulsi society had been the mosque, the city gates, and the central marketplace, Khan al-Tujjar.

Haj Taher's grandfather began his business carting crates of Nabulsi soap on mules down through Gaza and into Cairo, returning after weeks with huge rope-bound bundles of fresh Egyptian cotton, which he sold in the Nablus khan, using the profits to buy more soap, travel to Cairo, and repeat the circuit. When Haj Taher's father inherited the business, he began using local tailors and dyers, and in this way managed to expand the Kamal stall in the khan into a clothing shop. Then he established relations with textile producers in Damascus, who wove silks from Mount Lebanon with cotton shipped from Britain into one cloth, dyed indigo, scarlet, emerald, saffron yellow, vermilion; and, with leftover connections in Cairo, opened a Kamal department store on Bulaq Street, dispensing quilts, pillow and mattress covers, scarves, handkerchiefs, headkerchiefs, large bolts of white and coloured fabrics sold by the arm length. This was the business Haj Taher inherited. The Cairo store grew stronger as the market expanded, and in addition to the basics they were soon selling thobs and sadari waistcoats and sarawil pants, and abayas and the headbands that peasants wore to their weddings.

By the time Haj Taher had mounted his horse to make his way home towards Mount Gerizim, the sun was slipping back down again. A breeze flapped his shirtsleeves and cooled the sweaty hair around his ears, and already the houses and trees were losing their shadows as the wind whipped the sky with fresh clouds.

"Hamdillah as-salameh!" The housekeeper, Um Mahmoud, opened the door with her arms out. "Ahlan wa sahlan, ya Haj, ahlan wa sahlan."

"Thanks be to God. Um Mahmoud, I'm hungry."

"Your health, ya Haj, I'll put the water on to boil. Give me your coat."

In the entranceway Taher saw two letters on the table. He opened the first where he stood.

The Most Honourable Sir, Noble Brother, Haj Taher Kamal,

  After inquiring about that most dear to us, the health of your Noble Person, I put before you our hope that you will send us a dima cloth of pleasing form and fixed colour, a dark-coloured abaya like the one you sent us earlier, with a head cover, of good quality, of a length reaching below the knee. For the ladies, two and a half good-quality pieces of dima of fixed colour, so that they can tailor them into dresses at home. Four arm's lengths of mansuri cloth, two undergarments and four ladies' handkerchiefs. With the grace of God, Most High, we will send you its price after the holiday with the bearer, Husain son of Sulayman al-Muhammad. We implore you not to delay its delivery to us at all, for you are well aware of the wedding coming up at Abu Uthman's. God bless you.

                                                        Ibrahim Abd al-Wahhab

Such orders were usually handled by Hisham. But since he was here to receive it Taher could take care of it himself. It would be his first village visit as a patron since the war started, and he pictured briefly the enthusiastic welcome he would receive.

  The second envelope was a pale lilac colour. Written upon it were the words:

  Monsieur Midhat Kamal
  Maison de Famille Kamal
  Naplouse
  Palestine

Haj Taher could speak English and knew the Latin alphabet, so his son's name was quite apparent. He examined the two green postage stamps. They both showed the same image of a woman in a Grecian robe.

  Four years ago, he had received a letter from Midhat with an almost identical stamp, informing him of a change of plans: Midhat had left Montpellier and would complete his university course in Paris, returning home after the war had finished as originally agreed. He had also enclosed his new address, on the Rue du Four in Saint-Germain-des-Prés. The explanation for the change was vague: an opportunity had arisen by which he might gain greater and better experience. Haj Taher had not made a fuss. Why not Paris? All the better, have his son return with some more sophistication. After they had confirmed the transfer of funds the letters became infrequent once more. The last Taher received was in the spring: a postcard photograph of Midhat leaning on a cane with his hand in his pocket, glancing off into a corner behind the cameraman.

The lilac envelope was postmarked Port Said on the 13th of October, Haifa on the 17th, Jerusalem on the 18th and again on the 19th. Haj Taher tore it open along the upper fold with his big forefinger. Both sides of the page were thick with a stream of curved writing. He stared at it: he could not read it. At the end it was signed with a single letter: J.

What Haj Taher did not know, standing now at three o'clock in the afternoon on the 20th October 1919, in the entranceway of the family house, on the side of Mount Gerizim in Nablus, was that his son had already left Paris. And that earlier that morning, having stepped off a steamship onto the Egyptian shore, Midhat was this very moment in a carriage on his way to his father's house in Cairo, where he was hoping to surprise him.

Six days earlier, Midhat had boarded the *Caucase* bound for Alexandria. After sending his letter to Jeannette, he decided not to return immediately to Palestine. First, it would be a good idea to acclimatise. Egypt was the place to start, a place known to him but not the way Palestine was known. Cairo was not a part of him as Nablus was. Nablus was all smells and sounds, the rushing air between the mountains. The only other time he had visited Egypt, by contrast, was on his first passage to the Marseille steamship five years ago. He imagined the delight in his father's eyes when he saw him, unexpected and full-grown. He inhaled the sea air and smiled. The embrace would be full of spontaneous feeling.

Also six days earlier, a lilac envelope had left the Montpellier post office by mail cart and, also at Marseille, boarded a mail ship named the SS *Amboise*. There may have been a moment somewhere along the way in which Midhat and the envelope crossed paths. At the port perhaps, or somewhere in the Algerian basin or the Strait of Sicily, the two ships may have passed within view of each other. But regardless, the express mail boat docked at Port Said and the letter from Montpellier began its way overland to Palestine two days before the *Caucase* arrived at Alexandria.

In Alexandria the train station was closed. Other travellers who had alighted from ships gathered around a sign that announced track repairs; a few wandered to the entrance and peered through the glass. Scraps of paper and disused cloth banners were strewn on the lawns of the ornamental garden opposite, and around them the telegraph lines had been pulled down. A few hung loose from their poles like ribbons from a French liberty tree. Walking away from the crowd, Midhat found an idle caleche further down the road. A small man with a cigarette between his teeth was in the driver's seat, resting his feet on the doorframe. After some negotiation Midhat persuaded him to drive to Cairo for the extortionate price of five piastres.

The route to the capital exposed more broken telegraph lines, vacant tramways, abandoned banners at the roadsides proclaiming "Egypt for Egyptians," now trampled on and ripped. The horse pulled them alongside the railway track and Midhat glimpsed Egyptian workers hammering, under the watch of armed British soldiers.

The streets of the Abbassia neighbourhood were almost empty. It was that hour of the afternoon when the inhabitants lay in a stupor under shutter-strained daylight. He reached his father's house: a white villa with pillared balconies in the baroque Ismaili style. The orange trees in the front garden were in their final bloom. Half-brown flowers decayed on the grass.

Layla opened the door with a child on her hip and a thin black veil over her face. For a moment she said nothing. Then suddenly, she cried: "Midhat!" The child turned away and wiped his mouth on her shoulder.

She ushered Midhat in with her free hand, and peered out before closing the door, as if the street might hold more surprises. When she turned and removed her veil to kiss him, he laughed in spite of himself at her enthusiasm. Perhaps time and distance simply wiped away ill will. Layla smiled naturally, as if no malice had ever passed between them.

"How tall you are!"

She set the child on his feet, and he pulled at her skirt. Layla seemed smaller than Midhat remembered. He looked down at her thin wrists and her long black hair, and her fingers, which she still hennaed, pale red from a former ointment.

"You are truly a man."

This pleased Midhat not a little. She led him further into the house and shouted for more coffee. As she turned a door handle, the boy ducked under her arm and fled down the corridor.

Midhat recalled this room from his last visit, when it had been a bedroom. Now it contained two satin couches and a writing desk by a window, which was crowded with jasmine.

"Did you write? Your father is in Nablus, he said nothing about you coming."

Midhat was silent for a moment. Layla raised her eyebrows.

"Oh," he said. "I assumed he would be here. I suppose I thought no one was working . . . I heard about the strike."

"Yes, but it will soon return to normal. For that your father went to Damascus to buy more silks."

"Of course. Well, in that case I'm sorry to have interrupted you. I should take a train, and go to Nablus."

"Nonsense! Sit down. You must stay at least a night, you will have supper with me."

"No, thank you, I should go and see Teta, I should get back to Nablus."

"Midhat, I have not seen you in five years. Haram aleyk, you want to leave me after just hello? You must at least meet your brothers and sisters."

She opened the door to shout for the children. Then she sat again, and they did not speak for a few minutes. A maid entered with a tray of coffee, and the children followed.

There were five. The eldest, Musbah, was as tall as his mother's waistline and had a thick brow. He remained near the doorway, staring. The next eldest was a blonde girl named Dunya who reached forward for Midhat's hand. Then there were Nadim and Inshirah, both dark-haired, Nadim dressed as a sailor, Inshirah in a white dress. And then Nashat, the shy boy he had already met. Layla lifted Nashat and balanced him on her hip.

Midhat shook their delicate hands one by one. Nashat refused to look at him, sucked a finger, and hid in his mother's hair. As Midhat stepped back again, his stepmother fixed him with a determined look, and whatever rancour he had felt towards her suddenly vanished.

In Paris, he had often thought over his formative years in Nablus. Considering that each man was a product of his experiences, he thought that Layla's actions may indeed have done him some harm as a child. Too early she had exposed him to the shocking insubstantiality of the family, to the fact that parents are just two people who have been united.

When Musbah was born, Midhat had been thirteen. The baby, he recalled, was very small, with ridges under his eyes that made his cheeks bulge, and deep pleats in the flesh of his arms. Sometimes he looked demure and sometimes like an angry little man, punching himself with his tiny fists and yelping.

A load of furniture had followed the couple and the baby to Nablus from Cairo, in a convoy of three carriages pulled by chained horses. The house was soon full of trinkets, and the rooms became at once much bigger and more crowded. An ornate wooden table sat in the centre of the sitting room near a wardrobe covered in petals of mother-of-pearl; and identical octagonal side-tables perched all over the house like strange implements, tall, narrow, clawed. The European-style bedstead, carried in by three men, took four hours to assemble.

Because Taher was conducting business in Jerusalem, Layla supervised the workers. She did not rebuke Midhat when he peered around the door to watch. "There was a beautiful headboard, zey kida," she said, holding up her hands. "Fabric everywhere, silk. Bitjannin, haram. It would have been ruined on the journey." The men were clumsy in their bare feet, holding odd segments of wood and iron, bowing occasionally to the veiled mistress.

That was the first time Midhat had entered the bedroom since Layla and his father returned. The second time was after school when he met his friend Adel Jawhari on the road. Adel was weeping.

"They beat me in class."

"Why?"

"I laughed when Abu Nasir knocked his leg against his chair." Adel smiled, and showed Midhat the backs of his skinny calves. The dark bruises were red with wet slits.

"Teta uses alum. We have some, come inside."

As the door fell closed behind them, Midhat recalled that the medicine cabinet was in his father's bedroom. While Taher and Layla were in Cairo, of course, it was just another empty room in a house full of empty rooms, where, in addition to keeping medicine, they stored sweets and marmalade for guests. He motioned for Adel to be quiet, and tiptoed into the bedroom. The famous bedstead stood in the centre, covered in bright cushions. He approached the cabinet, unclicked the latch, and put his hand in to feel for the bottle. A dark-headed figure appeared in the doorway and screamed.

"Get out of here! How dare you come in here!"

Adel sprinted out the door. Before Midhat could follow, Layla had stopped the door with her body and raised her hands. Ten red fingertips.

Teta appeared behind her. "Habibi get out of there."

Midhat aimed for his grandmother. But Layla grabbed his arm and slapped him across the back of the head and neck, awkwardly and with force so that her long nails scraped the skin. He wrenched himself free and ran out through the front door, which Adel had left ajar. There was no sign of his friend out on the mountain. He cornered the building; no sign. Two sheets hanging on adjacent ropes formed a corridor; Midhat ran inside it and sat down, as the maid beyond pulled another sheet from a basket.

"Midhat?" came Adel's voice after a few moments. "Midhat?"

Then all that was left was the sound of the wet cotton rasping on cotton, and the flap of fabric as the maid slung the laundry onto the ropes. The sky grew dark, and the hairs rose on Midhat's legs. Rattling hooves announced Taher's return from Jerusalem; the door fell shut; Layla's voice began its uninterpretable squall, gusting out of windows as she passed them. The sounds settled. At last the maid called Midhat in for dinner, and they ate in silence around the low table.

He could never remember if this came before or after it was decided that he would leave for Constantinople. He remembered only that one night as Teta lay beside him on his bed she described the Turkish capital, and the new school he would be going to. He would say goodbye to his father, goodbye to the tiny baby, goodbye to Layla.

Midhat looked down at his stepmother, her hands on the shoulders of her sons, and recognised that above all she was extremely young. She could not be more than thirty. Which meant she had been approximately Midhat's age now when she married his father, if not younger. No wonder she had hated the heir of her predecessor. And no wonder she had preferred to live in Cairo near her family, and had used her energy to persuade Haj Taher to arrange it so. It had been necessary to claim her territory and expel the foreign boy when he trespassed into her bedroom. Marriage was her life's great venture, and, happily, she had prevailed.

The surprise that Midhat had planned for his father was all Layla's then, since immediately after he left the house she sent a telegram to her husband in Nablus. Haj Taher replied that he could of course stay in Palestine for a little longer than planned; it would do no harm to delay his visit to Damascus given the circumstances. By God's grace, how many times does one stand to welcome a returning eldest son?

In the Kamal house in Nablus, Um Taher was beside herself with glee. While Taher was out at the khan she went downstairs to tell Um Jamil, and instructed her to tell their neighbours; the news would travel around the rest of town through the whispers of the maids. Her grandson was returning, Doctor Midhat, from Montpellier and also from Paris. They must have a ladies' reception to celebrate. The following day Um Jamil came upstairs to help prepare the food, calling from the doorstep that Jamil was so pleased, so pleased! The years of the war had aged Um Jamil, and her birdlike face was covered with wrinkles that fanned out from the corners of her eyes. She sang in Um Taher as they rolled the kusa and crushed the garlic, and then left the rest of the work to Um Mahmoud as the other women arrived, kissing congratulations and sweeping through to the salon.

"Twenty-four years old? He has plenty of time!" said Um Dawud. "Let him play a little," she clucked, jiggling her shoulders.

"Dalia," said Um Taher. "Midhat is a nice boy."

"Shu nice boy?" said Um Dawud.

Um Taher looked astonished. A second later, she abandoned her piety, hooting as wholeheartedly as she had played her virtue, just before drawing her embroidery closer to her failing eyes, her belly wobbling beneath it.

"Um Mahmoud!" she shouted. "Are you making more coffee?"

"Yes Mama," came the voice of Um Mahmoud.

"And we need more chocolate ba'dayn!"

"Is Taher excited?" asked Um Burhan.

"Of course," said Um Taher.

The women exchanged looks. It was good to see her happy, meskina Um Taher.

"What will he do? Will he be our doctor in Nablus?" said Um Dawud.

"He must help his father first," said Um Taher. "He is the eldest, though his father's wife has more children."

"Bas I think we can expect great things, ya Khalto," said Um Jamil. "Throw him into the sea and he will rise with a fish in his mouth."

Um Taher bowed her head, as if she already knew.

While Um Taher entertained her ladies in the salon on Mount Gerizim, Haj Taher went to visit the British military governor of Nablus, in the old limestone municipal building on Northern Street, which was until last year the headquarters of the Turkish high representative and his advisory council.

Taher greeted the guard in English. He was here to see Colonel John Hubbard please, he had a special request. Please to tell him it is his friend, Mister Haj Taher Kamal. The guard bowed and gestured that Haj Taher should enter, then disappeared around a corner. After a few moments, Hubbard called:

"Kamal, come on in. Good morning, how are you today? Take a seat."

Hubbard was dressed in a khaki uniform with a red collar. He had a youthful face, which had at first caused some dissension among the Nablus notables, who took it as an insult to be sent a foreign principal who had barely grown his first beard. On a closer look, however, one could see the fine lines over Hubbard's forehead and grey hairs at his temples and in his moustache. Haj Taher first met Hubbard at a reception to inaugurate his appointment, ostensibly a celebration but really an attempt to curry favour with the local men of influence by making them feel included in the affair. After Hubbard made his speech the room relaxed into smaller groups, and Taher found himself in a corner with the governor himself. Hubbard told Haj Taher that until recently he was stationed in Cairo, and the pair spoke of the different neighbourhoods, and when Taher described his business and his patronage of various ventures in the town, including the new high school and the municipal hospital, Hubbard seemed impressed. A few days later he turned up at the Kamal store in the khan. He took coffee with Haj Taher and before he left purchased a small cotton bag with a red lining as a gift for his wife.

"Good morning Colonel John, a fine morning. How do you do today?"

"I am very well Mister Kamal. And yourself?"

"I am quite well, thank you." Haj Taher bowed and showed the tassel on his tarbush. "I have travelled from Cairo for the trade, and I will be leaving soon for Damascus."

"Excellent. It's extremely hot, isn't it?"

"Yes, it is very hot."

"So. What can I help you with?" Hubbard rested his lips on steepled fingers.

"I have a question."

"Fire away."

Uncertain what this phrase meant, Taher paused for an additional cue. When Hubbard said nothing, he continued.

"Do you speak French?"

"Yes, I speak French. Some anyway, not a great deal."

"Would you please read this for me?"

He reached into his pocket, and standing up from his chair handed Hubbard the lilac envelope.

"Of course."

Hubbard pulled out a folded pair of wire spectacles from his pocket, swung them open, and peered down through the lenses.

"Monsieur—Mister—Midhat Kamal, Kamal Family Home, Nablus, Palestine."

He looked up at Taher, then turned the envelope over, pulled out the letter, and cleared his throat.

"Dear Midhat."

It has been now four years since you left us in Montpellier. Four years!—I cannot believe it even while I write it. I find myself thinking about you often. Thank you for your letter. To tell you the truth it causes me a certain distress to discover that you have been in Paris—the thought that we might have communicated before now. You may also wonder why I have not tried to write to you—the truth is that for a long time I was angry and in pain. And I suppose that above all else I was muddled.

"Embarrassed or confused, actually. Sort of jumbled up that means."

I am afraid this might not reach you before you leave, so I am sending it to Nablus—which means that you are reading this at home. I hope the journey was safe and enjoyable.

Oh—I wanted to write to you for so long—and now that I am here at last with a pen I don't know what to write—All the things I had thought to say are suddenly difficult to

"Exprimer, to express."

When you left, the warmth of the house followed after you. I think we had not noticed how much your presence was a source of delight and joy. I wish I had behaved differently—if we could recover ground that has already been lost. But you are right, it is nonsensical to try. I wish only that what has happened is not definitive.

I have the impression that I am writing into a void—it is strange not to know how you will feel when you read this. I wish I could see your face. Oh, Midhat. Sometimes I think I feel you in my breathing. This is difficult to bear.

The long years of this war have been a weight on all of us, and now they are over I want to ask you one last thing: will you come back? I know you have just arrived so I wouldn't expect you immediately, and I don't want to beg, I want only to tell you how much I am longing

"Stop!"

Haj Taher's face was red.

"It appears to be a love letter," said Hubbard, putting it down and raising his glasses to his head. "Who is Midhat?"

Taher did not answer. He inhaled, bowed, and said decorously as he rose and reached out for the letter, "Thank you, Mister Hubbard," and, turning, mumbled: "A great kindness."

Hubbard half stood from his own chair, and bade Haj Taher goodbye.

"Salaam." Hubbard pronounced the word to rhyme with "alarm."

"Salam," said Haj Taher. "Allah yabarak fik."

In Cairo, Layla's chauffeur was driving Midhat to the Bab al-Hadid station. From the car window Midhat watched the locals and foreigners walking separately, the clatter and babble of the traffic dulled by the heat.

"One ticket to Jerusalem, please," he said to the ticket attendant in the booth.

"No Jerusalem train today."

"What?"

"Delayed. The tracks are being fixed."

"Damn. When is the next one?"

"It is the same train, it is delayed," said the attendant. "It is leaving in the morning, at six o'clock Frankish time. A ticket is seven piastres."

Midhat sighed, and counted out the money.

"Ya mu'allim," he called to the chauffeur. "Take my bag, and meet me in the morning here at half past five. The morning, not the afternoon. Mashi?"

"Yes, ya haj."

"Haj!" repeated Midhat, sardonically. "Ya'tik al-afieh." He handed the driver a piastre and turned back to the ticket attendant. "Are there any good restaurants nearby for lunch? Ishi baseet, ya'ni, not too heavy."

The attendant leaned forward at his desk and looked Midhat up and down. Then he disappeared from the booth and reappeared from around a corner in the foyer. He beckoned Midhat, shielded his eyes against the sun, and directed him to the Ezbekiya Garden, which was surrounded by restaurants and hotels where efendi will surely find something to his satisfaction. Then he waited for his tip. In the sunlight, Midhat saw that a thin layer of dust covered the blue uniform and grouted the crevices of the outstretched hand.

The path through the garden channelled the wind. Midhat dawdled in the shade of the beefwoods and gum trees, inhaled the breath of flowers beside the banyan trunks trailing hair with hollows like open mouths; he passed the spindly rubber trees and the royal palms, and reaching out across the pathway, the weird dangling fruits of an African sausage tree beside their big, crude red petals. The thicket opened onto a lawn where a band was assembling. The musicians wore galabiyas but their stringed instruments looked imported, and the sound they produced was definitely not Egyptian; nonetheless on the grass before them a trio of bare-bellied ghawazi women in billowing trousers began to swing their pelvises and beckon passersby as if to a native melody. Next he passed an empty Japanese pagoda, then a gabled building with a timber and mortar facade that resembled a chalet but whose signpost indicated the YMCA "Soldiers' Recreation Club." European couples in broad hats and white trousers danced on a terrace. The sun fell between the trees and Midhat's despondence lifted as the long hours of the night ahead began to appear rich with possibility. What had been lost by the delayed train was far outweighed by the gains of an evening suddenly unaccounted for.

For the past week he had walked every day over the decks of the *Caucase*, the engine pulsing under his feet, bitter air curling off the spume and pricking his cheeks with salt. Each turn roused a memory of his fearful self on the outbound trip, nineteen years old, with a shaky grasp of European manners, and sore with isolation. From his new vantage of self-possession and social grace, he could look back at that young man and laugh. But the pleasure of these thoughts was only a brief respite from the real anxiety of returning to Palestine.

Although his old fantasies of becoming French had expired, he still clung to a particular idea of cosmopolitan life. These circular walks, therefore, from the stern around the hurricane deck to the prow and back, or below deck between the velvet salon and the galleried halls, were not only a time to congratulate himself on his recent maturity; they were also a time to prepare for what lay ahead. A new era of prudence was upon him, and there would be no more retiring at daybreak from nights abroad, no more brandy to numb doubt, no more eight o'clock uncertainty over where or what he would be in a few hours' time. Gossip travelled fast in Nablus. Recklessness brought shame on families. But perhaps he might negotiate with his father over his future and go to Jerusalem, or to one of those port towns already loosened by pilgrim routes, perhaps, indeed, to Cairo; or perhaps they could even work out a way for him to return to France. He might expand the business in a westerly direction, and travel there for French fabrics.

There were things to look forward to in Nablus: his cousins, his grand-mother, the family at the diwan. But there would also be boredom, and deference to views not his own. The hours on the ship were therefore a time to meditate on the notion of duty, and on his place in that constellation of purpose and tradition which had for the last five years in France been suspended, when with a freedom born of strangeness he had bypassed the laws of family and dallied in the alleyways of chance and rapture.

Beside him, always, lingered the shadow of Jeannette. There had been no reply to his letter, and he told himself not to expect one. The act of writing had settled his yearning for the interim, and so it was his father and Nablus, the Bride of the North, that occupied him as he stepped onto the Alexandrian shore. And again his father, as he climbed into the back of the caleche outside the station. And again his father, as on the dust road the great pyramids emerged with their colossal geometry to shadow the desert horizon.

Yet by some strange arrangement of Providence he had been favoured. For here he was, the train delayed, Nablus delayed. Here, alone in Cairo, granted one last night of freedom.

He arrived at a lake fringed with white lights, and circling it passed through a gate back onto the crowded street. Ahead a sign announced the Grand Continental, and beside it a stream of café awnings shaded a cross-legged clientele. He walked a little further to the place with a French name: Le Grand Café Egyptien.

Inside, his eyes took a moment to adjust. A room lit with oil lamps, and crammed with circular tables, around which the patrons sat facing a stage. He chose an empty table near the front.

"Steak-frites. Et un verre du vin, s'il vous plaît."

The waiter frowned and conferred with a colleague. The oil lamps dimmed and a woman walked downstage. Her eyes were lined with black, and her hairpiece and bodice were draped with coins that twisted on their strings and glinted. The flesh of her midriff hung out from under her bodice; she churned it around her hips. A line of men at the back of the stage began clapping castanets; the woman revolved a veil with her raised arms and a new line of attendant dancers appeared. They twirled and arched their backs behind her, and just as the musicians exchanged their castanets for other instruments—a qanun, a tambourine, a violin, a darabuka—the woman opened her mouth and began to sing.

Her voice had a hard vibrato; at times she sang a single note and the oscillations were so pronounced she seemed to dance between them. Her chin turned, a secret half smile. Midhat glanced around the room. Some of the audience were certainly European—the blonds were probably Englishmen, others could be Greek or perhaps Italian, some were obviously Levantines, and a great many were aristocratic Egyptians, wearing elaborate clothes. The dancer teased them, stroking the air. Midhat watched her catching the eyes of particular men, inspiring expressions of envy from the other men at their tables, or claps on the back, hollers, and whistles. Midhat craved to be one of those chosen. He kept very still and stared as the dancer turned away from the audience and displayed two beautiful dimples in the flesh of her lower back. And then she turned again, and at last she looked directly at Midhat. He felt, immediately, the rush of glee and arousal he knew was intended.

By the time he had finished his fourth glass of wine, a table of young Egyptian men invited him to join them. They asked him where he came from and his reply, "Paris," sent a laugh around the circle. After that, there was little time for conversation. Midhat found himself on his feet with one of the girls from the stage while the men behind him cheered. The girl smelled of jasmine flowers and red wine. Her long black plait was smooth to the touch.

In the morning, alone in the train carriage, he wrapped his scarf around his eyes and drifted in and out of sleep. A good outcome from a conversation with his father, he thought, would be a position at the Kamal store in Cairo. In Cairo one could be almost as anonymous as in Paris. The line with Europe was thin.

Just after noon the train arrived at Damascus Gate in Jerusalem, where he hailed a taxi and drove north. Valleys of white rock, the wooded plains of Ayn al-Haramiya, stone terraces spilling fields of wheat down mountainsides crowded with harvesters. The sight of the hills had a peculiar effect on him, and he stared out of the car window at the deep shadows they cast in an unexpected state of high emotion. Nablus came into view, banked by olive groves. White houses, round terraces, the onion globes of minarets. The car slowed up the mountain road. Midhat paid the driver, and stepping out of the back, inhaled wild sage.

"Habib alby!"

"Teta! Teta, my God you've shrunk."

"And you have grown. You are so pale, are you ill? Yalla teta, come inside."

"Is my father here?"

"Waiting for you."

Indoors, he smelled onion and sumac, and beyond that a specific odour like cold plaster and mould, which plucked at a part of his memory grown numb with inattention. A whole section of his brain stirred to life. The shape of the kitchen windows, the one cracked pane, that silver dish, he had not remembered it before but recognised it now. Layla's short Damascene tables, even they were full of something he could not formulate, and all the latticed light from the strong morning falling on the embroidery. The objects erupted with pastness.

A fire was going in the brazier. His eye fell on a familiar calligraphic panel opposite the window, and as he approached the divan he wondered about a welcome party, whether Um Jamil and Jamil from downstairs or a couple of the other neighbours. But there was no sign or sound of anyone. Then from around a corner stepped the upright form of his father, dressed in a suit and tarbush.

"Father."

"Welcome home."

Midhat reached out to embrace him, and at first Haj Taher did not respond. But as his arms were falling Taher made a small sign, as though against his will, and with a slight incline of his head and a long blink he granted permission. The embrace was brief and stiff.

"Hamdillah as-salameh. I hope the journey was fine. Now, I must talk to you about something."

"Of course."

"Sit down here. Good. Now. We have to discuss some things, we have to make some decisions as soon as possible." He paused, assessing Midhat. His fingers were interlaced and one thumb was kneading the back of the other hand, wrinkling up the skin around his forefinger. "First of all, I understand that a young man has a certain amount of freedom. Should have a certain amount of freedom. This is, ya'ni, this is normal. Nonetheless, my understanding has always been, Midhat, that you would spend these years in Europe while the Turks were at war, obtain a European education. And after that, my understanding has always been that you would return home to our region as a well-educated and experienced man, ready to continue on the same path as your forebears and your peers. A path of honour, fhimet? Honour and . . . stability."

Haj Taher was using an elevated mixture of classical language and dialect that was quite strange to Midhat's ears. He longed for a glass of water. His father continued.

"Il-mohim, you will not be returning to France. If you attempt to go back there, you will be cut off. No money, no support, nothing. You understand? I will not tolerate any shameful behaviour."

Midhat sat in a shocked silence. Then he said: "Baba."

"You appear to have rented out the upper floor of your brain."

"What have I done?"

"I only hope, I only hope that you have learned at least something about being an adult during these five years abroad. Which I have entirely paid for."

"Yes. I mean, I hope so." His voice dropped. "None is perfect but God alone, from whom we ask forgiveness and aid."

"Praise be to God. And, now that you are a grown man, we must make arrangements for your future. Of course ordinarily I would suggest taking at least a few years to gain some experience in your profession, before we make further plans. But I feel that in your case these decisions must be made earlier. You have had all this experience, we cannot keep you . . . uncertain. First, it is my duty to acknowledge that having now trained as a doctor in France, you should be free to practise medicine here, if you wish. However, since you are my only grown-up son, I also present to you the option of learning my trade. With a view to taking over the family business when I am dead, or at least infirm."

Midhat waited. The silence persisted, and he realised that his father was expecting an immediate decision.

"I . . ." He stopped. He did not know what to say. At most, he had been prepared for some new constraints over what he could and could not do in his leisure time; he was not expecting such an absolute confrontation with his future. He had always imagined his father's business might be his eventually. But this was happening much faster than he had anticipated. The facts of his future career were commandeering their very reunion, which his father barely seemed to have registered. The additional notion that he might actually practise as a doctor began to cause Midhat some pain, and he broke out:

"But why can't I go back to France?"

Haj Taher's ears reared. "If you go back to France," he said slowly, "you will lose your inheritance."

"But what about—what about—Cairo?"

"Midhat, this is not a time to play."

"I'm not asking to play!"

"You are a man, and I am offering you a choice. Would you like to practise as a doctor, or would you like to learn the family trade."

Midhat looked away. "I don't understand."

"Answer me. You have had your education."

"I—I would like to learn the family trade."

"Good. We will begin that immediately then. I will send you down to work with Hisham after the weekend. And then after a year you will come to Cairo and learn how to keep the books, and deal with the customers on Bulaq Street. But we'll talk about that later. Now, as I said, we are hurrying things along in your case, since you clearly have strong energies that need diverting. Unfortunately I must continue on to Damascus tomorrow. And then I will return to Cairo, where I will stay for at least three months, probably. Otherwise, of course, I would have taken the matter in hand myself. But given these circumstances, I am leaving your grandmother in charge of selecting a wife."

"A *wife*?"

"Yes Midhat, a wife." Taher sucked his teeth. "My heart goes out for my son like fire, and my son's heart goes out for me like stone. That is my fortune."

Everything in Midhat's body rose to protest. He gaped, mute. Silenced by dread of his father—and also by a new and imprecise sense of shame and failure that was now rising and heating his ears.

Haj Taher stood up. Midhat, standing also, saw his grandmother in the corner of his eye. Taher left the room and Teta strode over, pulled Midhat back down beside her on the couch, and wrapped her arms around him. She smelled of olive soap.

"Everything forbidden is desired, ya sitti."

"I don't understand, Teta."

"He thinks you had too much freedom. But what can we do, there was a war."

"I don't understand. I haven't done anything wrong."

"You are tired. Sleep and bathe. Um Jamil is looking forward to seeing you. She will come up in a few hours, after you've had a rest."

Midhat pushed his way out of his grandmother's arms, though she was not resisting, and entering his old bedroom lay down immediately on the bed. He felt nothing at all, being in this room. At the sight of that old window, where he used to sit as a child: nothing. All his reactions were spent, darkened by his father's voice, which echoed in his mind, cutting him. What a fantasy to have expected any warmth, any show of pride, of care. Doors were slamming that he had not known were open; he knew not what lay beyond them, that he might have seen. Uncontrollable sense-memories of Montpellier started to fill his mind, seeping out of corners. A treacherous yearning uncoiled, it broke loose from Faruq's lessons in romantic narrative; it was ugly and incoherent, and it hurt. His head burned. He squeezed his wet eyes shut and thought of that house, every inch of it intimate; he thought of his first walk in the gardens with Laurent. How absurd it was that a single afternoon in which very little occurred should feel more vital to him now even than his homecoming, to the family not seen in five years, to the bed he slept in as a boy. How senseless, what a strain to his rational mind, to long this badly for a time that had in the end been so poor in pleasure, and so rich in pain.

4

"So, who will it be?" said Jamil.

"Who will what be," said Midhat.

Someone was having an argument outside the khan. Midhat craned his neck to peer between the hanging bolts of fabric but saw only the backs of people's heads.

"Your wife," said Jamil. "Who will she be? I mean, do you know yet."

"Oh. No idea. What's going on out there?"

"It's always like that. You'll probably have quite a good view working here every day."

Midhat stepped over the threshold of the Kamal store. On the edge of the square by al-Manara clock tower, a British soldier was gesticulating at the driver of a vegetable cart, encircled by a crowd of spectators. Midhat could only see the soldier's back: he wore a domed hat and a sand-coloured uniform with short trousers cut off at the knee. His lower legs were wrapped with a kind of bandage, a rifle was strapped over one arm, and he was waving a book in the air. The face of the driver, being elevated, was on display, and conducting the reactions of the crowd: irritation, amusement, exasperation. A third man spoke, another Nabulsi, standing on the far side of the cart.

"Bas ehkeelu," he shouted to the driver. "The tomatoes. Adaysh andak?"

"I didn't count the tomatoes. Why would I count the tomatoes? Hemar."

"Why is he not cooperating?"

"He . . . says . . . he did not count the tomatoes."

"God in heaven. Can you ask about the aubergines."

"What is aubergine?"

"This, that one."

"Adaysh andak betinjan, ya mu'allim."

"Adaysh andi betinjan? Hemar. B'arifish."

"He says he doesn't know."

"Fuck's *sake*. Wilson! Can you come here please, they're driving me up the wall."

"Yes sir, how can I help."

"Any luck with the others?"

"Got a list here."

"Good. Having trouble with this one—no, I'm not finished with you yet! Do not leave. Tell him not to leave please, we haven't finished with him."

"He says he needs to go the mosque now, sir."

"I don't care, we've not finished with him."

"Sir," said Wilson. "Sir it might be best to leave it now. They like to cause a ruckus. I've seen that one before."

The cart driver widened his eyes at the crowd and made a long face. It struck Midhat that perhaps he was only pretending not to understand English.

"What's his name," said the first soldier to the dragoman. "I'm writing it down."

"His name?"

"Yes, what is the name."

"His name is . . ."

"What is the name. Come on."

"Al-Harami!" shouted someone from the crowd.

"His name is al-Harami."

There was general laughter. The soldiers turned and marched out of the square, passing by the Kamal store where Midhat was standing. They both held notebooks, and the first soldier, whose badges suggested a higher rank, had a thick black moustache and spectacles. His cheeks were so highly coloured he appeared to be sunburnt.

"Who was that?" asked Midhat, as the crowd disintegrated.

"The driver? Abu Amin. Hilarious."

"No, the British."

"Oh, they're always making an inventory of things. They can't handle the Jews, so they handle the vegetables instead. Hang on, you haven't finished telling me about the French woman."

"You mean Jeannette? Well, to be honest with you, I really wanted to marry her. But I was young, I didn't know what I was doing." He fell silent.

"In the end, family is everything," said Jamil, with some unexpected tenderness. "We all owe our parents. You've really become a majnun though, haven't you ya zalameh, since you left?"

Midhat laughed. "Ya Allah I hope not. Tell me, what's the situation with the army?"

"Not good. Though, recently—look, do you have to stay here? Could we go to Sheikh Qassem?"

"Wait. Hisham?"

From the back of the stall, Hisham emerged with his arms extended, stretching between them a length of red fabric fringed with tassels.

"Yes, Midhat Bey?"

Midhat hesitated. "We are going to the café, Hisham."

Hisham blinked, eyed Jamil, and released a formless noise from his lips. "I will not be too long, I promise."

"Inshallah. Inshallah." Hisham bowed, the tassels shook.

Café Sheikh Qassem was the most popular café in Nablus and could be relied upon for company at all hours. Against the high, pale green walls a skyline of masculine heads was always visible, wafting clouds of nargileh smoke into the air, frantic with the commerce of voices. As Midhat followed Jamil over the threshold, a babble of voices reached their ears beneath the theme of a single baritone, and in a moment they saw some thirty or forty men, young and old, clustered around a table at the back. In the light of the nearby windows a newspaper was being read aloud.

"Thousands upon thousands have been demonstrating in the centre of Damascus, crying out slogans for war against the French. Rumours are already circulating that the Emir Faisal has struck a deal with Clemenceau . . ."

A young man, leaning over the back of a chair and tapping his toe on the floor behind him, caught sight of them and stood straight.

"Midhat Kamal!" It was Tahsin Kamal, one of Midhat's cousins. He pulled Midhat into an embrace. Behind him, another cousin, Wasfi, who had been at university in England; and Qais Karak and Adel Jawhari, famous best friends who had developed beards and broad chests since he saw them last; and there was young Burhan Hammad, youngest son of Haj Nimr, who couldn't be older than fourteen or fifteen but was already the tallest of the group, with a long neck and narrow face. And on the far side, lining up to greet him were two brothers from the Murad family, second or third cousins of Hani's: Basil and Munir.

Midhat's name spread through the crowd, and more faces turned, more people stood up to see him.

"Habibi Midhat, Midhat Bey."

In the light from the window, the baritone reader of the newspaper also rose to his feet. It took a moment for Midhat to recognise him, for he had also changed a great deal. It was Haj Abdallah Atwan, a lesser patriarch of the Atwan family, and owner of the Atwan soap factory.

There were several ways to map the social fabric of Nablus. Some described the city in terms of East and West, as two separate worlds that only ever met in the arcade of the textile market during popular festivals, when the young men of the opposing sides would stage play-fights, and draw off the tensions that had built up during the season. Some ascribed this rivalry to the ancient opposition of the Qaysi and Yemeni clans, dating from the early Islamic settlement of the land of Can'aan. That ancient opposition centred now on the specific rivalries between the Atwan, Omar, and Murad families, which had reached their apex during the civil war of the last century. Others would shrug and say it was a natural division of geography, the East stays with the East, and the West with the West; yet others would say the two sides possessed two different cultures, and that was the root of the division. For example, the people of the East ate their kunafe in a sandwich for breakfast, between two slices of bread, whereas the people of the West ate their kunafe as a dessert after lunch. Thus, the East-West rivalry was simply a natural polarity of appetite and custom.

In fact the city had not always been divided thus. But as wealth developed in Nablus at the turn of the century, and trade routes strengthened between Egypt, Damascus, and Beirut, the major families were bloated into different factions, and a variety of alliances were formed. These alignments were most often built on inherited stories of infighting, which, if they were recent, were claimed to be ancient, and used to buttress a current action. And if an Omar wished to do wrong by an Atwan and found no pretext at hand, he could always reach back to the campfire of his Yemeni ancestors and pull up some ancient tale.

And as the city developed its industries of soap and textiles, this became a common occurrence: the leisure time of the new capitalists expanded as their working hours decreased, and gossip started its ruinous motor into the salons of the wealthy. With such wealth came unhappiness, and with unhappiness intrigue, and the circulation of bitter jokes, and the women who had been free to cut wheat in the fields and carry olives in their aprons were locked at last in their homes, to grow fat among cushions and divert their vigour into childbirth and playing music, and siphon what remained into promulgating rumours about their rivals.

Abdallah Atwan was a pale-skinned man with thin hair and thick grooves either side of his mouth that made him seem older than his years, which could not number more than forty-five. He was renowned for his fondness for recalling the civil war between the Atwans and the Omars, and for reciting the litany of names of those who had committed crimes, and the names of their victims.

One tier below the landowning families were the ulema, scholarly families like the Hammads, who had begun to dominate politics as well. And below them were the newly rich mercantile families, who encroached now on the hard-won territory of those political ulema. There were mixed feelings towards this new set, the Kamal family among them, who were in the ascendant, attending the same parties, participating in the same conferences, and marrying their women.

A man might, of course, form a friendship in defiance of history. A man might lay history aside when kneeling on the floor of the Green Mosque. But Abdallah Atwan was not such a man. As he now put down his newspaper, less on account of Midhat than the disruption his entrance had caused to his rapt audience, Abdallah Atwan's demeanour, reaching across to shake Midhat's hand, was full of the ancient intersections of society and their forefathers.

"Hamdillah as-salameh," he said.

"Allah yisalmak," said Midhat.

"Your father's business is doing well," said Abdallah.

"You are a European," said Burhan Hammad. "Look at you."

It was true that without thinking much of it, that morning Midhat had pulled on his pinstriped suit from the Rue Royale, and walked into town with his steel-topped cane. He looked over at the local suits of the rest of the company, their ties sewn by the village women. He produced a pack of cigarettes from his jacket and offered one to Burhan. Though young, Burhan already flaunted a fashionable waxed moustache. He examined Midhat's suit admiringly.

"Yalla Midhat!" shouted Qais Karak. "All the characters are home at last."

"Keef I am European?" asked Midhat, once both cigarettes were lit.

"The way you hold yourself." Burhan laughed out his smoke.

Midhat sat at a table in the centre of the atrium, and a new circle formed around him as Jamil ordered coffee, and the young boys prodded Midhat for stories.

"What can I tell you?" said Midhat.

"Tell us about the women," said Tahsin.

All these men and boys, five years grown, had an alternative narrative of Midhat. Even from these few minutes' intercourse, they surely saw aspects of him invisible to those he had met in France. At the sense of exposure Midhat grew hot. He could not conceal, nor even detect, the survival of his child-self in his mannerisms, or traces of his characteristics as they had been popularly understood. A childish predilection for certain sweets, or certain games—the kinds of facts that were enlarged as personalities in Nablus were distilled into characters painted simply, so they could be picked out from a rooftop and fitted into stories. Midhat wished he could isolate those traces and remove them. Not because they were defects, but because they pinned him down.

Already it was clear from their amused expressions that the men around Midhat found him strange. And perhaps they had reason: to Midhat, this taste of coffee recalled the Seine, the bright window recalled chandeliers and women's faces.

"Midhat was just telling me about a love affair he had in Paris," said Jamil.

Midhat stared at his cousin. Jamil smiled back.

"It was not in Paris, Jamil."

"You said it was in Paris."

"No . . . I . . . in Paris there was . . ."

"Tell us, Midhat!" said Tahsin.

Midhat began to fabricate a composite woman made up of the features of a few he had regularly slept with. Maria with the canvas spats, Nicole with the red hair—he erased the odours of their bodies and sprayed them with violet, mixed their narratives with the plots of certain famous ballads, until someone cried out:

"I don't believe you."

Midhat chuckled, and they all slapped their knees. "Ça y est!" he said. Jamil watched with silent laughter. It struck Midhat that he should ask Jamil about his own adventures in Constantinople. His cousin had grown into a handsome man, with the regular features of a figurine—two straight dashes for eyebrows, a curl to his lip, an aquiline nose—and his chest was as broad as an officer's, his shoulders peaked with ganglions of bone as though his suit were sewn with the epaulettes of battle. Such a bella figura, he must have a score of conquests.

"Will you get involved in politics, Midhat?" asked Wasfi Kamal.

"I am already involved," said Midhat.

"Really?" said Jamil, knocking him on the shoulder with the back of his hand.

"In Paris, of course, there were a number of political activities. Discussions, conferences. Many people there in exile. Al-Fatat—"

"You're a member of Al-Fatat?" said Wasfi.

"No I wasn't a member. But my good friend Hani Murad was one of the original founders, ya'ni, and he writes to me sometimes. He is the emir's secretary at the Conference."

"Oh, very nice. Very impressive," said Wasfi.

At that piece of news, Abdallah Atwan spoke up for the first time since the group had relocated to their new table.

"And what is the news, then, if you are so well connected? Has Faisal made a deal with the French or not? Will Syria be independent? I should think Hani Murad has told you the latest, unless you are exaggerating your friendship."

"Calm down Amo, give him a chance," said Qais Karak.

"It's fine," said Midhat. "Well, the general picture from Hani's letter—"

"So there's only one letter."

"—was that the French and the British have already made their deals. That's what the British man Lawrence has been saying. So it was either . . . well, he had to make a deal with the French, or suffer their armies."

"I knew it," said Munir Murad.

"He's already made a deal?" said Wasfi. "Ya Allah, this is precisely the worst that could have happened."

Bodies bent away from the table at the impact, but Munir Murad bent even further towards Midhat.

"And Palestine? Did he say anything about Faisal's position on Zionism? The newspapers say nothing, only 'rumours are circulating,' blah blah blah."

Abdallah knocked his head back in displeasure and crackled the broadsheet in half, as though he were not only a subscriber to the paper but had written it himself.

"No," said Midhat, "he didn't say. My feeling is that Palestine should be part of Syria, because unity is stronger than independence."

This was not what he had consistently argued in Paris. But the tenor of the questioning suggested that it would be an opinion favourable to Nabulsi ears. And the refrain, "unity is stronger than independence," had been sounded out frequently in Faruq's apartment and was easy to parrot.

"Habibi, of course we should be part of Syria," said Munir Murad. "Remember you're in Nablus. That's not a feeling, that's a fact. All the oldies in Jerusalem who say otherwise, they're only worried about their tarabish. Pathetic. Who is more likely to knock off your tarbush, Emir Faisal or Lloyd George?"

"And what about you," said Midhat. "Are you all involved in politics?"

Munir and Basil Murad exchanged glances. Munir cocked his head.

"We are members of Al-Fida'iya, the Self Sacrifice Society."

Now it was Qais Karak and Adel Jawhari's turn to exchange a glance, and Adel rolled his eyes.

"What is that?" said Midhat. "I haven't heard of it."

"It's new," said Basil.

"It's a Jaffa society," said Tahsin Kamal.

"Yeah, well now it's a Nablus society too," said Basil.

"They work with the fellahin," said Burhan.

"Are you an authority on the subject?" said Basil.

"Basil, come on," said Qais Karak.

"Really? Like farm work?" said Midhat.

Jamil kicked Midhat under the table.

"No," said Munir. "We want to enlist the whole of Palestine."

"They have to take an oath that if someone is a traitor, then that person should be killed. Even if he is your own friend," said Tahsin, breathlessly.

Burhan Hammad clamped his teeth together and widened his eyes.

"Tahsin," said Munir. But he did not protest. If anything, he sat up a little straighter at the description.

"The problem with these societies," said Adel Jawhari, "is that they want money. And because Nablus is the richest city, we end up paying, and no one else does their share."

"I'm not sure that's true, Adel."

"It is," said Adel. "These societies are meant to be countrywide, but not everyone does their bit. As usual we have the most qawmiyyeh, and the others . . . I mean, the societies send petitions, they buy arms, I mean, little pistols, not exactly German rifles. Not that German rifles did the Turks much good, but the British have a ton of stuff and we've got nothing."

"As long as the Jews don't have anything, it doesn't matter if we don't have anything either. Fair is fair," said Tahsin Kamal.

"Fair is fair? Are you out of your mind?" said Munir Murad. "The Jews in England, do you know how much money they have? They have an empire. They've started colonizing here, they're messing with the peasants in the north, *that's* why there's no money—it's all going to the Jews. You can say it's the war, but the war has been over for more than a year now, and what has changed?"

Now, Abdallah Atwan took the reins.

"We must resist all of the Jews," he said. "Even our own Jews, the ones we have here."

"We only have about ten Jews in Nablus," said someone, "and they're Arabs."

"What about the Samaritans," said someone else.

"The Samaritans aren't Jews," said a third.

"Yes they are," said Abdallah.

The truth was that very few of the men sitting in Sheikh Qassem that day had ever met a European Jew. The Yishuv settlements were mostly quite far from Jabal Nablus, and as a result their only conception of European Jewish men and women was based on those devout incumbents of Jerusalem who were not even Zionists, and on the Samaritan Nabulsis, who claimed to be the original Israelites, and considered Mount Gerizim the sacred summit upon which Ibrahim was called to sacrifice his son.

But Abdallah Atwan's rage was general and his prejudice limitless. He was capable of seizing the hot zeal of indignation and, through a few words that reasserted his wisdom as an elder, impressing upon it the shape of tribal fury, that cared not for such subtle distinctions as those that existed between Jew and Jew.

When they left Sheikh Qassem it was already five o'clock, and darkness was beginning to rouse the evening winds that collected in the valley. Midhat raced back to the khan with numb cheeks. He reached the corner of the shop, and although the tailor's office was shut for the night he could see the glow from Hisham's oil lamp on the counter. He prepared an expression of friendly nonchalance, which he had honed for the craft of discarding vexed women. It was a technique based on the insight that an injured party will most likely forget the wrong done them if you pretended it had never happened, or that it was a trifling mistake

"Hisham, ya Amo! It was difficult to tear myself away," he said, stepping inside. "I was in a conversation with young Salim something or other, he was thinking of purchasing from us the fabric for his daughter's kiswa, it would be a big order, he said. Anyway, we were discussing for a long time outside Sheikh Qassem, and . . . he might come by tomorrow. Then again, perhaps he was only saying he wanted to purchase because he had not seen me in so long." He shrugged with mock humility. "But I guess that is the problem with being new in town, everyone is especially polite to you. Don't worry, I will soon become old news."

Hisham narrowed his eyes. "Salim who? I don't know of a Bint Salim getting married any time soon."

"Oh, they are from the East of Nablus." Midhat waved his hand. "You wouldn't know them."

Hisham nodded. "Tayyeb." Gently, he closed the accounts book. "You can go home now. It's late."

5

"Now Fatima," said Widad Hammad, on the way to the hammam, "Um Taher Kamal has invited us for coffee this afternoon."

Fatima and Nuzha walked a step behind their mother. Three figures in black muslin; the shortest, Nuzha, carrying a basket.

"Who, Mama?" said Nuzha.

"Not you. Just Fatima."

Fatima did not reply. Outside the storefront ahead, a group of men sat around a nargileh pipe in silence. The one holding the mouthpiece leaned back as they approached. Smoke furled up his face from the crack of his mouth. Widad, Fatima, and Nuzha marched, and the tacks in their heels sounded on the hard ground. They rounded the corner and Widad continued:

"Um Dawud says this Kamal lady has not stopped talking about her grandson since he returned. My grandson did this, my grandson lived in Paris. Hala' no, this way habibti. She will certainly ask you to marry him Fatima, so there is no need for your sister to come. Haram, Nuzha. It's pointless anyway because Fatima is going to marry Yasser."

"But Mama."

"We are not talking about this now."

The road narrowed as they passed the Yasmineh Quarter and came upon the khan. It was that hour after the midday prayer when the market was quiet, and shopkeepers rotated fruits in their crates to hide mould, or sat and chatted on chairs outside their stalls, watching children roll balls between the arches. Ahead, the clock tower; to the right, the Nasr mosque. The three black figures turned past the mosque and through a stone entrance into the hammam.

Widad took her daughters to the baths once a week. It was important for the health of the physical body, but even more important for a healthy social body, because aside from the istiqbalat held in private homes a hammam was a place for ladies to talk. It also gave one a chance to inspect the other daughters of the town for one's sons: at an istiqbal a girl would be covered in velvet and embroidered lace or whatever drapery best displayed her twin virtues of wealth and taste, as much as she had them—but here, unclothed in the steam, one could observe what nature had given her.

"Who is Kamal?" said Nuzha.

"Give me the towels, habibti."

Their mother led them into the darkness of the vestibule, and they removed their veils as she paid the attendant. In the first room they unbuttoned their gowns and pulled on striped wizra robes and wooden clogs, and in the second room the other bathers congregated in groups, glossy as creatures of the sea, clouded with steam. Widad ululated at her friends. Pretending to keep her gaze to the ground, Fatima transferred her eyes to where the women entered the private khulwa washrooms. She liked to watch as they dropped their robes. Don't stare, her mother always told her. How could one not stare? Displayed before her, the anatomies of all the ladies from town. Flesh shining with water and sweat, dimpled and variegated in the coloured light from the roof. She liked the backs of older women the most, the way the fat draped down over the hips in thick rolls like layers of cream.

Fatima followed Nuzha into a khulwa. She looked down at the stammer of her heart pushing her chest up down, up down, as the arms of the gown fell off her shoulders, and then she peered down at her feet, already wrinkled around the heel, the base flushed with walking, the black debris of stockings caught in the sweaty clefts between her toes. The only thing Fatima's mother ever told her about her body was that she must scrub it. Or be scrubbed, as the maids released the scrolls of dead skin in a froth of olive oil soap, leaving limbs and belly and back soft red with attrition. And that was it, the job was done, and they would leave the hammam into the dry air without another word said about it. When Fatima changed clothes at home she did so at speed and without much thought for the body she was covering and uncovering, but here at the hammam, where the hot dark rooms carried a religious charge, where the light from the tinted circles in the roof caught on the mist, and the slow women striped in wizra gossiped on benches around the walls, inhaling vapour as they picked at watermelon and cheese brought by the maids on cane trays—here Fatima looked down at her own naked legs with interest. Blue veins spread from her groin down her thighs. The blood pulsed in her feet.

Two maids dipped luffas in a copper basin. The water clicked in the walls, the marble floor blared heat. The sisters sat on the benches in the khulwa, and Nuzha's breasts swayed as she leaned forward. She was only fifteen but her breasts were already larger than Fatima's, though Fatima's were rounder. Fatima's veins dipped away from the surface, and her ribs showed through the skin, and below that her belly curved, the lacuna in the middle broad and deep as though the cord that once tied her to her mother was unusually thick. Her sister was wider in the hip, but otherwise their bodies were quite similar. It was in the tangle of hair below that lay the strangest accident of biology, and Fatima had never seen her sister's to compare. Another mouth hidden under there, ugly and red. Not only was that where the blood came from but other secretions appeared there also, or began there and spread elsewhere: briny odours, strange nocturnal aches that shuddered up her limbs. This body, with its hectic motions and sensations, was the central mystery of her life. Sweat crept down her forehead. She leaned forward for the maid to scrub her back, and one bead sped down the side of her nose.

Her mother was near the doorway, speaking to someone in her social voice. "Hakayt ma'a Um Hashim imbarrih." Fatima abhorred those false undulations. She thought they sounded servile. "An jad? Is that so?"

"Turn please, ya sitti," said the maid.

"Ma'roof," said Widad.

Nabulsi women were always proclaiming something was "ma'roof," that it was known. Out on the mountain road every house was visible, and it was a platitude that anyone who needed directions could be shown the spot from a neighbour's rooftop, though such a thing seemed unlikely ever to have happened, for who would ask who did not already know? Fatima's mother used the word interchangeably with "of course," so perhaps it had more to do with the way women related to one another, each as keen as the next to assert how much she knew.

Fatima's curiosity about the Kamal family was piqued. She had met Um Taher once at an istiqbal, but the little else she knew was based on details her brother Burhan brought home from Café Sheikh Qassem one evening two weeks ago. A man named Midhat Kamal had returned to Nablus from France, and was working in his father's shop in the khan. He had been involved in politics. And he wore beautiful clothes, and was very handsome. And he had had a lover in Paris, she was called Pauline—but at this point their mother had scolded Burhan for indecency and smacked the back of his hand.

Fatima and Nuzha rinsed, and wrapped again in their stripes returned to the main room for refreshments. Trays of food were laid out beside the fountain, and nargileh pipes set up along the walls, coiled around their cylinders. Their mother made a space for two on the bench beside her. When the girls were younger they always competed over food. Rather than trying to eat the most and most quickly, as one might in a household of need, the sisters had competed over who could eat the slowest, and leave the most food until last, because to consume was no longer to have, and she who had the most on her plate was king. Fatima watched Nuzha deliver a square of watermelon to her lips. Her teeth crushed the fruit, her lips glistened.

"I heard they are making their own soap, now," said someone to their mother on the other side.

"Ma'roof," said Widad.

Another woman was holding forth on a more interesting topic. "And she was so angry she said I won't sleep with you, I want a divorce, so, ya'ni, she went on strike, she wouldn't sleep in the bed, she moved to the floor of the bathroom, she said I will sit here in the bathroom until you divorce me. And she took in her blankets, ya'ni, and flowers, and she made it nice in there. And khalas she came back one day and he had gone in there and was sleeping on the floor where she put all her nice things, and she says shu sar? He says you made it so nice in here I want to sleep in the bathroom too."

The women leaned back into their laughter.

Fatima's fingers were wrinkled when they left the hammam. She and her mother walked Nuzha home, and then continued up to the Kamal house on Mount Gerizim. Her muslins were soft on her skin and the wind pushed the fabric against her mouth, so that as she exhaled the moisture warmed her whole face.

A maid answered the door; Widad addressed her as Um Mahmoud. Um Mahmoud led them to the reception room, where they sat beside each other on the sofa, and the wind rattled the window.

"As-salamu alaykum," said Um Taher in the doorway with a smile. Her red dress was stitched with black and her thin grey hair pulled back into a chignon. She had a round face and colourful lips.

"Wa alaykum as-salam," said Widad, rising to remove her veil. Fatima copied her.

"Mashallah, Fatima," said Um Taher. "You are much taller than when I saw you last."

They sat and Um Taher and Widad discussed the guests at a recent wedding in the town. Beside Fatima, on the windowsill, a fly was struggling on its back. Now it paused, tiny black legs kinked. Now it scrambled, fluttering its limbs.

"The girl has a beautiful singing voice," said her mother.

"Mashallah," said Um Taher.

"Fatima, would you sing?" said Widad.

"She doesn't have to if she doesn't want," said Um Taher. "Another time. Perhaps at the Atwan istiqbal. And you play the oud?"

"Of course." Fatima's voice croaked; she cleared it.

"She is very talented with the oud."

Um Taher said, "Oud is very good for the soul, ya'ni . . . it can be a relief for—especially for women. I mean, for God. You hear about this . . . God keep us all in his mercy." There was a long pause. Um Taher gave them another breathy smile. "Would you ladies excuse me, just one moment."

Although Um Taher was clearly advanced in years, her manner was not of the elderly. She moved slowly, but she was not frail. Her wrists were thick and strong, but not peasant-like; her skin was pale and her eyes were penetrating. As the door closed, Fatima's mother wriggled in her seat and sighed. She put a hand on Fatima's leg, as if to reassure her.

Beyond the window, two large black birds stood on the stone garden wall with scraps of something hanging from their mouths. One bent over to eat while the other remained on guard, and its down flashed indigo as it waddled along the wall, and then with a flourish of wings, hopped onto the gatepost and began to feast on its scrap. The pair flapped back and forth for a while, then abruptly departed, mounting the air and crying out. All at once, the limestone walls were marred with long white slashes.

"Look," said Fatima. "The birds left kaka all over their wall."

Her mother gasped. Fatima realised it must be some kind of omen. Widad hesitated, as if choosing how to react. She slapped Fatima's hand. "Fatima that is disgusting."

Fatima looked out again at the white slashes, and wondered if it was true that Um Taher was inspecting her for her grandson. She had not asked to hear her singing. Why, if her mother did not support the match, had she even brought her here? In an instant she recognised the path of her mother's logic. Her mother was showing her off, regardless that she was not on offer. She felt very aware of her face, and a little depressed. She asked:

"What was it she was saying, Mama, about God and the oud?"

"Not about God. About the wife of Haj Hassan, Yasser's mother. Unhappy for years, she was. She became fanatical."

"Nazeeha?"

"Yes. Hassan was gone too many years. When he came back she had . . . khalas, we shouldn't talk about it."

"Fine."

"Well, he gave her the oud. Hassan did. He made her play it, because she was seeing things. This Nazeeha, she was always religious, you know, she was seeing this and that every day. But it became more and more, and prayer was not enough to get rid of the religion in her. But the music worked. She became very good at the oud. Beautiful voice. She used to sing the Egyptian folk songs about Harun ar-Rashid with all the trills. But we shouldn't talk about it." A moment passed, and she added: "She is a *very* nice lady. She will make a good mother-in-law for you."

"Where did she go?" said Fatima.

"Zawata."

"No, I mean Madame Kamal."

Widad tapped her on the knee. "Shh."

Widad was correct about Um Taher's intentions: the moment their hostess closed the door, she had rushed along the corridor to find Midhat. Midhat was sitting on his bed with an open book on his raised knees.

"Quickly," she hissed. "We don't have much time."

Midhat followed her into the hall. She held a hand behind her to grip his wrist, and paused after each footstep. At the closed door of the sitting room, she pointed to the handle. He reached out.

"Hemar!" she hissed, and grabbed his wrist again. "Don't open the door, are you insane! Look through the keyhole. Quickly. Get on the floor."

Midhat tried not to laugh. He crouched on his heels and began to brush some of the dirt on the floor away with his fingers. His grandmother hit him on the back of the head. He looked up, incredulous; she widened her eyes and jabbed a finger at the keyhole.

The keyhole was not easy to peer through. It had not, as far as he could remember, ever actually been fitted with a key, and it had so clogged up with dust over the years that barely a crack of light came through, and it exuded the cold greenish odour of unpolished metal. He blew at it, to no effect. Above him, Teta produced a napkin from her pocket, twisted a pinch of the fabric between her fingers, sucked on the protrusion, and handed it down. Midhat inserted it into the keyhole and removed it to find the napkin twist grey with dust. He leaned his face against the door. Teta steadied the handle.

Two women sat on the couch on the far side. A mother and a daughter. The mother's hair was hennaed red-black, cropped close to her ears, and pinned back in waves like the Europeans. She wore a dark brown dress with a red-and-green bodice, and she had a sharp nose and a large bosom. The daughter was young, maybe seventeen, slight and pale, with dark hair parted in the middle showing a dash of pale scalp. Her eyes sloped down at the outer corners, and this she had accentuated with two lines of black kohl on her upper lids. Her cheekbones were round and prominent and seemed to elevate the edges of her lips, so that despite her sad angled eyes her mouth was taut with expressiveness. Midhat had never seen an unmarried Nabulsiyyeh of his own class without a veil before. He knew only the maids, and the women of his grandmother's generation. At best, the dancers in Cairo, Layla. This was an extraordinary view. It was like peering down a microscope at the secret structure of a cell. Above him, Teta sighed. The girl in the keyhole looked solemn, hands folded in her lap. The mother fidgeted. That was what they said: if you want to know how will the daughter turn out, look to the mother. In this case, however, the girl must take after her father, because there was no resemblance to the mother at all.

Again Teta sighed. But just as he was drawing away to ask about the father, the girl in the keyhole laughed. Though muffled by the door it was a deep laugh, and her whole body rocked. She was pointing at something outside the window, raising her arm from the shoulder like a little girl unused to the size of her limbs, and all at once her sad sloping face was changed totally, relieved of gravity by sudden joy. The mother snapped and batted a hand.

Then something odd happened. For one peculiar second, the girl turned her head and looked directly at Midhat. A straight gaze like an arrow aimed at the keyhole, those two sad eyes very large and very black. Midhat jerked away from the door.

"Tamam?" Teta whispered.

He took a moment. He nodded to his feet, rubbing his knees.

"Yalla, go," said Teta.

Tiptoeing into the kitchen he heard his grandmother announce: "I'm sorry I was so long." The door shut on her voice. "Maids! They drive you crazy, maids."

He walked to the bedroom, resumed his position on the bed, and opened his book. The words crawled over the pages. He did not know how much time had passed before Teta entered the room and sat by his feet. She was a little red in the face.

"So." She fixed him. "What did you think, habibi?"

"I think she is beautiful."

"Beautiful enough? Um Dawud told me her mother wants her to marry their cousin, Yasser Hammad. It's not the end, they aren't engaged. We can still do something. I have a few ideas."

"Who is her father?"

"Haj Nimr. A scholar, and the mayor last year. They have land in Zawata. He is one of the hospital founders, like your father. And she is beautiful. Very beautiful. Queen of Nablus, they call her. They say she is a little proud, but . . . I think she is an excellent match. I think her mother is . . . ya'ni, it's a good family. But, you know, I can't do this to every Nabulsiyyeh, invite her mother for coffee and put you by the keyhole. Habibi don't look so sour."

"You really think I can marry into the Hammad family?"

"Kamal is a good family, Midhat."

"Teta . . ."

"Your father's trade is doing well. I don't see why you can't marry who you like, you are a rich trader—or you will be. We can do it. You want us to try? You want to marry this one?"

"Teta."

"I'm just trying to make the best choice for you. This Fatima is very beautiful, and she plays the oud very well."

"But how do I . . . I can't marry someone I don't know."

"How would you know a woman before you married her? Ya sitti, you marry, then you get to know the girl. Hala' just think about it. If you want to marry her, we'll try to make arrangements."

"I will think about it."

"Baba says you will marry this year. It's this girl, or we pick someone else for you. There are plenty of Kamal girls of marrying age. And you, you are very, ya'ni, very desirable. You are a doctor, you are handsome, you are rich. I think we can be ambitious."

Midhat had been in Nablus for three weeks now. At night he had at first tried to will himself into unconsciousness, before he realised that whole hours could pass while he was still locked in the tedious purgatory between sleep and waking. Sometimes he lit a paraffin lamp, opened a book, and muttered French verses to himself like incantations. And there were other tricks, such as pretending to himself he was only temporarily shutting his eyes and would continue reading shortly, and at times this worked and he duped his mind into sleep with the pages of his book resting on each cheek, and when he woke found the leaves sadly crumpled and the gas lamp flame guttering beside him. But more often, even if his brain slipped into the first zone of unconsciousness, that soft membrane in which sounds were muffled and his breathing slowed—some rogue thought could easily drift into his ear and set his heart going again, and all at once he would be drearily awake. A thought of Jeannette reading his letter; an imagined expression of sorrow, or regret. At these times he yearned for a whisky. He might rise from the mattress and walk around the room, and if the sky was clear, observe the pockmarked face of the moon between the thick walls of his window. Sometimes he caught dawn blanching the peak of Jabal al-Sheikh, or in rare cases of bliss would lie back and fall asleep without knowing, without dreaming, and open his eyes to find the light had started without him.

His brain, deprived at night, was too elastic in the daytime, and interactions that should have been ordinary became incoherent. As he sat in the market and checked the accounting book, he seemed to be looking at the gridded page from underwater, and the inked digits stirred as if rippled by a breeze. But when evening fell, the exhaustion always pushed through to a new plane of being, and the lamps stayed on in his mind and would not let him rest.

That night he lay back and fixed his mind on the Hammad girl, her sad eyes surrounded by the remnants of keyhole dust. He twisted in the covers.

His stomach was disturbed and an odd tightness in his intestines articulated itself every so often into flatulence. The previous night, or was it the night before, he had been woken by painful hiccoughs, and after reaching the toilet in time to vomit returned and lay back on the mattress with a mouth full of acid. Tonight the cramp was further down. It occurred to him that he might have to see a physician if all this persisted. Fatima Hammad. Fatima Hammad would hardly marry such a weakling.

And yet, by some miracle, that night he did not even need to think of sleep. Sleep stole upon him while his thoughts were elsewhere, blending images, blurring the shapes of women into categories of pain. Those he had harmed: Jeannette, his mother. Those who had harmed him: Layla, Jeannette. And now, Fatima Hammad, her minuscule features perfectly focused by the keyhole lens. When the muezzin called, Midhat shifted on his pillow in the cold light, bewildered at how the night had passed. He crawled out of bed severely nauseated and prostrated himself in the direction of Mecca.

"In the mornings we check the register," said Hisham.

The air was mild for November, and the market was alive with dust and a jangle of glass and rocks under wheels, and voices calling out numbers and the names of objects. Bohemian crystalware shone between glass nargileh pipes, and with every drive of wind the German violins swayed and twisted from the wires attached to their tuning pegs. In the display at the front of the Kamal store the embroidered jackets also rotated, blocking and unblocking the columns of light that fell from the apertures in the khan roof as they turned their shoulders and backs. The rear of the shop, where Midhat sat with Hisham, was icy with shade.

"It is not so difficult. But sometimes we leave notes in the evening for things that must be written up the next day, so you must check, here, and see if the accounts are correct . . . heyk . . . and yes, we see the account was one digit off. That is the type of thing we check for. Next we check the orders that are in process, make sure the tailor is here, as-salamu alaykum ya mu'allim, ya'tik al-afieh, fine, Butrus is here. Now, the orders in process are listed on this side of the page . . . Midhat? Are you awake?"

"Na'am, Hisham. Sorry. You were saying. The tailor is here."

"Yes, and then we check the orders, we ask him how they are progressing. We'll do that in a moment. We have . . . not very many orders at present. But when Eid comes people always buy, it doesn't matter how hard the time is. And if there's a wedding, as you know. Hala' every transaction is recorded, and we mark here if they have paid or not. And the date, always put the date. Hala' on this page are the debts. And the interest is there . . . heyk, we calculate by how many days we've had the debt. See? Now, you do this calculation, I will ask how the order is going."

Jamil had been right to say Midhat would have a good view. The Kamal store was at the widest point of the thoroughfare and at the far Western end, making it easy to catch any Britishers peering into the marketplace, especially when they loitered by the shopkeepers near the exit, which they apparently loved to do, as though only with an escape route in sight would they actually take pains to address someone. Even from the rear of the store Midhat could look up and see quite a cross section of the khan, lit like a cinema screen by the sunlight. The soldiers were always writing in notebooks, and Midhat began to recognise their faces. There was one whose small chin retracted into folds like an accordion camera when he looked down at his notepad, and as he squinted up at his surroundings his mouth fell open. From afar one saw the glassy blue of his eyes.

Occasionally an English wife would appear and fondle items for sale. Such a woman was obvious a mile away, usually wearing some sort of veil over her hair and a grin of trepidation. Townswomen were not so common but there were usually at least a few, servants or the daughters of farmers buying for their families—not counting, of course, the rural fellaha women selling vegetables who did not wear the black veil. Peculiarly, or at least it now seemed peculiar to Midhat, the standard garments of the Nabulsiyyat could on occasion make it difficult to distinguish between a middle-aged woman, an old woman, and a young girl. A Nabulsiyyeh always wore a cloak, and above that her veil, and then a shawl. Midhat's eye was drawn to them, rare, dark figures in a crowd. From afar he would guess the age by size and gait, since a short one was a young girl, and a very large one had probably given birth many times but not yet reached the late female meridian of brittle bones and appetite loss, and then if the figure drew near he confirmed his guess or revised it according to what the eyes revealed in the gap between veil and shawl. On one occasion when a Nabulsiyyeh actually approached the Kamal stall he found he had guessed totally wrong, imagining her far older than she was, and when she spoke from the other side of that black fabric in the voice of a young girl, he realised with a blast that this person was only just now learning to perform from under her shroud, and that the delicacy of her footstep was not frailty but uncertainty.

"How are we getting on?" Hisham stooped under the lintel from the tailor's room.

"I . . . oh, I'm sorry Hisham. I was distracted."

"Ma'lish amo. We'll do it now, no matter. The date there . . . it has been another week. Which brings the Abd al-Wahhab debt to five pounds."

Midhat wrote a five in the debt column.

"What happens if they never pay?" he said.

"If they never pay?" Hisham hesitated. "First of all," he said finally, "we stop lending. And second . . . there are other things the merchants do. Sometimes there is . . . a coordination with the tax farmers, but you know your father is not so bad. Remember, it's a kindness to give credit. And sometimes these credit and debt habits go back, ya'ni, to our grandfathers."

Midhat had stopped listening, because a dark veiled figure was walking directly towards the store. Forceful strides. Her robe voluminous with air. She stepped from the light into the shadow, and then Midhat saw her strong brown eyes and caught a familiar homely whiff from her body.

"Teta! What are you doing here?"

"Ahlan teta," said his grandmother. "Habibi listen. We are going to see the Samaritans. Are you ready? Yalla, imshi."

"What?"

"Hisham, I am sorry we are leaving. This is very important. His father has asked."

"Of course, Um Taher. God keep you."

"Yalla Midhat. Get to your feet."

Midhat slipped off the stool. "But Teta, I'm doing the accounts."

Already she had turned and was out on the street again. He jogged to catch up. At the limit of the khan the sun warmed his face, dust rose at his feet, and Teta's dress ballooned out from under her shawl. He reached a level with her as they stepped through the arch.

"What has my father asked for? Why are we rushing?"

"As-Samariyin. It is something he would want, if he was here."

"The Samaritans?"

He hesitated. She swung down an alley.

"Te—ta," he called, following.

One more turn and she brought him to the outskirts of the Samaritan quarter, ducking into a clammy, narrowing passage of whitewashed rock. She tapped on a short wooden door to their right and rattled the handle. As she listened for footsteps she looked Midhat in the eyes, and then peered through the darkened window.

"I think we should talk about it." He could not keep his voice from rising. "I think you're being hasty."

A woman appeared from the alley behind them, dressed in pantaloons and unveiled but for a scarf over her hair. At the sight of Um Taher and Midhat, she started.

"Salam," said Teta. "Can you tell us where the priest is?"

Midhat squeezed the bridge of his nose. A headache was coming on.

"Yitzhak!" the woman shouted down the passage. There was no response; she sighed and considered Um Taher, then gestured for them to follow. Midhat dropped behind with his eyes to the ground, still squeezing his nose. They arrived at an uncovered stone stairway.

Teta thanked the woman and said to Midhat: "Yalla. Up."

The steps were slippery with wear, and far greater in height than in breadth. At the top, Teta put her hands on her hips and breathed heavily. Ahead was an empty, open courtyard. "I am old," she muttered.

Midhat's laugh echoed and reported back sounding far jollier than he felt. It was warm up here; the sun had heated the stone. The domed roofs of the town were visible on three sides over the low walls, and beyond them, the green mountains. Street noises were muffled by the elevation. The third, largest wall of the courtyard was the front of a building: the Samaritan synagogue.

"Why are we here?" said Midhat.

It was not really a question. There were three reasons why a Muslim Nabulsiyyeh would be meeting the Samaritan high priest, and Teta was not enough of a jealous type to set the evil eye on someone, and she could prophesy perfectly fine herself. Which left only one reason. She grasped his shoulder with one hand and with the other reached for her lifted foot.

"I don't want the magic," he said.

She met his eye with a shoe in her hand. "You don't want it?"

"No."

"But, habibi, you know it won't harm her."

"Bihimish, it's not the point. I don't want to do magic. Khalas. I haven't even . . . decided if I want . . ."

"Well we are here now, aren't we? Let us go inside and meet him. Then you can, whatever, it's up to you. But I'm telling you I am helping. I am on your side. It's up to you, but if I were you I would do it."

"I don't want it, Teta."

"I heard you. We are here now, we will meet him."

She removed the other shoe and groaned as she placed them both under the lemon tree. Midhat slotted a forefinger under his own shoelaces, slipped off the heels, and followed her inside.

He may have visited the courtyard before but he was now certain he had never entered the synagogue. Above him a vaulted ceiling; ahead, unadorned walls buttressed by pointed arches, which carved the space into rooms. Damp had left spots at the ceiling joints, and some of the paint was beginning to shred and fall. A large wooden timepiece like a severed grandfather clock was suspended near the high priest's chair. The minute hand jerked counterclockwise. Silently, barefoot, Teta led him under one of the arches, and stopped.

The high priest was sitting on another chair in an alcove, white-haired, black-browed, in a blue robe and turban. He was not alone. Beside him, on a carpet on the floor, a second man was kneeling. The kneeling man wore a grey smock coat buttoned up to his neck, the hem dirt-brown where his shoes poked out. Though his skull was totally bald, a copious wiry beard shot out from his chin like a hog-hair broom. He was staring at something on the carpet before him: a document with curling corners, a scroll perhaps, discoloured and covered in very fine calligraphy. The document lay in an open casing of red satin.

Moments passed. The kneeling man lifted the scroll from its edges and slid it away from him, revealing another page beneath. This one looked even more discoloured. The thick black brow of the priest twitched like a dog's with his shifting gaze. Finally, he lifted his eyes in the direction of Midhat and Teta.

"As-salamu alaykum."

"Wa alaykum as-salam," said Teta. "Abu Salama, keefak. Ana Um Taher. I'rifet hafidi? Midhat, ismu."

Midhat bowed at the high priest, and the priest rose slowly from his chair and bowed back.

"As-salamu alaykum."

The man with the enormous beard was also on his feet now. His smock had gathered up around his torso, and he flattened it before reaching out a hand to shake Midhat's, and nodded at Um Taher. His eyes were set so close he seemed to be frowning, his eyeballs pinkish and small.

Abu Salama introduced him. "Hada Abuna Antoine. Faransawi."

"Marhaba," said Teta.

"Marhaban," said Father Antoine. He pronounced his "r" in the French way.

"Bonjour," said Midhat.

Father Antoine blinked.

Enunciating pedantically, and using a few classical verb forms, Abu Salama said to the Frenchman: "I can ask this lady and her grandson to wait, if you believe you will be—quick. Otherwise, feel free to visit tomorrow, at the same time."

Father Antoine responded with equal meticulousness:

"With gratitude for your kindness, Abu Salama. I shall visit tomorrow."

The French priest knelt again on the carpet to replace the page he had lifted, then gently pulled the red satin over the four corners, and tied the black ribbon that lay beneath. The three standing watched. The Frenchman's thick fingers were gnarled and spotted and tufted with white hairs. On his feet again, Father Antoine nodded at the high priest, and rather than pass by Midhat and Um Taher to reach the door, turned through another arch-way around the far edge of the synagogue. His clacking footsteps circled around them, and as he came into view at the last moment Midhat adjusted his head to watch the figure and full beard silhouetted against the daylight. The clacks changed tone and receded.

"Um Taher, tell me," said Abu Salama. "How can I help."

Midhat stared at the closed parcel of satin.

"We need a charm," said Teta.

"Fine. For or against?"

"For," said Teta. "For love."

Midhat snapped his head back to look at his grandmother. The sharp movement sent a new pain down his temple.

"Have you brought any—" said Abu Salama.

"I have hair."

From the inside of her robe Teta produced a drawstring bag, and slid two fingers in. A single black hair appeared on her forefinger. The ends dangled: one curled, silver with light; the other was white-tipped. An entire root from Fatima's head. Midhat felt hot.

"No. Not possible. No, Teta." He put a hand on her back. "I am sorry for wasting your time, Abu Salama. But the fact is . . . no. Teta, put that away."

The black hair wobbled with the force of Midhat's breath, and Teta gripped it with her thumb to stop it falling.

"Well, if he doesn't want to," said Abu Salama, "I'm afraid we can't do it. It won't work, unfortunately."

Abu Salama opened his palm upwards and lifted his gaze to the ceiling. It was out of his hands, he seemed to be saying. The second she was released from the high priest's gaze, Teta turned her eyes on Midhat. Outlined by her veil, they skewered him. She slid the single hair back into the drawstring bag, and as she pulled the strings gave a long emphatic blink of irritation. Then she bowed at the priest. Midhat fought an impulse to laugh.

He led his grandmother back across the courtyard, and as they descended the steep steps, she said again: "It's up to you." He wished he could see her face. They walked back through the Samaritan quarter in exhausted silence, and she left him at the store. Hisham had placed a chair in the entrance. It was the time of afternoon prayer and the muezzin's voice sounded down the quiet khan. Midhat sat on the chair and two cross-stitched panels swung around his ears as Teta walked off. The pain in his temple was softer now, and had a rhythm. He squeezed the bridge of his nose, rested his fingers on his eyes.

Part of him did not object to the idea of a love charm. In fact, part of him was receptive to the idea. Yes, he had been educated in the sciences and rational argument, but superstition was a survival of childhood that was hard to erase. And when he thought of the supposed magic of the Samaritans, even now he felt a whisper of that old awe, standing on the dark threshold of knowledge. Superstition was not just for children and old ladies. Beliefs ran deep, and apparent sceptics were often secret zealots, murmuring in the high priest's office the names of fathers and mothers, unfolding palms to be tickled by a deciphering thumb, whispering astrological verdicts on the way home so they would not by forgetting lose what they had paid for. As a child he had heard rumours of dead birds encased in the plaster above doorways. As an adult, he retained some of the mystical sense laid down in infancy, that fearful curiosity, so that his heart still turned a little at a mention of the infamous book and its occult runes, even though he had since understood it was simply a set of religious texts written in their language. His thoughts dropped to the discoloured pages on the floor of the synagogue, and to the French Father Antoine and his beard.

When he opened his eyes, Hisham's thin figure was visible from the direction of the Nasr mosque.

"You can go for the day," he said, as he approached. "Khalas. There's no one here."

As Midhat climbed the mountain home he decided he had become too suggestible in his fatigue. He should not have let Teta take him all the way to the synagogue. Jeannette stepped into his thoughts: he could not imagine what she might say about all this. Or rather, he could—but he didn't want to.

They ate the kusa mahshi Um Mahmoud had prepared in silence. His mind relaxed, and forgetting the battle with his grandmother he remarked:

"Teta, you have to eat more. Have another kusaya."

Um Taher waited several moments before replying: "I am not hungry."

As though it were a normal evening, they repaired to the salon after dinner. Um Taher stitched, and Midhat tried to put his thoughts in order while pretending to read a novel. Um Mahmoud made a racket over the next day's breakfast in the kitchen and ducked her head in to wave goodnight.

The more his thoughts progressed, the more his headache, uncannily, receded. The pain lessened, and moved lower and lower in his skull until it seemed to disperse around his collarbone. If in the end he would have to marry someone, what held him back from saying yes to Teta, and conspiring for her choice? Fatima Hammad was indeed very beautiful.

The problem was Jeannette. It was remarkable that after years of silence his imagination was still able to invent reasons and ignore facts to preserve hope. He needed to concentrate, to run his fingers over the facts and make them real. He did not desire to revisit the episode with Sylvain Leclair and Frédéric Molineu. Yet how else could he be rid of her, except by recalling his suffering at the dinner table and her failure to defend him? She had transformed into a sticky substance, adhering to the walls of his brain. Faruq would call it forbidden love or some other cliché, but that was not it, not at all. Every description was like a sliding piece of ice that missed the point, and there she was below, darkly unexplainable. That house, its corridors, they trespassed onto the present—this must be why they called lovers insane. If a person lost everything that tied him to a place, no one could say that any of what occurred there was real. He had no photographs of Montpellier. Nothing but the coat he had bought, and the French hat, and his suits and ties.

Teta spun her panel round and pulled a thread tight. She licked a finger and caressed a new strand off the spool.

Nablus was where his duty lay. He was indebted to his father, and for that alone he must marry. This debt was arranged before he was born. His father's care was always based on this future sense, that Midhat would mature like a bond and yield to him. So although one might be convinced momentarily that family ties were petty, in the end, as Jamil said, they were everything.

Darkness rose in the windows, and the fire glowed more brightly. Midhat stopped thinking, and as the flame clarified in the corner of his vision, reflexively he played a game from his childhood. When he looked at the fire directly the edge receded into a blur: the game was to move his eyes fast enough to catch the flame when it was most clear, and there was no end, because it was impossible.

"You'll have to decide soon, ya Midhat," said Teta suddenly. She dropped her sewing into her lap. "You can't do nothing," her voice grew higher, "and not decide. Because we have to find another girl, and then it could be too late. Too late!"

"Teta, it has been one day since you asked me."

She picked up the fabric, lifted her eyebrows at the needle, and said mildly: "You are a stupid, stupid boy."

"Unbelievable," said Midhat. "You are pretending to give me a choice, but I don't have a choice. Clearly. Because you have already decided."

"Who do you think you are?" She cocked her head to the side. "You come here with all your . . . clothes—who do you think paid for this?"

She was pointing at his jacket, slung over the footstool. From the pocket, a silk handkerchief was hanging. Midhat turned his face to the window.

"I have given you a very good choice," said Teta. "Why are you making it difficult?"

She stood up, and something flew by. It was her sewing; she had thrown it onto the sofa.

"I'm finished. You do whatever you like. Fatima Hammad will be married to her cousin, your father will disinherit you, and then you'll be sorry, and alone, or with a stupid cow who will bear you no sons."

She bent and plucked up the sewing again, then slammed the door, leaving Midhat alone in the dark room. His breath was heavy. He looked straight at the blurred edge of the flame.

The following day was a Thursday. Dawn lifted on the khan as it filled with people, and shopkeepers from neighbouring stores dragged over their chairs to chat. A few customers touched fabrics but most lingered to talk and not to buy. As the shopkeepers swapped stories, Midhat watched the thoroughfare for veiled figures.

"Fa . . . when he talks, you know, really he believes what he did. He says when he arrived in Alexandria . . ."

"I remember this story."

"He found a soldier on the beach."

"Yes I remember this story."

"His eye is coming out of his . . . his . . ." The man telling the story lost his breath to laughter and slapped his knee.

"From his socket."

"He put it ba—"

"He put it back for him!"

The other man wheezed, and started coughing.

"Is there more coffee, amo?"

"Lahza," said Midhat.

He filled the coffeepot from the faucet, and as he struck a match to light the flame he slipped into a mechanical fantasy, in which someone ran through the khan calling his name.

In Paris, Faruq had expounded an idea that marriage could be a kind of romantic limitation, though not the province of romance itself. He extracted various such theories from his readings, When he first described this one to Midhat he was lying on his sofa in Saint Germain, shoeless feet on the armrest and head on one of his hands, in the manner of certain Western photographs of Arab women in staged repose. The more external restrictions, he said, the more profound true love becomes. It becomes pure—this is love for another woman, of course, not the wife. The stronger the limitation, the richer the life inside. At the time Midhat had nodded and made a mental note, desperate for any principles to steer his life by. But standing in the Kamal store in Nablus, coffeepot in one hand and stack of cups in the other, Faruq appeared to him in retrospect as guilty as the next man of parceling life off into pocket theories. He wondered what had changed, that his trust in Faruq, before so sound, should now falter. Was it simply the geographical fact of being back in Palestine? Or was it being faced with the prospect of an actual marriage, rather than some dream of it?

"Meen bidu qahwe?" he said to the circle of men. All raised their hands.

Every one of these men was married. Some had divorced and married twice, three times. Famously, the man telling the story of the eye, who went by the moniker "Abu Islam," had married a Christian woman from the east of Nablus. That was proof of a love match, if anything was.

Pouring the first cup of coffee, he wondered if it could be possible to defy his father, and at the same time obey his imperatives. The secrets of his life in France, the joys there but also the shame—that something large and dramatic had happened to him, leading him to abandon the course his father had chosen and begin anew, moving to Paris of his own accord, seeking other men to guide him, studying history instead of medicine, so that he knew the entire saga of Western Europe but nothing about healing a human body—he could see all of this taking on its own charge, so that his very privacy would become a kind of power. Never mind that much of what he was hiding was painful. His languishment would be more bearable because it was poetic, and suppression of the past would become a virtue, a secret source of grace.

The rest of the day passed unremarkably. The merchants packed up their wares and pulled the gates over their stalls. Midhat was bolting the green door when someone did actually run through the khan calling his name.

"Midhat! Midhaaat!"

Tahsin Kamal, his trouser legs riding up his knees.

"Habibi ta'al. There's a rawi at Sheikh Qassem."

Midhat shrugged, sliding on the padlock.

"Yalla. Ta'al."

"Wait a moment, I'm coming. Do you know what tale he's telling?"

"We'll find out."

They weren't the only ones walking in the direction of Sheikh Qassem. Before long they were in the middle of a nodding throng. Kufiyas trailed from the heads of fellahin, older men wore sagging shirts and belts around their soft bellies, the younger men slick-haired with cheap grease. Three shoeshine boys with dirty tarabish carried their equipment under their arms and shouted at each other like tiny adults. An old fellah in a red headdress and overlarge suit smiled at Midhat with a toothless mouth, his kinked fingers pointing at the café.

Sheikh Qassem was already crowded and dark. A circle of lamps in one corner indicated the rawi, sitting beside a qanun player with a stage space around them where the tables were pushed back. Behind him stood an idle gramophone, its silent horn like a huge black lily. The rawi was conversing with some nearby members of the audience, while his player plucked at the instrument in his lap and adjusted the pegs. Tahsin rested his head against the back wall and made a face: when are they going to start? Men from the major families occupied the chairs. By the window Midhat saw Abdallah Atwan hunched with a hand on the shoulder of his young son, and then a few tables nearer by he recognised Jamil's broad back. He slid between tables to kiss his cousin hello. A few people were singing along to the qanun music now, tripping in and out of a familiar melody. The rawi looked up: a little boy had entered, carrying a drum. The qanunist pulled up a third chair, and as the boy wriggled back on his seat the poet's practised face cooled the audience. Moving his head he hummed, and the qanun's notes ran like water around his voice. Men cheered and whistled.

"Abu Zayd al-Hilali," he sang. "Ana sa-aqool lakum qissat Beni Hila-a-al."

The qanun quietened, the little boy trilled his fingers lightly on the drum. The poet began to speak:

"In the name of God, the Almighty, this is the story of the Arabs of the Beni Hilal. In the time of the Sultan Sarhan, the mightiest warrior of Beni Hilal was Rizq the Brave, son of Nayil. Rizq the Brave had married eight women and sired many daughters. But not one of his eight wives had ever borne him a male heir. His soul grew troubled, and he began to sing:

Ah-ah-ah the World and Fate and Destiny
all I have seen with my eyes shall disappear
My wealth is great, oh men, but I am without an heir
and wea-alth without an heir after a life will disappear.

"Jamil," Midhat whispered. "Can we talk?"

His cousin sucked on his pipe and nodded. They slid along the back wall, and the boys by the door stood aside to let them pass. Outside, the light was leaving the sky.

"What's wrong?" Jamil looked back through the glass, on which scratches made yellow circles around the lamps inside.

"Where to begin. I have my own story to tell you."

The rawi's voice crescendoed: *A dark bird from the distance came to them.*

"This is Abu Zayd!" someone shouted, and people clapped.

A dark bird . . . ("Ayyyywa!" "Allah.") *. . . frightful to behold . . .*

"Don't tell anyone this, uh?" said Midhat. "My grandmother wants me to marry Fatima Hammad. The daughter of Haj Nimr. He's a judge, he was the mayor last year."

"I know him, of course."

"Teta invited the girl and her mother to the house, and then she showed me their faces through the keyhole of the salon door."

Jamil leaned his shoulder against the wall. "Mish ma'ool, Midhat. How did she . . . I mean, what did she look like?"

"Her face was—actually, you know, she looked like the moon." He laughed at the cliché, as he would have with Faruq, and observed a twitch of noncomprehension on his cousin's smiling face. A light flashed for an instant on a new gulf between them.

"A face like the moon," he repeated, looking out at the dark street, where a lone figure walked in the direction of the Western Cemetery.

Of course Jamil would not laugh; cliché was a French notion. There was no such thing as cliché in Nablus; there were only public channels for behaviour, the common currencies of desire.

And Khadra cried, the rawi's voice surged, *O how beautiful you are, O bird, and how beautiful your darkness . . .*

"Teta wants me to do a charm. I said no."

"You don't believe in that?" said Jamil. "Yeah, I suppose I don't either. It probably wouldn't hurt."

A musical interlude was beginning, with a light drumbeat.

"Listen," said Jamil. "I know you are fixated on this French woman, but that shouldn't stop you. I mean, Fatima Hammad? If you *can* . . ."

Jamil folded his arms at the window, and Midhat looked at the side of his cousin's closed face. Jamil was older than Midhat by almost a full year, which when they were children gave him an upper hand. Not only had he been ahead at school but his bones were always longer, his muscles more powerful, and when they fenced with branches he was always the victor and pinned Midhat to the ground with a faceful of twigs. Now time had levelled them and they were more or less the same height; still, Midhat was attentive to his cousin's tone. Was that disdain, or admiration, that made him say, "If you *can*…"? He had impressed Jamil with his stories of France, he could see that. He sensed his largeness vacillate in his cousin's eyes, with the weird embarrassment of reflected glory.

"I wrote to her," he said, after a while. "The French woman."

"Wallah?"

"Wallah. But she never wrote back."

The rawi's eyeballs were growing as he reached some climax. Smoke rose in long columns from the nargileh pipes.

"I feel . . ." said Midhat.

"What, habibi?"

"I don't know." He put his head in his hands. "You think I should do it? This Hammad girl?"

"Are you kidding?" said Jamil. "If you can. Definitely."

Inside, someone was shouting. "You can't leave him in prison!"

A young man upturned a chair. Others were rising to their feet. Some of the faces showed amusement; others, anger. Tahsin Kamal appeared at the doorway, straightening his tie and blowing out his cheeks.

"What's going on?" said Midhat.

"Everyone is angry because Abu Zayd was arrested."

"That comes much later. He can't jump around the story like that."

Tahsin shrugged. "Well, they're angry about it."

Midhat stepped into the café and saw the rawi waving his hands, one of which held a flute.

"Shwaya!" he shouted. "Stannu shwaya, I'll finish it. Lahza, lahza, itfadalu, please all sit down."

"Look at Haj Abdallah," said Jamil.

Near the window on the far side, Haj Abdallah Atwan was standing up. With one hand on his son's head, he was brandishing his other fist at the rawi and shouting.

"He has his son with him," said Midhat.

"I know. He frightens me sometimes."

The upright bodies strained to violence. Then the rawi's flute began to play, and the tension broke, and with scattered applause the bodies sat back down again for the poet to recite the next verse that would release Abu Zayd from prison.

6

Shortly after his return from exile in 1918, Haj Hassan discovered that his lands in the Jordan Valley, his twenty thousand dunums planted with wheat, had been sabotaged. The entirety of the crop was burnt, and there would be no return from the yield. His cousin, Haj Nimr, suggested the culprits were probably either vandals or thuggish foot soldiers returning from war. In any case, there was nothing to be done: the British were preventing Islamic courts from dealing with land disputes, even though they had not yet set up their own judicial system. In Zawata, Hassan fell into a depression, while his wife played all day long on the oud he had bought for her.

A year later, in November 1919, a representative from the Jewish National Fund visited and offered to buy the land immediately for ninety thousand pounds. Despite the extraordinary price, Hassan refused. The British military government had closed the Land Register, and he knew such transactions were currently illegal. Nevertheless, the event galvanised him to arrange an advance sale for when the ban was lifted, and he approached the Patriarchate of the Latin Church in Jerusalem. They struck a deal for four thousand.

"That was the right choice," said Haj Nimr.

They were sitting in the upstairs meeting room of his house, with the new mayor, Abu Omar Jawhari. The sunlight from the window was skipping around the floor at the whim of the fruit trees waving in the garden.

The seats were so slanted that each man was forced either to recline in full or to perch on the edge. Hassan was leaning back to Nimr's left. His large cream jacket augmented the impression that he had lost weight, and his short beard was salt-white. Even seated, there was some drama about the tarbush so upright on his head, his slow blink, his lower lip juddering with apprehension. Opposite him, and to the right of Nimr, Abu Omar Jawhari sat swinging prayer beads. A tight-fleshed man nearing fifty, he looked a deal more the bureaucrat than his companions: broad face, round glasses, cramped woollen suit.

Widad brought a tray of orange juice and glasses, to which Nimr now administered. His wife whispered: "You pour them all first. You hand them round after." Nimr waved her off, and as she left handed the first full glass to Hassan.

Abu Omar said: "This is happening a lot, you know, people selling to the Jews. But what are you going to do, when one guy is in Beirut and now there is a border . . ."

"Ya it is a difficult question. If you are like Hassan, then of course you will sell," said Nimr.

"I didn't sell to the Jews."

"Ya I know, I was saying you could have done. And that's when we get these problems with the fellahin, when they have no land, ya'ni. That Colonel Hubbard came to see me . . . khalas it's their problem." He poured a second glass.

Abu Omar, never one to let another appear more important than himself, said: "He came to see me too. I told him we need court jurisdiction to deal with it." He rolled his eyes. "He wouldn't listen to me."

"They won't listen to us," said Nimr, passing the next full glass to Abu Omar. "Jerusalem is the British capital. It's a local custom anyway, it's not in the law books. And more and more people care about what is on paper, and not just the British. As Ibn Abidin says . . ."

"So much on Ibn Abidin, ya Haj," said Abu Omar.

"He was a genius. Local custom must be included, or the people suffer. Bidna a balance between the written and the lived. This is where reasoning comes."

Abu Omar shook his head and swallowed. A small orange circle stamped his upper lip, which he wiped with a forefinger of the hand that held the prayer beads. "This is the problem. Philosophy and theology are so mixed up that even the kuttab schools are infected. Young Muslims are trained with these instruments of, ya'ni, unbelief." The beads clicked between his fingers.

"Listen," said Nimr, reaching for the third glass. "Last week I had to deal with one case, a dispute about a horse. The first party was a farmer from near Sabastia, I can't remember the village. He sold a mare to one of his usual clients, the transaction went through, the client bought the mare for so many pounds, and everyone was happy. Then, some weeks pass by, and the farmer is in Nablus for the harvest. And he is walking by the onion market, and whom does he see but his friend this client, the one who bought the mare. And the client has this expression of joy on his face, and he says, Thank you so much ya mu'allim for the mare, I am extremely happy. It gave birth yesterday to a young colt, and the birth went well, and the young horse is very healthy."

Nimr set down the jug on the tray, and Abu Omar gave a short laugh.

"So what we have here of course is two stupid people. One is the farmer who did not realise his horse was pregnant. Perhaps he thought it was just very fat, or something. Second is the client who did not realise it would upset the farmer to know he had sold a pregnant horse . . . ya'ni . . . two for the price of one. So of course this farmer is dismayed, he demands the client pay an extra sum for the second horse, which had been conveyed in this purchase without his knowledge. Or, he says, the client has the option of returning the second horse. So, what happens? Of course the client says absolutely not, the horse is mine, you sold it to me *fair and square* bi'ulu bil ingleezi, as one . . . package, ya'ni. And the farmer says, but if we count back to when the mare was impregnated, it must have happened in my care, the father would be one of my stallions, thus the offspring is rightfully mine, and and and, heyk heyk heyk.

"So we leave behind certain of the stupid aspects, this becomes an interesting case. Does one own a horse if it is not yet born? Remember, my role is to find the solution that is most just. And what is most just? That which makes the lives of men *less painful*. This is not something easily quantified, tab'an, for who can say the first farmer is not gravely hurt by the loss of this horse, now that he knows about it? Who is to say for the contingencies, perhaps his daughter is ill, perhaps he wants private treatment in Jerusalem. Of course, there are needs and needs, and these can be counted to a degree. And in this way, Abu Omar, such a case presents me with a *moral* question and at the same time a *logical* question. Logic is not divorced from life ya zalameh, and philosophy is what we live by, whether or not you are a philosopher."

"And what did you decide?" said Haj Hassan. "About the horse?"

"I hear you," said Abu Omar, and as he tilted his head his spectacles shone like mirrors. "But how do you apply this to the land sales? When you have some landlord in Beirut, and he wants to sell his land in the Galilee, because there is now a border and how is he supposed to get his yield. And the new buyers don't care about the fellahin. What would Ibn Abidin say, if the Quran says the owner is the one who ploughs. What I mean is there is logic and there is logic, and we can get lost in storytelling and lose sight of the truth. And this story about the horse . . . it could be used in fifty different ways, you could make any argument by twisting its limbs."

Haj Nimr sucked his lip, drank from his glass, and exhaled sharply through his teeth while looking at the juice. "In the end, it helped you to understand my argument. Therefore, it is a sound form of reasoning."

"And what did you say your verdict was, ya Haj? About the horse and its baby?" said Hassan.

Haj Nimr was about to respond when footsteps sounded on the stair, and he turned his head as the door opened on the veiled face of Widad Hammad.

"You have a visitor, Abu Burhan."

Haj Nimr stood and a pale young man entered, He was dressed in a slim navy suit and a dark red tarbush. His thick hair was black and his large green eyes shone, and, though it was cool outside, his brow was visibly specked with perspiration. He held his cane a little uneasily, the tip hovering near the ground as though he were uncertain whether to lean on or carry it. He glanced at the other men and jolted into a bow.

"As-salamu alaykum. My name is Midhat Kamal."

"Wa alaykum as-salam," everyone murmured.

"Nimr Hammad," said Nimr, reaching to shake his hand. "Would you like a glass of orange—Widad! Bring another glass, please. And more juice. Itfadal. Sit."

Midhat had already recognised the other men sitting there: the mayor Abu Omar Jawhari, of course, and the famous Haj Hassan Hammad. It had been enough to prepare for a meeting with Haj Nimr, and the sight of these other two was overpowering. He wished he could have brought his father with him.

"I am the son of Haj Taher Kamal," he began, and as he sat he immediately wished he hadn't, since it left Haj Nimr standing. "Grandson of Muhammad Kamal." He half turned in his seat to address Nimr, who was still waiting by the door for the juice and glass, but ended by announcing to the entire company: "My father owns the Kamal store in the khan and the Kamal store in Cairo. I have recently returned from France, from Paris, where I studied medicine, and philosophy, and history."

Abu Omar Jawhari turned down the corners of his mouth at Hassan as if to say, not bad. Midhat tensed his leg to stop it shaking.

"I know your father," said Haj Hassan. "He is my friend. Haj Taher is one of the municipal hospital founders, Abu Omar." He turned back to Midhat. "He helped me in the war."

"Did he?" said Midhat. This news of their families' alliance should have made him braver; and yet, knowing nothing of the episode, and with no one making any effort to explain it to him, he felt confused. And ashamed, as if his lack of intimacy with his father had just been exposed. There was a silence. He turned to Nimr. "I would like to ask—May I speak to you in private, ya Haj?"

"Oh yes, of course." Nimr glanced at the door. "Please, follow me."

As Midhat rose, Abu Omar poured himself the little juice that remained and held it up to the light.

Nimr led him to a narrow, humid room with a sloped ceiling. The window gave a view of the street, and Midhat peered down at the oval front steps that he had climbed only a few minutes before.

Haj Nimr folded his hands: Midhat saw a resemblance to Fatima. The eyes, the lips. He breathed deeply.

"I would like to ask for your daughter to marry me."

Nimr's expression did not change. Gradually, the eyebrows went up.

"Ah. Unfortunately, the answer is no."

Midhat looked down and tried to assemble a neutral face. He had failed, so fast. His mind ran in slow motion. He heard kitchen noises and women's voices from below, and when he looked up Haj Nimr was still watching him. The answer, unfortunately, was no. "If you *can*," Jamil had said of Fatima. The words echoed in Midhat's ears, hot with new meaning. At last, he managed:

"I see." His voice was very quiet.

Haj Nimr gave a genial grunt and smiled. "Thank you for your visit. How about that juice?"

"No. Thank you. Thank you for your time."

Midhat wished very much to bolt down the steps. But he bowed at Nimr's wife and stared at her hand as she opened the front door; a delicate hand, the wrinkles very fine, the fingernails sharpened and polished. When he reached the street he gave in, and broke into a run.

One person saw those little legs alternating, shuddering to a halt as a car passed; and on again, crossing the road. That person was at the top of the house, sitting in the third of three arched windows, using a tiny brush to rub olive oil into a basin of powdered kohl, and looking out over the town. Her sister Nuzha, half reclined on one of the beds, wiped a pale cream over her cheeks.

"What are you looking at?" Nuzha made an exaggerated sad face at a pocket mirror to stretch out the skin beneath her eyes.

"Nothing," said Fatima.

The figure disappeared and reappeared beyond the trellis. And then it ran, one arm raised, its hand on the tarbush.

7

Midhat started up the mountain at a run. As the road steepened, his momentum failed, and he lapsed into a jog. He had tried what they wanted. He did not belong in Nablus. This life, this system, it was not for him. He fell from a jog into a walk, and kicked a pebble. Of course, Teta would never see it that way.

"It's not my fault," he said aloud. "He's a snob. It's not my fault if she's going to marry her cousin. You want me to propose when she's already engaged? Teta, it's not my . . . I think it's actually *your* fault—"

A dark figure, like a tree with one thick branch, appeared against the twilit sky up the mountain ahead. It could have been a tree, only it registered in his vision as an alien shape on a known horizon. And it was moving. Midhat came out past a cluster of branches, and saw the figure one last time before it was engulfed by the mass of rising earth. The light was failing. Midhat increased his speed.

"Midhat!" came a voice from behind. "Midhat, wait!"

"Jamil?"

"Yes, yes, it's me." Jamil's tall body came up the path at an angle. "Why were you running?" He laughed, and burst into a sprint to catch up. "Are you scared?"

"No."

"Ça va?"

"Ça va bien."

"You don't look fine."

Midhat wrinkled his nose in protest. "I saw someone up there," he said at last. "With a big beard."

"It was probably the Brother of the Virgins."

"Who's he?"

"A priest. He likes to sit in odd places. Quite strange."

"Is he French?"

"Probably. Why?"

"I saw a Frenchman with a beard in the Samaritan synagogue."

"The synagogue—what were you doing there?"

"He was looking at something, I think. A page, or a book."

"What were *you* doing?"

Midhat hesitated. "I told you already. Teta wanted a charm."

Jamil did not reply. Midhat wondered if he ought to tell him what had happened at Haj Nimr's house. He was not sure he could bear Jamil's scorn.

"You know," said Jamil, leaning to pick up a stick from the roadside, "she's marrying him."

It was a moment before Midhat realised they were talking about Yasser. His stomach dropped. "What?"

"They signed the book already."

Midhat stopped walking. Jamil released a torrent of laughter, and Midhat waited for him to finish. Finally, Jamil wheezed, and said: "I'm joking." He raised his stick above his shoulder and lobbed it over the edge of the slope. He seemed to take no notice of Midhat's dismay. "I suppose they have been selling their old books. The Samaritans. These foreigners are coming to buy."

"What are they buying them for?"

"Money, habibi, what else. Times are tough. Oh by the way, I meant to tell you—"

"Do you mean money for the Samaritans, or money for the foreigners?"

"I'm working in the khan now, in a carpet store."

"Oh, well, that's good news," said Midhat. "We can eat lunch together."

"My father copied you. Or copied your father. I have to spend a year there and then I'll graduate to the offices. So I'm dealing with carpets all day. It's interesting." He did not sound convinced.

The bend in the road unfolded and they could see much further ahead. Coming down a narrow path that forked on the slope was the French priest. He was lifting his habit to climb over the rocks, and as he stepped at last onto the main track he opened the bag on his shoulder and slid a book inside. He was taller than Midhat remembered from the synagogue, and broader. The habit flicked up in front of his feet as he strode towards them.

"Bonjour," said Midhat.

To his surprise, the priest came to a complete standstill. "Bonjour."

The boys likewise stopped in the middle of the road.

"This is my cousin," said Midhat in French. "Jamil Kamal."

"Fursa sa'ida." The priest bowed his head. "Père Antoine." He reached out a hand for shaking.

"Fursa sa'ida," said Jamil.

Midhat looked at the pencil in Père Antoine's hand, and continued in French: "What were you writing?"

The priest regarded him. His eyeballs seemed quite pink. In Arabic, he said: "Notes. I am studying."

"At a university?"

"I am with L'École Biblique, in Jerusalem." He paused. "Je suis professeur. Though I am not teaching at the moment. You are a student?"

"No. I was a student. Now I am working, we are both working . . . in the market."

"Ah," said Antoine, blinking several times. "That is interesting."

"It is not particularly interesting," said Midhat at once. "In fact, I would say it is quite boring. Isn't it Jamil? I would say it is not interesting at all."

"I don't think it's *very* boring," said Jamil in Arabic. He wore an odd expression.

"I meant, only, that it is not *interesting* that one should be a student and then work in a market. It is . . ." Midhat shrugged, "commonplace. At the same time, I would not say it is particularly representative either."

There seemed to be no appropriate reply to this remark. A strong breeze ran through the grass on the mountainside. No one said anything, and Midhat knew the dissonance was his fault, that he had strained the exchange needlessly. The priest made a motion to go.

"It was nice to meet you," said Jamil.

Neither of the boys spoke on the way home. Then as they passed a thicket of trees before the house, Jamil said: "You know, I have forgotten most of my French."

"Have you?"

"Yes. If you don't use it, I think it just goes."

Teta was waiting in the kitchen. In his confession, Midhat angled the blame towards Haj Nimr.

"You are such an idiot," she said, unmoved. "You should have let me, why did you stop me?"

"You mean the charm?" he lashed back. "That doesn't even make sense! That was meant for Fatima, not for her *father*. You would have to have taken a hair from *his* head."

She marched out of the room. "And now I have to find you another girl. You are unbelievable. Unbelievable! You want to make me work like a donkey."

"It's not my fault," said Midhat, but she was already gone.

In bed that night he wondered whether Teta might have been right. Whether, had he said yes to the charm, Haj Nimr might have consented. Obviously, failing with the Hammads would not put an end to the question of marriage. If it was not her, it would be some other girl. In the morning, he rose early and left before Teta was awake.

To Hisham's bewilderment, Midhat threw himself into the bookkeeping that day with zeal. He exerted his mind all morning and all afternoon over the mathematics of debt and credit, in pursuit, not really of the ostensible goal—the completion of this or that task—but rather of the feeling afterwards. He wanted the used-up sensation, that ecstatic emptiness after concentrating. He wanted to be a body that did nothing but work, with no space left over in his mind to ruminate. He fell asleep quickly that night, and woke early again the following morning.

In this manner three weeks passed. It took that long for him to learn how to manage the accounts without Hisham's supervision. Several things must be done at once: he must monitor the interest accrued on the credit lines, while also remaining aware of the different family names, and the traditional allegiances that mitigated interest rates, or allowed one to speed up an order when the client came in person; and then keep an eye on the outstanding orders, the progress the tailor was making, and what stock, if any, was running low. As he became more adept at these details, however, he found they required less and less concentrated energy, and as more free time appeared in his working day the flurry of activity was breached with dangerous passages of stasis.

Teta made no further mention of brides, nor did Midhat broach the topic. He had still not told Jamil about his failure, and whenever he saw his cousin's long strides approaching the store, head dipping side to side in search of him, he adopted a languor he did not feel. He suspected Jamil was behaving stiffly around him too. Although this might only be a lingering shyness from their time apart, Midhat still felt their conversations had shallowed since that night at Sheikh Qassem when he first told Jamil about Teta's plan. It made him protective of his private feelings. Should Jamil ever ask, he was prepared to explain that he had not yet decided whether to speak to Haj Nimr. Jamil did not ask. Midhat tried not to think about it. But thoughts had a way of travelling back, like water on a skewed floor.

To distract himself, he spent time in the tailor's room. He brought Butrus cups of coffee, and watched reams of fabric develop into quilts and pillows and mattress covers, and the hemming of the silk belts and handkerchiefs under the biting tooth of the black and gold Singer sewing machine. Most of what the Kamal store produced was for clients in the hinterlands, so there was some limitation in type and style, although the fellahin did dress nicely for their weddings. But the store did not set out to provide for the upper-class market: those clothes were the domain of the Samaritan tailors.

The Samaritan store was located on a corner near their quarter. There were four staff, two women and two men, and at least three could usually be found sewing in a semicircle. The most gregarious was Eli, a tall, thin man with prematurely grey hair and a youthful olivey face. He was always happy to show Midhat what they were working on, and this became a point of interest in Midhat's day; sticking his head in after lunch he tracked the progress of the European-style woollen coats as they took shape, the way the gold embroidery was fitted over the jacket backs, and the gowns adjusted for the ladies to wear to their private parties. Finished items lay pressed and folded near the entranceway. Unless expressly forbidden by the client, items were also given a brief spell hanging in the window. Not long enough to attract the evil eye, but enough to advertise the design.

Though often ostensibly "Western-style," the clothes they produced were not precisely like Western clothes. The jackets were more square than those Midhat recalled from Paris, and though the fabrics were often imported—there was a recent flood of cotton from England, for example—they were habitually cut with local cloth, which meant nothing looked purely foreign. Nor did the Samaritans rely on European sewing patterns; their designs were based on local demand, with some influence from rare silent movies of Americans or Egyptians and even from the British women who peered into the khan. Little did those ladies know, the eyes travelling up and down their exposed forms were looking less at their bodies than at the fabric that wrapped them. And then the styles mutated from order to order, and each time an item was sewn it was adjusted to the preferences of that particular customer, and those changes were often applied to the next order. To Midhat, these stylistic compromises looked like errors. The tunic shape that was appearing at Parisian parties when he left, somehow preceding him to Cairo, was being tested now in Nablus in black silk and cotton, and at first he wondered if these tunics were for particularly large ladies, until he realised their sizes were being increased so they could be worn loosely after the local style, just in case, perhaps, some aspect of a woman's body should be indecently contoured.

In December the rains failed, and business at the khan slowed. Customers came into the Kamal store less to purchase fabric or visit the tailor than to repay their debts, or to beg for an extension until the harvest. On one particularly cold afternoon, a man with a dramatic stoop and a tarbush threadbare in several places stepped over the threshold and laid a bundle on the counter.

"What's this?" said Hisham.

"The order of fabric from last month."

That voice was familiar. The man's fingers lingered on his bundle, the tendons pronounced. Midhat crouched to see his face.

"Amo Ayman?"

"Midhat!"

It was a face from Midhat's childhood, the father of his little friend, the red-haired Hala Saba. Time had disfigured him, and long cracks ran across his temples.

"How are you, Amo?"

"I heard you had returned," said Ayman wearily. "Congratulations."

"The order?" said Hisham.

In a sharp movement Ayman released the bundle. Hisham started to unroll the fabric.

"Hisham, don't do that," said Midhat.

Hisham glanced up. Showing his palm Midhat said, in a voice not quite his own: "It's fine. I will deal with this."

Hisham contemplated him, and with an ambiguous bow at Ayman walked past them into the back room.

Midhat turned up one edge of the sacking. "You take this with you. There's no more debt. Khalas, it's finished."

Ayman's eyes ran down the buttons on Midhat's chest. "Oh no. Oh, Midhat, oh. God bless you, amo."

Midhat did not see Hisham for the rest of the day. The sky paled as he smoked by the door. Butrus came through on his way out, wrapped in an overcoat; Hisham had already left, he said. Midhat watched the shutters close over the other stalls one by one, the merchants waving to one another. Like his own, their families were said to depend on a hinge between the masses and the elite. But really, it seemed to Midhat, it was people like the Sabas who suffered. The Sabas had once been wealthy, that was known; and though the cause of their privation was unclear they were now the kind of Christians whose veiled women were the only marker left that they belonged in town. He wondered where Hala was now. He wondered if she was married.

"It's freezing," said Jamil, appearing from around the corner. "Will you hurry up please?"

"Give me a moment."

Jamil slid inside as Midhat continued to smoke, watching the ash creep up his cigarette and melt off. He heard his cousin say:

"What is this?"

"What is what."

"Mashallah. You are an artist."

"Oh no." The butt end flew from his fingers. "Don't, please." In two strides to the counter he reached for the accounting book, and as he tried to screen the page with his arm he raised his voice to invent what he thought was a better pretext for his indignation: "What the hell are you doing looking at our accounts?"

"You left it open."

The book was turned to the back. The left-hand page showed some waistcoats and a few variations on the cuffed trouser leg. On the right-hand page Midhat had attempted, several times, to draw a dress. He closed the book as Jamil withdrew, and then sank to his heels to unlock the cupboard where it belonged.

"You shouldn't look at other people's things," he said, pushing it onto the shelf.

"It was open!" Jamil laughed. "Why are you doing those drawings?"

"Why do you do anything?"

Midhat was not good at drawing. They were not taught to draw at school in Constantinople. In Montpellier there was some occasion for describing the cross sections of flora to annotate and memorise in botany class. In fact, that had been his first experience of observing and copying, the eye going back and forth from the specimen on the glass slide. But he had never drawn from the mind's eye before, and the results in the accounts book were clumsy. He had been trying to remember the guests at parties, mannequins in shop displays, the ladies' dresses that absorbed the fashions of military uniforms. He caught none of those nuances, however, and all the skirts were triangles. They looked like half-opened umbrellas.

He straightened up. Jamil was holding his stomach with mirth. Catching sight of Midhat's face, he fell slack. "What's wrong with you?"

"It's nearly dark."

"Oh, all right. I'll wait outside."

The cabinets did not take long to organise and lock. Midhat spent an extra moment cleaning the space around the counter, given that today for the first time he had exerted some authority over Hisham, and he felt unsteady about it. He took up the broom and performed a little sweep of the floor in front, where smears from muddy shoes dried off into dust, and threads sometimes lay sprinkled. Stepping into the open air with the padlock he caught Jamil, bowed against the cold, poking his finger into a crevice in the outer wall. He jerked up and met Midhat's eye. His forefinger was covered with white fluff.

"Cobweb," he said.

Without meaning to, Midhat smiled, and rolled his eyes to temper it.

"I wanted to ask," said Jamil, as they walked. "Did you see many motor-cars in Paris?"

"Of course."

"Did you see a Bugatti?"

"I don't know what that is."

"It's a race car."

"Maybe. I don't know."

"The Germans had many in Jenin," said Jamil. "In the base. Tahsin rode in one. He said it took three hours to Jerusalem."

"Why are you obsessed with cars suddenly?"

"Not obsessed. Not everyone has seen so many."

"You must have in Constantinople."

"I didn't see the Ford. Of course, I'm sure you saw every car ever made in Paris."

"Oh, Jamil, come on. This is stupid."

"What?"

"You have to stop this."

"Stop what?"

"Being . . ." He faltered. "You know, being jealous of me. The Paris thing."

Jamil made a sound in his throat.

"Not everything that has happened to me is so amazing."

"I don't know what you're talking about."

Midhat groaned. They had reached the edge of town and the trees were going black with sunset.

After several moments, he said: "I proposed to Haj Nimr, you know. He rejected me."

"Well, I'm sorry about that."

"No, you're not. That doesn't matter. My point is, not everything comes easy to me, either."

"I never said—"

"I said it doesn't matter. I shouldn't have brought it up."

Jamil did not reply. They went on up the slope, and as the road curved Midhat was seized by a memory. As though his thoughts had lagged, as though they had been searching for a long while for some association, and had only just hit upon it. It burst into his mind: the windy terrace in Montpellier, the lawn, the pond. Frédéric Molineu asking about the Samaritans on Mount Gerizim. He tugged at the scene, and other details clinging to the underside shivered into life. He stared at Jeannette's bare, wet legs. They came out through the trees.

"You know how you test a flat tyre?" said Jamil.

"How."

Again the road curved, presenting a view of the other mountain, dim with evening and distance.

"You wet your finger, heyk, and you feel for the air." Jamil rubbed his hands together. "You know I think you should try again."

"Try?"

"For Fatima."

"Fatima."

"Where are you, habibi?" Jamil touched his shoulder. "I can tell you're upset. How did he say no, Haj Nimr? Tell me his words."

"He said, 'Unfortunately the answer is no.'"

"Those were the words? Wallah. Well, even so. If I were in your position, I'd try again. He doesn't know you. You would be perfect."

"God keep you."

"And I'm not jealous. Mish ma'ool Midhat, I can't even believe you said that. I do think—"

Turning off the main track onto the road to the house they saw, between the branches of a low-hanging tree, the glass eyes of two unlit headlights. Just below, the curves of two front wheels.

"Ah," came a voice, and an upright shadow stepped onto the path. "Midhat."

Nerves snapped in Midhat's abdomen.

"Father. I didn't know you were here."

"And Jamil," said Haj Taher. "Ahlan wa sahlan, amo. I saw your father, you're working in the khan now."

"Ahlan, Amo, yes."

"I was at a meeting in Haifa. I came by on my way to Cairo, to see how things are going. Damascus is chaotic. Are you eating with us?"

"Yes he is," said Midhat.

"Yalla."

Teta was in the hall. Her eyes were bright, and her lips pressed hard against Midhat's cheek.

"Where is your mother?" she asked Jamil.

"Downstairs."

"You should have brought her, I miss her. Ta'alu." She took Taher's coat. "Mama," she said to him, "how was Damascus?"

"Demonstrations every day, I was just telling them." He lifted his tarbush and ran three fingers through his silver hair. "It makes life more difficult for everyone, including the merchants. You should have seen the crowds . . . oof."

"What was this meeting?" said Midhat.

"Ay meeting?" said his grandmother from the divan.

"A conference in Haifa. Is there anything sweet? I'm hungry."

"Wait for dinner," said Teta.

Taher made a gesture of impatience with his pursed fingers, and Teta rose. He turned to the boys. "It was al-Nadi al-Arabi, and the other societies. Haifa, Yafa, al-Nassira . . ." He waved a hand, already bored. But as he leaned back in his chair his demeanour changed, and he made a sucking sound through his teeth. His voice became public, explanatory. "We're setting up a committee for all Palestine, three centres, Haifa, Nablus, Jerusalem. We're talking about getting Palestinians to fight in Faisal's army, against the French."

Teta returned with a tray of baklawa. Taher pulled a piece from the edge, which clung to its neighbour with strings of honey.

"Where's the napkin."

"Army," said Jamil. "Is there a war?"

"Depends. They let Faisal have his government . . . but the people are unhappy. Have you heard from your friend Hani?" He pointed at Midhat with a sticky middle finger.

The question pleased Midhat, and he wished he had a better answer. "Not for a while. I should write to him, in fact."

Haj Taher leaned back again and crossed his legs. "And what about you, have we found you a wife yet?"

In the corner of Midhat's vision, Teta's eyes flashed.

"I think so."

Teta coughed.

"I was thinking I would ask Fatima Hammad. Daughter of Haj Nimr."

Jamil leaned forward for the baklawa, and Haj Taher turned to Teta. "She's a nice girl?"

Teta shrugged and nodded at the same time.

"Hammad is a good family," he said. "You should ask soon. She's how old?"

"I don't know, actually."

"Seventeen years," said Teta, with some force.

"Shu malik?" said Haj Taher. "What's up with you?"

"Nothing."

"Where's the food? Yalla."

"Um Mahmoud is cooking. It will be ready in half an hour." She eyed the door.

"Where's your watch, Midhat?"

It took Midhat a moment to process the question. He became aware of his hands, which he had placed on his thighs. He could not tear his eyes from his father's face, the black beard tipping as he rearranged his tie, the grey hair at his temples. The silence persisted. His father looked directly at him.

"It's being fixed," said Midhat.

"What's wrong with it?"

"Oh it's only the . . . mechanism . . . he said it would be easy to fix."

"Who's he."

"The watch . . . fixer. On the road to . . . the road in . . ."

"Jerusalem?" Jamil supplied.

"Jerusalem. Greek guy, he does watches, and clocks, cameras . . . and all of that."

"Well I hope it's not expensive." Taher extracted another piece of baklawa. "And how is the store? I saw Hisham."

"Good, yes, it's good. I'm enjoying it."

"Enjoying. Well, we'll get you to Cairo soon. You'll enjoy that much more."

To Midhat's relief, the conversation at dinner turned back to politics. Some of the notables in Jerusalem were not so keen on Faisal, his father said. They wanted Palestine to fight for independence on her own.

"And there have been some disturbances. You know what the people are like, when something catches fire . . ."

"What kind of disturbances?" said Jamil.

"I don't think that is going to help the cause," said Midhat. "We aren't strong enough to threaten anyone. The Europeans will always have better armies. If you're violent and you're also the weakest party, I don't think that works out well."

"How do you know we would be the weakest?" said Jamil.

"Look at the war."

"With the help of the Arabs, Britain and France won the war."

Midhat grimaced and shook his head. "That was something else. That was about being on the inside. It was a different situation."

"Mashi," said Haj Taher. "I agree with you on that last point. But about the violence, I mean of course that's *reasonable*. We are going about it on that basis, ba'dayn, all this in Haifa. Bas remember that not everyone is reasonable in a crowd. And how can you say this to someone when they're hungry. You and I, we're not hungry. *You* can afford to think the way you do. I'm not saying I don't agree with you, I'm just saying ash-sha'ab, ya'ni, the people work differently. It's economic, in a way."

Midhat nodded. He examined his father's face for any sign he might be irritated. All he could detect were the beginnings of a smile in his mouth and eyes, at which he experienced a minor thrill. In its glow he rushed over some new arguments, constructing a balance between the two perspectives, one for pan-Syrian unity, the other for Palestinian independence, trying to gauge, as he talked, what precisely his father's position might be in order to align himself with it. But after that initial speech about the people, Haj Taher became difficult to pin down. The smile had not materialised. He gave Midhat several long, inscrutable stares, and nodded occasionally, as though storing the information for a later judgment.

"But Palestine is tiny," said Jamil. "I don't see how we can fight without Damascus."

"My grandmother was from Damascus," said Teta, loftily.

"Since it's clear the Zionists don't want to mix with us," said Taher, "their economy is their own, then it means we have to work ourselves out on our own."

Midhat ran over this statement several times, but could not make sense of it. He realised he was frowning, and unclenched his forehead.

"And how is your wife, and the children?" said Teta.

"Fine, everyone's fine. Musbah is away at school."

"Habibi, give me the bread."

"And when will you be coming back again, Father?"

"To Nablus? The spring. The spring is the best time for a wedding."

The plates cleared, Jamil went home, and Haj Taher took his coffee in the salon. In the hall, Teta grabbed Midhat's arm.

"Why did you tell him that? He said no to you."

"Who?"

His father's legs were just visible through the salon door, one foot dangling over the other. A thread of cigarette smoke stretched across the doorway.

"Haj Nimr!" she whispered.

"Oh, just—Teta hold on. Let me try one more time."

"Castles in the air. You know this will be on my head."

"Why on your head?"

"Because I am supposed to be arranging it."

"Just wait. Let me try first. And if it doesn't work, then we'll talk."

In the morning, Taher refused Midhat's offer to accompany him to the station, but he did put an arm around him, and kissed his cheek. Midhat waited by the door as the footsteps died on the rocks. Memories of his father leaving coalesced into a single departure, like a stone hewed in one place by the repeated touch of water. This chill of being left behind, with the whole day ahead, this was a far stronger dose of childhood than anything he had recognised or recalled since his return.

Although his father's suggestion of a spring wedding would not leave long to secure a bride, Midhat did not immediately start planning a second proposal to Haj Nimr. Instead, over the next week he became preoccupied with the house in which the Hammad family lived. The building itself, with its three arched windows and grand entrance, began to feature in the landscapes of his dreams. He visited the road in secret, rising earlier than usual to walk by on his way to the khan. He stood on the dark morning street and stared up at the roof, then crossed over to the other side to catch the top of the front door. He did not investigate his reasons. Nor did he ever attempt to go beyond the wall. At first he tried to map out, from the configuration of windows, the room in which he had first proposed, with the sloping ceiling above the kitchen. But it was impossible to navigate the interior with only an external view. Sometimes, the slits of a shutter flashed as a body moved inside, but the house gave no other signals.

By the end of that week his resolve had hardened. He managed to forget the feeling of the first humiliation, and his courage was renewed. Sparing little time for self-reflection, his mind ran clearly. He worked well; he made cheerful conversation with Butrus in the back room and Eli at the Samaritan store. He did not pray; he thought too little about life beyond the present moment to give any thought at all for what might transcend it.

While doing the accounts one afternoon, he turned to the back of the book where his drawings were. The first was a page of waistcoats. He gripped the leaf at the seam, and began to tear. The sound was loud and pleasant. Gone the Parisian dresses. Gone the three-piece suits. As he was crumpling the ripped pages, his eye fell on the next. It was covered in drafts of the same woman's face. Dimple in the chin, little wrinkles under the eyes. He dropped the screwed-up balls of paper, and slid this page into the light. His heart fell. He had done the hair in different styles: short, long, pinned back. But he had accentuated those two features—chin and eyes—at the expense of the others. The lips were wrong.

"If we need more blue taffeta, we need more blue—" came Hisham's voice from the back room, where he was talking to Butrus.

Midhat blushed to think Hisham might have seen these. He placed his hands flat on the warm wooden counter. He was going to give in—just this once. Like falling into an illicit sleep: first, he summoned her chin. He waited for the rest. Broken lines came, movements, the shape of her face. Her lips. Sweet, soft, rounded at the bottom. His stomach twanged. The eyes had not come, and he was still waiting for them when Hisham's footsteps sounded behind him. He forced himself awake, tore the page three times with shaking hands, and threw it with the others into the bin.

"Before you say, 'I want to marry Fatima,'" said Jamil, "make sure you describe yourself. I am Midhat, I have lived in Paris, I am educated. Shayef? And then you say, I would like to marry your daughter, and so on, kaza wa kazalek."

"That's what I did last time."

"Well this time spend more time talking about yourself. And after that, don't forget to compliment the family. And maybe . . . dress up a little. What were you wearing last time? Try a nicer tie."

Midhat chose a blue mouchoir and a pair of matching blue silk socks, and had his shoes shined. He started sweating on the street below. He pressed the outer doorbell and the guard showed him up the steps, past the trellis, to the house itself.

Even after hours of talking it over with his cousin, he was unable to imagine this event happening in any other way than exactly as it had happened the first time. Widad would open the door, show him upstairs; he even anticipated the same group of men drinking orange juice. But it had been autumn then, and now it was the verge of winter, and the northern winds brought a whisper of snow. He climbed the steps and was about to knock when the door opened of its own accord. Haj Nimr was standing on the other side.

"I'm sorry, I didn't mean to startle you," said Midhat.

"Ah . . . Hello. How can I help? I'm leaving, I'm afraid."

"I would like . . . My name is Midhat Kamal."

"Midhat Kamal. As-salamu alaykum. I'm going to the diwan. Walk with me."

"I have studied medicine," his voice echoed under the arch to the gate, "as well as philosophy, and history also. And my father's business is doing extremely well in Cairo."

Nimr waved at the guard as they stepped onto the street.

"The name is becoming quite famous. Kamal. And he is involved in politics also, my father. He has just returned from Damascus, and he was at the general conference in Haifa. He will be one of the representatives for Nablus at the Palestine Committee meeting, with the aim of unification with Syria."

This last assertion was not exactly true, but it was a nice embellishment, which Jamil had said would leave an impression on Nimr's mind after he had forgotten the particulars.

"Oh, very good," said Nimr.

Midhat felt confident to proceed. "For these reasons, I believe I would make an excellent husband for your daughter Fatima."

They had reached the point in the street where the paving dipped over the shape of the mountain. Nimr stopped and turned his head. His mouth was slightly agape.

"You have already asked me this."

Midhat drew breath to interrupt. Nimr continued: "And I did tell you that the answer—unfortunately—is no."

"I know, I know," said Midhat. "I wanted to try again."

"The answer will still be no."

"Is she marrying Yasser Hammad?" Midhat had not planned to ask this, and knew he was blushing.

"Excuse me? No . . . no, she is not marrying Yasser." Haj Nimr considered him. And then, belatedly, seemed to take affront. "I am going to be late now," he said. "Ma'salameh."

Haj Nimr walked down the hill. Midhat stayed where he was, denied a second time. But at least he had learned that she was not marrying Yasser.

Even after this second rejection, he did not stop visiting the Hammad house. There was no snow yet, only rain, which came in heavy blasts, unpredictable and intermittent. Dawn shivered in the peaked windows that showed over the high wall. His morning visits became a secret compulsion, and over subsequent weeks he split into two people; one was the doctor of the other and made a point of checking his appetite. His doctor-self limited the visits to the Hammad house to every other day, and under this restriction he effected in his chest a strenuous longing on the days he was deprived. And on the days he surrendered and ran early down the mountain, he began to feel the same blissful consolation of running to meet a lover. Except that all he was meeting was a house, and not even an entire house: only what segments of window and roof were visible over the wall.

At least, this was the case until one morning, when he was waiting down on the street under a light drizzle, and the front door opened. Out stepped two figures in black. A shorter and a taller. One of them must be Fatima. On his tiptoes he squinted, the rain cold on his face. One of them half turned on the steps, and opened an umbrella. They disappeared behind the wall. The gate opened, and they slipped onto the road. He met the eyes of one, he did not know afterwards if she was the taller or the shorter, only that she met his eyes and he knew it was her. And then she had covered her head beneath the umbrella, and they were pattering away down the street.

The rain sharpened and crashed around him. Midhat felt sick. He looked at the stone wall, streaked with darkness by the rain, and vividly

Jeannette came to him. He saw her turning in the upstairs corridor, her soft rejecting cheek, and with a rush of loathing pulled the tarbush from his head. His shirt was wet. The puddles on the road were wide and deep and when he arrived home his feet were soaking, and Um Mahmoud shrieked at the footprints in the hall. On the table lay an envelope, addressed to him. He rubbed his arms with a towel and tore it open with a finger: the hand was Hani's.

9 February 1920

18 Jumada I 1338

Cher Midhat,

I write to you from Damascus—though I will be returning with Emir Faisal to Europe soon—I hope you are well—the last time I saw you, you were writing a letter—I hope that all worked out for the best. You must be happy back in Nablus with your family. I miss you dear Midhat—when the region is settled I hope we shall see each other again—for now as you may know it is a difficult time and the latest round of talks with Clemenceau has been a failure and yet there seems to be nothing else to do but continue to negotiate—even while the people of Damascus or really all of Syria are in distress.

After the withdrawal of the British troops the French have been in the coastal areas—there have been many clashes. Faisal has been corresponding with General Gouraud hoping to settle the tension and Gouraud has just now accused him of incitement. This is absurd of course—Gouraud is asking Faisal to deny rumours that the French want to invade. How can they expect him to do that when that is exactly what it looks like? How can they expect him to approve the imprisonment of Mahmoud Abd al-Salam and the other ones when in their demonstrations in Sidon they were calling out "Long live King Faisal"? How are we supposed to stop the newspapers from naming Faisal a king to whom Syria is his due kingdom? Tripoli expresses allegiance to Syria—how can they expect us to take action against them? Syria is in insurrection—it is imperative that we send Arab representatives to cool down the Western region. The French say this would have terrible consequences—how can it be terrible I ask you when they would be Syrians discussing with their compatriots the future of their country—reassuring them that they are all members of an independent Syria? The French say the Christians want to be separate from the Muslims—again this is not true—and they keep calling the Syrian army Sharifi when not one soldier is from the Hejaz—they are all Syrians! We are all Syrians. The French want to provoke religious warfare and now they have stopped the convoys of food from going to Aleppo. Would you call that the behaviour of an ally? I do not think so.

As for Palestine—the Zionist program is trouble for everyone. Faisal is trying to be honourable and naturally the French are putting pressure on him to compromise. I hesitate these days over whether to call myself Syrian or Palestinian—and what about "Arab"—when the Europeans use the word I am sure that in fact they only mean a Muslim—they often also seem to mean a man who lives in a tent. What does that mean for the Christians and the Jews and the people of the Levant in general? And while we're on that topic we should be clear about what exactly we ourselves mean by the term when we use it—is it simply a question of language or something larger—because in the end "Arab" might be no finer than "European"—and we know how different the French are from the Germans. This is why I think we should be called Syrians—were the Jews called Syrians at the time of Christ and before him? Yes—Herodotus had already called them thus.

In the end I hope we will be able to name ourselves—the American Commission reported that no solution that has only a single people in mind can prevail but on the contrary habibi Midhat we all know that the strongest power will prevail as it always prevails.

As for Faruq—when I left Paris he was continuing at the language school where the numbers had risen since the armistice—he misses you—he asked after his favourite lover and it reminded me to write—and of course I also miss you. I hope your journey was safe and Nablus is not yet too troubled by what is happening.

Your brother,
Hani

8

"Examine me," said Um Taher. "I'm sick."

"What?"

"I said, examine me."

"I can't," said Midhat. He hesitated, searching for an excuse. "I have none of the equipment."

"You can't do it without equipment?"

He closed his book. "Are you coughing at all?"

"Of course I'm coughing. You don't hear me at night?"

"Is there anything in the cough?"

"Sometimes." She tested her throat: nothing came. She whimpered. "Oh, I don't know."

"What about pain?"

"All the time."

"Where?"

"Sometimes here, sometimes here. I might be dying."

"You think if you were dying you'd be walking around? I don't think so," said Midhat, and roughly opened his book again.

With mock nonchalance, hand on the door handle: "In that case, I suppose I'll go to the clinic near the Green Mosque."

"No, you won't. You'll see the Ebal Girls at the hospital. I don't trust those clinics."

"Oh, Monsieur." She raised an eyebrow.

Um Taher did not ask her grandson to examine her again. Nor, however, did she go to the hospital; nor to the clinic as she had threatened. It was not that she was afraid, exactly. Only, she could count the times she had met a doctor with two fingers and a thumb, and that was including the birth of Taher.

A few days later, she found Midhat standing by the kitchen window staring at the wall between the cupboard and a rack of grimy spice bottles. When he was a child he had often walked in his sleep, and as she used to then at the sight of that small boy ghostly in the hall, Um Taher now made a hushing sound to soften her approach, feeling the familiar pang of terror that the grandson before her was not himself. His eyes met hers, red and tired, and as his lips trembled he pursed them stiffly.

"Teta I don't think I can do it."

"Do what?"

"Marry."

She clicked her teeth. "Everyone can marry. When I was a young girl, I was in love with a man who—"

"I know, Teta, I know this story."

"Sitti—yalla sit. Listen to me."

"I don't want to hear the story, I know."

"I'm not telling you the story. I'm telling you, you cannot see the length of your life. You only see these little things in front of you—I know you. Trust me. I am not choosing someone who will not be good for you."

"I—"

"Stenna, just listen instead of talking. Do you know how upset I was when I met my fiancé?"

He looked up. His eyes were watery. He shook his head.

"I screamed." Her hand swept the air. "Wallahi my mother was ashamed. But, sitti, believe, how quickly I loved him. Really. He was good with me. I was happy. My mother and father chose him well—"

Suddenly Midhat was on his feet. He bolted to the door.

"Where are you—what are you doing?"

He grabbed an ornamental copper pitcher from the sideboard and thrust it at the wall with both hands. It clanged off, crashed twice, and skidded across the floor.

"Stop!"

He leaned against the wall, his mouth opening like a baby's, trailing threads of saliva. Um Taher heaved down to pick up the pitcher; there was a dent in the belly.

"You've ruined my pot! Do you understand how lucky you are? Do you understand how people in this town are jealous of you?"

"Why do you *care*?"

"Why do I care! Majnun you are, are you trying to kill me? I will *hit* you."

"I can't do this, I can't . . . I'm sorry."

"Stop saying you can't."

"I can't, I need freedom."

That was too much. Um Taher slammed the unlucky pitcher down onto the table. "Freedom from *what*?"

He put his fingertips at his mouth and flung them forward.

"Teta help me, you have to help me. I'm so tired—I just want to stay on my own, I just—Teta, help me, I don't want some girl I don't know."

"As I explained to you—"

"Don't you see? I love someone else."

"You are the same as everyone, habibi," said Um Taher forcefully. "You have to forget. That is done now."

Midhat shot her a startled look. "What do you mean?"

"You are here now. You are making yourself sick from thinking—I see you thinking, it's not good for you."

Deep in her lungs Um Taher sensed the storm-crackle of an oncoming cough.

"I'll find you a beautiful woman, I promise. A beautiful, *intelligent* woman. You will live on your own with her, you will be independent. I promise you won't live with me—"

"Teta—"

"I'm not going to be here forever, and then who will look after you? Who will make sure your house is clean, feed you, help when you are sick? You think a ghost makes your bed? You think a ghost makes sure your clothes are clean?"

His chin was pitting; she changed course.

"Yalla habibi when we find you a wife your father will be very proud, very very proud—and *then*, habibi, you can do whatever you want. Go to Cairo, work with Baba, travel—whatever. And you will have this beautiful, lovely girl with you. And you will have children—as many children as you want."

She inhaled to continue. The cough shot up and rattled out of her mouth.

"Teta you have to go to the hospital."

"No," she managed to say, feeling his hand on her back. She took a breath, wheezed, hacked again.

"You know more about marriage, but I know medicine."

"Water."

The faucet hissed. "U ba'dayn," he called, "isn't the hospital owned by Dar Hammad?"

She made a scuffing noise of distaste. "Hammad family. Snobs, they are. Total snobs."

Everyone knew Haj Tawfiq Hammad founded the municipal hospital in a rage after an English missionary doctor tried to convert his sister. With the aid of other wealthy denizens—including Haj Taher Kamal—Tawfiq and his nephew Nimr renovated an old palace at the foot of Ebal, knocking through the walls to make four long wards, employing the French Sisters of St. Joseph, who did not evangelise, to be the staff.

Even though her son was one of the hospital founders, Um Taher preferred not to enter the strange building that smelled of death and surgical spirit. When she inhaled she continued to hear the sound of wheels being dragged over rocks but she stifled it and did not complain. If she coughed in company, she blamed the lack of rainfall, and the accumulation of dust.

Of late the rains had ceased entirely. The terraced fields on the mountains were turning grey, and when the trees thrashed, their fingers snapped quickly and fell. But while the imams were out praying for one final rain before the snow, the word among the ladies was that Madame Atwan would be hosting her istiqbal in the courtyard of her palace, safe in the dry evening. Um Taher was not in the mood for a party. But it was necessary she attend, since the task was upon her to find Midhat a wife before Taher returned in the spring.

Despite the winter sting in the air, the plants around the courtyard walls conjured an illusion of springtime. The wind quickened the leaves, which displayed their veiny undersides one by one. The servants filed out of the house bearing trays of coffee cups. The black contents shook and flashed.

At one end of the courtyard, women lined up to inspect a camera positioned on a tripod. In pairs they ran their fingers over the leather bellows, tested the black enamel around the lens with their fingernails, avoiding the glass as instructed. In turns they disappeared under the black fabric and cooed through the viewfinder. The owner of the contraption was an Armenian woman from Nazareth named Elmas, who stood guard to point at the various elements and announce their official names. She repeated the word "Kodak" several times.

From the other side of the courtyard, Madame Atwan observed the progress of the night's first spectacle. Or the second, since she herself was the first: hand still extended for the lips of the next arriving guest, moving it lower and lower as the hour advanced, so that the tardiest guests must practically kneel. The bracelets on her forearms slid floorward, the ones above the elbow indenting the flesh. The silk of her gown capped her bare shoulders, and her shoes, curved in the heel, alternately poked out from under her skirt as she shifted her weight between them.

She must be very cold, was Um Taher's first thought when she arrived and kissed the fingers. Coughing, she joined Um Jamil in the camera queue.

"Your health," said Um Jamil.

"The dust."

"Bitjannin!" cried the ladies around the camera. "Bitjannin!"

"My lungs have started to sing. Listen."

"It's hard to hear, Khalto," said Um Jamil.

"Bitjannin!"

"But you should see the Girls of the Mountain, if you're in pain."

"I don't like hospitals."

"Did you ask Midhat?"

"I did, he doesn't have the equipment, he said go to the Ebal Girls. I don't want to go to the Girls, shu bitsawi."

"How is he?"

"Wallah he needs a wife. Boys their age, this energy they have, they don't know what to do with it."

"Jamil is the same. He can be very moody."

They had reached the front of the line. Um Jamil approached the camera and Um Taher took a cup of coffee from a passing tray. It was already cold, and very sweet. She took one sip, coughed, and pressed her lips together. Water sprang to her eyes, and in a bid to conceal it she stepped forward to join Um Jamil by the lens.

"Yalla, go under, Khalto," said Um Jamil, lifting the black cloth.

Um Taher held Um Jamil's arm for balance, accepted the darkness, and positioned herself in front of the viewfinder. She gasped. Before her was a bright pane of glass. On top of the glass, on top or else somehow inside, the scene of the party floated upside down and reversed. She teetered, grasping Um Jamil's arm, and the image moved. It was a vision of phantoms: the women were walking suspended from their shoes, tapping up where their heads should be. Their heads hung below like black medallions around the fountain, which was itself hanging from the floor like a huge stone chandelier.

"Oh la la," she whispered.

Madame Atwan's voice rang out.

"Widad Hammad!"

The hanging faces turned. Blood rushed to Um Taher's cheeks and she was grateful for the privacy of the curtain. Into the upside-down scene walked Widad Hammad, smiling and holding out her arms to the hostess. Two girls followed. Fatima was the taller, or rather the longer, of the two, and God knew even capsized she was beautiful. It was enough to make Um

Taher dizzy; she reached for Um Jamil, who pulled the cloth off her head, and she came up for air.

There, across the courtyard, the real Hammad women stood the right way up. Fatima wore a black velvet dress and a collar of pearls. The second daughter was plainer, her eyes closer together; what was ripe about Fatima's mouth appeared too large on this one.

The arrival of the Hammads might have been a signal to the servant girls, because the moment Um Jamil stepped away from the camera two of them each lifted a leg of the tripod and carried it into an alcove where a third girl was ready with another, larger black cloth to cover it with. Disappointment passed over the faces of the women who had been waiting, but they soon dispersed into the circles that were breeding around the courtyard as coffee cups disappeared from the trays.

"His wife is beautiful. And the dress was very valuable ba'dayn," said a lady on one of the stools, adjusting an arm to keep her coffee level. "The collar. Like a half-moon. Silver. Kteer helu."

"Where did he get all the money from?"

Um Taher put a hand on her chest, and Um Jamil squeezed her arm. "You want my scarf?"

She shook her head.

"*She's* very beautiful," said Um Jamil, pointing at a girl with curly hair. "Who is her mother?"

"I don't know." Um Taher was still watching the Hammads and Madame Atwan. Widad Hammad was wearing an embroidered jacket, gold with red piping across the back, unusually close around the waist. Without warning, Widad swivelled round and saw her.

"Um Taher!"

"Marhaba," said Um Taher, majestically. "Aash min shafek." She commenced her slow approach.

Widad covered the remaining ground with an expensive clop of heels. "How are you." She kissed Um Taher three times. "What's your news?"

"Hamdulillah, and you, how are you."

"Hamdulillah, Nuzha, Fatima, say hello to Madame Kamal."

"As-salamu alaykum," said the girls.

"Mashallah," said Um Taher. "What beautiful girls you have." She shut her eyes to smile. She could not face Midhat's failure, she could not face it.

"We were discussing the French priest," said Madame Atwan, stepping from an adjacent circle and joining them. "Have you met him?"

"I have not," said Um Taher.

"What does he look like?" said Widad.

"Beard," said a lady in a draped green tunic, shaping a beard on her own chin. "Long gown. And asking questions," she scribbled in the air.

"Yes, he asks questions," said Madame. "They all ask questions. They all want to know how we live."

"I know him," said Um Taher suddenly.

Widad looked at her.

"Did you see him at the hospital?" said Madame Atwan.

"No, I saw him at the—" She turned her gaze to a window above the courtyard, where a light had come on. "I can't remember."

"Why are people interested, anyway," said the woman in the green tunic. "We have enough to think about. I am fed up with Europeans. I hate them, no one is more perfidious, I'll tell you that. At least an Arab lies to your face."

Widad was just parting her lips to speak when Madame Atwan cried: "We are going to take a picture now!"

Um Taher and Widad shared a startled look. They saw the direction of Madame Atwan's eyes: upward. The sky was molten dark. It was going to rain.

"Are we ready for the picture!" A tremor of panic, the herd of women shuffling. The camera was pulled out, its glass eye glittered aloft as two girls each held one of the tripod legs, and a third ran behind carrying the black cloth, which had slipped off.

"Elmas! Elmas?"

"I'm here, Madame. Who would you like me to photograph?"

Madame Atwan hesitated. "Me. And then the others. Where shall I sit."

Without waiting for an answer, she trotted across the tiles to select an unoccupied cushion, and placed it towards the centre of the courtyard as the guests fanned backward. She sat on the floor and arranged herself over the cushion, leaning sideways like a Roman.

"Keef," she said to someone. She felt for her earring, and turned it round to show the engraving. She doubled her chin to check her necklaces.

"Heyk, Khalto," said a young wife crouching to arrange Madame's skirt.

Elmas the photographer was ready with the camera. The ladies nearby observed as she adjusted the aperture and then ran the camera's head back and forth along its short jetty. "All right Mama," she called. "Move your head a little to the side."

She whispered to one of the servant girls, who ran indoors and returned with a device like an abbreviated dustpan with a wooden handle, and a small box. Elmas opened the box. In the manner of a performing magician or scientist she picked out two pots from inside, and held them up to show the labels: one said MAGNESIUM, the other B. N.

"Five spoons of this," she said loudly, measuring into the metal trough, "and six of this . . . five, six. One match, please."

The tiny match sizzled with a tang of sulphur. Elmas stepped forward, one hand on the buttoned end of a wire attached to the camera, the other holding her pan of powder aloft. On the cushion, Madame cleared her throat and lifted a stray hair from her forehead with one finger. Elmas dipped the trough to receive the match, and before they knew what was happening there was a bright flash of light. Just as quickly, darkness returned. The courtyard, cloudy, erupted with applause and whistles. Madame Atwan was getting to her feet with a smile and several women ran forward to help her, shouting, "Be careful!" Elmas gave an embarrassed half bow, pan aloft.

The light had left an impression on Um Taher's eyes. Over everything around her, over the women clapping and talking to one another, over the bodies of the young girls and the glittering jewellery, she saw her own capillaries magnified and white, like bolts of lightning.

"How are you Um Taher?"

Um Jamil was by her side.

"Tamam, tamam."

"Next, all the ladies!"

The rain commenced, little droplets. Around the courtyard, leaves began to twitch.

Um Taher was pulled into the second row beside Um Jamil. She glanced at the assemblage of unsmiling faces, then stared straight ahead as Elmas prepared a second flash mixture. A bang of light, and a loud shivering sound like breaking glass as the rain struck up in earnest. "Oh Mama!" Um Jamil said, and valiantly cast her shawl over Um Taher's head, as the three lines of ladies disintegrated. But although it was a disruption, everyone applauded the thunder just as they would another spectacle of the night, and whistled at the water rushing down while they ran for shelter by the doors, and the servants helped Elmas to protect the camera, calling: "Ya salam!"

Under the rain all formality dissolved. The laughing horde reassembled in the salon, shaking off clothes and drowning out the storm with their voices. A short woman with a veil entered through an internal door, strode to the centre of the room, bowed at Madame Atwan, faced the rest of the company and sang at the pace of a dirge: "Ishma'na – ya – nokh." A pause, and she completed the phrase: "Al-kukay—a—a—ayn – kokh."

The women applauded and whistled.

Ishma'na ya nokh al-kukay-ayn kokh
da akul al-mokh halakna
amilu ala ghee—eerna.

"Um Jamil," said Um Taher.

"Yes habibti."

"I want to ask you. Did you hear anything about Midhat, recently?"

Um Jamil tilted her head.

"I mean, has there been any, ya'ni—"

"Ah. No, no, I didn't hear anything. What are you worried about?"

She waved her hand, as though dispersing a smell.

"I did hear about Haj Hassan," said Um Jamil. "Did you?"

"No, tell me."

"Lost all his land in the valley. Sold very cheaply to the Jews."

"Why?"

"I heard three versions. One, he is worried about his wife, because she has gone insane. Two, the land was not producing enough and he needed the money. Three, he gambles. I don't know which is true."

In the middle of this speech, Um Taher noticed Widad and Fatima Hammad standing together a few feet along. Fatima was looking at the floor, but Widad was staring at them. Her face had gone grey.

"I feel sorry for his son," Um Jamil went on. "Nothing to inherit."

Only later, after Um Jamil left her on her doorstep, did Um Taher realise the party had been a failure for her. Of enquiries about available girls she had made none at all.

A cough hurtled up through her belly and out through her mouth. At least if she was dying, she would join Um Midhat in heaven. She pictured herself laid out across the board, and Um Jamil, weeping, ministering to her body. A dignified face, eyes closed. No: eyes open. Let them close the eyes before the burial, that was a lovely action. She raised a hand in the darkness and imitated the movement with her fingers. Then, swinging her weight to the side, she thought of Midhat. She could not leave him. She sighed, and a hock of phlegm caught in her windpipe, and coughing again she felt wisps of electricity conferring in her chest.

The morning was bleak. The storm last night had left nothing but cold behind. She wrapped herself slowly in many layers, resolved at last to visit the hospital.

The wind hurt her throat and tore the breath from her lungs. Taking the northern road that curved west she cleared the town and approached the foot of Mount Ebal. The first thing she noticed in the hospital foyer was the odour, sharp and chemical-sweet, penetrating to the back of her head. A large coffer with a slit for coins stood in the centre, and beyond it a row of tall windows showed a tree-filled garden and arable land. From the bottom of one window poked the ends of two posts, perhaps the ears of a chair—a veranda. She slipped a hand into her purse for the coffer, and a nurse materialised on her right. She gestured for Um Taher to follow.

The ward was long and dense with beds. Pictures hung crookedly on curved plaster walls and a large gas lamp swayed from the ceiling. Um Taher avoided looking at the occupants, but saw from the margins of her vision that all were girls, wearing nothing on their heads but a thin bit of fabric tied under the hair. The nurse's heels clapped across the tiles, and the bedcovers writhed as the patients watched her follow. Was this what they did all day, lie in bed surveying whoever came through? There must be another room, a private one, in which the older, distinguished ladies took their rest.

At the last bed but one, her gaze digressed. The bedclothes were so still that at first they appeared empty; there was, however, a woman lying there. On her back, staring up at the ceiling. It was not an attitude of repose.

"Keefek, madame?" said the nurse.

"Shu," said Um Taher, indicating the motionless woman. "Hayye?"

"Yes, she's alive," said a girl with an eye patch from the next bed. "She's mad."

From a lighted doorway a man called, "Could I have your name please?" and the nurse jumped into action. "Tfadali." She ushered Um Taher through the door and closed it between them.

A bald Arab man was washing his hands in a basin.

"I am Doctor Ibrahim. Your name?"

"Mahdiya Um Taher Kamal."

"Thank you." Doctor Ibrahim dried his hands on a flannel, and picked up a clipboard. "Please, sit."

The only place to sit was on a flimsy-looking bed with a white blanket. This room was both immaculate and crowded with objects. Um Taher fixed her attention on the shelves opposite, which held an assortment of translucent bottles with their labels facing her. As the doctor opened a drawer and shut it again, she reached out for a very small bottle at the end. The letters on the tag resembled grains of rice.

"You can read French?"

She looked up. The doctor had put on an apron.

"I cannot read at all."

"Ah, so it's the same. Don't worry, I won't be examining you. I am a surgeon. Here she comes, Sister Sarah. Bonjour Sister, meet Madame Kamal. La madame vient avec une maladie pulmonaire."

The nurse who had just opened the door was short, with black hair and a gaunt face. "D'accord."

The doctor swung a rubber pipe off his neck and handed it to her. "Fursa sa'ida, Madame Kamal," he said, raising a hand as he left.

Sister Sarah spoke slightly more Arabic than the other nurse. She asked Um Taher to remove her veil, and applying the cold metal plug at the end of the rubber pipe to Um Taher's chest, asked her to breathe in and out. Next, she told her to lean forward and lifted her gown to apply the metal to her back, warmed slightly by her skin but still cool, and asked her again to breathe in and out. Um Taher obeyed and heard the rattle of her lungs, amplified by the nurse's attention. Something hard and metallic tapped her around the spine. Her back went cold with exposure and she knew the nurse had moved away.

"Is it *sill*?"

"No," said Sister Sarah. She was writing in a large book. "No, it is not tuberculosis."

She would not need to stay the night. The nurse presented a small bottle of medicine with a rubber stopper and instructed her to put two drops in a big pan of hot water and inhale it in the evenings before bed.

As she was leaving, Um Taher saw a bald pate through the window in the foyer, ridges in the skull like sand dunes. Descending the outer steps she took a long route round the back. There he was, in the corner of the railed veranda, rocking on a chair. His whitish robe involved a kind of shawl over his shoulders, and on his head he wore a black hat with a wide brim. He had a blanket over his lap, and he appeared to be sketching the view.

She chose a chair beyond the remit of the window, and her heart began to calm as the animate landscape paused, the wind drawing breath before stirring the grasses again.

After a while the priest stood and approached. In careful, accented Arabic, he asked if he might sit nearby, pointing at a particular chair, not directly beside hers but a few chairs down. She nodded, shrugged her shawl a little closer and adjusted the veil over her neck. But instead of turning to her, or paying her any attention at all, the priest simply arranged his blanket, faced the landscape, and continued to sketch. Perhaps he had only moved to adjust his perspective. She wheezed. She listened to his pencil whisper over the page, and to some faint birdsong, and the clock ticking on the farther wall. After a few moments he asked, still drawing:

"Do you come to the hospital often?"

"No. I am not often ill. Ba'dayn, my grandson has trained to be a doctor."

"Oh really?" He was looking at her. "Where did he train?"

"France."

"Ah, I am from France! Where in France?"

"Paris. And . . . Montpeliano. Montpe . . ."

"Ah," said the priest.

They exchanged pleasantries about the hospital, the war, the British; the priest made her laugh with a joke about the rivalry between England and France. She was telling him a funny story of her own, a famous one about the Samaritans and a lascivious Greek pastor, when she noticed that the priest's pencil was writing words in the notebook, not drawing, and she cut herself off with: "What are you writing?"

The pen ran backward over the page and stopped.

"Something I wanted to remember. I'm sorry. Go on."

She would not go on. She must go and take her medicine, she said. She unlocked the gate on the veranda to depart that way, through the trees. From the lower path, she looked back and saw two figures on the balcony: the priest, and a woman. The black figure of the woman was moving, hands gesturing beneath her veil.

She returned two days later, and arriving half an hour before the clinic opened was shown onto the veranda. There was the priest, in a rocking chair with his book. He returned her nod and faced the view. Birds sang, the clock ticked. The priest did not speak. She watched the minute hand turn. Finally, she took a long, unsteady breath.

"I hear you have been talking to the Hammad family."

The long beard quaked with the movements of his face, and he blinked several times.

"Haj Nimr Hammad has been very kind to me," he said. "And of course, this is their hospital."

"How are they?" said Um Taher. "What is their news? I have not seen them for some time."

There was a pause. "Did you know about Haj Hassan's exile?" said the priest.

"Oh yes, yes, ma'roof. And he sold his land in the Jordan Valley. Poor man." She was quiet. "Anything else?"

"I'm afraid that may be all I know about the Hammad family. Let me . . . let me look in my notes." Pages sighed as he ran his hand over the corners.

"And what about, who has been . . . visiting the Samaritans lately?"

She challenged him with her eyes, thinking of her story about the Greek pastor. It was a transaction. She gave him one, he gave her one.

"Well, there was a lady who wanted to do a charm for her grandson . . ."

Her chest pounded.

"Apart from that, while I was there once I saw a man from one of the major families, but I wasn't allowed to sit in for that. They went into another room."

"Ah. And the family was?"

"The man was an Atwan."

"Atwan. And you don't know who the charm was for?"

"No. I remember something about a bird. I'm afraid I didn't write it down, I was trying to be . . . respectful."

The sides of his face spread apart and fell, and his arms shook as he made a hiccoughing noise. She realised he was laughing.

"Of course, of course," she said, hurrying to catch up.

The door opened. "Madame," said the nurse.

"Thank you, Abuna," said Um Taher, rising to her feet.

"You are welcome. I hope to see you again, Madame."

9

From an eastern peak of Mount Gerizim, Père Antoine watched the wind run through the valley, ruffling the trees and disturbing the grasses, and the whole landscape pulsed as the wind lost energy and mustered it again. He felt the alternating pressures on his sturdy body, pushing him gently back and forth, as the black cappa of his habit was tossed upwards like the skirt of a woman dancing.

The rock on which he sat was shaped like a gigantic molar, and the depression in the crown was so smooth it was easy to imagine that hundreds had used it as a chair over the ages, shepherds and wanderers and mendicants like himself. And there was another, smaller rock in front for one's foot to rest upon, before the declivity sharpened and the earth vanished, and a view rushed out of white citadels and walking figures. A vast and ancient olive tree stood rooted to his left, its bark so contorted and rivuletted that, squinting, one saw a crowd of figures stretched and crouching open-mouthed, like medieval lechers on a Last Judgment relief. All in all, the specimen had a girth of some three metres, which Antoine had estimated himself one morning by embracing it. More than once he heard it alleged the oldest tree in Palestine. Such allegations had to be taken with good humour; guides were always reporting prodigies they hoped would propel the hearer's arm a little deeper into his or her pochette. But quite rightly they perceived it was a marvel. Antoine found himself at this spot again and again on account of this tree, this beautiful crone, which made such superb company for the view.

Down there in the valley was Jacob's Well. The Russians had begun building a church around it more than a decade ago, but stopped when their revolution broke out, so the church resembled a ruin before it ever lived as an entire building, and Jacob's Well, though cleared of rubbish, remained half-exposed to the air. That was despite the fact that all the faiths of Abraham, which could squabble for eternity over relics and geographies, agreed at least on this one site, that it was Jacob's, which was where Jesus Christ met the woman of Samaria, and he, according to the Gospel of John, "being wearied with his journey, sat thus on the well" and asked that she might give him a drink. Yet no Nabulsi had gone out of his way to dress up the well for visitors, never mind the care they lavished on other shrines in the valley. No Nabulsi, aside from the odd enterprising guide, cared for European tourists at all. Other cities were forming whole quarters for pilgrims and artefact seekers. Nablus had not a single hotel for foreigners.

But this was why Nablus was perfect for Antoine's research: the city was nigh untouched. Her inhabitants did not perform, as he had watched impoverished Jaffans do, dressing up as shepherds to greet passengers from cruise ships with splinters of Christ's own cross. Never in Nablus. Despite or perhaps even because of the Christian and Samaritan elements, Nablus was a perfect specimen of the Islamic city. Antoine observed her lovingly from below as well as above, and noted down all the hearsay he gleaned from the patients in the municipal hospital.

Père Antoine's official position was Professor of Oriental Studies at L'École Pratique d'Études Bibliques in Jerusalem. He joined the school as a student some twenty years ago, around the time of the Dreyfus affair when France expelled the religious orders and the Dominicans left Lyon in a flood. On the clerical grapevine, young Antoine had already heard about Père Lavigne's new École in Jerusalem. Lavigne's school wanted to defend Catholicism against the Modernists. The method, however, was unorthodox: the scholars would actually try to satisfy the demands of science and history, contextualise the gospel using "modern" methods—but use what they found to *defend* supernatural faith.

Antoine was then nineteen years old and had never left France. He travelled by ship from Marseille to Port Said and thence to Jerusalem by train, and discovered on arrival that the strength of Lavigne's reputation had imputed to his project more substance than it had in reality. The priory was not yet built, though the priests had measured out the ground across the old tomb of St. Stephen. Along with three other seminarians who had arrived for the start of term, Antoine was directed to lodge in a temporary dormitory on the premises of the former Turkish slaughterhouse.

Père Lavigne, however, did not disappoint. A man of middling height, with a twisted friendly mouth, modest brown beard, and balding head, he infected the boys at once with his enthusiasm. His speech at the inaugural assembly gave Antoine the impression of a large-hearted visionary, striving, not without fear, but with courage enough to lead them all in their course towards truth.

Within a couple of weeks the impact was mutual: brother Antoine was star of his class in the Semitic languages, and in him Lavigne said he detected a capacious mind marked already by the anxieties of high ambition. Throughout the ensuing five years of his studies, and long after his anointment, Lavigne operated as Antoine's personal mentor. He encouraged Antoine's rigour, his independence, his virtue. Antoine's was a mind after Lavigne's own: that rare meticulous Catholic with a faith so pure he could keep one clear-sighted eye trained always on the earth.

The modernist crisis was a personal crisis for every exegete. Lavigne's courage was to bring this into the open, and steer the school to battle en masse. To defend the faith, he taught them, to seek out true meaning, they must fearlessly apply techniques of literary analysis to biblical text. Was it a camel that passed through the eye of a needle? Or was it, by a corruption of text and misunderstanding, a rope? Strengthened by their master's faith, and every day crossing the very ground that Jesus trod, living one storey above the sepulchred relics of Stephanos, the young brothers read the Gospels in Greek, studied and spoke Aramaic, closed in on the incalculable questions, confronted with valour the awful fact that the Latin vulgate they were raised on was itself a dilution. But in the mad breath of Jerusalem it was easy to visualize Christ's real body, the bony hands that healed and were maimed under the pale hot sky before that skull-white Golgotha stone, and these visions equipped them with courage where the Protestants, they knew, had already faltered.

Although the larger aim was metaphysical, therefore, Lavigne's vision for the school was absolutely local and material. He spent great energy seeking a faculty to develop the curricula of languages, archaeology, and geography. The school grew in size and sprouted a wing for another dormitory. The brothers and fathers considered themselves in Aquinas's image: all things in heaven and earth converged, and everything had its essence. As scholars they were stretching through their intellects to touch those essences, like pilgrims placing hands on the Anointing Stone.

The watchful eye of the papacy was not so sure. From that Latin vantage Lavigne's "historical method" looked suspiciously similar to the modernism it purported to attack. Lavigne's annotation of Genesis was banned. Far from discouraging the seminarians, however, this news of pontific suspicion actually spurred them on. A fever of devotion ran down the makeshift lecture halls. They were pioneers. First they had incurred the wrath of France, and now the wrath of Rome. They were a fellowship of brothers, navigating the rationalist storm together, aiming at the divine beacon of the Church's authority, with their minds.

At the farther edge of the city a motorcar appeared. It progressed like a beetle along the valley road and passed a tiny figure holding something; the figure moved to the side, and a puff of dust rose around the wheels as the vehicle turned a corner. A Brit's car, undoubtedly; no Arabs in Nablus owned cars, though chauffeurs were sometimes locals. Through the dust the figure continued walking. Antoine made a note:

"Ask ladies at the hospital—motorcars?"

The muezzins began to interrupt each other. He shifted his foot. A woman in a cloak was stepping off the path towards him. She wore a headdress—no, a wimple. It was Sister Louise.

"Sister! I didn't recognise you."

He stood and gestured at the vacated rock. She mimed a protest, then reached out for the back of the rock and circled her way around it, stepping carefully. With some difficulty, he crouched on the ground beside her.

"How are the patients today?"

"Another boy with influenza."

"You sound peeved."

Sister Louise tightened her lips. "Perhaps I am peeved." She sighed. "I have something to tell you. We have been debating it for some time, and now it is agreed. We will soon leave the hospital in Nabulsi hands."

"Truly?"

"This time, yes. We'll continue training the local girls, but eventually that will be enough. They want us to expand the girls' school. Don't look at me like that, it's by popular decree. They like the fact that we are very clean." In lieu of a smile, she pouted. "They see it as a Muslim attribute. So we will have a dispensary attached, and continue with the village visits. But the hospital . . . you know, Ibrahim is extremely competent. I don't know what that means for your research, father, but I imagine he won't mind you on the veranda. You see I'm tired. They accuse us of espionage, and then the moment the injured arrive from Jerusalem they are desperate for us to stay again. It is exhausting."

Sister Louise did look weary. She had a face like an elegant tortoise: wizened and close to the bone.

The Sisters of St. Joseph were a quiet, forbearing lot. They had tussled with the Nablus notables for years, accused of diverse crimes, from converting their patients to Christianity to taking business away from local doctors. But when they caught typhus during the war, the survivors among them were inoculated and therefore of value, so that the mayor at the time, Haj Nimr Hammad, urged them to stay and gave them the run of the new municipal hospital. The nuns had no funding from the British. Their tea tables were sparse, their bodies thin, they had the clean, drawn-out look of good household economists. Most admirably to Antoine, they did not cling to their Frenchness in any way. They truly did serve God alone.

"How is your work going?"

"Oh, this and that. I am worried that I have not achieved a cohesive . . ." He looked into her face. "It's like this, I look at my notes one day and I see things of interest, paths to follow. Another day, I look and I cannot remember what I thought was valuable."

He tapped the leather cover of his book with the pads of two thick fingers. His bond with Sister Louise was peculiar; in her company his reticence simply gave way. She seemed hard from the outside, and yet she always managed to pull confessions out of him, he who was ordinarily so guarded, and this she did apparently without judgment. And since Nablus was practically impenetrable to outsiders, she was also a great aid to his research. Sickness, hospitals, medicine—this was how one became familiar. She supplied Antoine with patients who were willing to talk, and his association with the hospital establishment was, in the eyes of the convalescents, greatly to his credit. Antoine had started wholly to rely upon her—and not only for learning about Nablus, but also about himself.

"Surely you are writing about the town," she said.

"Yes, yes, but my notes seem at the moment rather like an index of local gossip. I am concerned that the conclusions I should draw—though of course, that is running ahead of myself."

"Tell me what you have so far."

"Lists. Enemies and alliances. Family against family. Particularly this Atwan character," he flicked a forefinger against the book cover, "the one who owns the soap factory. Do you know him? He always has a vendetta against someone—but in general it is a very Naplousien phenomenon. This city . . ." He looked out at the buildings below and shook his head. "Between these mountains it is all jealousy and scandal."

"That is always the case, scandals are everywhere."

He hummed. "No, I don't think so. It is different here. It fascinates me, I must say. Something strong in the air."

On cue the wind pulsed, and Sister Louise's rosary snapped against the rock.

"In any case, I am looking for the shape."

"The shape."

"Of the work. If local intrigues do become my plot, what would they elucidate."

She opened her hands. "The life of the Muslim city?"

"Certainly that would be the premise. But . . . is that not a little trivial? Ideally one wants to elucidate—well, the teachings of the Church. I wonder if I was mistaken to choose the Islamic city . . ."

"Your last project was the Bedouin."

"Yes, but then you see the desert is a preserver. It was directly connected to biblical study, since the Bedouin are kept fresh from biblical times. And I did know that from the outset."

"Persist for now. It may become clear."

Antoine said nothing. He rubbed a finger along the edge of the pages.

"I should be sad if you change your mind." She gave him a quick smile. "If you choose to study somewhere else, I mean." She grasped the rock to get to her feet. "I have to prepare for the morning. You shouldn't stay long either, it is cold and will be dark soon. I hope you are staying with us tonight?"

"I should return to Jerusalem. I've been away too long, and they say snow is coming."

"Goodbye then, father. See you soon, I hope."

"Goodbye."

As she made her way to the path, he returned to his rock, breathing heavily. He opened the book and repositioned his leg on the little boulder in front.

Things had changed since the war. The numbers at L'École had grown, and the purity of Lavigne's vision for the school had become impossible to maintain. And although Antoine's colleagues in Jerusalem were pleasant, and he did have friends among them, he felt they now represented French interests rather more than they used to, and ought to. Quite unlike Louise and the other sisters in Nablus. Of course, the entire Holy City was currently under siege, and not just by the French: every European grappled for his quarter; a hospice here, a church there, a missionary facility around the corner, an archaeological chairperson two floors up. Flags waved from every cornice as though Allenby had done nothing, and while the diplomats pretended to be secular there was always an overlap with the general fanatics, who ran the gamut from saviours of their own souls to saviours of others', to those merely avaricious for anything ancient or well esteemed. In a word, there was no such thing as being disinterested. Even among those apparently present sola fide one struggled to extricate the throb of the mystical in their breasts from the national impulse, which was something that seemed to live in the bones these days. The blood rose in their faces at a newly discovered scroll, any mention of Byzantine legend or Mesopotamia, and amulets by the dozen were quarried daily, and inscriptions scrutinised at desks in offices overlooking the spice market, and though these types called themselves scientists and attached badges to their lapels, it was becoming hard to distinguish between a tourist and an academic when everyone had that same wild look in the eye.

But Antoine had persevered in his private rigour, with his monograph on the Bedouin communities. And now, his work on Nablus. With a zeal that belied his ivory beard his mentor Père Lavigne continued to stress the importance of ethnographic practice, even before one could perceive how it would illuminate faith. He laced his praise with reminders from across his paper-strewn desk: "Be precise, Antoine, while all around are vague. Never impute to the object of study what is not already there."

Antoine wondered whether scholars were always fanatics in some sense. Only, Jerusalem possessed a kind of chemical power to bring out what might otherwise lie dormant. The other day he saw a Swedish woman, generally known to be living on an academic fellowship from the Theological Society, actually howling in the wake of a cross reenactment, which comprised an Arab with a long nose dragging the burden of timber and trailing his feet like a marionette's down the Via Dolorosa. To be sure, even he sometimes felt it, a rustle of the desert baptism; and as the wind nudged the prongs of his beard, while he sat there by the oldest tree in Palestine before the valley of Nablus, he noted down in his long book how the appeal of the metaphysical had an amazing ability to reach all the way from the Judaean hills to the stacks of one's quiet library, where one could almost hear the British Zionists hurrying on the storm of progress with a thrill in their voices.

A massive cloud shadow, jagged like the shape of a continent, passed over the town and bent against the inclines of the mountains. Antoine could just about see the municipal hospital: a tiny oblong where the base of Ebal cradled an olive grove. He could not see the residence of the French sisters, however. Hidden, probably, behind one of those overgrown palaces.

As he packed his things and walked down to the bus station, he thought of what Louise had said about leaving the hospital. It was odd that the Nabulsis should miss the Turks so much as to continue worrying about espionage on their behalf. Had not the Turks been their tormentors, when all was said and done? A fellah passed him on the road, leading a packed mule up the mountain.

Perhaps men had an ability to forget the strictures of past law. The past appeared eternal: what had happened was inviolable; one did not keep forever the contingencies; what did not happen was forgotten. But in the present moment, one was made more aware of what would be possible *if only*; the bonds of present law held one by the wrists, and caused one to recall looseness where there was now firmness. Which meant it was natural that as the British soldiers paraded before the old prison houses, the Nabulsis would remember the amity of the Ottoman officers, and the marriages to their daughters, as it struck them that these British fathers would never bring a daughter to marry an Arab.

He found the first bus to Jerusalem and paid his fare. The sun was setting as they approached Damascus Gate.

10

That night, the snows began. In the morning, the sky smothered Nablus in a thick white smoke, which settled into thigh-high banks and silenced all the houses. No birds sang. Within days damp invaded stored grain and rotted the vegetables. Neighbours wrapped their legs in sackcloth to plough to one another's front doors, and any news that could not be transmitted in this manner was not transmitted at all.

Wrinkled deposits of ice masked the windows on Mount Gerizim. Midhat lurked in his bedroom and emerged only at mealtimes. Since their last exchange, Um Taher had not probed the issue of marriage. But with little to occupy her except sewing, she became obsessed by what the priest had almost told her about the Samaritans. Of course, that fragment of gossip might mean nothing at all; whatever curse he saw administered—a charm involving a bird was always a curse—might have been intended for anyone. And yet, on the blank snow beyond the kitchen window her brain painted images of jealous Nabulsis setting maledictions on her grandson. Against his ability to marry. Against his sanity. Her mind was incontinent: Midhat might struggle to see beyond the end of his nose, but Um Taher imagined future possibilities far too much.

By the middle of February 1920, the first globe thistles thrust their heads through the snow on the mountainsides, which melted in little circles around their necks. The white of the sky curdled and faded, and finally left the air a pale, empty blue. The blanket on the mountains became ragged, the streets turned grey, and the townspeople braved the thoroughfares and the children played in the open spaces.

One morning in March, everyone woke to find the cold had relented. The air was moving, birds singing, ice draining off the mountains into the valley, filling the streets with slush. The women of Nablus hiked out to Ras al-Ayn to sit by the waterfalls with their baskets of nuts, as their children washed lettuce in the icy water and cupped the leaves in their palms to stop them ripping in the flow. Newspapers were once more in circulation, telegraph lines were opened, and at last Nablus heard what was happening in Damascus and Jerusalem.

The negotiations between Faisal and the French that Hani had described in his letter to Midhat were soon public knowledge. So were the outbreaks of violence in the hinterlands. Agitation rippled into Palestine, and people in the coastal cities were photographed with placards saying: PALESTINE IS AN ESSENTIAL PART OF SOUTHERN SYRIA, and NO ROOM FOR THE ZIONISTS IN PALESTINE. "Violently suppressed by the British," wrote the reporter. "All rallies have now been banned."

"Have you heard anything yet?" said a voice.

Midhat had just arrived at the store and taken off his jacket; the speaker's shadowed head was visible through the gap in the display, but it was difficult to see his face.

"Burhan?" he suggested.

"Yes, yes it's me," said Burhan. "Have you heard anything?"

Adel Jawhari's face appeared beside Burhan's, along with a gas lamp that illuminated them both and shone a ray across the floor. "Are you guys talking about it?"

Midhat sucked his teeth and opened his hand.

"There's some news," said Adel. "I think Faisal is the king."

"King of what?"

"That's what we're trying to find out."

Burhan shrugged. "Hey, hey," he said, to someone out of view. "Is that a newspaper? Oh, sorry, ya'tik al-afia."

"Good morning Midhat," said Hisham, as Adel let him through. "Have you heard this thing about King Faisal?"

"What do you know? We haven't heard anything."

"Morning Midhat," said another voice.

"We don't know anything," said Midhat. "Oh, Qais, I didn't see you."

"You'll know in a moment," said Qais. He was grinning. "Look what I've got."

"Where did you get that from?" said Burhan.

"My father came from Jerusalem an hour ago."

Outside, someone shouted: "Qais's got the paper!"

"Zut alors," said Midhat.

"What did you say?" said Burhan.

"Quickly," said Midhat, "give that here."

The shout had already passed down the market and multiplied, and as men began to cram into the Kamal store, Qais was forced to one side. Midhat pushed some boxes back to create space and passed Qais an empty crate while everyone negotiated over chairs. Dawn was beginning.

"Are we ready yet?" said Qais.

"Yes!"

"Lahza, lahza." An old man shook an arthritic hand. "Does anyone have coffee?"

"Faisal!" Qais shouted. He spread his legs on the crate in the manner of an orator.

"Here you go, ya Haj," Midhat whispered to the old man, handing him a cup.

"The Emir Faisal Declared—King—of—Syria!"

Whistles and applause. Midhat looked over the sea of heads and caught sight of Jamil, leaning against the doorjamb with his arms folded. Their eyes met.

Midhat shouted out: "Does it say where Syria is?"

"Hang on!" said Qais. "Wait, wait everyone! Let me read the rest."

But the crowd was already too large to silence. A few people tried to lead them in an old farming song. Hisham lifted his bony arms and made a downward motion with his outstretched hands, but it was no use. Midhat forced his way over to Qais's corner.

"And it says Palestine?"

"Yes," said Qais. "Damascus is our capital."

"Give me," said a tall man, pulling out a pair of eyeglasses.

"So," said Qais, "we are now part of Syria." He turned to Adel. "Right?"

Adel blinked. "I don't know. Didn't they just ban our rallies?" He stared at the article. "Remember, we don't have an army."

"Faisal has an army," said Jamil.

That night the Murad brothers, Basil and Munir, enlisted Midhat and Jamil's help with what they titled an "operation." An uncle on their mother's side had fought with Faisal in the Arab Revolt against the Turks, and brought home as a trophy the Sharifian flag, red, black, green, and white, that he had waved from his horse. Close to midnight Basil and Munir, bearing this same ragged flag, climbed to the top of the municipal building and hoisted it onto the empty mast. As instructed, Midhat and Jamil circuited the building, nodding when they passed one another. At Basil's whistle, they met at the back to help the boys descend.

They saw it in the morning from the mountain path: the colours of the Arab Revolt, now the colours of Arab independence, rippling and unfolding over the town, exaggerating the wind.

"It's good to feel as though you're doing something," said Jamil. "Do you know what I mean?"

That day Midhat wandered back and forth from the edge of the khan watching the street until nightfall. Everyone was agitated. Every tiny action, each flick of a hand, shift of a trouser, amassed into a wave of motion, the way single leaves gesture in a forest until the whole becomes a single stirring animal. Next morning, the flag was gone. But it didn't matter. Everyone had seen it.

Although Midhat and Jamil had helped with the flag operation, over the next few weeks they spent most of their time not with the Murad brothers, but with Qais Karak and Adel Jawhari. Basil and Munir talked in slogans and always agreed with each other, but Qais and Adel liked to debate. After work, the four of them—Midhat, Jamil, Qais, and Adel—walked down together to Sheikh Qassem to decipher the newspapers. Adel, who was a member of the Muslim-Christian Society, was the one who first told them about the plan to demonstrate in Jerusalem in favour of Faisal, at the festival of Nebi Musa.

Midhat did not know when his father would arrive, but as April approached, Teta had still not found him a wife, and he was in no hurry to remind her. April was also the month when the region flared with religious festivals, and Nebi Musa, the Muslim pilgrimage to the tomb of Moses in Jericho, had recently become the most significant. Nebi Musa always coincided with Good Friday in the Orthodox calendar, but over the last few years the pilgrimage had taken on a secular weight with more and more Christians processing alongside the Muslims, or at least travelling down to Jerusalem on the first Sunday. Sometimes Jerusalem Jews joined in too—though presumably they would not do so this year. This year, by one further infelicitous overlap of calendars, the first day of Nebi Musa was also the first day of Passover.

"It is a fantastic opportunity," said Adel, forcing Midhat and Basil to quicken their pace. Jamil was already ahead of them. "They can ban our rallies, but they would never ban a religious event. They are always talking about maintaining the Status Quo—the reaction would be too enormous."

It was Friday, and they were walking to Ras al-Ayn with a nargileh pipe. En route they had come across Basil smoking on Qaysariyeh Road. Basil asked where they were going, and Adel told him to come along. When Basil said, could he bring Munir? Midhat and Adel exchanged a glance. One of the brothers was just tolerable; both might be unbearable. "Why don't you meet us there, then?" Adel had said, at which Basil let it go with, "I'm coming, I'm coming," and fell in step with Midhat.

"Are you going?"

"Nebi Musa?" said Basil. "Of course we're going."

He reached to scratch his lower back, and as he did so, opened his jacket. A pistol was tucked into his trousers. The grip bent over the waistline with a sheen of recent polish.

"Are you serious?"

Basil faced forward, chewing the inside of his cheek.

"What are you planning to do?"

"Have you heard of Jabotinsky?" he said after a moment.

"No."

"He's a Zionist. He's starting a Zionist army. If we want to beat them, we have to train ourselves."

Ahead, Adel burst out laughing. Jamil's long arms gesticulated, his shirt-sleeves blazing in the sun.

"And he had a tiny dog," Jamil said, "and he called it Naila!"

"Can I ask," said Midhat, "why you are taking it to Ras al-Ayn?"

"I'm getting used to carrying it."

"Which spring shall we sit by, guys?" said Adel, spinning round.

"Whichever you like," said Midhat.

A ring of women seated by the roadside shivered into motion and walked quickly off like a flock of blackbirds.

"Do you have others?" said Midhat.

"You want one?" said Basil. "We could probably get one before the festival. The person to talk to—"

"No no no, I don't," said Midhat.

"It's just in case, habibi," said Basil, with an indulgent smile. "Just in case."

The first day of the procession passed without incident. Pilgrims began their journey down to Jerusalem, prayed in al-Aqsa mosque, camped outside the city walls for a night, and continued on to Jericho. On Sunday morning, Midhat and Jamil met on the path in the dark, and as they walked down the mountain they heard the pilgrims singing in from the hinterlands. On the Northern Road they saw the festival convoy, ready with drums and cymbals, grainy in the colourless dawn.

Jamil and Midhat took the first train to Tulkarem and changed for Lydda. On the Lydda platform, the Englishwomen carried furled umbrellas. Common to all of them, Midhat noted a certain righteous bearing of the chin. After a while he became aware that none of the women would look him in the eye. He selected one at random. Straight pale orange hair, tucked under an ugly kind of cap. Cheap leather gloves, a camera.

"I'm already tired," said Jamil.

The orange-haired girl would not look at him. With a loud hiss the train pulled in, and she and her friend reached for the railing. All the women were boarding. Midhat recalled photographs of French trains bearing soldiers to the front, and looking at the points of their umbrellas saw the barrels of guns.

"I think Adel's over there."

Jamil gestured towards the end of the platform, before grasping the handrail and stepping up. He ducked his head under someone's arm and as Midhat slid in after him the attendants closed the doors. The engine whined, and the platform disappeared from the window. The carriage was close and warm. They saw the procession stretching far ahead to Jerusalem, winding through the valleys.

Over the next three hours, Midhat fell into a daydream. He thought of what Hani had said in his letter about naming themselves Syrians, and wondered what might happen next. Perhaps a war of independence. Which would do what to Nablus? He already knew how wartime could suspend the normal rules. It might free him from his father's command. Syria would be free—and so would Midhat. Jamil met his eye and winked. The mountains beyond the window interrupted the sunlight, sculpting his cousin's cheekbones with their moving shade. Beyond him, the foreign women hunched on the benches. And where would that freedom lead? Teta was right: he did not know what he wanted. His tableau vivant of King Faisal ruling Palestine lapsed into a vision of himself in Cairo, married with small children. He tried to work out where this image had come from, and was bewildered to realise that he was imagining himself married to Layla.

The echo of a drum fought discordantly with the rhythm of the crankshaft. In English a woman cried: "There are so many people!" The window was filled with heads and flags. The roar reached them dimly, like a waterfall across a canyon.

Midhat put an arm across Jamil to let the women alight first. Several thanked him, and as he bowed and lifted his tarbush, Jamil hit him on the chest with the back of his hand and laughed. Stepping down was like stepping into a thundercloud.

"Michael isn't that the Hebron procession?" shouted an Englishman in a boater. "I thought they weren't coming for an hour yet."

They followed the crowd towards the old city. One smug-looking tarbush was carrying a gramophone above his head, but its music was inaudible. The crowd thickened and slowed, and a horse appeared by the roadside bearing a stout man with a small block of a moustache. The middle two buttons of his waistcoat had popped open, and the separated seams disclosed a pointed ovoid of white shirt.

"Ya comrades!" His chins distended. "Behave peacefully! Ya comrades!"

At Jaffa Gate they came to a stop behind a group of young European men refusing to go further. Midhat took Jamil by the arm.

"We're going in?"

"Of course," Midhat shouted, and plunging through the group released Jamil's arm to clap, borne along under the arch of the gate.

The Europeans had moved to one side, and as the parade bent to fit through the entrance, Midhat saw that its tail was made up of Arab women. Many carried banners and placards like the men; a few even waved Sharifian flags. They were shouting something. "Falastin arad-na" was the first phrase; he could not make out the second. All at once the crush overtook them, and as they were impelled under the vault into the open air on the other side ("Stay with me," said Midhat, snatching his cousin's sleeve), they saw more women on the balconies above, throwing coloured handkerchiefs down onto their heads.

By a group of drummers, a Sufi dervish in a long gown and jacket of balding velveteen began to dance. His body torqued, first one way and then the other, so his garment spun out and the seams twisted. He rocked his head back and forth, patting the ground with his feet. Dust rose in a mist. The crush became an audience, dilating the space around him. A clap started, then one song caught over the discordance of the many and spread around their area, and as someone pushed him closer to the dervish, Midhat lost his hold on Jamil. The dancer's feet patted faster, faster, and

Midhat stepped close enough to hear the man's own voice: "La ilaha illa allah la ilaha illa allah."

Then something unexpected happened. Half propped up by people on either side, Midhat experienced a strange, dull explosion in his chest. Something close to joy but deeper, more serene. He moved his head to the pulse, his tongue ticked against his hard palate. Unable to see the dervish's feet, Midhat watched him revolving with mechanical smoothness, motored by the turbines of his tensed, upstretched wrists. A hand clasped his neck.

"Is everything all right?" Jamil's hair was matted, his forehead shining, a scum filmed his upper lip. "Look, look, dabke!"

The dervish gave way to a line of village men, grasping elbows and hopping up and down. One at a time they shuffled to the centre of the vacated ring, and jumped and kicked. From somewhere, pipes. Midhat looked down at his own legs. His shoes were pale with dust. He felt a shove from behind.

"You know dabke!"

"No I don't!" He gasped a laugh and pushed back.

The group of women at the rear had moved under the arch, and as the crowd compacted they settled by the wall and clapped along. One woman near the front, who was not clapping, caught Midhat's attention. She was looking directly at him. Staring, in fact, and standing very still. He tried to keep her level in his sight while everyone else jostled, then knew she had detected him because she quickly turned away. She remained in profile, motionless. Without even thinking of Jamil, Midhat pushed towards her. Although she did not move her head, he could see the white corner of her eye go black with her turning iris. Without the other eye, the single organ was like an object, and he did not have the feeling of meeting someone's gaze. Instead, he was watching her looking at him. A body blocked his view: he pressed against the next person along to take the woman into his sight again, provoking a knock on his shoulder as the dancing circle closed in on itself. The crowd began to shift. The horde of waiting pilgrims by the gate plunged towards him, and then she turned. He caught her: Fatima Hammad; both eyes, the downward slope at the corners, and though he could not see the rest of her face, the eyes were enough to summon the whole.

The current was too strong. He fell further to the right and Fatima dissolved into the wall of women. Midhat rotated to tell Jamil what he had seen, but all was motion, and his cousin was not there. He scanned faces as they passed.

"Midhat!" came a voice. "Midhat!"

It was Basil Murad. Waving, a few feet away, a distance of about seven or eight bodies. His section of the crowd was moving faster than Midhat's, sliding forward as the mass mutated. Midhat strained against the current, and considered running back for Jaffa Gate where the women were.

Pivoting round, he saw the place where the women had been was no longer occupied by women. He looked at the torrent ahead, chevronning to fit through the narrowing courtyard. People pushed from behind. Jamil must be somewhere there. He waved back at the place from which Basil had called, but Basil was no longer there either. There was nothing for it but to submit. He pressed forward with the multitude.

Before daybreak, Fatima and Nuzha had met Burhan in the hall to wave at the departing pilgrims. Their mother was in Lydda and would never know. Out on the dark street, they heard the trumpets and drums, and Fatima thought immediately of the Nebi Rubin festival. A shiver of memory: that sleepy excitement, waking early in the tent and hearing the musicians tuning their instruments.

The darkness magnified their footsteps. Along the Northern Road the music became louder until finally the dancing crowd came into view. In advance of dawn, lamps rocked from sticks and raised arms, their flames swaying like a blurred rash of stars.

The largest group of well-wishers was made up of townswomen. The sisters joined the group's flank, and, tentatively, Nuzha started to ululate. She laughed and looked back to check on Fatima, and for a moment Burhan dithered at the edge. Then he spurned the impulse and stepped off into the scattered strip of men. Feet apart, his hands rose to clap.

"Fatima? Is that you?"

"Meen?"

"Muna al-Jayyusi. Do you know me?"

A pair of eyes. Pale eyelashes.

"Muna? Of course I know you! How are you, I have not seen you since school!"

"*Ik*shif al*ay*ya, *ya* ta*bib* . . ." sang the pilgrims, stamping their feet.

"Come with us," said Muna. "We're taking the train from Tulkarem. The roads will be packed."

"To Jerusalem?"

"It's safe, we're just going to watch. Come."

"It leaves in twenty minutes," said a thin voice.

"If you want . . . Fatima," said Muna.

The group began to move off. Fatima grabbed her sister's arm. Nuzha stiffened.

"If he asks," said Nuzha, "I'll say you're helping at the school."

Fatima looked for Burhan. He was facing away, waving a handkerchief he had stolen from their mother's dresser.

On the platform their group made twelve in total. In the train carriage, they settled on three rows of wooden benches as dawn erupted across the windows.

Fatima's mind was sticky with anxiety. Although Nuzha would certainly keep her word, Burhan might tell their father, who would, of course, tell their mother. It was her mother Fatima feared. Her father was not the real lawmaker of the house; he was more like the law itself, a name Widad invoked as a spectre of wrath to make the children fearful.

Until recently Fatima had been persuaded by the myth of her father's great anger, and went quiet when he entered the room. But on the morning after the Atwan istiqbal, she had heard her mother's voice, voluptuous with emotion, coming from her father's office.

"I know," her father was saying. "Hassan told me. I advised him on the sale."

"You *advised* him on the sale?"

"Yes."

"Fazee'a! Men are proposing night and day, and you want to refuse them all."

"Night and day?"

"I know about Midhat Kamal. I was in the house. Don't look surprised."

"Enough."

"Enough, even though you decided not to tell me that also? His grandmother invited us round for coffee—ya Allah. Ya Allah. No one has such a husband." A clapping sound.

"I said enough."

"She is very wanted. She will not be wanted forever. You want her to marry the emir? Who exactly is your ideal husband? She is not that beautiful, Nimr, there are thousands of beautiful girls, beauty is not rare. I know you, I know you will wait until the family name is fallen and forgotten. You want me to die? Is that it, you want me to die, you want to kill me? No one in hell has such a husband."

Later on, Fatima realised she had witnessed a chink in her parents' alliance. It signified that her mother was not an exact conduit to her father, and that the threat, "Your father will be angry," might not always be true. Since then, it became not her father's but her mother's wrath that Fatima feared. Not the law, but the law's steward. And, watching her father, she started to wonder that she had been so easily duped. He seemed far too concerned with his life outside the house to pay them much attention, and though she may have attracted more of it over recent years, his concern for her marrying well was like an extension of his role as judge: he appraised her from a distance.

"Don't be frightened," said Muna. "We'll only stay a few hours, just to hear the speeches."

In the dawn Fatima noticed that the skin around her friend's eyes was delicately wrinkled.

"Are you married?" said Fatima.

"No," said Muna. Her eyes smiled. "I became a teacher. At the Fatimiyah School. Are you married?"

Fatima turned to the window. "Not yet."

They lingered on the platform as the carriages emptied. Among their group a leader emerged: an older woman with a veil and a white umbrella, which she held out before her like a staff. She steered them onto the street. Muna held Fatima's hand.

"I have missed you."

Fatima put her hand on her chest to communicate the same, and was surprised by how hard her heart was thumping.

The roads streamed with people. Night winds still ran through the air, and the women huddled together. Fatima wished she had worn sturdier shoes. At Jaffa Gate, beneath the clock tower, the stream fed into a sea, and dismounted riders led horses by the reins. The noise was extraordinary. She saw she had been wholly mistaken to think this would be like Nebi Rubin. Nebi Rubin was a festival of open-air beaches and children: this was a festival of men. She had never seen so many. She looked at their jagged movements, the jaws, exposed necks, and in her mind leaving for Nebi Musa and leaving home for marriage became one and the same thing. Both treacherous, both nauseating. Under her shawl she clutched her hands together and with her free thumb picked nervously at the tie on her waistband.

"Stay by the wall, ladies!"

They followed the white umbrella under the shade of the arch.

"I didn't expect so many!" said Muna, lifting her hands to clap.

Fatima stared at the men, and feeling her nose running, reached a hand up under her veil.

That was when she saw Midhat Kamal. Visible because of a space before him, in which someone was dancing dabke. She knew what he looked like because Burhan had seen him passing their house a few weeks ago, and called her to the window. Now he was laughing. He was lifting his arms to defend himself against another young man, a little taller, darker skinned, with an arrow-straight nose, who gripped him around the neck. The sight of Midhat was a balm on Fatima's temples. He was not frightening. The copperiness of his face, his smile. She watched him. Somehow, he managed to be both inside the scene and, like her, detached from it, observing. There was some freedom about him, laughing like that. He spoke to his companion. The laugh burst back onto his face and separated the features.

Then the drumbeats invaded her chest again and the cold thought struck that she was probably inventing. Led, as usual, by the repetitious longings of her imagination. She did not know Midhat Kamal. Having heard his name and conjured a picture from the things Burhan had told her, clearly it was she giving him a character and liberating him from the bonds of the scene. That was why he stuck out to her, distinctive and human over this sea of men.

He turned slightly from the dancing, and with a little frown that pulled his laughing eyebrows down—the sunlight strong on his features—she knew he had caught her. She switched her face away in surprise. Then, she could not help herself, but like a creature careful of its shadow she strained from the corner of her eye. He was still watching. And though her face was covered she felt sure he recognised her. He was, unmistakeably, making his way over. Every thought had its shadow, and it occurred to her that it was more likely she had drawn him by her staring. She had provoked him, he could not know who she was, she was simply a woman who had invited a man to move towards her. Divided by the possibilities, at the last moment she did both: she braved him with both eyes. And then she turned around, and retreated among the shawls and skirts and umbrellas of the other women.

A struggle started outside the Arab Club building as paper cups appeared above their heads. Midhat grabbed one, spilling contents that dried instantly over his fingers into something viscid and unpleasant. The cup held a few centimetres of lemonade. Saliva rose around his tongue. He opened his throat: it was warm and sugary.

The walls were draped with celebrants, and on the balcony of the Arab Club a line of tarbush-wearers in alabaster suits holding pieces of paper played with their ties. One man brandished a flag for their attention. There was Basil again, a few people ahead, punching the air and shouting.

The chant caught, strengthened by other voices: "Falastin arad-na, al-Yahud aklab-na! Falastin arad-na! al-Yahud aklab-na!" The words rushed through the crowd, mouth to mouth. *Palestine is our land, the Jews are our dogs.* They bored into Midhat's ears and pervaded his brain, and soon he lost his sense of discomfort, of dirt and sweat, of his thirst which the lemonade had awakened. His body was their body. And again in his chest, that weird swelling joy. The chant beat there without words, and this time the feeling spread to his limbs, which moved as if acted upon by reflex hammers. He clapped, his feet stamped.

Turning his head, Midhat saw a fist meet someone's face by the gate, and dark spatters on the wall, and in that instant he came unglued. A metallic taste arose in his mouth. His chest and ears hurt, and the percussion kindled a spurt of panic. Someone staggered and other faces changed, grooved like masks. Saliva flew, eyeballs flashed, limbs hardened into batons. The words were real now, in all their violence; his body peeled back into itself, and through his sweat-weakened shirt, his back and arms prickled with the wool fibres from his coat. At last the first speaker on the balcony began his oration, and the drumbeat went quiet like a dead breeze.

Behind the speaker a banner was unfurled with Emir Faisal's likeness, and Midhat looked back again. That cameo of violence he had witnessed was gone; he could not see the blood spatters, but the clock tower that marked Jaffa Gate was far off, there were so many people in the way. What a mistake to think he could find Jamil here.

The crowd started roiling again. The nearest wall was on his right. Midhat pushed, sweaty arms met sweaty backs. "Excuse me, excuse me." He put on a distressed face, which did nothing to expedite his passage. The wall was dank and rough. The unlucky ones nearest to it were so squashed he could see why many had resorted to climbing. One young boy was crying. Midhat pulled a handkerchief from his pocket and pressed towards him, but the boy did not register the cotton uncrumpling before his face. Tears continued to fill his eyes, breaking and falling.

The chant was up again. Beyond the boy, Midhat saw an opening in the wall.

"Amo, take it."

He reached to touch the boy's back. The boy flinched and hit him in the stomach. Midhat panted in surprise. He stared at the puckered face now turning from him, and then with a deep breath pushed past for the opening in the wall. It led to an alleyway crammed with people squeezing up into the square, but the gradient showed the crowd was not deep. He forced his way through, still mimicking his own dismay, his lip curving outward perversely like the crying boy's.

In the air of the street the sweat on his clothes ran cold and he gasped. His ribs were sore. The alley took him under a heavy arch and before long the crowd was nothing but a dim vibration in stone. He rested against the wall; it cooled his neck. Looking upwards he saw a patch of blue sky trapped between the buildings.

There was a new sound, coming from the other direction. Another rhythm, another drumbeat, coming closer. The beat clarified into the thud of marching. One two, one two, chopping the flagstones.

The first pair appeared from around the corner. Then like a ghost troop they filed past, paying him no attention. One two, one two. Beige jackets with ties, tan shorts. Military boots, one two. His first thought was that the British had brought in an army to guard the festival. But looking at the faces he realised they were not Englishmen, nor Indian colonials. He recalled Basil's comment about a "Zionist army." They continued to file past, there must have been hundreds, and not only men: he could see hair curled and pinned back from faces, all of them marching in rhyme, rifles on their backs, straps of bullets around their torsos. One, two, their feet smacked the ground. The last pair turned the corner, and they were gone.

Midhat fled. Perhaps if he had fought in the military he would have understood how so many people, all together, were no longer like people. He had read about crowds before, written about them in university essays on the French Revolution, seen photographs, heard reports—he had never been in one. What frightened him most, what made him shudder as his walk sprang into a run and he heard shouts behind him, was that *he* had felt something. That fever of unity, out there by the Arab Club.

Coming out through Zion Gate, he passed a few police by the city walls panicking inward, swinging their weapons. A noonday sun beat down. The taxi rank was all the way round by Damascus Gate, and his adrenalin faded at the prospect of the walk. He had only taken a few steps when a policeman in a pith helmet ran towards him, steadying his gun.

"I need to check you."

"Pardon?"

The policeman raised the gun. Midhat raised his hands.

"I need to check you."

"But—I'm leaving."

"Keep your hands up!"

The policeman's rough fingers woke the soreness in his ribs. He pressed the area around Midhat's waistband, then ran his hands down each of his legs, investigated the cuffs of his trousers, and finally asked him to remove his shoes. His socks were soaked in sweat and his soles were very tender on the ground.

"All right. You can go."

A taxi careened up the road. Midhat whistled, waved, and from the backseat breathed: "Nablus."

"We have to take the long route," said the driver.

"Mashi, take the long route."

He shut his eyes and rested against the leather. Honks, shouts. His breath became regular: he would sleep. On the red of his closed lids, Jamil appeared. Jamil, dropped into a pool of bodies. His eyes snapped open.

A line of pilgrims was straggling down the road parallel to theirs. Peddlers along the roadside held palms to their foreheads.

"Someone should warn them," said the taxi driver. He leaned across the wheel to look out the window.

"Yes," said Midhat.

The pilgrims struck their drums. Midhat summoned a new image of Jamil: several heads taller than everyone else, forcing his way through the crowd like a swimmer, sated, wading from a lake.

*   *   *

"What happened?" said Teta.

"I need some water."

"What happened?"

"I don't know. We shouldn't have gone, it was a stupid idea."

"Where's Jamil?"

Midhat gulped and wiped his mouth.

"You left him?"

"No, Teta, it was a crowd. You won't understand."

"What? What won't I understand?"

"It was a crowd, Teta! It was . . . it was . . ." He sat down and rested his head in his hands. "He will be fine."

"We have to tell Um Jamil."

"Why worry her? Just wait. A bit longer."

Teta fixed him. That "bit longer" was a concession, and he stood, in recognition of his defeat.

"Yalla," he said.

One look at Um Jamil's face and Midhat knew he would soften the truth for her. At the kitchen table the women besieged him with questions, and through his exhaustion he forced into a few coherent facts and images what he had seen: the crowd, the numbers; the heat, the chanting; being separated from Jamil; his decision, which he emphasised, that it was best to follow the crowd and find him, but which he afterwards realised was impossible; the speeches, which he could barely remember; the banner of Faisal; his escape. They gaped like children at a hakawati. After a while Um Jamil raised a hand and pressed her lips together. Midhat noticed her head beginning to tremble and wished she had not stopped him, he wished to correct what he had said, to intervene in the progress of her imagination. Now that he was no longer defending himself against Teta, it was striking him with full force what a terrible thing he had done, leaving Jamil. The facts he had shared, even in their censored form, admonished him for it.

"I will boil water," said Teta.

She tossed a bundle of dried sage onto the table, and Midhat picked the first leaf from its stalk. "Nothing has happened, I'm sure of it."

Tears pooled and dripped down Um Jamil's wrinkles.

"Nothing has happened," Teta sang.

The water boiled, the tea steeped into a gold liquid. Um Jamil's chest rose in fits. Teta poured three cups, and rummaged in the pantry for some bread and a jar of labneh balls in olive oil, and spilled a few onto a plate. Midhat mopped the oil slowly, watching it wander round the porcelain.

It was nearly seven o'clock when they heard the front door.

"Oh mama!" Um Jamil cried.

Their chairs screeched. Jamil had a black eye and his lip was cut, the collar of his shirt dark with sweat and dirt. He suddenly clutched the side of a dresser, as though he had seen it was about to fall.

"Oh my God," said Midhat.

"You're here," said Jamil.

Midhat tried to say something. To his horror, he found he could not.

"What happened to your face?" said Um Jamil.

"Someone elbowed me." Jamil winced. "They were dancing. Where did you go? I lost you, I was trying to find you."

"I'm sorry," said Midhat, "the police—I—I left."

"You left him!" said Teta. "You left him to be beaten up!"

"He was right," said Jamil.

"Sit, habibi," said his mother.

Jamil did not sit. "It was bad. They went straight to the Jewish quarter." He looked Midhat in the eyes, and Midhat perceived there was more he was not saying. "The British locked the gates. I had to wait until dark to climb the wall."

"Did Basil . . ."

"I didn't see Basil. I was just trying to get out of there. Honestly I have no idea what happened."

"You're hurt!" shouted Um Jamil, pointing at his shoulder. Um Taher gasped.

"No, Mama," said Jamil, shrugging her off. "It's not my blood."

There was silence.

"We shouldn't have gone," said Midhat.

"You should *not* have gone!" Teta shouted back, as though contradicting him.

"No, no," said Jamil. He raised a tired hand. "We were right to go. It is important to have seen this."

From the writhing crowd the women had retreated quickly in single file. Outside Jaffa Gate, the commotion was even worse. They pushed to the hem of the crowd, and Fatima, reckless with panic, ran from the hot sun under the awning outside the Christakis Pharmacy. Several women followed close behind, holding their veils to stop them from slipping, and crowded with her against the glass. The pharmacy was closed for Sunday, and the window display was a picture of stillness. The sunlight exposed the dust on a line of green medicine bottles; beyond the diagonal cast by the awning, the shadow was absolute. Then the dusty light was blotted with darkness, and English voices shouted over the din. Ten or so policemen came jogging down the road, red discs of field caps on their heads. They hovered as Jaffa Gate emitted a loud shrieking. Amid the motion it was difficult to make out any actual violence—until someone at the margin grabbed someone else's shirt, and one tall, seal-like Englishman with a heavy nose and sloping shoulders charged forward with his gun ready.

"Yalla ya banat," said the leader. She raised her umbrella over two companions. "To the taxi rank."

They clung together on the road and separated into the cars. Fatima put her face in her hands to recite the Throne verse. Suddenly she cried: "I don't have any money!"

"I have money," said Muna. "I'm sorry, I didn't know. I wouldn't have taken you if I'd known."

"I'm fine. Thanks be to God. We're all fine."

The taxi dropped Fatima first. She steeled herself to meet her mother, to formulate a least shameful version of the truth; for how would anyone believe a lie, covered as she was in dust? In the hall she listened, but heard nothing. Her mother had not returned.

In the bathroom she sponged her forehead, stripped, and rinsed her whole body. Her ears throbbed with the crowd. Images of the procession and riot, that churning sea of men, settled into mental drifts, and between them a conviction emerged, sculpted by their shapes, resolving in that space into something hard and intelligible.

In their bedroom, Nuzha lay on her stomach reading a magazine.

"Is Burhan here?"

"Oh, you're back. Yes he is, but he won't tell. How was it?"

"Violent."

Nuzha twitched in surprise.

"Do you want anything from the kitchen?"

Her sister shook her head. Fatima withdrew and descended the stairs, and whispered outside her father's study: "Baba." Silence. She let her voice into the breath. "Baba."

A chair creaked. "Meen?"

"Fatima."

The door resisted, caught on the carpet.

"You have to push."

It swished into an office warm with sunlight. Two large books lay open on the desk at which her father sat. The room was stifled with cushions and a musty smell of paper and bodies. A glaucous sheen covered the window glass.

"What." A pair of spectacles dimpled the skin on Nimr's forehead.

"May I sit?"

He looked slightly baffled, but did not object.

"Baba . . ." she breathed. "I want to ask you about . . ." She ran a fingernail across the skirt on her leg and looked up. Not at his face; at the shelf of books. A sound came from somewhere; music, from another room. "I'm frightened."

"Frightened?"

She looked down.

"Ah. Don't be frightened about *that*. And don't listen to your mother." He extracted his glasses from his forehead and sat sideways on his chair. "She doesn't know. Listen, habibti, we will find you a husband, don't worry. Someone wealthy, a good name, a good family."

"What about Midhat Kamal?"

He inhaled to speak. Then he released the breath, and shaking his head said, "The Kamal family is nothing, Fatima."

"Why?"

"Because I want better. I want—" His lips moved rapidly without sound, catching words and dropping them. "How dare you question me," he reached at last, a sharp note of surprise entering his voice. "I am your father. Really, shame, Fatima, shame."

"I'm sorry. I am just afraid, and I think that Midhat—"

"Why do you want him? Did your mother tell you to say this?"

"Burhan told me things about him. I would like—"

"You would like to marry this Kamal."

"Yes."

"He's not a good match for you."

"Why? Why is he not a good match?"

His mouth opened again. But this time she had startled him out of rage and into a quick answer. "Because he's not good enough. He's not good enough to be my relative! Who is Kamal? Nothing!" His throat rasped. "Yalla, what is it that you like about him. Tell me."

She hesitated. What a peculiar day! Making holes where she had not expected them. She tried to summon the features of Midhat that she knew, of which there were not many. "I like that he was in France," she said. "They call him the Parisian. He's very refined—they say. I like the way he looks. And I like . . ."

"You've seen him?"

"Burhan showed me," she said quickly, "through the window."

"I have to speak to Burhan."

"He didn't mean to, I asked him, in fact. I wanted to know, it's my fault, because I heard you talking about him, about Midhat, with Mama, and I wondered what he was like. And Burhan was with me and he pointed at the window when he was passing, with some other people, and Burhan said that one, that one is him."

"And you have decided you like him."

"Yes."

"Ya Rubbi. Ya . . . Rubbi. Where is the money from?"

"Clothing. There's a business. In Nablus and in Cairo, I believe."

"Well. I suppose the money will be safe. Not everyone's money is safe." He shook his head. "I have to think about it."

He slid back in his chair. It was some moments before she realised that this had been the signal for her to go.

"Thank you, Baba."

"Yalla."

The resolution Fatima had come to in the bathroom was this. Had she invented Midhat's difference from the other men, her invention still remained better than the pure unknown. Better to ride an ungrounded conviction and make her own choice, than to find herself being thrust by the neck, flung wide over the precipice, and out into the sea.

11

How did the riots actually begin?—that was one question people asked. Every account conflicted with another, and every eyewitness swore his own testimony was definitive. According to one version, the fighting started when a Jewish boy grabbed the Prophet's flag and tore a corner off the silk. Others said the flagbearer spat on an elderly Orthodox lady, and called her a Zionist son of a dog. Other accounts did not feature a flag at all, but centred on an event in the lobby of the Amdursky Hotel, where an old man was beaten to the ground with sticks. Some said the old man was Jewish, his assailants Arab; others said the man was Arab, his assailants Jews from Jabotinsky's army; all of them said that when someone came to help the man, whose head was bleeding over the marble floor, his helper was promptly stabbed by the assailants, and it was those savages who should be held responsible for the violence that immediately broke out in the street in front of them, in which four Arabs and five Jews were killed, and many more wounded.

One cause of the uncertainty was the nature of the old city of Jerusalem herself. Her alleys twisted unpredictably and her steps continually frustrated the passage of any horse or vehicle, and the stone of her buildings was so thick and unyielding that what happened in one street could not be heard in the next. Never mind that the British had spent months plotting a map of the town, and were in the process of dividing it into four quarters for the four main identities, a design that would become famous and presumed eternal by everyone, so that even the Arabs selling pendants demarked with the four quarters fifty years hence would by then have forgotten that it was a British invention, enforced so that the soldiers could navigate the roads more easily, and say of each man they met: you are a Christian, you are a Jew, you are Armenian, based on the nearest street name. But by April 1920, the Brits were still getting lost and asking for directions, and were so low on personnel on the morning of the Nebi Musa festival that the ensuing mayhem lasted for a full three days. For three days, feathers ripped from bedding flowed from windows like the snow that had lately thawed, and falling to the ground, mingled with the blood that shone black in the gutters, seeping at its touch into red. By the time the curfew was imposed at the end of those three days, the red was black again with muck, and the leaders who had ridden ahead of the crowds and urged them from the roof of the Arab Club to protest the Zionist program at all costs, or else to behave nobly and quietly in their protests, had fled to Egypt and were sentenced to imprisonment in absentia.

"This is no longer the twelfth century, father," said Père Antoine. "One does not expect to find oneself in a holy war."

Père Lavigne's beard swept over his desk, and he reached to trap a sheet of paper sailing forward.

"It is not a holy war, Antoine. It was a riot. Please don't be dramatic. The British haven't been here very long—but I don't know what's the matter with this pen, it does not want to give ink all of a sudden."

He pressed the nib onto the foolscap, leaving a thin scratch in the shape of an "I."

"I am worried for the Christians."

"The Christians, you are worried for?" said Lavigne, with a hint of a smile. "Ah, now this reminds me. The new Palestine Oriental Society is meeting next Thursday. Will you come? I am giving the keynote."

"How so?"

"They have elected me the president." His eyes had a watery tint. Perhaps it was the light.

"Wonderful. Congratulations."

"We are hosting it here, in the convent. Alors—don't go to Nablus, will you, just this once?"

"Of course, I will stay."

Lavigne bore down once more on his pen. "God with you, father," he said, without looking up.

Père Antoine ducked his head to don his hat and walked out into the heat of the cloisters. It was May, and Jerusalem was already baking. He clung to the slim shade of the walls towards to the dormitory.

Although the British civil administration over Palestine had just been ratified, Antoine remained disturbed by the Nebi Musa riot. He was here in Jerusalem when the rioters ran through, standing in the very courtyard outside the Holy Sepulchre when that stringy mass of men charged in through the high wooden doors. A gap had opened in the crowd and blasted him with the vision: a stretcher, borne out at a vicious angle. Blood falling on the stones. The body of a congregant, the lolling arm of an innocent, slaughtered at prayer.

In all his years here, he had never felt so ill at ease. Young Arabs on street corners set his heart racing. On the hospital veranda in Nablus he lost his nerve and struggled in his interviews. He had assumed it best to discuss this with his mentor. Now he saw he was mistaken, and the error was not a little painful. He climbed the steps to his room, considering how best to bring the whole thing up with Sister Louise.

He took a bus north that afternoon, and arrived at the sisters' house before dusk. In the hallway Sister Sarah said Louise was on an extended visit to a sick child in a village seven hours' walk away. No one knew when she might return. Antoine spent the next three days at the hospital noting down oddments of hearsay, feeling tender and strained. But with no sign of Louise, he returned to Jerusalem as he had promised Lavigne, deprived of his usual respite.

On Thursday afternoon, with half an hour to go before the meeting of Lavigne's society, Antoine looked up from his desk in the library at L'École to see he was no longer alone. Three British policemen were coming down the library steps. Had they not so rapidly removed their hats with the trepidatious postures of men on holy ground, Antoine might have thought he was under arrest.

"Good afternoon, Father Anthony," said the one in the middle. "Major Hodges here."

"Good afternoon," said Antoine.

"We've come to ask for your help."

Major Hodges was not a small man. Yet he gave an impression of smallness because his head was proportionately quite large. Hair grey and white; moustache dark and trimmed far above his top lip. A little chin—or, rather, a chin dwarfed by a hammock of flesh below, which protruded from his collar and curved underneath. As he cleared his throat and turned his whole stiff body to look at one of his officers, that pad of flesh rippled.

"We've heard, Father Anthony, that you have something of a special expertise in Nablus."

"Expertise? Oh, I don't know about expertise. An interest, certainly. I have an interest."

"Right. Thing about Nablus is—do you mind if I sit down?"

"Of course."

"Take a seat, gentlemen."

Three chairs screeched across the stone floor. Major Hodges sat nearest to Antoine and gripped the leather beak of his field cap.

"Thing about Nablus is they're unruly. Is there anyone in here by the way?"

"We are alone."

"Good. Nablus. Worst of the lot. Our trouble is, we've not got any . . ." he lowered his voice, "intelligence . . . from there since about nineteen seventeen or thereabouts. Asked the French nuns to keep an eye but . . . the thing about Nablus, as you probably know, well, it's a town of fanatics. Lot of troublemakers. What we in the CID, that's the Criminal Investigation Department, like to call mischief makers. Probably worse than Hebron, in fact."

Antoine inclined his head, not in agreement, but to show he was listening.

"Catch a troublemaker in Jerusalem and chances are two out of three he's from Nablus or thereabouts. That is not a lie. What I'm coming to is, it has been proving somewhat difficult to get many facts on the ground, so to speak. We recently set up a new department but if I'm honest with you, it doesn't matter if any one of us doffs the uniform. No one is going to talk to us."

Antoine glanced at the two other officers. One had big orange side-burns. The other had the tender features of an adolescent.

"We've been really struggling to get a local on board. But we've been doing the rounds and we heard you know a bit about the place. What we're trying to do is ascertain how much recent events were planned in advance. Nablus being one of the more organised in terms of, well, activities, as well as, like I say, more unruly. So if there is any sort of plan that is what one might call systematic on behalf of these mischief makers, to agitate the people, we need to keep an eye. Do you see? On the Jewish side we all know who's who. The Arabs are a bit different. Look, I'm going to level with you. We're behind and we're low on staff. We've started collecting fingerprints but what we really need is facts, names, alliances. Market gossip. We've got one report about the major families from about three years ago but things are always changing— and I'll tell you it's been bloody hard to find an Arab from Nablus who'll talk to us, and who we can trust. And one who speaks English." He took a breath, and fixed Antoine. "What we're wanting to know is—"

"Have I heard anything."

"Yes." He nodded. "And also," he gave a voluntary exhalation, "a bit more. We were wondering whether you might actually be willing to work for us. I know you're a holy man but it's quite common among your profession, believe it or not. And we know you speak the language, and about your considerable expertise in the study of Arabs." He gave a sardonic smile. "You will have some compensation, it will be small, but you will be honoured of course by His Majesty's Government for your services."

With an air of conclusion, he pursed his lips. His fingers were very tight on his cap, Antoine noticed, and the skin under the nails was going white. Antoine turned and looked through the window on the other side of his carrel.

"What would it involve?"

"Involve," repeated Hodges. "Lingering round the markets. Catching news here and there. Small is fine for starters, just to get a sense of . . . who the troublemakers might be. Next, make some friends."

Antoine took his time, looking at the sky. *Nablus was unruly.* Perhaps she was. She was complex, like a beautiful engine with different parts that conflicted to make the vehicle move. These were idiotic policemen, drawn from all quarters of their empire to treat each case of colonial disorder the same. And yet, against the very force of his disdain for them, Antoine felt a glimmer of—what was that? Possibility?

The truth was he probably already had the information they were after. He knew all about the families, who had feuded, who allied. He knew the kinds of crimes committed and how they were commonly avenged. It had not occurred to him that those acts of retribution he sometimes noted might be something the British should police; he simply observed them from the anthropological view. And yet there they were, listed in his book, ripe for such analysis. The bloody scene of Nebi Musa pulsed in his mind.

"O Jesu, vivens in Maria veni et vive in famulis tuis. Lord God, have mercy on me in your goodness." He placed his hands over his abdomen and bowed his head. "Hear me, O Lord. I am uncertain in my ways. Guide me on my path, in my next decisions. I am humbled before you."

The sergeant's eyes were wide.

"I am sorry. But, after all, I have nothing to give you."

"Ah," said the sergeant, in a tone of controlled surprise. "In that case. Well, if you wouldn't mind having a think about it anyway." He reached into his pocket, and pulled out a sealed envelope and a business card, "Major Hodges, I'm stationed at the police HQ in the old Russian compound."

"My answer is no."

Hodges hesitated. "Indeed. Indeed, no. Nonetheless, I'll be back in a few days to see, to see how you're . . . feeling." Before Antoine could interrupt him again, Hodges was on his feet. "All right boys, say goodbye to the father. Goodbye, Father Anthony. Off we go."

*　　*　　*

There were a few scholarly Jews and Arabs at Père Lavigne's meeting, but the audience seemed to be mostly Englishmen and Frenchmen, many from L'École, and some Americans, Greeks, and Armenians, among them the priests and rabbis conspicuous by their clerical robes and headpieces, and the archaeologists and diplomats distinguishable from one another only by degrees of tidiness and the use of pomade. Although the meeting had been advertised to the public, the only obvious non-researchers Antoine could detect were four women chatting in the back row. They were shushing each other as Père Lavigne assumed the rostrum at the front of the room. Antoine slid into an empty chair by the aisle.

Alone before his lectern, Lavigne's congenital tremor was magnified. His hand shook as it held his spectacles in place, and his head vibrated with something between a nod and a shudder.

"What are we doing?" he began, smiling widely. "We here present a truly strange spectacle. Europe, Asia, the world entire, has just been prey to the most horrific torments that history has ever known. Still, the earth trembles. Across the world, committees toil over how they shall provide the daily bread for their citizens. And here we are, gentlemen, gathered to discuss the meanings of words, and the rules of grammar, and facts of ancient geography, of wildflowers, of old melodies, of the engraved letters on the rocks of Palestine." He breathed a laugh. "But we know that this is important work. What we are embarking on is not useless. No, on the contrary. If anything can pierce the darkness of the future, if there is anything human that can illuminate the present, guide us on our way, strengthen us in these trials, revive our noblest hopes, it is the lesson of the past. It is the light of history." A pause as he turned over the page, and with his finger found the first line. "Only, we do not want any more of that type of history which is the child of the imagination, which paints large tableaux and tidies into a pretty sequence the melange of uncontrollable facts. No. Our method, gentlemen, is one of precision and accurate data, though these may be of a more mediocre appearance. Careful, patient study—that is the history of today. And for this, the strength of a single man will no longer suffice. Gone are the days of Herodotus, and even of Bossuet and Macaulay. We, gentlemen, will work together. Indeed, looking around me now I can say it would be assuredly difficult to assemble anywhere other than in Jerusalem such a diverse range of skills as those of you here present, on a terrain any more profoundly transformed over the ages, by such an extraordinary variety of civilisations."

With the applause Lavigne gripped one lens of his spectacles again. He waved off the man reaching to help him down the steps, and walked delicately to a seat in the front row. He raised a heavy eyebrow to smile at the person beside him.

There was another brief speech by the American consul, and then a break was announced, before the reading of the first papers. Tea was presented in the next room.

"Just milk for me," Antoine said to the server.

The boy looked blank.

"Bas haleeb." Antoine pointed at the jug.

Beside a pyramid of imported biscuits, a blond man with a centre parting exclaimed: "It is an abomination. The Turks had really terrible taste."

"It looks like a lighthouse!" said his interlocutor.

"Are you talking about the clock?" said a third, shorter man.

"Yes," said the blond. "Storrs wants it removed."

Antoine knew the clock tower well. It stood at Jaffa Gate, a relic from the old sultan's reign, constructed of factory-cut stone and markedly out of keeping with the style of the old city walls. Pale and rectilinear, with a pointed horseshoe arch aiming up at a balcony that circled the clock face. A crescent moon shot from the top, cradling a star. They said it was built when the time schemes were changing hands, as a sign of the sultan's modernity.

The end of the tea break was nigh. Someone announced the title of the first paper—"Noun Classes in the Hamitic Language"—and as the crowd began to shift, Antoine found Lavigne by the door. Holding one soft crooked hand between his own, he congratulated his mentor on the marvellous speech. It was, he said, a perfect introduction.

"You're not staying?" Lavigne's mouth hung open. His bottom lip was bleeding a little.

"I have things to attend to. I'm sorry. I promise I will be present at the next one."

When he arrived at the sisters' residence, Antoine found Sister Louise in the small dining room, alone at the table, drinking a glass of water.

The dining room of the sisters' residence had been extended some years earlier by the removal of a partition wall to a small conservatory, which, like the glass lid of a box turned sideways, gave them a view from the dining table of the plush garden beyond, dressed now in half-darkness, a little lawn and line of flowering herbs at the side. Each wall of the dining room bore a cross, and from the ceiling hung a bowl-like copper light fixture with a battered pendant and tarnished silver beads. It was unlit.

"Sister." Antoine sat in a chair, and the wicker squeaked. Hands on the marble tabletop, he felt a plummeting exhaustion. "Sister, I have suffered a moment of temptation."

Sister Louise was silent. Then she said, "You know, Antoine, I cannot provide you with absolution."

A circular mark was corroded into the marble near the edge. He touched it with his finger; it was rough. Someone had left a cut lemon face down.

"What is it you have done?" she asked.

"I have not done it." He could not suppress the sadness in his tone. "That is my victory." He rested his hand on the cold stone and listened carefully to make sure they were absolutely alone. Then he met Louise's eyes, which were, he noticed, far more fearful than her words sounded. "How do you manage it?" he said. "Manage, I mean, to remain so untouched."

"How?" She held his gaze. "I manage because I am not alone." He broke away, and she continued: "You must not lose courage."

"I have forgotten why I began in the first place." He heard himself whine and felt a need to cover his face. "Lord help me. I don't know what's happening."

"It is only because you are alone that you forget."

Antoine stared at her. "Alone?"

"Would you like to tell me what has happened? We can go elsewhere—"

"No. I mean . . . yes. I can tell you here. I will tell you here. Would you, could I close the door?"

Sister Louise was on her feet already, and in a second had twisted the key and was seated again.

"I was in the library." He looked up at the dark glass of the doors where, between the mullions and crossbars, their reflections were emerging. "Alone, yes. In Jerusalem, the monastery library, and a policeman came to see me. I was reading . . . it doesn't matter what I was reading. He had two other men with him." He glanced down. "Perhaps I should start further back—I don't know where to begin—"

"Beginning here is fine. You were in the library."

"In the library, yes, and the policeman came. With two other men. They asked me, would I help them. A question of expertise, you understand. They are worried about Nablus, he said, they are the most fanatical, the most . . . You know he said something, Sister, he said that two thirds of the troublemakers at Nebi Musa were Naplousiens. Do you believe that?"

Sister Louise was twisting a crust of toast idly on the saucer. She was not usually a woman who fiddled. "We have had problems with Nablus, as you know." She dropped the crust and dusted her fingers. "But I must point out, before I say anything else, that *we* are still here."

"But shutting down the hospital—"

"No we are not shutting it down, father, we are only passing it on. We are planning to remain, we will keep our clinic, and the school, and continue with the village visits. Father, you know our purpose has never really been to change them. We are not converting, not even preaching—we simply do the duty the Lord set in place." She made a quick sign of the cross.

"Yes, I know that. But this question of fanatical—I mean, you *have* had problems, you have told me so. And there is a fervour here, that I am sure of. I love Nablus. I loved her. But you know, when I saw that terrible scene in the old city, it made me feel I had been ignoring something, pretending it was not relevant . . . The sergeant gave me this."

From his habit he drew out the envelope, and opened it. Inside was a single page. At the head was typed: TOP SECRET.

Categories

Nationalist
Pro-French
Anti-British
Anti-Zionist
Amenable

"Amenable," said Sister Louise, after some moments. "Goodness me. Did you agree to it then? To help them?"

"No, I told you. I said no."

"But you were tempted?"

"Tempted—oh yes, I was tempted! Let me go back. First, before that, I was at Nebi Musa. I saw those awful things—I felt . . . Sister Louise, I felt that perhaps I had been wrong. I was so sure it was better not to be *involved*. But when I saw those things, how can I pretend—for it is a pretence! that I could look at civil custom only. As if civil custom existed alone. I mean, to look only at habits inscribed *within* the law—their laws, or British laws— as though to transgress were not also a part of communal life. But I was wrong—it is all a part of the whole!"

Sister Louise glanced at him quickly and then turned to face the garden doors.

"One cannot note down," Antoine went on, feverishly, "as if there were no frame—one always has a frame. I am from France, I *do* believe in France as protector of Catholics in the Levant, I am part of that, I am not separate—critical, yes. Not separate. I began to wonder if, in my work, if there might be a purpose, to aid some clarifying of the why, to accept my position as *part* of this mechanism, not to pretend I existed somehow beyond . . ." He broke off. "I don't know, Sister. I cannot locate my error. I am at a loss. Only I know I have erred. If it was in saying no, or if it is *this*," he gestured at himself, his body and his face, "this continued questioning. There was a temptation. Sister, I do not trust my own instincts."

"Oh come, father. Come." She leaned across, casting the list onto the table. "Don't weep."

"I am not weeping. I am simply at a loss."

"I wonder if you may have heard something."

"I have heard several things. The women at the hospital tell me all manner of facts, small in appearance, but together they give a glimpse, if not a picture, of the kinds of activities—whether criminal or not I don't know, certainly covert, certainly *of use* . . ."

"Certainly, yes, you have heard many things. But in fact I meant something else. I shall ask you outright. The fact is, I wonder father that you are confessing to *me*. And not to a priest who is properly ordained, which you might easily have done in Jerusalem."

"What? Do you mean—"

"You mustn't think I am rejecting you."

He examined her face. Despite the dark he could see she was flustered. She added: "Only it does beg the question."

The ceiling began to thump with footsteps. A loud creak, and the knock of something heavy being set down.

"When you said that I am alone," said Antoine quietly, after a pause. "What did you mean?"

"I was referring to my sisters, naturally, since we make our choices together. Of course you have L'École Biblique, but I know, since you have told me yourself, that it is not the same, that people come and go. There is not this same shared . . . it is not a vision, exactly, but a purpose, which we share. When one of us falls, there are several at hand to pick her up again."

"You did not mean to say I am alone, then, in the sense that I am without God."

"Oh." Her self-possession fell away again and she looked aghast. "No—gracious." She was apparently unable to go on. The knife went further into Antoine's shame.

The door handle began to shake, and someone called from the hallway: "Is there someone in there?"

"One moment."

Sister Louise rose and unclicked the door on a young woman wearing a nursing habit and a bewildered expression, a candle in her hand.

"I'm very sorry, Sister Marian. I must have locked it by accident."

"I came to light the lamps." Sister Marian peered in at Père Antoine.

He also stood, and reaching quickly for the page curving up from the table, bowed to conceal his face.

"If you would excuse us for just a little longer, Sister," said Louise, "we will be finished with our conversation in a few moments."

Sister Marian curtsied, and reached for the handle. Sister Louise locked eyes with Antoine and waited for Marian's footsteps to recede.

"My advice," she said curtly, "is continue with your work. It does have a value. Do not let thoughts of nations and laws and powers impinge on that. L'École Biblique has a reputation for remaining impartial, remember, and that is of consequence. If you can help it, do not become *involved*. Take it from me." Her glare was full of desperate meaning. "It is not worth it. If you will excuse me now, I must go to bed."

In the morning, as everyone took their coffee, the garden doors of the dining room were opened wide to admit a breeze. Sister Louise was returned to her impenetrable, capable self, though she was not, Antoine noted, among those leaving for the hospital. As they walked he heard Sister Marian say she was on another village visit.

Their conversation last night had not settled Antoine's dilemma. In fact, Louise's final words so surprised him that he had lain awake thinking over them. And over what Hodges had said, that this type of work was *quite common among your profession, believe it or not. We asked the French nuns to keep an eye.*

But for the chairs, the hospital veranda was empty. In the far corner Antoine's old rocker faltered in the wind. He sat back against its familiar ridges, opened his notebook to a blank double page, and began to sketch the view. He knew it so well he barely needed to look. In the foreground, three olive trees. A slope of earth with shadows and stones. In the back, Ebal rising. Above the mountain, the sky.

"Abuna," said a bright voice. "Zaman ma shoofnak."

The veranda door was open, and a small woman with a long neck trod out.

"Randa," said Antoine. "As-salamu alaykum, keef halek."

Randa was the wife of a soap factory labourer. She worked as an itinerant housemaid, and since she liked to gossip for gossip's sake had been a helpful source for Antoine's research. After their conversations he always gave her a few pennies. At first he had murmured the words: "for your trouble," but he had come to the conclusion that it was better to claim it was an act of charity from priest to pauper, separate from the information she gave him. It was not always easy to disguise the transaction: she spoke, he paid her. But Randa did her part by complaining of her back problems, how difficult the week had been, how expensive food was becoming, which all supplied pretexts for his payment as a spontaneous action.

"Oof, my back hurts," she said, as she took a seat beside him.

Antoine turned over the page.

"Salamtek. So. Have there been any stories, lately?"

"There was one blood feud," she said breathily, "between the Murad family and the Shawwaf. A Murad man went to visit the Shawwaf. The Shawwaf man chopped down his trees."

"Why did he chop down the trees?"

Randa looked dismayed. "Because he wouldn't pay the money!"

Antoine nodded. He wrote the date in the upper right-hand corner: 20 Mai 1920, and made a note: *Murad—Shawwaf.*

"And what else are people talking about in town, these days?"

"Oof," she said again. "Problems, problems."

"What kind of problems?"

"Ya'ni." She chewed her lip. "You heard about the riot? Riots in Nablus. In Yaffa, Haifa. All the country is in riots. It's very bad."

"Because of the Zionists."

"The Zionists are very bad. They want the land."

"What are people . . . what are people doing about it?"

"Ya'ni."

"What?"

"They will fight."

"Who will fight?"

"The boys."

Antoine turned the page back to his drawing, and lightly outlined a small rock in the foreground, and then another. He shaded with his pencil at an angle.

"Tell me . . . how did people feel after the events at Nebi Musa?"

"People argue."

He waited.

"Some people say, let's give the Jews something." She sighed. "Others say, you give them something, you'll give them everything, and we'll have nothing. Because in England there are many Jews. And the Mandoub es-Samme, the new Palestine governor, is a Jew. So it will be a Jewish empire. Arguing, arguing. This is always the way. Nablus is a city built on envy and intrigue." This old Nabulsi adage, "al-hasad wa al-fasad," stuck out from Randa's speech as a sudden eloquence amid the dialect.

"And what do you think, Randa?"

She played with her fingernail. "I don't know, ya Abuna."

"I have a question. Is Nablus, in your opinion, more—how shall we say . . . forceful than other towns in Palestine? More, I mean—"

"Of course!"

Antoine waited. Hodges's words, *a town of fanatics*, rang in his head. "In what ways?"

"In Nablus, they bring weapons." Randa stuck her lips out.

Antoine was astonished. "Weapons?"

"From the Bedu."

"I see. Only Nablus?"

She shrugged. A spider on the rail was lifting one gossamer leg, probing the air. Antoine struggled to think of another question.

Then Randa said: "I heard Marwan say they carry them inside lentil jars. They meet at a village . . ." She stopped.

"Marwan?" said Antoine.

But Randa would not continue. His pencil rolled to the seam of the pages.

"And how is your family?"

"We are very hungry. The chickens, we had trouble with the chickens. It was too hot for them last week."

Antoine reached for his leather purse, and pulled out a shilling.

12

In May 1920, while everyone else was discussing the Mandate, Midhat was thinking about Fatima Hammad. Specifically, he was thinking of her at Nebi Musa. Each time he summoned that hesitant figure he unbuckled a sharp, bodily feeling, close to the compulsion that used to draw him to pace like a sleepwalker outside her house in the early mornings, willing the windows to return his gaze.

It was almost dinnertime, and he smelled onions and heard the clink of porcelain. He stared up at his bedroom ceiling, resisting the edge of sleep. Some months ago he had wished to persuade himself to desire marriage, and it did occur to him now that he might have succeeded. But summoning the girl's eyes looking at him, the allure of fatedness remained, of recognising her and being recognised amid all those hundreds of people.

The remembered crowd throbbed in his chest, with its smooth disguising violence, and he sat upright. Across the windowsill lay his books, touched at angles by the late light. He rifled for a slip of paper and a pen. He did not even have a desk here. The only desk in the house was next door, in his father's unused study.

"Um Mahmoud?" came his grandmother's voice.

He perched on the mattress, plucked a book to lean on, and aimed the nib at the top left-hand corner of the page. This was an old impulse, to trace out the strands of event, draw up a diagnosis, and explain what had led to what. He wrote the title: FATIMA HAMMAD. He looked at the words, left to right, in the Latin alphabet. Should he not do this in Arabic? He wrote "Fatima Hammad" in Arabic. After that, however, he could think of no more words. Every one that came was French. He looked up and with a blast of nausea perceived the striped wallpaper of his bedroom in Montpellier, the window onto the green lawn, and felt the cold floorboards under his feet.

That movement of his mind, that dance of logic and contingency— surely it could not be forever marked by his experience at the Molineus'. He did not want to ride along life's surface without at least trying to work it out. He did not desire the part of himself that moved darkly at the sight of the dervish, in the heat of the chanting crowd. He hesitated, pen in hand, for a long time. After a while, he wrote: "Dear Jeannette." Dear Jeannette what? He looked stupidly at the page. His pen drew a circle, and he coloured it in with a zigzag of ink.

The following day, while Hisham was out, he sat reading at the store. The air was yellow with pollen. He had bought this book two years ago by the Seine, when while browsing the volumes for sale he chanced upon a passage about the Holy Land and immediately handed over the francs. Since then, it had become an illicit pastime to read descriptions of the place he came from, to be transported by a landscape so precisely drawn and tinted in this other language that he ended up longing for the sights of his childhood as though he were not already among them. A shadow fell over his page and he jumped.

"As-salamu alaykum," said Haj Nimr Hammad.

Midhat mumbled a response. Haj Nimr was wearing a summer coat, belted around the waist. He looked thin. With one stride he entered the corner where jackets were hanging ready for sale, then looked down at the small stove and coffee things. He approached a shelved wall stocked neatly with folded fabrics. He touched one at eye level, a print of blue flowers on yellow, and pulled it down like a doctor inspecting a bottom lip. He rubbed his thumb over the pattern.

"Can I help you with something in particular?" said Midhat. "If you are looking for a special occasion, may I recommend the Samaritan tailors." He was speaking too fast. His consonants became meticulous: "They work just around the corner. We," he shrugged, "mostly stock items for the fellahin."

Nimr returned to the fabric shelves. "The fellahin," he repeated. "And this is where you will be working?"

"Pardon?"

Haj Nimr faced him. The hollows of his eyes were very pronounced, and his moustache was full and grey.

"I'm training here," said Midhat carefully. "Ba'dayn I'll be in Cairo, where my father is." He paused. "The store in Cairo is larger, you know. Spacious."

Nimr nodded. "And you are not yet engaged?"

"No," said Midhat. "I am not engaged."

He nodded again. "In that case . . . in that case, if you wish to marry my daughter, you may."

Midhat gaped. A twitch of laughter advanced up his chest, and a hand appeared at his mouth, his own hand, to stop it.

"Thank you. God bless you, ya Haj." He slipped from his chair onto legs full of liquid. "Of course, yes," he heard himself say. "By God I would like to marry your daughter."

Haj Nimr's eyes slid away. "We will expect you soon, then, for the proposal."

"Yes."

"The wedding will have to be after Ramadan."

"Yes, yes, of course . . ."

"Ma'salameh."

After the last flap of Haj Nimr's coat in the yellow light, the silence in the store was enormous. Midhat laughed once, very loudly. Suddenly, he wanted to run. He sat down and crossed his legs. His arched top foot rapidly pressed and released an invisible pedal. At last a figure appeared in the doorway, and he jumped to his feet.

"Hisham, I have to go! I have to go!"

He sprinted up the mountain. Three fellaha women blocked the road as it steepened: he skirted them up the crag to the side, loose soil rolling, and ran along the path to the house.

"Teta! Teta! Where are you? Haj Nimr said yes!"

His grandmother appeared from her bedroom in a nightgown, her grey hair tied in a plait. She squealed and grabbed his ears, pulling his head down to her height.

"When when when?"

"Aha-ow!"

"We have to tell your father immediately!"

"He said we will wait until after Ramadan."

"What changed his mind?"

"I don't know."

"Tell Jamil, go, we'll tell your father after. Habib alby!"

She clapped her hands together, and gave a little scream.

"You are mad," said Midhat.

Um Jamil was slicing tomatoes in her kitchen, her fingers covered in juice and unbound seeds.

"Jamil is at the store," she said. A smile broke on her face. "What's happened?"

"I'll tell you later. I want to tell my cousin first." He squeezed her upper arm, and gave her a kiss.

He flew down the mountain. Near the bottom he stopped in the shade of a large tree and found he was out of breath. He turned his chin to the clear sky. Unburdened by the sun, he could see it glowing in the foliage above him, the green leaves fluorescent like the bodies of insects. He walked the rest of the way, straightened his tie, and pushed back the hair at his temples. Outside the market, men smoked pipes in the heat, and he saluted their rotating faces. A slew of water appearing from the entrance to a cheese shop caught his trouser leg, splashing dark grey. "It's nothing!" he shouted. He could smell milk fermenting. At a crossroads, four English policemen walked by. Behind them, three Arabs—also in uniform. Rifles. Cloth bandoliers of ammunition. One of the Englishmen nodded at him: his joy must be that obvious. Midhat nodded back, his love so general he could share it, even, in that moment, with them.

His thoughts had a long, smooth shape. What a city this was! He paraded down the alley, reflecting that children belonged de facto, webs of allegiance tied their little feet to the ground, their resemblances to others remarked upon, predictions made on such and such a basis. But for an adult, though allegiances from childhood might subsist they no longer constituted belonging. You needed something else—and now he had it. Now he would belong. The aims of his actions were clarifying, like a sturdy wall at midday. This was what was missing from his life in Nablus—how funny that he had barely a moment to recognise the absence before it was filled with the glorious flood of being known, of knowing, as he advanced towards the carpet shop. In those years of distance from Nablus, this being known was the subject of his nostalgia—how wrongheaded that was, since this feeling was not of the past. No, no, no, it was of the future! That was plain; it was fantastically coherent. Everything that had happened led to the present. All the hazards of Europe, all accident and wonder, even Nebi Musa, terrors seen and felt, all shame and pain, all objects in the corridors of that old museum pointed towards him at this moment. Yesterday he could not have teased his desire for Fatima Hammad from the other strands, from his father, from the need for what was denied, from the need for a woman. But with the prize virtually in hand he could see it all. That was a solid wall ahead of him; it was the foundations of a house. He had obeyed—and he had defied. He was of them, and he was his own. He with his strong body had laid the first stone, and others had seen it, Haj Nimr Hammad had seen it, and with him foresaw the edifice that would now arise.

Jamil's shop was dark with carpets that hung on every wall and in the windows. One step inside and Midhat's nose was overwhelmed by the animal fibres and the wool dyes cooking together in the darkness. Jamil, dressed in a thin chemise, held a brush and dustpan. A customer was describing a pattern with his hands in the air, and Jamil was nodding. At the sight of Midhat, he raised his index finger.

"Haj Nimr said yes," said Midhat, as the customer left. He bit his lower lip and grinned. "I'm going to marry Fatima."

"Congratulations."

Midhat waited for something more. Then it was he who stretched out to shake his cousin's hand. He looked into Jamil's eyes, and saw the smile had not reached them. A weight dropped in his stomach.

"Hey, Jamil," said a younger man at the back. "Do you want these or are we throwing them away?" He held up two rags.

"Well I'll see you later," said Midhat. He watched his cousin one more time, and seeing nothing, forced their cheeks together to hide his face. Under his hand, he felt perspiration on Jamil's neck. He must have his mind on other things.

As he walked back, however, Midhat wondered whether this final success with Haj Nimr had not unblocked that old spring of jealousy in his cousin. Clearly it was only staunched before, when he confessed his prior failure. Anger flickered. But the thought of his prior failure led again to the thought of his success, which was a thought hot with joy, and a rush of light entered his mind when he touched it. Nothing could overwhelm that now. His self had centred around his resolve, and he had won.

"Ya mu'allim." He waved at the telegraph operator. "I'm sending one to Cairo."

The operator passed him a slip from the pile. Midhat wrote: "Haj Nimr has accepted. I will marry Fatima Hammad. The wedding will be after Ramadan. Will you come to Nablus for the official proposal. Salamat. Midhat."

He paid, saluted, left. The thought of his father's praise poured a thrill down his spine, and he charged up the mountain path. The town below, the white buildings, the balconies and minarets.

He opened the door on women's voices. Um Taher was in the salon, fully dressed, drinking coffee with a group of friends. He raised his hand in the doorway.

"Salam."

"Join us, teta!" said his grandmother.

"Mabroo—ook," sang Um Dawud.

"Ah, thank you, Khalto. My grandmother told you all?"

"Why so sad?" shouted Um Taher.

"Not sad. Just tired. So much excitement! I told Jamil," he nodded at his aunt.

"Be happy, God doesn't always give," said Um Taher smugly to her companions.

"Fatima Ham*mad*!" said someone.

"Beautiful," said another.

Teta reached out an arm to welcome him. He sat beside her, sliding a nail under a chocolate wrapper. Um Jamil was in the middle of complaining about the carpet sales, which had been tapering off. Others hummed in agreement. It was not like a textile shop; the coming of Ramadan does nothing for carpets. Ba'dayn, she said, Jamil is not concentrating properly at the store. He has wandered away "fi aalam liwahdu," in a world of his own.

"What do you think?" she asked Midhat.

"To be honest, I have not seen him much myself. I have been so busy with . . ." He gestured in the air, as though already preparing for the wedding. "But I don't know, you may be right. He has seemed not himself. He spends a lot of time with those Murad boys."

"Since you two returned from that riot, nothing is the same."

"An jad nothing," said Um Dawud.

"Maybe Jamil needs to find a girl," said Teta. "It's not healthy, you know. You have to let it out."

"Teta," said Midhat.

"I think it's a question of age," said another woman. "Wallah al-azeem my son was grumpy till he was thirty. Wallah al-azeem."

"Get him a girl, he'll be fine," said Teta.

"Maybe he doesn't like the carpets very much," said Midhat.

Um Jamil turned her lip out. "You could be right."

The news of Midhat's engagement travelled fast. Over subsequent days old women he didn't know warbled at the sight of him, and old men chortled: "Dar Hammad! Dar Hammad!" Rumour had it that Abu Omar Jawhari himself would officiate at the signing of the betrothal contract. Haj Abdallah Atwan even gave him a nod one hot evening in the Manshiyah Garden.

"The Parisian," he called. "I heard the news."

"Thank you," said Midhat, with practised grace.

Abdallah laughed, one loud report of air, and the seams on either side of his mouth deepened. Midhat realised he had pre-empted Abdallah with thanks before any word of congratulation.

Presently Abdallah said, "Yes, well done. There is rarely happy news in Nablus these days. People love a wedding."

The other word on everyone's lips was the official beginning of the British Mandate over Palestine. Midhat frequently returned after work to hear women's voices asking questions such as: "Do you know what is the difference between the British and the French?" Leaflets from the Colonial Office fluttered through the streets declaring in both Arabic and Hebrew that the European mandates were confirmed by the League of Nations. France was to rule over Syria and Lebanon, and Britain over Palestine. No one was being given independence. The mandates were a temporary measure en route to self-government, a period of supervision "until such time as they are able to stand alone."

A telegram arrived from Midhat's father within days: a financial problem with the business, soon to be solved, required his continued presence in Cairo. As a result, he could not come for the official proposal to the Hammads. "I will be there for the ceremony in July," said the telegram, "and I will wire the money in a few days for the mahr and the wedding preparations. I am proud."

Midhat felt a cramp of longing. Only those words at the end conveyed any feeling: "I am proud." He folded the telegram in half. He walked into his father's darkened bedroom and with a deep breath continued into his father's office. He sat down at the desk.

The room was much smaller than Taher's office in Cairo. It contained merely this desk and chair, that cabinet by the door, and a small shelf of books beside a window facing the slope, where a bird was jumping between the branches of a hawthorn tree in the dusk. There was no lamp. Midhat opened a desk drawer and a pen rattled; he took it out and pulled a sheet from the stack of paper beside it, knocking the drawer closed with his foot. The ink had filled the cap; he looked at the blank page, rotating the pen by its barrel. Smudges bloomed on his fingers and thumb as he wrote the words: "My dear father." It was hard to see them in the darkness. He reached for a fresh sheet.

Cher Hani,

I am getting married to Fatima Hammad, daughter of Haj Nimr Hammad. I understand the situation is terrible in Damascus. We are all upset about recent events. But I hope you will be able to attend the ceremony—it will be around the third day after Eid al-Fitr. I hope you are safe. I miss you. I am happy about the marriage, but of course the mood in Nablus in general is not happy. We are worried about our fates. Wishing you all the blessings of the holy month of Ramadan. God be with you.

Yours,
Midhat

In the absence of Haj Taher, Teta insisted on attending the proposal. Quite possibly she would have insisted anyway. But on the morning of, she spent so long deciding what to wear—a blue gown and silver earrings—that she and Midhat arrived at the Hammad house to find the other Kamal men already waiting outside. Jamil leaned against the wall. His father, Abu Jamil, waved as they approached. Wasfi was there too, with both his brothers.

"Here's Tahsin," said Jamil, pointing over Midhat's shoulder at a skinny figure speeding down the hill.

"Don't run!" shouted Abu Jamil. "He'll ruin his shoes."

Midhat laughed nervously as Abu Jamil pressed the doorbell. The doorman appeared and they filed in, a nodding line of suits and tarabish. Um Taher brought up the rear with Midhat. He had forgotten how large the main hall was. It was like a church. The Hammads were more numerous than the Kamals, but at first sight, beneath that vast barrelled ceiling, they appeared a small group. Haj Hassan was at the back, there was Haj Tawfiq, a few other elderly men, several younger ones. Haj Nimr stood to the side with hands clasped. The Hammads were considerably whiter in beard than the Kamals, of whom Abu Jamil was the eldest. One by one, Kamals shook the hands of Hammads, nodding as-salamu alaykum, as-salamu alaykum, wa alaykum as-salam, as-salamu alaykum, wa alaykum as-salam.

He moved along the line and saw Fatima standing behind them, by the far couch, close to her mother. Her hair was parted down the centre and tied low on her neck, and she wore a thin white veil over her nose and mouth. A cream dress, a long necklace of pearls. Eyes heavily outlined. He smiled. She looked at him but did not smile back. Her shoes: aqua blue. With a force that did not belong to him, Midhat broke from the hand-shaking line and strode up to her. From his jacket pocket he pulled a poppy, which he had picked from the mountainside. The bright crêpe head lolled on the weakened stalk. Fatima reached out, and he was touched by the sight of her round fingers, broad at the hilt, tapering to the nail. A little laugh broke from her veiled mouth as she met his eyes. Everyone was watching: Haj Nimr, Widad, Fatima's sister, her little brother. Teta beamed.

A maid entered with the first tray of coffee, and the men shuffled into two orderly rows. Widad disappeared and reappeared with the second tray, and carried them between the rows so everyone could take a cup. Then Abu Jamil cleared his throat, and addressed Haj Nimr.

"Our son Midhat Kamal, son of Haj Taher Kamal, would like to ask for your daughter, Fatima Hammad, to be his wife."

The pause. Haj Nimr nodded at his family members, and they all tipped their cups to their mouths at the same time. They reached for the tray to release their hands for clapping and a few people whistled. Um Taher stepped forward to embrace Widad. Abu Jamil kissed Midhat on the cheek.

Midhat could not take his eyes off Fatima. She kept looking at the floor, but there was definitely a smile on her lips. He would have to survive off this for the whole of Ramadan.

After the proposal, Midhat only really saw Jamil across the dinner table on those evenings when he and Teta went downstairs after sunset. He whiled away most of the early Ramadan afternoons with Adel Jawhari and Qais Karak, amusing their minds while their bodies became accustomed to the fast. Following the iftar meal, the three of them would visit the midnight courtyards to see a karakozati pulling the strings of his marionette, or skirt the delta of an overpacked café where a rawi stood on his chair telling stories with an eye on the upturned tarbush that clinked through the crowd.

Adel and Qais were excellent company. They loved each other without envy, and accepted Midhat without question. Qais had an earnest, almost naïve air, coupled with the mannerisms of an older man; large hands, abundant stubble, and a tendency when laughing to frown slightly, as though he found everything a little preposterous. Having written four literary reviews for a newspaper in Jerusalem, he spoke of moving down there to develop a career in the field—though such a defection from the family trade of soap manufacturing would not be popular among his father and uncles.

Adel was wittier than Qais, but with a moral sense that weighed down many of his opinions. He had returned from university in Beirut a year prior, and in search of a purpose, alighted on the local branch of the Muslim-Christian Society. He was one of the society's youngest members, and half the time lectured Qais and Midhat about politics, having just signed the petition against the impending Mandate.

On the ninth day of Ramadan, the three of them left the mosque after evening prayers, and walked to Adel's house for iftar.

"I was going to ask you," said Qais, "are you still going to be a doctor?"

"A doctor, no," said Midhat. "Why? I gave up on that long ago."

"Politics, then."

"No. Not for me. I'll stay in the textile trade. Probably we'll live in Cairo, like my father."

"Even with your experience, ya'ni. Just the family business."

"Don't go to Cairo," said Adel.

"Why not?" said Qais.

"We need Midhat here, people like Midhat."

"Ya al-Barisi . . ." Qais half sang.

"We need the good characters," said Adel.

"Well, you know, I actually realised something," said Midhat. "Which is that it's not just about the family business. It's about something more, ya'ni, something . . . I haven't worked it out exactly. But if Cairo is the way the business is going, then we live in Cairo," he concluded. "That's simple."

"I understand," said Qais. "It's hard to be free here."

"No no, that's not what I meant. It's not about freedom. It's about . . . belonging."

"You know what they say about Nabulsi women," said Qais. "You take them out of Nablus, they become very willing. If you know what I mean."

Adel sucked his teeth. "Shu hada? He's about to get married."

Adel lived with his mother and father and siblings in the centre of town—though he maintained it was in the west—on the ground floor of a house built recently but in the old style, with a small internal patio and a pond for catching rainwater. They sat at a table outside, joined by Adel's two younger brothers and then by his father. The buildings around them were dark but the sky held onto an uncanny pale glow. Lucid in the cool, Midhat embarked on a story.

"One time, I was on a train in France."

"A what?" said Adel's father, who was hard of hearing.

"He said a train," said Adel.

"I was on this train, and I saw a man, sitting, over there."

He gestured at Qais, two chairs down. Qais's eyes encouraged him, wide in the candlelight.

"He was ikteer mratab," said Midhat. "Very chic. Suit, tie." He did the motions on his own body and sat up straight. "Moustache, very thin. Blond, cap. And we looked at each other, heyk," he closed his eyes and gave a half bow of formal greeting.

Consenting to take the role of the blond Frenchman, Qais did likewise and laughed.

"And after that, the train goes—"

"Where were you going?" said Adel.

"Oh, er . . . Lyon."

"Why?"

"This is another story," said Midhat, dusting the air with his fingers. "So the man gets up, alights. I have one more stop. I notice, as the train leaves the station, that he has left something on the seat. Small, leather, heyk. It is a wallet. I pick it up—ah, Monsieur, Monsieur! I wave through the window—khalas, he has already gone. Shu sar? I sit down with the wallet—I don't want anybody to steal it—"

"Was there money inside?" said Qais.

"A *lot* of money. Ten, fifteen hundred francs. Shu sar? I cannot take this money, that would be very dishonourable. So I look in the wallet, I see an address. A little card like this. Name, and address."

"What was his name?" said Adel.

"Laurent," said Midhat.

The moment he said it, a flush rose from within Midhat's abdomen and coursed up to his face. His scalp was on fire. Laurent. Dear Laurent. It was the first name that came into his head.

"Yalla," said Adel's father gently.

"So," he said, in quieter voice, bending his gaze up to the livid pallor of the sky, and exhaling slowly. "The address is such and such a place in . . . kaza mahal near Lyon. I get off the train, I cross the platform, ya'ni there is a little bridge over the tracks. I wait for the next train, it takes fifteen minutes, something like that. Then I stop at the station where the blond man got off. I take a taxi—there are many, many taxis in France—and I tell the driver, please take me to this place. Driver says—oh, you want to go to this place? I say yes, I want to go to this one. Tayyeb, it's a short trip, we arrive, what is it? It's a castle. A real castle, wallah al-azeem. Bisamuha *chateau*, bil faransawi. Long path like this, trees, and as I come up the path, I see horses running through the fields."

In a dark courtyard, the whites of the eyes will betray the direction of a person's gaze. As Midhat said the line about the horses, he caught Qais's doubting gaze sliding over to Adel. Adel made no attempt to stifle a convulsion of his chest. A modest shudder, it could have been a burst of air from his dinner; nonetheless, it hurried Midhat to the point.

"So I knock on the door, I ask for this Monsieur—Laurent. They tell me, but he is not a Monsieur! He is a Duke! It's not a lie, I swear to God—I see the blond man, coming through the far doors," he pointed at a window across the patio, drawn by a lamp glimmering there, "he comes out and embraces me, all the servants shake my hands . . . it became a great friendship. He was so grateful. He said he was sure all the money would have been taken. I stayed there three nights. Then I went back to Paris."

"Mish ma'ool," said Adel's youngest brother. "That's amazing."

Adel locked eyes with Midhat and started to laugh. Still stinging with the accident of Laurent's name, Midhat wondered, thus weakened, if Adel would challenge the veracity of his tale and embarrass him. Then something shifted; the muscles in his own stomach unfastened and he laughed, and Adel, set free, rocked backward and slapped his knee.

Perhaps it did not matter if he had invented the story. It was a good story, and that was plenty. This was the better way to tell his self; it was no use aiming directly. As the hilarity subsided, he experienced a rare moment of self-perception. He felt his presence from the outside, not only in space, but also in time. In a flash he saw this part he played for the men of Nablus as a kind of inverse of his persona in Paris—the part he used to play for women. He was always marked by his difference. Many times during courtships he had even purposefully weakened his French—which was then near fluent—and found he could play with ease the sweet buffoon and at the same time retain the glamour of hiddenness. There was always some kernel hidden in the folds, some mystery to long for. He could feel it again now, that double view.

He thought of Jeannette's piercing look, directed from across a table. He wondered what she would have thought of this fabrication, and noticed, as from a distance, the possibility of shame. It was replaced immediately by anger. He held the anger down, and the moment passed.

As the dark became total, talk gravitated as usual to Nebi Musa. Adel's father contended that the ratifying of the Mandate was a reaction to it, and that they had ruined their chances by that bloody scene. Adel, half in support of his father, repeated some of his usual polemic about using dialogue against disenfranchisement. It was a discussion had too many times before and did not take off beyond the usual circular arguments. They lost steam and Midhat suddenly thought of Basil's gun. Just like his thought of Jeannette, this image arose out of nowhere. How strange: he had forgotten the gun completely. Haj Nimr's acceptance came so soon after Nebi Musa it must have eclipsed everything else in his brain.

"Were there any shootings at Nebi Musa?" he said.

"Of course, there were shots," said Adel.

"What?" said his father.

Mistaking this for deafness, Adel shouted: "I said of course—"

"You didn't tell me that!" said his father.

"I didn't want to worry you."

"Who brought the guns?"

"Why should I know. Jabotinsky had guns. It was probably the Jews."

"Oh," Midhat broke in. "I remember . . ."

Another vision flickered. That army, or that militia, in Jerusalem.

"What do you remember?" said Qais.

But Qais was the only one who had heard; the others were talking among themselves. Midhat waved his hand. "Nothing."

He was surprised at himself. As he walked home he dwelled on the fact that he had blindly forgotten what he saw, Jabotinsky's men and women marching in formation. The version of Nebi Musa he gave Teta and Um Jamil had replaced his real memory of it. How peculiar. The edges of his brain felt alarmingly opaque. He wondered, dismayed, what else he might have forgotten, or was capable of forgetting.

The following day after work, Midhat climbed the mountain home, and in the doorway called for his grandmother. A telegram envelope lay on the table. From Cairo.

"Teta," he called, picking it up and walking into the kitchen.

The kitchen was empty. A cupboard door hung open; he closed it. She was not in the salon either, nor her bedroom. He walked to his own room, where a window exposed a red sun touching the horizon. He stood at his mat and began to pray, hands to his ears, bending, straightening, kneeling. After two prostrations he raised his head and started. Teta was sitting on his bed.

"You scared me! Are you a ghost?"

"I've made a mistake." Her voice was full of tears. "Forgive me. I was very angry with Um Mahmoud. She left."

"Why?"

"I don't know what happened." She threw her hands into the air and let them flop down again. "I don't know what's happening to me these days. She burned the dinner, she burned the bottom of the pot, I lost my temper. I never thought she would leave, like that."

"Oh, oh. Teta, it's fine, it doesn't matter." He sat beside her, and saw her fingers trembling in her lap. "Look, you have exhausted yourself."

"It matters! The wedding! Um Mahmoud, she is an excellent cook, usually she is excellent . . . we need her for the mansaf."

"It's going to be fine. We'll find someone else."

"I want Um Mahmoud. Don't tell your father."

"We'll find—you know, why don't I just go and see Um Mahmoud, and see if we can't make it better?"

"Oh, will you?" As she looked at him, the tears began to break. "I love her. She has been with us for so long."

"Of course I will. Everything will be fine."

"I know, I know. What's this?"

It was the envelope, he had thrown it onto the bed. In the old sunlight the white paper was going pink.

"The mahr, I think."

Through her tears, she gave him an ironic smile. "You didn't open it?"

"I was praying."

"God before money. Habibi is a good Muslim."

She ripped open the top, and pulled out the telegram. Her smiling mouth flattened. She frowned.

"I don't understand. What does it say?"

"Let me see."

Dear Um Taher and Midhat,

My dear husband has passed away. God have peace upon him. He had a heart attack. He was in his office. We were all asleep. Please come.

Layla

Midhat's mouth opened.

"No," said Teta.

"Baba."

A spasm, sharp and dark, ran up Midhat's spine. His eyes pressed shut, and he put his chin to his chest, as though to avoid a blow.

That was enough for Teta. Her weight slid off the mattress and onto the floor, and looking up he saw the shaking curve of her back. She started to wail. A low warning growl, then a long moan, gaining in pitch. One feeble hand percussed the wall. Something slippery was swelling in Midhat's head. The wailing was a song, a thing to hold onto. His arms and legs were painfully light. He watched her hand hit the wall, and the bed fell away. The floor was gone.

They would leave for Cairo in the morning. Midhat found some leftover rice, and after setting a pan to boil added some glugs of hot water. He stirred until the misshapen boulders crumbled into a watery mixture, and poured the clouded runoff into the drain by the back door. Teta entered as he was setting old vine leaves on a plate. Without a word she transferred the rice into a saucepan on the hob, and fiddled with spice bundles from the cupboard. The bread he had warmed up was hard by the time she finished. They ate in silence.

In the morning they woke when the musaharati came drumming by their house. After breakfast they took the train to Tulkarem and changed for the direct line to Cairo. Since it was Ramadan, travellers were few and they had four seats to themselves near the dining car. Midhat took the window seat. Teta prayed the entire journey, rocking back and forth, occasionally raising her head to the ceiling and holding up her hands. Midhat felt a strange dry desolation, as though all the moisture had evaporated from his body.

It was evening when they arrived in Cairo. The city had been repaired since his visit eight months ago, and seethed with people celebrating after iftar. The taxi from the station brought them down a wide boulevard lined with tearooms and bookshops, and men in tall boots guarded the glittering entrances to department stores. At the house in Abbassia they waited on the doorstep for several minutes before a maid opened the door. She showed them into the salon. Layla was dressed in black. She had gained some weight around her middle, and it was not the shape of a pregnancy. She looked angry as she reached out for Midhat, and up close he saw the red blur of recent weeping.

"It was a heart attack." Her upper lip shook. "God have mercy on him. He was eating . . . he was eating . . . pistachio nuts. In his office. Stupid man."

"Al-awda fi hayatek," Midhat murmured. His mind began to assemble the scene. He darkened it. He closed his eyes. "Allah yirhamo."

"Mama," said Layla, reaching out to the mother-in-law she had never loved.

Um Taher began to cry. "Where is he?"

"In the earth."

"You already buried him? Who washed him?"

"I washed him," said Layla.

Layla sent the maid to show Midhat and his grandmother the bedroom they would share. Teta ogled the gilded ceiling and the velvet cushions on the bed. A thin mattress curled up from the floor; Midhat placed his bag beside it as Teta asked the maid for the bathroom. On her return she whispered, "Go and see," and then seized slow possession of the chair in the corner. Consulting her compass she twisted the chair to the Qibla, at an angle to the window. Midhat lay on the mattress and was quickly asleep.

When he woke, the chair was empty. Voices drifted up through the floor. Half-moon creases rippled the back of his suit jacket: he opened his bag for a fresh one.

"It's very large, isn't it?" said a loud voice from below.

And another: "Marie! I didn't know you would come."

In the bathroom, a modern white toilet stood at the far end. Along one edge rose a free-standing bathtub, and opposite that the long neck of a basin reached through the floor. The three objects gleamed like clean teeth. Midhat knelt on the tiles, where some water had collected in the grouting, and put his head on the porcelain brim of the bath. It was hard and cold. Someone shouted his name. After a long pause he heard the soft footsteps and voice of a child.

"Midhat?"

"I'm coming," he replied, in a public voice. He stood and ran the tap, closed it again, and opened the door.

The messenger was Musbah, the dark-browed eldest of Midhat's half-siblings, leggy and afraid, with a downy upper lip. He waited for Midhat to put on his shoes, and then preceded him down the stairs. The hallway below was full of people, men and women both. Layla's voice said loudly:

"This is his son. Eldest son."

Musbah stepped off the bottom stair and there was a moment of confusion in which no one greeted anyone. Then the guests, discerning the difference between the two, turned to Midhat. He proceeded through the hall after Musbah, shaking their hands, not retaining a single name or face, and saw Layla accept a tray of food from someone and bear it out through a farther door. Chairs lined the walls. Children wandered in and out, Midhat's little half-brothers, Nadim and Nashat, in matching velveteen suits, and Dunya and Inshirah in checkered dresses. Musbah sat alone in a corner by the window.

"I knew your father very well," said an elderly man. He put a heavy silver Quran in Midhat's hands. "He was a good, kind person."

Too late the guests lingered, and respectful murmurs descended into lazy gossip. The children had long been in bed when Teta, at the edge of a circle of Cairene women, broke into a fit of coughing. One of the women rubbed her back, but Layla seized the moment to urge: "You must go to bed, Um Taher. To bed!" At last the final visitors pulled on their coats, and wrapping shawls around their necks bade them farewell.

In the middle of the night, something pulled hard on Midhat's earlobe. He opened his eyes to see Teta's big, pale face leaning over him.

"Don't lie on your back like that. You look dead."

"What?"

"I can't sleep. I'm frightened."

He had been dreaming. He did not know of what. Facts came crowding in.

"Yalla," she said in a tragic voice, sitting back on the bed.

He wrenched himself up and slid in beside her.

"Lie down."

Darkness closed over them again. A moment later, a vulgar sun inserted itself through the window and pressed down on Midhat's eyelids. In another room, a child was crying. The outside of the bedsheet was cold under his hand, and a little damp, and Teta was snoring with her back to him.

Without meals to rule the quarters of the day, Midhat strung himself by the prayer calls. He counted the hours and half hours between them. Each time the muezzin down the road started up again, he left the room where the family had congregated and went upstairs to wash and pray. Teta spent the entire morning in their bedroom, rocking in the chair, palms facing the ceiling. At noon she joined the rest of the family. The children wept on and off. How much the children understood, how much Layla had told them, was unclear, but at the least they were catching the sadness in the air, and conveying it in rotation so it never lapsed for long. Each time another broke out Teta turned her eyes to heaven. Musbah, who was certainly old enough to understand, hardly cried at all. He was also the only one old enough to fast, and he looked on miserably as his siblings plugged their tears with spoonfuls of food at lunchtime. Food was their only comfort, and even that was temporary. All other attempts to help, or embrace, or soothe, were rebuffed by striking arms. Occasionally they mumbled the syllables, "ma-ma," but they did not seem to want her when Layla picked them up.

Fair-haired Dunya looked the most like their father because of her broad cheekbones. Her nose was still sweetly curved with babyhood and her forehead often rumpled by a frown. Nashat had grown since the autumn, and Layla, huffing with exasperation, kept grabbing him to tug his shirt down over his belly. Inshirah and Nadim had Layla's eyes. Inshirah had her thin nose as well, but Nadim had a wide skull and little lips that did not resemble anybody's. Such mental observations consumed the hours between prayers. With any luck Midhat need not tread near the abyss today. And tonight there would be no time, surrounded by people. And tomorrow they would leave for Nablus, and by then all this would be shrouded in the past.

When evening fell and the next round of condolence-givers arrived, Midhat did not have an appetite.

"I'm fine," he said, turning away the plate.

"You have been fasting," said Teta, outraged. "You are too thin."

That might be true, but it was excellent, being hungry. It drew all energy to his stomach. He thought of nothing.

With night, he slept deeply. Some hours before dawn, however, he started awake. The low drumming of the pipes was loud in his ear, and at first he thought that was what had woken him. Then he realised how raw his stomach felt. It was making him dizzy, even where he lay. He crept out of the bedroom and downstairs. Just as he was about to enter the kitchen, he saw the door to his father's study. It was closed. He opened it.

The blinds of both windows were drawn, and the yellow fingers of a streetlamp slid in between the slats. The chair was slotted into the desk, and papers had been stacked around the edges, leaving an empty rectangle in the centre. The room held the smell of his father, the musk, the tobacco.

It all came in. There was nothing to stop it, he had not planned any defences in advance. Out of sight of his waking mind this scene must have been preparing itself with the details he was given, and now, unstoppable, it was beginning to play. He saw, he felt, in the middle of a mouthful of pistachio nuts, his father's chest beginning to squeeze. The absolute terror, imminent: his father's arms seized with that sudden grip and a deep, uncertain pain pulsing in the abdomen, an angel of death entering the room through the half-opened window as the nuts already chewed spilled from his lips and onto his shirt front. His gasp, his burning face. The body convulsing to vomit up those nuts so far ingested. And then still, the body lying where the life ended, slumped over the desk.

The blank desk stared at Midhat. He lifted one leg and kicked. It was heavy; it turned a little. He kicked again, harder. And again, grunting with all his weight and effort behind the motion of his right leg, and again, and the desk swivelled off wholly to one side, revealing white marks on the floor in the shape of its feet.

Rage flooded his body. He had done everything for this man. For this man's opinion, every choice. And he had succeeded! He was engaged to the Hammad girl! And where was his father? Midhat's whole life, stripped down to feeble reeds. They collapsed without him. He punched down, knuckles first. His fingers felt the ache, and, maddened by it, he pounded with the side of his fist, hammered a rhythm like Teta's song, and heard a moan seep from his grimacing mouth. He grabbed a piece of paper, observed without reading a title about licencing. All of it was business correspondence. With exaggeration he ripped it down the centre, severing the cushion of a letter Saad from its tail. Ripping the paper was like drawing blood and in the shock of the sound he was calm.

A noise came from the hall, and whatever Midhat was inside of, he fell out again. With a dizzy breath he pulled at the desk—first by the top edge, and when it refused to budge he bent over and grabbed the legs, causing one paper pile not weighted with an ornament to whisper upwards in a curve—and after roughly repositioning the feet he collected the fallen pages. He noticed his hand was bleeding as he opened the door.

A very pale Musbah was standing there. At the sight of Midhat, he looked relieved. He had been afraid, perhaps, of some returning spirit, some jinni of the passage out—and now he ducked his head and moved to go. Only then did Midhat realise his own face was covered in tears. He wiped them with his sleeves, calling: "Wait."

Musbah was already halfway down to the kitchen. Midhat ran a hand through his hair, checked the buttons of his pyjama shirt. He licked the blood off his hand.

"Wait. I wanted to tell you, to speak to you. Let's go in there."

They sat on the couch in the dark salon. He could hear Musbah breathing, and glanced at the small hands perched on his knees. The boy was already dressed for the day, and his velveteen was a little short in the sleeves. His jaw hung slack behind closed lips and his eyes bulged. He had a strange face: the brow heavy, the features as delicate as a girl's.

"I wanted to tell you." Midhat softened his voice. "You know, I lost my mother when I was very young. As young as Dunya."

Musbah's big eyes turned on him.

"Everything will be all right."

He waited. The boy said nothing.

"He will be happy in heaven. It is better there. He was a good Muslim, a kind, moral man. He will be rewarded. You see? He will be happy. Yes, I think he is already happy. Think of that."

"Yes."

"He was a good father," said Midhat, his voice cracking.

"Yes," said Musbah, and as he turned from Midhat a beatific expression broke over his features, as if he was remembering something.

Teta slept until sunrise on the third day, and then it was time to leave. In the shadow of the front door, with her children around her legs, Layla squinted as she waved. The taxi rolled off and Midhat awaited the first bitter comment, about Layla, or about the house. To his surprise, Teta didn't say anything. She stared out the window. It struck Midhat that he had no idea if she had even been to Cairo before.

On the train, Teta alternated between the usual motions of distant prayer and a very close kind of agitation, expressed in the way her hands, held rigidly open, fluttered from side to side, as though playing a tambourine. "What will we do," she said, with varying degrees of desperation and levels of address; sometimes to herself, sometimes very clearly to Midhat, other times halfway, the chant turning inward as she relapsed into prayer again, her words mixing with the voices of the ticket inspector and the station announcer who called out the names of places like wares for sale. Midhat repeated various empty mantras of comfort. "Everything will be fine," was one. "I'm with you," was another.

The train moved up along the Gaza coastline, and the sea sparkled beside them with white shards of sun. For the first time in his life, Midhat wished he were more religious. Of course he prayed, but though that was a private mechanism it sometimes felt like a public act, and the lessons of the Quran were learned by rote, one was steeped in them, hearing them so often. They were the texture of his world, and yet they did not occupy that central, vital part of his mind, the part that was vibrating at this moment, on this train, rattling forward while he struggled to hold all these pieces. As a child he had felt some of the same curiosity he had for the mysteries of other creeds—for Christianity with its holy fire, the Samaritans with their alphabets—but that feeling had dulled while he was still young, when traditional religion began to seem a worldly thing, a realm of morals and laws and the same old stories and holidays. They were acts, not thoughts.

He faced the water now, steadying his gaze on the slow distance, beyond the blur of trees pushing past the tracks, on the desolate fishing boats hobbling over the waves. He sensed himself tracing the lip of something very large, something black and well-like, a vessel which was at the same time an emptiness, and he thought, without thinking precisely, only feeling with the tender edges of his mind, what the Revelation might have been for in its origin. Why it was so important that they could argue to the sword what it meant if God had hands, and whether He had made the universe. Underneath it all was a living urgency, that original issue of magnitude: the way several hundred miles on foot could be nothing to the mind, Nablus to Cairo, a day's journey by train, but placed vertically that same distance in depth exposed the body's smallness and suddenly one thought of dying. Did one need to face the earth, nose to soil, to feel that distance towering above? There was something of his own mortality in this. Oh then but why, in a moment of someone else's death, must he think of his own disappearance?

"What will we do?" said his grandmother, as if she had just thought of it.

"Everything will be fine," he replied, gritting his teeth.

He had always had a schematic mind. That was the problem. He mapped one thing onto another. The vast barrel of darkness he had sensed was already collapsing under his mental fingers, he could not hold it, only muddy it with poor metaphors that turned it into something else. He tested, abstractly, the afterlife as described in the Holy Book. He could not picture his father in a garden. It was a false image. He did not have it.

"Habibi, don't cry," said his grandmother.

"It will be fine."

He trained his thoughts on Fatima, and mute illustrations of married life. The minutes accomplished the hours, and they were soon in Tulkarem, ready to change for Nablus.

They reached the house midafternoon. No Um Mahmoud was there to greet them. Something came into view on the doorstep: a white envelope. Half in the shadow, the circular stamp of the postal service. The sight of it was dreadful. An envelope had become a painful thing. Teta ignored it completely and wrestled with the lock. As she stepped over the threshold, Midhat picked it up.

18 May 1920
29 Sha'ban 1338

Dear Midhat,

A thousand congratulations—you must be extremely happy. I hope I will be able to come for the wedding—as you may have heard the French are building up their forces against us—I cannot say much—only that Faisal is nervous and there are demands on all sides. The people here actually think the Palestinians have more freedom than they do—after news of all these demonstrations and so on. We will see.

Dar Hammad is an excellent family—well done—I look forward to celebrating.

Your brother,
Hani

13

The official executor of Haj Taher's will was a lawyer from the Sinai who used to help him in the textile business. The unofficial executor, whose juris-diction was wider in effect than the official one, was Layla. Layla had always been astute about money matters, and the occasion of her husband's death was no different. Within a week of arriving back in Nablus, Midhat received his allotted inheritance by wire. Layla had already repaid Haj Taher's debts, and divided the remainder between herself, Midhat, and the other male children, with smaller portions for Dunya and Inshirah. Midhat used his share to pay the mahr for Fatima, and he also purchased a house on the southwest outskirts of town, in which they would live after the wedding.

The house was a single storey, and the elderly man who lived there before had taken his furnishings with him. The new household effects were financed by Haj Nimr, selected by Widad; since Um Taher was still grieving, Widad also took over the wedding preparations. The celebration, coming nigh after the fast ended, would consummate the Eid al-Fitr festivities with a three-day party, about which much bragging was perpetrated by those lucky enough to receive an invitation. The Samaritan tailors also profited from the occasion, and ran a brisk trade in garments for the bridal guests.

Hani could not come, after all. Their forces in Damascus had been routed by the French, and he and Emir Faisal were in exile: he sent a telegram from Amman to apologise. The wedding was marked in advance by the absences, and every joy in Midhat's head echoed with a hum of sorrow.

Eli the Samaritan helped choose Midhat's clothes: a tarbush of especial tallness, a foulard tie, his softest mouchoir for his pocket, and his shiniest, pointiest Italian boots, with a brown foot and black toe and a double zigzag stitch adjoining them. Fatima wore a white European-style dress with satin bows at the shoulders and elbows, and a dropped waist with a wide sash. Her sister had waxed her eyebrows with a paste of flour and molten sugar, and her hair was curled and stiffened around her face, the length braided and set into a chignon; at her crown her mother pinned a veil of rough netting. White silk stockings wrinkled around her ankles. She left her parents' house with her hennaed hands full of tokens: a fragment of wood, a mirror, a pair of scissors, a cube of sugar.

The night of the zaffeh procession was windy, and the candles kept blowing out. After the ritual washing in the hammam, and the dances at which the women tapped their mouths and fluttered their tongues like calling birds, and after the reading of the Fatiha and the blessings on the steps of the Hammad house, the young couple walked at the head of the parade, serenaded by the fife and tambourine, lit only by the harlequin glow of Venetian lamps, to the new house in the southwest, where the procession unfolded before the door singing songs and crying out their wishes for "green feet." Midhat and Fatima crossed the threshold, and, closing the door on the revellers, listened in silence as the party billowed back to town. They smiled, politely. She was wearing thick lines of kohl around her eyes, and her face was caked with powder.

"Hello," he said.

"Hello."

A large outdoor lantern stood on the floor; in a false show of certainty, Midhat crouched and opened the little glass hatch, and lit the wick with a match from his pocket. Then he picked up the handle and beckoned her to follow. And this was how, on an impulse, Midhat and Fatima spent the first part of their wedding night investigating their new garden.

The entire plot of land was situated on a slope, and the back garden flowed down a series of four narrow terraces. The first and widest held a wrought-iron table and three chairs. On the second and third, the arrangements of square beds suggested a former presence of flowers and vegetables, now berserk with weeds that violated the path. On the fourth and narrowest shelf, beside the tangles of a rosebush stripped of roses, stood a large cage with a cracked cement roof. Midhat raised the lamp and they peered inside. No birds. Only some ancient white scars on the ground. He circled back, and the swinging lamp sent a shuddering light over the low back gate and stretched a barred shadow on the lane behind. The silk on Fatima's dress shone. She started back up the garden steps, and Midhat hurried to guide her feet with the lamp.

"Would you like anything to eat?"

"No."

He considered saying: "Are you tired?" or "Ought we to go to bed?" Each phrase flipped over had a lewd underside, and he opted instead for silence.

In the hall he exchanged the lantern for an indoor lamp, and led the way down three shallow steps to the bedroom. The room was cold, half-sunk in the earth. The stone bricks of the walls were unpainted, and the only window was small and high and shuttered against the night. A cream silk coverlet adorned the bed, and on the opposite wall, between two green upholstered chairs, a mother-of-pearl inlaid cupboard stood on tall, bracketed legs. By the door hung a mirror in a curlicued frame. He watched Fatima absorb everything. The furnishings were not to his taste, being old-fashioned and feminine, but that was beside the point, since they were a gift from mother to daughter. Her hands were still covered in henna and he could see there were circles under her eyes. She was heavily perfumed. Midhat set the lamp on the bedside table, and whispered "Habibti," reaching for one embroidered palm.

Her lips parted on the teeth of a terrified smile. He stepped towards her and managed to kiss her forehead just as it was drawing away. Slowly, he took hold of her evasive chin, put his lips to one tired eye, then to the other. His left hand on his waistband, he tipped the top button of his trousers to the side, and released it from the hole.

"What are you doing?"

"Nothing. Undressing."

He leaned down for her lips. Hands met his chest.

"Habibti."

The elbows softened, and she allowed him to kiss her on the mouth, though her hands remained on his shirt. But the second button of his trousers made an even louder pop, and the arms straightened again. He took hold of them.

"Don't be afraid."

Her wrists slithered from his grip. Her smile was gone. With a quaver of indecision she took a false step and stumbled on the edge of the bed, falling into a sitting position with a loud snap. She lifted her skirt to reveal a heel had broken from one of her shoes.

"Let me help."

She was too fast. She had a musician's fingers; they unlaced the first shoe like a pianist rushing a toccata, and suddenly both were off her feet and she was bending down to slot them beneath the bed. Raised, her face was scarlet. Midhat had still only taken one step towards her, half-undone.

"It will be easier without the light." He stretched to twist off the flame. In the instant of darkness she gasped. He sat on the bed.

"Don't come near me."

To his bafflement, her voice came from several feet away.

"I will scream."

A weedy ray from the gap around the shutter, from the moon or some other remote source, was the only light available. It outlined Fatima's body but blotted her face. He saw her elbows bend, her fingers relaxed but ready. The silence tightened.

"You are my wife."

She drew a long, deep breath. In that moment, Midhat felt justified: she was steadying herself. Then the ten fingers tensed into a backward curve, and though he had not, indeed, come any nearer to her, Fatima wrenched from her lungs the scream she had just vowed to deliver. It tore through the air at whistling pitch and entered his ear like a needle.

"Oh God, no, please don't do that."

She did not deviate from that single, terrible note. One inhalation and she continued, though losing volume as she backed further away, another breathy cessation, and now that she was level with the window he could make out her face. Her eyes were wide and her chest was rising and falling.

"I won't come near you. I'm not doing anything to you, please just stop. Please."

She did not scream again, though he remained braced for the sound; adjusting now to the semi-dark, he watched her sit on the chair near the window. She lifted her feet onto the seat as if to hug her knees but instead stood up, holding the cupboard beside her for balance—or so it seemed at first, for a moment later, with a creak of woodwork, he watched the farthest cupboard legs lift off the floor as with one foot on the chair arm she pulled herself onto the top of it. The four legs wobbled, her dress rustled, she came to rest, pale hands gripping the finials.

"Now you cannot come near me."

He searched for her eyes, but saw only her hands.

"That is true," he said.

He looked at the empty chair and briefly imagined standing upon it to bring her down. His hands rested on his hips. A laugh escaped him; it sounded cruel. The bed nudged his shin and he sat on it.

"Allahu akbar," he said, to himself.

The dial of the lamp was stiff with rust and hurt his fingers as he worked it. The glow opened the room: there she was, cross-legged on the cupboard. He put one foot on the other knee. The heel of his right shoe gave quickly; the left required both hands, and his throat gave a little "phut" of exertion. He loosened his tie with a forefinger.

"Are you going to stay up there all night?"

He meant this to sound knowing, even haughty. But alas the question sounded plaintive and at once gave Fatima the power. She was silent. He, pulling off his jacket and then his shirt, uttered a series of dignified sighs, and so meticulously avoided looking at her that as he at last lay down in his underclothes it was his turn to flinch. Naturally, she had been staring at him the whole time.

"Do you need help getting down from there?"

"No."

"Shall I leave the lamp on?"

She did not answer. A draught entered from somewhere, and the flame, cavorting from side to side, blackened the glass where it narrowed into the flute. He reached out for the dial to lower the wick, which was easier on the way down. The darkness uncorked his fatigue, which had been suppressed for days, and engulfed him within moments.

The dreamless night lasted an instant. He woke on his back as he had fallen asleep. The ceiling above was so dim that at first he could believe only a few hours had passed—but sitting up he perceived the cold light of morning in the shutter crack. Fatima was asleep on the chair, curled so her wedding dress gathered around her thighs, her two hennaed feet pursed over each other like a pair of hands in prayer. He got out of bed, the better to observe her. Her mouth was open, and the hair at the back of her head bunched up unevenly out of her plait. Under his shadow a tremor passed through her eyelids and her mouth twitched. He turned on his heel. He would leave her to dress on her own, explore the house on her own, habituate herself to it, without him.

In the hall his trunk stood on end. He tipped it gently. This had been his sole companion on his travels, he thought ruefully; it still bore the bruises and scratches from the pitch of ships and luggage boys. Inside the top lay a pair of linen trousers. He put them on in the salon, a bright, narrow room that took all the light from the garden. Pulling on his coat, he set out for Mount Gerizim.

The plan was to sell the family house. Um Taher would move downstairs with Um Jamil, and the proceeds from the sale of the top floor would make up her living allowance. Although this was not due to occur until after the wedding, Um Taher was already spending most of her time downstairs. Midhat found her now in Um Jamil's kitchen, stirring honey into a cup of tea with her finger.

"What are you doing here?" she said. "Where is your wife?"

He heaved himself into a chair, and, with a sigh, confided to her the events of his wedding night. Teta listened patiently. Then she began to laugh.

"What did you do to her?"

"What do you mean what did I do?"

"Ya'ni, she was frightened. You have to go slowly, habibi. Um Jamil," she called suddenly, "Ta'ali."

Midhat assumed she wanted to ask his aunt something unrelated; to his dismay, Teta proceeded to recount to Um Jamil exactly what he had just told her. He tried to stop her with, "Do you have to," but she only picked up speed, dropping a gasp and pause in the right places. Um Jamil looked between Midhat and Um Taher with wide eyes, her birdlike head nodding, and as though she knew what was coming, her lips threatened to smile.

"So I told him," concluded Um Taher, "You have to go slowly, ya'ni, poor girl she was frightened. Saheeh wila la?"

"Have you tried caresses?"

"Oh Lord," said Midhat, "I can't do this."

"Lazim, you have to," said Um Jamil. "Ya'ni, kisses, ya'ni, very important."

"No that's not . . ." He groaned. "I'm going back. This was a mistake."

He hurried out. It was too soon to return to the new house, where Fatima awaited him. Or dreaded him. He took his old route down into town and walked through the khan.

There was no chair in the entrance, but from the outside the Kamal store looked empty. Inside, voices came from the tailor's room. Butrus was at his work desk, three other men standing around. They looked up as Midhat entered, and separated to greet him. His old friends, the Samaritan tailors. They smiled and Eli stepped forward to say congratulations, they had thoroughly enjoyed the wedding.

"Where's Hisham?"

"He has gone to find you," said Eli.

"What's wrong?"

Eli looked at Butrus, who was sitting at his desk.

"Wait for Hisham," said Butrus.

A peculiar half hour followed this exchange, during which Midhat repeatedly interrupted the conversation to press them for answers. Each time the tailors passed the same uneasy glance between each other, and shook their heads. "Wait for Hisham." Butrus made coffee, and the Samaritans drew up chairs to ask about the wedding. Midhat, so fixated on what they were withholding, examined their faces for clues and answered their questions without interest. He did not even watch out for Hisham, and was surprised when he appeared behind his chair.

"Did you already tell him?" said Hisham to the tailors.

"No, they didn't tell me," said Midhat, standing. "What has happened?"

Hisham looked afraid. "Your father," he said.

Midhat waited. "What about my father?"

"He, he . . ." Hisham swallowed and looked at the ground.

"What?" said Midhat.

"He wrote the business in Um Musbah's name."

"What?"

"The business. It's in his wife's name."

Midhat was silent. "*What*?"

Hisham raised his hands.

"What does that mean?"

The meaning was already clear. Their faces were bursting with pity. Eli grasped the ears of a chair, apparently in pain.

"We are contracted, me and him," Hisham gestured at the tailor, and Midhat saw that his hands were trembling, "to work for her. You, habibi . . . I'm sorry I'm I'm—"

"Did you know?"

"I'm sorry." Hisham's mouth crumpled.

Midhat gasped. "You knew, and you didn't tell me. Hisham!"

"I didn't want you to go to your father like that," Hisham pleaded. "I didn't want you to see him, feeling that, feeling angry."

"What am I supposed to do?" Midhat felt his face puckering. He wished the others weren't there. It was a stupid question, and of course no one answered. "For how long are you contracted for?"

"Our pay comes from Cairo. There are no sales in Nablus."

"Hisham, how long are you contracted for?"

Hisham shot a desperate glance at the tailor.

"I understand," said Midhat. "You need to be paid. It's fine."

It was not fine. Shock crested into anger as he walked onto the street. He looked around for something to kick. A loose stone from the paving.

An old tomato half-erupted from its skin. He hit the wall with the back of his fist, felt a good pain down the side of his hand, and then started off at a brisk pace. He couldn't risk one of the tailors coming out to console him.

How could he now go and face Fatima? Tell her his livelihood had suddenly come to an end? The livelihood which had been instrumental in convincing Haj Nimr he would make a suitable husband. All he had left to his name was the small dark house he had just purchased, with its empty shit-stained chicken cage at the bottom of the garden. He would have to divide the proceeds from the sale of the old house with Teta, and even that wouldn't last long. At the thought of Teta, he put his face in his hands. He caught one of the workers in the entrance to the carpet shop.

"Where's Jamil? Jamil, do you have a moment? I need to talk to you."

He led his cousin onto the street and explained what he had just found out.

Jamil looked aghast. "What? That's not possible. Surely she will at least employ you."

"What, like she employs Hisham? Do you know how much Hisham earns? I cannot support a family, my grandmother . . . anyway I wouldn't work for that woman if she paid—"

"But it's not possible. This isn't possible, Midhat. Have you made sure? I thought he promised you the business?"

Midhat opened his hands.

"I can't believe this. It must be her, she has persuaded him. What is *wrong* with that woman—"

"I don't know what I'm going to do."

"This is unbelievable."

"Yes, yes, it is unbelievable," Midhat snarled.

"But your father ba'dayn. I'm really surprised."

At that word, "father," a knot in Midhat's chest swelled and he screamed: "My father!"

Jamil shot a look down the road. "Yalla. Let's go for a walk."

Midhat let himself be led. Down the street alongside the Fatimiyah School. Past Rafidia by the upper outskirts. By the village of Balata, they took a route north through the mountains, and after a while Midhat lost the impulse to speak. Fury had left him like a flock of birds, and he felt sedated. He looked stupidly out across the plain. The blue sky was white by the brow of hills, where the green separated over raw pink. The slope beside them was pilled with wild round shrubs, and ahead a sharp light outlined the striations in the grey rock.

"I'm exhausted," he muttered. The words felt good. He said them again. "I'm exhausted."

It was not really true, however. The walking itself had begun to clear through his fatigue, disrupting the stagnant waters in which, left suspended, he felt at risk of drowning. The uphill motion made his thoughts fluid.

"You know how everyone calls me the Parisian?"

"Yeah."

"It's strange, it's only been a year. I already feel so far from it. I've been wondering. What would happen if I went back."

"You can't, habibi. Your life is here."

"What life?" He gave a humourless laugh. "I have nothing."

"Please. You just married the most beautiful woman in the town. You're a success. Everyone thinks so."

"I married her for *him*. I may as well have left for all the good I achieved. There was nothing to keep me here—"

"You did not only marry for him. I know you. You love her."

Midhat clicked his teeth. "You can't love a stranger. There's no such thing."

They had reached a kind of summit before the hill dipped again and rose. As they stopped moving, everything around them came to life.

"You want to know what happened last night? Fatima, she—she ran from me. She climbed on top of the cupboard and wouldn't come down."

He flicked his eyes onto his cousin and waited for the laugh. Jamil, who had his foot on a rock and was catching his breath, put a hand on his shoulder.

"It will get easier. She's a woman. She doesn't know anything yet."

"Don't tell anyone, will you?" said Midhat. "Though to be honest, Teta has probably told everyone already."

"You'll be fine. I know you'll be fine."

"Why do you only love me when I make a mistake?"

"My God," said Jamil, pulling his hand away. "That is not true. Midhat. You are so arrogant!" He burst out laughing.

"What do you mean? Arrogant how?"

"What do I mean. Really, you think you are in the centre of everything. Oh no, I don't mean like that. Shwaya, don't be angry."

"I'm not angry. I just don't understand."

"All right. Do you want to know what happened in my life the past two months? Are you interested?" Jamil made a strange lurching motion with his neck, and seemed, for a moment, to be in some kind of communication with himself. He resumed in a gentler tone. "First of all, I saw two people killed. First one, and then the other. Right before me, a few feet. All the blood, everything. I saw the last . . ." His lips pressed together. "The first one was a Jew, young guy, our age. Second one was Arab, killed by the Jew's friends. This has been in my mind, you know? It sticks there . . ."

"This was at Nebi Musa? I didn't know."

"You didn't ask! You didn't even ask. We got back and you were away in your world again, reading poetry. The Parisian, wandering around with your coloured ties. You didn't even ask me, you just left."

Midhat was trying to recall the period of time after Nebi Musa, what had happened, what he was doing, when his mind caught on the barb of that final accusation.

"I already said—you know I lost you in the crowd, how was I supposed to find you?"

"I know," Jamil waved his hand. Perhaps he had not meant to bring that up, it had slipped out in the fever of argument. "You should just look outside yourself a bit. The country is going to shit. We have starving fellahin walking around robbing people. You know how many people were robbed last week? Do you even listen to what people talk about?"

"Jamil, my father died. How you can say that, you don't know what I've been—you hardly even see me!"

"No one is buying carpets, but still they come in, they look, pretend they're going to buy things, and you know why? Because they have nothing else to do. I'm sorry about your father, but we've lost Damascus, now we're going to have a Jewish country, because that's what the British are making. Ya'ni, khalas. It will be the Turks in their worst years. Worse, probably."

Jamil continued walking, but Midhat stayed where he was. It took Jamil a second to notice, and he paused slightly further up the slope. Both were still out of breath.

"Why are you doing this to me?" said Midhat.

They were by a breach in the mountainside, a little hollow of a cave. The wind chilled Midhat through his shirt. Over Jamil's calm face, a lock of hair flew to the wrong side.

"I can't believe you could be so unsympathetic."

Jamil's bony arms jerked upward. "Sympathy!" he said.

Midhat pivoted away and started walking in the other direction, back down the hill. God bless gravity: if not for gravity, his body would have stopped and fallen. All he wanted was to disappear, to go back in time. The present was a bare rock without shelter. In the past all pain was finished, everything was known, nothing could hurt him any longer.

"Midhat!"

He kept going. The sun shone down with terrible clarity. There was no safety.

When he regained the path he saw that Jamil had not followed. By his foot, a lizard tongued over a rock and vanished. Then, as he faced the empty stretch ahead, it came back to him: that searing sensation he used to long for, safe in his dormitory in Constantinople. It was far stronger now. The outline of his body clamped down, burning his skin. The only way to relieve it was to run.

Fatima unpacked her clothes into the cupboard, and dragged Midhat's trunk down the steps to the bedroom. When the lid fell open, she laughed. This man had far more clothes than she had. She touched the first layer; something soft, a kind of house gown, it was thick and the lining was a deep maroon. Shirts, ties, satin and patterned cotton. She reached for the lid to close it, and as her right arm lifted, a sharp twinge in her neck forced her to drop it again. She rubbed the spot and stood looking at her reflection. One of her shoulders was noticeably higher than the other. She needed fenugreek.

The pantry was stocked with trays of food prepared by their relatives. Dishes of rice lay atop bowls of mulukhiyyeh and kusa and maqluba, and there were two bags of fresh tomatoes and cucumbers, and two bowls of fruit. No sign of fenugreek. She did find a bag of dried grape leaves. With the arm that didn't hurt she brought out the fruit, and set it on the table. The guavas were small and hard. Oranges, white dirt in the craters of their skin. She put a pan of water to boil, and reached for an onion and a large knife. On the table she halved the bulb, then sliced it crossways so it fell apart in glassy shards. She sang. When the steam filled the room she opened the window to the garden, where the iron chairs looked poorly with tarnish in the daylight. She plied her fingers into her neck.

The rice was cooling when the front door made a noise. She did not turn as Midhat entered; she set the naked leaves in a pile and released a pool of olive oil into a bowl. After a moment he walked out. She folded the first parcels, listening hard for anything else that might situate him in the house, any creaks or footfalls. But the next noise came from right behind her again, from the hall just beyond the kitchen. She was quick to hide her surprise.

"May I have coffee?" he said.

She wiped her hands on the dishcloth tucked into her belt, and opened a cupboard. Stacks of plates.

"It's in this one, here."

"And the pot?"

"This one—no, this one. You have . . . everything you need?"

"Fenugreek. We don't have." She untwisted the coffee jar. "But yes, I have everything. Oh, except . . ." She turned.

"Except what?"

"Who will fetch the water? At our house we had a well."

"The water carrier will come here," said Midhat. "We aren't so far. But will you be all right, I mean, will you be needing a maid?"

"Oh. I don't think so. At least, not for now."

The coffee was foaming. He accepted the cup she poured but did not, at first, drink from it. He sat at the table and looked at the opened window as Fatima's fingers worked. She set four vine leaf parcels on the plate with the others.

"What are you thinking about?" she said.

Midhat looked up at her. She wondered if he was affronted by her question. But in a moment he said: "I was thinking . . . about something that happened to me in France."

"It makes you sad?"

"Not particularly. It was—I had a friend who died. He was a very intelligent man. He had this idea about life. That it was all one thing, with death in it." He sipped the coffee. "I'm not sure it means much. What are you making?"

After a beat she replied, in a voice liquid with incredulity: "Vine leaves!"

"You're very good." He dipped his head low to the table, as if to get a view from the side. "They are very small."

"My mother taught me. In fact no, my mother didn't teach me, I learned from a Turk. You know there used to be Turks in the upstairs of our house."

She dipped a new leaf in the oil. She could feel him looking at her.

"I didn't know that."

The last rice grains were stuck into a cake along the bottom of the pan. She took a spoon to them, and they fell out onto the plate in the crammed shape of an oval.

"Now we are married," she said, and bit the inside of her cheek.

Midhat laughed, and she knew he had turned away.

"Yes. Now we are married."

By evening Fatima considered herself the victor. She did not feel particularly cheerful about it, however. Midhat had not touched her all day, nor made any reference to the night before. They continued to speak in the same genial, sidelong manner, but with none of the behaviour one might expect between a husband and wife in private. Fatima kept thinking about the laughing women in the hammam. They knew how it was supposed to be. This marriage really belonged to them, those naked figures gossiping in the steam, loitering in the corners of her mind. As afternoon progressed, she found she had used up all her self-possession in making those vine leaf parcels. She took a moment to cry weakly at the kitchen window. In retrospect, the terror of last night seemed easier than this footless unknowing of the waking day, now that the light was turned off the positions of a woman's body in one part of a room and a man's in another, and onto the vaguer profile of future uncertainties, in which time and space far exceeded what one girl's mind could map, and dwarfed by thousands her fear of a few inches, a few moments, the sound of his breath. Even standing there at the window, she did not know what to do with her hands. She ended by clasping them so tightly together the fingers blotched pink and white. She tried to concentrate on the hours ahead, but her unruly mind kept expanding to the panorama of years, years of this same unknowing, to which an end was swaddled in mist.

As night fell, Midhat read in the salon while she played the oud. This was taken for a virtue, a woman who could play the oud. She tried to play as though for her own pleasure, as if she barely knew he was there, and she even half sang the words, as though practising for another event. But there was no danger of him looking up, and this left her free to examine him. He looked tired, she thought. He was pale and his lids hung low. She quite liked the sight of his arms under his rolled-up shirtsleeves. After abandoning the halfway point of a few melodies, she rested the instrument on her legs, and touched the tuning pegs.

"What are you reading?" she said.

"Hm?"

That was the same look he gave her earlier, when she asked him what he was thinking about. His face was quite demonstrative. An appealing quality, but, perhaps, also one that spoke of a kind of carelessness. He lifted the spine of his book to show her. It was written in a European language. The woven cover was red, and a black silk bookmark dangled from the binding, heavily frayed.

"Flaubert," he said. "You speak French?"

"No. Some English. I know three words in German."

"What are these three words?"

"Abendessen. Mittagessen. Heisse. There were some others, I forgot."

He frowned, head to the side, lips parted. She answered:

"After the Turks left, we had Germans."

"Oh—yes, I remember this. My father told me that."

He lingered on her, then returned to the page. She wondered if the story was sad. He looked up again, apparently on the point of speech. For a second he held the position; she waited, unhappily, until he shook it off. She set the round back of the oud against the wall.

"Where are you going?" he said.

"The kitchen."

There was nothing to do in the kitchen. She ran a damp cloth along the edge of the table, where a little ridge might gather dirt. The cloth was clear; she had done the same thing earlier.

She made sure to precede Midhat to the bedroom, undressed before the mirror, and donned a nightgown. When he knocked and entered, he was already wearing a two-piece pyjama suit, blue with black piping. Last night, this was an image that might have terrified her. Now, she giggled: it meant he had anticipated her, and collected his pyjamas earlier. The shirt, not buttoned to the top, flapped open slightly beyond the lapel as he climbed into the bed. She slid in beside him. The sheets were heavy. They lay for a while in silence on their backs. Then Midhat said:

"Did you go to see the Nebi Musa procession in Jerusalem?"

Her breath stopped. "Yes."

"I saw you there."

Danger shot through Fatima's mind. Husbands were like parents, conscious of a woman's shame. She waited, frozen.

"Did you go alone?"

"Yes," she whispered. She felt a powerful urge to weep.

"Don't be afraid."

But all those words did was bring to mind the night before, which seemed no longer distant but rather very present, and her heart thumped hard. She longed for the darkness, she wanted to cover the heat rising to her neck and face, and she glanced, helpless, at the lamp beyond him. She felt exactly as exposed as she had before she climbed onto the cupboard.

"Why are you afraid?"

The sheet shifted. He was turning towards her. She could see his white eyeballs.

"I can feel you, you are afraid. I don't mind that you went to Nebi Musa. I was asking because . . . I wondered if you had seen anything. Anything terrible."

"I saw nothing. I was hardly there, I came, I left . . ."

"It was odd, though, didn't you think?" he said. "That crowd, all those angry people."

She inhaled too loudly. "They are uneducated. Ya'ni, poor people. Poor people are angry. This is why we have zakat."

Midhat turned onto his back. He switched off the lamp. Fatima's blush began to fade, and she listened to the soothing murmur of a draught. When she was calm she addressed him in a quiet voice.

"Will you tell me about Paris?"

"Paris?"

"I want to know."

He began, with slow, formal phrases. "I lived in Paris during the war. There were only a few men. Except for old ones. And, in addition, there were some Arabs."

Although at first he seemed reluctant, he soon relaxed into a mono-logue. His words drew pictures, and Fatima saw balconies and terraced cafés, heard voices and the sounds of glass and crockery as she walked down deserted streets and theatre aisles full of women in glitter pining for men at battle. Set free by the dark, she came closer to the vibrations of his voice, low in his throat, to the heat coming from his half-bared chest. She felt it on her shoulder as he turned over, surprised by how near his body was to hers. She was sensitive enough to realise that in this speech he was revealing some part of his inner life, and that it was a struggle to hold onto and translate it for her. It moved her to be taken into his confidence. With fresh temerity she put her hand on his chest, and under the silk of his pyjama shirt she felt his heart come to meet it.

"Might we one day go there?"

He pressed the back of her fingers. "We might."

He said something else she didn't hear. She had found his mouth and kissed it. Their foreheads touched awkwardly. There was some perspiration on his shaven lip. She immediately reached to touch him between the legs, amazed and shocked by her own courage. She was even more amazed at the weird shape of his anatomy that reared under the fabric, and snatched her hand away.

"Don't look at me," she said.

"I can't see you. It's completely dark."

That was clearly a lie, because she could still see him. She closed her eyes, boiling with shyness, and his fingers began, very gently, to wrinkle the nightgown over her legs. When it was necessary she raised her hips off the mattress, and then lifted her arms to help it over her head. Though her skin was flushed she was also pimpled over with cold, and when his hand met her hip she winced. Then she saw his shadow hesitate, and grasping him by the neck pulled him over her.

The pain was incredible. Whatever shame was left over, it evaporated at once in that unbearably specific heat. His arms trembled under his own weight, and his hair, flopping from his head, brushed her brow. Only when his eyes met hers and he said, "Are you all right?" did she realise how heavily he was breathing.

She smiled. "Yes. Thank you for asking."

In the morning, she woke alone. Two workers were shouting outside, instructing or greeting each other. She rose, and set the sheet to soak in the kitchen. The red stain lifted and clouded the water in the bowl. She jerked open the rickety window and the wind hurried in to startle the water's surface, cooling the skin on her neck.

Not at ease, precisely; she felt steady, that was it. The wind rifled through the garden, pushing the two trees near the bottom in circles and agitating the bushes. That space out-of-doors, both enclosed and open, all her own—she dashed to the bedroom and drew a coat from the cupboard, wrapped a cotton shawl around her head; below the coat her ankles were just visible above her slippers. She unbolted the salon doors to the first terrace, turned the handle, and tipped one of the iron chairs leaning against the table upright. Although all she could see beyond the garden was the mountain, nonetheless she stayed close to the back door.

Why, if there was no one to see her? They lived on the outskirts. That had been a worry at first, but now it seemed wonderful. Her anxiety about being far from the centre, from the famous houses, from her family, was fading—for perhaps, after all, this meant she would be liberated from the approval of others. Would it not be wonderful—thinking of the voices that had woken her from the fields—to be a fellaha, to be free like this? To shout in the morning alongside the men, as one set to work?

This view was indeed a spectacle. Even before the eye reached that churning froth of white and blue above, the wind below was magnificent, and as she watched it dismantle the garden's stillness, a washing rope on the patio began to swing from side to side like a necklace, and she had the thought that she should hang the sheet out here to dry. Inside, she wrung the fabric in the sink and carried it out. The uncoiled cotton smacked the washing line, and the wrinkles unravelled under her numbed fingers.

Perhaps it was the wind's noise that prevented her from noticing the figure at first. When it entered her awareness, it was standing perfectly still. She flinched, and the soreness in her neck reawoke. No gate had sounded, no footstep. The apparition was entirely in shadow, on the penultimate ledge, bottom half severed by the slant. She raised her hand to her forehead to block out the sunlight, and saw that whoever it was was now moving, climbing the steps. Her first terror was allayed when she saw it was a woman: heavy peasant dress; no veil. The woman stopped on the second terrace, and now Fatima could see her face. An old woman, too many teeth in her mouth. Her eyes were soft and large, her forehead long. She was holding her shawl over her chest with one hand.

"I knocked," she called out, in a low harsh voice.

Fatima took a step towards the chairs and the salon door, which she saw, to her horror, had swung open.

"You did not hear me," said the woman.

"Who are you?" shouted Fatima, but the wind snatched her voice away.

The woman continued to stand there, brazen, and Fatima was struck with the alien sensation that it was she, and not the woman, who was the interloper; this had something to do with her opponent's gravity, her fixedness, while Fatima felt as insubstantial as a piece of linen. She could be a previous incumbent; she might have worked for the old man. Or she might be a jinni. Fatima thrust out her arm and shrieked, as loud as she could:

"Get out of my house! My garden—get out!"

"Madame." The woman held her curved palms together as though catching something. "Madame, please."

Fatima stared. Was this woman here to beg? Should she try to run for the salon door—perhaps the woman had heard about her, the new young bride, and saw in her seclusion and youth a chance for robbery—one heard terrible stories. But instead of running for the house, Fatima was filled with blistering outrage that someone might think she could be taken advantage of. She pulled her coat tight across her body, fixed her scarf well around her head. She performed these small actions briskly and pointedly, in an attempt to display her aggression. Those few seconds gave the woman time to begin saying her part.

"Madame—I came to see your husband."

"Who?"

"Your husband." For the first time, the woman faltered. "Midhat Bey?"

"What do you want with him?" Fatima shouted.

"I wanted to say I am sorry."

The stranger took a step forward, as though to mount the terrace, and Fatima could see the skin around her eyes wrinkling around old folds as she dropped her glance to the ground. "Will you tell him for me? I am sorry . . ." Real tears appeared, silver on her face. "Tell him . . . Um Mahmoud is very sorry for leaving him. She is sorry for his father, Allah yirhamo. Tell him, please Madame." She met Fatima's gaze once, and resuming her grip around the shawl across her chest started to retreat down the steps, waving with her free hand, turning and bowing as she went. "Yislamo ideyki, Madame, yislamo ideyki, Allah ma'ek." She reached for the gate and pulled up the latch. "Allah yikhaleeki. Salam. Salam. Salam."

PART THREE

1

Half an hour before he was due to be hanged, Hani's uncle, Fuad Murad, composed a will on a blank page from the back of a novel. Sitting beside his warden near the gallows, he tore the sheet out very carefully. Then he leaned on the book cover with his back to the sun and wrote in the clarity of his own shadow.

> I write this commandment in the eighth hour and a half of the Saturday night on 14 Shawwal thirteen hundred and thirty-three by the Arab calendar where I am sentenced to death at the ninth hour of tonight mentioned. I mean I write this commandment half an hour before my death. I write as one of my companion convicts, Muhammad Abd al-Karim, is taken to be crucified, and I am glad for him that he has gone to meet the Lord Almighty. And I welcome death with an open breast, and if I leave this world I leave it as a Muslim, believing in God and the afterlife.
>
> See how my hand does not shake,

wrote the pen, tripping over the indents on the cover where the letters were gilded. He appointed his uncle the executor, and specified the money for each of his sisters, and the amount for his wife. The majority of his fortune would go to his daughter Sahar.

> And so that I shall greet death with a clear conscience, I also owe Rabea al-Dura, for fetching me those towels at the Hotel Continental, five and a half qurush.

That year, 1915, the year her father Fuad stood on the gallows platform in Aley, flanked by two other Syrians, necks in nooses and literally wrapped in their crimes, which had been written on huge pages and pinned under their arms like aprons, Sahar Murad was six years old.

Her memory went like this. At their home in Jenin, a messenger arrived with an envelope. Her mother fell to her knees outside the front door. It was summer, and very hot. Some days or possibly some weeks after that, they received a visitor.

"Good morning, sister," said a tall man, stepping into the hallway. He looked down at Sahar, bent to her height, and said, "Mashallah," and touched her hair. Eyes on Sahar, he addressed her mother. "We have things to discuss."

A few days after that, Sahar heard another man's voice in the hall. Thinking it was her father, she came to investigate.

"There she is," said the man. It was not her father. His arms reached out for her, and, cautiously, she walked into them. At once she was in the air, resting against the man's shoulder, his arm her seat. She was too large for this, and she could hear his breath. In a bright voice, he said: "I'll be seeing you in just a few years, habibti."

The third visitor Sahar remembered most clearly. There were circles under his eyes and he did not smell nice. He looked at her but unlike the others did not greet her. He simply turned to her mother and said: "Yalla. Talk." Her mother looked worried; that Sahar always remembered.

She was unsure when exactly she learned that her father was dead: whether it was a gradual process of understanding, or if there was a moment of revelation, which she afterwards erased. She remembered her mother's anxiety. The only times she left Sahar alone were weekday mornings, when a woman named Mariam came to teach her to read, and Saturday afternoons, when Noura the maid helped with the housework. Guests were rare, but Sahar knew if someone was visiting because her mother put on a veil and locked her in the bedroom. During those lonely hours Sahar opened the drawer that held her mother's scarves and wrapped them around her own head. There was no mirror in the bedroom to witness the effect.

In general, however, Sahar's childhood was not lonely. Under the aegis of the three women—her mother, Mariam, and Noura—she developed a noisy curiosity, and played for hours in the garden behind the house, examining the roots of the walnut tree, pulling at the grass, exploring the soil. Mariam provided books, gateways to distant countries and remote pasts, and as her reading ability improved Sahar plunged through the paragraphs of Islamic history on her own, and worked through the romantic plots of Egyptian novels, and in the evenings would summarise what she had learned for her mother, who could not read.

Of her father she remembered two things. One was sitting on his knee. The knee went up and down and she laughed as it jogged her, a bouncing kind of laugh, which was itself quite funny. The other was the feel of his large hands picking her up under the arms. The year she turned eleven, the year after the war ended, Sahar finally asked her mother why he was dead. To her surprise, her mother   sitting in a chair at the time, wiping dirt off a shoe with a damp cloth—gave her a direct answer.

"He was friends with people who did not like the Turks."

Sahar stood on one leg. "Why did they not like the Turks?"

Her mother rested her hands and looked straight ahead, wrists curling upwards to keep the shoe from touching her lap. "Because—it was an empire."

Sahar sighed. This was becoming familiar: this confused sensation of disappointment and pity, as she watched her mother reach a limit to her knowledge.

Then her mother said, "The Arabs, you know, we wanted independence."

Beneath the rag, a band of light stretched around the leather heel.

"And where are the Turks now?"

"In Turkey, I suppose."

"Now we have the English," said Sahar.

"Correct. They say it is only temporary, before we have independence. Inshallah. Inshallah it will be better than the Turks."

Sahar was thirteen when she began to menstruate. She was given plenty of warning. "You come and tell me," her mother had told her, "the moment it happens, you tell me." After such warnings, how could Sahar not be afraid, not knowing what it signified? She trudged to the bedroom and delivered the news. Whatever she might have expected, it was not this: her mother squeezing her hand so tightly it throbbed. She stared at Sahar, as though trying to look through her.

"What's wrong, Mama?"

Her mother drew long, emphatic breaths. "You will get married."

Another wave of that disappointed feeling came over Sahar, and she kept still, waiting for it to pass. Pity for her mother's limitations, her loneliness. Finally, she said: "I will allow you to live with me."

Her mother opened her mouth and looked as though she might laugh. But, alas, it was only the drawbridge to weeping.

"Oh no, no Mama, don't do that."

"Sahar I have to tell you something. First, get me a handkerchief."

When her father died, three uncles had visited. Did she remember?

Sahar thought of the rancid man with the dark circles. "Yes."

"Each of my brothers wants you to marry his son. Why? Because you are the heir to most of your father's fortune. They are bad men. They still visit us. Frequently. Every month I see them. I have not allowed them to see you. And now—no, we will not tell them you are ready. We will find a way—"

They decided to keep Sahar's puberty a secret. They even concealed it from Noura and Mariam, and unplucked the seams in Sahar's dresses to hide the breasts that would begin to grow.

In this way Sahar passed an entire year. For the first time the small world in which she lived had woefully shrank, and two of its three inhabitants she was no longer permitted to trust. In the daytime she looked at the garden from the doorway with longing, not daring to step out into that uncovered space in which someone might see her or snatch her. Though her curiosity was no less robust, it was mixed now with terror, and her preoccupation with her uncles verged on obsession.

Mariam showed no sign of being aware of what had happened, or was happening. Her lessons became conversations, since Sahar was nearly her equal in reading and required only practice. Sometimes they read the newspapers together and discussed recent events. There was not much to report on; after the riots the previous year the country was quiet, and most of the gossip Mariam brought was about the railway, which was being refurbished. And something called a telephone: there was one at the post office, you could have a conversation with someone all the way in Jerusalem, she said; the voices travelled through tubes. In the spring, Mariam brought a piece of news from even further afield. She had read about it in one of the local papers, and then came across a double-page spread in an Egyptian magazine to which she had a personal subscription.

On the twenty-eighth of May 1923 two women had descended from a train in Cairo. One was very famous, the wife of someone killed by the British. The women were returning from a congress in Rome, and as they stepped off the carriage, all the friends and admirers who had gathered on the platform to welcome them fell silent. Both women were dressed in black, with skirts that reached the ankle; one wore a large silver pendant on a thick chain; the other, a rosette. Their headpieces were pinned above their ears. Many people gasped. Neither woman was wearing a veil. One smiled. The other lifted her chin. And then, the crowd of women around them burst into rapturous applause. Several tore off their own veils and revealed their faces. The cameras flashed.

Sahar noticed a tremor in Mariam's fingers as she turned the page of the newspaper.

"What does it mean?" said Sahar.

"I don't know," said Mariam.

That summer, Sahar spent the hottest, most uncomfortable hours of the day reading on her bed. She set aside the history books and lived only in novels. One particular afternoon she was near the end of a novel about a queen of

Egypt who ruled many centuries ago. She was trying to stop herself from accelerating towards the climax, because she would mourn when it was finished, when she became aware that her mother had come into the room.

"They know," she said.

On her back, Sahar rested the book upon her chest. "Who does?"

"Your uncles. Two of them visited today. We can expect the third any minute."

When Hani Murad first arrived in Paris, he had yearned for a life of political significance. But after a year of working for Emir Faisal, he was already dreaming about a domestic one. As the delegation finally settled in Damascus to set up the new administration, he and the other aides encountered greater and greater obstacles, and as the French became progressively more violent and one by one the lights of their movement were snuffed out by censorship, and as the public despair became personal, and each one in the palace began to reflect on his private failures, this secret fantasy of Hani's started to grow. He pictured himself at a law firm. And writing—he could return to the history of Turkey he had been translating. He imagined a house. In Nablus? Jerusalem? A wife. The comfort of knowing that he might reasonably guess the content of each hour of the day.

In 1920, the Arab resistance against the French in Syria had failed in toto, and they lost their war of independence almost immediately. Hani and the emir, fugitives from Damascus, parted ways with four kisses on the cheek in the back of a taxi. Faisal was accepting a British appointment as king of Iraq, with an Englishwoman as his chief advisor. In the spring of 1923 Hani returned to Palestine, a Palestinian. As he had predicted, he had no choice in the matter. Their dream of a united Levant was scuppered, at least for the moment.

Jerusalem was quiet when he arrived. Or as quiet as she ever was. Hani entered salons and slapped old friends on the back, grinning as they kissed him; he caught conversations midway, and gave sophisticated monologues when asked for his opinion. Should they cooperate with the British and their quasi-democratic systems, if that meant accepting Zionism? Or should they boycott entirely, and continue to strive for independence without compromise—which was what they were owed, by both previous promises and natural right?

"What do you think, Hani," they asked. "Could the English be persuaded to reverse their commitment to Zionism?"

Hani was tugged down to the tables, forced onto the couch, and his voice grew hoarse with his point of view. He rented an apartment in Jerusalem. He arranged to meet with the heads of the major families, unburdened himself of the various pieces of wisdom and experience he had collected, asked them which side they fell on, to cooperate or to boycott. He ordered all the newspapers, caught up on local opinion. He purchased a desk and pushed it up against a window in his new study, with a view of Damascus Gate. He watched the crowds file in and out.

He took a train north to visit his family. Uppermost in his thoughts that day was his aunt Um Sahar: he had long feared that he was to blame for her widowhood.

Years ago, during that naïve early period in Paris, Hani had sent a letter to Jenin urging his uncle Fuad to join his band of exiled Arab thinkers, who were gathering in the evenings in one another's houses and debating with exhilaration. The war had begun, his friends were fired up by new currents of influence, and Hani, young and bursting with ideals, wanted to share his new world with his uncle. Usually his group corresponded using numerical ciphers, but since Fuad would not know the code Hani wrote to him in plain Arabic. He never received a reply. A short while later, news reached him of Fuad's execution. That letter of invitation haunted Hani, dropped so carelessly into the postbox on the Rue du Four.

For years he had rehearsed an apology to his aunt. On arrival in Jenin he found her much changed: her wrists stuck out from the sleeves of her gown, her delicate back was curved. And at the sight of that thin, solitary figure in the unlit corridor, the selfish nature of his desire for forgiveness flashed upon him, and he knew he must say nothing. It would cost her too much to pull up that atrocity so far in the past. How odd that he had imagined she might remain as she was, trapped in forty days of mourning while he passed away years. She smiled as Hani held her hands and asked how she was. Oh, this and that, she said. She mentioned a daughter. The sunlight pulsed behind clouds, brightening the room so the bookshelf and furniture glowed and dimmed. He said he was delighted to see her, and that he missed her. But the truth was the house weighed on him, and he was relieved when it was time for him to go.

At the door, she remarked: "You remind me of him."

"Who?"

She smiled.

"I sent a letter," he began, unable to stop himself, "from Paris—"

She shook her head, still smiling.

"If there is anything I can do for you," he said, "you must tell me."

On his way back to Jerusalem, Hani stopped in Nablus to see his old friend Midhat Kamal.

Since his marriage three years earlier, Midhat had been living with his wife and child in a small house on the edge of town. The child was named Massarra, and she was a year old.

In contrast to Hani's aunt, Midhat had changed little since their last meeting. Except for his belly, which was rounder. His hair was thick and long, and although at first his boyishness seemed to have gone, once they were seated in the salon and the niceties were over, he began to joke, and his eyebrows stretched northward as they used to, with that familiar mischievous look. At first he made a point of holding his baby daughter on his knee, but when she struggled and whined Fatima appeared and silently collected her, swinging her in her arms back to the kitchen.

"I was sorry to hear about your father," said Hani. "God bless him."

"Oh," Midhat pawed the air to brush it off, but then seemed unable to say anything else. Fatima had made some ma'mool biscuits, which were still warm, and very crumbly, and they ate these in silence. Then Midhat said: "We started a new business. Tailoring clothes. I'm working with one of the Samaritans. And Butrus, our old tailor. We make suits."

"That's wonderful," said Hani. "Congratulations. May God keep your business in good health!"

Midhat grinned. "Ba'dayn we are importing some women's clothes from Cairo."

"Well, you know I am looking quite tatty myself," said Hani. "Perhaps I shall come to you. This suit is ancient. I bought it in that place, do you remember?"

"The one with the blonde?"

"Exactly. They had those fantastic cravats."

"I still have three or four."

"You don't!"

"I do." Midhat chuckled. "They have half a drawer to themselves. Fatima thinks I'm mad. But anyway—tell me about the political life. How is it?"

"Ya'ni . . . the Zionists are in less of a fever, so the Arabs are just fighting each other. Nashashibi, Husseini, you know how it is."

"Same in Nablus."

"But I am optimistic about the next delegation to London. I am optimistic."

There was nothing to be optimistic about. Hani didn't know why he was performing in this way for Midhat. Perhaps it was something that occurred between friends parted for a long time: first impressions after the hiatus were more important than true firsts because they were weighed down by expectations born of memories. A true first meeting required modesty; a first meeting after time had passed required boasting. The fact was that the new delegation to London had been advised by their British supporters to soften their demands. Don't ask for independence, they were told: you won't get it. Curry favour, show you are peaceful. Ask to have a say in immigration. Then you'll appear reasonable, and the powers that be might take pity.

A few days later, the Arabs boycotted the elections for a legislative council. To accept any British institution was to accept British rule. Hani was sitting at his desk looking over the crowd at Damascus Gate when his telephone rang.

"Operator speaking," said the receiver. "Hani Murad?"

"With you."

"Madame Murad on the line."

A click, a rustling sound, and a different voice said:

"Amto will you come back?"

"Aunty, hello. What's wrong?"

"Will you come? I don't . . . I don't want to . . . to speak on the . . ."

"Understood," said Hani, to whom secrecy was now second nature. "I'm on my way."

In the hallway, his aunt looked even more frail than she had the last time.

"You said if I need anything. Did you mean it?"

"Absolutely," said Hani.

"My daughter is fourteen years old. She is Fuad's only heir. Three of her uncles . . ."

Before she had progressed very far into the story, Hani realised what was being asked of him and reached for the back of a chair.

"Ah of course!" His aunt gestured that he should sit down. "I am so much a mother I forget to be a host. I will boil water for coffee."

"There is a big difference in age," said Hani, as his aunt rummaged in a cupboard. "You know how old I am? Thirty-four. When she is twenty she'll realise . . ." He rested one hand on top of the other. "I can see you are in a predicament, but I don't know that this would be the right—"

"I know how I raised her," said Um Sahar, facing him with the coffeepot. "She'll never feel that way. I beg you amto. I have no alternative."

Every nicety was gone; she put the ghallaye on the stove and sitting beside him pressed her fingers on top of his. His eyes roamed her face. He had killed her husband. He had left these women unprotected. He bent his eyes to her hands, so thin the knuckles were like coins.

"May I see her?"

When her mother called for her, Sahar was already listening at the door. She hung back before entering. This was a nightmare. Was it possible? Another uncle.

"He is a good man," said her mother.

The good man was already grey. He was tall and thin, and his heavy eyelids gave him an ironic expression. He smiled at Sahar. She wanted to be sick.

They put the veil on her that night. Her mother prayed loudly and wept. After dark they took a car all the way to Jerusalem, and Sahar slept on the backseat, waking every now and then to the noise of the engine and reaching for her mother's hand.

They must have carried her upstairs for she woke in the morning beside her sleeping mother. A man's voice came through the wall in isolated bursts. Sahar crept out of bed and opening the door a crack saw the good man standing at the table by a window, speaking into a shiny object she knew at once must be a telephone.

The sheikh was even shorter than Sahar, and his head looked like a shiny nut. When he arrived at eleven o'clock, he set a lump of papers on the table and opened his Quran. The mother would act as the agent, he explained, with barely a glance at Sahar. Like a heroine submitting to fate, Sahar sat soundless at the other end of the sofa while her mother and Hani repeated the Fatiha and responded to the sheikh's legal recitations. Within a few minutes, they had signed the book of marriage.

"We will send you to school," said Hani, when the sheikh left, touching Sahar's head.

11 February 1924

Dear Sahar,

First of all I want to tell you, and I hope you don't mind, but in your last letter I noticed two grammatical errors. When you write: "Of the twelve girls in my class, only four of us are Muslims," you put "twelve" in the accusative, but you should remember that "twelve" shows case agreement, so it must be in the genitive. However, you write "four" correctly, in the masculine—because of polarity for the cardinal numbers. The other error is in your use of the subjunctive—remember to drop the nuun.

I am busy with politics as always. There are many arguments. Do they talk about this much at school?

Salamat,
Hani

15 March 1924

Dear Hani,

Thank you for your corrections. The lessons are fine. I enjoy my classes in Geography and English and History. I thought that I would like the Literature classes because I enjoy reading, however I do not like the teacher. She is always very certain that she is correct, and she does not like to hear other points of view!

My favourite teacher is Miss Schmidt. She teaches Geography. She is not friendly at first but I believe she is a conscientious person. In addition to this, she is intelligent.

The teachers do not talk about politics in the school, however the students talk. Most of the girls here do not like the Mufti. Even the Muslim girls talk about not wearing the veil. Please do not tell my mother.

Is your work very difficult? What is your opinion of the Mufti?

Salamat,
Sahar

23 December 1924

Dear Sahar,

I am sorry for this delay, I have been busy as usual. We have failed to convene another Congress, the divisions are very deep. Zionist immigration is increasing, land is sold all over, and the Arabs still have not formed a united front. I am not sure if it is appropriate to share my opinion of the Mufti. In fact, I have not yet decided. I prefer not to take a position and stick to it as though upon it my honour depended, since this is a habit I see everywhere, to the detriment of the national movement. Men claim to have principles but really they only care about keeping power. They do not try to see the larger picture, which is that while we are squabbling with each other the land is being taken from under our feet.

I know you prefer stories and novels, but I recommend that you read poetry, even if they are not teaching it to you. Start with al-Barudi, he is full of moral wisdom. Also I like the Egyptian poet Hafiz Ibrahim very much. And here is some of Ahmad Shawqi for you to enjoy:

And the star stared at us like an eye unmoving, unblinking
So that at parting's call our bond dissolved.
Now a sea separates us, and beyond the sea a wilderness.
My night is now here in Egypt, hers there in the West,
How content with her company must her night be!

Yours,
Hani

17 January 1925

Dear Hani,

I enjoyed reading what you wrote about the problems facing the Arabs at this time.

I find this poem very beautiful. I know some al-Barudi and Shawqi but I will read more.

We heard about the protests when Lord Balfour visited. Is this not an example of the ability to suspend squabbles in the face of a greater cause?

Sorry this letter is short. Today is sports day, and I am playing tennis.

Sahar

26 May 1925

Dear Sahar,

It pleased me very much to see you at your mother's house. You are growing fast, and I admit it was a shock to see how tall you are! And you are well spoken.

I am writing to you from Amman. I have come to visit my friend King Faisal of Iraq at a meeting about the new uprising in Syria. It is pleasant to be with him, he is an example of an honourable man, so careful of the fates of others.

Hani

29 June 1925

Dear Hani,

We have finished our end-of-year examinations, and now it is the holiday. Since my mother did not want me to return to Jenin we are staying in Jaffa until August.

Are you in Syria? We have been hearing about the uprising against the French. I hope you are in Jerusalem. Since I am sending this letter to Jerusalem, however, whenever you read that question you will be in Jerusalem! I pray you are not in Syria.

Now I am not at school I have been reading the newspapers. Did you hear that after the British government diverted all the water from an Arab village to give to the Jews building houses in Jerusalem, the Arabs took the government to court, and they won? I think this is a sign that the British government is a just government, that they will relent before their own legal system when the proper argument is made.

Salamat,
Sahar

2 October 1925

Dear Sahar,

Your reaction to the water dispute made me smile. Sometimes the law can seem boring but sometimes, yes, law is the stuff of life. As to whether the British government is just, we shall have to see.

Thankfully I was not in Syria. We have been organising a Central Committee for the Relief of Syrian Victims since the uprising started, however, and we have written to the League of Nations to protest the brutal French bombardments of Damascus.

I begin to wonder whether a revolution is what we need in Palestine, as they have in Syria. There are some people promoting this in the North. Our tragedy is that the Palestinian national movement currently has no strategy. More than a thousand Jewish immigrants enter the country each month and it is clear they wish to create a Jewish state. We might be the majority but we are treated as a minority, and I see they intend to make us one. This alleged British policy of maintaining the Status Quo is totally false.

I am building a new house in the Musrara neighbourhood which I hope will be pleasing to you. The architect is Turkish and has designed several other houses nearby. Meanwhile I am working with domestic disputes and land issues, and it seems that while we enter a political malaise there is an atmosphere of sociality with the Brits. There are many parties, for example.

You are back at school now. How is the start of your final year?

Salamat,
Hani

15 November 1925

Dear Hani,

Entering the final year of school I have an unusual feeling. I will be sad to leave my friends, particularly Margo and Lamees. I know I will still see them although not every day. However, I am also excited. Tonight we have a concert in the courtyard and Lamees is playing the piano.

How is the house in Musrara? It is strange to think there are only a few months left. Today we had a sewing class and I have been making a turban hat for myself. I am afraid these details are boring to you, but they are all I have to tell, so forgive me!

Sahar

9 January 1926

Dear Sahar,

The details you share are not boring in the slightest. It is always wonderful to hear what you have been doing, day by day. Very soon you will be telling me this over dinner, God willing. I hope I have already told you this, but your Arabic has improved tremendously and your handwriting is also very nice.

Excuse me for being brief, but I must now prepare for a reception tonight with the new High Commissioner, and tomorrow I will be attending a meeting with a few of my colleagues in the Old City. I very much look forward to seeing you in May. The house is ready.

Salamat,
Hani

When Sahar walked out through the school gates for the last time that spring, unveiled, she took a taxi straight to her husband's new home in Mus-rara, a West Jerusalem neighbourhood not far from the Old City walls. And there he was, waiting at the top of the steps before the open door. He was not as tall as she remembered. Certainly, he looked older. At school this man had been the envy of her classmates and source of her quiet pride. But her first sensation, as she stepped over the threshold, buttoned up in her new dress and carrying her bags of books, was that Hani did not quite match the picture she had created and shared and adored.

The house had two floors and plenty of bedrooms, and the windows onto the street were arched. The ground level was centred in the traditional style on a courtyard with a pool and fountain, and a floor of ornate black, red, and blue tiles. The tiles made a deep smacking sound as Sahar followed her husband to view the living rooms.

One year later, when the Jericho earthquake shook through Jerusalem, a fault appeared in these tiles, spining across the courtyard and stopping just before the pool in the centre. Once the dust had settled on the city and the casualties had been counted, Sahar took on the responsibility of restoring the floor. She and her maid collected the broken pieces, cracked and poking upwards from their places, leaving a rough diagonal of cavities across the floor. Hani, preoccupied as always, could not recall where the architect had sourced the tiles. Sahar borrowed copies of Egyptian homeware catalogues from her colleagues in the Women's Association, and donning one of her turban hats visited the ceramics shop in the Armenian quarter, bringing with her a small bag of fragments to show as examples. The shopkeeper knew who she was because of her husband, and, instantly deferential, covered his counter with scores of samples in terracotta and porcelain with various varnishes. None were suitable: all were too bright, and those with patterns were completely wrong, internally coherent and repetitious, rather than part of a design that would stretch across the floor. The shopkeeper, now perspiring, insisted on searching his back room, until Sahar said the name of the architect quite fiercely and asked if that man had ever purchased any ceramics from his shop.

"Oh Madame," he said. "I would be greatly honoured if that were so."

"I suppose that means no."

As she turned to leave, the shopkeeper threw out that if she wanted to ask the architect himself, she would find him at al-Aqsa mosque. He was leading the repairs there after the damage caused by the earthquake.

The architect was crouching at the western corner of the mosque compound dressed in a dark blue suit. Upon seeing Sahar beside him, he stood and smiled. He held a ruler in one hand and a dirty piece of paper in the other. His waxed black moustache was threaded with grey, and his mottled hair swept up into a peak on one side.

"You built my house," said Sahar. "I am trying to find the tiles you put in the courtyard."

At first, the architect pretended to recall the house she described. But it was quickly obvious that he was pretending, and he confessed that having constructed so many buildings in that neighbourhood, he had delegated cosmetic decisions like tilework to his trainees and assistants, who were innumerable, and on constant rotation.

"I believe," he said finally, "they may have been ordered from Italy."

"Italy?"

"Yes. But I can't remember where."

She thanked him, sadly, and he asked for her name, holding her hand an instant longer than necessary and looking into her eyes. Sahar withdrew and wound her way back to the Armenian ceramics shop, where the shopkeeper, at the sight of her, burst out from behind the counter.

"May I see those tiles again?" she said.

She chose a stack of plain black, plain blue, and plain red ones, examining them next to her broken chips regretfully. The new reds were the worst;

slotted into place on the courtyard floor beside the soft orangey originals, they glared with a vulgar, burnished discordance.

Within the year, however, the new tiles began to fade. Hani had barely noticed them, and when she pointed them out merely said: "Well done." Within two years, the sight of the mismatched tiles did not even bother Sahar anymore; she became used to and even fond of them. One day during the autumn of 1929, their courtyard was packed with two hundred female delegates of women's organisations from all over the country, wearing hats and heeled shoes that multiplied the dull sound of the tiles into a cannonade. The Jerusalem women with the highest-ranking husbands sat in chairs while the rest stood around the walls listening and raising their hands to interject.

Everyone was in a fury about the riots over the Wall. It was the Jews' Wailing Wall and the Muslims' Buraq Wall, where the Prophet ascended to heaven. The Jews had set up a gender partition that violated the Status Quo of Holy Sites, as established by the Ottomans and maintained by the British, and looked like a step towards taking possession of the whole. Riots ensued: Arabs died, Jews died; but the Arabs were treated far more harshly in the aftermath and several were sentenced to hanging.

The women elected Madame Husseini to the chair. She raised her hand for quiet. They would march on the Government House. A delegation—Sahar, only twenty years old, among them—would go straight to the High Commissioner and his wife with their list of demands and announce their plan to demonstrate.

("And they threw their veils back," said Hani, reciting the story to Midhat, "like this, and they told him, we are going to march, we are protesting the Balfour Declaration and the maltreatment of Arabs. What does the Commissioner say—he says, I'll stop the protest by force if I have to. So, what did the women do?"

"What," said Midhat.

"They would still demonstrate. But—they would demonstrate in *cars*."

"No," said Midhat, smiling.

"Yes. One hundred and twenty cars.")

*   *   *

Sahar sat in the back of a Buick 154, behind the chauffeur; beside her was a Christian woman from Jaffa named Jamila. From the passenger seat, elderly Mrs. Abdul reached across the steering wheel to pump the horn. Cars before, cars behind, the pavements on either side crammed with police officers. The women streamed past Damascus Gate in a honking convoy, screaming slogans from their opened windows. At each of the foreign consulates five women exited the foremost vehicles and walked as one to deliver their memoranda. By half past six, the hot red sun descending, the formation of cars splintered into banners that fluttered apart through the city towards their neighbourhoods and towns and villages.

One evening in 1933, Hani told Midhat this story again. It was one of several about his wife that, proudly, he seemed always to have at hand. That night he had just returned from Iraq and, fatigued, was walking out to buy cigarettes when he caught sight of his friend at the top of Jaffa Street near the new King David Hotel. He knew Midhat's silhouette at once: the upright posture, the idle progression along the street as though taking in his surroundings at leisure and quietly judging them, a pair of gloves flapping from his hand. Hani reached him in ten long strides.

"What are you doing here?" he said, taking Midhat by the shoulder.

They stood before the hotel, vast and many-windowed like an office of state.

"Hani!" said Midhat. "We came to the cinema." His look of wonder contracted into a smile. His eyelids hung low; his moustache was waxed finely on his upper lip. "My grandmother and the children—they went in, but I needed some air. But, Hani I miss you, it has been over a year since I saw you last. Where have you been?"

"Just recently I was in Baghdad. King Faisal's funeral."

"Bravo," said Midhat, nodding his approval as though Hani was fulfilling a task he had assigned him. "Allah yirhamo, a great man. Shall we, what do you think, get a drink?"

A woman in a grey ball gown passed into the hotel lobby on the arm of a man in tails. Midhat and Hani followed, and the woman glanced anxiously over her shoulder. They turned down a corridor into the hotel bar. Piano music floated out from a gramophone in the corner. The walls were dark and the barman's shelf was mirrored at the back, giving a chandelier-like impression of endless bottles and faces. Midhat chose a pair of stools beside the window, which displayed the lush enclosure of a hotel garden, electric lamps among the bushes illuminating tables of flushed tourists and grey journalists.

"Two whiskies."

"You'll never guess who I saw," said Hani.

Midhat shook his head, as though clearing his ears to hear better.

"Faruq al-Azmeh."

"Oh my goodness. In Baghdad?"

"He was travelling to meet a woman. You remember how he was."

Midhat leaned away from the bar, holding the edge for balance.

"He asked after you," said Hani. "He wanted to know if you were still reading, and still in love."

"Oh, well then, you may tell him I am in love."

"Do you know, he is going bald? He is not married, of course."

"I'm surprised."

"Are you? His entire philosophy was against marriage."

An attractive middle-aged figure in a black dress appeared in the mirror behind the bottles. Midhat watched her wander out again through the back door. "I don't think Faruq was *against* marriage," he said. "He just particularly liked the idea of the extramarital."

Hani chuckled and took a sip. "Look at us. Two married men."

This was the preamble to Hani's story, into which he plunged after a lengthy sigh. Midhat had heard several versions of this tale, but this was the first time Hani described with such detail the way he saved his young wife from the clutches of three miserly uncles, and brought her, in the dead of night, to Jerusalem.

The entire affair, recounted thus in Hani's words, became a tale of action that verged at points on absurdity. For most of its duration Midhat grinned and chuckled at appropriate moments. But as Hani went on to describe his wife's role in the women's committees and demonstrations—facts so well known that Midhat's expressions of surprise were completely feigned, though conversationally necessary—certain earlier parts of the story continued to strike him with an eerie force. In this account of Sahar's uncles something lay untapped, some other mood or meaning. Even the parts that were comical, or, perhaps, especially those parts—the three men, the phone call from the aunt, the nighttime journey—glinted with something sharper, something deeper than a mere question of power thwarted. It occurred to Midhat that a tragic story told quickly might contract easily into a comedy, and without the measure of its depths make the audience laugh. His friend carried on about the newspaper reports in praise of his wife—"And the speeches she makes, about unity, about freedom—really, I am proud of her"—but Midhat was only half listening, because he was thinking about the way his own charade might be told after he was dead, when he no longer held the reins on his memories, and they galloped off into the motley thoughts and imaginations of others.

"The tragedy," said Hani, "is that three Arabs were still hanged. Far fewer than were sentenced in the first place. But it's enough to burn in the memory and make a martyr. Death creates these myths, you know."

"Yes," said Midhat. "Terrible. Do you remember that story of the man nicknamed Barbar in Nablus?"

"No," said Hani. "I don't know it."

"You don't? Well, I'll tell you. It is said this man hated his nickname. It was given to him because he was very talkative when he was young."

In the mirror between the gin bottles and the brandy, the woman in black briefly reappeared, accompanied now by a wraithlike man in a tweed suit.

"So when he grew up, he founded a mosque in Nablus in his real name. Salim Basha or something, I can't remember. And then he left for many years to as-Salt, and when he returned to Nablus he asked a little boy in the street, where is the mosque of Salim Basha? And the boy replied, 'You mean Barbar's mosque?'"

Hani laughed hard and slid back on his stool. The barman flinched; then he saw that they were laughing, and he snickered.

2

Midhat never felt guilty about nights like this, spent drinking in a café or a bar populated by Jews and Europeans. He needed a little freedom from Nablus, from her stuffy, fervent atmosphere. He needed respite, truthfully, from his own home, from Fatima's increasingly tart replies, and from the children's easy leap to violence, which had turned the house into a kind of martial zone in which he was constantly disentangling their limbs and delivering verdicts as to who was in the right and who in the wrong.

Midhat and Fatima had four children. Massarra came first, followed by Taher. Khaled, the third, was born the year of the Jericho earthquake, and was the only one who did not cry in the midwife's arms.

The fourth child arrived in 1929, two years after Khaled. That was the year of the Wailing Wall riots, of the massacre of Jews in Hebron, of Sahar Murad's march to the High Commissioner, and Fatima, desolate on the cusp of yet another pregnancy, forced to concede at the age of twenty-eight that she had never been the mistress of her own body, lay in secret in the bathtub one day and ate with a spoon the entire contents of a bottle of powdered harmal seeds, which smelled and tasted foully of earth. She had acquired the bottle at great expense from one of the few remaining quack doctors in the old city, who handed it over with a euphemism and an unpleasant wink. Within a few hours the nostrum resulted in some hot and painful diarrhoea, but no sign of blood or a foetus, and several months later the red skin of baby Ghada met the cool spring air of the municipal hospital, to Midhat's delight and Fatima's exhaustion.

In preparation for one of his wife's receptions, which she held once a month, year in year out, for all the important ladies of Nablus, Midhat would usually deposit the children with his grandmother and travel by taxi down to Jerusalem to spend a night with his friend the journalist Qais Karak and the dancing girls at the Ma'arif Café. He no longer invited Jamil, who only ever scoffed at the suggestion, but he did sometimes persuade Adel Jawhari to join, and the three men motored to the seaside and swaggered along hotel balconies overlooking the water. Midhat would smoke one of Adel's cigarillos, his double-lined robe de chambre flowing open, around his neck one of the printed scarves he had imported from France heavily scented with his Farina Gegenüber cologne.

In the coastal towns there existed an unspoken shift between the attitudes of the night and those of the day, between the animosity of the working man with his needs, and the freedom of the dancing one. This, at least, was how Midhat conceived of the contradictions, which did not trouble him as much as they troubled Adel. One night at the Casino Café in Jaffa, in the summer of 1934, they fell into conversation with a man who revealed himself to be a fervent Zionist.

"I can't believe I was even talking to him," said Adel, stepping after Midhat onto the lamplit pier. "Can you believe it? I can't believe it."

Midhat patted his back and embarked on a soft utopian argument, as the dark sea crashed nearby. To prevent intermingling was impossible, since they were living in the same country; and tonight they were watching the same dancing troupe, and the music was playing and the wine was flowing, and someone had just told a joke, so why not enjoy the camaraderie even if it would end at daybreak?

"Habibi Midhat," said Adel, beneath a streetlamp. "You are naïve."

Midhat was silent. He was thinking of Jamil. He still occasionally saw his cousin at family meals, and knew the basic facts of his life, but since that argument after Midhat's wedding they had not been close and rarely saw each other. Since Nebi Musa, even. Jamil was unmarried, and had devoted the last fifteen years of his life to "the Cause," rallying support for a boycott of the Mandate and its institutions. Midhat could tell that Fatima admired Jamil for his commitment, and he took this as an implicit criticism of his own lack thereof. The children, on the other hand, seemed wary of their uncle when they sat near him at Eid. Except for Khaled, who studied Jamil with a fascination that made Midhat feel ashamed.

He signalled the waiter as they went back inside, and within the hour Adel was kissing a black-haired Russian girl named Polinka. Midhat saw them from the corner where he sat with one of the dancers on his knee.

Although he took pride in being a bon vivant, by the age of thirty-nine Midhat could no longer truthfully call himself a healthy man. The doctor said he ate too much. He also drank too much coffee, and smoked too many cigars. And he was very fond of arak—though this last was a secret vice, which even the doctor did not know about.

For a period of about a week and a half after Ghada was born, he had suffered from a weird nocturnal paranoia: every time he closed his eyes to sleep he felt the bed shaking. At first he accused Fatima of doing it, and when she denied this, he started to imagine the entire room was shaking, and that someone was walking on the roof. Logic lost authority after midnight, and the next evening the shaking was so strong he was certain it was a tremor from the earth itself, prelude to another earthquake. He was so alert, awaiting and registering every tiny vibration, that he barely slept at all. Nor did he suffer in silence, but repeatedly woke his wife to ask her if she had felt that one, or that one. In the morning, Fatima took charge of the investigation. She forced Midhat to lie down on the sofa and then to lie on the grass. These experiments yielded nothing, but the next night Midhat spoke suddenly into the darkness above their bed.

"There is a specific rhythm. Dun-dun, dun-dun."

The bed rocked as Fatima sat upright and glared down at him. Her eyeballs glowed. Her shadowy hair was spiralled into a pile.

"That's your heartbeat," she said. "You are an *idiot*."

Very carefully, Midhat listened. She was right. The shaking coincided, at a slight delay, with each of his heartbeats. It was the blood in his own body. Fatima struck his shoulder, and Midhat exploded with laughter. She hissed: "You'll wake the children!" But a moment later she surprised him. She giggled, melting back against the bedhead, and her legs bent under the blanket from the convulsions. It was an intimate moment, which prolonged itself into a happy hour or two, during which the bed shook even more than usual. The following day the doctor told Midhat he must reduce his coffee and sugar consumption in the hours before sleep. But what really happened was that he grew accustomed to the rhythmic shaking, which did not seem so pronounced now that he knew its cause.

Mornings were the more common occasion for intimacy with Fatima, particularly after a night apart, he in Jerusalem or along the coast, she at one of the Nablus istiqbals. Midhat believed the spark was most likely the change in routine, which made each a little stranger to the other, and revived some nostalgia for the early, more mysterious days of their marriage. Returning home from an evening abroad he would find his wife softened by the breath of change and released from her customary irony, which he assumed she had expended in great quantities of wit the night before. In addition, she seemed pacified by the taste of society which reassured her that the rest of the world, by which she always meant the rest of Nablus, was not better off than they. At these times, desire was tangled with an awareness that other people had seen their spouse, had seen and judged what they now saw, lying on the bedsheets in the sifted morning light. And each welcomed and coaxed the jealousy this thought summoned from the dark, because, in this instance, jealousy was a rise to desire, which by bringing the whole world into the bedroom made it easier to be alone.

November 1935. Midhat heard voices as he approached the kitchen. His shoe clicked on the terracotta tile, and the voices stopped.

A morning haze curtained the farther mountain from the kitchen window, and under it the things of the garden—trees, furniture, bushes, wall—were the colour of ash. Fatima was at the table, knees bent to her body, heels balanced on the edge of the seat. Her neck was stringed with tension, which suggested she had only just rested back against the wall. Beside her, Nuzha was leaning over something flat on the table.

Though younger than Fatima, over the past fifteen years Nuzha had aged much faster than her sister had. She could not be more than thirty and yet the hair around her face was already greying and the sides of her mouth were lined. Behind her back, Fatima often called her sister a simpleton; but Nuzha was not simple. She had only remained carefree, in a way Fatima never had been.

"Look here," said Nuzha. "We found this among my mother's things."

Two bony fingers rotated the picture so Midhat could see it the right way up. It was a photograph, faded with age, showing two rows of women in party dresses, a few kneeling in the front. Most of the faces were blurred, mouths and eyes smoky lines and holes, but here and there part of a dress or a jewel was caught perfectly. In the background, the engravings of foliage on the flowerpots were pristine. Above them drifted a blotchy mist of real leaves.

Midhat pointed his little finger at a figure in the second row, one of the only perceptible faces. "There's you," he said. A girlish Nuzha looked dead at the camera. Beside her stood a grey smudge.

"Yes that's me. Doesn't it look like we're dancing?"

Midhat studied the figures, trying to see them in motion.

"Where are you? Where was it taken."

"I don't know. Isn't that funny? People didn't really have cameras in those days, so I can't think . . ."

"Atwan istiqbal," said Fatima, in a jaded voice. The window light polished her nose and forehead.

"Oh," said Nuzha. "Yes, Atwan. But why are we moving like that?"

Midhat said, "It must have been the—"

"Must it?" said Fatima.

He looked over at his wife's strained neck, then picked up the photograph and drew it close to his eyes. He examined the plant pots.

"It's raining." He put it back on the table.

Of all his wife's habits, the one that irked Midhat most was the effort she put into not appearing interested. It was an aristocratic trait that he abhorred, and towards which she had a natural advantage, being able to express boredom simply by keeping her face immobile. When the muscles of Fatima's face were slack the corners of her eyes and mouth drooped south, as though she could hardly bother to keep her eyes open. Sometimes he liked to provoke her, and for this reason he had placed the photograph far away from her on the table. But, as usual, Nuzha blithely interfered and handed the picture to her sister, so that Fatima did not need to move for a view. She eyed it and said nothing.

Midhat knocked on the girls' bedroom door, and Ghada ran out to meet him.

"Baba Baba Baba I dreamt we were in an earthquake."

"Oh dear," said Midhat. "Massarra are you finished with the comb?"

Massarra, who was plaiting her hair, passed the comb behind her while keeping eye contact with her reflection in the mirror.

"We were in the earthquake," Ghada continued, while Midhat sat on the mattress and drew her between his knees, "and then we went on holiday."

"Why are you so messy." He touched the big knot of hair on one side of her head. "Did the earthquake roll you around in bed?"

Ghada clucked and tipped her head back, gurgling as he turned her by the shoulders to see the rear. He teased the biggest knot by combing lightly several times until the threads began to separate. Ghada gripped her hands over her crown as he laboured, and when the knot fell apart he combed through the bent threads. Two clean socks lay across a chair. He crouched to Ghada's feet, and she held his head for balance as she stood on one leg.

"Shoes." He pointed to the line of shoes beneath the window. "Taher, good morning habibi."

His eldest son often approached before anyone had noticed him. Taher was tall for an eleven-year-old, with a silent manner and a bald stare, his long rectangular head drenched in black curls. He ignored his father, walked through the door, and disappeared.

"Massarra, are you ready? Khaled? Where is he."

"Give me four and a half minutes," said Massarra.

"Where is Khaled?"

"He's in my bed."

"You didn't wake him? Khaled, get up."

"I did wake him!" Massarra twisted round indignantly, and the completed plait coiled around her neck as she held the other steady. "He went back to sleep, didn't he!"

After a quick breakfast of bread and za'atar, the boys set off for school. Midhat waited in the hall while the girls said goodbye to their mother and aunt. Then he reached for Ghada's hand.

The mist was clearing, but it had rained in the night and a rind of dirt soon gripped his boots. A splatter appeared on the toe of Ghada's shoe: he lifted her under the arms and balanced her legs over his stomach, arms around his neck.

Massarra tugged at Ghada's skirt. "I can carry her."

"She's too heavy."

"No she's not. You're making a mess of it."

He didn't respond. They had reached paved ground near the school and it was time to set her down anyway.

"Just take her hand."

Massarra seemed satisfied. "Come on little one," she said.

His daughters disappeared and reappeared between the bills posted on the gate. Seven or eight bore the same message: "Right Is Above Strength and People Are Above Government." From a farther street a wind called, and as it reached him the bills flapped like bunting from the railing. "Fight the British, Fight the Jews, Fight the Arab Traitors—Signed, The Rebellious Youth."

Across the concrete path, the schoolgirls crowded up the steps.

When they were first married in 1920, Midhat and Fatima had intended eventually to leave Nablus. But the dream each had entertained of Europe, or of Cairo, grew dim the longer they were entrenched here, in this town with its webs of subtle comfort, of knowing and being known, all of which made departure for new territory seem too severe a breach.

The truth was that without his father's business everything Midhat had of worth was in Nablus. To begin from scratch in another country, even in another city, would mean starting with nothing at all. Nouveautés Ghada, the shop he had opened with the Samaritan Eli after the local Kamal store closed, was in the new town between Barclays Bank and a sports equipment store. For all the usual fluctuations Nouveautés had been doing well: a high-water mark in sales coincided five years earlier with a surging interest in women's fashion, when at last Nablus seemed to be catching up with the other cities. Veils, though not gone entirely, had thinned into vapours of chiffon, as in more conservative parts of Jerusalem and along the coast; skirts concluded at the knee, and the black stockings on the shelves of Nouveautés disappeared almost as soon as they were laid there.

Not everyone in Nablus was glad about their good fortune. Over the course of the last decade, several of Midhat's acquaintances had turned cold, and more than once a group of women paused in front of his shop and, believing themselves invisible, glowered at the dresses on display. Teta remarked that it was the same in his father's time: a self-made man was more vulnerable to the evil eye than he who inherited his privilege. "This is partly why he moved to Cairo."

"Really?" said Midhat. It never occurred to him that his father might have wished to escape Nablus.

"They say the bite of a lion," said Teta, "is better than an envious look."

And, of course, when people looked at Midhat, they saw a man who had married above his station, a sybarite, an optimist, a success with women, a carefree lover of the West. Regardless that he had hardly made fortune enough to take his family abroad, Midhat and his wife rapidly became local objects of jealousy. Chic, charming, well educated; their house was no Atwan palace, but Fatima's istiqbals were renowned for their flair, for the studied nonchalance of the hostess on the Armenian chaise. Her talent at the oud was itself an occasion for spite, and replacing the instrument in its velvet-lined case she would whisper the Daybreak Sura to repel the evil eye as her guests relinquished their last cups of lemonade and trailed out through the garden gate.

By 1935, fear was afoot in Nablus, and with fear came ill will. The finger levelled at the enemy swung inexorably round to the apostate nearer by, and by "apostate" one meant any neighbour who might be considered wanting in ideological zeal. Armouries had been installed in Jewish settlements, and as the Arab elites continued bickering over degrees of cooperation, their national movement was grinding to a halt. Alarm bells rang in Europe, and Jewish immigration swelled with refugees. Without a proper channel for their anger the Nabulsis became nasty in the markets, so that to walk through the onion souq was to hear voices raised with a passion quite out of proportion to any of the transactions at hand. Even the women's groups became forces of rage, and thin-veiled Nabulsiyyat took to the podiums before the post office to point at the sky and unleash their fury at British hypocrisy, and at every local person too weak for the Cause.

Adel bemoaned the infighting. Basil Murad had even accused *him* of not being radical enough. But often, he added, twisting his glass on the table, one could see that long-standing enmities were rising to the surface and adopting the guise of political indignation. More than once Midhat came home to find Fatima wafting burning sage into the corners of the living room and muttering incantations. He tried to laugh it off. It did not help Fatima's fear of the evil eye that her husband was not a political activist, and had gone into business with a Samaritan.

Although Nouveautés remained relatively prosperous, Eli attributed a recent decline in sales to the political situation. People did not want to give the appearance of having money to spend. It wasn't good for the resistance. Only last month barrels of ammunition for the Jews were discovered in Jaffa, and the Arabs had called a daylong strike all over Palestine. Massarra insisted Midhat take her on the march, but then Ghada had tripped in the garden and hurt her knee, and begged him not to leave her, after which ensued a loud and pointless argument, so in the end the children spent the strike day sulking in their bedrooms while Midhat took a nap.

The soap industry especially suffered. The Egyptian market withered, and then the Jews set up their own factories for export, selling "Nabulsi-style soap" but using castor oil, instead of olive, which was far cheaper. One night in Jerusalem Qais Karak admitted to Midhat and Adel with a half-amazed laugh that his father, the famous soap manufacturer, now relied on the income from his journalism. Many times Midhat had passed the open front of the Atwan soap factory and heard Abdallah Atwan shouting at someone about the Jews. Penned in by her two mountains Nablus was not, in any case, growing at the rate of other towns. Compared with Jaffa and Jerusalem and Haifa and Akka—all open to the sea, to Christian pilgrimage routes and tourism, electrified and full of cinemas—this town was decaying in her provincial backwaters, subsisting on memories of former glory, her inhabitants recalling with artificial frequency the days when she used to be called "the little Damascus."

"When Nouveautés grows," Midhat sometimes told Fatima late at night, "then we can think about Cairo."

Everyone, however, even their children, felt the urgency of staying in Nablus. They had a duty to remain. Forget local rivalries, in the end it was as the Bedouin said, the enemy of one's enemy was a friend; and though Midhat might not be active the way Jamil and Adel were active, he was a Nabulsi, and everyone in Nablus breathed the same haunted air.

He did not often pause to reflect on what might have been, but every now and then he looked up from the inventory books and heard a sound like a strong wind whooshing past his ears, and with a vertiginous feeling, as though standing on the prow of a ship, his life slipped into view. Suspended there on the bright blade of the present moment, he turned his head and glimpsed from a distance how his fate had rolled out. The shape of his marriage, his profession, his family, his house. Viewed from this angle, the question of choice seemed quite irrelevant.

It was mostly Adel who brought him news of Jamil. Jamil was debating in the nationalist clubs, making speeches, writing petitions, amassing allegiance, employing connections across the Jordan River to collect arms from the Bedouin. Sometimes Midhat saw in his cousin's life another path for his own. He thought about his youthful days as a student, caught up in the drama of "exile" in Paris with Faruq and Hani and the others, drunk on the notion that to argue was important, with a productive end, and that he, gesticulating at his friends with a glass of liqueur, was engaged in a significant path of thought, a small piece of a wider picture of men arguing in rooms. Now, speech clogged with arak, he murmured and smiled at his cousin and compatriots. That was not his life.

* * *

As Midhat approached Nouveautés Ghada, he saw Eli hunched at the counter. Eli's ears poked out under his tarbush, and he was running two fingers through his beard.

"Good morning, Abu Taher," said Eli, lurching upright, eyes wide. A newspaper sighed as he shifted it across the counter. Midhat angled to see the headline.

"What happened?"

"No, not there," said Eli. "We had an accident."

"An jad?"

"Come and look."

He followed Eli into the tailoring room. Butrus had not arrived, but the window shutters were open. Positioned on the table between the flywheel of the sewing machine and a stack of cottons stood two naphtha lamps. The glass of each flute was broken, jagged all the way around.

"Ah, what a shame." Midhat touched a peak. "It isn't a disaster. Where are the pieces?"

"This is not about expense," said Eli, in a warning voice. "It's about how did this happen. Why are these broken."

Midhat was well acquainted with the symptoms of superstition, since it was an affliction from which his own wife suffered, as well as his grandmother. He had recognised them before in Eli's behaviour: that eye lingering on a dark corner, a twitch of the lips murmuring a protection. Unusual, however, was for Eli to admit something like this so directly.

"You think someone did that? I don't think so, Eli."

"I'm telling you. Both lamps? To me, that's a signal."

The shards of one, Midhat saw, were as regular and upright as the tines of a mock crown. "We have a third. Where is it?"

The shutter banged the outer wall as Eli pushed the casement bar, and in the tiny extra light the window afforded, Midhat opened the cupboards.

The lack of electricity in Nablus had, like many things, a political basis. More than a decade ago the council voted to boycott the Electric Company, a Zionist enterprise backed by the British. This abstinence from electric light remained a point of pride: nowhere in Palestine was such cohesion in evidence. Not in Haifa, not in Jaffa, not in Jerusalem. Fortunately for Midhat and Eli, the breadth of their shopfront windows meant they had little need for oil lamps during the day; Butrus, however, used them a great deal in this back room, where he often hemmed into the night.

Midhat mounted the stairs to the storeroom. He stacked one empty crate on top of another, and moving along the banister caught sight of Eli hovering between the shelves below. Presently he landed on the lowest step, and contorted his body to send his voice up to Midhat.

"Abu Taher I have to tell you something."

He twisted further to meet Midhat's eyes. His skin was so clear that in certain lights he looked like a child. As though he had coiled too tightly, his body swung back round and he spoke to the display shelf of cravats.

"There was—years ago now—I heard that someone put the evil eye on you. I remember . . . I remember Abu Salama telling my mother."

Midhat took a moment. In spite of himself, his body went limp.

"Do you know who?"

"No."

"But you think it was this person?"

"I don't know. People see you, they think . . . these are difficult times, Abu Taher." Eli looked back, beseeching. "People are angry . . . what? Why are you laughing?"

Midhat had put his head in his hands. "Because, habibi, we can't blame everything bad on the evil eye."

"It's not funny."

"I'm sorry. I've stopped." He showed his palms. "Anyway, didn't you just say it was years ago?"

"It was."

"Well then, there's probably not much we can do about it, is there?"

"Yes there is. You can find the curse."

"Where?"

"It will be in your house somewhere. A bird, probably. And a token."

Midhat's head swung from side to side. "I'm sorry habibi but I just don't believe that. I'm sorry. Two lamps! Ah, but—if it makes you happy

I'll have a look when I get home." He hooted, and made his way down the stairs. "Yalla, let's get to work."

Midhat was exaggerating his humour, exactly as he did with Fatima. The more paranoid and mystical his wife became, the more Midhat, with a grin, insisted on the evidence of their senses. But as the business of the day began in earnest, uncomfortable thoughts began to gyre. Was it possible that someone in Nablus bore such ill will towards him that he or she had resorted to magic to make him suffer? Regardless of whether one believed such things, bad feeling was bad feeling and caused damage in myriad ways. He ran over the characters from town. He thought of Jamil. But Jamil was family, and would never do such a thing.

Midhat's collaboration with Eli had been Eli's doing: he said the idea came to him because of Midhat's sense of style, and because of the interest he showed in their work at the Samaritan store. After Midhat agreed and they began planning the venture, Eli asked him whether he still had that album of drawings.

"Album of drawings? What album?"

"You used to draw clothes, when you came back from Paris," said Eli. "I heard about it from, I can't remember who."

The only drawings Midhat had ever produced were those doodles in the back of the old accounts book at his father's store. He had ripped out and destroyed those long ago. Was it possible those crude sketches had been so magnified beyond their merits into an "album"? It must have been Jamil. Or Hisham. Nothing went unnoticed in such a town.

"Oh yes, that one," Midhat had said airily. "Yes, I threw that out long ago. I could make another. I might be able to remember the designs. With your help, of course, cher Eli."

Coming on the tail of the news about his father's business, Midhat took pains to ward off any feeling that Eli was taking pity. One did not go into business with someone out of charity, of course, but it still felt necessary to accentuate his expertise as artist and businessman and intellectual, rotating a pencil between his fingers and staring into the distance, in support of the fiction that it was he condescending to work with Eli. Thus the relationship began with a kind of pretence, and continued in the same vein, since each man tended not to say precisely what he meant. For Midhat, this was born of a desire to impress and not to offend; in Eli's case it was the inveterate caution of a member of an endangered sect trying to survive in another culture. It was not exactly customary for a Samaritan to go into business with a Muslim.

Although Midhat never had any evidence that Eli kept secrets, he interpreted secrecy in many aspects of Eli's behaviour. That tendency to wait before answering a question; that preference for silence over saying no. He found he longed for Eli's confidence almost the way he longed for Fatima's. In the end he resented his wife for reserving it; but if Eli was cautious he at least had cause. Only last week, he told Midhat, the Samaritans had woken to the sound of rocks showering their houses. "We are not even Jews!" he said, waving a necktie Butrus had asked him to examine. The more fearful among the Samaritans were leaving their quarter in the old city and joining the new settlement on Mount Gerizim. It was not as though one could take a pointer to the vandals and show them that in the annals of Greek and Aramaic the Israelites had splintered from the Samaritans as far back as the time of Moses. To a dispossessed farmer they were all the same, all "Jews."

One evening in the spring before the earthquake, Eli had invited Midhat to dinner. The last time Midhat had been to the Samaritan quarter was with his grandmother on that abortive trip for a love charm seven years prior, and indeed it had taken almost as long for Eli to invite him. On the way, they stopped to call on the old high priest, and found the front door to Abu Salama's house open. The priest was not in the first room. Eli led the way into the second, calling out:

"Good afternoon, Abu Salama."

It was quite possible, since Abu Salama was an old man, that he simply did not hear them approach. Or he may have been too slow to hide what he was doing. Either way, the instant they entered the room Midhat saw they had interrupted something.

Abu Salama was sitting beside a young boy at a table on which a series of objects were arranged. In the centre, a long piece of parchment was held down with stones at the top and bottom, its four corners curling. A bowl of clear water on one side held a lace of colour; beside it slouched a pile of murky rags; on the other side, a pestle and mortar stood near a bottle of dark liquid. The residue on the neck of the bottle had a sticky sheen. At the edge of the table near Midhat and Eli lay an open paper of saffron threads. A rag hung from Abu Salama's hand. Rather than greeting them the old man stared, his mouth a crack in the withered rock of his face.

Midhat glanced at Eli for a cue. Eli's skin had lost colour. He bowed at Abu Salama, murmured his greeting, and hurried Midhat out of the house.

At the appalled look on his colleague's face, Midhat realised he had witnessed something he should not have. He had long learned by example not to record what he must not see, but as Eli led the way in silence to his own home, Midhat's instinct to ignore was overridden by some force of attraction. Part curiosity, part something less easy to define. Recognition—or, perhaps, affinity. That was a glimpse of a wider operation. The high priest was dyeing that parchment. There had been a smear of colour on the paper. And that was saffron he had seen, and in that sticky bottle some kind of juice or pigment.

Throughout the meal Eli refused to meet Midhat's eye. His bottom lip twitched and he stared so incessantly at his elderly mother serving the stuffed potatoes that at one point she asked, "What is wrong with you? Do I have something on my face?" Midhat was grateful for the silence. His colleague's panic spoke transparently of shame. Which might signify that some documents the Samaritans sold to foreigners were faked—which might, of course, indicate some charlatanry in their other activities. Was it shameful? Not necessarily. He envisioned a foreigner, a Frenchman, holding the counterfeit document, interpreting the Samaritan specimen in his European library, sliding his authentic facts into the bookcase. And with that view in mind the real Samaritans went sliding about beneath the indices. They fabricated in order to be free, that was it: materially, because they were poor, but in other ways too. To invent one's self was to resist the inventions of others: to forge was to author. It made perfect sense that the high priest did the dyeing, for instance, and not someone of a lesser stature. One needed to be precise in one's fakery. It took delicacy, an artist's eye, to choose the marks that would conceal.

*   *   *

When Butrus arrived at the store, an hour after Midhat was presented with the broken lamps, it took him three minutes to uncover the third. He had hidden it, entire, under a lump of fabrics, which he confessed was his habit in case the others went missing. Of the broken lamps he said: "It was probably a bat." He took off his coat and set about scrutinising the body of the first customer with a tape measure dangling from his teeth.

The rest of the day passed unremarkably, and Midhat excused himself ahead of closing time because they had guests for dinner. He reached home at five thirty; at six, the doorbell rang.

"Good evening habibi!"

Hani Murad stepped through the opened door in an overcoat shining with rain.

"Good evening," echoed Sahar, poking her head in.

Midhat embraced them, and Fatima appeared from the bedroom wearing a black dress with a round neck. Droplet earrings sparkled from her earlobes, and a tiered silver necklace shone over the black silk on her chest.

Fatima and Sahar had of necessity developed a strained sort of bond. There were only six years between them—one less than the gap between Fatima and Midhat—but it was enough for Fatima to feel some conflict about treating Sahar as an equal. Over the years she had become as obsessed with status as her mother once was, and at times appeared to lord it over Sahar, a tendency which Sahar, an expert at managing condescension, and preternaturally capable of appearing both deferential and at ease, politely ignored.

Although their family originated in the hills of Nablus, Sahar and Hani were the perfect type of free Jerusalemites. In fact, one might argue that the ultimate free Jerusalemite was someone who came from elsewhere, being unfastened in that metropolis by the distance from their kin. Sahar, who still worked as an activist both for the national movement and for women's rights across the Arab world, including raising the marriage age and removing the veil, had become famous for speaking at rallies and demonstrations. The women she associated with came from all parts of society, including the fellahin; all classes, all religions.

Whenever they spent time with Hani and Sahar, Midhat fancied his wife became, by contrast, more emphatic in her Nabulsi pride, more uncompromising even than she usually was, as though to embody the very spirit of the town.

"Keefek, shu akhbarek," said Fatima stiffly, kissing Sahar on each cheek.

"How was the journey," said Midhat, helping Hani with his coat. "Was it fine?"

"Oh yes it was fine."

Fatima pointed a languid finger at the dining room.

"Would you like to sit in here, please."

Fatima took Sahar's bag to the guest bedroom, and Midhat saw Hani's eyes follow her. His wife had dressed more glamorously for the evening than Sahar, who wore only a simple cotton dress.

They sat in the lamplit dining room, Hani opposite Midhat, Sahar opposite Fatima's vacant chair. The window showed a black sky, and they heard the rain like wings beating the glass. Fatima returned with a tray of salads on her best porcelain, a set of reticulated German plates. She was protective of these, with their gold butterfly edging and chain of yellow and pink flowers around the rim; they were a gift from her mother. Since they could not afford new china, it was imperative they take care of the ones that would never go out of fashion. The German plates had their own cupboard, with a double lock.

"Where are the children?" said Hani.

Fatima delivered a spoonful onto his plate. "At my mother's."

"You miss them?" Midhat grinned, and winked at Sahar. "Maybe it's a sign."

"So Sahar, tell us," said Fatima. "This argument the ladies have been having in Tulkarem. Do you know anything about it?"

"What argument?" said Midhat.

"It's just a silly rivalry." Sahar smiled. "If I'm honest, I don't know much either."

Fatima squinted as she served herself, and looked about to ask something else when Hani interrupted.

"The thing about the women," he addressed Midhat, wiggling his body a little from side to side as though digging a hole in his chair, "is that they are generally much better at cooperation than we are. We could learn a lot from them. These factions are a mess. Don't pretend Nablus isn't just as bad. I have to say. I try to find a road between my principles and cooperation but . . ."

"It's hard, I believe," said Sahar, "for some of these people to imagine the future. They are worried about losing out. Whereas we women have always cooperated behind the scenes. So it makes sense that we would be able to put aside our . . . our . . ."

"Selfishness?" Midhat supplied.

"Yes, you could say that." Colour came into Sahar's cheeks. She had a kind of genial radiance that made everything she said sound pleasant. "But there is still competition, even with women. What I mean is that sometimes to cooperate is difficult in the present, because you can't imagine the other side." She made a motion with her hand to express an other side, as though folding dough. "Since we've never had independence, we don't know what it's like."

"Of course, that's not what she says in her speeches," said Hani. "You have to give a unifying message."

"Well, I don't make many speeches anymore."

She smiled at Fatima. Fatima eyed her for a moment, then returned the smile with a demonstrative blink.

"But people have learned from you," Hani went on, addressing his wife. He turned to Midhat. "And it's the way you say it. You know that's more than half of it. Sometimes it's just perfect coming from a woman. A woman can say anything."

"Can she?" said Midhat.

"What about Qassam?" said Fatima.

"What about Qassam," said Hani.

"What about the way he says it."

"Well that's different obviously. Qassam is a preacher."

"But he's effective," said Fatima. "Especially after they found the weapons in Jaffa. People want to listen to him."

Midhat looked at her in surprise.

"Among the fellahin, yes," said Hani. "But of course it has a different . . . effect. I mean, having a woman speak," he gestured at his wife, "It's good for the Europeans. And for us. It's a sign of enlightenment, a progressive society. It shows we can rule ourselves. That's why I said a woman can say anything."

Fatima persisted. "But of course the British are frightened of Qassam."

"Oh absolutely," said Hani, his eyes widening. "And they're not frightened of women."

"So," said Midhat, jumping aboard, "have you been much involved with Qassam then?"

"We have had contact, yes," said Hani. "He might be a potent ally." He lifted his shoulders and opened his hands as he said this, as though excusing himself. "Besides Qassam's group, nowhere, except perhaps Nablus, are people ready to rise against the British . . . militarily, ya'ni, but also with civil disobedience, which for years I've been saying is the best way to resist. You've seen the reports, you know the numbers. The Jews are armed. If it comes to that, Qassam will turn out to be much stronger than these democratic so-and-sos."

There was a long silence. Midhat tore a piece of bread, and the steam whiskered off in the lamplight.

"The house is beautiful," said Sahar.

"It is difficult to heat," said Fatima. "We get a draught from the mountain."

"Good for the laundry."

"You've seen the garden before, haven't you?" said Midhat.

"Yes, yes," said Sahar. "I remember from last time. It's lovely."

"It's a shame it's too dark now, or I'd take you down to see the chickens."

"Why would she want to see the chickens?" said Fatima.

"And the roses, and the trees, etcetera." Midhat waved the bread in the air. "But I think the chickens are marvellous."

Sahar and Hani shared a smile. As they returned to their meal, Fatima stood up and walked into the kitchen.

"It has stopped raining," said Hani.

"Well, we won't go down to the chickens in the dark," said Midhat. He waited for laughter, and when there was none added: "Shall I put on music?"

"Wait until after dinner," shouted Fatima.

"She has the ears of a bat," said Midhat.

"You know we heard some wonderful music in Cairo," said Hani.

"Oh yes, it was wonderful," said Sahar.

There was no time to pick up this thread, however, because Fatima was returning, and it was necessary to coo over the meat steaming in its bed of spiced rice and pine nuts. Fresh plates thudded onto the table. Fatima said to Sahar:

"So you are having a family?"

Midhat, reaching for the serving spoon, frowned at her.

"How did you know?" said Sahar.

"You said you weren't making any more speeches," said Fatima. "I wondered."

After dinner, the women took tea in the salon. Midhat waited until they were out of sight, then raised an eyebrow at Hani. "Arak?"

"Of course."

Hani turned in his chair and Midhat crouched before the cupboard.

"Fatima doesn't know."

"Know what."

"She thinks it's milk."

"Does she!"

"Some things you have to keep private. Ah—music, I forgot. Let me see, let me see."

Though weighed down by the meal, one sip of arak untied a cord around his brain and he felt lighter. He moved slowly over to the cabinet and slid his fingers through the pile of records. He chose a singer from Aleppo and dropped the lever. The strings commenced.

"Sometimes I think . . ." he said.

Above the orchestra, the voice was starting.

"Tell me habibi, what do you think."

His friend leaned back, legs crossed, one arm over the chair. Hani had known him for years. Not only that, he had known him in Paris. He had not been in Montpellier, but still he was the only one who grasped something of the full shape of Midhat's life. It might even be better that he saw it at a distance, always living in a different city. Distance allowed a special clarity, the outline of a coast viewed from the sea. Midhat sat in Sahar's chair, and began in abstraction.

"Things are never perfect. And there is usually some separation between inside and outside. In our lives. The way we behave. Don't you think?"

Hani made a recognisable gesture, which had hardened now into a full-blown mannerism: tipping his head to one side with his mouth open, closing both eyes tight and then opening one of them, looking up into the corner of the room as if trying to do some mental arithmetic. "Um, I mean, actually no I don't agree. I believe in being consistent. I think—well ideally I believe in consistency." He turned his glass little by little on the table as he spoke. "You know there are those people who stick to their position as though their honour depends on it, so, regardless of the situation, they will cling to this position because—their family says they should, or whatever. It's a question of honour. Apparently. But in the end those people are nearly *always* corrupt. They say one thing, they do another. Of course everyone makes mistakes, but half the time those ones who are so emphatic—that's because they feel the need to cover their tracks." He jabbed the air with a finger. "Having *said* that, I also think that when you find something you believe, you have to stick to it." His hand sliced horizontally, clearing a surface. "For example, we must maintain a policy of non-cooperation with the English. Absolutely. And I still believe we should have a united Syria— eventually, at least. That's what we're owed, we fought alongside the English, and that's what we're owed. And we almost, *almost* had it. The main point though is that we shouldn't be *dogmatic* at the expense of—possibly changing our minds. It's a different kind of consistency, to be flexible. I suppose I have always believed that. Believed in . . . doubt."

This had deviated so far from Midhat's original intention that he was momentarily flummoxed. Just as he was angling for a way back in, Hani continued:

"Take the issue of women, for example. I believed, and I'm sure you believed, that women should never, ever enter politics. I believed that, absolutely, I thought it was a bad idea, women have their role, their duties end at the door. And now, I'm proven wrong. What can I say. I stand corrected. Why was I saying—oh yes, because one should be flexible, not dogmatic. Of course, I wasn't married back then. And marriage does change everything . . ."

"Yes," said Midhat with energy, grappling for the reins, "marriage changes everything. In fact I wasn't actually thinking about politics when I made that remark—though I think you are correct, that is a very—observant philosophical point." He laughed. He felt they had gone back twenty years; they were in Paris, in Faruq's sitting room. "I meant something more simple, about the life inside. When your life isn't . . . per-fect . . ." He eyed Hani, wary of discomfiting him. "The things you wished for as a young person—I mean, the past becomes a kind of private philosophy, the things you remember. I remember things . . ." He shook his head theatrically.

Hani's mouth opened in a grin. "Oh, I see. The old Midhat!" He swirled the arak around his glass. "My philosophe, my amoureux . . ."

Midhat had misfired again. Silent, he met his friend's smile. The recorded strings crescendoed, and after the scratchy break a new, slower song began. He uttered a laugh and flourished his hand. "I miss you, habibi." He poured more arak, followed by a cloud of water from the jug.

"I miss you too."

They shared a fond look. He saw Hani only once or twice a year, and yet nothing about their friendship had ever faded. It was the opposite of Midhat's relationship with Jamil. With Jamil it was all physical proximity and emotional distance.

"But what you were saying," Midhat began, in a new serious voice— for if he could not speak from his heart, all the same he could avoid being trapped in the role of romantic clown—"could also be a result of the radical turn, could it not? When people stick to their convictions, ignoring reality. Perhaps, could it be, the nature of religion itself. To see the unity underlying the discord."

"Oh, I wish, habibi. I wish," said Hani. "*If only* that were true." He shook his head. "Actually I think it's the discord that makes someone like Qassam so appealing. An outsider, a preacher, accessible to everyone. Ya'ni, imagine you are a poor Muslim farmer. What is the word 'nation' to you? You never had one before. You have never travelled, don't read, why would you want one now? Ya'ni, it's quite abstract—you have your land, your livelihood, and your religion. So the question—how to get these people involved—we show them, there is a threat to your land, you deserve to be a citizen, you deserve rights. This is what we have tried. But now what Qassam is doing, appealing directly to their *faith* . . ."

They heard the front door. Then, the voice of Midhat's youngest daughter:

"Ahlen!"

"Hi baba," said Midhat, leaning back and placing his hands on his chest.

"Stop it. I said stop it."

"What's going on?" said Midhat.

Nuzha poked her head through the door. "They're fine, just squabbling. Good evening, oh Hani keefak, I didn't see you, shu akhbarak." She grinned with her head to the side. She was out of breath. "Where's Sahar?"

"Salon," Midhat replied. "Hi baba—oh but what's happened to your shirt?"

Khaled had appeared under Nuzha's arm, with a face of thunder.

"Ghada put dirt on me."

Midhat glanced at Hani, and then back at his son. "Yalla, wash it quickly before your mother sees."

"I'll do it," said Nuzha.

The telephone rang in the salon. Midhat heaved to his feet and nudged Khaled aside. Fatima looked up from the sofa as he walked in.

"The children are here?"

He nodded and reached for the receiver. This was a gesture he loved to make, the one strong hand stretching out to the instrument clearing its brassy throat. But the instant the disc met his ear this pleasure was sapped by an odd, arak-infused sadness, a passing vision of a man proud of his telephone.

"This is the operator. Eli Kahen is calling for Midhat Kamal."

"Midhat Kamal with you."

The line crackled.

"Midhat!"

"With you."

"Midhat there's been a fire!"

"What?"

"A fire! Fire in the shop! Someone set fire to the shop!"

"No."

"Yes!"

"I'm coming now."

The mouthpiece rattled on the hook.

"What's happened?" said Fatima.

"Baba tell him to stop it," shrieked Ghada. She ran into the room. "Baba!"

"NOT NOW," boomed Midhat.

Ghada flinched by the doorway.

"What's happened?" said Fatima, getting to her feet.

"*Nothing*," said Midhat. "There's just a problem at the shop."

Hani drove. The sky hung like a black liquid on the point of bursting. Already Midhat was imagining Fatima's reaction when he told her. Her shame, always her shame. For himself, failure did not mortify him the way it once had; he had some sense now that the broken edges were part of the whole, and the future narrowed to a point. If there was only one outcome, what was the point of being afraid? But Fatima—she was balanced so precariously between her notions of what was done and not done, of who had seen and not seen, that such a disaster would drive her to the floor in a rage. Two roads from the shop, a burning smell reached the passenger seat. Was that smoke, floating in the dark above the rooftops?

"No no no no." He clasped his sweating hands together. "No no no no."

They turned the corner on a crowd of people. The blaze appeared to be quenched. British police uniforms; dismounted horses; two Model T Ford Tenders parked at angles with spent hosepipes unfurled. Hani pulled up and Midhat clambered out, peering through the foggy darkness. A terrible, acrid smell hit him, at once sweet and sour, and as he walked down the incline, scraps of burnt matter flew erratically through the air around him like black butterflies. Someone called his name. Eli ran forward, the thinness of his legs exposed as the wind drew his trousers back. His hands were black, and Midhat saw he had been weeping.

The building looked blinded. The window glass was broken, the stonework charred with vast upward streaks. A sedate plume of smoke billowed up, unfurling into a shapeless fog and smothering the stars. A fireman waited

for them to unbolt the warm metal safety door and then led the way into
the interior. It was hard to see, the beam of the fireman's wind-up electric
torch kept catching on swirls of grey. The room smelled, peculiarly, of old
meat. The boxes at the top of the stairs appeared untouched, the char reaching only partway up the banister. But as they entered Butrus's room, the
stench doubled with a sourness of destroyed fabric. A policeman pointed
at the table, collapsed into a pile of cinders, and said: this was where the
fire started. Then he pointed at the back window through which they had
forced the hose: a thick shaft of black soot covered the gap between the
top ledge and the ceiling. Eli gripped Midhat's upper arm.

"Everything will smell so terrible."

Midhat saw Hani had followed them in, and avoided his gaze. Cinders
disintegrated under their feet as they walked out again. On the street, the
crowd had dispersed.

"And the other buildings weren't affected?" said Midhat, taking a step
towards the sports equipment shop.

"No, and the bank is fine too," said Eli. He lowered his voice. "That
lamp. I knew something like this would happen."

"Does Butrus know?"

"He doesn't have a telephone, I called his mother. Go home and sleep
now, Abu Taher. We'll deal with it in the morning."

"I'll be here at daybreak."

"Oh no, *you* won't." Eli turned to face him. "You will look in your house
for that thing I told you about."

"Let's go home," said Hani. "Yalla habibi. Imshi." As they opened the
car doors, he said: "I am so sorry, I can't tell you. This is terrible. If there
is anything I can do—or even if you just want us to go, if you need time
on your own—"

"No, absolutely not," said Midhat. He managed to smile. "It's a shock,
I'm sorry. You mustn't leave. *I'm* the one who should be sorry. This is not
what you expected after a long journey."

"Khalas, I'll do anything to help. I'm in Jenin tomorrow in the morning,
but if there's anything I can do when I come back . . ."

There was a clean feeling in the air when they arrived at the house, and the car doors made a clapping sound in the darkness. The house was quiet, and as Midhat descended the steps to his bedroom, sprung with nerves, he heard his wife moving inside. A fire, and the evil eye: hazard and scandal, two things that would set Fatima alight.

3

That their life was not more illustrious was clearly a source of pain for Fatima. That she was married to the co-owner of a shop, and not someone of high rank. In the early years they had rehearsed the myth of their romance, how Midhat proposed once, twice, and the third time she had chosen him. This story was the bedrock of all that came after, all the things they had imagined about each other from afar—most of which had transpired either not to be true or to be complicated by other factors, so that the foundation tilted and required extra work to balance. Fatima no longer liked to go over those early days. Apparently it tormented her to recall the time before her future was foreclosed. What was it she had wanted from her marriage, exactly? In what exactly had Midhat failed? To be rich? To take her abroad? To be, simply, different?

The first crack came with the news that the Kamal business was written in Layla's name. At first, Fatima did not seem to understand what it meant. But as the years went on and she watched Midhat struggle to build something from nothing, she exaggerated his achievements among her friends, and opened the gap between her wish and the reality, a gap in which a violent disappointment resided. At the same time, he was certain her fibs boosted the popularity of Nouveautés Ghada among the Nabulsiyyat, and for that he was grateful. Women admired Fatima. Unlike Midhat, they fell for, and wished to emulate, her attitude of ornamental boredom. If Fatima told a few choice persons that the Cairene suits her husband sold were the height of fashion, then they quickly became so.

That night Midhat did not tell Fatima that someone may have put the evil eye on him: the fire was quite enough news for one evening. He downplayed it as they undressed for bed, he said it was small, he ascribed his involuntary sighs to Eli's overreaction, he said these Samaritans, they are always hosting huge funerals for tiny animals. There was nothing destroyed that could not be replaced.

He woke in the morning full of dread. Hani left for Jenin, and when Midhat returned from taking the girls to school he found a note in the hall explaining that Fatima and Sahar had gone to a friend's house. When he telephoned Eli, Eli's wife picked up: her husband was taking care of the wreckage, she said, but had left a message: begin with the doorways. After that, look between the roots of trees, near beds, and beneath loose floorboards or stones. Also, although the clients who paid for Samaritan magic were advised against using storage spaces, he must inspect them anyway, because if the client had panicked they may have hidden something quickly in a cupboard.

Their house had eight doorways. He found no loose stones or any cracks in the plaster. He could see nothing hidden above or below the thresholds. He recalled one of the paving blocks at the back door had been unstable for years, but kneeling before it with a kitchen knife he found the cement would not give, and after a while he decided it was pointless.

Getting down to his knees, holding the rails of each bed to peer underneath, he soon wished he had a leaner companion to help him. He should have gone to the shop and insisted that Eli join and advise. Apart from anything else, if there had been someone to witness this he might have found it in himself to laugh.

Ten years after the opening of Nouveautés Ghada, Midhat had received a letter from his half-brother Musbah. They had not spoken since their father's funeral, and the voice of this letter was the voice of a grown man, with a grown man's sense of guilt. He was writing to explain, belatedly, that at the time of his death their father had been very much in debt.

Midhat was reading the letter in the salon, and at this point steadied himself against the wall by the door. Musbah went on to describe how Haj Taher had paid a large sum of money to bail a friend out of prison in Cairo, and died before he could be reimbursed. He and his mother had spent much energy and time trying to extract a reimbursement from this man, but owing to a variety of legal perversities their endeavour was to no avail; the family business was depleted in value, and they had moved out of Abbassia into a smaller house in a cheaper neighbourhood.

The letter did not end there. Guessing perhaps that Midhat's sense of injustice was acute and enduring, Musbah seemed to find this present misfortune an occasion for further reflection upon their circumstances. Even before his eye travelled down the page Midhat saw the direction this was going. He shut the door before sitting in the chair by the telephone. A fire was dying in the brazier, and the smell of Fatima's cooking wafted in through the cracks in the doorframe.

> Our father was proud of you. He said this more than once to me, and I have to tell you he often said it in front of my mother and she was not always pleased. He was proud of your education, he was proud that you were trained as a doctor, and he was proud that you were well esteemed by your peers. For this reason I believe, and in fact I have to say that I know, that he felt you were capable of standing on your own, now that you were equipped with your fine education and your excellent engagement and for these reasons you did not require the support my mother did. My mother was burdened with five young children. I am sorry that the inheritance was not more equal, but given how little money there was left I can also understand why he decided that she needed what stability the business might still be able to provide, in our diminished circumstances.

It was a groping kind of apology; part excuse, part defence. Unclear also was how much of this explanation of their father's actions was being expressed with authority and how much was speculation. Midhat looked at the phrasing of the statements about their father's pride, his belief that Midhat was "capable." It was impossible to divine the degree of certainty from the syntax.

He folded the letter three times, scoring it with his fingernails. Why even revisit these old injuries? Death had long solidified his father's command; after that, nothing else would ever be known for certain. That he had acted as Musbah claimed seemed plausible, and might mitigate the blackness of his cruelty. But no explanation, however convincing, could entirely close the wound that, unvisited, remained untended, and lay as one of several open sores in the back of his mind. Any pleasure at his father's pride was swamped too fast by sadness, and historic shame at the unchallenged fiction, propagated by Teta, that Midhat was trained as a doctor. And shame always summoned anger, and he was done with anger. He folded the letter once more and tossed it onto the fire. The coals ate the paper and it curled directly into a cinder.

Cold comfort, indeed, that his father was proud. Fatima was calling for dinner, her shout echoed in the corridor. He waited for the pain to pass, but it was severe, and he pushed his fist against his forehead. Yet again his time in France had determined what came after. How perfect, that his father should have thought that period had endowed his son with strength.

He never spoke of Musbah's letter to anyone. But as the months accumulated, he began to wonder whether his father was not entirely wrong. Having stood alone perhaps he was indeed better off than his half-brothers and -sisters. After living abroad, unprotected, acquainted early with the frailty of life and its relations, he might be more equipped than they to face catastrophe when it came.

After no luck with the cabinets, Midhat approached the tree in the garden. Lacking a spade he applied a dinner spoon to the soil around the roots. He sweated; beneath his shirt the heat was rising on his chest. He found an old newspaper to kneel on and scrabbled with his hands. The previous morning's mist had returned with less force, and as the sun squeezed through the clouds, baking the back of his neck like a fever, the chickens in the coop at the bottom of the terrace burst into a clamour. He sat back on one foot in a crouch, wiping his face with the heel of his palm. The cement roof of the coop was visible from here. As the disturbed birds settled down, it occurred to him their lodging might be a perfect place to hide a curse. So near to the gate—someone could easily climb over unseen and bury something amid the hay.

The smell of chicken faeces was always a surprise. Midhat slipped through the crack in the wire door with his neckerchief pulled over his mouth and nose, and the birds crowded on one side, yapping and jerking and treading absurdly in the fashion he adored.

"Yalla, ya shabab, yalla," he said. "Tell me, yalla, where did he put it?"

The shelves where they roosted dripped with hay, empty of eggs. One bold chicken came to investigate his foot, snatching her head in different directions and peering from the side. Midhat kicked the tray of seed with his toe.

"Abu Taher," came Fatima's voice. "What are you doing?"

He turned. Fatima and Sahar were standing by the lower gate, squinting at him from beneath their scarves.

"Are you collecting eggs?" said Sahar.

Fatima's face was white.

"Habibti," said Midhat, lifting his trouser legs by the knee to climb out. He rubbed his grimed fingers together, shifted a lock of hair off his face with a bent wrist. His wife was trying to control her breathing. He saw a choice: either to weather her fury, or to tell her the truth, and by appealing to her superstition gamble that he could divert her rage into needy fear. Telling the truth seemed kinder, to both of them. "I have to talk to you," he said.

Sahar took the cue. The gate squeaked; she mounted the steps to the house. Fatima's ears drew back and her forehead tightened, as though she were ready to charge or back away. There was no time to gauge whether she would in fact take his part or blame him, but he had begun now, and must continue.

"Eli told me there was a curse," he whispered. "Someone put the evil eye on me. On us."

Her eyes ran very fast over his face. Her breathing shallowed, and he knew he had succeeded.

"Are you sure it's this house?"

"What do you mean?"

"When was the curse made? If it was a long time ago it could be in your old house."

"Ah yes. Yes, you might be right." He opened the wire door, as the chickens crooned and nodded forward. "Yes, habibti that's an excellent thought. He did say it was a long time ago."

"Excellent?" said Fatima. "No. No. This is not excellent."

She winced, and her eyes darted to the terrace, as if she had just seen something move.

The old house now belonged to his cousin Wasfi. Um Taher still lived downstairs with Um and Abu Jamil and Jamil, and collectively they had decided to sell the upper part to a family member: choose the neighbour before the house, as it was often said. Um Mahmoud was working there again, employed by Wasfi and his wife. Despite her age Um Mahmoud had remained agile, and cuddled Midhat each time she saw him. The house thus occupied, when Midhat visited one he visited all, and although he now tiptoed to Wasfi's front door, hoping to go unnoticed, someone soon shouted out to him from a lower window.

"Khalto!"

Um Jamil was waving enthusiastically from behind a vase of flowers.

"Oh hello, Khalto," said Midhat. "This is a nice tree over here." He pointed vaguely, then reversed his steps to the downstairs door.

"Hi teta," called his grandmother.

Teta was draped over the sofa beneath a quantity of embroidered fabric, and on the seat beside her lay a jumble of coloured spools stabbed with needles. An uproar of pans and boiling water issued from the kitchen; above them, Um Jamil called:

"We heard about the fire!"

"Yes what happened?" said Um Taher. "Sit down."

"Oh, dear." Midhat sighed into an armchair and set his tarbush on the table.

"Well?"

"We don't know what happened, Teta."

"Is it bad?"

"No, it's not bad. Eli is sorting it. It's just an accident. With the lamps, you know."

"Ya Allah," said Um Jamil, gliding in with hot coffee on a tray. "It would be better if we just got the electricity."

Um Taher sucked her teeth. "Ta'awun," she said to her stitches, pulling the needle like a violin bow and rotating the fabric. *Cooperation*: it was now one of those words even ladies in their eighties could recite with an air of righteousness.

"Jamil is at a meeting," said Um Jamil to Midhat.

"I see."

"Something, you know, nationalist. Something about a strike?"

She cocked her head hopefully. She still reported Jamil's activities to Midhat, apparently in the hope that he might have some other information to contribute. She also often expressed her worry that Jamil showed no interest in getting married. Sometimes she said, "People don't marry so much nowadays," but in a voice that lacked conviction, her eyes lingering on Midhat for a confirmation or a denial. At times he felt sympathy; he saw the struggle to understand her son's behaviour from the limited facts she could accrue in her living room. But even Midhat's strongest sympathies could be tested by overuse.

"Mashi." He smiled, and was saved from spouting an inanity by Teta, who said suddenly:

"Mashallah you look like your father."

"Do I? Oh, Teta."

"Usually you look like your mother, but today you look like Taher. Allah yirhamo. It's your face. You have a bigger face now."

"Thank you. How is your health?"

"I'm always dying. Will you pass the sugar. I have pain in my lung, and in my bladder, thank you, but that's life. Fatima didn't want to come?"

"She is at home, we have guests. Hani and Sahar."

"Hani! How is Hani? Habibi Hani. I like him."

"He is well, he is well. Busy, busy."

"Busy." Um Taher sucked her teeth. "Everyone is busy."

"Is Wasfi at home?"

"Oh Wasfi, he is the worst," said Um Taher. "He barely comes to see us. Does he khalti?"

Um Jamil grimaced blandly and shook her head, sipping her coffee as she eyed a crack in the wall.

Neither Wasfi nor his wife was at home, but their front door was unlocked. Much of the furniture from Midhat's childhood had remained, and the changes imposed by Wasfi and his wife were mostly imperceptible— bar the elaborate porcelain ornaments on the walls about which Teta still complained, because the blue and white did not go well with the Damascene chairs. Midhat always felt he was trespassing, especially when peering into his own childhood bedroom—into which a second bed had been squeezed for Wasfi's younger son—in part because of all the known objects. They no longer held any magic from the past. They only made him feel his age, his distance from the time when they were familiar.

He ran his fingers over the plaster of the kitchen doorway. He stared down at the slabs on the threshold, and poked the edges with his toe. He entered his old room. Wasfi's boys were tidy, and nothing lay under their beds except their shoes. The cupboards held only clothes, spare sheets, and blankets.

He stepped into his father's bedroom, which Wasfi now shared with his wife. It amazed Midhat that they still slept on the same European-style bedstead that Layla had brought from Cairo, back before the roads were even paved, before the trains ran direct. He glanced at the floor, the walls. He opened the cupboard and felt around among the clothes as quickly as possible, then, finding nothing, pushed the cupboard doors closed to enter his father's study.

This room had changed even less than the others. The same desk stood before the window; the same chair. The same bookshelf, though the books it held were different. An old copy of Montesquieu's *De l'Esprit des Lois* lay on top of the others, as though studied recently and carelessly returned. It was a dun-coloured volume with vertebral ridges above and below the title. He tipped it from the shelf, and let it fall open in his hand.

> The motion of the people is always either too remiss or too violent. Some-
> times with a hundred thousand arms they overturn all before them; and
> sometimes with a hundred thousand feet they creep like insects.

His brain moved stiffly through the words. He had not read French
in years. His bookshelves at home were full of French books, but he had
stopped opening them because it tired him to push uphill through their
pages.

A few years ago, he tried to speak French to one of the Catholic Sisters
of St. Joseph. The "Ebal Girls," as some people still called them, had long
before relinquished the management of the municipal hospital, and handed
it over to a few local Western-educated doctors and nurses they themselves
had trained. But with an affection for the building and its regulars the Ebal
Girls still made visits now and then, imparting odds and ends of obsolete
advice. His grandmother, who for all her initial mistrust had come to adore
the hospital, visited for a checkup at least once a week. Occasionally he
accompanied her, and on one of these occasions had attempted to address
an emaciated elderly nun who was bedridden with illness. Her name was
Sister Louise. Beyond "Bon soir," however, Midhat found he could not
say anything. The words were like dry objects in his mouth that he could
not chew. Teta's embarrassment made him feel even worse—and when he
returned home he reached for the old poets he used to like. Fatima said she
found him asleep in his chair half an hour later, glasses on his head and the
pages of the book squashed on his chest.

He forced his way through the paragraph of Montesquieu. He was
shifting heavy sand, trying to uncover something hard beneath. He felt the
pieces of his mind like the wheels of a clock running too slow.

The daylight was full now. Glancing up he saw rays stretching indoors;
and yet it was cold, his shoulders were hunched, he was holding the book up
to his face. A low sun shone in through the window at a blinding angle and
lit his fingers so they glowed red. All along its path dust sparkled, washed
around in the air's current. A sharp beam outlined the shadows on the floor,
and he caught sight of a tiled corner. An object used to stand there. A chest
of drawers, perhaps; or a shelf, or a chair. How odd, you could know a room

for years, be familiar with its contents, but when something was removed, you could not for your own life recall what it was. And there, that tile where whatever-it-was used to stand was sharpened by the light. An outline of black. He set Montesquieu aside and, crouching in the corner, noted with his fingers that it wobbled. He needed a blade.

The kitchen was the same; the cutlery in the drawer was different. He selected a knife with a bone handle, and kneeling once more in the study, slid the knife's rounded end into the side of the tile. It yielded with a scraping sound. The fingers of his left hand grabbed the edge: it was heavy, he felt the blade suffering and bending under the weight. The tile was deeper than it looked, and when he managed at last to draw it upward, a small puff of dirt and crumbled cement flakes flashed in the air. He put his hand into the hole, felt the edges of something smaller and lighter than the stone, and drew up a wooden cigar box.

He wiped off the dust. The broken halves of two grey-green labels lay across the opened edge. The coloured paper around the perimeter was tattered. The lid opened easily, and the box exuded a strong smell of tobacco, sharp and sweet, full of cedar. He smelled his father. He felt his father's beard scratching his cheek.

Inside the box lay several objects. He wiped his fingers on his trouser legs to touch them: two bronze figurines, Grecian women, with a pale green tarnish caught in the folds of their hammered robes and obscuring their faces. Beside them, a twisted length of fabric. He unravelled it: it was soft and cream-coloured. There were no marks upon it and the edges were not hemmed. A rag for polishing the figurines? A tiny cardboard box, inside it a ring, for a woman—a silver ring with an engraving. He held it between his thumb and forefinger and felt genuinely shocked. Could these trinkets belong to Wasfi? But he was sure, sure by the smell, that they were his father's. Then whose was this ring? His mother's? He was perplexed. Without his father these objects had no meanings, their threads had all been cut. But already in the light of them, that man named Haj Taher Kamal was changing shape; the side of him that lay in shadow loomed larger in the darkness. Never would his father have struck him as superstitious; on the contrary, he was highly rational, he had turned the business he inherited

into a lucrative enterprise, observed jealously by many ungenerous neighbours. But this hoarding and hiding—this was the behaviour of a suspicious person. A silver ring in a cigar box hidden under a stone? There was
no jewel, the item was not valuable enough to warrant concealment. And
what else was there—he put his hand in. A series of documents. A thin
and worn-out leather strap, punctured with holes for buckling. The paint
on the leather was cracked and disintegrating; it left a brownish dust on
his fingers. He turned to the documents. The first envelope contained a
tintype of a house he did not know. He tilted it in the light, and the metal
shone. It was not a Nabulsi house. The entrance was of striped stone, the
windows were barred. There were no people in the picture. He turned to
the second envelope. It was lilac-coloured. Written upon it were the words:

Monsieur Midhat Kamal
Maison de Famille Kamal
Naplouse
Palestine

He stared at the handwriting. In a practised motion, he pressed the
edges together to open the top, and pulled out the letter. His hands started
to shake. Unlike Montesquieu's, the words entered his head with no difficulty at all.

7 October 1919

Dear Midhat,

  It has now been four years since you left us in Montpellier. Four
years!—I cannot believe it even as I write it. I find myself thinking about
you often. Thank you for your letter. To tell the truth it causes me some
distress to discover that you were in Paris—the thought that we might have
spoken before now. You may also wonder why I have not tried to write to
you—the truth is that for a long time I was angry and in pain. And I suppose
that most of all I was confused. I am afraid this might not reach you before
you leave, so I am sending it to Nablus—which means you are reading this
at your home. I hope the journey was safe and pleasant.

Oh—I have been wanting to write to you for so long—and now I am here at last with a pen I don't know what to write!—All the things I had thought to say are suddenly difficult to put into words.

When you left, the warmth of the house followed after you. I think we had not noticed how much delight and joy were supplied by your presence. I wish I had behaved differently—if we could recover ground that has already been lost. But you are right, it is senseless to try. I wish only that what has happened might not be final.

I feel as though I am writing into space—it is strange not knowing how you will feel when you read this. I wish I could see your face. Oh, Midhat. Sometimes I think I feel you in my breath. This is difficult to bear.

The long years of this war have been a strain on all of us, and now they are lifted I want to ask of you one last thing: will you come back? I know you have recently arrived so I wouldn't expect you immediately, and I don't want to beg, I want only to tell you how much I long for your company. I have wronged you—please know that the error was not only yours—and I hope, and wish, that we might remake some of what was broken during that incident over dinner. I cannot tell you how mortified I was to wake and find you had gone. I cannot tell you—I am still so filled with remorse, and pain, even four years on. At first I don't think I knew it was remorse, I distracted myself, I went to join Marian at Divonne-les-Bains. I was useless as a nurse, truly, but they needed hands even to help with the cleaning, and though there wasn't much time with so many wounded coming in, I liked to read to them in the evenings, especially the ones who were certain to die.

Divonne was not a happy place, but I had not been in the company of so many people for a long time and that was a distraction. I am glad also for Marian's sake that she did not have to witness this devastation on her own. And there was a garden, a little way from the hospital, which was usually empty, and where I would feel peaceful, and sit very still and think of you. When I left, when the war ended, which had been a cloud on everyone's vision, all I know is it was suddenly quite obvious to me what I had done.

I do not know what exactly happened between Sylvain and my mother, but my understanding is that she was probably in love with him. I do not think he behaved dishonourably; in fact, it was he who severed the connection. He was like an older brother to her, I think, and he certainly cared about her. I only know that when my grandfather asked if he would marry her, he declined. That is all I know. That is probably all I will ever know; Sylvain is difficult, and as he gets older he gets more difficult, and the few times I have tried to ask him, he was unkind to me. I sensed some soreness there, which it was not my right to touch. And besides, these days he is spending much more time in Paris, so we hardly see him.

I'm sorry for drawing you into this story of my mother, and for making you think I wanted you to solve it. Really I just wanted comfort, and someone to talk about it with. It was an unhealthy obsession. That awful night, before you left, I did not defend you—and I am so sorry. The only excuse I can suggest is that I was shocked and not strong enough to handle my own mind, and morals, and desires. In that moment it was my loyalty to my family—to my father—for it is, in the end, only him and me together, I have no other family—that dictated my actions in the face of a rupture. It was instinctive, though on reflection I know I was in the wrong. As for my mother—I feel very strongly now that it is beyond time to close off the past, and to stop trying to find out why she died. My obsession with her has prevented me long enough from fully experiencing the present time. I feel my mind has snagged on that mystery, as on a broken hook, and it has been and will be hard to tear it off without suffering—but I must do so or I will never go anywhere. I refuse to hang there forever. How many of the things I ascribed to her are really true about myself—not wanting to live, making herself sick so she would not have to step out into the world. I believe this could just as easily be said of me—because above all I feel it has prevented me from appreciating you, dear Midhat. But how many times shall I say "I feel" in this letter! I am not a good writer of letters—.

It is winter here, and the pond has frozen over. Montpellier is quiet; I don't know if we shall have any more parties. We tuned the piano yesterday, and I have been practising. I miss you very much. Come back, please.

Yours ever,

J.

As he read, Midhat was not aware of being in any pain at all. Nearing the final page, however, and sensing the moment when he would have to come back into the room, he immediately turned to the first sheet and started to read it through again. Then he read it a third time, and then a fourth, until the words were like an incantation and he lost count.

He dropped out of the present time. Jeannette was beside him, speaking. It was a miracle. This piece of paper had transferred him absolutely to that other time and place. He was with Jeannette in the garden, by the pond; he was walking down a street in Montpellier, he was sitting in a lecture hall, sure of returning to her in the evening, he was waking before dawn and finding her in the corridor. He heard her breath in his ear.

There was a noise. His trance snapped open, and he put the letter on the floor.

"Midhat? Are you all right?"

A man was standing over him, blocking the light.

"What's wrong with you? What's wrong with him?"

Jamil's face, darkened by the sun. He looked afraid, or angry.

"Midhat?"

Midhat looked around. He was in his father's room. It was bright. He looked between Jamil's legs at the desk and the window, he saw their undersides, the sky from low down, and the room smacked him in the face. The cruel transparency of the present time, this searing whiteness. A section of his brain, suppressed for too long, shot through with spasms of pain. He moaned. He felt the heat of Jamil's body crouching near him, and his cousin's face came properly into view.

"Why did he keep it?"

"Keep what, Midhat?"

"Why did he keep it?"

"Midhat?"

A second person had arrived. He could see legs approaching.

"What's he doing?"

What superstition made his father keep it? Midhat looked at Jamil's face in wonder. Had his father thought it was a Samaritan thing? One of those things they made and dyed a fake colour—did he think it was an amulet because it was in another language? He put his hands on the floor.

"It's not real!"

"What's not real?"

The moan was coming out of his mouth. "Stop touching me."

"What's not real, Midhat?"

Had he thought it held some power beyond him, simply because he could not read it? Yes. He could see why his father might have thought that. Even he could see that.

"Midhat, habibi, you have to get up."

Here was something beyond nature. He clutched his stomach. Hanging on the wall was a large translucent object, like a pool of water suspended sideways. His heart began to thump.

"Midhat, can you hear me?"

Hani was beside him. His eyes were full of love and concern. Oh Hani, he wanted to say. He could not say it. The tears streamed down his face.

"Can you pick him up?"

"Midhat, you have to help us. Can you take his hand?"

"I need to go back, I have to go back. Don't stop me."

"Go back where, habibi?" said Hani gently. "I'm not stopping you. Can you stand up? Take his arm—gently."

Just then, as they brought him to his feet, a high ringing sound erupted. It was like a sharp blade of silver being inserted into his eardrum. Midhat clutched his ears and moaned. It was pretending to be benign, it pretended to be beautiful. But it was pain, that high ringing sound was pain. It was entering his ears like a virus. It was interfering in there, it was doing things it shouldn't. Someone needed to take things in hand and put an end to that sound.

"Cut it off!" he said, as they led him from the room.

Time moved slowly in the corridor. He was aware of being led, he felt the ground hitting his feet. But now there was a little tear in the fabric and he was peering through. Someone was forcing him to peer through it. He thrust his arm out, he felt a distant throbbing in his leg.

"Midhat, Midhat, will you sit in there? It's Hani. Will you sit down?"

"Hani!" said Midhat. "You are my friend."

"Yes! Yes I am here," said Hani. "How are you feeling? Are you . . ."

"Je suis complètement lucide. Une lucidité absolute. Qu'est-ce que c'est, qu'est-ce que c'est cette folie?"

As though he had just caught sight of himself, he collapsed back into the leather seat, and began to laugh.

4

Fatima saw the aeroplane on the way to her parents' house. It was flying beyond Mount Ebal, an insect with a marking on its tail, the propeller at its nose audible even from this distance. It moved up and down slightly, as if on a gentle wind, and then, progressing forward, circled and tipped sideways, exposing its marvellous wingspan.

Today was Wednesday. Usually she would visit her parents on Fridays. From the doorstep she saw exasperation pass over her mother's face.

"We have guests," said Widad, stepping back to let her in.

"Who?"

"Amo Hassan. And the French priest."

"What French priest?" said Fatima.

"Friend of your father's. Yalla we're having coffee."

"Could we speak alone?" said Fatima, but her mother's back was already turned, ascending the stairs.

On the landing, Widad pushed the door open so that one muffled voice became clear: her father's.

"This is my understanding, and I honestly believe . . ."

There was no formal recognition of the two women as they entered the room, but Haj Hassan, wearing a dark maroon tarbush, acknowledged his niece with a slight duck of his head, and the French priest tipped his glance to her very quickly before adding to something her father had said. Widad offered Fatima the remaining chair and sat on a footstool. Fatima looked curiously at the Frenchman. His black robe had a dirty hem, and his beard, entirely white, was stiff like the bristles of a brush, and his brow wiry and expansive. The sky was grey in the windows, though outside it was blue; on the table lay a tray of biscuits and coffee, and on the stool beside Haj Nimr a large unbound book with uncut pages.

"Some of the women are going to take food and bullets," said Widad.

"Who are?" said Nimr.

Widad shut her eyes.

"I hope that you, at least, are not," he said.

"Take bullets where?" said Fatima. A glance passed between Hassan and Nimr, and she was swift to add, in a languid tone that belied her intention: "I saw the aeroplane, outside."

The effect was achieved. Hassan turned to look at her. "You could see it?"

"Yes, it was flying over that way."

"Fa . . . they killed one of them, you know." He turned back. "One of the British."

"And where are they now?"

"Hiding," said her mother.

"The point I wanted to make," said Nimr, with the tone of one who has suffered a long interruption, "is that one cannot be too stringent about these things."

"What things?" said Hassan.

"Just as it is better to decentralise a government," said Nimr, "so it is better to decentralise the application of religious laws, according to the needs of the civil society."

"We have literally been having this conversation for years," said Hassan, reaching for a biscuit.

Fatima appealed to her mother with her eyes. Widad refused to look at her, and lifted her chin.

"When you exist *within* the state, civil laws, religious laws, they are like laws of nature," said her father.

He was now addressing only the French priest, who appeared to be the sole person listening. Hassan was brushing crumbs off his chest, oblivious to the piece of stewed fig lodged on his chin.

"Only when we step beyond and observe the edges, can we see they are buildings made by men, and they do not extend to infinity."

"B-buildings!" Hassan sputtered, "made by, by men!" He looked to the French priest to share his incredulity—but the priest had eyes only for Nimr.

"The fellahin have this love," Nimr went on, "of local saints and walis and leaders that are not, ya'ni, halal. But this is how laws stretch and change shape at the edges of the Islamic world."

Fatima stopped longing for the conversation to end. She had collected the necessary pieces, and now she dived in headfirst. "Baba, Haifa is not the edge of the Islamic world," she said. "And the followers of Qassam are not only fellahin."

Her father studied her. Over the years, Fatima had earned the right to hold opinions that differed from his. She had become renowned for her reason, and her status during such discussions approximated that of a widow, who had earned her authority by age and the death of others. Except that no one had died, and Fatima was only thirty-two. Nuzha, by contrast, was never present during conversations like these and presumably would not know what to say if she was. All the same it was an expression of her youth that Fatima occasionally went too far. To contradict her father outright, and in company, even if that company consisted only of a relative and a holy man. She caught her breath, unsure if she should feel encouraged by the fact that the Frenchman beside her was nodding vigorously.

"She is correct," pronounced the French priest. He had a heavy accent. "In truth, I was in Haifa only last week, and I found that most people who are interested in the sermons of Qassam are workers. Railway workers, harbour workers, postal workers. It is only recent, this support among the villages."

Haj Hassan squinted at the priest's beard, and his own jaw wobbled in anticipation of speech. "I can assure you, Abuna Antoine." He raised a hand. "That these workers were originally fellahin. Fa, they are villagers who moved to Haifa when they lost their land. Hata I don't know if worker is the right word, fa, most of them are unemployed. Mish heyk?"

The Frenchman's eyes rose to the ceiling as he digested this remark.

"What I mean, baba," said Haj Nimr to Fatima, smoothing with his tone the corner of her last remark, "is that they like a local leader. This is the fellahi mentality. They like a sheikh, a wali. Hala' the two are combining fi Qassam, religious and political. This was not the way before."

"You're not going to like me saying this," said the Frenchman. On cue, Haj Hassan frowned. "But there are some studies on this at my school."

As though he had not heard, Nimr said brightly: "You will stay with the Ebal Girls in Nablus?"

"Yes." The Frenchman smiled. "But I'm not sure they are girls any longer."

Fatima saw a twitch pass through her father's forehead.

"Khalas Fatima." Her mother was on her feet, making a big gesture with her hand, as though to a recalcitrant animal. "Ta'ali, we'll make the tea."

Fatima rose. To conceal her irritation at being taken away, she adopted a blank expression, just as she had done when she arrived at the front door twenty minutes ago, concealing her distress.

After her morning with Sahar, Fatima had been unable to return home alone, so frightened was she of the building that might or might not have the evil eye upon it. She was also smarting from the incident in the garden, that view of her husband in the chicken coop with his earth-stained hands, Sahar a witness over her shoulder. Envy jostled shoulders with the evil eye, and yet Fatima coveted envy, and dreaded the loss of it. And who would envy the picture of her marriage that Sahar had seen? When Sahar left for Jenin, Fatima sought shelter in her parents' house.

She often came here when she felt perturbed, even though the house never turned out to be the shelter she needed. Of course it was unreasonable to expect the place to remain unchanged after she married, or somehow to revert to its old nature, yet she always hoped against the evidence of her last visit there that she might step through the doorway and find the mood of the building, the behaviour of its inhabitants, the colour of the ornaments, exactly as they were when she was seventeen. She yearned for the place where her status was secure, and where, most importantly, she was not responsible for maintaining it. Until she married, Fatima had been a prize, famous for being not yet won. Marriage meant someone had named her price. It did not matter that she herself chose her mate: in the eyes of Nablus she was appraised and evaluated, stripped of the precious mystery of being young and undefined. This was the reality she was forced to live under. Forgetting how much as a girl she had hated feeling amorphous, she looked back at her youth and saw, with what she thought were clear eyes, that the anticipation of glory had itself been the real glory, and should have been treasured.

In such moments of distress, the changes in her parents' house impressed Fatima powerfully, but the needs of her heart always prevailed over any memory of disappointment, and she never retained the facts. Ah, now she recalled: her mother, petulant where she used to be passionate. Her father, ossified where once he was flexible. Today he was belabouring his point about Qassam through the same old contours of his rigid cosmology, ignoring those facts even Fatima was aware of. After all these years of learning, of striving for clarity, Nimr had frozen halfway up the summit, and his ideas set in stone at some stage of their development, to be applied now to everything without discretion.

Her mother sneezed as they entered the cold kitchen.

"You wanted to talk alone?"

"Yes."

"What is it then. Yalla."

"I am just worried. And I'm tired."

"What's happened?" Widad picked up a plate that was leaning on the sideboard and touched with her fingernail a fine crack in the lip.

"There was a fire in my husband's shop."

Her mother jerked up. "Mish ma'ool, a bad one?"

"He says it is a small one."

"You think someone did it."

"I don't know," said Fatima, defensive. She circled the table. "I'm just nervous, that's all."

"Don't be. Inshallah kheir."

"Yes, yes."

Widad put down the plate. "What did your husband say?"

"He said it was not a big problem," said Fatima. She hated discussing Midhat with her mother. Midhat, in the field of their relations, was Fatima's expression of free will. "I don't know, Mama. I feel . . . I don't know what."

"How are the children, then?"

"Fine, the children are fine."

"You never bring them here."

"What do you mean? I brought them last night."

"But you don't bring them with you, when you visit. You always come alone."

"Well, sometimes I need a rest, I don't see why—"

"You think there is a rest in my life?"

"*Leh* Mama, why, you are so irritable . . ."

"Excuse me Mama," came the small voice of Selma, the maid, hunching in the door to the dining room. "There is someone outside."

As Widad reached for the door handle to the hall, Selma added:

"No, sorry Mama, over here." She gestured behind her, at the window that looked onto the kitchen garden.

Widad followed her as far as the doorway, and then abruptly withdrew.

"Who is it?" said Fatima.

"I don't know."

Fatima took her place and saw the long legs of a man pacing backward and forward along the flowerbed. The legs stopped, and the man stooped down to peer in through the window.

"Jamil?" said Fatima. "That's Midhat's cousin."

Jamil jumped off the raised bed onto the ground, and waved at Fatima without smiling. He had the rangy, hollow-cheeked look of all the young radicals, with a scarf wrapped tightly around his neck.

Widad appeared in a coat, and pushing past Fatima, unbolted and opened the casement window. "Why didn't you come in the main door?" she shouted.

"No one was answering," said Jamil. "May I speak to your daughter?"

"What's happened?" said Fatima.

"I'm sorry, Madame." He addressed Fatima over her mother's shoulder. "Can we speak a moment?"

"Do you want to come inside?"

"Midhat's had an accident."

"A what?" said Fatima.

"An accident. You understand?"

"Is he alive?" said Widad.

"Yes yes, he's alive."

Fatima tried not to run. She buttoned her coat with trembling fingers as she made her way to Jamil, who had gone to the front door and was waiting on the terrace.

"Where is he?" said Fatima.

"Take it slow," said Jamil, speaking very fast. "He's at my mother's house, he's fine now, he's sleeping. We don't know what happened." They reached the lower gate and Fatima lifted the latch. "I think he hit his head. He is not . . ."

"Not what?"

"He is not . . . clear, ya'ni. He is a bit . . ." He whipped a hand in front of his face.

"What do you mean?"

"Khalas you'll see."

As they turned the corner onto the southern road to Gerizim, Fatima felt a great urge to hit Jamil.

"Can't you just tell me what happened?"

"I don't know what happened, I told you. You'll see him in a moment."

Um Jamil opened the front door. Um Taher and Hani were sitting in the salon; Um Taher was rocking backward and forward on a chair.

"He's asleep!" she cried at the sight of Fatima. "You mustn't wake him!"

"What happened to him?" said Fatima.

Hani leapt up. In the daylight his hair looked very grey, and she noticed a bruise on his cheekbone. "We found him up there," he said gently. "We found him, he was very distressed. Come."

He led her down the hall and stopped outside Um Taher's bedroom. She turned the handle. "I'll wait out here," said Hani. Fatima nodded.

The bed lay under the window on the far wall. She could see Midhat's body rising and sinking with deep, regular breaths beneath the blankets. The glossy tip of his black head was just visible at one end. She approached. He was turned so entirely towards the window that she could see only the end of his eyebrow, and the bent cavity of his nostril, and his parted lips pressed onto the pillow. The mattress sighed with her weight. She touched the hair that had fallen over the side of his face and uncovered the slit of his closed eye.

"What happened," she whispered. She put her palm on his warm head: his eyelids flickered, but otherwise he did not stir. She ran her fingers around his hairline, examining it gently, as though she might find a wound.

When she emerged, everyone in the salon turned to look at her. The men were standing, the women were sitting. She steeled herself and addressed Hani.

"How did he hurt himself?"

Hani exchanged a glance with Jamil. "We should see how he is in the morning."

"Probably the shock is a part of it," said Jamil. "The fire, and so on. We heard him upstairs, he was very upset."

"What had he found?" said Fatima. She was thinking of the evil eye.

Hani's features were suddenly disfigured by surprise. For a moment he didn't say anything. His eyes conferred with Jamil's. "I'll take her up there."

The light outside hurt her eyes. The sky was pale blue and the wind constant, so that what leaves there were left on the trees wiggled continuously. They circled the perimeter to the upper house and Wasfi answered the door.

"Marhaba Fatima. How is he?"

"Sleeping," said Hani. "I want to show her the box."

"Tfadalu," said Wasfi, and led them down the hall.

Fatima rarely came to this house. When they visited Midhat's family they went to Um Jamil's, and Wasfi, if he was home, joined them down there. Now that she knew the story of Midhat spying on her in the salon, this house held for her a particular aura associated with that incident, so that she felt sensitive to its warren-like design, and the impression that every closed door was an aperture. Wasfi led them to Haj Taher's old study and waited outside as Hani reached for something on the desk. It was a cigar box.

"I found him looking at these things." He spread his bony fingers over the top and opened the lid with his fingertips.

Several items lay inside. She shook the box a little as she poked them. Two bronze models of women. A ring. A blank rag. And an envelope. She opened the envelope. Inside was a tintype of a house.

"What are they?"

"I have no idea," said Hani.

"There was nothing else?"

"Nothing."

"Hani," said Fatima. "Did he hit you?"

Hani put his hand over the bruise on his cheek with a feminine gesture of recollection. "Yes," he said. "I don't think he meant to."

A current of shame shut Fatima's eyes. On her closed lids she saw, with the exactitude of a real memory, a vision of her poor husband, lashing out, deprived of grace.

Père Antoine left the Hammad house shortly after Haj Nimr's daughter. The aeroplane was still weaving back and forth over the mountains: the English had not found the brigands yet. Certainly they would kill them when they did, if only as a lesson to the others.

He sighed, and started walking. This visit to Haj Nimr Hammad was supposed to be a terminal milestone in his project: putting a published copy of his study of Nablus into the hands of a Nabulsi who would—or at least could—read it. During the research years, Haj Nimr had been one of his few aristocratic sources of information. As one of the hospital's founders, he was on good terms with the sisters and, unlike some, quite willing to answer their friend's questions regarding the town and its families. Although Nimr accepted the book with grace, however, Antoine detected his disinterest. It was the Nabulsi way of course, not to be direct. And since the manhunt for Qassam began only yesterday they had plenty of reason to be distracted, though that did nothing to abate the recurring sadness that nobody cared.

As the road to the bus station sloped, the plane ducked behind the buildings. It purred loudly, mingling with the din of Antoine's own body, his breath catching on the back of his throat, shooting through the piston of his nose, the tacks in his boot soles ringing out on the paving stones. He crested the hill and the noisy aircraft came again into view: a small white fleck, angles shadow-grey, beyond the sprawl of the mosque.

He was put in mind of the Graf Zeppelin, which had looked even more bizarre when it flew over Jerusalem a few years ago. Everyone at L'École Biblique turned out to watch when at the culmination of a rainstorm the gigantic machine appeared at the edge of the sky. The weather gave the whole event the appearance of a miracle: the sun's path through the thunderous firmament, the silver airship emerging from the mist and circling the old city four times, a vast tumescent pipe gliding over minarets and domes. One brother remarked that Jerusalem looked as though she was sunk beneath the sea, and this was a submarine coming to investigate the wreckage. A hundred metres above the Church of the Holy Sepulchre, the zeppelin shut off its engines and unfurled a German flag, to applause and tumult all over the Mount of Olives. How much had changed in four short years. There was no chance the British would let the German zeppelins fly over Jerusalem now, with those black hooked crosses painted on their fins.

The bus reached Jerusalem at dusk. The police station was quiet when Antoine arrived.

"Evening, father." The guard set down his newspaper. "You're here late."

The lamp on the front desk wore a fur of dust.

"I would like to hand in my report."

"Michaels is in the back office."

Antoine breathed heavily along the corridor. Now that his scholarly work on Nablus was complete, his work as an informant should also be coming to an end. He was sixty-seven, and considering retirement in Nablus. Sister Louise had died of typhoid three years ago, and he was the only one who fought to keep her body there. Nablus was her home, he urged Sister Marian: it was only right to bury her in the Catholic cemetery, here at the foot of Mount Ebal. But the sisters had been given their instructions from the family, and would not deviate, and so the body was shipped at great expense back to France. Since then, Marian had taken Louise's place as Antoine's primary contact in the Order, but of course she could never provide him with the same solace and companionship. Reflecting upon it now, Antoine considered Louise the only person he was ever truly familiar with. He may have lost the battle over her burial, but to stay in Nablus with the sisters these days was the same to him as to visit her graveside and lay flowers by her name.

Naturally, Père Lavigne would expect him to retire at the convent in Jerusalem. But Lavigne's health was deteriorating rapidly, and now that Antoine no longer had Louise, he was not sure he could bear to watch his mentor age and die also.

Michaels glanced up as he entered. His spectacles looked very small on his face. The lamp cast a sharp yellow circle on his desk.

"Father, good evening. You're here late."

"Good evening, Inspector. I have brought my report."

"Pop it over there, would you."

"I want to add something—to do with this sheikh, Qassam."

Michaels set down his pen.

"I have been visiting with a high family in Nablus today, they were discussing the sheikh and the hunt for him and his men. There was mention of women carrying weapons to the mountains."

"This is in your report?"

"No, I only heard it this afternoon."

"I see." He looked thoughtful. "And is there any more on the arms trafficking?"

"In the report. One source, a patient in the hospital, says weapons are being brought over the Jordan River. From the Bedouin tribes. I need to acquire more details."

"Try to get some dates. And times. I'll put the other agents on it as well."

Antoine had never told Sister Louise about agreeing to help the British. This was despite the fact that her very allusion to doing likewise had convinced him to. "Take it from me," she had said, "it is not worth it." It was also that allusion, however, that set in motion his withdrawal from her confidence. Her words had provoked in him a feeling of shame, which soon afterwards became intolerable. In those few seconds Louise had demonstrated the steep imbalance in their intimacy: how much he had always shared with her, and how little she with him.

Michaels was Hodges's replacement, and he began their alliance by asking for quite basic information about Nablus: local demography, economic activity, famous personalities. As the situation became more heated, Antoine supplied more targeted intelligence. But in general the Brits seemed too concerned about Communism among the Jews to pay much heed to intelligence about the Arabs. They were not at first perturbed, for instance, by Antoine's report on arms shipments from Transjordan, which he had drawn from snippets overheard at the hospital. "Just keep an eye," said Michaels. "You mean an ear," said Antoine.

Do not get involved, it is not worth it. Antoine still returned to the words, heard them again in her voice, half-murmured, like an afterthought. He often wondered what her role had been, whether for the British or the French, and what about it so enervated her that she should warn him off. For the truth was that although he considered the British a little incompetent, Antoine did not find their work a burden per se. It rather relieved him of a burden—that of observing Nablus, of witnessing the ferment of unrest and permitting its path to violence unbridled. Informing was a moral valve: he helped keep danger in check. Last month, for instance, he had reported a conversation between four upper-class Muslim ladies in which one woman suggested a secret plan was afoot. It soothed his soul that he might have played even a small role in the path of that aeroplane flying over the trees.

Fifteen years had passed since he began his monograph on Nablus. The final writing, the terminal act of composing into chapters and indices the product of ten years' notes had sent him into a rapture, a particular concentrated bliss that only heightened the loss of it, and made of his return to self a fall. Although in the end, despite Lavigne's encouragements, the study had no ostensible bearing upon the Christian faith, Antoine's analysis was nevertheless precise and thorough, and he was proud of how clearly he had portrayed the city's preservation by its two mountains, analogous to the way the desert preserved the Bedouin. His research about female oppression was also highly original, especially given the many obstacles to direct contact with Nabulsi women. His secret weapons were, of course, the hospital and his priesthood. Christian or no, everyone in this place trusted a holy man. Indeed most of his intelligence for Michaels came from the same sources.

None at L'École had remarked upon the publication, however. Returning from France with printed copies he had presented a condensed version of the monograph at the Palestine Oriental Society on a panel alongside the flora of the Galilee and the grammatical qualities of various ancient verb forms. Attendance at these meetings had shrunk; the age of observation that Père Lavigne had inaugurated was already over. What had it been? Some sense of common purpose, was it? Or was he already misremembering? There was a polite discussion in the tea break afterwards, and Lavigne, long beyond ability for any serious debate, drawn from his shell to hear his old pupil speak, smiled and kissed his cheek. That was all.

Now his gaze must turn upwards. Louise was gone; heaven was the place of honour. He had wished to remain outside of society in Palestine, and thus he had remained. Every clue, followed as though he was going to *find out*, had led, where? To a publication which very few, in all likelihood, would ever take the time to read. And yet, by God, how halcyon even the research years seemed from this distance! That Muslim town had run a plumb line through his life. He was exhausted, he needed to retire—and yet at the prospect of ending his informing also, of cutting off his final path through Palestine, a pall hung over everything and he couldn't help it, he hankered after his last illusions of duty as for a return into grace.

Candles adorned the tables in the convent dining room. Over stew and rice, a Franciscan and a Dominican were debating the unity of the Church before an audience of wide-eyed seminarians. Père Lavigne dripped brown sauce down his beard and stared glassily into the distance. After dinner, Antoine skipped Mass, and dragged his feet to the dormitory building. A messenger caught him in the shade.

Qassam dead. Please go back to Nablus. J.M.

He left early the next morning. The bus reached Nablus just after eleven o'clock, and after alighting, Antoine passed the Atwan soap factory and noted that its advertising pillars of soap had been dismantled and the storefront was padlocked. The post office was also barricaded. He crossed the rickety bridge over the railway line and in minutes was among the well-scrubbed buildings, late-flowering beds, and fruit trees of the northern quarter. This was a chic neighbourhood now, relatively unspoiled by the earthquake. Lights shone in the windows of the sisters' residence: Antoine had a sensation of returning. Jerusalem was strange, France even stranger; Nablus was his home.

Hand on the gate, he caught a spasm of voices from inside. The door opened at his first knock and Sister Marian wafted him in. Two other sisters flew like pigeons up the stairs and the icons clattered on the walls.

"What is going on?"

"Oh—Père Antoine." Marian thumbed the wimple at her temples. There was a basket at her feet, covered in a blanket.

"Sister Marian I need the—" said a younger spectacled nun with sharp, modelled features. "Oh goodness." In her arms she was carrying a cloth bandolier of bullets.

Antoine's vision sharpened. He stared.

"Father, I'll explain," said Sister Marian. "But—you must be discreet when the soldiers arrive, or we're in danger."

"Yes, of course."

"When they come," she said, directing him into the dining room, "we will all be serene."

Antoine sat at the dining table, as beside him Sister Marian pressed her hands into a prayer. He watched her murmuring lips. With a shift of horror, he realised he had made an error.

As Sister Marian had predicted, in the morning there was a hammering on their door. Seven soldiers arranged themselves along the banister.

"Might we ask a few questions?"

The nuns *were* serene. Above all, Antoine was struck by how off guard the young soldiers seemed, how unsettled and at a loss, grasping their hats beside their guns. Nestled in that request for information, he fancied he heard a yearning for comfort rather more general; comfort of the kind men usually sought in a holy woman and the folds of her habit. And in that, naturally, he recognised a spectre of his younger self. It pained him, thinking of Sister Louise, and he receded with a glow of anguish and his usual facility at disappearing into an inconspicuous corner of the dining room.

This room. It was at this table, around which the soldiers were drawing out chairs, that Antoine had confessed to Louise he was tempted to inform for the British. Why it never occurred to him, then or afterwards, that she might have already taken the opposite stance, he didn't know. But then, why had she never told him? Perhaps she knew about his decision and kept her secret accordingly—he bowed his head—yes, that did seem likely. One could not, in the end, fault her for that.

Sister Marian was pulling a sympathetic face. As capable as Sister Louise had been, Marian was, if possible, an even more perfect performer. She supplied some platitudes about the nature of the Arabs while pouring coffee into seven tiny cups.

When at last the soldiers departed, Antoine mounted the stairs without a word. Beyond his bedroom window a goatherd was coaxing a sluggish flock along the alley, and behind his closed door the sisters whispered in the hall. He wondered if he had mistaken them, if their Order was propelled by French interest after all, and intent on undermining English rule. That did not seem plausible.

He pressed his fingers against his mouth and faced the thought he had been avoiding. At root there must exist some profounder alliance between the sisters and the Arabs. Louise saw something in them he had not seen. With a cold rush he cast his eyes up at the Virgin propped above the window, cloaked in her painted rays of yellow light, and wondered whether, had he known the truth earlier, he might have felt differently about Nablus. How strange all this was! He covered his stinging face with his hands. That his opinion of an entire people could in the end be so mutable, so subject to the opinions of his peers. No, not his peers: Louise.

The funeral for Qassam was held the following day at the mosque on Haifa's docklands. Antoine and the sisters read about the thousands who trooped towards Haifa from all over the country, delaying the ceremony by over an hour.

"A sign of what is to come," said Sister Celine, squeaking against the wicker of her chair.

The French-language broadsheets were spread over the dining table. Now that he was in their confidence, the sisters held back nothing. Antoine marvelled at Sister Celine's prophesy. A sign of what is to come?

"What was he like?"

"Qassam?" said Sister Marian. "Quite intelligent. Frightening. Charismatic, obviously."

"You know," he said, "the Palestine Oriental Society have been rather foolish. I have often heard them claim the Arabs have no public opinion. They picture them as a crowd of morons ruled by their elites." He pointed at the aerial photograph. "And now look. The inert multitudes have organised of their own accord."

But his grimace belied his frame of mind. He listened with perplexed clarity to several memories of himself reciting adages that bore a painful affinity to those opinions he was now claiming to disdain. This Muslim city, "lost in the mountains." "Divided"—the remembered words moved again on his lips—"from the great movement of the world."

Sister Celine was correct. Over the course of that winter it became clear the Brits had accidentally made this Qassam into a martyr, and now their object, a population of biblical peasantry and Levantine crooks, diseased with desire for a nation, stirred uncannily into life. In January 1936, local politicians met in a Nablus soap factory to discuss a general strike. Qassam-inspired armed bands continued to roam the countryside. Attacks on Jewish civilians were followed by retaliations against Arabs. In April, the Arabs set up strike committees across the country, agreeing on a list of demands and aims—proportional representation, a stop to Jewish immigration—and embarked on a countrywide refusal to pay taxes or to trade. In the hills, violence heaved against soldiers and Jewish settlers.

The British possessed neither sufficient manpower nor adequate knowledge of the terrain. As winter turned to spring, Antoine received multiple telegrams from Michaels. "Waiting for your report. J.M." "Report to HQ. J.M." "Shall we send someone? J.M." To the fourth telegram, Antoine sent the reply:

"My apologies but I have lately become very sick and am confined to bed. I will soon go to the hospital. Yours A.K."

At least that last statement was not a lie: he set out for the hospital that afternoon. It was May, and in the silent streets, severed telegraph lines swung in the breeze. Outside the post office, sandbagged against bombs, a bloodstain coated the pavement. Around the corner a British army car lolled on its back, windows smashed, the horseshoe on the dashboard pointing its tines to the ground. A demolished house crouched between mounds of rubble, as though ready to emerge at any moment to its full stature.

He nodded at the nurses in the hospital foyer and took his old position in the corner of the veranda. His rocking chair had gone. On one of the ordinary chairs he sat facing the grove, thinking of Louise. When they laid her on the dining table in her shroud, he had spent a long time looking at her. He thought of her hands, placed over each other on her chest, the skin draped over the bones of her fingers like a thin yellow fabric.

Men's voices leaked from the hall, louder and louder, until the veranda door shook open and a nurse bolted it in place. A dozen men sloped onto the balcony. Bandaged arms, bandaged legs, plenty of crutches, one man with a head wound, another apparently without a hand. They sat noisily, chatting. One or two nodded at Antoine; he nodded gravely back. He could not recall so many patients taking the air at once before. Two chairs down from his, a man with flame-blue eyes and grey hair cracked his knuckles. "Sharp and then dull," he said. He spoke with a refined urban accent. The next man along said nothing. This one, despite the gauze around his arm and head, had the bearing of a ready fighter, and looked as though he might at any moment reach out and grip the peeling wooden rail that separated them all from the wilderness, launch himself over it as over a vaulting horse, and disappear among the bushes. Next along, an elderly white-turbaned gentleman with a chiselled nose was drinking coffee. Someone switched on a wireless. It droned, then began to speak. ". . . An attack on the road between Nablus and Tulkarem at approximately oh eight hundred hours. Two casualties have been reported . . ." An hour had passed, and a nurse knocked on the windowpanes. At the signal, the sunbathers swung upright from their stations of repose, and surrendering the blankets to their chairs, trundled indoors in single file.

The following morning, Antoine arrived to find the veranda occupied by female patients. He walked behind their chairs and stationed himself in the corner. He had not been sitting long when a whisper shot down the balcony, and propelled everyone into an animal silence. A crowd of Arab men had appeared in the grove below. They carried a motley array of weapons— full rifles, kitchen knives, some sharpened sticks. In an instant they raced up the slope and separated to scramble over the rocks. British soldiers came in pursuit, but their vehicles could not pass through the woodland, and after an ungainly dismount they trooped under the branches in their big boots, hesitating and swivelling to study the vantage, disappearing and re-emerging back and forth between the bushy hair of the olives. When they finally made their way up the hill, so Antoine was later informed, they found only peasants, tilling the land and pursuing ordinary farming work.

Returning on every day of fine weather, Antoine heard all manner of stories. Who fought here, who fought there, who was a traitor, who killed that Jewish settler, who killed that policeman. Aref Abd al-Razzaq was a well-known character, famous for turning up in one place and appearing ten kilometres away a moment later shooting at something else. Rumours about the Jews ranged from plausible to outlandish: rumours of slaughter, of designs to occupy the Haram, of other deep, disgusting perversities which the fighters imbibed like fuel. Vivacity of story was an elixir to violence. The strongest tonics concerned the British, source of all evil and oppression, of which the flogged and weeping bodies in the hospital provided sufficient proof.

None of the patients seemed particularly bothered by Antoine's presence. He credited his tie to the "Ebal Girls," who were still held in great esteem by the hospital establishment, and, of course, were so recently helping the rebels, though one did wonder how thoroughly that was *ma'roof*.

Also possible was that since he was French rather than English, they considered him comparatively benign. They might even think he was another inmate in the ward, soon to return to bed. Or perhaps they didn't mind him because they thought he was a mad old man. One could get away with a great deal, being a mad old man.

He held neither book nor pen in his hands. He made no notes. He simply observed as the premise of his monograph disintegrated before his eyes. His premise had been that Nablus, shielded from the world by her two mountains, possessed some qualities of amber: liquid first but hardening into a preservative, and presenting to the curious eye a picture of essences. But now look, how fast custom could degrade from its pure form. Even this habit on the veranda, people of all classes sitting side by side—for although sickness had always levelled station, the hospital had previously been the haunt only of Christians and the lower classes. And with the local clinics in Nablus obsolete, beliefs in modern medicine absolute, plus the hospital facilities enlarged, catering improved, midwives trained, and especially with these novel habits of taking the air—one would be forgiven for construing the changes in the municipal hospital as a microcosm of larger shifts in the town. That was not necessarily unusual, of course; war changed habits, and this was beginning to feel like war. Above all, the strike itself, the fact that the Arabs could undertake a cooperative action so far-reaching and long lasting—it was all completely remarkable, and completely beyond the compass of Antoine's understanding.

One afternoon in May, he sat steadying the brim of his hat against a strong spring wind. The weather had not deterred the patients, however, who came out as usual for their sunbath. Not that there was much sun. Antoine peered at the gradations of white over the sky, blending tinges of yellow and blue.

"Good morning tout le monde!"

A large man in a light wool three-piece suit strode onto the veranda, beaming at the patients with his hands behind his back.

"Ya Haj," he addressed the old man by the door with a frown. "How is your lung? Better?"

"Better, better," said the old man.

"Thanks be to God."

The next invalid twisted around in his chair. Though he could not hear the doctor's response, Antoine saw his head shaking in sympathy. Apparently fearless in the face of contagion, the new doctor rested his hands on the chair backs as he passed, and Antoine caught snippets of conversation in a variety of accents. Several fellahi men and boys, villagers from outside Nablus, and upper-class patients, who seemed, judging by their intonation, already well acquainted. A flicker of irritation passed over the features of one middle-aged man with an ear infection.

"What?" said a bandaged fighter. "Of course I'm in pain. Two of them shot me, up close. Not more than a metre. Thank you, yes." He nodded and turned aside, wincing dramatically as he touched his elbow.

"And sometimes it is sharp," said another voice. "And sometimes it is dull."

"I'm sorry to hear that."

"They gave me ice, but the ice felt very hot, which worried me."

"Don't be worried, that's normal."

An uproar of bushes announced another onset of wind, which drove the voices in the other direction.

"Bonjour, Monsieur."

The three-piece suit was beside him, face dark against the sun. A pair of hands asked if the chair was vacant. Antoine held out his palm.

"Merci."

"Vous parlez français?" said Antoine.

"Bien sûr." The man sniffed. "J'ai habité en France depuis longtemps. Pendant la guerre."

"Pendant la guerre—en battaille?"

"Non, non. Pour les études."

"De médécine?"

"Oui. J'ai pris le serment d'Hypocrite." He began to pat his pockets. The maroon tie around his neck was patterned with green hoops.

"D'Hippocrate," corrected Antoine.

"Oui, le même."

"Ah," said Antoine, gently hitting his own knee. "Now I know who you are. You own the clothing shop. Kamal."

There was a silence. Monsieur Kamal drew a long handkerchief from his front pocket and blew his nose. Antoine looked out at the orchard as if out at sea, listening to the trees.

"La Provence," said Midhat. "C'est tellement belle."

"C'est vrai," said Antoine. "Mais moi, je préfère ici. Le paysage de la Provence me rappelle cette vue—mais vous parlez français très bien, Docteur."

Midhat replied in Arabic. "I am not a doctor."

Antoine glanced at him. The joviality had gone, and the face, full-cheeked and slender browed, sharpened. A wind swarmed down the valley and thrust itself over the veranda rail. Midhat's hair blew back from his forehead and he shut his eyes. The pockets of soft flesh above his cheeks seemed to press back into his skull, his mouth assumed a grim horizontal, and the threads of his small moustache ruffled minutely in the current.

"Which bed are you sleeping in?"

"Oh—" said Antoine. "*I* am not a patient." He laughed.

Midhat tutted. "No bed for a holy man! What are we coming to."

And then, with extraordinary slowness, Midhat wrapped his fingers around the arm of the chair and stood up. He moved off behind the others, and stopped dead before the door. A nurse rushed out.

"There you are!" She grasped his arm. "Why are you dressed? Come on. Come back, Amo, come back."

It rained on the way home. Drops, invisible and fast, fell cold on Antoine's hands and face. He found Sister Marian outside the chapel, holding an umbrella and stretching out one of the lapels of her overcoat. She smiled when she recognised him.

"Are you very happy, Sister?"

She held the umbrella over his head and fell in step.

"It is odd that one's mood should be so affected by the behaviour of one's pupils."

"You have been teaching."

"Children can be so unpredictable. Today they were very enthusiastic."

"How old?"

"Seven and eight. They drew flowers mostly, except—look at this one. Isn't it marvellous."

He took charge of the umbrella as she revealed the bundle of papers hidden under her coat. She held up the first page: a childish depiction of Mary's Immaculate Heart, red and small and pulsating with gold daggers of light. On the page beneath he could just see the tip of a purple flower with a strong green stem.

"Very accomplished."

"She is a Muslim." Sister Marian pressed her lips together and elongated her jaw, suppressing a smile. "They gave them to me as gifts. I'm going to hang them in the dining room. How was the hospital?"

As Antoine was contemplating how to describe his day, he nodded at the driver of a two-horse cart trotting past.

"We are having lamb for dinner," said Sister Marian.

"Very good."

"Sister Margareta was given a sheep by one of the villagers who was wounded outside Jenin."

"Did she heal him?"

"I think he lost an arm."

The door was at hand. Sister Marian turned the key, and as they stepped into the cool shade of the hall, she asked: "Have you decided, yet, what it is you will write next?"

This, at last, unlocked him. "I don't suppose, Sister," he said expressively, "that I shall write anything."

As the words left his mouth he felt their significance. But this was lost on Sister Marian, whom, yet again, his heart had mistaken for Louise. Marian did not have the field of reference to read or take an interest in Antoine's meaning; her questions were pleasantries. She held out a page wrinkled with gouache and raindrops.

"We must all retire at some point," she said, drawing it aside and picking up the next. "We were visited last week by the education director's assistant, Mister Jerome. He was very eager to suggest our curriculum should not be too literary. They are worried we will give the girls ideas."

"What does that mean, *literary*?"

"They would prefer we taught them to embroider and left it there, I think. And hygiene, which they are obsessed with. The inspector calls it maintaining the status quo, keeping Arab girls at home . . . or maintaining tradition, he said. What's comical"—she said this without smiling, she had noticed a stain on the tablecloth and hunched over to scratch it with her nail—"is that it has become rather fashionable to send them to school. We have hardly enough staff to keep up. Every father in Nablus seems to want his daughters to learn history, and do you know why? To make appealing wives. Nabulsi men like good conversationalists. So in the end," she sighed, straightening up, "I suppose they all have the same purpose in view."

She set the paintings on the sideboard and gathered the cloth, revealing the burnished brown nakedness of the table beneath, scarred in places by a less fastidious housemistress.

"In any case," she said, opening the cabinet for a fresh one, "controlling the history books didn't stop them."

"How long, Sister, have you been helping?"

"The Arabs?"

"Yes."

"Me, personally?"

"All of you."

"Since the end of the war." She met his eye. "You know, Father, help can be very broadly defined. This with Qassam . . . at first, it was only a question of keeping quiet. Then, little by little, one realises one has taken a side. To help one party can simply mean not helping the other."

"Yes, of course," said Antoine coolly. But in a few seconds his wish for knowledge overrode his desire to prove he already had it, and he said: "And Sister Louise? Was she . . ."

"The same. We all did. We all do. If our purpose is here, why would we act against the local people?"

"Why indeed. And where—can I ask, where did you acquire the arms?"

"Oh father, that was only a bit of ammunition." She thrust the new cloth over the table. The linen fluttered and sank heavily past the edge, and she stretched across to push out the furrows with the flat of her hand.

He turned to go. In the doorway, he could not help throwing out:

"I'm interested, you know, in how much all of this is inevitable. The fighting, and the . . . situation." He watched for her reaction. "One people in need, trespassing on the rights of another, I wonder how much . . ."

Sister Marian's frown rose into an expectant triangle.

Antoine said, "I have spent the latter part of my career"—to his surprise, the word pained him—"trying to construct a pattern of this town. According to my training, all that is was there to begin with. But is one always to simplify, to make a picture more coherent?"

She opened the cutlery drawer.

"To impose . . ." He was losing her. He could not stop. "Sister Marian, I am literally watching them. I don't know why. I don't know why I am here. Nablus has become my whole life, I cannot leave it. But there is no discernible *point* to watching them. I am not helping anyone."

"Do you need to help?" said Sister Marian, counting forks. "You are not a missionary."

"I am not."

"You are in the service of knowledge," she said simply, and the forks in her hand crashed onto the table.

5

The ward was smaller in Midhat's mind. Every time he opened his eyes the space surprised him, measured out by the beds that pulled the walls apart. All the others stirring, sleeping, blinking, coughing, praying—but when he closed his eyes his ears blocked up, and a curtain drew around his cot, and it was warm and quiet.

Opening his eyes on the huge ward, Midhat twisted his neck to look through the window behind him. An olive grove. In rows the trees stood, frozen in the act of passing along their loads. The young ones were thin and sprightly, the crones squat, volute. He extended a hand and grabbed one around the waist, and with a roar of soil pulled it up out of the earth, churning a thick brown fog. The problem with objects is that even when they fall they leave something behind, and the tree remained standing although it was also in his fist, and he grabbed at the tree that remained standing undisturbed in the field, but now it was made of thin wafer that melted in the heat of his hand and passed through his palm.

The olive harvest was just completed, but the trees already carried new green fruits, little hard things amid their leaves. Obviously, everything was always growing.

The nurse, Jumana, helped him into a seated position. She unbuttoned his shirt with her dry fingers and slid it off his back. He heard the patter of the sponge as she squeezed it over the bowl, and his anticipating flesh tingled. The wet warm began first over his shoulders, then entered the soft, haired places under his arms, tinkling back into Jumana's bowl. She drew the sponge along his wrists where the rough edge tickled, and at last reached his hands—this was the part that made him laugh. Someone else washing his hands, a sensation never dreamt of. Next the chest, the rolls of his torso, squeezing into those crevices for dirt; then the neck, the area expressive above all the others of cleanliness, for when your neck was scrubbed you felt so clean you might not even need a bath; why was that? Perhaps because it was close to the brain—and down his lower back went the knifing heat, the warmth already cooling in the air.

There were times, while the rest of the ward moaned and coughed and spoke and prayed, and he turned his neck to look out the window at the moonlit grove, for at night Jumana left the shutter open a crack for him, especially for him he thought, that Midhat believed he had never been more lucid in his entire life. He had arrived in the hospital some time ago, he was not sure exactly how long. Months, possibly. He had recovered in himself a great facility for thinking, which he supposed must have lain dormant for years. Who knew why such things happened. Perhaps he had been sleepwalking; emptied out by days that revolved and disintegrated, by his family, by the shop, by other little things that absorbed time like grains of rice in water. Lying in this hospital bed, however, surrounded by coughing and spluttering and weeping and raving, but released from the nets of those daily facts, he engaged in thinking and felt relatively placid. Problems arose when his mind stopped and he became a body, because he could not do both activities at once. When he stopped thinking, his flesh started to inflate. There was nothing to be done, it was a great pink thing and he looked at his hands with horror. Think; think; a balm—achieving nothing—an action only, a soothing motion over things that threatened, breeding in corners of the ward. Thought flowed from thing to thing, he wrapped his hand around them and fingered their textures. The content of these thoughts? Mostly himself. He danced between two, three, four ideas of himself, that is to say of Midhat Kamal, and these ideas overlapped like conflicting maps of the same place. He looked at the inconsistencies in his thoughts and did not come to any conclusions. Sometimes his father entered them. For short bursts he looked at the man sidelong, he did not look at the box, he did not agitate those things that did not make sense.

To his right lay a boy named Sami with two broken legs who wept during the night.

"Can you hear that noise?"

"What? What noise?"

"It's loud. It keeps me awake."

"I can't hear anything."

"It's unbearable."

Midhat said: "It must be the plumbing."

It occurred to him that he was someone who often said things like that: "It must be the plumbing." "Oh, it must have been the weather." "It must have been this, it must have been, must have been—must it have been?" Yes, it must.

Her long thin fingers, and round fingernails like full moons. And why did he remember her chin so well? The chin was very small, and there was a dimple in it. A light fixture swayed from the ceiling.

Seized at once by a shaft of terror, he grasped at the bedsheets: she wouldn't look like that any more. He gripped the sheets and stretched his arms. How many years—one two three four five six seven eight nine ten eleven twelve thirteen—fifteen years he counted. More than fifteen! Twenty years. Twenty years. She turned her face. Pity cramped his stomach, his face hot and wet, drenched in tears—poor Midhat. He said aloud: "Poor Midhat." Sheets whispered and he knew someone was turning to look at him. "Habibi Midhat," said Midhat. "Ayuni. Poor, poor Midhat . . ." He started to weep again. In that moment, wound up in self-pity, happiness did not seem far off.

He dreamt about Jeannette's mother, Ariane Molineu, and that Ariane was Jeannette. He woke and checked the olive trees—still there, dawn lurid—and recalled the dream and the fact that the two women were one person. Something might be cleared up by this. At the same time it went black with fog, like the glass on the inside of a lamp.

The light began changing on the lawn. He walked up the steps of his back garden, he felt the familiar rhythm of his footfall, leading with the right leg and switching halfway to lead with the left, and on the top terrace he came across the day he had found the letter, like a playing card mislaid and recovered. He looked at the day and his limbs moved, striking hard things and soft things. He thought about his horror—approaching it side-on, not to expose too much surface area—the first horror of the dream materialising, his innards crossing the boundary of his skin into the exposing air. At that stage, he felt mostly disgust.

Now that he had regained his ability to think, the invasion of the past no longer horrified him so much. The new horror, surpassing that first, was the fact that everyone *pretended* the past didn't do that. Everyone lived on this skin of life and pretended they didn't know what they were standing on. How could he, Midhat Kamal, go back to pretending, now he knew how flimsy it all was?

"Hello," said Teta.

He was surprised to see Teta sitting at the foot of his bed. On a chair, facing him. It was daytime. He was a little hungry. He heard a footstep in the hall. His grandmother was wearing a mingled expression of fatigue and fright. He examined her appearance as if from a photograph. An extremely wrinkled face. Far more wrinkled than it was in his mind, if he were to summon it separately. Upper lip hidden by a moue, lower lip pink and flat and shiny, little wrinkles below leading up, as though the chin was being sucked up into that pink skin-ledge. Watery eyes, bluish brown, mixed. Creamy heavy cheeks collapsing into wrinkles at the jawline. Hair grey, long, thin, tied back from her face. Body large and small: large on the breast, but also diminished, shrunken. She looked weak and if it weren't for her cheeks her face would articulate her skull. It struck him that life does not usually leave a person at once but that it gutters, slowly thins and lengthens, like a tall flame.

"Don't leave, Teta," he said.

Her lips pursed, drawing lines over her face. "I have to go eventually. You don't want me to eat?"

Midhat sank back into the mattress. He wondered whether he might disappear. It was hard to cling onto himself when there were so many others, there were so many other people and they were crowding him out. He tried to summon one of his four ideas of himself that he had had only a few moments ago, a few days ago, but he couldn't even locate one. All he had left was this strange cut-out. He was a likeness in reverse. He was a cameo.

Weeks passed. Teta visited again. Midhat adopted smiles and phrases of the old formula, tinned exasperation at his grandmother's foibles, such as rolling eyes, and other habits of expression. Observing her frown he felt a movement of sympathy in his breast. She was excessively wrinkled. He began to put on a most reasonable, doctorly voice, but it soon turned false and impracticable. He became tired after a while and wanted a nap.

A memory appeared at the front of his mind. His daughter Ghada stamping in the garden in a pool of water. She lifted her arms behind her to jump, and the water reached up and stroked her legs. A banner unwound and fell.

It was winter when Teta announced that, in a few months, they would be taking him to the psychiatric hospital in Bethlehem, which was run by the British. The nurses there were properly trained to deal with cases like his.

"Yes," he said. "Good idea."

Hani had pulled some strings to move him up the waiting list. These facts entered his mind like hearsay, and later he wondered where he had learned them.

Another time, he said: "I'm feeling better. I don't think I need to go to Bethlehem."

"Yes, yes you do. The nurses here—"

Teta's brow quivered, and she looked scared. A dollop of fear dropped into Midhat: what had he done to scare her?

"You have misunderstood," he said in a gentle voice. "I am not sick. I am not majnun. I am only very sad. That is all."

"Yes," said Teta faintly.

Fatima visited. She sat where Teta had sat and fixed him with a look of glazed fury.

"Where are the children?"

"At home."

"How are they?"

He watched her, the clenched hands in her lap, and felt, as he had for Teta, an incredible pity. His feelings were at a distance. He said nothing. Rather, as he lay there pitying his wife, Midhat felt his self dissolving again. To survive the wave he gripped the edges of the mattress with both hands. When the wave broke, he opened his eyes and saw a woman sitting where Fatima had been, wearing a thick black veil that exposed only her eyes.

"Why are you wearing a veil?"

"We all have to wear the veil," said Fatima.

"This is a hospital," said Midhat. "Not a mosque."

She sighed. A nurse walked past, carrying a roll of lint.

"I'm surprised they let you in here," he went on. "They're very unhygienic."

"Midhat, the thuwwar have ordered us all to wear the veil."

"Thuwwar?"

"To make us different from the Jewish women probably."

"*Thuwwar?*"

"Yes. There is an uprising. We are led by the glorious fellahin."

"What happened to the shop? There was a fire in my shop, Fatima."

"There is a strike. All shops are closed."

He did not remember the rest of this conversation. He knew he had struggled because he was tired afterwards, and when he woke he found they had strapped him into the bed by pulling the cover very tightly, securing its edges under the mattress. The air was warm, and the stretched cover, consisting only of a double sheet, displayed the contour of his legs and stomach. A glissade of sheet connected the high point of his belly with his knees, like a tight sail in wind.

The next time Fatima came, she was wearing a scarf but it was under her neck, so that her entire face, and not just her eyes, was exposed. He laughed humourlessly.

"You are changing your fashion, my dear."

Whether she replied to this comment he had no idea. He was absorbed entirely into a thought, with only a vague awareness that he was still speaking and she responding, and when he woke she was gone and he could not remember any of it.

Since the weather was growing mild, Jumana allowed him to take the air on the balcony. He felt awake with the draught on his face, and some of his more lucid moments occurred here, out of doors. He exchanged remarks with other convalescents and visitors, and watched in shock as spring usurped winter over the fields.

One day, after Jumana had helped him into his suit and tie, Midhat stepped out towards the rail, leaning on his cane. He turned his head, and caught sight of a man sitting at the far end of the veranda. His heart swooped below his stomach. He heard a sharp ringing sound.

"What is he doing here?"

"Who?" said Jumana, turning to look.

It was Docteur Molineu. Aged a great deal, and certainly no longer with that elastic, limber body. Fuller, bearded—but it was him, unmistakeably. Midhat looked into Jumana's eyes.

"Get me away," he whispered.

At the instant he said those words, he was struck by a new thought. His heart rose up from beneath his stomach. If the Docteur was here, he might convey a message to Jeannette.

"Away from who?" said Jumana, stroking his arm. "What did you see?"

"A man I knew—" said Midhat, beginning to tremble. His mind frothed. What should he ask him to say? He lifted his arm to point. "There."

"Where?"

He looked again, and fell silent. The man sitting at the far end was not Docteur Molineu. In fact, it was an old priest. With a big white beard, and a large-brimmed black hat.

They took him to Bethlehem in a hot car.

"Where is Hani?" he asked.

"Sarafand."

"Sarafand?"

"Yes."

"And Fatima?"

"Looking after the children."

On either side of him in the backseat, Teta and Um Jamil began to pray.

Two nurses were waiting for them outside the Bethlehem hospital. One of them addressed Um Jamil as she helped Midhat into a wheelchair.

"You can visit on Tuesdays."

Midhat spluttered into tears. Teta appeared from the other side of the car and steadied herself against the bonnet.

"What is the treatment you will give him?"

"There is no treatment," said the taller nurse.

"What?"

"We have no treatments."

"If you want treatment, go to the Jewish clinics in Jerusalem."

"What was the point in putting him here?" said Teta to Um Jamil.

"Do you want the bed or not," said the taller nurse. "There is a very long waiting list, there are at least a hundred people—"

"How long will he have to stay?"

"It depends."

They kissed Midhat many times. He did not conceal his weeping. The corridor they wheeled him down was dark, and voices rumbled from behind doors. When they tried to remove his suit he insisted on doing it by himself. To his surprise they consented. He wondered, bitterly, as he unbuttoned alone in a small room and laid his trousers on the bed, if this would be the final dignity bestowed by his association with Hani Murad. He placed his jacket and shirt neatly on the thin-sheeted mattress, and then his socks, and pulled on the green gown they had given him. They weighed him and wheeled him to a bed at the far end of a ward between a cold plaster wall and a man with a prominent forehead, who was also quite fat. At the sight of Midhat, this man looked gleeful. One glance at the man's inert other neighbour and Midhat guessed he had been deprived of company. Aware of his own physical volume as his wheelchair neared the bed, he felt a stab of revulsion that this insane person might perceive some similarity between them.

"Bon soir, Monsieur," said Midhat. As the nurse turned over his cover, he muttered: "Thank you, Mademoiselle."

"Oh la la," said the man. "Al-Barisi."

"Yes," said Midhat, sitting on the mattress. "I have lived in Paris."

This did not discourage the man from talking, and before long Midhat was apprised of the rumours that had been travelling between the beds, including one about the previous matron, Miss Whitaker. Miss Whitaker had *innhablat*, gone what the British nurses called "off the rails," and locked a Palestinian nurse in one of the maniacal cells. Miss Whitaker had been deported and admitted into an asylum outside Beirut.

"And the British had to pay for it," he said. "They pay for her but they can hardly pay for us. How long were you on the waiting list?"

"Not long," said Midhat coldly.

At last, silence. After a while, Midhat heard him accost his other neighbour, but he could not make out any replies.

He did not feel calm in this ward. Over the next few days he noticed smells lingering when they returned from the dining room, and in order to avoid a sticky residue on the floor by his bed it was necessary to bend his leg and aim with his foot when standing up. He spent his energy trying to ignore the sound of moaning, as well as the more sinister wails that penetrated from the hallway at night. When the wails stopped abruptly, Midhat wondered whether his mind had triumphed, whether he had so successfully blocked out the noise that he now could no longer hear it even when he tried. But presently he heard the bits and pieces of other sounds, shufflings and murmurs, and then he worried why the wailing had ended, what vile sedations and other narratives it implied. He missed the benign muttering in the municipal hospital in Nablus, and when a British nurse came to his bed to tell him he had been selected for a private interview with the matron, he could not help replying: "Please, do let me out of here. I am not actually mad." The nurse helped him into the wheelchair as he continued to explain how he would rather take the opportunity to walk, and then drove him through the dank corridor of his arrival into an office at the farther end.

The matron was a tall, bronzed woman with freckles and erratic black hair pinned beneath a white hat. In English she informed him from across her steel desk that the nurses had diagnosed him as "docile." Midhat parsed her words and translated them into French, and she eyed him with something like suspicion. Understanding that a response was required, he nodded and interlaced his fingers in his lap. It was a gesture his muscles knew well, the gesture of a shop owner condescending to listen to his client. He experienced a strong wave of humiliation and pressed his fingertips into the spaces between his knuckles.

"We are upgrading you, Mister Kamal," said the Matron, "to the rehabilitation ward."

She had a mouth, he noticed, somewhat like a beak, with a space between the front of her teeth and the inside of her lip, where grain might be stored for her offspring.

The new ward received more daylight, even though the barred window by his bed only gave the view of another internal wall. To his left lay Yusef Qadri of Hebron. To his right, a Pole named Henryk. Henryk was very thin and blond and his feet poked out between the posts. He was a violin player, and he had suffered in the pogroms. Yusef was likewise thin, and never said a word. Henryk said many, many words. He spoke perfect French.

On the second day, Henryk said: "Do you know why we are here?" He shot a glance at the window, and the tendons lifted from his neck like the treble strings of a piano.

"Why," said Midhat.

"Because we have an inner life."

"A what?"

"This is the disease of being civilised. That is why there are more mad Jews than mad Arabs."

Midhat looked at Henryk's face. The sharp corners of his cheekbones brought out the largeness of his eyeballs, whose lids hung halfway down like a pair of waxy shades.

"No."

"Yes. We are alienated from nature," said Henryk. "We are civilised. Whereas the Arabs—you are one with nature."

Midhat groaned, and pulled his pillow over his head. He shut his eyes and followed the rhythm of his footfall in the garden, going up the terraces.

Right left, right left. Halfway up, he switched: left right, left right. He woke with a start, and the top of his bare foot hit the cold enamel of the bedpost.

It was morning, and there was a nurse beside his bed.

"You have a guest. Come to the visitors' room. Come on now," she said again, in a bright voice that did not match her expression.

He put on his slippers and followed her out into a corridor with beds against one wall and chairs along the other. He wondered what it was like to lie there, with people walking back and forth along your feet. Next, a set of stairs led to a small, unplastered room with doors open onto a dry garden. He was stunned to realise it was summer. Two other patients were sitting with visitors, and Teta was near the door, twisting her fingers in her lap. He took the empty chair beside hers and saw, reflected in her eyes, that the hospital was dreadful.

"Oh, Teta," he said.

He felt as ashamed as if he were the hospital's representative. She leaned over to whisper something to him, and he caught a glimpse of the cotton dress she was wearing under her coat, with its close pattern of stars, stitched in navy blue. After a moment he realised she had still not spoken, and looking in her eyes again he saw, with a snag in his chest, that she had decided he would not understand. A wall arose between them. Badly, he wished to say: I understand. But every time he tried to speak something hot and low and laden with pain surged up and stopped his mouth. He could feel the tension in his face. He wanted to tell her he did not belong here. He watched her conducting her distress on the chair across from his, inhaling deeply and then letting the breath go. Behind him, a woman was saying:

"And Bassima is going to start school next week…"

Suddenly, Teta was struggling onto her feet. He fell in her shadow as she bent for a kiss. She addressed the nurse beside the door, then waddled out on her bad hip, and every point of his body stretched towards her.

When he returned to the ward, Henryk was wearing a pair of spectacles and reading a book. The title was hidden under his fingers.

"Qu'est-ce que vous lisez?"

"Un roman."

He waited for more. Light from the window shone bluish on the wall ahead, and it struck Midhat as a shame they had not positioned the beds to give the patients a view. Not that it would be much of a view. Perhaps the nurses did not want to put ideas into their heads. His neighbour in the previous ward had told him about the ones who attempted to escape.

"It was very cold on the boat," said Henryk.

At first, Midhat thought he was reading aloud from his book. Then he noticed the novel was face down on Henryk's lap.

"Pardon?"

"And so cramped." He met Midhat's eyes. "I'm talking about the boat. How I came here, we came here, my family and I."

"Ah."

"It was September. So we thought the weather would be mild. The weather was terrible." He said this with the rhythm of a joke, and smiled. "There were hundreds of us, we took the train, my wife and I and our son Aleksander, to Bulgaria. The quota for that year was exceeded already, so we were tourists. We were coming to Palestine for the holidays. We did not have many things. The guards, I'm sure, knew we were not on holiday. In fact, I think they were told to help us along. But we were due to set sail from Bulgaria on this ship, and my wife said I could not bring my violin—because who brings a violin on holiday? And at first, you know, I resisted her. I was determined to bring my violin. Then we met one of the representatives, Lejba his name was. We paid . . . we paid seven hundred fifty zlotys each, so with my son that is over two thousand, that is two thousand two hundred fifty zlotys. Can you imagine? They gave us passports with new names. We became the Wolmarks. Henryk Wolmark is my new name. I will not tell you my old one, because that belongs in Poland with my violin. Then, this representative, he also said I could not take my violin. Tourists with musical instruments are suspicious, he said. But if"—Henryk turned and looked at Midhat again, and for the first time his eyelids lifted, displaying the immaculate whiteness around each grey-blue iris—"if the border guards knew what we were doing, what was the problem with taking my violin?"

He seemed genuinely waiting for an answer. Midhat said nothing. He
had decided he did not wish to hear this story.

"The British," said Henryk at last, "is the answer to that question. But
I'll come to that. First we set out on our pleasure cruise." He cackled. "My
wife and I, we each brought two coats, and we wore both of them all the
time." Another laugh. "Aleksander—poor Aleksander. *Papa*, he said to me.
Papa, I am so cold, will you share your coat with me? I do not know why, if
they were so intent on moving us here, they did not make the experience
more pleasant. The food—the captain, I swear, was deliberately screwing us
over. I put Aleksander under my coat, and we sat together like that, singing."

There was a silence. Yusef Qadri gave out a moan, and Henryk sighed.
Midhat waited. Henryk picked up his book and looked at the cover. Midhat
could see the title, and that it was written in Polish.

"The situation was already bad for the Jews," said Henryk at last. "But
it was not this bad. We were lucky. I had an aunt and uncle who lived in
Danzig."

He turned away and his pyjama top rode up over his bony flank. Midhat
wondered whether Henryk had admitted himself, or whether, like Midhat,
his family and friends had brought him. He decided to pay attention next
Tuesday to see whether a nurse took Henryk to the visitors' room. Obvious
symptoms of instability in him Midhat could not detect, but then, perhaps—and thinking this he slid down so he was completely horizontal—
his own predicament might affect his ability to distinguish sanity from its
inverse in other people.

Now, that was a fearful thought. Locked in his brain, Midhat could
not trust his own perceptions. He thought of the sharp ringing sound that
sometimes burst into his ears, and considered, unguarded, the nature of
his own case.

He had had twenty years to think over what happened at the Molineu
house. Long ago he had diagnosed his accusation of Sylvain Leclair as the
fatal misstep, the final act that pushed Jeannette away in the instant she
might have been his ally. And this he had accepted as one accepts the ending
of a story about someone else—already assimilating that ending when he
wrote to Jeannette from Paris to say goodbye, expressing himself at last in

good French as he wished to express himself, deliberately and with grace, reading his declaration aloud to Hani on Rue Spontini, making sure each comma was correct. Then he had returned to Palestine and erased, gradually but with determination, every vestige of hope. He had faced forward with valour—yes, he commended himself for it— addressing the onward thrust of time. And as time went on, the past had receded. He married, he had children, an income, social standing—was, in effect, a self-made man.

Hard, then, not to see this letter as a weapon sent across the barrier to skewer him. If he had stayed in Montpellier, if he had not been so proud, everything might have been different. That gesture when she turned from him in the hall was branded on his brain; she would not look at him. How could he have known—it was not final! His anger rose and shot towards Jeannette. She was incredibly selfish. How like her it was, really, to stretch out her arm and ruin his life at this late stage.

For a moment, he allowed himself. He closed his eyes and imagined. He felt the barricade he had been holding up against this fantasy, and as he lowered it his entire body sighed. Here he was, in Nablus. Fresh from the ship. And here, in the hall, was the letter with his name on it. He picked it up, his finger tore the flap. He heard Jeannette's voice, and her words had different meanings now, they filled him with a sense of imminence, of chance, of hope —he grabbed his still-packed bag with his heart bursting and stepped back onto the mountain. Train to Tulkarem, train to Alexandria. He was leaving it all—Teta, his father, his family, everything. He was on a train to Egypt, he was boarding a ship to Marseille. And there she was, waiting for him, on the docks. He saw her from afar, her dark hair. And now, her face, he could see her, and now he was holding her real body, and his nose was in her hair. Tears filled his eyes and his whole self smiled, gazing up at Jeannette on the hospital ceiling.

Something squeaked: a nurse's rubber footstep. A few beds along a patient sneezed. Midhat blinked, and wiped the tears from his face.

His thoughts, he noticed, had gained facility. He logged his sensations: calm, no discomfort in his eyes, no blurry vision. He interlaced his fingers on his stomach and concentrated. Was it possible? Had his storm of confusion reached an apex and withdrawn? There was a cramp in his foot, and lifting his leg he twirled his ankle to unlock it. The leg was weak and sore. He shifted to look over at Henryk, who was also on his back, arms folded, chewing his bottom lip. He looked over at Yusef Qadri; Yusef was sleeping.

Onto this new clear stage of his mind stepped Fatima, and then Teta, and Eli and the burnt-out shop, and all the facts of home, his children. His heart lunged. He needed to go back. They required him. He had assimilated pain before; he would do so again. The only thing Jeannette's letter actually revealed was that his father was cruel and had betrayed him. And, of course, that love was not lost when he thought it had been. But now it was, so it meant nothing.

"We loved our fathers too much," he said aloud.

He extended his lower jaw, trying to stopper his tears. He thought of Ghada, of lifting her up: would he do to her what his father had done to him? Would he leave her? It was agony, it would not end, but in the light of that, what was there to revise? He could not write back, call her on the telephone, say: Jeannette, here I am, would you like to meet? He could not board a ship to Marseille. He could not cover that distance.

He caught a darkened flash of his younger self—there, standing on the other platform. A residue of Henryk's story, the pattern and tone of it, that part about his old name, left in Poland with his violin—something about that property of distance, blending time and place, gave form to a vision of a young man stepping off a train in Montpellier. Look at him: awash with fatigue, dragging a vast trunk, blank with the richness of an unmarked future, full of enthusiasm and fear. How did one get from there to here? The gap was too enormous. With his foot Midhat felt the edge of a gorge dividing that life, possessed of that old future sense, from what had transpired, from the bank he stood on. He was two men: one here, one there, that one, he saw, young and slender, guileless, untrained for battle. He felt sorry for that young man; he did not know what he was in for.

"It is very different here," he said, "from what I had been led to expect." Henryk exhaled. "Quite."

The ceiling began to secrete noises, rumbling feet, a clash of plates. Brandishing a clipboard a nurse ushered them up for lunch. Midhat pushed his feet into the rectangular slippers by his bed, and shuffled after Henryk.

The dining room steamed with the aroma of stew. Midhat stood behind Henryk in line for the tureen, and observed the faces of those carrying their plates to the tables. He wondered if any were as sane as he was, likewise imprisoned because they had witnessed some part of the world's cloth slashed and corrupted. Some, to be sure, resembled lunatics of the type a child might recognise: singing, or torpid and silent, incapable of sitting up properly in their chairs. But many, like Henryk, gave an appearance of civility and control.

"Wakey-wakey," said the woman with the ladle.

The green-brown liquid careened to film the plate-sides with a gritty spume as he made his way towards Henryk. Yusef Qadri followed close behind. They sat either side of a plate of buckwheat, and Yusef's fork trembled between his fingers.

Midhat hated the way the nurses watched them eat. He had learned it was best to eat slowly and inconspicuously, since he who refrained from eating, or he who ate with appetite, was he who attracted their eyes and their scribbling pencils. The chief matron, the giantess, strolled between the tables like the captain of a ship. Midhat inserted his bread into the stew.

"I like to listen as they chat," said Henryk. Midhat noticed three nurses talking together on his other side. "They think we can't hear them." Henryk lifted his spoon. "I can. A demonstrative theatrical line, that one just said. What a phrase."

Everything had its proper order. First the nurses scraped the leftovers off the plates into a bucket, then they stacked the plates on their steel contraptions and wheeled them away, and only then did the chair legs squeal as the patients were allowed to file out.

In the ward, someone had switched on the ceiling lights against the gloom, and the barred patch of sun on the wall had stretched to the right and almost faded. Midhat removed his slippers and slid under the blankets.

"In the Dardanelles," said Henryk, "the British caught us."

Midhat listened without speaking. He did want to know the story of Henryk's demise. He wanted to know how Henryk had arrived here. He closed his eyes and saw giddy pictures, a violet sea, and a fine powder, particles of water, stirred and swooped over his bed. He confronted his body in the darkness, his blood beating. He opened his eyes and sent his energy to his ears.

"They pursued us and stopped us from reaching port. So we had to go back to Greece. We were so dejected, you can imagine. My wife was crying. We docked at Tinos. By this time, we had made some friends among the others, there were more than three hundred of us. Three hundred fifty, I think. In particular we liked this man Julian, young, very enthusiastic about the Hehalutz movement. We, not so much. My wife she liked it, but mostly you know it was that we were poor in Poland, life was not good, we had the pogroms, she did not want to raise Aleksander there, she was frightened that what was happening nearby was going to happen at home. We heard these stories about Palestina, the life here . . . Julian, he was a real enthusiast. He taught me a lot about Zionism I didn't know. We stayed in Greece one month, and set out again in November. Oh, Midhat. It was terrible."

At the direct address, Midhat shifted to view his storyteller. Henryk was on his back, gazing straight up, gesticulating with his hands.

"Ten weeks at sea. I wondered why we had come in the first place. Why did we come? I remember." He tapped the fingers of one hand on the back of the other. "It was my wife. My wife wanted us to come. We tried to go back to Greece, but this time Greece didn't want us." Midhat watched Henryk's hands move like seaweed in the weak sun from the window. "We tried once more at Tel Aviv, but no, and now, can you imagine, I have been at sea for months, I am longing for my violin. This is not a small thing. I ache, all I see is water. Not blue water. Dirty, grey, sick green water. It is winter, the sky goes black, and we have bought one more coat for Aleksander to wear from Greece, but we do not have enough money for anything else. We did not imagine we would be at sea for so long, remember." Forefinger and thumb extended, the right hand wagged. "The rations, little portions, worse than here. Stale bread. Horrible.

"Finally, one night, we are lingering in the Mediterranean close to shore, and Julian wakes us up in our bunks. He says, we are going to go alone, will you come with us? How, I say. The lifeboats, says Julian. I say, what about the lookout boys? And Julian says, the boys know, they are coming with us. We were perhaps forty, fifty persons in total, everyone got on the deck, some still in pyjamas but wearing boots. We did a terrible thing, taking the lifeboats. We rowed in the dark, it was so cold, and we left most of our things, since these are small boats, you cannot take your luggage. That night on the sea, my God it was dark, and there, us, trembling towards the lights of the shore."

He was silent.

"And what happened next?" said Midhat.

"Well, here I am," said Henryk. He lowered his hands onto the bed-cover, arms straight, like a child.

Midhat had the feeling of being forcibly ejected from the story. He wondered if he had somehow missed the climactic event that explained Henryk's presence in the asylum. He tried to think of some way to ask about the wife and child. No words seemed appropriate. The patch of light on the wall presently disappeared, and on the ceiling the yellow circles from the lamps grew brighter. A mosquito cried, lethargic with someone's blood, and carried its legs to rest on the wall by the bed.

"Thank you for your letter," said a voice.

A hand smacked, and a streak of blood emerged from the plaster.

Midhat did not need to look around for the speaker. He could sense her beside him. He felt a glow of excitement.

"Oh, yes, the letter," he said. "You are most welcome. Really. It was my pleasure. I have to say"—he chuckled—"I am relieved that it reached you."

He twisted round to look at her face. How extraordinary. Far more precise than he had ever remembered her. She smiled, and little soft creases appeared in the skin under her eyes. He reached out and touched her shoulder, and gasped at the familiar pressure of her body under his hand. All his anger was gone.

"When you left," said Jeannette. She looked down, struggling for the words. "The warmth of the house followed after you." She smiled. "I was useless as a nurse, but they needed help even with the cleaning."

"I'm sure you were better than you think you were."

She touched his hand, and her cold dry fingers sent another flutter to his chest. He inhaled, feeling the heat from her body. This was really happening.

"It has been four years since you left us in Montpellier," she said. "Four years! I cannot believe it."

"Nor can I. Your voice . . ." He shook his head. "I missed your voice."

"I wish that what has happened might not be final."

Puckers of anguish travelled over Jeannette's forehead, her cheeks, slid down from the corners of her eyes.

"For a long time I was in pain," she said.

"I know."

That face! How often he had tried to picture it, and grasped only a thin residue of associations. He fastened his grip on her shoulder, felt the hard bone, with his other hand touched his finger under her chin, felt the miraculous cold soft of her cheek, and a rush of sensation met his ears, nose, and palate—sunlight on a lawn, the crystal of a chandelier, a tree through a window—the echo of a high dark church, the smell of must, voices clattering off walls—and he felt a burning in his stomach, a heat ascending to his neck. There was a high ringing sound.

"I wish I could see your face," said Jeannette.

He reached for her hands and pressed them together.

"But I'm here," he said.

The panic was starting to rise.

"Sometimes I think I feel you in my breath."

"I wish I could be in the clinic in Jerusalem," said Henryk.

Midhat looked round. Henryk was sitting up in his bed, rubbing his eyes.

"I heard they have treatments there that send you into a coma. I am so tired of being awake."

"Jeannette?" said Midhat.

"Who is Jeannette?"

Midhat held out his hands. He felt the air.

"Well, why did you not go to Jerusalem, then!"

"It was too expensive," said Henryk. He sounded offended.

Midhat looked over and saw Henryk draw his hand under the cover and pull it out again. In his palm lay a gold disc. He rubbed his thumb along the edge. It was a pocket watch. He popped the clasp to reveal the face and began to wind the tiny crown. Midhat stared. The mechanism rasped and ticked. He could see the numerals from here—they were written in Arabic. His heart pummelled against his lungs.

Slowly, he said: "Where did you get that?"

"Get what?"

"That." He pointed. "That watch."

"Oh, this?" said Henryk. "This was a gift."

"Who gave it to you?"

The surprised expression on Henryk's face was mixed with something else. Interest. He was looking at Midhat with interest.

"Why do you ask?" he said. "It was a gift from a friend." His pompous mouth hung much further open than was necessary.

"Can I see it?"

"No."

Midhat waited a moment. Then: "Please."

"Why would I give it to you?" said Henryk. "I don't want you to take it."

Midhat's entire body propelled round in his covers until he was facing Henryk fully. "What was your friend's name?"

"Serena."

"No it wasn't."

"You are manic," said Henryk. He looked delighted.

In a much cooler tone, as if it had just occurred to him, Midhat repeated: "Who gave you that watch?" But the ruse was sabotaged by the hand that now reached out uncontrollably from his bed. "Let me see it. Let me see it."

"It's mine." Henryk laughed. "You can't have it. You think I would give something as precious as this to a mad Arab? Are you out of your mind?"

"Give it to me! Give it to me!" He was out of the bed. His fingers found Henryk's neck, he pressed hard on the clavicle and the eyes bulged and the face began turning red. Hands pushed up at Midhat's chest but they were too weak. His enemy strained in Polish, and then in French.

"LÂCHEZ-MOI! LÂCHEZ-MOI!"

Someone grabbed Midhat's wrists, someone else his torso. He was dragged back to the bed, his ankles and arms were pressed down into the mattress.

"No, no, no." His voice gurgled in his throat. Four nurses were holding him down. His chest was burning. "I killed him, I killed Laurent." He gulped the air. "For nothing. I killed him for nothing."

6

Ghada Kamal loved funerals. When school finished at three o'clock she listened for the sound of drums, and if passing out through the school gates she heard them—even faint, far-off—she would follow. Surveying the road for any hint of unusual commotion, straining over the motorcars for the report of sad voices—there, the pace of traffic slowing, pedestrians diverted down an alley—Ghada, scampering along with her empty sandwich case clutched to her chest; one corner turned and then another, coming at last upon the mourning procession in their black and dark blues, men first, women second, drums third, the chief mourners by the body taking turns to lead the others in the chant, "There is no god but God," and the echo from the rest, "There is no god but God," Ghada slipped into their ranks and, overwhelmed by the sheer immensity of noise, jubilantly stalked the coffin all the way to the cemetery.

One good thing about staying at Sido Nimr and Teta Widad's house while Baba was away was that it was closer than home both to her school and to the centre of town. The bad thing was there was only one entrance. At home she used to climb the bottom gate and pretend she had been in the flowerbed the whole time, but Sido's garden wall was too high, which meant that when she rang the doorbell she gave herself away; and when she did not ring it she also gave herself away, since her mother consulted the members of the family over whether or not they had heard the bell, and thus found out with ease whether her youngest daughter was in the house. Massarra would equivocate on Ghada's behalf: "I don't know, perhaps I heard it, perhaps I didn't," but Taher kept an ear out on purpose. "Where is Ghada?" her mother asked. "Is Ghada home yet?"

"Ask who died today," Taher replied. "Ghada will be with them."

The truth of the matter was, their mother did not actually seem to mind that much. What bothered Ghada, rather, was that it seemed increasingly she couldn't do anything without everyone knowing about it. She supposed this must be a hazard of growing older.

Her mother had informed them, drifting into their bedrooms at Sido's in a beige nightgown, that they would continue staying at their grandparents' house until their father returned. Ghada puffed without speaking, then threw herself onto her bed. She heard Massarra ask when he was coming back, and the answer: "I don't know."

Baba had already missed Ghada's seventh birthday. "You know you are only one day older, not one year older. It's an illusion," Khaled had said. It was also the day they announced the general strike, which meant her birthday was completely ruined, since of course that was all any of the guests talked about when they came round for cake. The calamity of Ghada's life was that when she wanted to be noticed she was ignored, and when she wanted to be ignored she was noticed.

But other than gunfire at night, since her birthday the streets had been unusually quiet. When she went out funeral-walking Ghada found the shops closed, their metal shutters pulled across and padlocked, the ground cleared of refuse and the husks of merchandise, the ribbons and papers and empty boxes that ordinarily littered it at close of market day. And apart from the occasional band of armed fellahin marching through the town, there was no sign of anyone striking anyone else. She wondered, dragging the skein of wool she called her "cat" up an empty hill towards the Eastern Cemetery, whether the men of Nablus had gone to Jerusalem to strike people there. She pictured her father at Damascus Gate, hitting someone with his stick. Whatever the cause, the new quiet made it easier than usual to pick out the funereal drums, and catch up with the coffins before they reached their graves.

Christian funerals she loved most of all, because they played music as well as the percussion. She gazed at the faces of the musicians, transfixed by the lightning movements of their fingers. She strode with confidence and no one doubted that she knew the dead. With the cemeteries she was certainly familiar; she knew the profiles of their headstones as one might know the skyline of town on the ride home. She knew the Christian grave-yards around the different churches, the Orthodox and Roman monuments and cenotaphs, and the Western Muslim Cemetery where her mother's family were buried, their tombs regularly replastered white, and the Eastern Cemetery, to the north near Ebal and the railway station. After the coffin containing the dead person had been lowered into the earth, and the sheikh or priest had emitted some holy words, Ghada trod out between the head-stones and walked back to her grandparents' house through the quiet street.

One afternoon in June, after the congregants had departed, Ghada remained peering in through the archway of the Greek Orthodox Church. A late rain conjured a rich smell out-of-doors and her shoes were muddy from the graveyard. But from inside the church the fumes of incense still emanated, dregs from the tinny censers which minutes before had been swinging up and down the aisles. The priest was the only one left. In long black robes and hat, beard sprawling from the curtains of his habit, he was lighting the tapers, stroking the wicks with the end of his thin candle to impart the flame.

The days were getting longer. And yet, owing to a lingering warmth in the wet air, Ghada did not anticipate the onset of night. Only when the call to prayer reverberated from the minarets did she notice the light changing behind her. She gasped. Her first instinct was to run, and she would have done so, had not the street before the church filled up at that very moment with other people running.

She took a breathless step back under the arch. In the half-dark the runners accumulated. Kufiyas whipping behind their heads, feet hitting the ground. She could hear the clothes rustle against their bodies, and the clicks of things they were carrying. She gripped her sandwich case and kept still. The runners thinned, now only two or three passed at a time. There was something weird about the scene, and it was a moment before she understood that it was because no one was speaking. A fusillade of gunshots started up in the distance, and a few fellahin ghost-men increased their speed. Across the way a woman appeared in a doorway. She stepped to the side, and three running men passed into her house without dropping pace.

"What are you doing here, little one?"

Ghada looked up. The priest was pressing the heel of one hand against the armpit of the arch. His eyebrows were big and put his deep eye sockets in shade.

"Where are your mother and father?"

Ghada's face stretched open.

"Don't cry. No, no, no."

Tutting and pouting the way childless people pouted at children, he crouched to pick her up, and then she was in the air with his arms around her waist, being carried into the church. Tears erupted forcefully from her eyes, her only dam against fear crumbling at this first sign of kindness.

"Do you know where you live?"

"Of course I know where I live!" she broke out, full of scorn.

"We will wait," he whispered, gesturing at the door, "until the rebels are hidden."

Two big armoured vehicles appeared in the proscenium of the door-way, mounted with torches that beamed along the road. At last, voices. English shouts.

The hard polished wood of a pew met Ghada's backside, and the priest, after closing and bolting the doors, crouched again before her with an agility one did not associate with priests; he was talking again but she could not hear him, she was too preoccupied with her tears, which were relentless and very tiring. The harsh fibres of a rag rubbed the underside of her nose. And then he was beside her, sitting on the pew. Gunshots screamed beyond the doors; he tried to put his big old hands over her ears but she pushed them away. By the time silence fell and she had stopped crying, nighttime was absolute. The priest dragged open the door on the black night, and gestured for her to climb into his arms.

As they walked, he sang loudly. "Irahamna ya Rab—iraham-na. Li-an-nuna mutaha-yru-un-a an ku-u-u-ul-i jawab." A slow, plodding melody, very solemn. Ghada, hugging his neck, experienced the deep vibrations in her side, as the sandwich case, which he was holding in one hand beneath her legs, beat against his thigh. They passed a group of soldiers peeping through the windows of a house, and the priest increased his volume. The soldiers glanced up like animals and stared; the priest added some English words to the song, which Ghada recognised from school: "Glory to the Father, the Son, the Spirit—Holy." The soldiers lost interest.

When he dropped her at the gate, she whispered: "Thank you, father."

"Goodnight." The sandwich case dangled from his fingers. For a brief second he touched the top of her head. She was halfway up the steps when his singing restarted. In the thin light from the windows the skirt of his black robe swayed from side to side.

Her mother opened the door. "Where in God's name have you been!"

"The priest brought me home."

"Priest?" She slammed the door. The wings of her nose flared. "No more funerals! No more! If you don't come home immediately after school the Ghuleh will follow you and she will eat you. She will *eat* you."

Ghada eyed her mother's features. That neck, stretched by rage. She looked terribly ugly.

"Where has Ghada been?" Taher was in the hall, dressed in a tweed suit and tarbush too large for him.

"Go away," said Ghada.

"Don't tell your brother to go away."

Taher cracked a smile and walked off singing in English: "*Ghada* had a little mare, its coat as white as snow. And where that mare and *Ghada* went, we're jiggered if we know."

"Where did you learn that?" said Fatima.

The boy shrugged. "Oozelbart, Oozelbart, where have you been? I've been to Damascus to see Haj Amin."

"Stop speaking English."

Ghada pushed her way past her mother, and when she met no resistance, ran up the stairs to the bedroom. Massarra was sitting in the window, darning a hole in her skirt, which was hitched over her thighs. She glanced up as Ghada entered.

Ghada lay flat on her back, awaiting her punishment. She listened for footsteps, and, each time they approached, held her breath. Each time, they travelled past the door. She turned to face the wall. The wind crooned and a light rain ticked over the windowpanes.

When she woke, it was morning. Her sister was gone. A blanket lay on top of her, and lifting it Ghada saw she was still in her clothes. Someone had taken her shoes off and put them on the floor.

She changed her knickers, and without touching the caked mud on her shoes slipped them on, took a piece of cheese from the kitchen, and left the house. There was no sign of her mother. The morning was cool and bright. A few cars travelled down the road; there were no pedestrians. A tangle of armed soldiers adorned the back of a Ford Tender, draped over their guns. They ignored her. She paused at the tip of the road from Sido's house. Then she turned up the higher road, which led to their old home.

As she walked, she imagined Baba would be there. Her evil mother was keeping her from him. Partway down the street, the force of longing took hold of this fantasy, so that as the corner of the house came into view she started to run, ready to jump into his arms. She slowed, laughing, breathless, at the door.

The shutters were closed. The air cooled in the shadow of the tree. The blank door goaded her. Yet her craving for Baba was strong, and she ran a hand against the rust and peel of the iron rail and mounted the steps to try the handle, but the cold iron sweated in her fingers and would not give. Then something made a noise. In the house, near the house, she didn't know—she scuttled down the stairs and ran. The road felt longer this time, and her legs hurt, her shoes smacked the ground. At the junction she slowed to a walk, her heart still going.

"I was looking for you," said Sahar, on the doorstep. "Your neighbour told me you were here."

It was early afternoon, and Fatima was not expecting visitors. Sahar was visibly sweating from the heat.

"Are you sure you should travel like that?"

"There are many things I probably shouldn't do." Sahar sighed, and spread her fingers over her pregnant belly.

They sat in the large main room, Fatima on the couch facing the door, Sahar in a chair at an angle. The swelling had reached her neck and she had the heavy, bovine look of one overwhelmed by the activities of her body.

"Please." Fatima pointed at a bowl of dates. "Were there many soldiers?"

Sahar nodded. "On the road from Jerusalem. I saw a train overturned."

"Al-hamdulillah. How is your husband? Is he still detained?"

"Yes. I have only heard a little. I know he is active. Writing to the British, and the Higher Committee. Working, in other words. He told me," she began to laugh, "he told me they are meditating every day. That it is the only way to cope."

"Do they get fresh air?"

"Yes, they go outside," said Sahar.

"I heard this is important."

"And Midhat?"

"Midhat does not write," said Fatima. She paused. "His leg is healing well."

"Ah good, good."

Fatima scrutinized Sahar. The person she really yearned to talk to was Hani. She longed for his reassurance that everything would be fine, it would be over soon, Midhat was only temporarily disturbed and would soon recover. For, apart from his famous wisdom, Hani knew Midhat better than anyone else did. She needed to be told there was a rational cause. Midhat was usually the one who would tell her that. It was becoming hard to keep her balance without him, paying for paltry vegetables in other people's living rooms, the constant fear of disaster, teetering on the edge so that she rose breathless in the mornings without appetite. Although she was living with them now, her parents brought no solace. Her father was too detached to discuss anything with her, and her mother's historic reserve against Midhat was transparent and abiding.

She could not formulate any of this into a question. She was so used to wearing her polished social armour, requiring nothing, that though she desired Sahar's comfort she did not know what to do with her desire. After several seconds of contemplating, she realised Sahar was smiling, and understood that something on her face must have conveyed proximity to speech. She said:

"How long do you think the strike will last?"

"I think they will make concessions in a month or two."

"They?"

"The British." Sahar shifted her leg with a heavy jerk and released a breath. "You know some people say, well, if we are in the right then of course they must see sense. They have this idea of British justice, you know. But to be honest with you Fatima, I think they are shocked, the British, we have shocked them, and this is the only thing that may make them relent. They call it crime. Mish ma'ool. If to want a nation is a crime," she laughed, and for the first time her weary voice rose in pitch, "we are all criminals! They should lock us all up."

"Oh God, no." Fatima suddenly felt sorry for Sahar. A moment later, this was overtaken by a burst of self-pity. "Only have one child," she said.

"One?"

"Four is too many."

"Are they difficult?"

Fatima shook her head and breathed: "Ghada."

A voice came from outside: "Fat-meh? Fat-i-ma! Open the door!"

"Lahza, lahza."

Um Taher was standing at the bottom of the steps, with a thin bit of chiffon tied under her hair. She looked exhausted. One hand reached upwards, snapping open and shut. Fatima jumped down two steps and stuck out an elbow to assist her.

"What's happened? Is everything all right?"

"Fine mama." Um Taher heaved in slow motion, dragging one leg. She was barely putting any weight on Fatima's arm. "Except that Wasfi and Jamil have filled our house with fighters and there is dirt everywhere everywhere. Fazee'a. I am sick to death. The noise. The *boots* they wear." She exhaled into the room. "Sahar! Where is your husband? Ooh la la, you are very pregnant."

"He is in the prison camp. Keef halek?" Sahar wobbled onto her feet and leaned forward for two kisses.

"Still? God give you strength habibti." Um Taher patted her arm. "I saw Midhat today."

"How is he?" said Fatima in a low voice.

Um Taher spread her lips, unsmiling. "Where is Ghada?"

"Ask who died today," said Massarra, walking into the room and reaching out her arms. "Hello Teta."

"Who died today?" said Um Taher. "Where's your grandmother?"

"I'm still alive," said Widad, mock-weary, clopping into the room. In her social voice she sang: "How are you, how are you," kissing each guest. "Mashallah," she said to Sahar's stomach. "How many months?"

"Many people died today," said Sahar. "At Ayn al-Haramiya. Seven. Months, I mean, not the dead. How many dead I don't know."

"Who?" said Fatima.

"Oh it's the same as usual," said Um Taher, sitting down. "The rebels, bihuttu stones in the road, the army car, phut, stops, English come out, and then from the hills the fighters shooting down. Some rebels died, the others they went to our house."

"Those are the fighters in your house?" said Fatima.

"Yes, yes."

"Massarra go upstairs."

"Why, Mama?"

"Let her stay," said Um Taher. "The children should know. We are all fighting, even you and me."

"Except me," said Sahar. "I'm not fighting."

"Pregnancy is fighting. You will give birth to a fighter. Inshallah he will be a boy," said Um Taher.

"And how is your grandson?" said Widad.

Um Taher narrowed her eyes. "His leg is healing well."

"You don't need to . . ." Widad began gently, and broke off.

"Massarra, go upstairs," said Fatima.

"*Why*," said Massarra.

Um Taher folded her hands. "Well he is doing better."

"*I* know where Baba is," said Massarra.

Everyone glanced up at the girl. Her new bobbed haircut would have made her quite grown-up looking, were she not twisting back and forth on one leg.

"He is in mustashfa al-majanin," said Massarra.

"Baba is not majnun," said Um Taher. "Baba is just sad."

"But why is he sad?" said Massarra. "That's what no one will tell me. Is he sad about Palestine?"

Um Taher laughed. "Maybe. Maybe he is sad about Palestine."

"How is the hospital?" said Widad.

"I don't want to talk about this anymore," said Fatima. "Mama don't make that face."

"I made no face."

"We need to take him out," said Um Taher.

"Why?" said Fatima, but she shook her head to thwart Um Taher's reply. "The more we talk . . ."

"I won't tell anybody, I promise," said Sahar. She put a hand on her heart, the other still resting beneath her belly, as though propping it up. "I have no one to tell. I live alone, more or less."

"You live alone? Like this?" said Um Taher. "Ya salam what is happening to us. Someone should be with you. You should come and live with me."

"Thank you, Teta," said Sahar. "After my mother died—"

"Allah yirhamha," said Um Taher.

"Thank you, Allah yirhamha, after that I have no more family in Jerusalem except for my husband, and now that they have imprisoned him . . ."

Widad tutted theatrically and shook her head. "They strip us. They strip us down."

"Of course I have a maid," said Sahar, "so I don't really need anything."

"Needs needs. There are needs and there are needs," said Um Taher. "There's someone at the door."

"Is there?" said Fatima.

"Yes there is, I just heard it."

This time they all did: a loud rap like the bark of a dog. Fatima walked to the window and made a tunnel of her hands to peer through the glass.

"It's a man. Where is my scarf."

Um Taher made a snoring noise. Widad pulled a scarf from around her own neck up onto her head and, wrapping it around twice, tucked the ends under her chin; Fatima picked up Sahar's black veil among the coats, and selected a brown one for herself.

"I don't have one," said Massarra.

"I told you to go upstairs," said Fatima. "Teta."

"Yes," said Um Taher.

"Would you like to borrow a veil?"

A salvo of harsher knocks erupted from the door.

"No thank you," said Um Taher, closing her eyes with emphasis. She turned her head slightly to the side, as if to show off the small piece of fabric already slung over her hair. She had fastened it at the back, leaving both her neck and large swathes of grey hair free.

"Upstairs, Massarra," Fatima called, hurrying to the door.

Massarra made the same snoring sound as her great-grandmother, and sloped out of the room.

A rebel tha'ir was standing outside. He had a bulbous nose and hard, demarcated cheekbones. His kufiya was secured on his head with a black i'qal around the crown, and he wore a khaki Ottoman-style military jacket paired oddly with some dirty brown qumbaz trousers. The nose of a rifle strapped to his back poked up above his head.

"Good afternoon," said Fatima. "May I help you."

"Where is your husband?" He flicked a hand over his chest and his fingers rippled down the bullets.

"The hospital," said Fatima.

"Is he a doctor?"

"No."

He considered her without reserve. "We want to know if you have any ammunition, or if you have any men who can fight." In this speech his accent emerged, and she guessed the Northern Galilee. He peered into the room behind her, where the women sat perched on the chairs and sofa, utterly still, all veiled except for Um Taher.

"Is that a Jewish woman?" said the rebel.

"No," said Fatima. "That is my husband's grandmother."

He frowned. "So. Any men?"

"Only my father," said Fatima. "And he is too old."

"Your sons?"

"My sons are aged twelve and ten."

"Brothers?"

"My brother has joined the fight already. Burhan Hammad, perhaps you know him."

"No I don't," said the tha'ir. There was some lapse in his military attitude, as though he were lost in thought, and he snagged his head to the side. After a moment Fatima realised he was listening. He shifted round and shouted down at someone. "No one here." Turning back to Fatima he raised a fist, showing her the base of it.

She nodded. "Ala rasi."

"Allah ma'ek Sitti."

"We have been raising money," said Sahar, as Fatima shut the door and pulled the scarf off her head. "For the fighters."

"Bravo," said Fatima. "I am worried about Ghada. Does anyone know where she is?"

There was another knock on the door.

"They can't keep coming in here!"

"Maybe it's your daughter," said Sahar.

As Fatima put her veil back on, she heard her mother say: "And how is your health, Um Taher?"

"I am always dying."

"I think you will outlive us all." Widad gave a dry laugh.

It was a different rebel this time. The first rebel was still there, however, standing a few steps down, and since the new rebel was considerably shorter, their heads were on a level.

"Sitti I must come in," said the new rebel. He had a gruff voice. His hair was grey and his body sinewy, and there were blemishes from the sun across his forehead.

"Please, tfadalu." Fatima stepped aside.

"Name?"

"Is he coming in too?"

"He'll stay outside."

Shutting the door, she saw the first man flick his tails out and reach a hand onto the steps to sit down.

"Name?" said the new rebel.

"Hammad."

"Profession?"

"What? Oh . . . my father is a scholar and a judge."

"Which school?"

"Hanafi."

His bottom lip turned down and he nodded.

"Married?"

"Me? Yes."

"Name?"

"Kamal."

"Profession?"

"Shop . . . shop owner. Clothes."

"They are shut, of course, striking."

"Yes, of course."

"Is he here, your husband?"

"No."

He waited for her to elaborate.

"He's in the hospital. He broke his leg."

"Ah, fighting."

"Something like that."

"Right, I need to look around." The rebel began to tread across the floor towards the three seated women. Sahar ostentatiously caressed her belly.

"Please wait a moment sir," said Fatima quickly. "I must tell my children."

From the stairs, she heard her mother offer the man a cup of coffee, and the rebel's reply: "Actually Madam I am very hungry, we have been running for hours. Just a piece of bread, or . . ."

She went to the boys' room first. Taher was reading on his bed, lying on one side. Khaled, on the floor, was writing digits in an exercise book with a blunt pencil.

"There's someone here who needs to look around the house. Get yourselves tidy and put your things away."

"Who, Mama?" said Khaled.

She looked down at her son. Reluctantly, she said: "A rebel."

Khaled's mouth dropped open and curved into a grin.

"Don't get excited. You will both stay up here. You will be very, very quiet."

The girls' room was across the hall.

"Massarra, where is Ghada?"

"I'm here Mama!"

Ghada was on the windowsill, legs tucked under her arms.

"Where on earth have you been?"

"She's been here," said Massarra.

There was no time to ask questions. Fatima addressed Massarra in an adult tone of voice. "They are going to look around the house. I need your help. You must be quiet."

Massarra nodded officiously.

The door to Haj Nimr's study swished open, and Fatima saw her father slumped at the desk. His right hand was coiled up into his wrist like a sleeping animal, and his mouth, hanging open, was marked along the bottom with a rim of dried spittle, which plastered the corners between his lips. The lamp beside his book was almost out of oil and the flame was low.

"Baba," she whispered.

He whimpered and his head lolled to the side.

"Baba."

His eyebrows rose. "Habibti I am sleeping."

"I know, I'm sorry. But there are two rebels downstairs. They want to look around the house. Do we have any money around? Or—or weapons."

There was a silence. Then he shifted upright in his chair and blinked awake. "There is a German gun. In the kitchen cupboard. It's old, though." He squinted at her, as though facing a bright light. "At least twenty years old."

"Will you come, Baba? We are all women there."

He shifted sideways in his chair and shut his eyes again. "Tell them I am sleeping."

Downstairs, both rebels were sitting on the sofa. From a silver tray Widad was serving coffee, alongside a plate of biscuits and another of bread with za'atar. At the sight of Fatima, the first rebel said, somewhat apologetically: "We will just eat first."

"Sahtayn," said Fatima. She was about to add, "Bon appétit," a phrase often used in their household on account of Midhat, but checked herself in time.

"What villages are you from?" said Sahar.

"Me, I am from Sha'b, in the Galilee," said the first fighter. He tore at a piece of bread with his teeth, a motion that seemed to require his whole body. Widad moved the plate of olive oil a little closer to him.

"Tayiba," said the second, shorter one. With apparent reluctance, he added: "It's near to Tulkarem."

There came the sound of feet, and Fatima's sons materialised in the doorway behind her. Khaled had put on a tweed jacket, too short for him in the sleeves. Taher was wearing his tarbush and carrying a book. Fatima shut her eyes in exasperation.

"What are your names?" said Khaled, leaning forward on his toes.

The rebels gazed at him. Khaled returned the gaze with something like longing, but Taher, Fatima noticed, looked somewhat disturbed. He was holding his book very firmly up to his chest, and his jaw was clenched.

"I am Abu Raja," said the tall one from Sha'b.

He turned to his companion. The shorter one from Tayiba shrugged and shook his head. He swung a cup to his lips and downed the contents in a single gulp.

"Are you Aref Abd al-Razzaq?" said Khaled.

"No," said the shorter rebel. "But Aref is my cousin. Where did you hear about him?"

Khaled glowed. "Everybody knows about Aref . . ."

"All right, all right," said Fatima. "Let's get this over with. Boys go upstairs. *Go.*"

Taher dragged Khaled by the elbow. Fatima waited until she heard their feet on the landing before, in a quiet voice, addressing the short cousin of Aref.

"We have one gun. It's downstairs in the kitchen. Would you like to come and see, or shall I bring it?" Sending a glance over the others she caught a look of dismay on Um Taher's face, which confused her.

"*I'll* get it," said Widad. "Excuse me please."

They waited in silence. The sunlight petered out in the window above the door. Sahar's expression dulled; her eyes, unfocused, fell to the ground. Fatima considered asking the men to give them privacy, but there was an icy tension in her legs. Why did she not simply ask? Surely they would not be so inhumane as to say no. On the contrary, they were here to fight on their behalf, ready where the ulema and politicians had failed. Where was her father? Asleep upstairs. Her husband? Never touched a gun in his life. And Hani was in a detention camp, and yes Wasfi and Jamil and the others helped, and many wives of famous men were orating at the protests, but still most of the brave, the armed men and women, were peasants.

She felt a headache coming on. There lay Sahar, pregnant and exhausted, wrapped in the veil she had been fighting against. This forced rebel lore, the songs the shoeshine boys sang about the whores who wore Western clothes, all of it had some quality of revenge, disguised as ardour. Was that such a heavy price to pay, though, for their freedom? She looked at the cousin of Aref, sitting closest to her. His fingers were entwined, and he was staring down between his arms at the ground. She inhaled and smelled something sour. It was, she believed, the odour from his body.

In contrast to Sahar, Um Taher seemed unusually alert. She was pouting with what could be either disapproval or approval, hands clasped, staring at the rebels. Once they left, Fatima would ask her about Midhat. Abu Raja surveyed the room, twisting to view the tall sparsely decorated walls, the closed doors, and in his open mouth his tongue was visibly folded among his back teeth. When his eyes fell on Fatima he looked, she thought, slightly abashed. At last, Widad's high heels clopped on the stair.

She carried the weapon, wrapped in hessian, at a ceremonious height with two hands. Fatima relinquished her chair and her mother sat to unwind the bundle, revealing a gun so large that Fatima was astonished she had never come across it during her entire childhood in this house. A long silver barrel, a worn wooden handle; from the way the tendons moved in her mother's hands she saw it was very heavy. A small brass loop on the bottom tinkled as Widad delivered it in both palms to the cousin of Aref Abd al-Razzaq.

He rattled it with difficulty. "No bullets?"

"Unfortunately," said Widad.

But it was the gentler one, Abu Raja, who handled the gun with confidence, peering down the barrel and checking the sight line. He shared a look with his companion, opaque to the rest of them.

The long-awaited inspection of the house was cursory. The snack and the gun seemed to have softened the rebels' manners, and they spoke with a hint of regret of the other houses they still had left to search, and said of course they wished to leave the ladies in peace. Aref's cousin stepped out first through the front door, and Abu Raja addressed Sahar as an afterthought.

"Where is your husband?"

"Sarafand," said Sahar.

He cocked his head. "Name?"

"Hani Murad."

"Bismillah," said Abu Raja, and his companion gasped and stepped back inside. "Why didn't you say so! Hani Murad. Ya Allah, your husband is a great man, a *great* man."

Fatima clenched her fingers around the door handle.

"Thank you," said Sahar.

"She is pregnant," said Fatima.

"Mashallah," said the cousin of Aref, now pole-upright and bowing with a hand on his chest. "Allah yikhaleeki, ya Sitti. Allah yikhaleeki."

Fatima watched the rebels creep away under the darkness. On feet silent as paws they scudded over the terrace and down the steps to the road.

The women took off their veils without speaking. Widad led Um Taher upstairs to the spare bedroom, and Fatima stared after them, her thirst for comfort dashed against Um Taher's receding back.

"How are you feeling?" she said to Sahar. "Do you want anything? You must stay here, you'll sleep in my bed."

Sahar frowned. She said: "Thank you. I'd like a glass of water, if I may. I'll come with you."

"No no no, you stay. Have you eaten enough?"

"Plenty."

Fatima ran the faucet in the kitchen far longer than necessary. She gripped the cold edge of the sink, and the touch sent a chill down her body. The porcelain around the drain was covered in long scratches and a string of something green draped over one of the bars between the holes. At the sound of steps behind her, she roused herself and quickly filled the glass.

"You should be resting," she said, and then with surprise: "Oh, Teta."

"Habibti." Um Taher limped into the glow from the window. The tautness of her face upstairs was gone; her cheeks were slack and her eyes shining. "I have to tell you." She was out of breath. "We need to bring him back to Nablus. We need to bring him back . . ."

"Sit, sit, take a seat."

Teta's hands were shaking. "He said he killed someone."

"What?"

"Don't worry." She managed a condescending smile. "He didn't actually kill anyone." The muscles in her face twanged flaccid and the smile dropped off. "He is just mad."

"How do you know?"

"Trust me. I know."

"Who did he kill—or say he killed?"

"He is not a murderer," she said again with that same smile, as though Fatima had brought up this idea. "An idiot, maybe, not a murderer. Anyway, we need to get him out."

Fatima's eyes fell from Um Taher's face to her fingers resting on the table, firm and capable, as if the wrinkled layer were only a glove she had put on. She whispered: "How will we get him out?" and glanced up to check her expression.

Um Taher's voice rose, edged with a whine. "Why do I always have to do these things alone?" She opened her hands. "Why weren't you with me, mama?"

"I'm sorry," said Fatima. "The children—"

"You can leave the children with your mother! I hate that place, I hate . . . why Hani thought it was a good idea, why! We know whatever the ingliz make is not good, nothing is good that they make. Stupid." She continued murmuring, until her eyes met Fatima's and her screwed-up face relaxed. "Don't cry," she snapped. "If I thought you'd cry I wouldn't have told you."

Fatima lurched. In a tone of glacial anger, she replied: "Um Taher, I said I'm sorry. I will come next time if that's what you want. But Sahar is waiting for me upstairs, and she needs water. So, if you will excuse me."

"Oh, go," said Um Taher, with a flap of her hand.

Upstairs, Sahar was asleep. The weave of her fingers beneath her belly had collapsed open, and her unravelled hair lay down the chair back. Before Fatima could fetch a blanket, she pulled herself upright. "Ah. Thank you."

"It's nothing." Fatima set down the glass. She hovered as Sahar reached for it. "Has your husband said anything to you?" She heard her words as if spoken by someone else. "About my husband. About what happened?"

Unless Fatima's eyes were deceiving her, Sahar winced. But a moment later the discomfort appeared more likely physical than moral, given the desperation with which she drank the water, holding the glass with both hands in a manner that reminded Fatima of Ghada. Sahar finished and frowned. "What sort of thing do you mean?"

"Anything," said Fatima, desperately casual. Standing with one hand on the back of the chair, she gesticulated randomly with the other. "Anything you might remember."

"I'm sorry. It must be, I imagine, very difficult."

Fatima gave a voluntary smile. "It is difficult, yes. I'm sure you can see that. I'm sure it's obvious."

"No, you manage very well. It's only that I imagine it must feel hard. I find it hard, and I have only . . ."

"I have my mother. And a grandmother-in-law." She made an ironic face. "I am beset, in fact, with mothers."

Sahar smiled, and Fatima remembered with a flush that Sahar's mother was recently deceased. She chased the silence with a rapid, unprefaced: "Allah yirhamha," which did nothing to cool her hot brow. Though Sahar betrayed no sign she had noticed, and her smile resisted all projection, once more Fatima wondered at her own slipping social grace.

"How is the shop?" said Sahar. "What happened after the fire? The damage must have been considerable."

"Eli—you know Eli? He came by the day before yesterday. They are almost finished with repairs, but the stock . . . the smell is too bad. They will throw it away. Not that it makes a difference. They can't open." In her neck and shoulders Fatima could feel the ghost of her mother's mannerisms. That transparent overeagerness. She concentrated, and stripped her face of expression.

"It is difficult," said Sahar sympathetically.

"I'm not complaining. This is more important. We all make sacrifices for sake of the larger . . ."

"Yes, that's exactly right."

Fatima was silent. "I should take you to bed."

"There was a letter," said Sahar.

It was a moment before Fatima understood what she was referring to. "From who?"

"A woman. From a long time ago."

The words hung in the air. Fatima stared without seeing. The point of a needle slid into the soft patch of flesh between her ribs. From a distance, she heard herself say:

"Was she from France?"

Sahar nodded. "It was in French," she said quietly. "I didn't read it. Hani . . ."

"I don't want to know about it," whispered Fatima.

A great weariness had come over her. She closed her eyes, and saw Midhat lying in his hospital bed. Of course, there would have been other women. Her chest ached.

But, in a moment, all thought of Midhat was eclipsed by her awareness of the pregnant woman sitting before her. She turned her gaze back on Sahar, lying like a royal animal on the Damascene chair. Why had Sahar decided to tell her this? What was her motivation? Her mind scrawled charts of insidious narrative: Sahar was trying to poison her against her marriage, because her own husband was imprisoned. She was lonely, and loneliness made women vicious. Face turned aside, eyes still on Fatima, forehead troubled by a frown. She knew she should be leading Sahar up to bed, but Fatima couldn't move. Something heaved and froze inside her. It was getting dark, the lamps needed lighting. Her ringed hand looked pale on the chair back.

"Mama," came a voice.

Massarra was at the bottom of the stairs, one leg bent with a lingering foot behind her.

"We're hungry."

"What do you mean you're hungry?"

"We didn't eat."

She followed her daughter's eyes to the silver tray on the coffee table, the empty cups, the torn scraps of bread and the dish of oil and za'atar, the plate of fig biscuits. Ghada appeared behind her sister on the stair and shouted with effortless volume: "Mama I'm hungry!"

A noise exploded from Fatima's mouth.

"GO AND MAKE SOMETHING THEN!"

Massarra did not flinch. She gave her mother a piercing look, and only a tremor passed through her lips.

"You're not a child," said Fatima.

"I know," said Massarra.

Fatima reached out and slapped her daughter across the face. Behind her, Sahar gasped. Ghada, on the stair, looked suddenly very small and wan. Massarra's face went scarlet, and not only where the handprint was materialising on her cheek, but all over. A muscle pulsed in her jaw. She turned, saying: "Come on, Ghada." Ghada hesitated. Then, accepting her sister's hand, she followed her down the lower steps.

Fatima remained with her back to Sahar, watching the spot where her daughters had been.

"I'm sorry if I upset you," said Sahar. "I thought it was good to tell the truth."

Fatima's face started to mangle. She had no control, she half turned, hoping the dark was a sufficient shield. A staccato thud struck up in her chest.

"You should rest," she murmured. "Let me show you . . . your room."

In the sights of Jamil's rifle, the back door to the Sports Club was opening. He drew a breath, pushed all the air from his lungs, and deflated his body against the side of his weapon. His heart clanged. The wood panels on the door dropped slowly into shadow. He aimed at the widening column of darkness in the frame, his finger on the trigger. The door stopped. And then, with the same controlled slowness, the panels veered forth again into the sunlight. A final shove sent a minuscule shudder through the wood. Jamil lifted his finger. Beside him, Basil Murad blew out his cheeks.

They were in a bedroom on the second floor of a house owned by the Karak family, two streets from the Sports Club. Madame Karak had pushed the beds against the walls, from which she also withdrew a mirror and several pictures. Jamil did not take well to this last gesture, and scoffed as Madame hurried out, hands full, eyes down, promising breakfast.

Jacketless, he was lying on the floor before the open double doors to the balcony. The chequered locks of his kufiya hung down over his shoulders, and the barrel of his gun was nosed through the lowest curl of the balcony rail. His elbows were propped against a sandbag stolen from the post office. Basil—contrary to Madame's wishes—lay belly down on the last bed abutting the casement window, which he had fractionally opened for the passage of his own rifle. On the floor between them lay a plate of quartered figs.

It was June 1936: the third month of the general strike. The morning was overcast, the streets empty. The week before, they heard the British had bombed the old city of Jaffa, which, with its winding alleys and matrix of courtyards and back doors, had been rebel-ridden and impossible to occupy. Evacuation notices flew from the sky before the bombs did, describing the demolitions as "improvement measures." After the first blasts, a road ten metres wide was paved from the Ajami police station to the sea. The Jaffa Strike Committee announced the damage was worse than that from an earthquake.

In Nablus, the British had seized the shari'a court and the Sports Club. The latter building, at whose back door Jamil was currently training his rifle, had been the headquarters of the Nablus Strike Committee. Fortunately, no documents or equipment had been left on the premises. In fact, the resistance was so decentralised that no list of the committee members even existed: almost everything was word of mouth. This British triumph had not then struck the heart of the movement; nevertheless it was an insult and bad for morale. The Committee was now forced to meet in the auditorium of the disused cinema instead.

"The roof," said Basil.

Jamil turned his eyes, sore from the blank sky. On the bed, Basil was steadying his gun with one hand and holding a pair of field glasses to his face with the other. They clashed lightly against his spectacles.

"What's there?"

"Machine guns."

Jamil lifted his head and squinted at the Sports Club's flat roof. Outlined against the sky, two black circles of machine gun barrels eyed him. He said nothing. He lowered his head back to his gun and stared at the door. Basil reached for a fig quarter.

"They think we are getting help from the Italians." Basil flicked the stem away. "I heard it from Issa, in the police." He shut one eye and peered down his carbine. "Issa's mother, actually."

With a tiny violent gesture, the back door of the Sports Club opened again. Jamil inhaled and exhaled fast, gripping the barrel.

"Wait," said Basil.

"What?"

"Roof."

In the doorway, a policeman appeared. Full garb: hard hat, gun ready, bare legs and putteed ankles below short trousers running to open the door of a military car parked a few metres off. One leg inside, the other gone, car door slam audible over the quiet distance. The engine revved.

"Shit," said Jamil. He turned his body fully and opened his hand. "Why did you stop me?"

"The roof," said Basil steadily. "There's someone there."

Jamil tipped his gun up and stared along the barrel at the sockets of the machine guns. One sky-filled gap between the nearest barrel and the roof suddenly blacked, and the dark half-moon of that gun's upper curve grew slightly. A person, casting a shadow. Without thinking twice, Jamil aimed at the gap and squeezed the trigger. The gun reported with a slap.

"Shu!" said Basil. "What are you doing?"

A cry: a body slumped over the gun and into view. Jamil shot the bolt back and forth and the spent cartridge rang on the tiles. He took aim again.

"*That's* what I'm doing."

"Shit," said Basil through the binoculars. "That was perfect."

The man's hand dangled. His five white fingers, visible even to Jamil's naked eyes, did not stir. Something else moved on the Sports Club roof. It slid along the ledge, a slender brown extension of the stone. The arm of a soldier in uniform. Jamil aligned the sights, fired.

"Stop!" Basil hissed.

"Did I get him?"

Jamil reached for the binoculars, dragging Basil towards him by the lanyard around his neck, and turned the lenses on the place where the second soldier's arm had been. Drips of red glanced down the stone. His heart jumped: no sign of the dead man's hand, nor his mate's. Yes, that was foolish.

Basil slumped against the wall, careful with his boots on the bed. The bags under his eyes cast dark shadows, doubled by his glasses.

A loud crack in the hall shot him to his feet. Jamil pulled the butt of his rifle against his shoulder. The door opened.

"Bravo, ya shabab," said Madame. She ignored the gun and crouched to set a tray between them. Two yellow glasses of mint tea, a pile of hot bread, a plate of cheese. She rubbed her hands on her apron, and wavered. "How long do you need to stay?"

"Half an hour," said Jamil. He reached for tea. "Maybe an hour."

"Thank you so much, Madame," said Basil. "Really, God keep you safe."

"Not at all. Sahtayn."

Basil cleaned his spectacles on his shirt, and ripped a piece of bread.

Jamil and Basil considered themselves crossover figures. Crossed between town and country, Nabulsi and fellah, strike and rebellion. Some newspaper editorials argued that where the civil disobedience of the general strike was the urban struggle, the armed uprising was the rural one, and the separation between the two both inevitable and lamentable. Jamil was determined to rectify this misconception. Young men from noble families had indeed taken up arms, and more were doing so by the day—especially in Nablus. Sure, most of the major battles were still in the mountains, but that was a question of terrain, of playing to their advantages as an agile people on the known crags, where the British blundered with their boots and bad maps. Until last week, was not Jaffa, that city of indecipherable streets, a rebel stronghold? A question of terrain: the British could not infiltrate. Ergo, they bombed it. Sure, some new reluctance was sprouting among the wealthy, some resentment at being ordered around by peasants, who were starting to threaten landowners and merchants with defamation and damage to property unless they handed over funds that only a month ago they had been donating with pride. If only they *were* being helped by the Italians: they were strung out on the dregs of their resources, grain stores ran low, Nablus was hungry. But since the army had made this incursion the townspeople were not waiting to be saved. The roads of Nablus were strewn with nails and broken glass to puncture English tyres. Under the arcades of the old city, people looked alert and touched their holsters. These two were not the only ones firing from upper bedrooms.

Among other notables, Jamil and Basil were original members of the Nablus Strike Committee when it first convened in April. They still helped coordinate with committees in other towns, and with ancillary local ones that distributed grain, rice, and sugar across Nablus, that funded the poor, prevented bankruptcy, monitored strike exemptions—including the cafés that opened at night for exchanging news, and pharmacies, which rotated so that one was available every twenty-four hours. But they also bore weapons. Jamil Kamal and Basil Murad were thuwwar. This was their third sniping operation, undertaken at their own initiative. Chief among the tactics they had learned from those refined veterans flowing in from Syria and Jordan and Lebanon was: after the shot, don't move. They are watching for movement. Jamil had taken a big risk by shooting twice.

Basil wrapped half a round of bread over a slice of cheese and resumed his vigil at the window, looking through the binoculars.

"That was stupid."

Jamil rolled his eyes. They ached: he shut them. "Ya'tik al-afieh."

"Allah ya'afik."

He sipped his cooling tea. He had no appetite. He had risen earlier than necessary, and running the faucet in the dawn dark to splash his face woke his mother, who crept into the kitchen to berate him for not sleeping enough. "I sleep like the dead, Mama," he said. But she was right. He had so feverishly compounded his duties as a bridge between the city and rebel commands, undertaking tasks that could have been delegated, that although he dropped off at night under a warrior's fatigue he woke in the mornings with a chemical jolt, disturbed by a spectral image of victory. When he wasn't plotting with Basil, he was on the telephone with leaders in Jerusalem, or with forces in Syria, tallying losses against victories and tracking arms deliveries over the Jordan River, where Arab patrols were bribed with hashish brought on camels from Latakia. He was not a public figure. He was not Hani Murad. He saw himself as a quiver of darkness; an actor and also a ligament; the fibre between fighter and fighter.

Ever since he first saw death at the Nebi Musa riots sixteen years earlier, Jamil had longed to be *doing*. That pair of dirty corpses still lay in his memory. The moment he bore the weight of that dead Arab aloft, and the still-warm blood soaked into his jacket, was a tremendous, altering moment. With a great slow force over subsequent months this experience gradually changed Jamil's sense of responsibility. And finally, now, the time for witnessing and suffering, of debating in assemblies and composing memoranda, was over. His arms grew full of blood; his stomach sharp. He so dissolved into his mission that the strains in his body became idiomatic of the struggle: the energy in his feet was Arab energy, his mind's determination was Nabulsi determination, the weakness of his ankles Palestinian weakness, the ache in his bones a Palestinian ache. News of British violence gusted through him and flowered out as anger. Images remained: he saw the policemen flogging student protesters on their bare buttocks in a line outside the mayor's office. Peasant women being searched for arms on the roadside and lewdly gestured at. A house demolished, the family holding their belongings beside the soldiers on the hillock, forced to watch as their home exploded. His rage pulsed. He tended carefully to the hearth of his fury: well-kept it fuelled him, but he was no help to anyone if his whole self went up in flames. His irritation at Basil about the second shot was really irritation at himself, because he could not afford to be rash. He bowed, penitent, over his tea, and forced himself to eat a piece of bread. His grateful stomach unclenched.

The escape route was laid out in advance. After eating, they washed their hands in the Karak bathroom, slung their weapons, and left by the kitchen door into the sheltered hawsh courtyard. With a silver flash, an upper window opened along the stretched arm of a young girl. She peered down as Jamil and Basil slipped into the tunnel beneath the house, where a door on the corner stood purposefully ajar. The owner, waiting in the vestibule, bowed as they darted through his living room. Basil led them up a rear staircase. At the head of the stairs, through an open window, they heard the clamour of a police patrol. Basil hugged the wall, but Jamil slid his weapon off his shoulder and went to look. Three vehicles rolled by, reflecting blades of sunlight.

"They're going in the wrong direction," he said.

"You can leave those here," came a woman's voice.

Jamil jumped round. A veiled figure was standing in the doorway.

"Under the bed," she added.

Basil unslung his rifle and Jamil held out both guns by their barrels. "Thank you, Khalto."

"We'll collect them this evening," said Basil.

"Inshallah," said the woman wearily, a rifle in each hand.

The external staircase took them into a back alley, darkened by high stone. At the intersection, Basil gripped Jamil's neck. Then he turned, hunched, in the direction of his brother's house.

Jamil took the fastest route from the old city and was soon on the mountain, unarmed but for a small old dagger in his waistcoat. His alertness began to ebb. He thought of the first man, that shadow, featureless until the moment of death, when his body had blossomed forth and his hands slipped into view. He forced himself to conjure a portrait of him. A hackneyed image of an officer with a brutal moustache, alive, death-marked. Then the simple pleasure of the act returned: aiming, firing, seeing the hand fall. He bristled. It was an excellent shot.

His mother's living room smelled strongly of burnt sage.

"Ah habibi." She rose from the couch. "Khalto, weinek?"

"Ah mama," said Um Taher, stepping from the bedroom, straightening the lapels of her gown over the steep hill of her breasts. "Ah khalti, ah he's here. Yalla habibi we need to talk. Abu Jamil?"

"He's sleeping. Leave him." Um Jamil dusted her hand, meaning: he wouldn't help us anyway. She faced her son with a hungry expression.

Jamil dropped onto the sofa. He was his family's conduit to the struggle, and though he knew his duty was to help them by explaining, the task wearied him. Sometimes he considered the contrast between his duties outside the house, which, though larger, he undertook without complaint, and those smaller ones at home that he resisted, as if a muscle in his mind had only one direction in which to move when faced with his mother, and that direction was against.

"We need to talk," said Um Taher again, sitting opposite.

"Mashi," said Jamil.

"About Midhat," said his mother.

"I," said Um Taher, and putting her hands on her knees she let out a gust of air, "I went to see him in the hospital."

"Mm," said Jamil.

"And I didn't like it," said Um Taher. "I don't like it at all. Habibi, will you help us? We need to take him out."

"I don't see how I can help."

"We need, ya'ni, more people." His great-aunt began to move in a manner familiar to him, her white eyebrows tensed and her fingers grasping after her words: the manner of someone constructing a plot. "The more family who come to help, the more we can make them feel, ya'ni—we're going to go there in two cars, Fatima is coming, your father—we need everybody we can get. Men, especially. We need you."

"That's not how it works with these places, Khalti," said Jamil. "If they think he's dangerous they won't release him."

"But we're going to try," said his mother, nodding vigorously.

"You shouldn't have put him there in the first place," said Jamil. "You should have left him with the Ebal Girls."

"That's what I said," said Um Jamil. "We could have got a sheikh, we could have tried another way. It's the mixture of things, I heard, it's the mixture that makes you mad, that draws in the jinn." She made a fist and swerved her extended thumb from side to side: "Love plus sorrow. Love plus grief. Grief plus fright. It's mathematical. One man can take only so much. This fire at the shop came at a bad time—grief plus . . ."

"We're not getting a sheikh." Um Taher looked irritated. "He's not possessed."

Jamil nearly smiled. Um Taher had always been the superstitious one in the family, but his mother appeared to have overtaken her. Perhaps it was a stage women passed through in their journey towards obsolescence, a phase of murmuring born of panic, grappling at trinkets and ancient tricks, from which they finally emerged white-haired, rational, and resigned.

"I know, Jamil," said Um Taher, "that this is not the time for this. You have other things to think about. But think. He's your cousin. He's your brother. And he is suffering in there." Her mouth melted open. She cupped a hand to her face and swallowed her next words.

"Listen," said Jamil heavily, though he did not know what he was going to say.

"We will take him out," said his mother, "and when he is well he will become a fighter."

"Mama, Midhat will never be a fighter." The telephone was ringing. "Give me a moment."

"Basil Murad for Jamil Kamal," said the operator.

"Jamil is with you."

"Ah habibi," said Basil. "We need to go, the road between Anabta and Nur Shams. Are you ready? Abd al-Rahim al-Haj Muhammad is leading. Munir has gone to collect the rifles."

Jamil glanced over at his mother and great-aunt, who were watching him. "Do you have that thing we were talking about?"

"Yes. The English called for help—that's where the patrols were going."

"Anabta exactly?"

"Just before."

"I'll see you at your brother's." He replaced the telephone.

"You're not going," said his mother.

"Going where?"

"Battle. You are not going."

"Mama. Relax."

"He wants to fight, let him fight," said Um Taher.

"He's my son!"

"Look, what time is it now—eleven o'clock. I'll be back for dinner. I promise. Mashi?"

His mother released a moan, and kneaded the knuckles of one hand into the other palm. "God keep you safe. God keep you, God keep you."

Jamil pulled on his jacket and left the house.

In general, he avoided thinking about Midhat as much as possible. The day he found his cousin trembling on the floor of Wasfi's study, he had wept briefly in front of Hani. But he did not visit Midhat in the Nablus hospital where he was all winter, nor in the Bethlehem one where he was moved last month. Nor had he made plans to.

Over the past decade, their contact had been minimal. News of his cousin was mostly mediated by Um Jamil and Um Taher, and by Adel Jawhari and other activists who knew him, and sometimes by those in town who did not know Midhat well but imitated his gestures and referred to him as "the Parisian" with an affection that slid into derision. "I'm going to the *banque*," was something still said among Jamil's colleagues, with a flipping of the non-firing hand. But Jamil always had the impression, even from afar, that Midhat exaggerated this image for the fun of it. So he was not exactly the dupe of these jokes, but rather, with one further remove might be extracted from "the Parisian" entirely, which was not him precisely but some other person whom he took the liberty to play. Still, as the years passed Jamil felt shame and irritation when his cousin's name was mentioned. Respectful affection in Nablus had shaded into malice once the Syrians rose up against the French Mandate. Everyone knew France was a cancer of imperial force, leaching life from Arab households. To be a Parisian in Nablus was to be out of step with the times, locked in an old colonial formula where subjects imitated masters as if in the seams of their old garments they hoped to find some dust of power left trapped. This was not precisely the case with Midhat, who seemed rather blind to the deep meaning of his costumes, and was certainly not striving for power or superiority when he meticulously crimped a mouchoir in his pocket and said, "Voulez vous?" Blinking when they talked of politics, agreeing mildly and continuing on his way, so literally in love with the pattern on a scarf that he would spend great fortunes behind his wife's back in order to import it from Europe.

When Midhat had first returned from Paris after the war, Jamil remembered him full of quick energy, with a varnished way of formulating his ideas. France had turned him into a man quite different from the shy schoolboy of their childhood. Many in Nablus even speculated that Midhat might go into politics, given how naturally he discussed Faisal and the Syrian question. Midhat, a politician! Within a year of his return he became so self-absorbed that he jumped when you spoke to him, and between the pair of them a constriction commenced that neither tried to ease. For a while Jamil went on craving the lost affinity of their youth, until it was clear that this quality of sympathy would be impossible to revive. Divided from his cousin in the crowd, Jamil's resentment decayed into scorn.

In the full sunlight he began to sweat. In a way, it made sense that Midhat was now in a hospital for mad people while Nablus was in revolt. How else would al-Barisi have coped with wearing patched trousers? Where would be that man's fortitude, confronted with the scrawny limbs of his nieces and nephews, the hunger and tiredness in the eyes of everyone? Anger was making Jamil walk too fast: he cooled his final thought. Not everyone could be a fighter. When Midhat returned from hospital he would probably manage as well as most.

He ducked into the old city and shrank against the wall. The most dangerous rage of all was the rage against impurity. Condemnation of strike-breakers had lately reached the pitch of fever: last week, a group of youths between eight and fourteen had badly wounded a vegetable merchant by stoning him, after giving him a black eye and pouring a bucket of muck over his head. The man's crime? Suspicion of *wanting* to break the strike. The Committee were setting up a system of rebel courts allowing witnesses to testify before an audience. They hoped this theatre of persuasion would induce the accused to ratify his or her allegiance to the cause—but mostly they meant to placate the accusers, and conjoin everyone in a spirit of common struggle. Unless they handled it properly, this kind of rage would be the death of them.

Jamil turned the corner to Munir Murad's house, and in his mind saw Midhat on the floor, holding a letter. He saw his cousin's devastated stare. He felt the return of that ancient fundamental love that had shoved up inside him and turned his own eyes wet with surprise. Munir opened the door.

"Ta'al," called Basil from another room.

On the dining table lay a flaccid canvas bag with leather straps and a small wooden box lashed to two cylinders with copper wire.

"I didn't pack it yet," said Basil.

Jamil raised the bomb with both his hands. An expert from Damascus had helped them assemble it in the cinema last week with supplies smuggled in on the back of a vegetable cart. Basil held up the flap of the bag, and Jamil slid the box inside and levered the bag onto his back. Though it would not explode until the fuse was lit, at the weight his stomach lifted with apprehension. Basil passed over a rifle and a cloth bag of ammunition.

"You collected these in daylight?" Jamil checked the chamber and slipped in three bullets.

"They've all gone to the mountains," said Basil. "Honestly, if we weren't needed—I'd say we should take the Sports Club."

"Munir, are you coming?"

"Next time, boys. Next time."

They reached Zawata in half an hour. On the parched street, four fighters ran to catch up, wishing them peace. Two were young and beardless. One slim older man carried only a stick. After the greetings, no one spoke. The pale rumble of machine guns echoed from the distance, where a grey balloon of smoke was rising.

"I'll take the bag for a while," said Basil, and the younger heads turned. "Don't wait for us."

By the time Basil was digging his thumbs under the straps and their boots were thudding softly again on the dirt road, those four figures had shrunk where the road twisted to the main square of the village, halfway to the hillside of the battle. Two warriors vaulted past on whinnying horses, and as the hooves contracted into silence the gunfire thickened. At the edge of the village, peasant women were filling jars from a well. Three bowed and joined them, jugs sloshing on their shoulders, and they travelled the road in a silent line between the villages, and the shallow basin that preceded the wadi, stepping ably over the rocks. The rumble resolved into shots and human shouts. They held their rifles and began the climb.

Partway up, Basil slipped and gasped, seizing at a bush. Jamil lunged for his arm, careful not to touch the pack, heart high in his neck, and as Basil found his footing there was a racket of displaced branches ahead. A man in Turkish uniform complete with medals skidded down towards them. His arms flew up and a woman cried, "Ya Allah!" Blood was flowing down his face: his ear had been blown off. They swung apart to let him by. Guns snapped from the other side of the hill.

They had reached the summit. Prone rebels shielded by boulders were firing down the steep valley wall; some were throwing rocks. Jamil dived for shelter into a small ditch fringed with bushes, and pressed his face low to the earth to see.

Beneath the veils of gun smoke, some ten metres below, the convoy was stopped in the valley behind a roadblock of stones. The Lewis gun mounted in the foremost car was silent, presumably out of ammunition—or perhaps the gunman was down; but the car windows were alternating fire up at them. Behind three military vehicles stood the few civilian cars under their protection, but the rear of the convoy wound out of sight where the valley turned. Beneath Jamil's courage, fear glowed. He broke the dry spray of a bush with his hands to make room for his body, and shifted his gun into the cleft beneath a boulder at the top of the ditch. He aimed at the windows of the second car. He worked the bolt back and forth, fired. Worked the bolt, fired. He had no idea if his shots were landing. There was a scream from further off. Someone ran past his left and a rock hurtled down onto one of the car roofs. The man fled the return fire, and stumbled, bellowing in sudden pain.

Jamil refilled his chamber and aimed at another window. On the opposite side of the valley, the snout of a machine gun was rising. The body of the tank came crawling into view. At once, it commenced its continuous shuddering stream, turning up squalls of dust all over their summit. Jamil spun round and made himself as small as possible in his ditch. He could not see Basil anywhere. Others were tucking their legs up and hugging the ground. The red of fresh blood adorned the rocks and wet-blacked the earth. Nearby, one with a wounded thigh continued shooting; beside him lay a dead man, and another dying further down. A young bareheaded woman scrambled up and grabbed the dead man's feet, pulling him after her down the slope. The man still alive cried: "Me! Me!"

A military plane appeared and disappeared, and as the bomb thundered Jamil swivelled onto his front over the shuddering earth. His head knocked on the rock and pain cascaded down his skull. He saw Basil. The rifle was limp in Basil's hands; the backpack was on the ground beside him. The lenses of his spectacles were opaque with dirt and his lips were moving in prayer.

"Go over there!" Jamil screamed, pointing at an unoccupied cluster of rocks. "Use the gun! And the bomb—careful—"

Someone in the valley had spotted them: gunfire increased in their direction and Jamil dug his feet for purchase into the soil, trying to narrow his body while arranging himself to shoot. His rage blazed, and he was glad. The power increased in his hands. Another bomb, further away, sent debris stinging onto his face. He stopped to wipe his eyes with his fingers, and then with his shirt. More rebels were coming up from the rear, clean and vigorous.

"Khalto, drink!" said a voice.

He turned his head carefully. Among the trees, a woman of about his mother's age was holding out a jug of water.

"Get back!"

"Courage!" she shouted.

"Get back!"

A bearded fighter appeared behind her, dressed ambitiously in three bullet bandoliers and a cartridge belt. He shrank into a firm crouch a few feet off and began firing down with great speed and refilling the chamber of his carbine.

Jamil rearranged his knee on the ground, toes behind him flexed on a stone, the other leg crouched, the rifle butt in his shoulder. He aligned the sights on the windscreen of another military car mounted with a machine gun and squeezed the trigger. His bullet glanced off the steel; he shot the bolt, fired again, shot the bolt, fired. An older man passed by bearing a sword and ran down the slope towards his death, brandishing the blade over his head like a believer on the Prophet's birthday. Jamil whispered a dua at the sight of him, his heart slipping in pity. He reached into his bag for bullets. Two left.

"Can you spare some ammunition?" he shouted at his neighbour.

The man did not hear. Three bandoliers might be ambitious, but it looked as though he would use them all. Basil had moved off to the suggested rock cluster and was finally firing his gun. The pack with the bomb was nowhere to be seen.

"Basil!" Jamil shouted. His courage was swiftly disbanding. A second tank appeared on the opposite hilltop. He put his fingers around a stone and threw it at the convoy. It landed on a bush by the roadside. He was shaking. He lay on his front behind the rock.

Today was going to be his death day. He, like those other sacrificial peasants, must now run down the hill with a stick. He wrenched a yell into the earth. His lips were gritted with soil, his voice was painful. Gunfire echoed in the chamber of his stomach. He was seized with the desire to stand up and run away. What would he tell those women waiting at the bottom of the slope, when they saw him? That he was out of ammunition? "Courage!" they would say. Courage meant throwing rocks against artillery. Courage meant descending into the valley unarmed.

"Basil!" he shouted again, desperately.

Basil glanced up. He saw Jamil and drew one arm across his body. The canvas bag appeared in his lap: he placed it as far from himself towards Jamil as he could without exposing himself to the valley. His face glistened with concentration. Jamil heaved a vast inaudible howl and rolled into clear view. He hauled the bag back to his nook and unfastened the buckles. Kneeling, he unwound the fuse, which was tucked into a top corner of the box. He put his shaking hands into his pockets for the matches. He lit the frayed wire. He stood to full height, took a running start, and hurled down his gift. As the smoking box pirouetted towards the convoy, he threw himself onto the ground.

There was a cracking roar. The front car with its grilled maw and her-ringboned tyres rose in the air as on a wave, and the second car rose behind as the roof of the first car lifted. Heat swept up the valley wall, followed by a stream of fumes. The engine was aflame. A cloud of hard dust began to rain down, and Jamil covered his face. He waited for the pelting to stop. Then, through the dust, he shouted: "Basil I have no bullets!"

Basil was firing at a soldier who was trying to extricate himself from the wrecked car. The filth on his spectacles was streaked with fingermarks. Jamil crawled over and grabbed his arm.

"Come when you have none left," he said. "I have nothing. I—I—"

"I have," said Basil, "take—"

"No, no."

Basil fixed on him. "I understand," he said. "Go."

There was enough smoke to obscure Jamil's passage. He was not the only one: three men at different times ran past him down through the thicket towards the road. As he footed the slope a sharp gash of pain in his back made him stagger. He leaned breathless against a tree, and reaching a

hand to his left shoulder fingered a rip in his jacket and shirt. In the patch
of exposed skin a wound stung. His fingertips were wet, and red. He rolled
his shoulder and kept walking; it moved easily, which meant the bullet had
only grazed him. But as the trees thinned out he jumped at the sound of
women's voices and grasped his arm. He squeezed, pulling a face of pain
and dismay. It was a mask, a performance of agony. And at the same time
it was a genuine expression of horror at the direction his feet were taking
him in. Not today. No, not today, unarmed on the battlefield. To die here
was a waste. He wasn't just a fighter; he was needed elsewhere. He was a
vital link. He squeezed his arm. His left hand was going numb.

Two women were trying to lift a man covered in blood. At the sight of
the Ottoman khakis Jamil stopped. He had seen this man earlier. The hair
and kufiya were drenched scarlet where his ear had been.

"Abu Rami, Abu Rami," wailed one of the women. She grasped the
fabric on his shoulders. "I know his daughters. He is a good man."

"He is from your village?" said Jamil.

"Yes, yes."

"Why is he wearing this uniform?"

"They gave it to him," she said, and finally, as though this comment
had brought her to, relinquished her tough and useless grip on his jacket.

"I think—I think he is martyred," said the younger woman. She reached
for his holster and drew up a heavy pistol. It was old, with a silver barrel
and wooden handle.

Jamil looked at the dead man. The mouth was open in a bloody snarl,
the eyes grimaced shut. A chill of cowardice ran over Jamil's skin and his
gullet rose with animal disgust. That was what a noble death looked like.
Poor Abu Rami. His brains lay so close to the air. All that blood, draining
into the ground—something must have struck Jamil blind on the hilltop
for he could no longer see in the blood what he was supposed to see. Where
in that red muck was the move transcendent? Where the doubled symbol
of faith, the brave struggle for the homeland and its heavenly reward? He
could only see an ugly mess, a vile human content. He loathed himself. The
virtue of his own desire to live appeared strongly in doubt.

"Allah yirhamo," he said. His voice was thick in his throat.

"Allah yirhamo," repeated the elder woman.

What made him better than this ill-shod peasant? Recruited with nothing to lose on the jobless docks, or else a simple farmer answering the call to mobilize, as these women had, united with their fellows by the doctrine of self-sacrifice. Jamil was not better than them: only arrogance told him he was. On the contrary, Abu Rami was three times as pure as he, Jamil Kamal, sullied by his upbringing among fine things in Turkish halls.

"Take his weapons, take his bullets," said the older woman, lifting the man's rifle. Her eyes were polished by tears. "Take them. Yalla. Yalla. Go back khalti, go mama."

"Ah—but you're bleeding," said the young woman.

"It's nothing." Jamil weighed the guns in his grip, and examined the leather pouch of bullets. "A scratch only. Thank you. God keep you safe."

He turned, and walked back up the slope. A man with a club charged past, emitting a belly-deep roar. Jamil knew that sound. That was the sound of anger, summoned to drown out terror.

When Basil saw him, he touched Jamil's arm affectionately. Jamil began firing with the dead man's gun. But it wasn't long before a commander brought news that they were encircled by tanks, and it was time to hide. Jamil and Basil followed the other survivors across the hillside towards a cave. They waited for nightfall, drinking water from jars and washing their faces and wounds. Jamil sat sentinel for a while at the edge, and as the battle heat cooled he rested on his heels and thought of Midhat. He felt again the weight on his arms as they had carried him to the car, when Hani had asked, with a grave look, whether Jamil could read French.

"I used to," he replied. And Hani, with a look almost of apology, folded Midhat's letter and its envelope into his breast pocket.

Jamil could form a rough idea of what was in that letter. He did not feel curious about it. In part, he was sure that whatever it was would not translate; but mostly, with his ears flooded by his cousin's sobs, there had been little room to feel anything in that moment besides impotence and fear. He clenched his jaw and looked up at the trees. The sun was declining, and in the chill of the aging day the branches began to shake.

8

The detention camp at Sarafand was one converted corner of an active British military garrison. The cells were a series of pitched-roofed wooden barracks, separated by tall fences of barbed wire. At the beginning of Hani's detention, only five of the camp beds in his barracks were occupied. But as the summer progressed, and more and more senior personnel were arrested, the beds filled, until by the hot dark of August each room was crammed with men accused of inciting violence, snoring side by side in the close night. Several times a day the barracks doors were thrust open, and two or three soldiers would march in and take a register. This happened at intervals of a precise inexactitude seemingly designed to surprise the detainees in the act of "gathering in large numbers," which, as they were repeatedly informed, was against camp regulations.

At Hani's request, Sahar had sent him a white kufiya and white abaya, which like the other urban detainees he wore as a gesture of solidarity with the rebels. He grew his beard long, and spent his days in a folding chair out on the small perimeter of earth they jokingly referred to as the "garden," between the walls of the barracks and the barbed wire fence, shuffling round the barracks with the sun to keep in the revolving shade. The barracks' single desk was reserved for the eldest among them, Hussam Effendi from

Jaffa, and as the day went on the others would help Hussam Effendi carry the desk with his book and papers in pursuit of the shadow. Everyone else rested Qurans on their knees and wrote letters leaning on the covers. They never mentioned the tedium. Sometimes their eyes met, and without the usual relief of a burden shared, the inmates silently communicated to one another the same dull and tenacious sadness. Meanwhile they knew the rebels were organising, and military leaders from Syria dressed in old Ottoman regalia were setting up regional commands and courts in the mountains to judge traitors. But God gave every man his own particular battle to fight, and this was theirs: the same bland food, the same view of walls, the same worn faces, the same eyes shut in prayer, the same prayers for patience forming on the same lips.

Besides studying the sacred text, Hani spent his days reading the newspapers and writing—to his wife, to his friends and colleagues, and to British government officials. Trusting that everything he wrote would be read by the prison officers, he took the opportunity to administer any small barbs of spite that he could muster without incurring further punishment.

Aziza Sahar,

I cannot believe you are the one who gave me the idea to prove my arrest here is illegal. In your letter you said—"You think you're being detained, but actually you are locked up." And I was surprised at first—but now—I admit that I am in fact imprisoned and not arrested or detained—because a detainee should be detained only until he is brought to court. And from this idea I have immediately progressed to the fact that neither the Governor of the Brigade nor the High Commissioner himself has any right to imprison anyone. In any case—the detention of around fifty of us is due to end on about the 22nd or 23rd of this month—but I do not know if the authority will renew the detention period—we shall see. It would not surprise me—everything here is insulting.

Although the August heat had not abated, something in the air began whistling of autumn, and the sun seemed always to be setting. Hani started writing letters to a newspaper in Jaffa for publication, as a more formal outlet for his frustration. With plenty of time to think in Sarafand, he had been contemplating how adept the British always were at naming: they bombed Jaffa, and named it urban renewal. They arrested a nationalist, and named him a criminal, and naturally Palestinians were all known as Muslims. And since they had announced a plan to declare martial law, and reinforcements were arriving at Haifa in the thousands, with no other weapons at his disposal but the power of his mind and his pen, this was one more battle Hani might try to fight. He began to spend the hours between the bland lunch of bread and tomato sauce and the bland dinner of rice and meat sauce constructing dispassionate arguments in Arabic, describing with phrases borrowed from legal records and Arabic rhetorical tradition the most striking examples of British injustice.

He was in the garden one afternoon writing one of these letters, on the difference between a prisoner and a detainee, consulting Sahar's correspondence for inspiration, when he looked up from his lap and saw, through an aperture between the neighbouring barracks' walls, a procession of Arabs in single file with their hands behind their backs. In one of the split seconds allowed by the aperture, Hani saw and recognised the compact body and bright eyes of Abd al-Hamid Shuman, and groaned.

"What is wrong now?" said Hussam Effendi, putting his hands down on his desk.

"They've got Shuman," said Hani. The last soldier vanished behind the wall, and a cloud of dust filled the breach.

Abd al-Hamid Shuman was the founder of the Arab Bank, and Secretary of the Strike Fund Committee. The detainees in Hani's barracks had often comforted each other by remarking that the British might cut off "organisers" like Hani all they wished and have no discernible effect on their struggle. Once the spirit of revolution was abroad in the chest of the fellah, it would not be repressed. But now it looked as though they had finally gone for the coffers. A wiser strategy; one must at least give them that credit.

Abd al-Hamid did not seem in low spirits, however. During the exercise hour he greeted Hani with four kisses and a grin, and asked for his news in a non-particular way as if they had happened to run into each other on the street. Then, with a spurt of energy, he turned on his heel and approached one of the guards. The sun baked down. Hani watched; they seemed to be laughing. The guard addressed his colleague, then a fourth man joined them, and within a few minutes, Abd al-Hamid emerged from the exchange carrying a football.

"What are you doing with that?" said Hani.

"Yalla everyone," called Abd al-Hamid.

Across the yard, heads lifted.

"I need two teams."

The arrival of Abd al-Hamid thus inaugurated a strange period in the detention camp when, at any one time, one could find at least fourteen men playing football on the sports field under his umpirage.

Hani did not participate in these games. Occasionally he would sit and watch, but increasingly he took advantage of the peace in the garden while everyone was on the field. One day in the middle of August, he was composing a new letter to the newspaper on the topic of martial law when he developed a terrible toothache.

He assumed it was a muscular injury. But over the course of the afternoon the ache narrowed its focus to three particular teeth, around which the gum became so inflamed that at dinner he was forced to chew exclusively on the other side of his mouth. The doctor at the medical centre gave him a bag of salt with which to gargle, but even gargling every hour did nothing to improve his condition. Over the next few days, biting his food without fully closing his mouth, Hani had the unpleasant impression that he resembled a dog at the dinner table.

"Ask special permission," Hussam Effendi called suddenly from across his desk.

Hani dropped the hand grasping his head; he had not realised Hussam was watching him.

"Go to Jaffa," Hussam went on. "I know a very good dentist. Greek."

"God keep you," said Hani. He cleared his throat. "Perhaps I will."

"Ask," said Hussam, sliding the glasses he had pulled onto his head back down to his nose. "No harm in asking."

Hani looked at his newspaper. "Outdo others in patience," he murmured. "Remain resolute, and be mindful of Allah, that you may succeed."

Was there no harm in asking? Hani did not want to ask. He doubted the wisdom of it, and if one doubted, one must not do. Over the next two days, the pain expanded along his jaw and annexed two more teeth. Incapable of much beyond reflecting on the pain and his unwillingness to ask for a dentist, he concluded that he was hesitating less at the prospect of being refused permission to leave, and more at the idea that he might be spared before the other detainees. It would not do to break their solidarity; this was simply another battle he must fight. Besides, regardless of how excruciating it was, there was something a little ignominious about a toothache.

"Mister Murad."

"Yes?"

"Someone here to see you."

It was so rare to receive visitors that at first Hani thought they must have called a dentist for him, and his chest softened with relief. The soldier's steps heaved and clanked with his weapon-laden uniform, and behind him, Hani flowed in his white abaya on silent, sandalled feet.

Six soldiers stood to attention at the entrance of another barracks. Hani ducked his head to enter, and as his eyes adjusted to the darkness he perceived two men seated beside a third empty chair. The first man rose, a heavy figure with large eyes: it was one of his colleagues in the diplomatic leadership of the revolt, Elias Darwish. Hani reached out and kissed his friend. He rarely saw Darwish except during the exercise hour, in which there was little time or privacy to talk. As the two top "ringleaders," he and Darwish had been deliberately separated by the British, and kept in barracks on opposite sides of the camp.

"Hani Bey!" said the other man, who was wearing a suit. It was the Iraqi Foreign Minister, Nuri Said.

"Nuri." Hani stepped forward for a handshake and a kiss. "It has been a long time. I heard you were in Jerusalem—how are you, what's your news? You look exactly the same."

This was almost true: Nuri had put on quite a lot of weight since Hani last saw him in Baghdad, both around the middle and under his chin, which he ducked with an arch smile of greeting. But his curly side parting remained in place, grey at the temples above where his ears stuck out. He was wearing a thick blue knitted tie.

"Welcome, welcome," he said, "please, please."

Darwish grunted at the guards: "Will you leave us?"

Nuri folded his hands, and threw Hani a significant look. Hani had known this man for almost twenty years. Nuri's career began with the Hejazi Revolt against the Ottomans during the war. After that he had remained one of Faisal's men, first in Paris at the Conference, where he and Hani became acquainted, and afterwards in Damascus, and then in Iraq.

"The Iraqi people are in despair," said Nuri smoothly, plucking the tops of his trouser legs as he sat. "It is the same in Saudi Arabia, and in Transjordan. We are all agitated by the situation in Palestine."

Hani had the strong impression of a prepared speech, perhaps on its third or fourth outing.

"I have in mind an Arab brethren," Nuri went on. "In view of the national ties between Palestine and Iraq, and in view of the sound friendship between the Iraqi and British Governments, in agreement with their Majesties, we will seek to resolve the Palestinian issue. We will look after you. The British want a Royal Commission as soon as possible to investigate the causes—"

"We cannot stop the strike," rumbled Darwish, "without an end to immigration. That is the first condition."

"Of course," said Nuri, flicking his tie. "Now, in June I spoke with Weizmann. Yes, I spoke with Weizmann. And he said the Zionists would stop immigration for a year. That was in June."

Darwish's face remained blank.

"Are you sure?" said Hani.

"Yes, I'm sure."

"He said they would stop immigration for a year," said Hani.

"He said they would be willing to consider it."

"All right, there's the difference," said Darwish. "Willing to consider."

"Look," said Nuri, leaning forward in his chair. "You are going to have to end the violence at some point. It can't go on forever. I know, I know, that the harvest is soon. And I think the Brits have enough of your critical people here now to make supplying the rebels difficult. Listen, Hani, listen to me."

Hani's jaw throbbed.

"They will win," said Nuri. "One way or another they will win. Don't you see? Your little armed force getting ready around Nablus is not an army. It's not a real army. But if you get out now, if you announce an end to the strike *willingly*, without being forced, then you can tell your men, you can tell Palestine, that you have won *something*—a stop to immigration before the Commission arrives—and then you'll be heroes."

Darwish's face was tightening into a scowl.

"If we call off the strike," said Hani, "and they do not stop immigration, the rebels will actually kill us. I have no doubt." He held his jaw. "We cannot give in, Nuri."

"Are you all right?"

"It's nothing. My tooth, I have a toothache."

"Salamtak. They must have a doctor here."

Hani waved his hand.

"The people are suffering," said Darwish suddenly. "This is the truth."

Hani looked at him in surprise.

"What?" he said.

Darwish raised his eyes to Hani, with an almost apologetic expression. Delicately, he said: "A full strike for six months. No activity at all . . . " He raised his hands. "Nuri does have a point. It will not be sustainable for much longer. Perhaps we should—take advantage of the circumstances. And twist them to suit the struggle, as best we can."

In an instant, Hani revised his understanding of Darwish's scowl. He had assumed his colleague was unconvinced, angered, but in fact the opposite was true. He had never heard Darwish express doubts like these before; he thought rather that everyone in Sarafand understood that they were all sacrificing for the larger project, and they would never back down, they must preserve their solidarity. It was for that very reason that Hani had decided not to see a dentist. But looking at his colleague now he experienced an upwelling of energy, not anger precisely, but something like alarm, and it crossed his mind that, of course, since they were all in different barracks, varying reactions and revisions and objectives would be burgeoning between those other beds. Divide and conquer: that was the design. A cord snapped in his chest as he realised both Nuri and Darwish were waiting for his assent. He wondered whether Darwish had already agreed to Nuri's plan before he arrived.

"What's in it for you?" he said to Nuri, allowing some spite into his tone.

Nuri blinked. "It is my duty, my sense of duty, my Arab—but what do you mean, what's in it for me?"

Hani raised an eyebrow, preparing his verbal weapons. Even if he must eventually accept this plan to end the strike, he would not capitulate without at least probing Nuri's virtue, which now seemed to him to be very much in question. But as he was opening his mouth to deliver his accusation, an unbearable pain shot through his lower jaw, and he bent forward, holding his cheek.

"Salamtak," said Darwish again.

"I'll tell you what," said Nuri. Hani could tell from his voice that he was smiling. "Come to the meeting in Jerusalem. Next week. We'll get you out of here, Hani Bey. We'll get you home to your wife. And we'll get you to a dentist."

When Midhat saw Abu Jamil and Jamil standing at the foot of his bed, both wearing suits and ties, he assumed he was hallucinating.

He had been downgraded to the acute ward since the incident with Henryk, and here, in addition to enduring the noises, he was keeping a constant vigil against hallucinations. He had deduced that the pocket watch in Henryk's hand was illusory—though less because of its own logic than because, using the internal logic of a dream, he understood that the vision of Jeannette could not have been real. And if that was not real, then *that* was not real either. At the sight of his uncle and cousin, therefore, his heart sank: he had been so sure he was improving. Then he noticed that Abu Jamil was fatter than before, and his moustache was big and grey. Jamil was thinner, hair slicked back with pomade. He stared at Midhat.

"Excuse me sir," said an English nurse. "You cannot be in here."

"What did she say?" said Abu Jamil.

Jamil shrugged.

"Midhat, what did she say?"

Midhat grinned—he couldn't help it—and croaked: "You can't be in here." He had not spoken in days.

"Forbidden," said a Palestinian nurse, striding forward. "You must leave immediately."

"That is my nephew. That one. We want to take him out."

"No."

"What do you mean, no?"

"He is a patient, he . . ." Her voice fell into a whisper.

"Majnun!" Abu Jamil burst out, opening his fingers from his mouth, as if throwing the word at her, "*You* are majnuna!"

Three more nurses and two uniformed men appeared. Jamil caught Midhat's eye and winked, and then the crowd of staff escorted him and his father out. Abu Jamil's voice still carried from the hall, however, where it was clear they were making a scene. A chorus of rustling bedsheets indicated the other patients turning to listen. Midhat's heart pounced; he thought he discerned Wasfi's voice, and then Um Jamil's thin fast chatter. Next came Teta's wailing: unmistakeable, dramatic. After that, a silence. The man to Midhat's right gave him a questioning look. The ceiling pressed down. Midhat gripped his fists on nothing.

"Put your slippers on."

It was the matron. She was standing beside his bed. The angle magnified her jaw and the black cavities of her nostrils.

"I said, get up."

Midhat eased himself upright and followed her out of the ward.

Abu Jamil, Jamil, and Wasfi stood along the far wall of the corridor. Wasfi was wearing a bright red tie. They stood erect as Midhat entered; Abu Jamil puffed—"Ho ho!" Jamil opened his mouth, then took a deep breath and grinned; Wasfi punched the air. Two veiled women stood beside them—Teta and Um Jamil. Teta rushed towards Midhat and her gown, separating from the outline of Um Jamil's, revealed a third woman behind.

"And now that we have agreed on the transfer," said the matron, "please all of you leave the vicinity. Show them where he can change his clothes."

"Fatima," said Midhat.

Slowly, Fatima raised both her arms. But Teta had already reached for Midhat's face, and was moving her thumbs across his cheeks. "Your wife is very clever," she whispered. "Abu Jamil give me the bag. Suit, shirt, socks, shoes, tie. Yalla habibi put your clothes on." As Midhat stepped towards his wife, Teta patted his arm. "You'll see her after. Go."

The nurse took him to a small room containing a narrow medical bed with a cross on one wall and a chart of numbers on the other. A long spotted mirror rested between a chair and a dusty glass-fronted cabinet, and he saw, beneath the window, a pair of scales. The latch clicked. This was the room where they had weighed him when he first arrived. Here, he had surrendered his clothes. He remembered this thin, sheeted mattress, where he had laid his trousers and arranged his socks. He looked across at the mirror and saw a gaunt unshaven man with longish hair, and hairy arms and ankles sticking out of a green gown. A reflected section of window showed an empty road.

"Abu Taher."

The door was open. Before he saw Fatima he smelled the scent of her body; the scent of their home. When she didn't move, he pulled her across the threshold by the arms.

"Please," he said. "Sit."

She did not sit. She kept to the spot where he had let go of her, staring at the chart on the wall. Her eyes were large and shining.

"Please take that off," said Midhat. "Let me see you."

For a moment he thought she would refuse. Then she flipped the veil back from her temples and walked into the light. Instead of the fear he had come to expect he saw a face folded with distress, and though he could not see tears the muscles around her eyes were so strained she must be keeping them back.

"How is the shop?" he said at last, and heard, with regret, the wound in his voice.

Fatima covered her eyes with her hands, tapered like a pair of wings, heavy veined from the heat. Midhat took one wrist and her body followed, and she pushed against his chest.

"Oh no no," he said, touching her quivering hair.

She separated herself, wiping her eyes with the knuckles of her forefingers. "You need to dress."

"I missed you," said Midhat. "Why did you never come to see me here?"

A noise of wheels outside half eclipsed the latter part of his question, but Fatima had heard him. She made no attempt to stop her face from seizing up like a child's. Midhat's hands extended, far apart, fingers outstretched as if to catch or to embrace, or perhaps he was reaching, for her, for a word to undo what he had just said. Fatima's storm gradually subsided. She looked exhausted, tensed on the brink of speech. But without saying anything she bent from the waist and started to unbuckle his bag. She placed his garters on the mattress and, wrinkling up a dark blue sock, crouched at his feet.

"Yalla." She waved the sock at him, and he lifted his gown. Once the elastic had sprung to his calf she took up the second one. Next, the trousers: fly unbuttoned, she opened the legs into two puddles on the floor. He put a hand on her shoulder and sought out the flagstone with his feet, and she helped the fabric over his ankles. She tugged off the gown and eased him into a shirt, flipping the buttons into their holes from bottom to top. She let him fasten his belt by himself. Right arm into his jacket, left arm in, and as she was relaxing the laces of his shoes, pulling up the tongues, she said: "You want the tie too?"

Midhat chuckled. She had never dressed him before. It was funny how quickly that sticky silence smoothed, and this renewed habit of company sent the unspoken accusation that he had abandoned her floating off above his head. He pressed his heel past the leather of the shoe. Here it came, the first breeze of relief. He was leaving this place.

But as Fatima rolled up his hospital gown, he was overwhelmed with the contrary heaviness of a strong, physical loss at the prospect of leaving. Some trace of that virus must be surviving inside him, tempting him even now with the amnesiac allure of that other woman. Like waking in a chilled bed and yearning after the disappearing scraps of a dream, even while knowing the object of yearning was a part of his own mind. A fraudulent allure, an ignis fatuus, and yet, and yet: that vision of her in the ward was—he slipped his heel into the second shoe, and with the thud his stomach dropped and he experienced an echo of his rise to that summit, the very real sensation of Jeannette's living shoulder beneath his hand, her voice, her breath—if that was a hallucination, then hallucinations were a kind of heaven.

He watched his wife approaching with the tie, holding the two ends in her hands to noose it around his neck. There in the mirror stood a haggard man in a suit, a second column of silver buttons appearing under his pale fingers. He bent his head to accept the tie. As if by this motion of his head he had tipped the balance of fluids in his ear, the bronze sound of bells thronged through the air. He jerked back and searched Fatima's eyes.

"Can you hear that?"

"Hear what?"

"Bells," he breathed.

She frowned. "Yes, I can hear bells," she said. "Bethlehem is full of churches."

She reached again to put the tie around his collar. He gasped and grabbed her hands—soft, small, damp—and prised them open to cover the palms with kisses.

"Thank you, thank you."

"Stop it!" said Fatima. But her fingers were yielding to his lips, and she was laughing.

Jamil drove faster than normal, and Wasfi watched through the windscreen for British army cars. Um Jamil and Abu Jamil had arrived separately. ("Will you be all right?" said Wasfi. "Your aunt has the eyes of a fox," said Abu Jamil.) Fatima sat behind Wasfi, Midhat in the middle holding her hand, Teta on his other side.

"Hani meant well," said Teta, pulling her skirts between her legs and arranging her feet. "But how is he to know? He has other things on his mind. Heyk az-zuruf. But look, Midhat is not mad, is he? Are you habibi? Just sad."

"Yes, I'm just sad."

"Good good," said Teta. And looking out the window: "Horrible place."

"How did you get me out?" he said.

"Fatima did," said Teta. "She told them you were a doctor. Trained in France. Then she said you had taught her how to care for the sick. Then she said—what did she say? She said you were grieving for your father, and that she would look after you. Then she said, the conditions in that hospital are shameful, much worse than in your house, where she is with you the whole time. But, ya'ni, she didn't say it like that, she said it in a way that made it impossible to argue. She made that woman, the tall one, embarrassed."

"We call this an attack of multiple angles," said Wasfi.

"She did it in English?"

"No," said Fatima quietly. "Wasfi translated."

Midhat wrapped his hand around her fingers. "God bless you."

Everyone looked out of the windows. They were cautious of him, that was obvious. In all honesty so was he, watching himself, nervous, fearing that something illogical might at any moment emerge onto his field of vision and once more disrupt the fabric he shared with everyone else, expose that his senses still could not be trusted, that all the parts that allowed him to speak and be understood were only superficially restored, and beneath them lay other parts whose damage was irreparable. He watched Jamil's hands, brown and knuckly, mastering the steering wheel.

"How is the strike?"

Wasfi turned in his seat. "Shu mn'ulak . . . busy. Jamil is organising a lot."

"Really?"

Jamil nodded in the rearview mirror.

"And what about fighting?"

"Jamil is fighting," said Wasfi, "and what's his name, Basil Murad." He turned back as they passed a group of houses and ducked his head to look. "Wait, wait." He held an arm out to Jamil. "Slow. Bas . . . anyway yes—most people help with money and organising. Also to enforce the strike . . . ya'ni it's hard. It gets hot, it gets harder. When the harvest comes . . ." He sucked his teeth. "But Khalto—did you see all those Jews in the hospital?" He glanced at Teta. "What are they thinking."

"I know," said Teta. "Stupid. Stupid al-ingliz."

Midhat looked through Fatima's window. "Everyone gets sick."

At the Jerusalem-Nablus highway, a stationary army car came into view. A group of soldiers were nudging rifles into the ribs of fellahin, who held their arms in the air as their bodies were searched. Everyone in the car, including Fatima, faced mechanically forward, except for Midhat, who watched the scene revolve as they passed. A soldier in shorts and helmet was patting one of the Arabs all the way down to his shoes.

The hills gathered round. Olive trees laced the rises, terraced with white rock. Nablus appeared in the windows and Jamil drove past the disused railway line and the empty streets.

They parked in front of the house. Wasfi opened the rear door and Midhat, kissing his grandmother, slid out after his wife, embracing Wasfi and thanking him. Jamil stepped out of the car but remained waving from the other side. His oiled hair shone in the sun.

"Give him a kiss!" said Teta.

He rounded the bonnet at an awkward, lurching jog, wrapped his bony arms around Midhat's neck, and kissed him quickly on each cheek.

"God with you."

Midhat looked Jamil in the eye. That urgent stare from the hospital was gone. Everyone was watching them: their distance was a public affair.

"Don't go out at night," said Teta, poking her head out the door as Jamil returned to the driver's seat. "They fight at night."

The car was pulling away. Fatima started up the steps.

"Where are the children?" said Midhat.

"My parents'. They'll be back in an hour or so. We need a siesta."

"I don't."

"Well, I need a siesta. You do what you like."

In the daytime gloom, the bedroom furnishings seemed strange. The chairs, the high window, that mirror, the cupboard, this bed—their familiarity was uncanny. Fatima faced the cupboard to undress, the bones of her back slipping around beneath her skin as she pulled on a nightgown. Everything would be better tomorrow. After a night's sleep, this strange familiar furniture would have impressed itself on his brain, having been plunged into darkness and recreated in the new day. And before long he would escape his sense-memories of those cold, painted bedposts, which struck the tops of his feet when he turned in the night. He faced the ceiling and thought of Jeannette. He tried to summon the rush of touching her shoulder. It was too faint. It would not rise.

Fatima was opening a drawer in the nightstand. She pulled out a cigarette and struck a match.

"I am happy to be home," said Midhat.

She swung her legs onto the bed, and the rotating strings of smoke ascended.

"I am happy too. We have been at my father's house."

"Oh?"

"Yes. The rebels came for money. In the end, we gave them an old gun." She inhaled. "Hani Bey is in a prison camp."

"Hani?"

"Mm. Poor Sahar, she is pregnant you know. I hope it will end soon, the strike, I want to go back to normal. Every night we hear gunfire. Khaled comes and sleeps with me, sometimes."

"Hani's in prison," said Midhat, "Oh—" He put his hand to his lips. "I think I knew that. Someone told me. At Sarafand."

"And Uncle Hassan sold more land to the Church," said Fatima, "to fund the cause."

"Wallah."

"The last time I saw him was . . . last year." She closed her eyes; she was talking randomly. "There was a priest there. French."

"Oh, yes, I know him. Brother of the Virgins."

"He wrote a book about Nablus."

A memory blurted across Midhat's mind. He saw the Nablus hospital in the fog of his derangement, and there, Frédéric Molineu, sitting beyond the other patients on the far edge of the veranda. He looked at the memory in astonishment; anger flooded him, pursued by a kind of holy terror. Then, quite as abruptly, he recalled a desire to speak with his old enemy. He turned his head, and Docteur Molineu had vanished. In his place sat a priest.

"Are you all right?"

He made a noise. "I was just remembering something at the hospital. A man."

"A man?"

"A—yes. A Jewish man." He cleared his throat. "I met him, I mean. In the bed next to mine."

She tapped into the ashtray, and Midhat wondered how much she knew about his psychosis. How much did any of them know? Who knew what one let slip in a delirium? He teetered, exposed, as though a gale had forced open his greatcoat. He looked over at his impenetrable wife.

"Fatima."

"Yes."

"How did you really get me out?"

"The way Teta said."

"By telling them I was a doctor?"

"Among other things."

She shrank down against the pillows.

He said, "You look so sad."

She closed her eyes. Tears slid down her lashes. He did not try to comfort her. He returned onto his back, and as her breathing slowed the mattress shifted under her slackened muscles. He still had a strong desire to talk. It had been so long since his last clear conversation, and he was remembering the pleasure of it. He looked again at his wife's face, her breaths short and light from her open mouth.

"Fatima," he whispered. A long silence followed before the next breath, which came like a gasp, in, out. His energies gathered to a point. "I know," he said, "this was not what you expected."

He arranged his head in his palm, propped on his elbow. A crease quivered down her brow, and he waited before resuming: "I'm sorry. When the strike is over, when we have money again, I promise we'll leave Nablus. We'll go to the sea. We'll go to Beirut, we'll go to Jaffa. *Alexandria—*"

Her lips started to tighten. Her cheekbones emerged into distinctness. She opened an eye.

"Salut," he whispered, smiling.

She twisted to face the ceiling.

"Sorry." He closed his eyes as if to sleep. But the need to speak remained caught in his chest, like an unexpressed cough. So much had happened, was still happening. He wanted to say how peculiar it was to wake up after having been asleep for months. Though physically only a couple of hours' drive from Nablus, really he had been abroad, in another country, while in his hometown a kind of war was going on—he wanted to talk about the strike; what it might achieve; what it meant to walk down these empty, menacing streets. He wanted to ask Fatima questions, he wanted their words to come out and meet in the middle. He wanted to tell her about his delusions, and by telling them draw out what remained of their poison—he wanted to tell her how changed he felt. That he could see himself a little more clearly from the outside. And he could see Fatima, beside him. Her nightgown had risen above her knees, above the gentle curve of her whalebone shins, crossed like the arms of musical instruments; she had taken off her stockings, and from her locked ankles, wisped with pale hairs, her pinkish feet protruded, her slender-necked big toes. She inhaled slowly. He felt her weariness, he knew she was blinking at the ceiling. Beside him, this breathing, opaque body. No, he would not tell her any of this. The wave crashed.

"I think," he said, "that I should go on a walk."

"You need to rest."

There was fear in her voice. He reacted to it as he always used to: with a ludic grin. "You know how long I have been in bed for?" he said. "I need to walk."

"No."

"What do you mean, no?"

"They are fighting out there—they are sniping. It's not safe."

"But, Fatima, I have to see Eli. He has been without me for months and months. Imagine."

"You need to rest. No."

He rasped his palate and raised his hands. "Oh, *fine*," he said. "Out of the rule of the doctors, under the rule of the wife. This is my fate."

"BABA! BABA!"

Fatima groaned. Ghada skidded into the room.

"Habibti!" said Midhat. "Habibet alby—why is your hair so long?"

"Baba Baba Baba."

"Baba *misses* you."

"You weren't here for my birthday." She held out her arms to be lifted. "You weren't there."

Taher and Massarra hovered in the doorway. "Baba," said Khaled, barging between them.

"Mama is sleeping," said Midhat. "Oof, you've grown!" he said, putting Ghada down. "Yalla, ruhu."

He led them into the kitchen. Through the window the trees shone grey-green. A flock of birds charged across the sky.

Khaled put his elbows on the table. "Where have you been?"

"That's none of your business," said Massarra.

"Is there any fruit?" said Midhat.

One old and dry orange, was the answer. They watched him force a knife through the skin and pull the strips of rind one by one from the rounds.

"Salt," he said, extending a hand across the table with mock ceremony. Khaled passed the little pot, and Midhat crushed some over the slices, flourishing his arm up and down. Ghada laughed.

"Don't be sad, Taher," said Midhat, rising to rinse his fingers.

"He's not sad," said Massarra.

"What have you all been eating?"

"Bananas," said Khaled.

"Bananas?"

They watched him dry his hands on a dishcloth. As he turned to the window, an alien sound entered his ears: a hoarse, voiceless tinkle, like a high key on an out-of-tune piano. There was no piano in the house. His posture slumped. The whistle tickled his eardrums.

On the red screen of his closed eyelids the priest appeared. The Brother of the Virgins, on the balcony, asking questions. His desire to speak with the priest was immediate and profound. He recalled meeting him in the Nablus hospital, though not what they spoke about. A rare creature, this man of France, of faith: the foreigner who knew Nablus. He did not know yet exactly what he would tell him, only that they must speak.

"Sahtayn my darlings. Eat."

"And there's cheese," said Massarra. "And there's figs in the garden."

"Oo-ooh," said Midhat, with singsong enthusiasm. "My favourite."

"I'll get them. The birds ate a lot when we weren't here, but there are still a few."

"Later, my love. Why is no one eating?"

Khaled lifted a slice. "I need a napkin."

That first night home in Nablus, Midhat was woken every few hours by gunfire crackling from the mountains. When at one point the din became particularly acute Fatima reached beneath the duvet and put her warm hand on his arm. She did not apply any pressure; she was simply reassuring herself that he was there. Or, perhaps, reminding him that she was.

In the morning, Widad Hammad bustled into the hall.

"Where is your husband? I am here to wish him good health."

"He's coming," Midhat heard Fatima say, before her voice was swallowed by the corridor.

He held down his irritation. He took his time to bathe and shave, and whisk his neck with his French badger brush, and smack his chest with his old cologne, and trim and file his fingernails, and pluck the longest hairs from his nostrils, and do up the buttons on his linen suit, and oil and comb his hair, and wash his hands before joining his wife and mother-in-law in the salon. Widad was in the chair beside the window. At the sight of him, she pronounced, "Hamdillah as-salameh!" and stuck out her neck for three kisses. Without waiting for his response she reverted to a story she was in the middle of telling.

"They arrested three and shot four."

Midhat took a cup from the tray. "Where?"

"Beit Dajan."

"Did they leave the bodies?" said Fatima.

"Selma heard it from Muhammad Saka, who says that the police report says they were running away. What an accusation! Of course they were running away. They weren't hiding in the lentil jar. They always do this," she explained, turning to Midhat. "They come into the village, they arrest people, then they smash everything. They mix all the food together, the flour with the rice and the sugar wa kaza into a pile wa ba'dayn they usually add olive oil or petrol. Disgusting."

Teta, Um Jamil, and Abu Jamil arrived within the hour. They stared intently at Midhat from the doorstep, and Teta gave a satisfied nod. "You look good. Um Mahmoud wishes you health."

"Do you want coffee?"

"We're not staying long."

"With or without sugar?"

"With, please, thank you habibi," said Um Jamil, following Um Taher, who was already walking into the salon and calling her hellos.

A tapping on the salon window announced Nuzha and their brother Burhan, who had come up the path. A weary look passed over Fatima's face, but Nuzha anticipated her and said to the opening door, "We're not staying for lunch." Voices rose, and the conversation splintered. Taher and Khaled appeared in the hall, and Fatima sent them to fetch extra chairs from the kitchen. Midhat dozed in and out of attention.

"And now he's in Transjordan."

"Why?"

"He goes to visit these groups—I'm not sure . . ."

"Can you swim? I'm very good at swimming."

"But since Hani Bey was released—" said Nuzha.

"What?" said Midhat.

"Yes," said Nuzha, sitting back to include him. "They released him yesterday. And a few others. They are negotiating in Jerusalem, with the kings and Nuri Basha."

"That's the first I've heard of it," said Abu Jamil.

"Ya salam," said Midhat. "Is the strike ending?"

"No one knows. Not yet, I don't think," said Nuzha.

Midhat stopped listening again and looked at his hands. He saw Hani's legs in his father's study, and then his face coming into view. He had no idea what Hani thought of him now. For the duration of their friendship Midhat was always relatively confident of Hani's perception of him—since it was, after all, a picture half of his own creating—but there was no way to be sure any longer, not since Hani witnessed Midhat's moment of collapse, when he had become so utterly unknown to himself.

The thought that followed this one struck him full force between the brows: Hani must have seen the letter from Jeannette. And so, therefore, must Jamil. His throat burned; he glanced at his grandmother, who was pouting and nodding, and then at Um Jamil. He looked at Fatima, stunned that it had not occurred to him before. Did they all know? His wife was playing with a button on her sleeve and listening to Nuzha. He could see no way to find out without directly asking, and thereby revealing himself. As for the letter itself—there was no way to ask where that was either. Not without reopening the chasm he had just crawled out of. He shuddered: either Jamil or Hani must have it. Surely both would protect him. They loved him; they would not reveal him. Fatima noticed him looking at her, and questioned him with her eyes. He pushed his face into a smile. Of course, he had already been revealed. He had no idea what they had seen; but they had seen him.

"I will be sad when the revolt is over," said Khaled.

"Will you?" said Fatima.

"There will be nothing to focus on. Ordinary life is *boring*."

His mother swatted his leg. "Shame."

"I don't want to go back to school," Khaled replied, with dignity.

"When was the last time you saw Hani?" said Nuzha.

Fatima winced.

"Last year," said Midhat.

Here they all were, watching him return, gently, to this world. Ready to press him back into the shape of a person. Their impressions glanced off him like beams of light. There had been times in his life when he thought the need for them was illusory, this group of people, living in the same place, tied by their names and inherited stories. But if that was illusory, what was real? Without them, he was a body floating in the air—he stuck his foot out onto the cold tile, and struck a match to light Abu Jamil's cigar.

As Fatima repaired to the kitchen, he pulled out some olive wood misbaha beads and began counting them off to calm himself. He maintained his sociable smile; he did not want them to see him ruminate. His old schematic way of thinking was quite gone. Gone that ability, or propensity, to map one thing onto another. Nothing would ever again be contained by a map.

Fatima appeared in the dark hall bearing a tray. She nodded at him, and he felt a twinge of anger that she should take it upon herself to approve his behaviour. But in a moment his anger was swept off by love, and love was flooded with sorrow. So it was. After one thought arose another soon overtook it, and they fell back one by one, like the breathy concessions of the sea.

He spent the afternoon reorganising his bookshelves. For many years his books were arranged with a false economy in two rows, leaving the second row completely hidden behind the first and all of its titles forgotten. Today he was rediscovering them, wiping pelts of dust off their top edges with a cloth. Several he had brought back from Paris, some were gifts from Faruq. One he remembered picking up beside the Seine; it fell open at a well-thumbed page on a description of Jerusalem, shimmering in the distance. The telephone rang. The operator announced his aunt's house, and then Teta came on the line, hiccoughing.

"I have to tell you something," she said. "But don't—don't be sad. Mama? Be strong."

"What is it?"

"Jamil is . . . Jamil is gone."

In the background, Um Jamil wailed.

"I'm coming immediately," said Midhat.

He set down the telephone, and stood motionless for a long moment. He could hear his children laughing in the other room. He looked at the cloth in his hands, covered in dust.

He stumbled on his way to the car. His aunt and uncle's house was dark, the shutters were closed and they had not lit the lamps. Um Jamil backed into the corner by the kitchen as he entered, her mouth an open hole.

Jamil was on the table. The heels of his boots, tanned with wear, were just visible beneath the sheets. He was wrapped in two of them, through which large bands of blood had soaked and dried and turned brown. Only the top part of his torso was uncovered. His buttoned shirt was heavily bloodied, and his pale chin was lifted. Midhat's heart swung violently as he approached. Jamil's mouth was open, his eyes were closed, and the weight of his face was already sinking into his narrow cheeks. His long nose pointed upward, as though he were taking a deep breath: it was a figure of pain, and of release.

"Oh," said Midhat. His eyes filled with tears. He traced a finger over the torn fibres of Jamil's necktie. The bristles of the unshaven neck touched his fingertips and he drew back in shock. Then, with conviction, he placed his palm on the dead cheek. The certain cold of the flesh beneath his hand made him cry out: "Oh no." He heard his voice shaking.

Abu Jamil showed him the piece of paper.

This man was killed in an altercation with British soldiers, who acted in self-defence.

Teta was holding his arm with two hands. Cords tightened in her wrists. He met her eye and, trying not to weep, blinked: I'm fine.

It fell to Midhat and Abu Jamil to wash the body. Midhat, who had never done this before, watched his uncle set about the task with rags and bowls of water without bothering to wipe the tears that ran off his chin. They unwound the sheets, and covered Jamil with a fresh sheet from navel to knee, and then set about dressing his wounds. After washing him five times, and covering him in his shroud, they took turns to bathe. Midhat fetched his aunt and grandmother from upstairs, and they sat together praying around the body. Munir Murad arrived to give his condolences, and to tell them that Basil was still alive, and going on trial.

"Basil?" said Midhat.

"They were driving back from across the Jordan River," said Munir. "They were on a mission for the cause. Basil told me, before they came to arrest him."

Jamil had left Nablus with Basil after bringing Midhat home from Bethlehem, and driven through the night over the Damiya Bridge into Transjordan. At Ajlun, someone from the Adwan tribe was waiting. They paid for some hundred or more rifles, pistols, and shotguns, along with ammunition, then rested until afternoon and set out for Nablus at dusk. At about one in the morning, near the village of Beit Furik, they realised they were surrounded. Basil managed to escape.

"His trial is in three days," said Munir. "Here, in Nablus." He nodded, blessing the house.

Three days passed. Three days of wailing and condolences and agitation, the body interred, the funeral prayers spoken before the mound of displaced dirt in the Western Cemetery.

At the trial, the policeman said Jamil had shot at the soldiers. Basil's lawyer asserted that this could not possibly be the case, since they were clearly ambushed. But the judge averred that the greater crime was Basil and Jamil's, and that in the absence of witnesses there was nothing to corroborate the lawyer's argument. Basil was sentenced to nine years in Akka prison for the possession of explosives and firearms.

People gossiped about betrayal. How else could the army have known where their car would be, and at what time? These things did not happen in the dead of night by chance. Of course there were myriad ways a plan might leak without deliberate malfeasance: an indiscretion on the telephone, a chance word to a taxi driver, a peasant who saw the car and told a policeman without knowing what he did.

Hani arrived on the fourth day to give condolences. He had had an operation on his jaw, with several teeth extracted, and was struggling to speak. Regardless of this, he was quickly besieged by other guests, who wanted to know about the progress of the talks in Jerusalem. It became clear over the course of the afternoon that something more was expected of Hani, whose presence conferred a particular solemnity onto the occasion. And so he took it upon himself to deliver a few words, in the phlegmatic, professional manner of one whose opinion is always in demand. His words on Jamil's martyrdom had a far greater effect on the mourners than any of those delivered by the imam, who stood aside, nonplussed, while this gentleman in a kufiya spoke softly from one side of his mouth.

"Our brother Jamil joins the souls of Sheikh Izz ad-Din al-Qassam," said Hani, "of Mohammed Bashir, Sheikh Yassin, Sadiq Zakaria, and Ahmad Maalouani, Ahmad Sheikh Said and Sa'id al-Masri, and countless others. All men who have fought bravely in the name of freedom against oppression. Jamil is a soul of great fortitude, and commitment, and bravery, and he will be rewarded by God in Paradise, and, as in the words of Ibn Masud, the Believer will have no rest until he meets God."

After his speech, Hani came to kiss Midhat. It was the first time they had seen each other since that day in Haj Taher's study. Hani smiled, and neither spoke.

The trouble must have shown on Midhat's face because Hani reached and held his cheek. As he did so, Teta caught Midhat's eye: she was in the hallway, watching him. So, he noticed with alarm, were Wasfi and Abu Jamil. Tahsin was speaking to one of the neighbours, moving his hands in wide circles, but his eyes shifted upwards and he looked at Midhat. Teta questioned him with a tiny shake of her head, and he forced a smile.

"Is the revolt really ending?" he said.

"It seems that way," said Hani. "We hope so."

"I slept through it all," said Midhat. He examined Hani's tired face, thinking of his cousin. He wondered whether Jamil had thought of him at all, during his last days. He hoped not. He did not think he deserved Jamil's thoughts.

Hani smiled and opened his mouth, but whatever he was about to say, he seemed to decide against it. With a chill, Midhat looked into his friend's eyes and understood very clearly that Hani had seen the letter. But instead of shame, he felt, to his surprise, an almost unbearable sensation of relief. As though an immense wall were in the act of falling. The wall fell, and there he was. Standing on the other side. He felt the air on his face. He tried to speak, but could not.

"Everything will be better from now on," said Hani. "The worst is over."

Midhat nodded. Finally, he mumbled: "Praise be to God."

Hani kissed his cheek. Midhat looked down, stunned. With the energy of a new bad habit he reached into his mind for Jeannette. The vision of her in the hospital grew colder each time he reached for it, but he could not stop himself. He concentrated, trying to see her. He squeezed Hani's shoulder.

"Thank you for coming."

"God with you," said Hani.

Midhat moved off towards the window. Her fading from his memory might, it occurred to him, simply be in the nature of the mystical. These things did not stay. Or was it rather—he touched his eyes with his fingers— was it that calling delusions by divine names was just a way to cope with yet another unutterable loss? He looked up as Fatima appeared in the doorway. Her powdered face, her knee-length blue dress, her brown leather shoes, all lit by the garden behind him. Time was a treacherous distance, and it would not be crossed but through the dangerous substitutions of the imagination. He reached. His hand brushed her neck. Fatima eyed him, appraising. No, it could not be resolved. For there she was, and there she was.

Ghada had been tracing her finger over the leaf design on the hall tiles to disguise the fact that, really, she was watching her father as he moved about the room, talking to different people, standing alone and staring. Every so often, she wiped her finger on the back of her sock.

He was quite as elegant as she remembered, dressed in his black suit with a blue tie. He did seem older, and a little less fat—but that might have been because of the photograph in the salon, which had, during his long absence, replaced her memories of his real body. In the photograph, Baba was sitting at a table, looking quite stout. She knew enough now about perspective to recognise that this was in part because of the angle. One of her recent discoveries was that when things were further away they were smaller, and when they were nearer they were larger, and her father's legs loomed in the foreground of the photograph, and his foot was huge. He wore a linen suit and was reading a book, with a cat beside him. He was staring at the camera, head resting on his hand, but he did not look as though he were really seeing. Rather, his mind seemed elsewhere, although at the same time, when she pulled the photograph close to her face, she could see that his lips were a little stuck out, as though about to say something. Perhaps the word "and." Once, while she was holding the picture close to her face, she did not notice her aunt Nuzha entering the room. Nuzha whipped the picture from her hand, ignoring Ghada's outrage, and said: "I think this one was staged by the photographer. He is dressed too elegantly for reading. And that cat is sitting too perfectly. It must be fake." Although

Ghada knew her aunt was not deliberately trying to annoy her, she sucked her teeth and huffed her breath. How poorly Nuzha understood her father, who always dressed elegantly, even for bed.

She lifted her gaze, holding this photograph in her mind to compare it with the man before her. Baba laughed softly at something Hani said and the expression she recognised from the picture returned. He looked up at the distance, lips slightly pursed as if to say "and."

Khaled was the one who told her where he had been all this time—and at first she did not believe it. Then a new nightmare had taken hold that Baba might never return. Or he might return a madman, or another person completely, pretending to be him.

She looked up again, with an instinct that he might run away. He was talking to a man she didn't know now, with a tall tarbush and grey in his hair. Baba's lips began to move, and from the way he was waving his hands she knew he was telling a story.

"Where are you going?"

"I have to run an errand." Midhat touched Ghada's hair. The guests were gone; the afternoon was almost over. "But now, you know if Mama asks where I am, you must tell her I'm in the garden. Mashi? I'm looking at the chickens."

Ghada covered her mouth with both hands. Midhat put on his coat and selected a cane, and stepped out of the house.

The street was hot, and the air, alive with flies, smelled strongly of wild, dry thyme. At the intersection, the thoroughfare was as quiet as a Friday. He walked quickly in the shade. Something thin and black on a rooftop caught his eye. It moved, and revealed itself as the shadow of something pushed by the wind.

The route to the hospital took him near the road to Nouveautés Ghada. He hesitated at the bend with the corner of Barclays Bank just in sight. The fire at Nouveautés seemed so remote—now every shop in Nablus was closed, and that was the least of their worries. This, he supposed, must be catastrophe's slim gift, to make other terrors seem from its vantage comparatively light.

A pattering struck up behind him and he turned. Something white was running down the hill.

"No, Papi, go home!" he shouted.

"I'm coming with you!"

"Ghada, *go home.*"

Ghada's scrubbed, flushed face expanded into view, and as she reached his side he saw she had combed her hair into a centre parting. He gripped her shoulders and the white puffed sleeves of her dress rose like meringues.

"Papi." He let out a breathy syllable of exasperation. "I can't take you with me, it's too dangerous. And now I have to take you home. You are very naughty, do you know that?"

Her lip trembled; she avoided his gaze. "*No.*"

"I'm very angry with you," he added softly, touching her chin.

While his daughter tried to summon tears, Midhat considered whether he should go to Eli's house, and under pretext of discussing the shop leave Ghada in the care of Eli's wife. Then her posture transformed: she stuck a hand on her waist, and turned her watery eyes on him with a supercilious expression.

"They don't shoot in the daytime, silly, they shoot at night. And anyway, a man walking with a little girl is much safer than a man walking on his own."

"I think not, sweetheart," he said, though it occurred to him that she might be right.

"I'll tell Mama."

"Excuse me? Is that a threat? Shame on you, Ghada."

"I'm not letting you leave again," she said. "Where are we going?"

"*I'm* going to the hospital."

"You have just left the hospital!"

"A different hospital," said Midhat. "Calm down. And walk quickly."

Her short legs slowed his pace so much that he soon picked her up and carried her. Ahead, a car crept slowly across Mount Ebal. They climbed the hospital steps.

A patient was leaning on his crutches in the foyer. He lifted his head and locked eyes with Midhat just as another stepped in from the veranda, and a shadow flitted over both their faces. Then Midhat greeted them by name—Iyad, Abu Marwan—and they brightened. Iyad set his crutches against the wall.

"Abu Taher!" he said, hobbling forward. "We missed you."

"And I missed you!" said Midhat. He addressed two weather-beaten fellahin behind Iyad: "As-salamu alaykum, I am Midhat Kamal. Has everyone been sitting outside?"

"Yes," said Abu Marwan, "as usual."

Beyond them, another man was waving—an old regular from Nouveautés. Midhat nodded, feeling graceful, and in all their faces seeing reflections of his grace.

Père Antoine was surprised to see Midhat Kamal on the veranda. The last occasion had been during the spring. Only afterwards had Antoine learned that this Kamal had lost his mind and was being sent to an asylum. He wondered whether Midhat would recognise him.

A few variants of Midhat's story had been in circulation, but female patients tended to remark upon the plight of his wife, with the words "Meskina Fatima." It became a kind of refrain, spoken in a way that suggested a pity not unmixed with pleasure. Others expressed clearer disapproval, gesturing at the lint-wrapped heads and splinted limbs on the veranda as if at the patent shame of being hospitalised for any ailment other than those sustained during armed struggle. One woman had mentioned it was "ma'roof" that Midhat Kamal had made his fortune by illegal means. Ergo, someone cursed him, and set fire to his shop. Ergo, he went mad. "Hatha mantiqi," this woman had concluded her analysis, with a satisfied pout.

Midhat raised a hand in greeting. He was wearing a double-breasted suit and carrying a cane. The wind flipped his tie over his shoulder, and a little girl appeared beside him, dressed in white.

"Good to see you again!" Père Antoine called. "Please, join me."

"Thank you very much." He strode along the railing, and the girl ran to the opposite corner and sat on the floor.

"You'll dirty your dress."

"Oh."

Midhat swatted the air. "It's done now." He sat in the chair beside Antoine. "Marhaba, keef halak."

Up close, Midhat looked quite as drawn and pale as one might expect of someone lately released from an asylum.

"I realised," said Antoine, injecting a smile into his voice, "that I never told you my name."

"Father Antoine," said Midhat. He looked him straight in the eye. "We did meet before."

Antoine paused, then nodded carefully. "Ah. Yes we did. Here, a few months ago."

"Non non," said Midhat, "Avant ça. Years ago. I think you are the Brother of the Virgins." His eyebrows began to rise, followed by the corners of his lips. His eyes became slivers.

"Is that what they call me?" said Antoine.

"They used to."

Antoine laughed and ran his fingertips through his beard. "You are visiting?"

"Yes. Have a cigarillo," said Midhat. "My cousin brought them from Beirut."

Only one cigarillo was missing from the line-up. Antoine rolled the next into the vacancy and pinched it by the gold seal; Midhat held another with his teeth and drew a packet of matches from his pocket. He lit Antoine's first. Antoine sucked, exhaled, and watched the ends of the leaves crisp. Not often did a layman offer him a smoke. He looked out at the orchard and imagined, for a moment, that he was another person, with another life.

"What is your opinion of the uprising?"

Midhat uncrossed his legs, nostrils fuming. "I wish I had not missed the beginning."

The implied candour of this remark took Antoine off guard. He stole another look at his companion. Midhat was gazing at his little girl. Perhaps he took it as a given that everyone knew of his confinement.

"Yes," said Antoine. "The beginning was quite beautiful. Now, people seem rather tired. I doubt they will want to miss the harvest." Midhat opened his hand—agreeing, qualifying?—and Antoine tipped his head back and blew into the air: "I hope they will succeed. That some good will come of this."

"Well," said Midhat. "We deserve it."

He had put no pressure on that "we." Nevertheless, Antoine felt the force of his correction.

"Of course you are justified, there's no doubt about that," said Antoine. "All I meant was, now the British are bringing more troops, and there is talk of martial law, and, you know, if there is anything I have learned in my life—and though I am an old man the truth is I have only learned a few things! But I do know we can never predict the future. So I only meant—that it might go either way, if you see." He sucked the cigar and rotated it as he held his breath, looking at the smouldering end. "More and more, I find, I struggle to hold the larger picture in view. Every year, my . . . mind," he drew his palms together, "becomes smaller."

Somewhere, someone was playing scales on a piano. The sound brought the cicadas on the mountain to life, so that the silent veranda was abruptly full of noises. The pianist wavered between two notes.

"Do you work with the nurses?" said Midhat.

"Oh no," said Antoine. "I was a researcher. I wrote a book."

"Bravo."

"So-so." He tipped his head from side to side. "I am also a priest," he gestured at his robes, "and once, I taught at L'École Biblique. In Jerusalem."

"Now I really envy you."

"Really?"

"I would love to be at a university. In France, I went to two universities. I loved them. The classes, I loved . . ." Midhat shook his head, lifting his eyes again to his little girl, who, seeming to sense his gaze, also glanced up. "You know this sense that everyone around you is arguing," he said. "When you are writing you are writing to one another, even to people who are dead. Even to people who are not alive yet."

"Well now," said Antoine, "this is really the dream of the university! My experience was usually of a bleaker sort of monastery. Of course, L'École Biblique is attached to a convent. But, actually, convents are not bleak places to live, generally speaking. Contrary to popular opinion perhaps."

Midhat's eyes grew round. "*Bleak*?" He laughed in disbelief. "But at a university, where every man can think for himself—"

"And can count on being wrong half the time."

Midhat was shaking his head.

"*At least* half the time," said Antoine. "Probably more."

"That's the point."

"To be wrong?"

"To be . . . sharpened against others, against their . . . you know."

Down in the grove, a ragged cat pranced out from under the veranda, tail erect, stalking something too small to be seen.

"You had a wonderful time at Montpellier, then," said Antoine.

"And the Sorbonne."

Antoine chuckled.

"I have forgotten everything now. I remember some things. I remember I loved . . . the medicine bottles." He contracted his lips around his cigarillo, puffing repeatedly before exhaling through his nose. "I can't explain."

"The bottles?"

"No, not the bottles. That's not what I meant."

"Tell me. I'm interested."

"Are you?"

"Very much."

Midhat met his eye. "Are you going to write it down?"

"What?"

"I said, are you going to write it down?"

Here, it seemed to Antoine that several moments passed. He was quite unable to speak. His skin ran cold. His mind was bursting with Louise.

"I know you have been writing about Nablus," he heard Midhat say. "My wife told me."

"Your wife?"

"Fatima Hammad. The daughter of Haj Nimr."

Very slowly, Antoine released his breath and shut his eyes. "Yes. I did write about Nablus. I am not writing anymore. So—no, I will not write it down." He pretended to laugh. Only now, as the conversation was slipping against him, did he recognise how he craved the approval of this francophone Nabulsi. A crescendo of footsteps indoors heralded the end of their exchange, with its little window of sympathy: any moment now, more patients would be coming out for air. He cleared his throat for the goodbye. The footsteps vanished, and the doors did not open. Midhat tapped the ash of his cigarillo and flattened his tie, and the girl looked up.

"Is that your daughter?"

"Yes."

There was another long silence. When Midhat spoke again, he did so with a formality that suggested he had been considering his phrasing.

"When I look at my life," he said, "I see a whole list of mistakes. Lovely, beautiful mistakes. I wouldn't change them."

That same expressive intensity had returned to his face. In the space of a few seconds Antoine assessed this sociable, humorous man as rather evasive—a person who ordinarily withheld a great deal. But it quickly struck him that he was probably being influenced by those rumours of Midhat's psychosis, by the idea that a man would not enter an asylum without some discrepancy in his soul's architecture. That might seem reasonable, but Antoine nevertheless pulled back on the collar of his presumption, which, after everything, still strained to race off down paths of cause and effect. Pensively, he listened for the piano. He heard only the cicadas.

"I would change—perhaps I would change a few things," said Midhat. "But how are we to know? We make the biggest decisions when we are young."

"You are still young."

Midhat raised an eyebrow.

"You cannot be more than thirty-five."

"I am forty-one."

"Oh, that's young. You have plenty of time to make more errors."

They both laughed, and whatever tension had emerged, or that Antoine had imagined into being, departed.

"Go on," he said. "Tell me more about this woman."

Midhat gave him a shocked grin. "How did you know it was a woman?"

It was Antoine's turn to raise an eyebrow.

"Well. It was a very, very long time ago. In fact, I don't even know if she is still alive. And if she is, she has probably forgotten. She might remember me. We always hope people remember us, but I'm not sure they do for very long. Maybe something reminds them, once in a while. Some object or other. But that would be only a brief breach—or at least, it should be brief, if one is to continue. The past comes back to me now and then." He smiled. "But I do not live there."

Antoine faced forward, with a priest's instinct that he must allow Midhat to speak unobserved.

"One thing I would change is the mistake I made about your country. I had an idea about France, you know. I had a kind of fantasy of virtue. *That* I would change, or maybe," his tone twisted, he skewed the thought, "maybe that is just the only thing I could have changed. The other things, it was all . . . just . . . out of my hands."

"You are not the first to make this error," said Antoine. He adopted a pastoral air and interlaced his fingers: "But you know that a *place* cannot be virtuous. An idea may be virtuous. Not a place."

Down in the grove, the cat was snatching its way up a tree trunk.

"You will go back?" said Midhat.

"Oh, France does not love me. After the uprising, I think I will go to Cairo."

Midhat made a noise of interested surprise.

"I would like to live more in the world," said Antoine, "from now on."

"A worthy ambition."

"I have found it rather difficult, rather taxing . . ." He left off.

Midhat did not ask him to complete the thought, and Antoine regretted his personal turning. He imagined Midhat was put off by it, that having come here to confess he did not expect his confessor to reciprocate. He took a last breath of his cigarillo, holding it very hard, and in his chest felt a now familiar bending inward of shame. After more shuffling noises from inside, the door opened. Out stepped an old man, followed by a younger one with a broken leg.

"As-salamu alaykum."

"Wa alaykum as-salam."

The old man led the younger to a pair of seats further along, and pulling out a pipe, began stuffing it with tobacco. Antoine pressed the stub of his cigarillo onto the stone below the railing.

"How many are dead?" said Midhat quietly.

"I couldn't tell you. Many. Probably many more have gone unrecorded. It has not been a bloodless revolution. Did you hear about the battle at Anabta? Dawn till dusk. Several *women* were martyred."

"You probably know more than most Nabulsis know," said Midhat. "I should come to you for the news, one never hears it straight from anyone directly involved. My cousin . . ." He stopped. "My wife thinks someone in Nablus has a grudge against me. Do you know anything about that?"

Antoine considered. This had occurred a few times during the years of his research—a Nabulsi asking *him* for information about Nablus— albeit few enough to count on one hand. It was a long time since he last examined his notes from those days. He scoured his memory. Beyond the recent remarks about Midhat being in hospital, he could vaguely recall some sidelong expressions of resentment but could summon no particulars.

"I can't think," he said. "Prejudice is common."

"Yes, yes," said Midhat, wearily. "I don't care so much, anymore, what other people think of me."

"That's good."

"We need a bit of it, it's not nothing." Midhat stretched one leg to put his ankle on his knee. "But I think my family is enough. My wife is the measure of my life. And I am always falling short. Ha! Then, my cousin . . . he was my *moral* measure. And I always fell short. My children are my family measure: but I fall short. By their expectations I am always a compromise, I always fail. On the other hand, I think," unexpectedly his voice cracked—he leaned forward, his ankle slipped awkwardly off his knee, "without them, I would be nothing at all."

At this eruption of feeling, Antoine started. Midhat was staring wide-eyed at the olive grove. Without warning, his whole body lurched, and as though something were rising and forcing its way out of his mouth, he choked: "Father."

Antoine glanced at the door, wondering if he should call a nurse. Neither of the other men noticed Midhat's agitation. But the girl—the girl's eyes were fixed on him. Her arms had seized up, as one afraid of making a sudden move.

Midhat held his knees with his long fingers, gaping at the distance. "Father," he said again.

"Yes." Antoine put a hand on Midhat's back. "Yes, I'm here."

With one long deep inhalation, as if surfacing from underwater, Midhat said: "I forgive you."

Antoine's breath stopped. "What?" he said.

He tried to stop the hand on Midhat's back from shaking.

At the valley's edge, the sun plunged towards the mountain. A wide strip of sky was turning red. The heat thinned on the air, and the conflagration spread across the glass of the windows.

In Midhat, something heavy gave way. He heard, or felt, the lapping of a black lake below him, and a sigh of stone-chilled air just released, and the tinkle of a deep well, shooting glances of light up at a man kneeling with his roped bucket. He felt the warm consistent pressure of the priest's hand on his back.

He moved his head, ready to thank him—and was surprised by what he saw. Antoine's pinkish eyes were stretched in shock, and the soft lips amid the white beard were parted. Midhat took a deep, resigned breath. But his initial assumption—that the priest thought he was mad—faded as Antoine's expression of terror transformed into one of searching, the pupils flicking side to side as he switched his focus between Midhat's eyes. The adhan started.

"Are you all right?" said Midhat.

"Baba," said Ghada.

"Yes, habibti."

Ghada stood and wiped the back of her dress.

"Yes yes," said Midhat. "Yalla, we're going home."

Looking back he caught a tiny contraction of the priest's eyelids, which did not close completely, but rather, like the lens of a camera, reset their focus. Antoine nodded. He retracted his hand.

"God," he said, raising the hand in farewell. He did not complete the phrase.

**Key events in the development of the Palestinian
and Syrian national movements**

1882–1903 First wave of Jewish immigration (aliyah): around thirty-five
thousand Jewish immigrants, mostly from Eastern Europe,
settle in Palestine and establish agricultural enterprises.

1904–1914 Second wave of Jewish immigration (aliyah): around forty
thousand immigrants with a strong ideological commitment
to Zionism arrive in Palestine.

1911 Foundation of the Arab nationalist organisation al-Fatat
(the Young Arab Society) in Paris.

1913

18–23 June Arab National Congress: Arab reformist organisations and
students living in Paris meet in the hall of the French Geographical Society to discuss the future of the region in the
face of Ottoman policy, increased Zionist settlement, and
British and French colonial interests.

1914

2 August Ottoman-German Alliance: Ottoman Empire secretly agrees to enter the war in alliance with the Central Powers once Germany declares war on Russia.

6–10 September Miracle of the Marne: First World War battle fought along the Marne River in France resulting in an Allied victory against German armies.

29 October Ottoman Empire officially enters the First World War.

1915

17 Feb (–9 Jan 1916) Dardanelles Campaign: British and French military campaign on the Gallipoli peninsula against the Ottoman Empire, resulting in an Ottoman victory.

24 April (–1917) Armenian Genocide: Ottoman government systematically exterminates and deports its Armenian population.

July (–March 1916) Hussein-McMahon Correspondence: in an exchange of letters, the British government agrees to recognise Arab independence after the war in exchange for the Sharif of Mecca's help in launching a revolt against the Ottoman Empire.

21 August Executions announced of eleven Arab nationalists, reformers, and members of the Decentralisation Party on the orders of Ottoman military leader Djemal Pasha (Jamal Basha).

1916

6 May Executions announced of twenty-one more Arab nationalists, reformers, and members of the Decentralisation Party on the orders of Djemal Pasha.

16 May Sykes-Picot Agreement: secret agreement between Britain and France defining future spheres of control in the Middle East, premised on an Ottoman defeat. Borders defined of future Syria, Lebanon, Palestine, Transjordan, and Iraq (hitherto known collectively as "Greater Syria").

10 June (–Oct 1918) Great Arab Revolt against the Ottoman Empire, led by the Sharif of Mecca in collaboration with T.E. Lawrence largely in the Hejaz.

1917

2 November Balfour Declaration: public statement by the British government of support for the establishment of a national home for the Jewish people in Palestine.

9 December Jerusalem surrenders to British troops.

1918

19–25 September Battle of Nablus: British victory and Ottoman and German retreat.

31 October Defeat of the Ottoman Empire. British and French Occupied Enemy Territory Administration begins in Ottoman territories, including Palestine and Syria.

11 Nov (–July 1919) Egyptian Revolution: countrywide uprising against the British occupation of Egypt and Sudan, leading to later British recognition of Egyptian independence in 1922.

1919

(–1923)	Third wave of Jewish immigration (aliyah): around forty thousand Zionists settle in Palestine. This wave is triggered by the British conquest of Palestine, the Balfour Declaration, and the October Revolution in Russia and ensuing pogroms there and in Poland and Hungary.
18 Jan (–21 Jan 1920)	Paris Peace Conference: post-war discussion at Versailles, centring on German reparations and allocation of previous German and Ottoman territories. Concludes with signing of peace treaties and creation of the League of Nations (precursor to the United Nations).
27 January	First Palestinian National Congress in Jerusalem sends memoranda to Versailles rejecting the Balfour Declaration and demanding independence.
June	King-Crane Commission: survey, appointed by President Woodrow Wilson, of public opinion in the former Ottoman Empire regarding partition under a mandate system. Recommends an American, non-imperial government to guide the Arab peoples towards self-determination; concludes that most Palestinians oppose Zionism and that Zionists intend "a practically complete dispossession of the present non-Jewish inhabitants of Palestine, by various forms of purchase." Report is submitted to Paris Peace Conference but goes unheeded.
2 July	Syrian National Congress is convened in Damascus.

1920

8 March	Syrian National Congress declares an independent Arab Kingdom of Greater Syria under the rule of King Faisal.
4–7 April	Nebi Musa riots occur in Jerusalem.
19–26 April	British mandates over Palestine and Mesopotamia (modern-day Iraq) and French mandate over Syria and Lebanon are confirmed by the League of Nations.
5 May	Nablus Muslim-Christian Association lodges a protest with military governor against Zionism and the impending Mandate over Palestine.
June	Haganah, a Jewish paramilitary organisation, is founded.
1 July	British military rule in Palestine ends and civil administration begins, led by High Commissioner Herbert Samuel (until 1925).
24 July	Battle of Maysalun: French victory over Faisal's Syrian forces. The Arab Kingdom of Greater Syria is disbanded and Faisal is expelled from Syria.
14 December	Third Palestinian National Congress in Haifa calls for Palestinian independence under the same terms as the Mandate of Iraq, with a parliament elected by a one-citizen-one-vote system.

1921

11 April	Emirate of Transjordan, a British protectorate, is established.
	British appoint Haj Amin al-Husseini the Grand Mufti of Jerusalem, a new religious position.

1–7 May   Jaffa Riots: violent clashes between Arabs and Jews in Jaffa. The investigative commission concludes the cause is Arab discontent with Jewish immigration for political and economic reasons.

19 July   First Arab Palestinian delegation leaves for London to negotiate with Secretary for Colonies Winston Churchill for independence.

23 August   Kingdom of Iraq founded under British administration (until 1932) with Faisal ibn Hussein as king.

December   Wooden crate bursts open on the Haifa docks, leading to the seizure of three hundred pistols and seventeen thousand rounds of ammunition smuggled from Vienna by the Haganah.

1922

3 June   Churchill White Paper: document drafted in response to unrest calls for limiting Jewish immigration and stresses that the British government never

> at any time contemplated, as appears to be feared by the Arab Delegation, the disappearance or the subordination of the Arabic population, language or culture in Palestine. They would draw attention to the fact that the terms of the [Balfour] Declaration [...] do not contemplate that Palestine as a whole should be converted into a Jewish National Home, but that such a Home should be founded in Palestine.

Nevertheless, the government continues to support Zionist immigration.

1923

February–March Elections for a proposed Legislative Council fail, owing to a Palestinian Arab boycott.

May Egyptian feminist Huda Sha'rawi removes her veil in public when returning to Cairo from the Women's Suffrage Alliance Congress in Rome.

29 September British Mandate over Palestine and the French Mandate over Syria and Lebanon legally come into effect.

1924

(–1928) Fourth wave of Jewish immigration (aliyah): around eighty thousand Zionist Jews immigrate to Palestine, largely from Poland.

1925

25 March–1 April Anti-Balfour demonstrations: demonstrations and general strikes all over Palestine to protest the visit of Arthur James Balfour (Lord Belfour).

July (–June 1927) Great Syrian Revolt against French rule in Syria resulting in French victory.

November General strike in Palestine in support of the Syrian Revolt.

1926

16 February British authorities give retroactive legal recognition to land sold or negotiated during prohibition period (1918–1920) and accept unofficial Zionist land books.

16 May Collective Punishment Ordinance: British authorities formalize principle of collective punishment in Palestine.

1927

11 July   Powerful earthquake hits Palestine, affecting Jericho, Nablus, Jerusalem, Ramle, Lydda, and Tiberias, and destroying several villages.

1928

20–27 June   Seventh Palestinian National Congress in Jerusalem affirms demand for a democratic parliamentary government.

1929

(–1939)   Fifth wave of Zionist immigration (aliyah): between two hundred twenty-five thousand and three hundred thousand Jewish immigrants arrive mostly from Germany, increasingly in response to the rise of Nazism.

23–29 August   Worshipping Jews bring furniture to pray at the Wailing Wall / al-Buraq Wall, which Palestinian Arabs fear signifies a change to the Status Quo of Holy Sites, as established by the Ottomans. Following political demonstrations by militant Zionist groups, Palestinians riot in several towns. Shortly after this, rioting Arabs perpetrate a massacre of Jews in Hebron.

26 October   First Palestine Arab Women's Congress is held in Jerusalem.

27 October   Delegation from the Women's Congress demonstrates in Jerusalem against the Balfour Declaration, Collective Punishment Ordinance, and maltreatment of Arab prisoners.

1930   Under the leadership of Sheikh Izz ad-Din al-Qassam, the Black Hand Islamist group begins a militant campaign against Jewish civilians and the British Mandate.

1931

April Irgun, a paramilitary group and right-wing revisionist breakaway from the Haganah, is established by Ze'ev Jabotinsky and others.

August Demonstrations in Nablus against the storing of weapons in Jewish settlements are broken up by police baton charges.

1932

3 October British Mandate over Iraq is terminated; Iraq gains independence.

1933

January–July Nazi Party comes into power in Germany. With increasing anti-Semitism in Europe, Jewish immigration to Palestine rises dramatically.

8 September King Faisal of Iraq dies.

27 October General strike in Palestine to protest Jewish immigration and British pro-Zionist policy, with disturbances in major towns.

1934 Organised illegal Jewish immigration (Aliyah Bet) to Palestine begins, without permission of the Jewish Agency or British authorities.

1935

15 September Nuremberg Laws: German laws institutionalising the racial theories of Nazi ideology strip German Jews of their rights. Jewish immigration to Palestine rises dramatically.

16 October   Cement Incident: large shipment of weapons, concealed in drums of cement, is discovered at Jaffa harbour destined for Tel Aviv. The Arab Executive calls for a general strike, and a demonstration in Jaffa turns into a riot.

20 November   Sheikh Izz ad-Din al-Qassam is ambushed and killed by British soldiers in the hills of Ya'bad above Nablus.

December   High Commissioner Arthur Grenfell Wauchope proposes a twenty-eight-member Legislative Council, with Palestinian Arabs holding fourteen seats. Palestinians accept in principle, but the proposal is defeated by pro-Zionist members of the House of Commons.

1936

15 April   Following the murder of three Jews in a robbery incident near Tulkarem, two Arabs are murdered near Petah Tikva.

17 April   During the funeral of one of the Jewish victims, rioting breaks out and three Jews are murdered. The Mandate authorities institute Emergency Regulations and impose curfews across Palestine.

20 April   Arab National Committee forms in Nablus, followed by committees in all other Arab towns and villages, calling for a general strike.

25 April   Arab Higher Committee, consisting of members from all Arab political parties, calls for the strike to continue indefinitely.

May   "Village searches" begin: British pre-emptive campaign of terror to discourage Arabs from resisting British rule.

6 May   National Committees announce a tax strike.

11 May	British army reinforcements arrive from Malta and Egypt. Haganah and other organisations guarding Jewish colonies are legalized as the Jewish Settlement Police.
23 May	British arrest sixty-one Arab "agitators" and intern them in detention camps; thirty-seven more are arrested at the beginning of June.
May–June	Jaffa port is closed; sporadic attacks occur on the railways and Jewish settlements. Armed bands appear in the hill country.
17–29 June	British army demolish large areas of Jaffa.
6 July	British military "comb-out," using four thousand troops, machine guns, and tanks, begins in the region between Nablus and Jerusalem.
4 August	Collective Fines Ordinance: law issued by British authorities imposing collective punishments such as fines, mass destruction of property, curfews, and mass administrative detention.
August	Jewish acts of retaliation begin.
30 September	Martial law is declared in Palestine.
11 October	Arab Higher Committee calls an end to the strike, and thereby the revolt.
November	Casualty figures from hospital records give the number of fatalities in Palestine during the six months of disturbances: 1,195 Arabs, 80 Jews, 21 British Army, 16 Police and Frontier Police, and 2 non-Arab Christians.

ACKNOWLEDGMENTS

Thank you to Ghada Hammad; to the unfailingly generous Said Kanaan, Musbah, Randa, and Nour; to George Hintlian, for his encouragement and guidance; to Naseer Arafat; Albert Aghazarian; Kamal Abdulfattah; Nazmi Juubeh; Samih Hammoudeh; Qais Hammad; Aroub Bayazid; Abir Hammad; Ali Hammad; Faruq and Mona Hammad; Sami Hammad; Iyad Hammad; Khaled Kamal; Bassima Abu al-Huda; Waddah Kamal; Rami Kamal; Farid Kamal; Emad Kamal; Nejad Kamal; Nasser Kamal; Waddah Zuaiter; Rima Tarazi; Salim Tamari; Haifa Khalidi; Sharif Kanaana; Sahar Huneidi; Malak Husseini; Malak Abd al-Hadi and Samir Abd al-Hadi, on the will of whose grandfather, Salim Abd al-Hadi, Fuad Murad's will is based; Faiha Abd al-Hadi; Beshara Doumani; Ted Swedenburg; Sonia Nimr; Azzam Abu Saud; Samih Abdo; John Tleel; Ghada Khoury; Nazeeha Tuqan; Rima Keilani; Siham Abu Ghazaleh; Fuad Shehadeh; Adel Abu Amsha; Salwa Masri; Fuad Halawi; Abdul Rahman al-Haj Ibrahim; Abdul Sattar Qassem; Mohammad and Rola Zomlot; Mamdouh al-Aker; Uhud al-Aker, Rakefet Zalashik, and Raphael Koenig; thank you all for putting up with my questions, and sharing your knowledge and memories. And thank you, Zena Agha, for the maps.

To the best and most generous readers I could have asked for: Katharine Hammad, Joseph Minden, Allison Bulger, Coco Mellors, Steve Potter, Liz Wood, and Saad Hammad. For the conversations, advice, and wisdom, thank you Xanthe Gresham-Knight and Arthur Fournier.

Thank you to the adjudicators of the Harper-Wood Studentship at St John's College, Cambridge, and particularly Ruth Abbott; thank you to Amy Hempel, Bret Johnston, and Rick Moody, and to everyone at NYU, especially Zadie Smith, Nathan Englander, and Deborah Landau. Thank you to the board of the Axinn Foundation, to Beatrice Monti and Andrew Sean Greer at the Santa Maddalena Foundation, and to the MacDowell Colony for the Arts.

I am especially indebted to the following books: *Nablus: City of Civilizations* by Naseer Arafat; *Rediscovering Palestine: Merchants and Peasants in Jabal Nablus, 1700–1900* by Beshara Doumani; *The Nation and Its "New" Women: The Palestinian Women's Movement, 1920–1948* by Ellen Fleischmann; *Coutumes Palestiniennes: Naplouse et Son District* by Antonin Jaussen; the memoirs of Muhammad Izzat Darwazeh, and of Awni Abd al-Hadi; *Tarikh Jabal Nablus wa al-Balqa'* by Ihsan Nimr; *The Journal of the Palestine Oriental Society* (1920), especially the speech of Marie Joseph Lagrande; *Memories of Revolt: the 1936–1939 Rebellion and the Palestinian National Past* by Ted Swedenburg.

With special thanks to Georgia Garrett, Laurence Laluyaux, Stephen Edwards, and the rest of the team at RCW, Melanie Jackson, Michal Shavit, Elisabeth Schmitz, Morgan Entrekin, Katie Raissian, and Ana Fletcher.

To David Bradshaw and John Coulter, in loving memory.

Thank you to everyone who told me stories about Palestine. And thank you to Arthur, for listening to mine.

GROVE PRESS

Ⴤ

Reading Group Guide

by Kirsten Giebutowski

THE PARISIAN

Isabella Hammad

ABOUT THIS GUIDE

We hope that these discussion questions will enhance your reading group's exploration of Isabella Hammad's *The Parisian*. They are meant to stimulate discussion, offer new viewpoints, and enrich your enjoyment of the book.

More reading group guides and additional information, including summaries, author tours, and author sites for other fine Grove Atlantic titles may be found on our website, groveatlantic.com.

QUESTIONS FOR DISCUSSION

How does this fictionalized account of real historical events add to your understanding of the region? Talk about Hammad's choice of a main character in light of this.

———

What did Midhat hope for from France, and how does it satisfy and betray his hopes? Would he have been better off not going to France, given the pain it causes him and the way the experience marks him as "other" back in Nablus? Or does his status as "the Parisian" suit him?

———

In the shop one day in Nablus, Midhat opens a book from Paris that describes the Holy Land: "It had become an illicit pastime to read descriptions of the place he came from, to be transported by a landscape so precisely drawn and tinted in this other language that he ended up longing for the sights of his childhood as though he were not already among them" (p. 323). What are the hazards and gifts of seeing one's home through the eyes of an outsider? Discuss the role of longing in Midhat's life. Does it interfere with his happiness or augment it?

———

Midhat looks at the adaptations of Western clothing in the Samaritan store and sees their "stylistic compromises" as "errors" (p. 243). How does this point to the challenge Midhat faces in straddling two cultures with different aesthetics and values? Is evaluating one in terms of the other's standards always going to result in unfair judgment? By the end, how has Midhat's vision changed toward both cultures?

———

When Midhat says he can't marry Fatima because he needs freedom, Um Taher demands, "Freedom from *what*?" (p. 262). Consider her question.

———

What draws Jeannette and Midhat to each other? Would they necessarily have been better suited than Fatima and Midhat?

———————

Midhat compares his friendships with Hani and Jamil: "He saw Hani only once or twice a year, and yet nothing about their friendship had ever faded. It was the opposite of Midhat's relationship with Jamil. With Jamil it was all physical proximity and emotional distance" (p. 409). Is Midhat's assessment fair? Jamil is provincial by comparison to Hani's (and also Faruq's) cosmopolitanism—what does each friendship offer to Midhat?

———————

During his breakdown, Midhat feels lucid. In the hospital, "the invasion of the past" no longer bothers him so much; instead, "the new horror, surpassing that first, was the fact that everyone pretended the past didn't do that. Everyone lived on this skin of life and pretended they didn't know what they were standing on" (p. 457). Do you think in some sense we have to throw a veil over reality, or live with a degree of illusion, in order to maintain mental stability?

———————

Reflecting on her youth, Fatima considers that her real value had been as a potential prize for some man, and that "marriage meant someone had named her price. It did not matter that she herself chose her mate: in the eyes of Nablus she was appraised and evaluated, stripped of the precious mystery of being young and undefined. . . . the anticipation of glory had itself been the real glory" (p. 434). Does this favoring of the potential over the actual connect her thinking with Midhat's? Though Sahar's more evolved views perhaps make her a more like-able character than Fatima, is Fatima more complex? What are her internal struggles?

———————

What do we learn about Hani from the manner in which he corresponds with Sahar?

———————

How does Hammad show us the class differences within the revolt? Revisit the encounter between the fighters and the women at the Hammad's home (pp. 486–493) and also the paragraphs about Jamil and Basil's role as crossover fighters, bridging the urban/rural divide (pp. 501–503). Do you see a mix of respect and suspicion on both sides? Look at the summary on page 201 of how Nablus's social classes came into being: How has the growth of industry been a blessing and a curse, and who has benefited least?

How does Père Antoine's project and attitude toward the Arab world relate to Frédéric Molineu's? What was his main premise about Nablus and how is it shaken? Do you think his actions are a betrayal of his priestly office?

Um Taher and Ghada are both fiercely devoted to Midhat. How are they humorous as well as determined, estimable figures?

We are shown a society in which men and women occupy different spaces outside the home: the men gather at the café and marketplace, the women at the hammam and istiqbal. What kinds of things are accomplished in these spaces? Though they may be seen as traditionally masculine or feminine spaces from the outside, is there a way in which within them, each sex is free to express both gender roles? Have experiences of same-sex spaces been of value to you in your own life?

In their final conversation, Midhat tells Père Antoine: "When I look at my life, I see a whole list of mistakes. Lovely, beautiful mistakes. I wouldn't change them" (p. 545). How has Midhat arrived at this reconciliation with his life? What are the possible readings of the forgiveness Midhat offers Antoine at the end of their conversation? How does Midhat's declaration affect Antoine? Why doesn't he complete his farewell phrase?

Reviewers have pointed to this book's kinship with classic nineteenth-century novels, citing its seriousness and comprehensiveness, its tracing of its hero's moral development within the context of broad historical change, and its achievement of a realism that can only be accomplished by painting detailed pictures in unhurried fashion. Against the backdrop of much contemporary fiction, do these conventions from the past end up feeling new and refreshing?

SUGGESTIONS FOR FURTHER READING

Arabesques by Anton Shammas

Season of Migration to the North by Tayeb Salih

Mornings in Jenin by Susan Abulhawa

Salt Houses by Hala Alyan

Sentimental Education by Gustave Flaubert

The Cairo Trilogy by Naguib Mahfouz

Teta, Mother, and Me: Three Generations of Arab Women by Jean Said Makdisi

Palestine Collection by Joe Sacco

Orientalism by Edward Said

Palestinian Walks: Forays into a Vanishing Landscape by Raja Shehadeh

The Red and the Black by Stendhal